'Peter Temple is deservedly the leading lig
fiction and it's time the rest of the world caught on ... The writing
is lean and muscular, but also effortlessly elegant ... This is crime
writing at its very best'

Mark Billingham

'Great locations, hard-nosed dialogue and a twisting plot combine to
create superb entertainment'

Evening Standard

'We can see why he is one of Australia's leading crime-writers ...
characterisation, dialogue and the quality of the prose are all top-
class'

Sunday Telegraph

'Peter Temple's prose is brusque and tender, according to need, his
characterisation subtle yet strong, and his themes urgent and
universal. Put simply, Temple is a master'

John Harvey

ALSO BY PETER TEMPLE

Shooting Star

THE JACK IRISH BOOKS

Bad Debts
Black Tide
Dead Point
White Dog

THE PETER TEMPLE OMNIBUS

THE BROKEN SHORE
IN THE EVIL DAY
AN IRON ROSE

Quercus

First published in Great Britain in 2008 by

Quercus
21 Bloomsbury Square
London
WC1A 2NS

A CIP catalogue reference for this book is available
from the British Library

ISBN 978 1 90520 472 4

10 9 8 7 6 5 4 3 2 1

Printed and bound in Great Britain by Clays Ltd, St Ives plc.

CONTENTS

THE BROKEN SHORE

To Anita:
for the laughter and the loyalty.

CASHIN WALKED around the hill, into the wind from the sea. It was cold, late autumn, last glowing leaves clinging to the liquidambars and maples his great-grandfather's brother had planted, their surrender close. He loved this time, the morning stillness, loved it more than spring.

The dogs were tiring now but still hunting the ground, noses down, taking more time to sniff, less hopeful. Then one picked up a scent and, new life in their legs, they loped in file for the trees, vanished.

When he was near the house, the dogs, black as liquorice, came out of the trees, stopped, heads up, looked around as if seeing the land for the first time. Explorers. They turned their gaze on him for a while, started down the slope.

He walked the last stretch as briskly as he could and, as he put his hand out to the gate, they reached him. Their curly black heads tried to nudge him aside, insisting on entering first, strong back legs pushing. He unlatched the gate, they pushed it open enough to slip in, nose to tail, trotted down the path to the shed door. Both wanted to be first again, stood with tails up, furry scimitars, noses touching at the door jamb.

Inside, the big poodles led him to the kitchen. They had water bowls there and they stuck their noses into them and drank in a noisy way. Cashin prepared their meal: two slices each from the cannon-barrel dog sausage made by the butcher in Kenmare, three handfuls each of dry dog food. He got the dogs' attention, took the bowls outside, placed them a metre apart.

The dogs came out. He told them to sit. Stomachs full of water, they did so slowly and with disdain, appeared to be arthritic. Given permission to eat, they looked at the food without interest, looked at each other, at him. Why have we been brought here to see this inedible stuff?

Cashin went inside. In his hip pocket, the mobile rang.

'Yes.'

'Joe?'

Kendall Rogers, from the station.

'Had a call from a lady,' she said. 'Near Beckett. A Mrs Haig. She reckons there's someone in her shed.'

'Doing what?'

'Well, nothing. Her dog's barking. I'll sort it out.'

Cashin felt his stubble. 'What's the address?'

'I'm going.'

'No point. Not far out of my way. Address?'

He went to the kitchen table and wrote on the pad: date, time, incident, address. 'Tell her fifteen-twenty. Give her my number if anything happens before I get there.'

The dogs liked his urgency, rushed around, made for the vehicle when he left the building. On the way, they stood on station, noses out the back windows. Cashin parked a hundred metres down the lane from the farmhouse gate. A head came around the hedge as he approached.

'Cop?' she said. She had dirty grey hair around a face cut from a hard wood with a blunt tool.

Cashin nodded.

'The uniform and that?'

'Plainclothes,' he said. He produced the Victoria Police badge with the emblem that looked like a fox. She took off her smudged glasses to study it.

'Them police dogs?' she said.

He looked back. Two woolly black heads in the same window.

'They work with the police,' he said. 'Where's this person?'

'Come,' she said. 'Dog's inside, mad as a pork chop, the little bugger.'

'Jack Russell,' said Cashin.

'How'd ya know that?'

'Just a guess.'

They went around the house. He felt the fear rising in him like nausea.

'In there,' she said.

The shed was a long way from the house, you had to cross an expanse of overgrown garden, go through an opening in a fence lost beneath rampant potato-creeper. They walked to the gate. Beyond was knee-high grass, pieces of rusted metal sticking out.

'What's inside?' Cashin said, looking at a rusted shed of corrugated iron a few metres from the road, a door half open. He felt sweat around his collarbones. He wished he'd let Kendall do this.

Mrs Haig touched her chin, black spikes like a worn-down hair brush. 'Stuff,' she said. 'Junk. The old truck. Haven't bin in there for years. Don't go in there.'

'Let the dog out,' he said.

Her head jerked, alarmed. 'Bastard might hurt im,' she said.

'No,' he said. 'What's the dog's name?'

'Monty, call them all Monty, after Lord Monty of Alamein. Too young, you wouldn't know.'

'That's right,' he said. 'Let Monty out.'

'And them police dogs? What bloody use are they?'

'Kept for life-and-death matters,' Cashin said, controlling his voice. 'I'll be at the door, then you let Lord Monty out.'

His mouth was dry, his scalp itched, these things would not have happened before Rai Sarris. He crossed the grassland, went to the left of the door. You learned early to keep your distance from potentially dangerous people and that included not going into dark sheds to meet them.

Mrs Haig was at the potato–creeper hedge. He gave her the thumbs up, his heart thumping.

The small dog came bounding through the grass, all tight muscles and yap, went for the shed, braked, stuck its head in the door and snarled, small body rigid with excitement.

Cashin thumped on the corrugated iron wall with his left hand. 'Police,' he said loudly, glad to be doing something. 'Get out of there. Now!'

Not a long wait.

The dog backed off, shrieking, hysterical, mostly airborne.

A man appeared in the doorway, hesitated, came out carrying a canvas swag. He ignored the dog.

'On my way,' he said. 'Just had a sleep.' He was in his fifties perhaps, short grey hair, big shoulders, a day's beard.

'Call the dog, Mrs Haig,' Cashin said over his shoulder.

The woman shouted and the dog withdrew, reluctant but obedient.

'Trespassing on private property,' said Cashin, calmer. He felt no threat from the man.

'Yeah, well, just had a sleep.'

'Put the swag down,' Cashin said. 'Take off your coat.'

'Says who?'

'I'm a cop.' He showed the fox.

The man folded his bluey, put it down on his swag, at his feet. He wore laced boots, never seen polish, toes dented.

'How'd you get here?' Cashin said.

'Walking. Lifts.'

'From where?'

'New South.'

'New South Wales?'

'Yeah.'

'Long way to come.'

'A way.'

'Going where?'

'Just going. My own business where I go.'

'Free country. Got some ID? Driver's licence, Medicare card.'

'No.'

'No ID?'

'No.'

'Don't make it hard,' Cashin said. 'I haven't had breakfast. No ID, I take you in for fingerprinting, charge you with trespass, put you in the cells. Could be a while before you see daylight.'

The man bent, found a wallet in his coat, took out a folded sheet of paper, offered it.

'Put it in the pocket and chuck the coat over.'

It landed a metre away.

'Back off a bit,' Cashin said. He collected the coat, felt it. Nothing. He took out the piece of paper, often folded, worn. He opened it.

Dave Rebb has worked on Boorindi Downs for three years and is a hard worker and no trouble, his good with engines, most mechanic things. Also stock. I would employ him again any time.

It was signed Colin Blandy, manager, and dated 11 August 1996. There was a telephone number.

'Where's this place?' said Cashin.

'Queensland. Near Winton.'

'And this is it? This's your ID? Ten years old?'

'Yeah.'

Cashin found his notebook and wrote down the names and the number, put the paper back in the coat. 'Scared the lady here,' he said. 'That's not good.'

'No sign of life when I come,' said the man. 'Dog didn't bark.'

'Been in trouble with the police, Dave?'

'No. Never been in trouble.'

'Could be a murderer,' said Mrs Haig behind him. 'Killer. Dangerous killer.'

'Me, Mrs Haig,' said Cashin, 'I'm the policeman, I'm dealing with this. Dave, I'm going to drive you to the main road. Come back this way, you'll be in serious trouble. Okay?'

'Okay.'

Cashin took the two steps and gave the man back his coat. 'Let's go.'

'Charge him!' shouted Mrs Haig.

In the vehicle, Dave Rebb offered his hands to the dogs, he was a man who knew about dogs. At the T-junction, Cashin pulled over.

'Which way you going?' he said.

There was a moment. 'Cromarty.'

'Drop you at Port Monro,' Cashin said. He turned left. At the turnoff to the town, he stopped. They got out and he opened the back for the man's swag.

'Mind how you go now,' Cashin said. 'Need a buck or two?'

'No,' said Rebb. 'Treated me like a human. Not a lot of that.'

Waiting to turn, Cashin watched Rebb go, swag horizontal across his back, sticking out. In the morning mist, he was a stubby-armed cross walking.

'NO DRAMA?' said Kendall Rogers.

'Just a swaggie,' said Cashin. 'You doing unpaid time now?'

'I woke up early. It's warmer here, anyway.' She fiddled with something on the counter.

Cashin raised the hatch and went to his desk, started on the incident report.

'I'm thinking of applying for a transfer,' she said.

'I can do something about my personal hygiene,' Cashin said. 'I can change.'

'I don't need protecting,' she said. 'I'm not a rookie.'

Cashin looked up. He'd been expecting this. 'I'm not protecting you from anything. I wouldn't protect anybody. You can die for me anytime.'

A silence.

'Yes, well,' Kendall said. 'There are things here to be resolved. Like the pub business. You drive back at ten o'clock at night.'

'The Caine animals won't touch me. I'm not going to go to an inquiry and explain why I let you handle it.'

'Why won't they touch you?'

'Because my cousins will kill them. And after that, they'll be very nasty to them. Is that a satisfactory answer, your honour?' He went back to the report but he felt her eyes. 'What?' he said. 'What?'

'I'm going to Cindy's. Ham and egg?'

'I'll let you face the savage bitch? On a Friday morning? I'll go.'

She laughed, some of the tension gone.

When she was at the door, Cashin said, 'Ken, bit more mustard this time? Brave enough to ask her?'

He went to the window and watched her go down the street. She had been a gymnast, represented the state at sixteen, won her first gold medal. You would not know it from her walk. In the city, off duty, she went to a club with a friend, a photographer. She was recognised by a youth she had arrested a few months before, an apprentice motor mechanic, a weekend raver, a kicker and a stomper. They were followed, the photographer was badly beaten, locked in his car boot, survived by luck.

Kendall was taken somewhere, treated like a sex doll. After dawn, a man and his dog found her. She had a broken pelvis, a broken arm, six broken ribs, a punctured lung, damaged spleen, pancreas, crushed nose, one cheek-bone stove in, five teeth broken, a dislocated shoulder, massive bruising everywhere.

Cashin returned to the paper work. You could get by without identification but Rebb had been employed, there might be some tax record. He dialled the number for Boorindi Downs. It rang for a while.

'Yeah?'

'Victoria Police, Detective Cashin, Port Monro. Need to know about someone worked on Boorindi Downs.'

'Yeah?'

'Dave Rebb.'

'When's that?'

'1994 to 1996.'

'No, mate, no one here from then. Place belongs to someone else now, they did a clear-out.'

'What about Colin Blandy.'

'Blands, oh yeah. I know him from before, he got the bullet from the Greeks, went to Queensland. Dead, though.'

'Thanks for your time.'

Cashin thought that he had made a mistake, he should have fingerprinted Rebb. He had cause to, he had allowed sympathy to dictate.

Could be a murderer, said Mrs Haig. Killer.

He rang Cromarty, asked for the criminal investigation man he knew.

'Got a feeling, have you?' said Dewes. 'I'll tell them to keep a lookout.'

Cashin sat, hands on the desk. He had threatened Rebb with this, the fingerprinting, the long wait in the cells.

'Sandwich,' said Kendall. 'Extra mustard. She put it on with a trowel.'

An ordinary shift went by. Near the end, the word came that the first electronic sweep found no David Rebb on any government database in the states and territories. It didn't mean much. Cashin knew of cases where searches had failed to find people with strings of convictions. He clocked off, drove out to the highway, turned for Cromarty.

Rebb had walked twenty-three kilometres. Cashin pulled in a good way in front of him, got out.

He came on, a man who walked, easy walk, stopped, a tilt of shoulders, the tilted cross.

'Dave, I've got to fingerprint you,' Cashin said.

'Told you. Done nothing.'

'Can't take your word, Dave. Can't take anyone's word. Got to charge you with trespass,' Cashin said.

Rebb said nothing.

'That's so we can take your prints.'

'Don't lock me up,' said Rebb, softly, no tone. 'Can't go in the cells.'

Cashin heard the fear in the man's voice and he knew that once he would not have cared much. He hesitated, then he said, 'Listen, you interested in work? Dairy cows, cow stuff. Do that kind of thing?'

Rebb nodded. 'Long time ago.'

'Want some work?'

'Well, open to offers.'

'And garden stuff, some building work maybe?'

'Yeah. Done a bit of that, yeah.'

'Well, there's work here. My neighbour's cows, I'm clearing up an old place, might rebuild a bit, thinking of it. Work for a cop?'

'Worked for every kind of bastard there is.'

'Thank you. You can sleep at my place tonight. There's a shed with bunks and a shower. See about the job tomorrow.'

They got into the vehicle, Rebb's swag in the back. 'This how they get workers around here?' he said. 'Cops recruit them.'

'All part of the job.'

'What about the fingerprints?'

'I'm taking your word you're clean. That's pretty dumb, hey?'

Rebb was looking out of the window. 'Saved the taxpayer money,' he said.

CASHIN WOKE in the dark, Shane Diab on his mind, the sounds he made dying.

He listened to his aches for a time, tested his spine, his hips, his thighs – they all gave pain. He pushed away the lovely warm burden of the quilts, put feet in the icy waiting boots, and left the room, went down the passage, through Tommy Cashin's sad ballroom, into the hall, out the front door. It was no colder out than in, today the mist blown away by a strong wind off the ocean.

He pissed from the verandah, onto the weeds. It didn't bother them. Then he went inside and did his stretching, washed his face, rinsed his mouth, put on overalls, socks, boots.

The dogs knew his noises, they were making throat sounds of impatience at the side door. He let them in and the big creatures snuffled around him, tails swinging.

Thirsty, he went to the fridge and the sight of the frosted beer bottles made him think he could drink a beer. He took out the two–litre bottle of juice, eight fruits it said. Only a dickhead would believe that.

He held the plastic flagon in both hands, took a long drink, a tall glass at least. He took the old oilskin coat off the hook behind the door, picked up the weapon. When he opened the door to the verandah, the dogs pushed through, bounded down the steps, ran for the back gate. They jostled while they watched him come down the path, shrugging into the coat as he walked. Gate open, they ran down the path, side by side, reached the open land and made for the trees, jumping over the big tufts of grass, extravagant leaps, ears floating.

Cashin broke the little over-and-under gun as he walked, felt in his side pockets and found a .22 slug and a .410 shell, fed the mouths. He often had the chance to take a shot at a hare, looked through the v-sight at the beautiful dun creature, its electric ears. He didn't even think of firing, he loved hares, their intelligence, their playfulness. At a running rabbit, he did take the odd shot. It was just a fairground exercise, a challenge. He always missed – his reaction too slow, the .410's cone of shot not big enough, too soon dissolved and impotent.

Cashin walked with the little weapon broken over his arm, looking at the trees, dark inside, waiting for the dogs to reach them and send the birds up like tracer fire.

The dogs did a last bound and they were in the trees, triggering the bird-blast, black shrapnel screeching into the sky.

He walked over the hill and down the slope, the dogs ahead, dead black and light-absorbing, heads down, quick legs, coursing, disturbing the leaf mulch. On the levelling ground, on the fringe of the clearing, a hare took off. He watched the three cross the open space, black dogs and hare, the hare pacing itself perfectly, jinking when it felt the dogs near. It seemed to be pulling the dogs on a string. They vanished into the trees above the creek.

Cashin crossed the meadow. The ground was level to the eye but, tramping the long dry grass, you could feel underfoot the rise and fall, the broad furrows a plough had carved. The clearing had once been cultivated, but not in the memory of anyone living. He had no way of knowing whether his ancestor Tommy Cashin had planted a crop there.

It was a fight to get to the creek through the poplars and willows, thousands of suckers gone unchecked for at least thirty years. When he reached the watercourse, a trickle between pools, the dogs appeared, panting. They went straight in, found the deepest places, drank, walked around, drank, walked around, the water eddied weakly around their thin, strong legs, they bit it, raised pointed chins, beards draining water. Poodles liked puddles, didn't like deep water, didn't like the sea much. They were paddlers.

Across the creek, they began the sweep to the west, around the hill, on the gentle flank. In the dun grass, he saw the ears of two hares. He whistled up the dogs and pointed to the hares. They followed his arm, ran and put up the pair, which broke together and stayed together, running side by side for ten or fifteen metres, two dogs behind them, an orderly group of four. Then the left hare split, went downhill. His dog split with him. The other dog couldn't bear it, broke stride, swerved left to join his friend in the pursuit. They vanished into the long grass.

After a while, they came back, pink of tongues visible from a long way, loped ahead again.

Walking, Cashin felt the eyes on him. The dogs running ahead would soon sense the man too, look around, turn left and make for him. He walked and then there were sharp and carrying barks.

The man was out of the trees, the dogs circling him, bouncing. Cashin was unconcerned. He saw the hands the man put out to them, they tried to mouth them, delighted to see their friend. He angled his path to meet Den Millane, nearing eighty but looking as he had at fifty. He would die with a dense head of hair the colour of a gun barrel.

They shook hands. If they didn't meet for a little while, they shook hands.

'Still no decent rain,' said Cashin.

'Fuckin unnatural,' said Millane. 'Startin to believe in this greenhouse shit.' He rubbed a dog head with each hand. 'Bugger me, never thought I could like a bloody poodle. Seen the women at the Corrigan house?'

'No.'

They both had boundaries with the Corrigan property. Mrs Corrigan had gone to Queensland after her husband died. No one had lived in the small redbrick house since then. The weather stripped paint from the woodwork, dried out the window putty, panes fell out. The timber outbuildings listed, collapsed, and grass grew over the rotting pieces. He remembered coming for a weekend in summer in the early nineties, hot, he was still with Vickie then, a big piece of roof had gone, blown off. He asked Den Millane to contact Mrs Corrigan and the roof was fixed, in a fashion. Roofs decided whether empty houses would become ruins.

'The Elders bloke brung em,' said Den, not looking up. 'He's a fat cunt too. The one's got short hair, bloke hair. Like blokes used to have. Then they come back yesterday, now it's three girls, walkin around, they walk down the old fence. Fuckin lesbian colony on the move, mate.'

'Spot lesbians? They have them in your day?'

Millane spat. 'Still my bloody day, mate. Teachers in the main, your lessies. Used to send the clever girls out to buggery, nothin but dick-heads there couldn't read a comic book. Tell you what, I was a girl met those blokes, I'd go lessie. Anyway, point is, you ever looked at your title?'

Cashin shook his head.

'Creek's not the boundary.'

'No?'

'Your line's the other side, twenty, thirty yard over the creek.' Millane passed a thumb knuckle across his lower lip. 'Claim the fuckin creek or lose it, mate. Fence that loop or say goodbye.'

'Well,' Cashin said, 'you'd be mad to buy the place. House needs work, ground's all uphill.'

Millane shook his head. 'Seen what they're payin for dirt? Every second dickhead wants to live in the country, drive around in the four-wheel, fuckin up the roads, moanin about the cowshit and the ag chemicals.'

'No time to read the real estate,' Cashin said. 'Too busy upholding the law. Still need someone to take the cows over to Coghlans?'

'Yeah. Knee's getttin worse.'

'Got someone for you.'

'There's a bit of other work, say three days, that's all up. No place to stay, though.'

'I'll bring him over.'

Den was watching the dogs investigating a blackberry patch. 'So when you gonna leave the fancy dogs with me again?'

'Didn't like to ask,' Cashin said. 'Bit of a handful.'

'I can manage the fuckin brutes. Bring em over. Lookin thin, give em a decent feed of bunny.'

They said goodbye. When Cashin was fifty metres away, Den shouted, 'Ya keep what's bloody yours. Hear me?'

THE CALL came at 8.10 am, relayed from Cromarty. Cashin was almost at the Port Monro intersection. As he drove along the coast highway, he saw the ambulance coming towards him. He slowed to let them reach the turn-off first, followed them up the hill, around the bends and through the gates of The Heights, parked on the forecourt.

A woman was standing on the gravel, well away from the big house, smoking a cigarette. She threw it away and led the paramedics up the stairs into the house. Cashin followed, across an entrance hall and into a big, high-ceilinged room. There was a faint sour smell in the air.

The old man was lying on his stomach before the massive fireplace, head on the stone hearth. He was wearing only pyjama pants, and his thin naked back was covered with dried blood through which could be seen dark horizontal lines. There was blood pooled on the stones and soaked into the carpet. It was black in the light from a high uncurtained window.

The two medics went to him, knelt. The woman put her gloved hands on his head, lifted it gently. 'Significant open head injury, possible brain herniation,' she said, talking to her companion and into a throat mike.

She checked the man's breathing, an eye, held up his forearm. 'Suspected herniation,' she said. 'Four normal saline, hyperventilate 100 per cent, intubation indicated, 100 mils Lidocaine.'

Her partner set up the oxygen. He got in the way and Cashin couldn't see what was happening.

After a while, the female medic said, 'Three on coma scale. Chopper, Dave.'

The man took out a mobile phone.

'The door was open,' said the woman who had been waiting on the steps. She was behind Cashin. 'I only went in a step, backed off, thought he was dead, I wanted to run, get in the car and get out of there. Then I thought, oh shit, he might be alive and I came back and I saw he was breathing.'

Cashin looked around the room. In front of a door in the left corner, a rug on the polished floorboards was rucked. 'What's through there?' he said, pointing.

'Passage to the south wing.'

A big painting dominated the west wall, a dark landscape seen from a height. It had been slashed at the bottom, where a flap of canvas hung down.

'He must have gone to bed early, didn't use even half the wood Starkey's boy brought in,' she said.

'See anything else?'

'His watch's not on the table. It's always there with the whisky glass on the table next to the leather chair. He had a few whiskies every night.'

'He took his watch off?'

'Yeah. Left it on the table every night.'

'Let's talk somewhere else,' Cashin said. 'These people are busy.'

He followed her across a marble-floored foyer to a passage around a gravelled courtyard and into a kitchen big enough for a hotel. 'What did you do when you got here?' he said.

'I just put my bag down and went through. Do that every day.'

'I'll need to take a look in the bag. Your name is…?'

'Carol Gehrig.' She was in her forties, pretty, with blonded hair, lines around her mouth. There were lots of Gehrigs in the area.

She fetched a big yellow cloth bag from a table at the far end of the room, unzipped it. 'You want to dig around?'

'No.'

She tipped the contents onto the table: a purse, two sets of keys, a glasses case, makeup, tissues, other innocent things.

'Thanks,' Cashin said. 'Touch anything in there?'

'No. I just put the bag down, went to the sitting room to fetch the whisky glass. Then I rang. From outside.'

Now they went outside. Cashin's mobile rang.

'Hopgood. What's happening?' He was the criminal investigation unit boss in Cromarty.

'Charles Bourgoyne's been bashed,' he said. 'Badly. Medics working on him.'

'I'll be there in a few minutes. No one touches anything, no one leaves, okay?'

'Gee,' Cashin said. 'I was going to send everyone home, get everything nice and clean for forensic.'

'Don't be clever,' said Hopgood. 'Not a fucking joking matter this.'

Carol Gehrig was sitting on the second of the four broad stone steps that led to the front door. Cashin took the clipboard and went to sit beside her. Beyond the gravel expanse and the box hedges, a row of tall pencil pines was moving in the wind, swaying in unison like a chorus line of fat-bellied dancers. He had driven past this house hundreds of times and never seen more than the tall, ornate chimneys, sections of the red pantiled roof. The brass plate on a gate pillar said The Heights, but the locals called it Bourgoyne's.

'I'm Joe Cashin,' he said. 'You'd be related to Barry Gehrig.'

'My cousin.'

Cashin remembered his fight with Barry Gehrig in primary school. He was nine or ten. Barry won that one, he made amends later. He sat on Barry's shoulders and ground his pale face into the playground dirt.

'What happened to him?'

'Dead,' she said. 'Drove his truck off a bridge thing near Benalla. Overpass.'

'I'm sorry. Didn't hear about that.'

'He was a deadshit, always drugged up. I'm sorry for the people in the car he landed on, squashed them.'

She found cigarettes, offered. He wanted one. He said no.

'Worked here long?'

'Twenty-six years. I can't believe it. Seventeen when I started.'

'Any idea what happened?'

'Not a clue. No.'

'Who might attack him?'

'I'm saying, no idea. He's got no enemies, Mr B.'

'How old is Mr Bourgoyne?'

'Seventy something. Seventy-five, maybe.'

'Who lives here? Apart from him?'

'No one. The step-daughter was here the day before yesterday. Hasn't been here for a long time. Years.'

'What's her name?'

'Erica.'

'Know how to contact her?'

'No idea. Ask Mrs Addison in Port Monro, the lawyer. She looks after business for Mr Bourgoyne.'

'Anyone else work here?'

'Bruce Starkey.'

Cashin knew the name. 'The football player?'

'Him. He does all the outside.' She waved at the raked gravel, the trimmed hedges. 'Well, now his boy Tay does. Bit simple, Tay, never says a word. Bruce sits on his arse and smokes mostly. They come Monday, Wednesday and Friday. And when he drives Mr B. Sue Dance makes lunch and dinner. Gets here about twelve, cooks lunch, cooks dinner, leaves it for him to heat up. Tony Crosby might as well be on a wage too, always something wrong with the plumbing.'

The male paramedic came out. 'There's a chopper coming,' he said. 'Where's the best place to land?'

'The paddock behind the stables,' said Carol. 'At the back of the house.'

'How's he doing?' Cashin said.

The man shrugged. 'Probably should be dead.'

He went back inside.

'Bourgoyne's watch,' said Cashin. 'Know what kind it was?'

'Breitling,' said Carol. 'Smart watch. Had a crocodile-skin strap.'

'How do you spell that?'

'B-R-E-I-T-L-I-N-G.'

Cashin went to the cruiser, got Hopgood again. 'They're taking him to Melbourne. You might want to have a yarn with a Bruce Starkey and his young fella.'

'What about?'

'They're both part-time here.'

'So?'

'Thought I'd draw it to your attention. And Bourgoyne's watch's probably stolen.' He told him what Carol had said.

'Okay. Be there in a couple of minutes. There's three cars coming. Forensic can't get a chopper till about 10.30.'

'The step-daughter needs to be told,' Cashin said. 'She was here the day before yesterday. You can probably get an address from Cecily Addison in Port Monro, that's Woodward, Addison & Cameron.'

'I know who Cecily Addison is.'

'Of course.'

Cashin went back to Carol. 'Lots of cops coming,' he said. 'Going to be a long morning.'

'I'm paid for four hours.'

'Should be enough. What was he like?'

'Fine. Good boss. I knew what he wanted, did the job. Bonus at Christmas. Month's pay.'

'No problems?'

Eyes on him, yellow flecks in the brown. 'I keep the place like a hospital,' she said. 'No problems at all.'

'You wouldn't have any reason to try to kill him, would you?'

Carol made a sound, not quite a laugh. 'Me? Like I'd kill my job? I'm a late starter, still got two kids on the tit, mate. There's no work around here.'

They sat on the steps in the still enclosure, an early winter morning, quiet, just birdsounds, cars on the highway, and a coarse tractor somewhere.

'Jesus,' said Carol, 'I feel so, it's just getting to me … I could make us some coffee.'

Cashin was tempted. 'Better not,' he said. 'Can't touch anything. They'd come down on me like a tanker of pigshit. But I'll take a smoke off you.'

Weakness, smoking. Life was weakness, strength was the exception. Their smoke hung in sheets, golden where it caught the sun.

A sound, just a pinprick at first. The dickheads, thought Cashin. They were coming with sirens.

'Cromarty cops'll take a full statement, Carol,' he said. 'They'll be in charge of this but ring me if there's anything you want to talk about, okay?'

'Okay.'

They sat.

'If he lives,' said Cashin, 'it's because you got to work on time.'

Carol didn't say anything for a while. 'Reckon I'll keep getting paid?'

'Till things are settled, sure.'

They listened to the sirens coming up the hill, turning into the driveway, getting louder. Three squad cars, much too close together, came into the forecourt, braked, sent gravel flying.

The passenger door of the first car opened and a middle-aged man got out. He was tall, dark hair combed back. Senior Detective Rick Hopgood. Cashin had met him twice, civil exchanges. He walked towards them. Cashin stood.

The whupping of a helicopter, coming out of the east.

'End of shift,' said Hopgood. 'You can get back to Port.'

Irrational heat behind his eyes. Cashin wanted to punch him. He didn't say anything, looked for the chopper, walked around the house to the far hedge and watched it settle on the paddock, a hard surface, a dry autumn in a dry year. The local male medic was waiting. Three men got out, unloaded a stretcher. They went around the stables and into the house through a side door.

'Take offence?'

Hopgood, behind him.

'At what?' said Cashin.

'Didn't mean to be short,' said Hopgood.

Cashin looked at him. Hopgood offered a smile, yellowing teeth, big canines.

'No offence taken,' said Cashin.

'Good on you,' said Hopgood. 'Draw on your expertise if needed?'

'It's one police force,' said Cashin.

'That's the attitude,' said Hopgood. 'Be in touch.'

The medics came out with the stretcher, tubes in Bourgoyne. They didn't hurry. What could be done had been done. After the stretcher was loaded, the local woman said a few words to one of the city team, both impassive. He would be the doctor.

The doctor got in. The machine rose, turned for the metropolis, flashed light.

Cashin said goodbye to Carol Gehrig, drove down the curving avenue of Lombardy poplars.

'CAUGHT HIM yet?'

'Not as far as I know, Mrs Addison,' said Cashin. 'How did you hear?'

'The radio, my dear. What's happening to this country? Man attacked in his bed in the peaceful countryside. Never used to happen.'

Cecily Addison was in her after-lunch position in front of the fireplace in her office, left hand waving a cigarette, right hand touching her long nose, her brushed-back white hair. Cecily had been put out to graze in Port Monro by her firm in Cromarty. She arrived at work at 9.30 am, read the newspapers, drank the first of many cups of tea, saw a few clients, mostly about wills, bothered people, walked home for lunch and a few glasses of wine.

On the way back to the office, she dropped in on anyone who wasn't quick enough to disappear.

'Sit down,' she said. 'Don't know what the world's coming to. Read the paper today?' She pointed at her desk.

Cashin reached for the Cromarty *Herald*. The front-page headlines said:

ANGER MOUNTS
ON CRIME WAVE
Community calls for curfew

'Curfew, mind you,' said Cecily. 'That's not the way we want to go. Can't have Neighbourhood Watch calling the shots. Old buggers with nothing better to do than stickybeak. Neighbourhood bloody Nazis.'

Cashin read the story. Outrage at public meeting. Call for curfew on teenagers. Epidemic of burglaries and car thefts. Five armed robberies in two months. Sharp rise in assaults. Shop windows broken in the Whalers Mall. Lawless element in community. Time for firm action.

'Aimed at the Abos,' said Cecily, 'always is. Every few years they get on to it again. You'd think the white trash were all at choir practice of a Saturday night. I can tell you, forty-four years in the courts in Cromarty, I've seen more Abos fitted up than I've had hot dinners.'

'Not by the police, surely?' said Cashin.

Cecily laughed herself into a coughing fit. Cashin waited.

'I hate to say this,' Cecily said, taking the newspaper. 'Don't mind telling you I've voted Liberal all my life. But since this rag changed hands its mission in life is to get the Libs back in Cromarty. And that means bagging blacks every chance they get.'

'Interesting,' said Cashin. 'I want to ask you about Charles Bourgoyne. I gather you pay his bills.'

Cecily didn't want to change the subject.

'Never thought I'd say something like that,' she said. 'Hope my dad's not listening. You know Bob Menzies didn't have a house to live in when he left Canberra?'

'I didn't know that, no. I'm a bit short of time.'

A lie. Cashin knew how hard the ex-Prime Minister had done it because Cecily told him the story once or twice a month.

'Paid for his own phone calls, Bob Menzies. Sitting up there in the Lodge in Canberra, when he rang his old mum, he put a coin in a box. Little money box. When it was full, he gave it to Treasury. Went into general revenue. Catch today's pollies doing that? Take a coin out more likely. Rorters and shicers to a man. Did I tell you they wanted me to stand for Parliament? Told em, thanks very much, I'm already paid for being involved with crooks.'

'Charles Bourgoyne,' said Cashin. 'I've come about him. You pay his bills.'

Cecily blinked. 'Indeed I do. Known Charles for a very long time. Clients of the firm, Dick and Charles, Bourgoyne & Cromie, we did all their work.'

'Bourgoyne & Cromie's a bit before my time. Who's Dick?'

'Charles's dad. Bit of a playboy, Dick, but he ran the firm like a corner shop, argue the toss over a couple of quid. Not that he needed to. Go anywhere in this country, all the Pacific, bloody New Zealand, B&C engines everywhere. Put the lights on all over the outback. Powered the shearing stands, made a mint after the war, I can tell you. Whole world crying out for generators.'

'What happened?'

'Dick kicked the bucket and Charles sold the business to these Pommy bastards. They never intended to keep the factory going. Just wanted to cut out the competition.'

Cecily was staring out of the window, smoke curling through her fingers. 'Tragedy,' she said. 'I remember the day they told everyone. Half Cromarty out of work at one fell swoop. Never worked again, most of them.'

She scratched where an eyebrow had been. 'Still, can't blame Charles. They gave him assurances. No one blamed him.'

'About the bills.'

'Bills, yes. Since old Percy Crake had his stroke. Attend to matters on his behalf. Not that Charles couldn't do it himself. Just likes to pretend he's got better things to do.'

Cecily took a final vicious drag on her cigarette and, without looking, inserted the butt into the vase of flowers on the mantelpiece. A hiss, the sound of silk brushing silk. Mrs McKendrick, her ancient secretary, put flowers in the two rooms twice a week, first emptying urns full of foul beer-dark water and Cecily's swollen cigarette ends.

'Who'd try to kill him?' said Cashin.

'Some passing hoon, I suppose. Country's turning into America. Kill people for a few dollars, kill them for nothing. Thrills.' A bulge moved in her cheeks, suggested something trying to escape. 'Drugs,' she said. 'I blame it on drugs.'

'What about close to home? Someone who knew him?'

'Around here? If Charles Bourgoyne departs, it'll be the biggest funeral since old Dora Campbell kicked it, now that was a send-off. A lovely man, Charles Bourgoyne, lovely. They don't make gentlemen like that any more. He was a catch, I can tell you. Still, the girls all had long teeth by the time he married Susan Kingsley. They say old Dick told him to get married or kiss the fortune goodbye. Said he'd give it to the Cromarty old-age home.'

'What happened to Erica's father?'

'Erica and Jamie's father. Bobby Kingsley. Car smash. Had another woman with him unfortunately.'

'Charles have enemies?'

'Well, who knows? Bourgoyne Trust's put hundreds of kids through uni. Plus Charles shells out to anyone comes along. Schools, art gallery, the Salvos, the RSL, you name it. Bailed out the footy club umpteen times.'

'How does attending to Bourgoyne matters work?'

'Work?'

'The mechanics of it.'

'Oh. Well, all the bills come here, credit card, everything. Every month, we send Charles a statement, he ticks them off, sends it back, we pay them out of a trust account. Pay the wages too.'

'So you've got a record of all his financial dealings?'

'Just his bills.'

'From how far back?'

'Not long. I suppose it's seven, eight years. Since Crake's stroke.'

'Can I see your records?'

'Confidential,' she said. 'Between solicitor and client.'

'Client's been bashed and left for dead,' said Cashin.

Cecily blinked a few times. 'Not going to get me in trouble with the Law Institute this? Don't want to have to ask bloody Rees for advice.'

'Mrs Addison, it's what you have to do. If you don't, we'll get a court order today.'

'Yes,' she said, 'I suppose that changes things a bit. I'll tell Mrs McKendrick to make copies. Can't see what help it'll be. You should be out looking for bloody druggies. What's stolen from the house?'

'The people who work at Bourgoyne's,' said Cashin, 'what about their pay now?'

Cecily raised her pencilled eyebrows. 'He's not dead, you know. They'll be paid until someone instructs me to stop. What would you expect?'

Cashin got up. 'The worst. That's what police life teaches you.'

'Cynical, Joe. In my experience, and I say that with …'

'Thank you, Mrs Addison. I'll send someone for the copies. Where's Jamie Bourgoyne?'

'Drowned in Tasmania. Years ago.'

'Not a lucky family then.'

'No. Money can't buy it. And it ends if Charles dies. The line's broken. The Bourgoyne line's ended.'

The street was quiet, sunlight on the pale stone of the library. It had been the Mechanics' Institute when it opened in the year carved above the door: 1864. Three elderly women were going up the steps, in single file, left hands on the metal balustrade. He could see their delicate ankles. Old people were like racehorses – too much depending on too little, the bloodline the critical factor.

The Cashin bloodline didn't bear thinking about.

'I CAN'T fix stuff like this for you, Bern,' said Cashin. 'I can't fix anything. Sam's in shit because he's bad news and now he has to cop it.'

They were in a shed like an aircraft hangar at his cousin Bern Doogue's place outside Kenmare, a town twenty kilometres from Port Monro with a main street of boarded-up shops, two lingering pubs, a butcher, a milk bar and a video hire.

Farmland had once surrounded the village of Kenmare like a green sea. Long backyards had run down to paddocks with milk cows oozing dung, to potato fields dense with their pale grenades. Then the farms were subdivided. Hardiplank houses went up on three-acre blocks, big metal sheds out the back. Now the land produced nothing but garbage and children, many with red hair. The blocks were weekend parking lots for the big rigs that rumbled in from every direction on Saturdays – Macks, Kenworths, Mans, Volvos, eighteen-speed transmission, 1800-litre tank, the owners' names in flowery script on the doors, the unshaven, unslept drivers sitting two metres off the ground, spaced out and listening to songs of lost love and loneliness.

The truckies had bought their blocks when land was cheap, fuel was cheap, freight rates were good and they were young and paunchless. Now they couldn't see their pricks without a mirror, the trucks sucked fifty-dollar notes, the freight companies screwed them till they had to drive six days, some weeks seven, to make the repayments.

Cashin stood in the shed door and watched Bern splitting wood on his new machine, a red device that stood on splayed legs like a moon lander. He picked up a section of log, dropped it on the table against a thick steel spike, hit the trigger with a boot. A hydraulic ram slammed a splitter blade into the wood, cleaving it in half.

'Well, Jesus,' said Bern, 'what's the use of havin a fuckin copper in the family, I ask you.'

'No use at all,' Cashin said.

'Anyway, it's not like it's Sam's idea. He's with these two Melbourne kids, city kids, the one breaks the fuckin car window with a bottle.'

'Bern, Sam's got Buckley's. I'll ring a lawyer, she's good, she'll keep him out of jail.'

'What's that gonna cost? Fuckin arm?'

'It'll cost what it costs. Otherwise, tell him to ask for the duty solicitor. Where'd you get this wood?'

Bern put fingers under his filthy green beanie, exposed his black widow's peak, scratched his scalp. He had the Doogue nose – big, hooked. It was unremarkable in youth, came with age to dominate the male faces.

'Joe,' he said, 'is that a cop kind of question?'

'I don't care a lot about wood crime. It's good-looking stuff.'

'Fuckin prime beef, mate. Beefwood. Not your rotten Mount Gambier shit.'

'How much?'

'Seventy.'

'Find your own lawyer.'

'That's a special fuckin family price. Mate, this stuff, it runs out the fuckin door.'

'Let it run,' Cashin said. 'Got to go.' He walked.

'Hey, hey, Jesus, Joe, don't be so fuckin difficult.'

'Say hello to Leeane for me,' Cashin said. 'Christ knows what she did to deserve you. Must be something in another life.'

'Joe. Mate. Mate.'

Cashin was at the door. 'What?'

'Give and take, mate.'

'Haven't been talking to my mum, have you?'

'Nah. Your mum's too good for us. How's sixty, you tee up the lawyer? Split, delivered, that's fuckin cost, no labour, I'm takin a knock.'

'Four for two hundred,' Cashin said. 'Neatly stacked.'

'Shit, takin food out of your own family's mouths. He's up next week Wednesday.'

'I'll ring with an appointment time.'

Bern smacked on another log, stamped on the trigger. There was a bang, bits of wood went everywhere. 'Fuck,' he said. He pulled a big wood sliver out of the front of his greasy army surplus jumper.

'This place's a model of workplace safety,' Cashin said. 'Be on my way.'

He went out into the grey day, into Bern's two-acre backyard, a grave-yard of cars, utes, trucks, machinery, windows, doors, sinks, toilet bowls, basins, second-hand timber, bricks. Bern followed him to his vehicle, parked in a clearing.

'Listen, Joe, there's somethin else,' he said. 'Debbie says the Piggot kid, I forget his name, there's hundreds of em, she says he's sellin stuff at school.'

Cashin got in, wound down the window. 'Got something against drugs, Bern? Since when?'

Bern screwed up his eyes, scratched his head through the beanie with black-rimmed nails. 'That's totally fuckin different, we're talking about sellin hard stuff to kids here.'

'Why'd she tell you?'

'Well, not me. Told her mum.'

'Why?'

Bern cleared his throat and spat, bullethole lips, a sound like a peashooter. 'Leeane found some stuff. Not Debbie's, just holdin it for this other girl bought it from a Piggot.'

Cashin started the vehicle. 'Bern,' he said, 'you don't want your cousin the cop cracking down on teenage drug-taking in Kenmare. Think about it. Think about the Piggots. There's an army of them.'

Bern thought about it. 'Yeah, well, that's probably the strength of it. Mark me for the dog straight off, wouldn't the bastards. Boong dog. Mind you, comes to Doogues against Piggots, they wouldn't take a round off us.'

'We don't want it to come to that. I'll call you.'

'Wait, wait. You can do somethin else for me.'

'What?'

'Put the hard word on Debbie. She won't listen to her mum and I'm a fuckin non-starter.'

'I thought she was just holding the stuff?'

Bern shrugged, looked away. 'To be on the safe side,' he said. 'Can't hurt, can it?'

Cashin knew there was no way out. Next he would be reminded of how Bern had risked death by jumping onto the back of mountainous, cretinous Terry Luntz and hung on like a chimp on a gorilla, choking the school bully with a skinny forearm until he relaxed his deadly squeeze.

'What time's she get back from school?' Cashin said.

'About four.'

'I'll come round one day, point out the dangers.'

'You're a good bloke, Joe.'

'No, I'm not. I just don't want to hear about fucking Terry Luntz again. He would've let me go.'

Bern smiled his sly, dangerous Doogue smile. 'Never. Blue in the face, tongue stickin out the side of your mouth. You had fuckin seconds left.'

'In that case, what took you so long?'

'Prayin for guidance, mate. What excuse you cunts got for takin so long to catch our beloved Mr Charlie Bourgoyne's killer?'

'The victim's not being squeezed by a fat boy. There's no hurry. What've you got against Bourgoyne?'

'Nothin. The local saint. Everyone loves Charlie. Rich and idle. You know my dad used to work there, Bourgoyne & Cromie? Charlie sold it out under em. Shot the fuckin horse.'

Cashin passed three vehicles on the way home, knew them all. At the last crossroads, two ravens pecking at vermilion sludge turned on him the judgmental eyes of old men in a beaten pub.

IT WAS darkening when Cashin reached home, the wind ruffling the trees on the hill, strumming the corrugated iron roof. He got the fire going, took out a six-pack of Carlsberg, put on *L'elisir d'amore*, Donizetti, sank into the old chair, cushion in the small of his back. Tired in the trunk, hurting in the pelvis, pains down his legs, he swallowed two aspirins with the first swig of beer.

Life's short, son, don't drink any old piss.

Singo's advice, Singo always drank Carlsberg or Heineken.

Cashin sat and drank, stared at nothing, hearing Domingo, thinking about Vickie, about the boy. Why had she called him Stephen? Stephen would be nine now, Cashin could make the calculation, he knew the day, the night, the moment. And he had never spoken to him, never touched him, never been closer than twenty metres to him. Vickie would not bring him to the hospital when Cashin asked her to. 'He's got a father and it isn't you,' she said.

Nothing moved her.

All he wanted was to see him, talk to him. He didn't know why. What he knew was that the thought of the boy ached in him like his broken bones.

At 7 pm, on the second beer, he put on the television.

In what is feared to be another drug underworld killing, a 50-year-old Melbourne accountant, Andrew Gabor, of Kew, was this morning shot dead in front of his fifteen-year-old daughter outside exclusive St Theresa's girls' school in Malvern.

Footage of a green BMW outside the school, men in black overcoats beside it. Cashin recognised Villani, Birkerts, Finucane.

Two gunmen fled the scene in a Ford Transit van, later found in Elwood.

A van being winched onto the police flatbed tow truck to be taken to the forensic science centre.

Police appealed to anyone who saw two men wearing dark clothing and base-ball caps in the van or at or near the scene around 7.30 am to contact CrimeStoppers.

*It is believed that police today questioned Mr Gabor's nephew, Damian
Gabor, a rave party and rock concert entrepreneur. In 2002, Mr Gabor was
found not guilty of assaulting Anthony Metcalf, a drug dealer later found
dead in a rubbish skip in Carnegie. He had been shot seven times.*

On the monitor behind the news reader Cashin saw The Heights filmed
from the television helicopter, vehicles all over the forecourt, the search of
the grounds in progress.

*Following another crime of violence, the seventy-six-year-old head of one of
the state's best-known families is tonight fighting for his life in an intensive-
care unit after being brutally assaulted at his home outside Cromarty.*

*Charles Bourgoyne was this morning found near death in the sitting room
of the family mansion. He was flown to King George's Hospital by helicopter.*

*Mr Bourgoyne, noted for his philanthropy, is the son of Richard Bourgoyne,
one of the founders of Bourgoyne & Cromie, legendary engine manufacturers.
Charles Bourgoyne sold the family firm to British interests in 1976. His twin
older brothers both died in World War II, one of them executed by the Japanese.*

*Homicide investigators believe Mr Bourgoyne, who was alone in the house,
may have been the victim of a burglary turned vicious. Items of value are
missing from the house.*

Hopgood on camera, outside The Heights, wind moving his straight hair.

'This is a savage attack on a much-loved and defenceless man.

*We are committing all our resources to find those responsible for this terrible
act and we appeal to anyone with information to come forward.'*

*King George's Hospital tonight said that Mr Bourgoyne's condition was
critical.*

Cashin reached for the envelope with the business statements from
Cecily Addison. This has nothing to do with me, he thought. I'm the station
commander in Port Monro, staff of four.

Old habits, curiosity. He started with the most recent statement. Then he
heard the name.

*Australia's newest political party, United Australia, today elected lawyer and
Aboriginal activist Bobby Walshe to lead it into the federal election.*

Cashin looked at the television.

*The new party, a coalition of Greens, Democrats and independents that has
drawn support from disaffected Labor and Liberal supporters, will field candi-
dates in all electorates.*

Bobby Walshe appeared on camera. Handsome, sallow, hawk-nosed, just a hint of curl in his dark hair.

'It's a great honour for me to be chosen by so many dedicated and talented people to lead United Australia. This is a watershed day. From now on, Australians have a real political choice. The time when many Australians saw voting for one of the small parties as a waste of a vote are over. We're not small. We're not single-issue. We offer a real alternative to the tired, copycat policies of the two political machines that have dominated our political lives for so long.'

Bobby Walshe had been the smartest kid in Cashin's class at primary school and that hadn't stopped him being called a boong and a coon and a nigger.

The Bourgoyne payment statements didn't make any sense. Cashin's attention wandered, he put them back in the file, opened another drink and thought about what to eat.

THE HILL was lost in morning mist, a damp silence on the land. Cashin took a route towards the Corrigan boundary, visibility no more than thirty metres, the dogs appearing and disappearing, bounding patches of dark in the pale-grey world.

At the fence, there was a path, overgrown. He had walked it often as a boy, it was the direct way to the creek. In childhood memory, the creek was more like a river – broader, deeper, thrillingly dangerous in flood. The dogs were behind him when he made his way through the vegetation, crossed the puddles. On the other side, he whistled for them and they rushed by and led the way up the slope to the old Corrigan house.

Trespassing, Cashin thought.

The dogs had their heads down, a new place, new scents, interested-puzzled flicks of tails. He walked around the house, looked through the windows. Doors, skirting boards, floorboards, mantelpieces, tiles – all seemed intact. The place hadn't been looted like Tommy Cashin's ruined house. If there were new owners, they wouldn't need to spend much to get it liveable.

They walked through the yellow grass as far as Den Millane's fence, went down. Above the creek, Cashin found the remains of a fence, rusted wire, a few grey and riven posts lying down, possibly the boundary Den talked about. It was around two hundred metres, a bit more perhaps.

Did he want to claim this line?

Ya keep what's bloody yours.

Yes, he did want to claim it.

He walked across the creek, down the narrow twisting path through the poplars, into the rabbit grounds, then turned for home. It was fully light when they approached the house, but still an hour before the sun would burn off the mist. He was thinking about Kendall. What did being raped do to you? A male cop, off-duty, had been grabbed by three men in Sydney, out in the western suburbs, taken to an old drive-in. They handcuffed him to a screen pylon, cut off his jeans with a Stanley knife, carved swastikas into his buttocks, his back.

Then they raped him.

A cop called Gerard told Cashin the story one night, in the car. They were parked, eating kebabs.

The bloke never came back to work. Went to Darwin. They say he topped himself up there.

Gerard, dark-faced and handsome, dead-black hair, a mole on his cheek.

Got the cunts but. Done it through a ring, big fucking stupid lead thing, home-made ring. Melted sinkers. The cop could draw it.

What'd they get?

Death penalty. The one drowned in the river. Homebush. Other two, murder-suicide. Very ugly scene.

Gerard had smiled. When he smiled he showed some inner-lip, an intimate colour, vaginal.

Before Cashin did, the dogs saw Rebb sitting on the old garden bench. They charged.

Rebb was smoking a hand-rolled, flat, as much paper as tobacco. He was shaven, hair damp.

The dogs were all wag and twist, they liked Rebb, but then they liked most people.

'Put stuff in the wash machine,' Rebb said, cigarette in the corner of his mouth, a big hand for each dog. 'That okay?'

'Any time,' said Cashin. 'Up early?'

'No.'

'I'll make some breakfast when I've showered.'

'Got food,' said Rebb. He didn't look at Cashin, he was intent on the dogs. He had said the same thing the night before.

'Scrambled eggs,' said Cashin. 'You make it for one, might as well make it for ten.'

When he was clean and dressed, he put cutlery, bread and butter, Vegemite, jam, on the table, cooked the food, found Rebb outside with the dogs. Rebb didn't eat like a swaggie. He kept his elbows at his sides, ate with his mouth closed, slowly, ate every morsel.

'Good,' he said. 'Thank you.'

'Fill up on the bread.'

Rebb cut a thick slice. He spread butter, put on a coal-dark seam of Vegemite.

'You can stay here if you like,' Cashin said. 'Won't cost you. Ten minutes' walk to the cow job.'

Rebb looked at him, nothing, black eyes. He nodded. 'Do that then.'

They drove around to Den Millane's, not a word spoken. Den heard them coming, he was at the gate. He shook hands with Rebb.

'Pay's nothin fancy,' he said. 'Do it myself, bloody knee wasn't crook. Know cows?'

'A bit, yeah.'

Cashin left them, drove to his mother's house, twenty minutes. The roads were thin strips of pot-holed bitumen, lacy at the edges, room for one vehicle, someone had to give way, put two wheels on the rutted verge. But, generally, both vehicles did, and local drivers raised their hands to each other. He passed potato fields and dairy farms where the sliding-jawed animals turned soft eyes. From Beacon Hill, the land sloped to the sea, peaty soil the colour of chocolate when ploughed, lying naked before the south-westerly wind and the wild winter gales off the Southern Ocean. Early settlers planted cypress trees and hedges as wind-breaks around their houses. It worked to some extent but the displaced wind took its revenge. Trees, shrubs, sheds, tanks, windmills, dunnies, dog kennels, chickenhouses, old car bodies – everything in its path sloped to leeward.

Cashin parked in the driveway, went around the back, saw his mother through the kitchen window. When he opened the back door, Sybil said, 'I've been thinking about you, living in that ruin. After what we put in with you kids, your dad and me.'

She was arranging flowers in a large squarish pottery jug, brown and purple. 'That vase,' Cashin said. 'Could that be a rejected prototype for storing nuclear waste?'

His mother ignored the question. Outside, his stepfather appeared from the shed, wearing white overalls, gloves, a full-face mask, a tank on his back. He began spraying the rose arbour. Mist drifted.

'Do the roses like Harry bombing them with Agent Orange?' Cashin said.

She stood back to admire her work, a small, trim woman, strong swept-back hair. All the size genes in Cashin and his brother, Michael, came from their father, Mick Cashin.

'Charles Bourgoyne,' she said. 'What are you doing about that?'

'Doing what can be done.'

'I'll never understand humans. Why didn't they just take what they wanted? Why did they have to bash an old man? What could he do to resist them?'

'I've given up on the understanding part,' said Cashin. 'The question you want answered isn't why, it's who.'

His mother shook her head. 'Well, on another matter,' she said, eyes on the arrangement, moving her fingers. 'Michael's bought a unit in Melbourne. Docklands. On the water. Two bedrooms, one-and-a-half bath-rooms.'

'A clean person, Michael,' said Cashin. 'Very clean. What do you do in the half bathroom?'

'Pour the tea,' she said. 'Just made.'

He poured tea into handmade mugs that tilted when at rest. His mother bought things at outdoor markets: terrible watercolour paintings, salt and pepper cellars in the shape of toadstools, placemats woven from plastic grocery bags, hats made of felted dog hair.

'Michael's in Melbourne so much he says he might as well have some-where to keep his clothes,' she said.

'The spare set of clothes that would be.'

31

His mother sighed. 'Give credit where it's due, that's what you haven't learned, Joseph.'

'Take credit where it's offered, I've learned that. Why do roses need that chemical shit Harry's spraying?'

'You never swore. Michael picked it up at school, the first day, came home and said a swearword. I went down there, gave that Killeen man a few words of my own. Never trusted him and proved right. Mother's instinct.'

'I should have learned to swear early,' said Cashin. 'By now I might have half a bathroom at Docklands. I'm going to fix up the house.'

'Are you mad? Why?'

'To live in. As a step up from living in a ruin.'

'It's haunted.' She shuddered in a theatrical way. 'Built by a madman. Leave it alone. You should sell it.'

'I like the place. I'm going to clear up the garden.'

'I thought this was temporary? For you to get better.'

Cashin finished his tea. 'Life's pretty temporary. How's uni?'

'Don't change the subject. I should have gone earlier. Wasted years.'

'Wasted how?'

She came to the kitchen table and patted his cheek twice, gave it a final sharp slap. 'I only want the best for you,' she said. 'You set your sights so low. The police force, I ask you. Stay here a moment longer than you need to, you'll be stuck forever. Game over.'

'Where do you get that from?'

'What?'

'Game over?'

'Old before your time,' she said. 'Why don't you sign up for a course at uni? Be among young people. Stay fresh.'

'I'll kill myself first,' Cashin said.

Sybil put fingers to his mouth. 'Don't say that. The closed mind. It's the older generation's supposed to have that.'

'Got to go,' he said. 'Be among young people. Arrest them.'

'Turn it into a joke, you get that from your father, that's pure Cashin. Even a tragedy's only a tragedy for five minutes, then it's a joke.'

They went out. Harry was misting the arbour, the cattle dog standing behind him, looking up, faithfully breathing in the fumes.

'So the dog's expendable?' said Cashin. 'Collateral damage.'

At the gate, his mother said, 'It's a pity you don't have children, Joseph. Children settle people down.'

The sentences stopped Cashin in his tracks, filled him with wonder. How could she of all people say that?

'How do you know I don't have children?' he said.

'Oh, you.' She held his arms and he bent to kiss her on the cheek. For many years, he could not kiss her.

'Did I ever tell you I thought you were going to be the bright one?' she said.

'I am the bright one,' he said. 'You're confusing me with the rich one. One of Bern's boys is in trouble in Melbourne.'

'It'll be that Sam, right?'

'Right.'

'What kind of trouble?'

'Theft from a parked car. Him and two others.'

'What can you do?'

'Nothing probably.'

'The Doogues. I always thank the Lord I've got no ties with them.'

'You're a Doogue. Bern is your nephew. He's your brother's son. How can you not have ties with them?'

'Ties, dear, ties. I don't have any ties with them.'

'Game over,' said Cashin. 'Bye, Syb.'

'Bye, darling.'

Harry waved a gloved hand at him, slowly, like a polar explorer saying a final sad goodbye.

DRIVING TO Port Monro on a cold day, overcast, Cashin thought about his mother in the caravan, saw her sitting at a fold-down table topped with marbled green Formica edged with an aluminium strip. She had a plastic glass in one hand, yellow wine in it, a cigarette in the other hand, a filter cigarette held close to her fingernails, which were painted pink, chipped. Her nose was peeling from sunburn. There were blonde sunstreaks in her hair and it was heavy with salt from swimming, pieces fallen apart, he could see her scalp. She drank from the glass and liquid ran out of her mouth, down her chin, fell on her teeshirt. She wiped her chest with her cigarette hand and the cigarette touched her face, the glowing tip dislodged, stuck to her shirt. She looked down at the burn opening like a flower. She seemed to wait forever, then she carefully tilted her glass, poured wine over it. He remembered the smells of burnt cotton and burnt skin and wine filling the small space and how he felt sick, went out into the sub-tropical night.

Some time after Cashin's father's death, he didn't know how long, his mother had packed two suitcases and they left the farm outside Kenmare. He was twelve. His brother was at university on his scholarship. At the first stop for petrol, his mother told him to call her Sybil. He didn't know what to say. People didn't call their mothers by their names.

They spent the next three years on the road, never staying anywhere for long. When he thought about those times later, Cashin realised that in the first year Sybil must have had money: they stayed in hotels and motels, in a holiday shack near the beach for a few months. Then she started taking jobs in pubs, roadhouses, all sorts of places, and they lived in rented rooms, granny flats in people's backyards, on-site caravans. In his memory, she always seemed to be drinking, always either laughing or crying. Sometimes she forgot to buy food and some nights she didn't come home till long after midnight. He remembered lying awake, hearing noises outside, trying not to be frightened.

The turn-off to Port Monro. Light rain falling.

Cashin's shift started at noon, there was time for coffee. He bought the paper at the service station, parked outside the Dublin, hadn't been there for a while. You couldn't go to the same place too often, people noticed.

The narrow room was empty, summer over, the long cold peace on the town. 'Medium black for the cop who pays,' said the man sitting behind the counter. 'My customer of the day.'

His name was Leon Gadney, a dentist from Adelaide whose male lover had been found knifed to death in a park near the river, possibly killed by one of the sexual crazies for which Adelaide was famous, possibly killed by policemen who thought the crazies were doing a public service when they killed homosexuals.

'You could close in winter,' said Cashin. 'Save on electricity.'

'What would I do?' said Leon.

'Go to Noosa, chat to other rich retired dentists. It's warm up there.'

'Fuck warm. And I'd like to go on record that I'm not a retired dentist. Ex-dentist, former dentist, now impoverished barista and short-order cook.'

He delivered the coffee. 'Want a nice almond bickie?'

'No, thanks. Watching the weight.'

Leon returned to his seat, lit a cigarette. 'In a certain light, you're not bad looking,' he said. 'And here we are, virile single men marooned on an island of old women in sandals.'

Cashin didn't look up. He was reading about police corruption in the city, in the drug squad. The members had been selling drugs they'd confiscated. They had originally supplied the ingredients to make the drugs. 'You're very distinguished, Leon,' he said. 'But I've got too much going on, I couldn't concentrate.'

'Well, think about it,' said Leon. 'I've got good teeth.'

Cashin went to work, dealt with a complaint from a man about a neighbour's tree, a report of a vandalised bench in the wetlands. A woman with a black eye came in – she wanted Cashin to warn her husband. At 2.15, the primary school rang to say a mother had seen someone lurking on the block across the road.

He parked a way from the school, went down a driveway and looked over the fence. High yellow grass. Someone had thrown a concrete slab and got no further, weeds covering the heap of building sand. There was a small shed, a panel van parked behind it.

Cashin walked back down the drive and onto the block, approached the vehicle. The windows were fogged glass, no one visible in the cab. He rapped on the roof with knuckles.

Silence. He bounced his fist.

'Fuck off!' A male.

'Police,' said Cashin.

The vehicle moved. He stood back and he could see a figure climbing over the bench seat. The driver's window came down a few centimetres: eyes, dark eyebrows, strands of black hair.

'Just takin a nap.'

'This your property, sir?' Cashin was showing his badge.

'I'm the builder.'

'Not much building going on.'

'Startin soon as he gets his finance.'

'You local, sir?'

'Cromarty.'

'I'd like you to step out of the vehicle, sir, and show me some ID.'

'Listen, takin a nap on a buildin job, what's the fuckin crime?'

'Out of the vehicle, please, sir. With your ID.'

The man turned, reaching backwards. Cashin saw skin colour, the man was half-naked, he was looking for his pants.

Cashin stood well back, hand inside his jacket, eased the gun in the clip.

The man moved, struggled, he couldn't get his pants on. 'Listen,' he said through the gap. 'Somethin a bit private goin on here, y'know. Gissus a break, will you?'

'Get out and put your pants on,' said Cashin. 'Sir.'

The door opened. A thin man, late twenties. He moved his legs out, open flannel shirt over a teeshirt, no shoes, hole in a red sock, one leg in his denims, stood in the weeds to pull them up, zip. He had a pimple on a thigh.

He reached inside, found a wallet, offered it. 'Driver's, credit, all kinds of shit.'

'Put it on the roof,' Cashin said, 'and stand against the shed.'

'Jesus, mate, I'm just a fuckin brickie.'

He obeyed. Cashin took the wallet, looked at cards. Allan James Morris, an address in Cromarty. He wrote it down. 'Phone number?'

He gave Cashin a mobile number.

'Now if you'll help the person with you get out, I'd like some ID there too,' said Cashin.

Morris walked back to the van, opened the back door, there was an exchange. A girl in jeans and a short pleated pink jacket got out. She was no more than fifteen, dark hair, pretty, it wouldn't last. Her lips were puffy, lipstick smeared.

'ID, please,' said Cashin.

She opened a wallet, offered a card. Cashin looked at it.

'Not you,' he said, flicked the card back across the bonnet. 'Got some real ID? We can do this at the station. Get your mum and dad in.'

She pouted, eye-flick to Morris, produced another card, school ID with a photograph: Stacey-Ann Gettigan.

'Fourteen, Stacey,' he said. 'In the back of a van with a grown man.'

'Just waggin,' she said. She folded her arms under her breasts. 'Not a crime.'

'What do you reckon, Allan?' Cashin said. 'Crime to be jumping a fourteen-year-old in your van?'

'Just kissin and that,' said Morris.

'Take your pants off to kiss? Kissing with your bum? You married, Allan?'

Morris scratched his head. He was in sunlight and Cashin saw dandruff motes fly into the still air. The girl was looking down, biting on a painted nail. 'Listen,' said Morris, 'no harm done, I swear.'

'Married, Allan?'

'Yeah. Sort of.'

'Sort of? They got that now? Do a sort of ceremony in church?'

Morris didn't want to look at Cashin. Cashin motioned to the girl to follow him. They went around the shed. He said, 'Got a complaint you'd like to make against this man, Stacey? Made you do something against your will? Threaten you? This's your chance.'

She closed her eyes, shook her head. 'No. Nothin.'

'Sure? I'm going to write all this down, that I asked you. Want to talk somewhere else, on your own? A woman cop?'

'No,' she said.

Cashin went back and beckoned to Morris, walked down the block a few paces. The man came, not easy in his skin, a rabbitty look. They stood in the weeds. White clouds moved across the pools of rain on the concrete slab.

'What's she to you, then?' said Cashin.

'Cousin, some kind, I dunno exactly.'

'Yeah?'

'She's on at me all the time, come to me work even. I done nothin. Today's the first … anyway, nothin happened. I swear.'

'Not Deke Gettigan's granddaughter, is she?'

Morris scratched his head with both hands as if suddenly attacked by lice. 'Mate, they'll fuckin kill me,' he said. 'Please, mate.'

'Don't bring any more kids here to root, Allan,' said Cashin. 'Nowhere near here. There's an alert on your van from now on. And you're not the builder here, are you?'

'Me mate, he's kind of, he's the …'

'You come down this way to do a bit of building, that's building I'm talking about, not fucking under-age girls, you let me know, Allan. Then I'll tell the school they don't have to worry about a man with his cock out, he's just having a piss. Okay?'

'Right, sure. Thanks.'

Cashin looked back as he walked away. The girl held his eyes. She knew she was out of this, he wasn't going to dob them, and she smiled at him, bold, sexual, ancient wisdom.

AT THE station, Carl Wexler came out of the front door making flexing bodybuilder's movements. He was a year out of the academy, not stupid, third in his course, but a city boy, resentful about being posted away from the action.

Cashin lowered his window.

'Cromarty rang, boss,' Wexler said. 'Senior Hopgood for you.'

Cashin went in and rang.

'Your mate Inspector Villani sends his love,' said Hopgood. 'How is it that wogs have taken over this force?'

'Natural selection,' said Cashin. 'Survival of the best dressed.'

'Yeah, well, he's given me the benefit of his wog opinions. He wants you to ring.'

Cashin didn't say anything. Hopgood put the phone down.

The city switch put Cashin straight through.

'How's retirement?' said Villani. 'I went down there once. Very nice. I hear the surfies call it the Blue Balls Coast.'

'Wimps,' Cashin said. 'What?'

'Joe, listen, this Bourgoyne was news to me but the media put that right. Then Commisioner Wicken yesterday explains to me how connected the step–daughter is, senior partner at Rothacker Julian, the Labor Party's legal wing.'

'That now carries some weight in a homicide?'

'I'm finding out all kinds of stuff. Today Mr Pommy Commissioner Wicken gives me hints on conducting myself in public. Fashion tips too. What suit, what shirt, what shoes. I enjoyed that so very much.'

'So?'

'I want you on this.'

'I'm the cripple running Port Monro now. Send that prick Allen.'

'Joe, we are thinner than the Durex Phantom. Jantz, Campbell and Maguire, all retired in one month. DePiero quit, Tozer's on stress leave, your mate Allen, his wife buggered off with a butcher from Vic Market, took the kids. Now he's found some mystical shit, living in the fucking moment. I wouldn't send him to a Buddhist domestic.'

A pause.

'Also,' said Villani, 'when the newspapers get down there in a few days, you'll see the former drug squad's criminal mates are again killing each other. The big boss woman's supposed to have sacked all the dirtbags and elevated the cleanskins but whoopy do, here we go again. So I've got a number of people committed to the utterly pointless shit of trying to find out which particular cunt killed some other cunt for whose death we should be grateful. As a city. As a state. A country. As a fucking world.'

'I think you're over-excited,' said Cashin. 'On Bourgoyne, what's to show for the forensic geniuses you had here?'

'Bugger all. The alarm was off. No break-in, no prints, no weapon. No strange DNA. Don't know what's gone except the watch. There's locked drawers broken open in the study and his bedroom.'

'And him?'

'It's likely to be murder. Lives, he's a cabbage.'

'Did you ever ask yourself why they hit on the cabbage? What about the carrot? How about the Brussels sprout?'

'Let's leave the philosophy for the pub, gentlemen.'

It was a Singo saying, from the time before Rai Sarris.

'So what am I supposed to do?' said Cashin.

'This Rothacker Julian connection, we need a senior officer on the job. I don't want any fuck-ups. I'm new in the tower, Joe, I can feel the wind. This'll end up some dumb *In Cold Blood* thing, I feel it in my dick, it's just the in-between shit we have to manage.'

'What about Cromarty?'

'Fuck them. This is the commissioner speaking.'

'And I say no?'

'Listen, son, you are still a member of homicide. You're a member on holiday. Remember duty?'

'Some things about it, yes.'

'I'm glad I don't have to say any more.'

'You arsehole.'

'Come around to my office and repeat that to a senior officer,' said Villani. 'First, a talk with Ms Bourgoyne, the step-daughter. She's been asked to go down and take a look, should be there in about an hour. Cromarty's opening the place.'

'She's been interviewed?'

'Not really. What we need is for you to be with her when she sees the house. Find out what was in the drawers, if she can see anything else missing, anything unusual while she was there, any ideas she can give us.'

'Sure you need a senior officer? Why don't you just give your marvellously detailed instructions to some prick from traffic?'

'Sorry, sorry, sorry. Jesus, don't be so touchy.'

'What about other family?'

'No one close. There was a step-son, Erica's brother. She says he drowned in Tassie a long time ago.'

'She says?'

'We'll verify that. Okay? We'll get some prick from traffic to check that out. Give him detailed instructions.'

'Just asking.'

CASHIN DROVE out to the Bourgoyne house, up the steep road from the highway, through the gates, down the winding poplar drive, and parked in the same place as before. The gravel showed the marks of many vehicles.

He parked and waited, listened to the radio, thought about being on the road with his mother, the other children he met, some of them feral kids, not going to school, beach urchins, the white ones burnt dark brown or freckled and always shedding pieces of papery skin. He thought about the boy who taught him to surf, in New South Wales, it might have been Ballina. Gavin was the boy's name. He offered the use of a board with a big piece out of it.

'Shark, mate,' said Gavin. 'Chewed the bloke in half. He don't need it no more, you can have a lend of it.' When they left, Gavin gave him the board. Where was Gavin now? Where was the board? Cashin had loved that board, covered the gap with tape.

I'm bored here, love. We're going.

His mother had said before every move further north.

Cashin got out of the car to stretch his spine, walked in a circle. A vehicle was coming.

A black Saab came around the bend, parked next to the cruiser. The driver eased himself out, a big man, cropped hair, wearing jeans and a leather jacket, open.

'Hi,' he said. 'John Jacobs, Orton Private Security Group. I'm ex-SOG. Mind if I see the ID?'

Police Special Operations Group membership was supposed to bestow some kind of divinity that transcended being kicked out for cowardice or for turning out to be a violent psychopath.

Cashin looked at the cruiser. 'That's my car. Your idea is I could be a dangerous person stole a cop car?'

'Don't take anything for granted,' Jacobs said. 'Used to be standard police practice.'

'Still is,' said Cashin. 'And I'm the one who asks for ID. Let's see it.'

Jacobs gave him a closed-lips smile, then a glint of left canine while he took out a plastic card with a photograph. Cashin took his time looking at it, looking at Jacobs.

'You're keeping the lady waiting,' said Jacobs. 'Need better light? Sure you don't want back-up?'

'What's your job today?' said Cashin.

'I'm looking after Ms Bourgoyne. What do you reckon?'

Cashin gave back the card. Jacobs went around the car and opened the passenger door. A woman got out, a blonde, tall, thin, the wind moved her long hair. She raised a hand to control it. Early forties, Cashin guessed.

'Ms Bourgoyne?'

'Yes.' She was handsome, sharp features, grey eyes.

'Detective Cashin. Inspector Villani spoke to you, I understand.'

'Yes.'

'Do you mind if we have a look around? Without Mr Jacobs, if that's okay?'

'I don't know what to expect,' she said.

'It's always difficult,' said Cashin. 'But what we'll do is walk through the house. You have a good look, tell me if anything catches your eye.'

'Thank you. Well, let's go in the side door.'

She led the way around the verandah. On the east side was an expanse of raked gravel dotted with smooth boulders, ending in a clipped hedge. She opened a glass door to a quarry-tiled room with wicker chairs around low tables. There wasn't any sun but the room was warm.

'I'd like to get this over with as soon as possible,' said Erica.

'Of course. Did Mr Bourgoyne keep money on the premises?'

'I have no idea. Why would he?'

'People do. What's through that door?'

'A passage.'

She led the way into a wide passage. 'These are bedrooms and a sitting room,' she said and opened a door. Cashin went in and switched on the overhead light. It was a big room, curtains drawn, four pen-and-ink drawings in black frames on the walls. They were all by the same hand, suggestions of street scenes, severe, vertical lines, unsigned.

The bed was large, white covers, big pillows. 'There's nothing to steal here,' Erica said.

The next two rooms were near-identical. Then a bathroom and a small sitting room.

They went into the large hall, two storeys high, lit by a skylight. A huge staircase dominated the space. 'There's the big dining room and the small one,' said Erica.

'What's upstairs?'

'Bedrooms.'

Cashin looked into the dining rooms. They appeared undisturbed. At the door to the big sitting room, Erica stopped and turned to him.

'I'll go first,' he said.

The room smelled faintly of lavender and something else. The light from the high window lay on the carpet in front of where the slashed painting had hung. The bloodstain was hidden by a sheet of black plastic, taped down.

Cashin went over and opened the cedar armoire against the left wall: whisky, brandy, gin, vodka, Pimms, Cinzano, sherries, liqueurs of all kinds, wine glasses, cut-glass whisky glasses and tumblers, martini glasses.

A small fridge held soda water, tonic, mineral water. No beer.

'Do you know what was kept in the desk?'

The small slim-legged table with a leather top stood against a wall.

Erica shrugged.

Cashin opened the left-hand drawer. Writing pads, envelopes, two fountain pens, two ink bottles. Cashin removed the top pad, opened it, held it up to the light. No impressions. The other drawer held a silver paperknife, a stapler, boxes of staples, a punch, paperclips.

'Why didn't they take the sound stuff?' she said.

Cashin looked at the Swedish equipment. It had been the most expensive on the market once.

'Too big,' he said. 'Was there a television?'

'In the other sitting room. My step-father didn't like television much.'

Cashin looked at the shelves of CDs beside the player. Classical music. Orchestral. Opera, dozens of disks. He removed one, put it in the slot, pressed the buttons.

Maria Callas.

The room's acoustics were perfect. He closed his eyes.

'Is this necessary?' said Erica.

'Sorry,' said Cashin. He pushed the OFF button. The sound of Callas seemed to linger in the high dark corners.

They left the room, another passage.

'That's the study,' she said.

He went in. A big room, three walls covered with photographs in dark frames, a few paintings, and the fourth floor-to-ceiling books. The desk was a curve of pale wood on square dark pillars tapering to nothing. The chair was modern too, leather and chrome. A more comfortable-looking version stood in front of the window.

The drawer locks of two heavy and tall wooden cabinets, six drawers each, had been forced, possibly with a crowbar. They had been left as found on the morning.

'Any idea what was in them?' said Cashin.

'No idea at all.'

Cashin looked: letters, papers. He walked around the walls, looked at the photographs. They seemed to be arranged chronologically and, to his eye, span at least seventy or eighty years – family groups, portraits, young men in uniform, weddings, parties, picnics, beach scenes, two men in suits standing in front of a group of men in overalls, a building plaque being unveiled by a woman wearing a hat.

'Which one's your step-father?' he said.

Erica took him on a tour, pointed at a smiling small boy, a youth in school uniform, in cricket whites, in a football team, a thin-faced young man in a dinner jacket, a man in middle age shaking hands with an older man. Charles Bourgoyne had aged slowly and well, not losing a single brushed hair.

'Then there are the horses,' she said, pointing. 'Probably more important than the people in his life.'

A wall of pictures of horses and people with horses. Dozens of finishing-post photographs, some sepia, some tinted, a few in colour. Charles Bourgoyne riding, leading, stroking, kissing horses.

'Your mother,' said Cashin. 'Is she still alive?'

'No. She died when I was young.'

Cashin looked at the bookshelves: novels, history, biography, rows of books about Japan and China, their art, culture. Above them were books about World War II, the war against Japan, about Australian prisoners of the Japanese.

There were shelves of pottery books, technical titles, three shelves.

They moved on.

'This is his bedroom,' said Erica Bourgoyne. 'I've never been into it and I don't think I'll change that now.'

Cashin entered a white chamber: bed, table, simple table lamp, small desk, four drawers open. The lower ones had been broken open. Through a doorway was a dressing room. He looked at Bourgoyne's clothes: jackets, suits, shirts on hangers, socks and underwear in drawers, shoes on a rack. Everything looked expensive, nothing looked new.

There was a red lacquered cupboard. He opened it and a clean smell of cedar filled his nostrils. Silken garments on hangers, a shelf with rolled-up sashes.

He thought of asking Erica to come in.

No.

Beyond the dressing room was a bathroom, walls and floor of slate, a wooden tub, coopered like a barrel, a toilet, a shower that was just two stainless-steel perforated plates, one that water fell from, one to stand on. There were bars of pale yellow soap and throwaway razors, shampoo. He opened a plain wooden cupboard: three stacks of towels, six deep, bars of soap, bags of razors, toilet paper, tissues.

He went back to Erica. They looked at another bedroom, like a room in a comfortable hotel. It had a small sitting room with two armchairs, a fire-place. There was another bathroom, old-fashioned, revealing nothing. At the end of the passage was a laundry with a new-looking washing machine and dryer.

Beyond it was a storeroom, shelves of heavy white bed linen and table-cloths, napkins, white towels, cleaning equipment.

They went back the way they had come. 'There's another sitting room here,' said Erica. 'It's the one with the television.'

Four leather armchairs around a fireplace, a television on a shelf to the left, more Swedish sound equipment to the right. Cosy by the standards of this house, thought Cashin.

'Well,' said Cashin, 'that's it. We needn't go upstairs, I gather it's undisturbed.'

There was a moment when she looked at him, something uncertain in her eyes.

'I'd like to go up,' she said. 'Will you come with me?'

'Of course.'

They crossed the house to the entrance hall, walked side by side up a flight of broad marble stairs to a landing, up another flight. All the way, he shut down his face against the pain, did not wince. At the top, a gallery ran around the stairwell, six dark cedar doors leading off it, all closed. They stood on a Persian rug in a shaft of light from above.

'I want to get some things from my mother's room, if they're still there,' said Erica. 'I've never had the nerve before.'

'How long have you waited?'

'Almost thirty years.'

'I'll be here' said Cashin. 'Unless ...'

'No, that's fine.'

She went to the second door on the left. He saw her hesitate, open the six-panel door, put out a hand to a brass light switch, go in.

Cashin opened the nearest door and switched on the light. It was a bedroom, huge, twin beds with white covers, two wardrobes, a dressing table, a writing table in front of the curtained window. He walked on a pale pinkish carpet, lined like a quilt, and parted the curtains. The view was of a redbrick stable block and of treetops beyond, near-leafless, limbs moving in the wind, and then of a low hill stained with the russet leaves of autumn.

He went back to the gallery and went to the balustrade and looked down the stairwell at the entrance hall, felt a flash of vertigo, an urge to throw himself over the barrier.

'Finished,' said Erica behind him.

'Find what you wanted?'

'No,' she said. 'There's nothing there. It was stupid to think there might be.'

They went back to the sunroom and sat with a glass-topped table between them.

'Notice anything worth mentioning?' said Cashin.

'No. I'm sorry, I'm not much use. I'm pretty much a stranger in this house.'

'How's that?'

She looked at him sharply. 'Just the way it is, detective.'

'Everything locked at night, alarm switched on?' he said.

'I don't know. I haven't been here at night for a very long time.'

Time to move on. 'About your brother, Ms Bourgoyne.'

'He's dead.'

'He drowned, I'm told.'

'In Tasmania. In 1989.'

'Went for a swim?'

Erica shifted in her seat, crossed her legs in corduroy pants, twitched a shiny black boot. 'Presumably. His things were found on a beach. The body wasn't found.'

'Right. So you were here on Tuesday morning.'

'Yes.'

'Visit your step-father often?'

She rubbed palms. 'Often? No.'

'You don't get on?'

Erica pulled a face, looked much older, lined. 'We're not close. It's our family history. The way I grew up.'

'And the reason for this visit?'

'Charles wanted to see me.'

'Can you be more specific?'

'This is intrusive,' she said. 'Why do you need to know?'

'Ms Bourgoyne,' said Cashin, 'I don't know what we need to know. But if you want me to record that you preferred not to answer the question, that's fine. I will.'

She shrugged, not happy. 'He wanted to talk about his affairs.'

Cashin waited until it was clear that she wasn't going to say any more. 'On another subject. Who'll inherit?'

Widened eyes. 'No idea. What are you suggesting?'

'It's just a question,' Cashin said. 'You didn't discuss his will?'

A laugh. 'My step-father isn't the kind of person who would talk about his will. I doubt whether he's ever given dying a thought. It's for lesser beings.'

'Assuming that he knew the person who attacked him …'

'Why would you assume that?'

'One possible line of inquiry. Who might want to harm him?'

'As far as I know,' she said, 'he's a much respected person around here. But I don't live here, I haven't since … since I was a child. I've only been a visitor.'

She looked away. Cashin followed her gaze, looked out at the disciplined gravel that ran to the hedge. Nothing lifted the spirits about the grounds of The Heights – hedges, lawns, paving, gravel, they were all shades of green and grey. It came to him that there were no flowers.

'He had all the garden beds ripped out,' she said, reading his mind. 'They were wonderful.'

'A last thing. Do you know of anything in your step-father's life or your life that might have led to this?'

'Such as?'

'This may become a murder investigation.'

'What does that mean?'

'Nothing will be left private in the life of anyone around your step-father.'

She straightened, gave him the unfazed gaze. 'Are you saying I'll be a suspect?'

'Everyone will be of interest.'

'What about perfect strangers?' she said. 'Is there a chance that you might take an interest in perfect strangers who got into the house and attacked him?'

He wanted to echo her sarcastic tone. 'Every chance,' he said. 'But with no sign of forced entry, we have to consider other possibilities.'

'Well,' she said, looked at her watch, a slim silver band, 'I'd like to get going. Are you a local policeman?'

'I'm down here for as long as it takes.'

There was truth in this. There was some truth in almost anything people said.

'May I ask you why you brought the bodyguard?' said Cashin.

'It's a work-related thing. Just a precaution.' Erica stood up.

Cashin rose. 'You've been threatened?'

Erica held out her right hand. 'Work-related, detective. In my work, that makes it confidential. Goodbye.'

They shook hands. The ex-SOG man, Jacobs, walked onto the forecourt to see him go. In the mirror, Cashin saw him give a mocking wave, fingers fanned, right hand held just beside his tough-guy smile.

Cashin gunned the cruiser, showered Jacobs with gravel, saw him try to protect his face.

CASHIN DROVE out on the road behind Open Beach, turned at the junction with the highway, went back through Port Monro, got a coffee. He parked above Lucan Rocks, below him a half-dozen surfers, some taking on the big breakers, some giving it a lot of thought.

It was a soothing thing to do: sit in a warm car and watch the wind lifting spume off the waves, see the sudden green translucence of a rising wall of water, a black figure's skim across the melting glass, the poetic exit into the air, the falling.

He thought about Gavin's shark-bitten board, paddling out on it, the water warm as a bath. The water he was looking at was icy. He remembered the testicle-retracting swims when he was a boy, when they had the family shack above Open Beach and the Doogue shack was over the next dune, rugged assemblages of corrugated iron, fibro sheet, salvaged weatherboards. In those days, the town had two milkbars, two butcher shops, the fish and chip shop, the hardware, a general dealer, one chemist, one doctor. Rich people, mostly sheep farmers, had holiday houses on the Bar between the sea and the river. Ordinary people from the inland had shacks above Open Beach or in South Port or in the streets behind the caravan park.

Cashin remembered his father stopping the Falcon on the wooden bridge, looking down the river at the yachts moored on both sides.

'This place's turning into the bloody Riviera,' his father said.

'What's a Riviera?' said Joe.

'Monaco's on the Riviera,' said Michael.

Mick Cashin looked at Michael. 'How'd you know that?'

'Read it,' said Michael. 'That's where they have the grand pricks.'

'Grand pricks?' said Mick Cashin. 'You mean the royal family? Prince Rainier?'

'Don't be rude, Mick,' said Cashin's mother, tapping his father's cheek. 'It's pronounced pree, Michael. It means prize.'

Every year there had been more city kids on the beach. You knew city kids because of their haircuts and their clothes and because the older ones, boys and girls, wore neck chains and smoked, didn't much care who saw them.

Cashin thought about the winter Saturday morning they had driven up to their shack and Macca's Shacca next door was gone, vanished, nothing there except disturbed sand to show where the low bleached building had stood, gently leaning backwards.

He had walked around, marvelling at the shack's absence. There were marker pegs in the ground, and the next time they came a house was half-built on a cement slab.

That summer was the last in their shack, the last summer before his dad's death. Years later, he asked his mother what became of the place.

'I had to sell it,' she said. 'There wasn't any money.'

Now you would have to be more than just rich to own a place in the teatree scrub on the Bar and no shacks broke the skyline above Open Beach; on the once worthless dunes stood a solid line of houses and units with wooden decks and plateglass windows. Nothing under six hundred grand.

A fishing boat was coming in, heading for the entrance.

Cashin knew the boat. It belonged to a friend of Bern's who had a dodgy brother, an abalone poacher. Just six boats still fished out of Port Monro, bringing in crayfish and a few boxes of fish, but it was the town's only industry apart from a casein factory. Its only industry if you didn't count six restaurants, five cafes, three clothing boutiques, two antique shops, a book-shop, four masseurs, an aromatherapist, three hairdressers, dozens of bed-and-breakfast establishments, the maze and the doll museum.

He finished his coffee and went to work the long way, through Muttonbird Rocks, no one in the streets, most of the holiday houses empty. He drove along two sides of the business block, past the two supermarkets, the three real-estate agents, three doctors, two law firms, the newsagent, the sports shop, the Shannon Hotel on the corner of Liffey and Lucas Streets.

In the late 1990s, a city drug dealer and property developer had bought the boarded-up, gull-crapped Shannon. People still talked about a bar fight there in 1969 that needed two ambulances from Cromarty to take the injured to hospital. The new owner spent more than two million dollars on the Shannon. Tradesmen took on apprentices, bought new utes, gave their wives new kitchens – the German appliances, the granite benchtops.

Two men in beanies were coming out of the Orion, Port's surviving bloodhouse, still waiting for its developer. In Cashin's first week in charge, three English backpackers drinking there at lunchtime gave some local hoons cheek. The one took a king hit, went down and stayed down, copped a few boots. The others, skinny kids from Leeds, were headbutters and kickers and they got into a corner and took out several locals before Cashin and his offsider got there.

The bigger man on the pavement was giving Cashin the eye. Ronnie Barrett had various convictions – assault, drink-driving, driving while suspended. Now he was on the dole, picking up some cash-in-hand at an auto wreckers in Cromarty. His ex-wife had an intervention order against him, granted after he extended his wrecking skills to the former marital home.

Cashin parked outside the station, sat for a while, looking at the wind testing the pines. Winter setting in. He thought about summer, the town full of spoilt-rotten city children, their blonde mothers, flabby fathers in boat shoes. The Cruisers and Mercs and Beemers took all the main street parking. The men sat in and outside the cafes, stood in the shops, hands to heads, barking into their mobiles, pulling faces.

But the year had turned, May had come, the ice-water rain, the winds that scoured skin, and just the hardcore left – the unemployed, under-employed, unemployable, the drunk and doped, the old-age pensioners, people on all kinds of welfare, the halt, the lame. Now he saw the town as you saw a place after fire, all softness gone: the outcrops of rock, the dark gullies, the fireproof rubbish of brown beer bottles and car skeletons.

Ronnie Barrett, he was Port in winter. They should put him in an advertisement, on a poster: GET TO KNOW THE REAL PORT MONRO.

Cashin went in, talked to Kendall. It was overlap time, the two of them on duty for a few hours. He wrote the report on his visit to The Heights, sent it to Villani, printed two copies for the file.

Then he rang homicide and spoke to Tracy Wallace, the senior analyst.

'Back in harness, are you?' she said. 'I gather it's titsoff down there.'

Cashin could see the flag, plank-stiff in the arctic wind. 'Nonsense. Only people with over-sensitive parts say that. What's the word on Bourgoyne?'

'Unchanged. If you're recovered, please come home. The place is filling up with young dills.'

'Be patient. They'll turn into older dills.'

THE SHIFT went by.

Cashin went home, along the country roads. Newly milked dairy cows, relieved for a time of their swaying burdens, turned to look at him, blessed him with dark, glossy eyes.

No sign of Dave Rebb.

He walked the dogs, made something to eat, watched television, all the time the pain getting worse. It took revenge for the hours he was upright. For a long time after he left hospital, he had been unable to cope without resorting to pethidine. Getting off the peth, the lovely peth, that was the hardest thing he had ever done. Now aspirin and alcohol were the drugs of choice and they were a poor substitute.

Cashin got up and poured a big whisky, washed down three aspirins. Callas, Bergonzi and Gobbi always helped. He went to the most expensive thing he owned, two thousand dollars worth of stereo, and put on a CD. Puccini, Tosca. The sound filled the huge room.

He owed opera and reading to Raimond Sarris, the mad, murderous little prick. Opera had just been rubbish arty people pretended to like. Fat men and women singing in foreign languages. Books were okay, but reading a book took too long, too many other things to do. There were few spaces in Cashin's days before Vickie and, afterwards, he left home early, came back in the dark, ate at his desk, sitting in cars, in the street. His spare time he spent sleeping or someone, a cop, would hoot outside and they'd go to the races, the football, fishing, stand in some cop's backyard eating charred meat, drinking beer, talking about work.

Then came Rai Sarris.

After Rai, he had many hours of the day and night in which he had no capacity to do anything except read or watch television. At night, when they were trying to wean him off painkillers, the aches in his back, his pelvis, his thighs, would always give him a moment to drop into sleep. He would fall away from himself for a while, to a deep and dreamless place. The pain would wake him slowly, pain as a sound, far away but insistent, as with a crying baby, part of a dream of hearing something unwelcome. He would move, not fully awake, lie every way, trying to find a position that lessened the pain. Then he would give up and lie on his back – sweaty, now aching from neck to knees – and switch on the light, prop up, try to read. This happened so many times in a night, they blurred.

One day a nurse called Vincentia Lewis brought him a CD player and two small speakers and a box of CDs, twenty or thirty. 'My father's,' she said, 'he doesn't need them anymore.' They sat on the bedside cabinet untouched for a long time until, waiting for the dawn one morning, pain shimmering, Cashin put on the light, picked out a disk, any disk, didn't look at it, put it on, put on the headphones, put out the light.

It was Jussi Björling.

Cashin did not know that. He endured a few moments, gave it a minute, another. In time, the day leaked in under the cream blind, the morning-shift nurse came and ran it up. 'Look a bit more peaceful today,' she said. 'Better night?'

What did Rai Sarris call himself now? For months, they had tapped everyone Rai knew. He never called anyone.

Cashin got up with difficulty and poured another whisky. A few more and he'd sleep.

THEY WALKED around the western side of the house, through the long grass, dogs ahead, jumping up, hanging stiff-legged in the misty air, hoping to see a rabbit.

'Where'd you grow up?' Cashin said.

'All over,' said Rebb.

'Starting where?'

'Don't remember. I was a baby.'

'Right, yes. Go to school?'

'Why?'

'Most people know where they went to school.'

'What's it matter? I can read, I can write.'

Cashin looked at Rebb, he didn't look back, eyes front. 'Like a good yarn, don't you? Big talker.'

'Love a yack. How come you walk like you're scared you'll break?'

Cashin didn't say anything.

'Confide in anyone comes along, don't you? Why's the place's like this?'

The dogs had vanished into the greenery. Cashin led the way down the narrow path he'd cut with hedge clippers. They came to the ruins. 'My great-granddad's brother built it, then he dynamited this part of it. He was planning to blow the whole thing up but the roof fell on him.'

Rebb nodded as if dynamiting a house was an unexceptional act. He looked around. 'So what do you want to do?'

'Clear up the garden first. Then I thought I might fix up the house.'

Rebb picked up a piece of rusted metal. 'Fix this? Be like building that Chartres cathedral. Your kids'll have to finish the job.'

'You know about cathedrals?'

'No.' Rebb looked through an opening where a window had been.

'I thought we could do it in bits,' said Cashin without enthusiasm. He was beginning to see the project through Rebb's eyes.

'Easier to build a new place.'

'I don't want to do that.'

'Be the sensible thing.'

'Well, maybe cathedrals didn't look like a sensible thing.'

Rebb walked beside the wall, stopped, poked at something with a boot, bent to look. 'That was religion,' he said. 'Poor buggers didn't know they had a choice.'

Cashin followed him, they fought their way around the building, Rebb scuffing, kicking. He uncovered an area of tesselation, small octagonal tiles, red and white. 'Nice,' he said. 'Got pictures of the place?'

'They say there's a few in a book in the Cromarty library.'

'Yeah?'

'I'll get copies.'

'Need a tape measure. One of them long buggers.' Rebb mimed winding.

'I'll get one.'

'Graph paper too. See if we can work up a drawing.'

They walked back the long way, it was clearing now, pale blue islands in the sky, dogs ranging ahead like minesweepers.

'People live here before you?' said Rebb.

'Not really. A bloke leased it, ran sheep. He used to stay here a bit.'

'Cleaning up the garden's going to take a while,' said Rebb. 'Before you start the big job.' He found the makings, rolled a smoke as he walked, turned his back to the wind to light up, walked backwards. 'How long you planning on taking?'

'They know how long a cathedral would take?'

'Catholic?'

'No,' said Cashin. 'You?'

'No.'

The dogs arrived, came up to Cashin as if to a rendezvous with their leader, seeking orders, suggestions, inspiration.

'Met this priest done time for girls,' said Rebb. 'He reckoned religion's a mental problem, like schizophrenia.'

'Met him where?'

Rebb made a sound, possibly a laugh. 'Travelling, you meet so many priests done time for kids, you forget where.'

They were at the front entrance.

'Help yourself to tucker,' said Cashin. 'I'm getting something in town.'

Rebb turned away, said over his shoulder, 'Want to leave the dogs? Take them to Millane's with me, stay in the yard. He likes them. He told me.'

'They'll be your mates for life. Den's has to be better than the copshop.'

Cashin drove to Port Monro down roads smeared with roadkill – birds, foxes, rabbits, cats, rats, a young kangaroo with small arms outstretched – passed through pocked junctions where one or two tilted houses stood against the wind and signs pointed to other desperate crossroads.

In Port, Leon made him a bacon, lettuce and avocado to take away. 'Risking the wrath of Ms Fatarse here, are we?' he said. 'I'm thinking of having a sign painted. By appointment, supplier of victuals to the constabulary of Port Monro.'

'What's a vittle?'

'Victuals. Food. In general.'

'How do you spell that?'

'V-I-C-T-U-A-L-S.'

'I find that hard to accept.'

Cashin ate his breakfast at Open Beach, parked next to the lifesaving club, watching two windsurfers skimming the wave tops, bouncing, taking off, strange bird-humans hanging against the pale sky. He opened the coffee. There was no hurry. Kendall was acting station commander while the Bourgoyne matter was on. Carl Wexler didn't like that at all, but the compensation was that he could bully the stand-in sent from Cromarty, a kid even rawer than he was.

Bourgoyne.

Bourgoyne's brother was executed by the Japs. How could you be interested in Japanese culture when your brother was executed by the Japs? Did executed mean having his head cut off? Did a Jap soldier cut off his head with a sword, sever the neck and spine with one shining stroke?

Some fucking *In Cold Blood* thing. How did Villani know about Truman Capote? He couldn't have seen the movie. Villani didn't go to the movies. Villani didn't read books either, Cashin thought. He's like me before Rai Sarris. He doesn't have the standstill to read books.

Before Rai, he wouldn't have known what *In Cold Blood* meant either. Vincentia gave him the book. She was doing a literature degree part-time. He read the book in a day and a night. Then she gave him *The Executioner's Song* by Norman Mailer. That took about the same time. He asked her to buy him another book by Mailer and she came in with *The Naked and the Dead*, second-hand.

'All about dying?' he said. 'I think I can read other kinds of stuff.'

'Try it,' she said, 'it's about a different kind of senseless killing.'

Shane Diab shouldn't have been there. Nothing could change that. He was just a keen kid, he was in awe, so rapt at being in homicide he would have done anything, gone anywhere, worked twenty-three-hour days, then got up early.

There was no point in thinking about Shane. It served no purpose, cops got killed in all sorts of ways, he could just as easily have been shot by some arsehole brain-dead on Jack Daniels and speed. That was the job.

Cashin's mobile rang.

'Joseph?' His mother.

'Yes.'

'Michael rang. I'm worried.'

'Why?'

'It's the way he sounds.'

'How's that?'

'Strange. Not like him.'

'Rang from where?'

'Melbourne.'

'The one-and-a-half bathrooms?'

'I don't know, what does it matter?' Irritated.

'How does he sound?'

'He sounds low. He never sounds low.'

'Everyone gets low. Life's a seesaw. Up, down, brief level bit if you're lucky.'

'Rubbish, Joseph. I know him. Will you ring? Have a chat?'

'What do I say? Your mother asked me to ring you? We don't have chats. We don't have any chat.'

Silence. A windsurfer was in the air, hanging beneath his board. He disconnected, man and board vanished behind the wave as if dropping into a slot.

'Joe.'

'Yes.'

'It's Mum, not your mother. I brought both of you into the world. Will you do that for me? Ring him?'

'Give me the number.'

'Hang on, I'll find it. Got a pen?'

He wrote the number in his book, said goodbye. The windsurfer had reappeared. I'll ring Michael later, he said to himself. After a few drinks, I'll make up a reason. We'll have a chat, whatever the fuck that is.

In the main street, Cashin bought groceries, milk, onions and carrots, half a pumpkin and four oranges and a hand of bananas. He put the bags in the vehicle, walked down to the newsagency. It was empty except for Cecily Addison looking at a magazine. She saw him, replaced it on the stand.

'Well, what's happening?' she said. 'What's taking you so long?'

'Investigation progressing.' Cashin picked up the Cromarty *Herald*. The front-page said:

RESORT COULD BRING 200 NEW JOBS

'They call the man a developer,' said Cecily. 'Might as well call hyenas developers. Hitler, there's a developer for you. Wanted to develop Europe, England, the whole damn world.'

Cashin had learned that when Cecily got going, you didn't have to say anything. Not even in response to questions.

'Going to the mouth since I don't know when,' said Cecily. 'My dear old dad made little cane rods for us, two bricks and a biscuit high the two of us. There's that little spit there, a bit of sand, perfect to cast a line. Mind you, you had a walk. Park the Dodge at the Companions camp, best part of twenty minutes over the dunes. Seemed like a whole day. Worth it, I can tell you.'

She paused to breathe. 'What do you think this Fyfe jackal is slinging the pinkos?'

'I'm not quite with you, Mrs Addison.'

Cecily pointed at the newspaper.

'Read that and weep. The socialists are talking about letting Adrian Fyfe build at Stone's Creek mouth. Hotel, golf course, houses, brothel, casino, you name it. If that's not enough, this morning I find my firm, my firm, is acting for the mongrel. No wonder people think we're lower than snakes' bellies.'

'Why does he need lawyers?'

'Everyone needs lawyers. He'll have to buy the Companions camp from Charles Bourgoyne. Well, could be the estate of Charles Bourgoyne now. What this rag doesn't say is buying Stone's Creek mouth's no use unless you can get to it. And the only way's through the nature reserve or through the camp.'

'Bourgoyne owns the camp?'

'His dad gave the Companions a forty-year lease. Peppercorn. That's history, been nothing there since the fire. Companions are history too.'

Cashin's mobile rang. He went outside. Villani.

'Joe, Bourgoyne. Two kids tried to sell a Breitling watch in Sydney yesterday.'

CASHIN SAT at a pavement table. 'You heard this when?' he said.

'Five minutes ago,' said Villani. 'Cash Converters kind of place. Your pawnshop, basically. The manager did the right thing, sent his offsider out after them and he got a rego, reported it. And that lay on some dope's desk till now.'

'So?'

'Toyota ute, twincab. Martin Frazer Gettigan, 14 Holt Street, Cromarty.'

'Jesus,' said Cashin, 'not another Gettigan.'

'Yes?'

'A clan. Lots of Gettigans.'

'What are we talking? Aboriginal?'

'Some are, some aren't.'

'Like Italians. Find out about this ute without spooking anybody? Can't trust the Cromarty turkeys. Turkeys and thugs.'

Cashin thought about the building site, the trembling panel van. 'I'll have a go.'

'From a distance, understand?'

'Not capiche? Out of fashion, is it?'

Villani said, 'Don't take too long about this. Minutes, I'm talking.'

'Whatever it takes,' said Cashin.

He rang the station, got Kendall. 'Listen, there's an incident report on Allan James Morris, me, complaint from the primary school. His mobile number's there.'

It took more than a minute for Morris to answer. Pulling up his pants on a building site somewhere, thought Cashin.

'Yeah.'

'Allan?'

'Yeah.'

'Detective Sergeant Cashin from Port Monro. Remember me?'

'Yeeaah?'

'You can help me with something. Okay?'

'What?'

'Martin Frazer Gettigan, 14 Holt Street. Know him?'

'Why?'

'I'm in a hurry, son. Know him?'

'Know him, yeah.'

'Is he in town?'

'Dunno. Don't see him much.'

Cashin said, 'Allan, I want you to do something for me.'

'Jeez, mate, I'm not doin fuckin cop's work ...'

'Allan, two words. Someone's grand-daughter.'

Cashin heard the sounds of a building site: a nailgun firing, hammer blows, a shouted exchange.

'What?' said Morris.

'I want to know who's driving Martin's Toyota ute.'

'How'm I supposed to fuckin ...'

'Do it. You've got five minutes.'

Cashin drove to Callahan's garage at the Kenmare crossroads, filled up. Derry Callahan came out of the service bay, cap pulled down to his eyebrows, unshaven. Cashin knew him from primary school.

'You blokes got nothin to do except drive around?' he said. He wiped a finger under his nose, darkened the existing oil smear. 'What's happenin with the Bourgoyne business?'

'Investigation proceeding.'

'Proceeding? You checkin out the boongs? Curfew on the whole fuckin Daunt, that's what I say. Barbed wire around it, be a start. Check em comin and goin.'

'Lateral thinking,' said Cashin. 'Why don't you write a letter to the prime minister? Well, spelling'd be a problem. You could phone it in.'

Derry's eyebrows disappeared beneath his cap. 'They got that?' he said. 'Talkback?'

The mobile rang while Cashin was paying Derry's sister, fat Robyn, slit eyes, mouth permanently hooked into a sneer. He let it ring, took his change and went into the cold, stood at the vehicle, in the wind, looking across the highway at the flat land, the bent grass, pressed the button on the phone.

'Well, he's here,' said Allan Morris. 'Workin over at his old man's place.'

'The ute?'

'Had to make up a fuckin stupid story.'

'Yes?'

'Says he lent it to Barry Coulter and Barry's kid buggered off in it. He's not fuckin happy, I kin tell you.'

A sliver of pain up from his left leg, the upper thigh, into his hip. He knew the feeling well, an old friend. He shifted his weight. 'What's the kid's name?'

'Donny.'

'That's Donny Coulter?'

'What else?'

'Buggered off where?'

'Sydney. He rang. Got another kid with him, Luke Ericsen. He's the driver. They're cousins. Sort of. Donny's not too bright.'

'Been in trouble, these kids?'

'Black kids? In this town? Ya phonin from Mars?'

'Yes or no?'

'Dunno.'

'We never had this talk,' said Cashin.

'Shit. And I'm plannin to go around tellin everyone about it.'

Cashin rang Cromarty station, got Hopgood, gave him the names.

'Donny Coulter, Luke Ericsen,' said Hopgood. 'I'll talk to the boong affairs adviser. Call you back.'

Cashin pulled away from the pumps, parked at the roadside, waited in the vehicle thinking about a smoke, about having another try at getting Vickie to let him see the boy. Did she doubt the boy was his? She wouldn't discuss the subject. He's got a father, that was all she said. When they had their last, unexpected one-night stand, she was seeing Don, the man she married. Seeing, screwing, there were men's clothes in the laundry, muddy boots outside the back door. A vegetable patch had been dug in the clay, seed packet labels impaled on sticks – that sure as hell wasn't Vickie.

You'd have to be blind not to know who the father was. The boy had Cashin written on his forehead.

His mobile.

'Typical Daunt black trash,' said Hopgood. 'They've got some minor form. Suspected of doing some burgs together. Means they did them. Luke's older, he fancies he's a fighter. Donny's a retard, tags along. Luke's Bobby Walshe's nephew.'

'How old?'

'Donny seventeen, Luke nineteen. I'm told they might be brothers. Luke's old man fucked anything moving. Par for the boong course. What's the interest?'

'Looks like one of them tried to sell a watch like Bourgoyne's in Sydney.'

A pause, a whistle. 'Might have fucking known it.'

'New South's got an alert for a Toyota ute registered to Martin Gettigan, 14 Holt Street. The boys are in it.'

'Well, well. Might go around and see Martin,' said Hopgood.

'That would be seriously fucking stupid.'

'You're telling me what's stupid?'

'I'm conveying a message.'

'From on fucking high. Suit yourself.'

'I'll keep you posted,' said Cashin.

'Gee, thanks,' said Hopgood. 'Do so like to be in the fucking loop.'

Cashin rang Villani.

'Jesus,' said Villani. 'Plugged in down there, aren't you? I've got news. Vehicle sighted in Goulburn, three occupants. Looks like your boys are coming home.'

'Three?'

'Given someone a lift, who knows.'

'You should know Luke Ericsen is Bobby Walshe's nephew.'

'Yes? So what?'

'I'm just telling you. Going to pick them up?'

'I don't want any hot-pursuit shit,' said Villani. 'Next thing they're doing one-eighty on the Hume, they wipe out a family in the Commodore wagon. Only the dog survives. Then it's my fault.'

'So?'

'We'll track them all the way, if I can get these rural dorks to take KALOF seriously and not spend the shift keeping a look out for skirt to pull over.'

'If they come back here,' said Cashin, 'it'll be Hopgood's job.'

'No,' said Villani. 'You're in charge. You've done enough malingering. I want to avoid a Waco-style operation by people watched too much television. Understand?'

'Capiche,' said Cashin. 'Whatever that means.'

'Don't ask me. I'm a boy from Shepparton.'

AT 3 PM, Hopgood rang.

Cashin was in Port Monro, looking at the gulls scrapping in the backyard, no dogs to chase them away.

'These Daunt coons are on their way,' Hopgood said. 'Don't stop somewhere for a bong, they should be here about midnight.' He paused. 'I gather you're the boss.'

'In theory,' said Cashin. 'I'll be there in an hour or so.'

He went home, fed the dogs. They didn't like the change in routine; food came after the walk, that was the order of things. There was no sign of Rebb. He left a note about the dogs, drove to Cromarty.

Hopgood was in his office, a tidy room, files on shelves, neat in and out trays. He was in shirtsleeves, a white shirt, buttoned at the cuffs. 'Sit,' he said.

Cashin sat.

'So how do you want this done?' Hopgood affected boredom.

'I'll listen to advice.'

'You're the fucking boss, you tell me.'

Cashin's mobile rang. He went into the passage.

'Bobby Walshe's nephew,' said Villani. 'I take your point. We do this thing by the book. There's a bloke coming down to you, on his way now. Paul Dove, detective sergeant. Transferred from the feds, done soft stuff, no one wanted him but he's smart so I took him. He's learning, takes the pains.'

Takes the pains. That was a Singo expression. They were both Singo's children, they used his words without thinking.

'He's taking over?' said Cashin.

'No, no, you're the boss.'

'Yes?'

'Yes what?'

'Oh come on,' said Cashin.

'He's Aboriginal. The commissioner wants him there.'

'I'm lost here. Night has fallen.'

'Don't come the naïve shit with me, kid,' said Villani. 'You told me about Bobby Walshe. Plus Cromarty's record's fucking appalling. Two deaths in cells, lots of other suspicious stuff.'

'Go on.'

'So. When these boys get there, they'll be knackered. Let them go home. You want them asleep. Go in two hours after they pack it in, more. Gently. I cannot say that too strongly.'

The conversation ended. Cashin went back into Hopgood's office.

'Villani,' he said. 'He wants the boys lifted at home.'

'What?'

'At home. After they've gone to bed.'

'Jesus Christ,' said Hopgood, running both hands over his hair. 'Heard everything now. You don't just go into the fucking Daunt at night and arrest people. It's Indian territory. Excellent chance we end up being attacked by the whole fucking street, the whole fucking Daunt, hundreds of coons off their fucking faces.'

Hopgood got up, went to the window, hands in pockets. 'Tell your wog mate I want confirmation that he's taking all responsibility for this course of action. The two of you both.'

'What's your advice?' said Cashin.

'Lift the cunts on the way into town, that's no risk, no problem.'

Cashin left the room and rang Villani. 'The local wisdom,' he said, 'is that going into the Daunt for something like this is inviting a small *Blackhawk Down*. Hopgood says to lift them on the way in is easy. I say let him run it.'

Villani sighed, a sad sound. 'You sure?'

'How can I be sure? The Daunt's not the place it was when I was a kid.'

'Joe, the commissioner's on my hammer.'

Cashin was thinking that he wanted to be somewhere else. 'I think you might be over-dramatising,' he said. 'It's just three kids in a ute. Can't be that hard to do.'

'So you'll be the one on television explaining what happened to Bobby Walshe's relation?'

'No,' said Cashin. 'I'll be the one hiding in a cupboard and letting your man Dove explain.'

'Fuck you,' said Villani. 'I say that in a nice way. Do it then.'

Cashin told Hopgood.

'Some sense,' said Hopgood, face in profile. 'That's new.'

'They're sending someone down. The commissioner wants an Aboriginal officer present.'

'Jesus, not enough coons here,' said Hopgood. 'We have to import another black bastard.'

'Is there somewhere I can sit?' said Cashin.

Hopgood smiled at him, showed his top teeth, a small gap in the middle. 'Tired, are we? Should've taken the pension, a fucked bloke like you. Gone up where it's warm.'

Cashin willed his facial muscles to be still, looked in the direction of the window, saw nothing, counted the numbers. There would be a day, there would be an hour, a minute. There would be an instant.

IT WAS the usual mess: desks pushed together, files everywhere, a draining board full of dirty mugs. Someone had left a golf bag in a corner, seven clubs, not all of one family.

Cashin was eating a pie, meat sludge, when Hopgood showed Dove in.

'The supervisor's arrived,' he said and left.

Dove was in his early thirties, tall, thin, light-brown head buzz–cut in homicide style, round rimless glasses. He put his briefcase on a desk. They shook hands.

'I'm here because they want a boong present when you arrest Bobby Walshe's nephew,' Dove said. He had a hoarse voice, like someone who'd taken a punch in the voicebox.

'You can't be plainer than that,' said Cashin.

Dove looked at Cashin for a while, looked around the room. 'Heard about you,' he said. 'Where do I sit?'

'Anywhere. You eaten?'

'On the way, yeah.' Dove took off his black overcoat, underneath it a black leather jacket. 'Got stuff to catch up on,' he said, opening his brief-case.

Cashin didn't mind that. He wrapped the remains of the pie, put them into the bin, went back to Joseph Conrad. *Nostromo*. He was trying to read all Conrad's books, he didn't know why. Perhaps it was because Vincentia told him that Conrad was a Pole who had to learn to write in English. He thought that was the kind of book he needed – writer, reader, they were both in foreign territory.

Cashin's mobile rang.

'Michael called again.' His mother.

'Bit hectic here, Syb. I'll do it first chance I get. Yes.'

'I'm worried, Joe. You know I'm not a worrier.'

Cashin wanted to say that he knew that very well.

'You could do it now, Joe. Won't take a minute. Just give him a ring.'

'Soonest. I'll ring him soonest. Promise.'

'Good boy. Thank you, Joseph.'

Ring Michael. Michael came to see him in hospital, once. He stood at the window, spoke from there, did not sit down, answered three phone calls and made one. 'Well,' he'd said when he was leaving, 'chose a dangerous occupation, didn't you.' He had a thin smile, a boss smile. It said: I can't get close. One day I may have to sack you.

Hopgood stuck his head in. 'Cobham. The BP servo. Three in the ute.'

The boys were 140 kilometres away.

Cashin went out for a walk, bought cigarettes, another surrender. A cold night, rain in the west wind, the last of the leaves flirting with bits of paper in the streetlights. He lit up, went down the street of bluestone buildings, past the sombre courthouse, the place where young men finally found the stern father they'd been looking for. Around the corner, uphill, past dark shops to the old Commonwealth Bank on the next corner, now a florist and a gift shop and a travel agency.

Here on the heights of Cromarty the rich of the nineteenth century and after – traders in wool and grain, merchants of all kinds, the owners of the flour mill, the breweries, the foundries, the jute bag factory, the ice works, the mineral water bottling plant, the land barons of the inland and the doctors and lawyers – built houses of stone and brick.

Coming to town was a big thing when Cashin was a boy. The four of them in the Kingswood on a Saturday morning, his father with a few shaving cuts on his face, black hair combed and shining, his mother in her smart clothes, only worn for town. Cashin thought about her touching the back of his dad's head, the tongue-pink varnish on her nails.

He turned the corner at the Regent pub, a noise like a shore-break behind the yellow windows. When the shopping was done, Mick Cashin met his brother Len at the Regent for a drink before they went home. He dropped Sybil and the two boys on the waterfront and went to the pub. They bought chips at the little shop and walked out on the long pier, looking at the boats and the people fishing. Then they went up through the town, up the street he was now walking down. Cashin remembered that Michael always kept his distance from them, hanging back, looking in shop windows. It wasn't hard to find the car, always near the pub. They got in and waited for Mick Cashin. Michael had his school case, he did homework, it would have been maths. His mother read from a book of riddles. Joe loved those riddles, got to know them off by heart. Michael didn't take part.

Mick Cashin crossing the road with Uncle Len, laughing, hand on Len's shoulder. Len was dead too, an asthma attack.

Cashin felt the wind on his face, the salt smell in his head. He was a boy again, the child lived in him. He turned the corner and went back to the stale air of the station, two elderly people at the counter, the duty cop looking pained, scratching his head. Someone in the cells was making a sad singing-moaning sound.

Hopgood and four plainclothes were in the office. One of them, a thin, balding man, was eating a hamburger and dipping chips into a container of tomato sauce, adding them to the mix. Dove was at the urn, running boiling water into a styrofoam cup.

'Welcome, stranger,' said Hopgood. 'The bloke at Hoskisson's just logged the ute. We've got fifty minutes or so.'

Hopgood made no introductions, went to the whiteboard stained with the ghosts of hundreds of briefings and drew a road map.

'I'm assuming these pricks are going to Donny's house or Luke's,' he said. 'Makes no difference, a block apart. They're coming down Stockyard Road. We have a vehicle out there, it's had a breakdown, it'll tell me when they pass. When they get to Andersen Road, that's here, the second set of lights, they can turn right or they can carry on to here, go down to Cardigan Street and turn right.'

Hopgood's pen extended the road out of Cromarty. 'That's too hard. So we have to take them here where it's still one lane.' He pointed at an intersection. 'Lambing Street and Stockyard Road.'

He put an X further down the road. 'Golding's smash-repair place. Preston and KD, you'll wait here, facing town. You're group three. I'll let you know when to get going so you'll be in front of the ute. When you get to the Lambing lights, they'll be red. They'll stay red till we're done. With me so far?'

Everyone nodded. The hamburger-eater burped.

'Now when the ute pulls up behind you,' he said, 'you blokes sit tight. Wait, okay? Lloyd and Steggie and me, that's group one, we'll pull up behind them in the Cruiser and we'll be out quick smart.'

Hopgood ran a finger under his nose. 'And Lloyd and Steggie,' he said, 'I hereby say to you and everyone else I have received a message from on high and nothing, that's absolutely nothing, can happen to these … these dickheads.'

He looked from face to face, didn't look at Cashin or Dove.

'Right,' he said. 'Anything stupid happens, we run away and hide. We will starve the pricks out. This is not some kind of SOG operation. Detective Senior Sergeant Cashin, you want to say something?'

Cashin waited a few seconds. 'I've given Inspector Villani and the crime commissioner an assurance that seven trained officers can pick up three kids for questioning without any problems.'

Hopgood nodded. 'Detectives Cashin and Dove, you will be group two in the second vehicle behind the ute. Your services are unlikely to be needed. Any questions? No? Let's get going. I'll be talking to all of you. Code is Sandwich. Sandwich. Okay?'

'If they've got a scanner?' said Preston. He had a big nose and a small, sparse moustache, the look of a rodent.

'Have a heart,' said Hopgood. 'These are Daunt dickheads.'

A uniformed cop came in. 'The third one in the ute,' he said, 'it might be another cousin. Corey Pascoe. He's been in Sydney for a while.'

They put on their jackets and went out to the carpark behind the station, a small paved yard carved out of the stone hill.

'Take the Falcon,' said Hopgood to Cashin. 'It's in better nick than it looks.'

They drove out in a convoy, Hopgood's Landcruiser in front, then Cashin and Dove, behind them the cops called Preston and KD in a white Commodore. It was raining heavily now, the streets running with the lights of cars and the neon signs of shops, blurs and pools of red and white, blue, green and yellow. They crossed the highway and drove out through the suburbs, past the racecourse and the showgrounds, turned at the old meatworks. They were on Stockyard Road. The boys were out there, coming towards them.

'This bloke know what he's doing?' said Dove. His chin was down in his overcoat collar.

'We hope,' said Cashin. The car smelled of cigarette smoke, sweat and chips cooked in old oil.

'Sandwich,' said Hopgood on the radio. 'Group three, station's coming up, should hear from me again inside twenty-five minutes.'

'Group three, roger to that,' said a voice, possibly KD.

Golding's Smash Repair came into sight on the right, a big tin building, a scarlet neon sign. In the rearview, Cashin saw the white Commodore turn off.

The rain was heavier now. He upped the wipers' speed.

'Sandwich group one,' said Hopgood. 'Turning left.'

'Group two, roger to that,' Cashin said. He followed the Cruiser into a dirt side road, muddy. It stopped, he stopped. It did a U-turn, so did he. It stopped. He pulled up behind it, killed the lights.

A knock on his window. He ran it down.

'Keep the motor running, follow us when we go,' said Hopgood. 'No more radio talk from now.'

'Right.'

'Don't like this fucking rain,' said Hopgood and went into the dark.

Window up. They sat in silence. Cashin's pelvis ached. He settled into his breathing routine but he had to shift every minute or two, try to transfer the weight of his torso onto less active nerves.

'Okay if I smoke?' said Dove.

'Join you.'

He punched the lighter, took a cigarette from Dove, dropped his window a centimetre or two. Dove lit their smokes with the glowing coil. They smoked in silence for a while, but nicotine loosens the tongue.

'Do a lot of this?' said Cashin.

Dove turned his head. Cashin could only see the whites of his eyes. 'Of what?'

'Be the Aboriginal representative.'

'This is a favour for Villani. He says he's been leaned on about the Bobby Walshe connection. I quit the feds because I didn't want to be a showpiece boong cop.'

'I was in primary school with Bobby Walshe,' said Cashin and regretted it.

'I thought he grew up on the Daunt Setttlement.'

'No school there then. The kids came to Kenmare.'

'So you know him?'

'He wouldn't remember me. He might remember my cousin. Bern. They teamed up on kids called them names.'

Why did I start this, thought Cashin? To ingratiate myself with this man?

A long silence, no sound from the engine. Cashin touched the pedal and the motor growled.

'What kind of names?' said Dove.

'Boong. Coon. That kind of thing.'

More silence. Dove's cigarette glowed. 'Why'd they call your cousin that?'

'His mum's Aboriginal. My Aunty Stella. She's from the Daunt.'

'What, so you're a boong-in-law.'

'Yeah. Sort of.'

In the hospital, he had begun to think about how he'd never stood with his Doogue cousins, with Bobby Walshe and the other kids from the Daunt when the whites called them boongs, coons, niggers. He'd walked away. No one was calling him names, it wasn't his business. He remembered telling his dad about the fights. Mick Cashin was working on the tractor, the old Massey Ferguson, big fingers winding out sparkplugs. 'You don't have to do anything till they're losing,' he said. 'Then you better get in, kick some heads. Do the right thing. Your mum's family.'

By the time his Aunty Stella took him in, no one called any Doogue kid anything. They didn't need help from anyone. They were big and you didn't get one: they came as a team.

Cashin watched the main road. A vehicle crossed. No move by the Cruiser. Not the one. He put on the wipers. The rain was getting harder. Now was the time to call this thing off, you couldn't do stuff like this in a cloudburst.

Another vehicle flicked by.

Glare of taillights on. Hopgood moving.

'Here we go,' said Cashin.

IT WAS raining heavily, the Falcon's wipers weren't up to it.

Hopgood didn't hesitate at the junction, swung right.

Cashin followed, couldn't see much.

They were at fifty, eighty, ninety, a hundred, the Falcon went flat, it couldn't do more than that,something wrong.

He felt a front wheel wobble, thought he'd lose control, slowed.

Hopgood's taillights were gone into the sodden night.

This wasn't smart, this wasn't the way to do it.

'Get Hopgood,' said Cashin. 'This is bullshit.'

Dove took the handset. 'Sandwich two for Sandwich one, receiving me. Over.'

No reply.

Golding's Smash Repairs on the left, neon sign a red smear in the wet night. Car one, group three, Preston and KD, they would have pulled out, they would be ahead of the ute now, closing on the traffic lights.

'Abandon,' said Cashin. 'Tell him.'

'Sandwich one, abandon, abandon, received? Please roger that.'

Four vehicles, speeding in the rain on a pitch-black night.

The lights would be red. Preston would stop.

The ute would stop behind him. Three kids in a twincab. Tired from a long trip. Yawning. Thinking of home and bed. Were they Bourgoyne's attackers? At least one of them would know who took the watch off the old man's wrist.

'I say again, abandon, abandon,' Dove said. 'Roger that, roger that.'

'Say again, Sandwich two, can't hear you.'

Coming up to the last bend, driving rain, the Lambing Street intersection coming up. Cashin couldn't see anything except the yellow glow of street lights beyond.

'Sandwich one, abandon, abandon, received? Please roger that.'

Cashin slowed, in the bend now.

Red glare. Cruiser taillights.

Stopped.

Cashin braked, the Falcon's back wanted to slide away, he had to go with it, straighten out gently.

'Fucking hell,' said Dove. 'Sandwich one, abandon, abandon, I say again, abandon. Roger that, roger that.'

Cashin stopped behind the Cruiser, couldn't see anything. Three doors open.

'Let's go,' he said, something badly wrong here.

Dove was around the car first, Cashin bumped into him, they almost fell, both blind in the pouring rain.

A vehicle had slammed into the traffic lights on the wrong side of the road. A ute. He could see three or four figures, milling about.

Gunshots.

Someone shouted: 'PUT THE FUCKIN THING ...'

A shotgun fired, the muzzle flame of a shotgun, reflected by the wet tarmac.

'DROP IT, DROP THE FUCKIN GUN!'

'BACK OFF, BACK OFF!'

Two more bangs, handgun, tongue-tips of flame, quick, SMACK-SMACK.

Silence.

'Fuck,' said Dove. 'Oh my sweet fuck.'

Someone was moaning.

Hopgood shouted, 'KD, GISSUS THE FUCKING SPOTLIGHT!'

A few seconds and the light came on, the world turned hard white, Cashin saw the broken ute, thousands of glass fragments glittering on the road.

Three men standing. A body behind the ute, a shotgun beside it.

He walked across the space, wiping rain from his face.

Lloyd and Steggie, guns out, pale faces. Steggie's mouth moved, he was trying to say something. Then he was sick, a column of fluid. He went to his knees, to all fours.

'Get an ambo!' Cashin shouted. 'Maximum fucking speed!'

He went to the person on the ground, a slim youth, his mouth was open. He was shot in the throat. Cashin saw a glint of teeth, heard a gurgling sound. The youth coughed, blood poured out of him, ran in the road, thicker than the rain.

Cashin took the youth's shoulders in his hands, raised him, knew he was going to die, felt it in the thin arms, the little shakes, heard it in the rasping sounds.

'The fucking idiot,' said Hopgood from behind him.

Cashin let the boy down. There was no help he could give. He got up and went to the ute. The driver was pinned by the steering wheel and the dashboard, his face covered in blood, blood everywhere.

Cashin put a finger on his neck, felt the faintest pulse. He tried to open the door, couldn't. He went to the other side. Dove was there. The passenger was another boy, he had blood flowing from his mouth but his eyes were wide.

'Oh fuck,' he said softly. He said it again and again.

They got him out, laid him down. He would live.

The ambulance arrived, then another, the second with a doctor, a woman. She'd never done gunshot but it didn't matter, it was always too late.

When they lifted the boy, Cashin saw a shotgun in a black puddle beside him, single-barrel pumpgun, sawn off.

The driver was still alive when they got him into the ambulance. The cops stood around.

'Nobody touches anything here,' said Cashin. 'Not a fucking thing. Close the road.'

'Who the fuck do you think you are?' said Hopgood. 'This's Cromarty, mate.'

VILLANI PUT the tape in the machine and gave the remote control to Hopgood. 'This is the media conference two hours ago,' said Villani. 'Be on telly at lunchtime.'

The assistant crime commissioner's pink baby face appeared on the monitor. He was prematurely bald. 'It's my sad duty to report that two of the three people involved in the incident outside Cromarty late yesterday have succumbed to injuries received,' he said. 'The third person has a minor injury and is in no danger. The events are now the subject of a full investigation.'

A journalist said, 'Can you confirm that police fired on three young Aboriginal men at a roadblock?'

The commissioner remained blank. 'It was not a roadblock, no. Our understanding is that police officers were fired upon and responded appropriately.'

'If it wasn't a roadblock, what was it?'

'The persons involved are suspects in an inquiry and an attempt was made to apprehend them.'

'That's the Charles Bourgoyne attack?'

'Correct.'

'Did both victims die of gunshot wounds?'

'One of them. Unfortunately.'

The journalist said, 'And is that Luke Ericsen, the nephew of Bobby Walshe?'

'I'm not yet in a position to answer that,' said the commissioner.

'And the other boy? What did he die of?'

'Injuries sustained in a vehicle accident.'

Another journalist said, 'Commissioner, the officers involved, were they uniformed police?'

'There were uniformed police at the scene.'

'So if it wasn't a roadblock, was this a chase gone wrong?'

'It was not a chase. It was an operation designed to avoid any danger to everyone involved and ...'

'Can you confirm that two police vehicles were travelling behind the vehicle that crashed. Can you confirm that?'

'That's correct, however ...'

'Excuse me, commissioner, how is that not a chase?'

'They were not pursuing the vehicle.'

'It wasn't a roadblock and it wasn't a chase and you have two dead Aboriginal youths?'

The commissioner scratched his cheek. 'I'll say again,' he said. 'It was an interception operation designed to minimise the possibility of injury. That is always the intent. But police officers in danger have the clear right to act to protect themselves and their colleagues.'

'Commissioner, Cromarty has a bad reputation for this kind of thing, doesn't it? Four Aboriginal people dead in matters involving the police since 1987. Two deaths in custody.'

'I can't comment on that. To my knowledge, the officers involved in this incident, and that includes a highly respected Aboriginal police officer, behaved with the utmost respect for protocol. Beyond that, we'll wait for the coroner's verdict.'

Villani gestured to Hopgood to switch off the monitor. Cashin was standing at the window, looking at the noonday light on the stone building across the street, having trouble focusing. He was thinking about the crushed boy in the ute. Shane Diab looked like that, the life squeezed out of him.

Pigeons and gulls were walking about, some drowsing, apparently living in amity. Then full-on violence broke out on the parapet – wings, beaks, claws. The peace had only been a lull.

'The position is,' said Villani, rubbing his face with both hands, ageing himself, 'that this operation has brought upon me, upon you, upon this station and upon the entire fucking police force an avalanche of shit. We are buried in shit, the guilty and the innocent.'

'With respect,' said Hopgood, 'how can you know that a driver will be so dumb? What kind of stupid cunt swerves around a car at red lights and loses control?'

'You can't,' said Villani. 'But you wouldn't have had to if you'd listened to me and taken them at home. Now you'd all better pray these kids are the ones attacked Bourgoyne.'

'Ericsen had no reason to fire on us,' said Hopgood. 'He's a violent little arsehole, he'd likely have done the same if we'd waited till they were home in the Daunt.'

'My understanding,' said Villani, 'is that Ericsen's in an accident, he gets out, sees two civilians jump out of an unmarked car and come at him. Could be mad hoons. Three years ago four such animals did exactly the same thing, beat two black kids to pulp, the one's in a wheelchair for life. Also in this town a year ago a black kid walking home was chased down by a car. He tried to run away and the car mounted the pavement and collected him. Dead on arrival.'

Villani had been looking around the room. Now he stared at Hopgood. 'You familiar with those incidents, detective?'

'I am, boss. But …'

'Save the buts, detective. For the inquiry and the inquest. Where you will need all the buts you can find.' Villani sighed. 'Two dead black kids,' he said. 'Bobby Walshe's nephew. Shit.'

'Walshe's never been near his nephew,' said Hopgood. 'He's too good for his fellow Daunt …'

He didn't say the word. They all knew what the word was.

'I wish I was more distant,' said Villani. 'Mars, that would be good. Maybe not far enough.'

Cashin coughed, it caused a scarlet flash of pain.

'I'm just a country cop,' said Hopgood, 'but it's not clear to me that the presumption of innocence lies with arseholes who try to run red lights, hit a pole, climb out with an unlicensed sawn-off pumpgun and fire on police officers.'

He rubbed the stubble on his upper lip with a big finger. 'Or is it different when they're related to fucking Bobby Walshe?'

'That's well put,' said Villani. 'The presumption of innocence. You might think about retraining for the law. For something anyway.'

He took out cigarettes, flicked the pack, lipped one, lit it. There was a sign prohibiting smoking. His smoke stood in the dead air.

'The procedure here is going to be a model for future cock-ups,' said Villani. 'Two feds plus ethical standards officers plus the ombudsman's office. They're here. All officers involved are now on holiday. Any contact, that's the phone call, the little chat, the fucking wink over the bananas in the supermarket, those concerned will turn in the wind. Understand? The family, the brotherhood, that shit, that is not going to operate. Understood?'

Cashin said, 'Could you go over that again?'

Villani said, 'Well, that's it, you can go. Cashin stay.'

Hopgood and Dove left.

'Joe,' said Villani, 'I don't appreciate smart shit like that.'

He smoked, tapped ash into his plastic cup. Cashin looked away, watched the birds across the street. Sleep, shuffle, shit, fight.

'For presiding over this cock-up, I am branded,' said Villani.

'It was my advice. What else could you do?'

'You passed on Hopgood's considered opinion. That's what you did. Passed it on. I decided.'

Villani closed his eyes. Cashin saw his tiredness, the tiny vein pulsing in an eyelid.

'I shouldn't have brought you in,' said Villani. 'I'm sorry.'

'Bullshit. No sign of Bourgoyne's watch?'

'No. Probably flogged it somewhere else. They're looking. They haven't found Pascoe's place in Sydney.'

'Sydney detection at its best,' said Cashin.

'I wouldn't point the finger,' said Villani. 'Not me.'

Silence. Villani went to the window, forced it open, shot his stub at the pigeons, crashed the window down.

'I've got a little media appearance to do,' he said. 'How do I look?'

'Ravishing,' said Cashin. 'Nice suit, ditto shirt and tie.'

'Advised by experts.' At the door, Villani said, 'If it were me, I'd say as little as possible. Innocent stuff comes back to haunt you. And this cunt Hopgood, Joe. Don't do him any favours, he'll sell you without a blink.'

IT WAS mid-afternoon before Cashin's turn.

In an overheated interview room, audio and video running, he sat on a slippery vinyl chair before two feds, a fat senior sergeant from ethical standards called Pitt and his puzzled-looking offsider Miller, and a man from the police ombudsman's office.

Cashin took the first chance to say that he'd had to convince Villani to approve the operation.

'Well, that's a matter for another time,' said Pitt. 'Not the matter at hand.'

The feds, a man and a woman, both stringy like marathon runners, took Cashin through his statement twice. Then they picked at it.

'And I suppose,' said the man, 'with hindsight, you'd see that as an error of judgment?'

'With hindsight,' said Cashin, 'I see most of my life as an error of judgment.'

'Are you taking the question seriously, detective?' said the woman.

Cashin wanted to tell her to fuck off. He said, 'In the same circumstances, I'd make the same decision.'

'It resulted in the deaths of two young men,' she said.

'Two people died,' Cashin said. 'The courts will decide who's to blame.'

Silence. The interrogators looked at one another.

'What was your initial opinion of conducting an operation like this in heavy rain?' said the woman.

'You can't choose the weather. You take what you get.'

'But the wisdom of it? What was your opinion?'

'I had no strong opinion until it was too late.'

It had been too late. He had waited too long.

'And then you say you instructed Dove to call Hopgood and order the operation abandoned?'

'I did.'

'You believed you had the authority to order the operation abandoned?' said the man from the ombudsman's officer.

'I did.'

'You still think so?'

'I thought I was in overall command, yes.'

77

'You thought? It wasn't made clear who was in command?'

'I'm in charge of the Bourgoyne investigation. This operation flowed from it.'

They looked at one another. 'Moving on,' said the woman. 'You say you made three attempts to call it off?'

'That's correct.'

'And they weren't acknowledged?'

'No.'

'Dove asked for the calls to be acknowledged?'

Cashin looked away. He was in pain, thinking of home, whisky, bed. 'Yes. Repeatedly. After the first message, Hopgood asked for a repeat, said he couldn't hear us.'

'That surprised you?'

'It happens. Equipment malfunctions.'

'To go back to the moment you rounded the vehicle,' said the male fed. 'You said you heard shots.'

'That's correct.'

'And you saw a muzzle flash beside the ute?'

'Yes.'

'You heard a shot or shots and then you saw the muzzle flash?'

Cashin thought: he's asking whether Luke Ericsen was fired on and fired back.

'An instant in a cloudburst,' he said, 'I heard shots, I saw a muzzle flash at the ute. The order, well ...'

'It's possible the muzzle flash was Ericsen firing after the other shots?' said Pitt.

'I can't make that judgment,' Cashin said.

'But is it possible?'

'It's possible. It's possible the shotgun fired first.'

'I'm sorry, are you changing your statement?' The woman.

'No. I'm clarifying.'

'A person of your experience,' said the male fed. 'We'd expect a little more precision.'

'We?' said Cashin, looking into his eyes. 'Does we mean you? What the fuck do you know about anything?'

That didn't help. It was another hour before he could go home. He drove carefully, he was tired, nerves jangling. At the Kenmare crossroads, he remembered milk and bread and dog food, there was only a bit of the butcher's sausage left. He pulled in to Callahan's garage and shop.

The shop was unheated, smelling of sour milk and stale piecrust, no one behind the counter. He got milk, the last carton, went to the shelves against the wall to get dog food. One small can left.

'Back again.'

Derry Callahan, oil smears on his face, was standing behind him, close up. He was wearing a nylon zipped-up cardigan, taking strain over his belly.

'Good to see you blokes earnin yer fuckin money for a change,' he said.

Cashin looked around, smelled alcohol and poisonous breath, saw Callahan's pink-rimmed eyes, the greasy strands of hair hand-combed over his pale spotted scalp.

'How's that?' he said.

'Takin out those two Daunt coons. Pity it wasn't a whole fuckin busload.'

There was no thought, just the flush. Cashin had the can of Frisky Dog, Meaty Chunks in Marrow Gravy, in his right hand. He turned his hips and brought his arm around close to his body and hit Derry in the middle of his face, not a lot of travel, they were close. The pain made him think he had broken his fingers.

Callahan went backwards, two short steps, dropped slowly to his knees, at prayer, hands coming to his face, blood getting there first, dark red, almost black, it was the fluorescent lighting did that.

Cashin wanted to hit him again but he threw the carton of milk at him. It bounced off his head. He stepped over to kick Callahan but something stopped him.

At the vehicle, Cashin realised that he was still holding the dog food can. He opened his hand. The can was dented. He threw it onto the back.

Rebb heard him arrive, a beam of light, the dogs jumping, big ears flapping, running for him. He fondled their ears, hand hurting. Dogs went between his legs, came around for more.

'Thought you'd buggered off,' said Rebb. 'Leaving me with your mad dogs and your debts.'

THE DOGS woke Cashin a good way out from dawn and, blind, he crossed the space, let them into the cold, dark room, went back to bed. They snuffed the kitchen for dropped food, gave up, jumped onto the bed, spoilt rotten.

Cashin didn't care. They sandwiched him, pushed against him, lay their light heads on his legs. He went back to sleep, woke with a start, a sound in his memory, a scrape, metal against metal. Head raised, neck tense, he listened.

Just a sound in a dream. The dogs would hear anything unusual long before he did. But sleep was over. He lay on his back, fingers of his right hand hurting, hearing the sad whimpering pre-dawn wind.

The boys in the ute.

In the same circumstances, I'd make the same decision.

It resulted in the deaths of two young men.

Until that moment in the stale room, it had not fully dawned upon him that the line ran directly from the bleeding and dying boys to him on the phone talking to Villani.

I think you might be over-dramatising. It's just three kids in a ute. Can't be that hard to do.

Would it have been different if Hopgood had spoken to Villani? Would Villani have rejected the advice if it came directly from Hopgood?

No matter how much they might have botched raids on the boys at their homes, there wouldn't be two dead.

He tried to think about something else.

Rebuilding Tommy Cashin's blown-up house, lying ruined since just after World War I. How stupid. It would never be done, he'd waste his spare time for a while, then he'd give it away. He'd never done anything with his hands, built anything. How had the idea come to him?

It had somehow developed on his walks with the dogs as they returned to the house in its tangled wilderness. And then one morning on the way to work he met Bern at a crossroads. A load of uncleaned old red bricks was on the back of his Dodge. Sitting beside Bern was a local ancient called Collo who cleaned his bricks, sat outside in all weathers covered in a grey film of cement dust, whistling through the gaps between his teeth, utterly absorbed in chipping at mortar.

They pulled onto the verges, got out. Bern crossed the road, smoke in his mouth.

'Bit early for you,' said Cashin. 'Pull down a house in the dark?'

'What would you cunts know about honest labour?' said Bern. 'All got these fat flat arses.'

'Student of arses, are you?' Cashin said. And then he said the fateful words. 'How many bricks you got there?'

'Three thousand–odd.'

'How much?'

'What's it to you?'

'How much?'

'For a valued customer, forty a hundred, clean.'

'Let's say twenty-five.'

'I'll sell you bricks for twenty-five, I can get forty? Know how scarce old bricks are? Antiques, mate.' He spat neatly. 'No, you don't know. You know fuck all.'

'Say thirty.'

'Whaddaya want with bricks?'

'I'm fixing Tommy Cashin's house,' said Cashin. The words came from nowhere.

Bern shook his head. 'You're another fuckin Cashin loony, you know that? Done at thirty. Delivery extra.'

Now the bricks were stacked near the ruin.

Cashin got up, pulled on clothes, made tea. On the edge of dawn, he set out for the beach with the dogs, a fifteen-minute drive, the last few on a dirt track. Under a sky of streaked marble, he walked barefoot on hard rippled sand against a freezing wind.

His father's view had been that you didn't wear footwear on the beach no matter what you were doing there. Not thongs, not anything. If the sand was hot, well, shut up or go home. Cashin thought about the summers of having his soles burnt, cut from broken glass and sharp rocks. He must have been seven or eight when he stood on a fish hook. He hopped and sat down hard, tears of pain flowing.

His father came back, lifted the foot. The hook was in the soft flesh behind the pad of his big toe.

'No bloody going back with hooks,' Mick Cashin said and pushed the hook through.

Cashin remembered the barb coming out of his skin. It looked huge, his father took it between finger and thumb and pulled the whole thing through. The skin bulged before the eyelet emerged. He remembered the feeling of the length of pale nylon gut being drawn through his flesh.

The dogs liked the beach, weren't keen on the sea. They chased gulls, chased each other, snapped at wavelets, ran from them, went up the dunes to explore the marram grass and the scrub for rabbits. Cashin looked at the sea as he walked, his face turned from the grit blowing off the dunes.

A strong rip was running parallel to the beach, just beyond the big breakers. They went all the way to the mouth of Stone's Creek. The outgoing tide had divided the stream into five or six shallows separated by sandbars, perfect finger biscuits of different widths. This was where Cecily Addison told him Adrian Fyfe planned to build his resort.

Hotel, golf course, houses, God knows what else. Brothel, casino, you bloody name it.

On a wild polar day like this, the idea was lunacy.

The dogs went to the first rivulet, wet their feet, thought about crossing to the first biscuit. Cashin whistled and they looked, turned, ready to go home for breakfast.

When he had fed them, showered, found a clean shirt, he went in to Port Monro to clear his desk. There was no knowing how long the suspension would last. Forever, he thought.

Outside the station, a woman sat in an old Volvo wagon, two young children imprisoned in the back. He parked behind the building and by the time he unlocked the back door, she had her finger on the buzzer.

He looked through the blinds before he raised them: thirtyish, many layers of garments, weak and dirty hair striped in red and green, a sore at the corner of her mouth.

Cashin unlocked.

'Keep fucking easy hours here,' she said. 'This a copshop or what?'

'Not open for another half an hour. There's a sign.'

'Jesus, like fucking doctors, people only allowed to get sick in office hours, nine to fucking five.'

'Missed an emergency, have we?' He went behind the counter.

'I've fucking had it with this town,' she said. 'I go into the super last night, they reckon they seen me taking frozen stuff out of me trackie at the car. So I'm gonna walk around with fucking frozen peas down me trackie, right? Right?'

'Who said that?'

'The Colley slut, she's history, the bitch.'

'What did she do?'

'Sees me coming in, she reckons I'm banned. Half the fucking town there, hears her.'

'Which super are we talking about?'

'Supa Valu, the one on the corner.'

'Well,' Cashin said, 'there's always Maxwell's.'

She thrust her chin at him. 'That's your fucking attitude, is it? I'm guilty without trial? On their fucking say so?'

Cashin felt the tiny start of heat behind his eyes. 'What would you like me to do, Ms…?'

'Reed, Jadeen Reed. Well, tell that Colley bitch she's got no right to ban me. Tell her to get off my case.'

'The store has the right to refuse admittance to anyone,' Cashin said. 'They can tell the prime minister they don't want his business.'

Jade widened her eyes. 'Really?' she said, a grim smile. 'Fucking really? Don't give me that crap. You telling me I park a Mercedes wagon outside the fucking super the bitch would try this on? Reality fucking check, mister.'

Hot eyes now. 'I'll note your complaint, Ms Reed,' he said. 'You might also like to take your problem up with the Department of Consumer Affairs. The number's in the phone book.'

'That's it?'

'That is it.'

She turned, walked. At the door, she turned again. 'You wankers,' she said. 'Looking after the rich, that's your fucking job, isn't it?'

'Got a record, Jadeen?' said Cashin. 'Any form? Been in trouble? Why don't you sit down, I'll look you up?'

'You cunt,' she said, 'you absolute fucking cunt.'

She left, tried to slam the door but it wasn't that kind of door.

Cashin went to his desk and worked through the papers in his in-tray, looked for matters that needed his attention. The dogs were walking around the enclosure like prisoners in an exercise yard, walking because it was less boring than the alternative.

I'm not suited to this work, Cashin thought. And if I can't handle this station, I'm not suited to any kind of police work. What else did Rai Sarris do to me? It wasn't just the body. What neural cobweb did the mad prick cause to fizzle? Once I had patience, I didn't get hot eyes, I didn't punch people, I thought before I did things.

Constable Cashin is good at dealing with people, particularly in circumstances where aggression is involved.

Sergeant Willis wrote that on Cashin's first assessment, showed it to him before he sent it. 'Don't get up your fucking self about this, son,' he said. 'I say it about all the girls.' At his cubicle, he turned. 'Course, in my day, a report like this, they'd say put the wuss on traffic.'

Kendall arrived. She was making tea, her back to him, when she said, 'The business in Cromarty.'

'Yes. A monumental stuff-up. I'm now on holiday. You're in charge. The relief kid'll stay on.'

'How long?'

'Who knows? Till ethical standards get the blame sorted out. It could be permanent.'

'They the Bourgoyne ones?'

'Looks like it. Them or someone they know.'

'Good riddance then,' she said.

Cashin looked out the window at the sky, hated Kendall for a while, her quick stupidity. He saw the sparks, the crushed ute, the rain, the blood in the puddles. The boys, broken, life leaking away. He thought about his son. He had a boy.

'It only looks like it, Ken,' he said. 'Nobody should die because we think they might have done something wrong. Nobody gave us that power.'

You fucking hypocrite, he thought.

Kendall went to her desk.

He finished, took the files and his notes and went over, put them in her in-tray. 'Pretty much up to date,' he said.

She didn't look at him. 'I'm sorry I said that, Joe,' she said. 'It just, shit, it just came out, I wanted to say ...'

'I know. Solidarity. That's a good instinct. Call me if you need anything.'

He was at the back door when she said, 'Joe, feel like a bit of company. Well, any time. Yes.'

'Take you up on that,' he said, went out.

He walked around to the Dublin. A new four-wheel-drive was parked outside and Leon had two customers, a middle-aged couple having break-fast. Soft-looking leather jackets hung on the backs of their chairs.

'Takeaway black,' said Cashin. 'The overdose.'

'Either you sit down or you get one of those vacuum cups,' said Leon. 'Polystyrene does nothing for expensive coffee.'

Cashin had no interest. 'I'll bear that in mind,' he said.

Leon went to the machine. 'Your muscle boy was in yesterday. Very fetching but not keen on paying. Long and pregnant pause before he shelled out.'

Cashin was looking across the street at Cecily Addison talking to the woman outside the aromatherapy shop. 'He's a city lad,' he said. 'They treat officers of the law differently there. Like royalty.'

'Message received. Roger. Do you say that? Roger?'

'We say Roger, we say Bruce, we say Leon, it all depends. Case by case.'

Leon brought the container to the counter, capped it. 'Bringing in rein-forcements for the march?'

'The march?'

'Could be ugly. Feral greenies, rich old farts pulling up the drawbridge.'

'I could be missing something here,' Cashin said. He had no idea what Leon was talking about.

'The march against the Adrian Fyfe resort? Been away, have we?'

'Can't keep up with events in this town. It's all go, go, go. Anyway, I'm on holiday.'

'Why don't you try Noosa, chat to rich retired drug cops? It's warm up there.'

'Don't care for the victuals in Noosa,' Cashin said. As he said the word, he saw the strange spelling. 'Listen, an ordinary old toasted cheese and tomato?'

Leon raised his right arm in a theatrical way, drew fingers across his forehead as if wiping away sweat. 'I take it you don't require sheep-milk fetta with semi-dried organic tomatoes on sourdough artisan bread?'

'No.'

'I suppose I can find a gassed tomato, some rat-trap cheese and a couple of slices of tissue-paper white.'

Cashin bought the city newspaper and drove to Open Beach. One surfer out on a big, heaving sea.

The headline on page three said:

TWO DIE IN CHASE
CRASH, GUNFIGHT

It had happened too late for the previous morning's newspaper. The three youths were much younger in the photographs. The captions didn't mention that. And the reporter didn't buy the interception line. It was a chase gone wrong. Luke Ericsen, he said, 'apparently died in a hail of gunfire'. The conduct of seven officers was under investigation.

Another story was headlined:

UNITED AUSTRALIA LEADER SLAMS POLICE

Bobby Walshe was quoted:

Shock and grief, they are my emotions. Luke Ericsen is my sister's boy, a bright boy, everyone had great hopes for him. I don't know exactly what happened but that doesn't really matter. Two youngsters are dead. That's a tragedy. And there's been far too many of these tragedies. Right across Australia, it's a police culture problem. Indigenous people get the sharp end. Who needs courts when you can hand out punishments yourself? And I'm not surprised this happened in Cromarty. The present federal treasurer entrenched the culture there when he was state police minister. He helped the local police to cover up two Aboriginal cell deaths. I'll remind him of that disgraceful episode in the election campaign. Often. That's a promise.

The toasted sandwich wasn't bad. Flat and tanned, leaking cheese, something yellow anyway.

Would Derry Callahan complain? Punched with a can of dog food. Cashin thought that he didn't care. Hitting him was worth the damage to his fingers. He should have kicked him too, it would have been a good feeling.

His mobile rang. It took time to find it.

'Taking it easy?' said Villani. 'Lying on the beach in the thermal gear. The striped long johns.'

'I'm reading the paper. Full of good news.'

'I'll give you good news. The pawnshop bloke, he's ID'd Pascoe and Donny.'

The surfer paddled on a great wall of water. It seemed unwilling to break, then it curled, he stood, an upsurge from a sandbar caused it to crash. He shot out the back, towed by his board.

'I just talked to the commissioner,' said Villani. 'Actually, he talked to me. Non-stop. The spin doctors say we're playing into our enemies' hands. I think that means Bobby Walshe and the media. So it's just Lloyd and Steggles suspended. You are no longer on holiday. And Dove's coming back to you, he'll be your offsider.'

'What about the rest?'

'Preston to Shepparton, Kelly goes to Bairnsdale.'

'And Hopgood?'

'Stays on the job.'

'So the idea is to load the other ranks?'

'The commissioner's decision, Joe. He's taken advice.'

'That's what I call leadership. In Sydney, the pawnshop, it was just Pascoe and Donny?'

'Ericsen was probably waiting outside.'

'So what happens to Donny?'

'He's still in hospital, under observation, but he's okay, bruises, cuts. He'll be charged with attempted murder, interview at 10 am, lawyer present.'

'On this? Well, excuse fucking me, that's a pretty thin brief.'

'With luck, he'll plead it,' said Villani. 'If not, we'll see. You'll see.'

'This is the post-Singo attitude? Winging it?'

'It's what we have to do, Joe,' said Villani, a flatness in his tone.

THEY SAT in the interview room, waiting. Cashin hadn't worn a suit since coming to Port Monro.

'In a very short time, I've grown to hate this town,' said Dove. His forearms were on the table, cuffs showing, silver cufflinks, little bars. He was looking at his hands, his long fingers stretched.

'The weather's not great,' said Cashin.

'Not the weather. Weather's weather. There's something wrong with the place.'

'Big country town, that's all.'

'No, it's not a big country town. It's a shrunken city, shrunk down to the shit, all the shit without the benefits. What's the hold-up here? Since when do you sit around waiting for the prisoner?'

A knock, a cop came in, followed by the youth Cashin had seen in the passenger seat of the ute at the fatal crossroads, then another cop. Donny Coulter had a thin, sad face, a snub nose, down on his upper lip. It was a child's face, scared. He was puffy-eyed, nervous, licking his lips.

'Sit down, Donny.'

Another knock, the door was behind Cashin.

'Come in,' he said.

'Helen Castleman, for the Aboriginal Legal Service. I represent Donny.'

Cashin turned. She was a youngish woman, slim, dark hair pulled back. They looked at each other. 'Well, hello,' he said. 'It's been a while.'

She frowned.

'Joe Cashin,' he said. 'From school.'

'Oh, of course,' she said, unsmiling. 'Well, this is a surprise.'

They shook hands, awkward.

'This is Detective Sergeant Dove,' said Cashin.

She nodded to Dove.

'I didn't know you lived here,' said Cashin.

'I haven't been back long. What about you?'

'I'm in Port Monro.'

'Right. So who's in charge of this?'

'I am. You've had an opportunity to speak to your client in private.'

'I have.'

'Like to get going then?'

'I would.'

87

Cashin sat opposite Donny. Dove switched on the equipment and put on record the date, the time, those present.

'You are Donald Charles Coulter of 27 Fraser Street, Daunt Settlement, Cromarty?'

'Yes.'

'Donny,' said Cashin, 'I'm going to tell you what rights you have in this interview. I must tell you that you are not obliged to do or say anything but that anything you say or do may be given in evidence. Do you understand what I've said?'

Donny's eyes were on the table.

'I'll say it again,' said Cashin. 'You don't have to answer my questions or tell me anything. But if you do, we can tell the court what you said. Understand, Donny?'

He wouldn't look up. He licked his lips.

'Ms Castleman,' said Cashin.

'Donny,' she said. 'Do you understand what the policeman said? Do you remember what I told you? That you don't have to tell them anything.'

Donny looked at her, nodded.

'Will you say that you understand, please, Donny,' said Cashin.

'Understand.' He was drumming his knuckles on the table.

'I must also tell you of the following rights,' said Cashin. 'You may communicate with or attempt to communicate with a friend or a relative to inform that person of your whereabouts. You may communicate with or attempt to communicate with a legal practitioner.'

'At this point,' said Helen Castleman, 'I'd like to say that my client has exercised those rights and he will not be answering any further questions in this interview.'

'Interview suspended 9.47 am,' said Cashin.

Dove switched off the equipment.

'Short and sweet,' Cashin said. 'Would you care to step outside with me for a moment, Ms Castleman?'

They went into the corridor. 'Bail hearing at 12.15,' Cashin said. 'If Donny was to tell his story, there might not be opposition to bail.'

Her eyes were different colours, one grey, one blue. It gave her a look somehow fierce and aloof. Cashin remembered studying her face in the year twelve class photograph long after he left school.

'I'll need to get instructions,' she said.

Dove and Cashin went down the street and bought coffee at a place called Aunty Jemimah's. It had checked tablecloths and Peter Rabbit pictures on the walls.

'Old school mates,' said Dove. 'Lucky you.'

'She was too good for me,' said Cashin. 'Old Cromarty money. Her father was a doctor. The family used to own the newspaper. And the iceworks. The only reason she didn't go to boarding school was she wouldn't leave her horses.'

On the way back, Dove opened his cup and sipped. 'Jesus, what is this stuff?' he said.

'Some of the shit you get without the benefits.'

Helen Castleman was outside the station, talking on her mobile. She watched them coming, looked at them steadily. They were near the steps when she said, 'Detective Cashin.'

'Ms Castleman.'

'Donny's mother says he was at home on the night of the Bourgoyne attack. I'll see you in court.'

'Look forward to it.' Cashin went in and rang the prosecutor. 'Bail is strenuously opposed,' he said. 'Investigations incomplete. Real danger accused will interfere with witnesses or abscond.'

At 11.15, Dove and Cashin headed for the station door.

'Phone for you,' said the cop on the desk. 'Inspector Villani.'

'What's wrong with your mobile?' Villani said.

'Sorry. Switched off.'

'Listen, the kid gets bail.'

'Why?'

'Because that's what the minister told the chief commissioner, who told the crime commissioner, who told me. It's political. They don't want to take the chance Donny so much as gets a nosebleed in jail.'

'As their honours please.'

'Donny's bail not opposed,' Cashin said to Dove.

'Pissweak,' said Dove. 'That is capitulation, that is so pissweak.'

The desk cop pointed at the door. 'Got a reception committee. Television.'

Cashin went cold. Somehow he hadn't thought of this. 'You speak to them,' he said to Dove. 'You're from the city.'

Dove shook his head. 'Hasn't taken you long to turn into a flannelshirt, has it?'

They went out, into camera flashes and the shiny black eyes of television cameras, furry microphones on booms thrust at them. At least a dozen people came at them, jostling.

'What's Donny Coulter charged with?' said a woman in black, blonde hair immobilised with spray.

'No comment,' said Dove. 'All will soon be revealed.'

They made their way down the stairs and the camera crews ran ahead and filmed them walking down the winter street under a grey tumbling sky. Rounding the bend, they saw the crowd outside the court.

'Ms Castleman's spread the word,' said Dove.

The crowd parted, allowed them a narrow corridor. They walked side by side between the hostile faces, silence until they neared the top of the stairs.

'You murderers,' said a man wearing a rolled-up balaclava on Cashin's left. 'All you cunts are good for, killin kids.'

'Bastards,' said a woman on Dove's side. 'Mongrels.'

The lobby was crowded, the small courtroom was full. They made their way to the prosecutor, a senior constable. 'Change of mind,' said Cashin. 'Not opposing bail for Coulter.'

She nodded. 'I heard.'

They took their places on the Crown's seats. Dove looked around. 'Just the two of us representing the forces of law and order,' he said. 'Where's Hopgood, the friendly face of community policing?'

'Probably on the firing range breaking in the replacements for KD and Preston,' said Cashin.

Dove looked at him for a second, the round glasses flashed.

Helen Castleman arrived with an older woman. Cashin thought he saw a resemblance to Donny.

At 12.15 exactly, Donny was brought up from the cells to a hero's welcome from the spectators. He didn't look at anyone except the woman with Helen Castleman. She smiled at him, winked, a brave face.

The audience were told to be silent, then to stand. The magistrate came in and sat down. He had a chubby pink face and the grey strands combed over his bald scalp made him look like an infant suffering from a premature-ageing disease.

The prosecutor identified Donny, said he was charged with attempted murder. The audience had to be hushed again.

'This is obviously a show-cause situation, your honour,' she said, 'but there is no objection to bail.'

The magistrate looked at Helen Castleman and nodded.

She rose. 'Helen Castleman, your honour. I represent Mr Coulter and would like to apply for bail. My client has no criminal record, your honour. He has been charged in the most tragic circumstances imaginable. A few days ago, he saw his cousin and a close friend die in an incident involving the police …'

Applause from the gallery, a few shouts. More silencing by the clerk of the court.

'In this court, Ms Castleman,' said the magistrate, a baby with a gruff voice, 'it is not a good idea to grandstand.'

Helen Castleman bowed her head. 'That was not my intention, your honour. My client is just an innocent boy, the victim of circumstances. He is traumatised by what has happened and he needs to be at home with his family. He will give and honour all undertakings the court may require. Thank you, your honour.'

The magistrate frowned. 'Bail is granted,' he said. 'The accused is not to leave his place of residence between the hours of 9 pm and 6 am and must report to the Cromarty police once a day.'

Applause again, more shouts, more silencing.

Cashin looked at Helen Castleman. She tilted her head, gave him a suggestion of a smile, lips just parted. Cashin felt like the teenage boy he once was, full of lust and full of wonder that a beautiful and clever rich girl would kiss him.

THEY WALKED past Helen Castleman being interviewed on the court steps and the television crews caught up with them before they reached the station. Dove declined to answer questions.

'There's a room organised, boss,' the desk cop said to Cashin. 'Upstairs, turn left, last door on the right.'

When they got there, Dove looked around, shook his head. 'Organised?' he said. 'They unlocked the fucking junk room, that's organised?'

Tables pushed together, two computers, four bad chairs, piles of old newspapers, scrap paper, drifts of pizza boxes, hamburger clams, styrofoam cups, plastic spoons, uncapped ballpoints, crushed drink cans.

'Like a really bad sitting room in an arts students' shared house,' Dove said. 'Disgusting.' He went to a window, unlatched it, tried to pull the bottom half up, failed, banged both sides of the frame with fists, tried again. Cords showed in his neck. The window didn't move.

'Shit,' he said. 'Can't breathe in here.'

'Need the nebuliser?'

It was provocative and it worked. 'I don't have fucking asthma,' Dove said. 'I have a problem with breathing air circulated ten thousand times through people with bad teeth and rotten tonsils and constipation.'

'Didn't mean anything. People have asthma.' Cashin sat down. He had to live with Dove.

Dove pulled a chair out, sat, put his polished black shoes on the desk. The soles were barely worn, insteps shiny yellow and unmarked. 'Yeah, well,' he said, 'I don't have asthma.'

'Glad to hear it. I'm assuming what will happen here is the defence will want Luke Ericsen loaded with Bourgoyne. Luke's dead, it's not a problem for him.'

'If Donny was there, he'll share the load.'

'Placing Donny there,' said Cashin. 'That's a challenge. And if it happens, the story then will be led astray by his older cousin, didn't take part, that sort of thing.'

A crash, his heart jumped. Unlatched by Dove, its sash cords rotten, the top half of the window had waited, dropped. The big panes were vibrating, wobbling the outside world.

Cold air came in, the sea – salty, sexual.

'That's better,' said Dove. 'Much better. Delayed action. Smoke?'

'No thanks. Always fighting the urge.'

Dove lit up, moved his chair back and forth. 'I'm new to this but if you don't place Donny at the house, all you have is he went to Sydney with Luke and they tried to sell Bourgoyne's watch. A half-way solid story about where he was on the night, tucked up in bed, he'll walk.'

'I suppose he should. That's the system.'

Dove eyed him briefly, narrow eyes. 'The smartarses who walk. You see them look at their mates, little smirk. Outside, it's the high fives. How easy was that? Fucking shithead cops, let's do it again.' Pause. 'What's Villani say? Your mate.'

Cashin felt a powerful urge to smack Dove down. He waited. 'Inspector Villani says nothing,' he said. 'The solicitor says Donny's mum's giving the alibi. There may be others to confirm it.'

Dove's head was back. 'Some women amaze me. They spend their whole lives covering up for men – the father, the husband, the sons. Like it's a woman's sacred duty. Doesn't matter what the bastards do. So what if my dad beat my mum, so what if my hubby fucked the babysitter, so what if my boy's a teenage rapist, he's still my ...'

'We don't have anything that says Donny was there on the night,' Cashin said.

'Anyway, it's academic,' Dove said. 'Hopgood's right. Bobby Walshe's made them go soft-cock on this. First it's bail, next they drop the charges.'

'You should tell Hopgood that. He'll want you on the Cromarty team. You could be spokesperson.'

Dove smoked in silence, eyes still on the ceiling. Then he said, 'I'm black so I'm supposed to empathise with these Daunt boys. Is that what you're saying?'

There was a gull on the sill – the hard eyes, the moulting head, it reminded Cashin of someone. 'The idea is to keep an open mind until the evidence convinces you of something.'

'Yes, boss. I'll keep an open mind. And in the meantime, I have to live in the Whaleboners' Motel.'

'The Whalers' Inn.'

'Could very well be.' Cigarette in his mouth, Dove looked at Cashin. 'Just tell me,' he said. 'I accept reality. I'll read a book until it's time to go home.'

'The job is to build the case against Donny and Luke,' said Cashin. 'I don't have any other instructions.'

'I'm not talking about instructions.'

The sagging chair wasn't doing anything for Cashin's aches, his mood. He got up, took off his coat, spread an old newspaper on the floor, lay down and put his legs on the chair, tried to get into a Z shape.

'What's this?' said Dove, alarmed. 'Why are you doing that?'

Cashin couldn't see him. 'I'm a floor person. We'll have to see where we can get with Donny's mum.'

Dove appeared above him. 'What's the point?'

'If she's going to lie for the boy, she'll be worried. They don't know what we've got. Getting Donny to plead guilty to something would be a good outcome.'

Cashin heard the door open.

'Just you, sunshine?' said Hopgood. 'Where's Cashin?'

Dove looked down. Hopgood came around the table and studied Cashin as if he were roadkill.

'What the fuck is this?' he said.

'We missed you in court,' said Cashin.

Hopgood's chin went up. Cashin could see the hairs in his nose. 'Not my fucking business.'

'We need to talk to Donny's mum.'

'Thinking about going to the Daunt, are you?'

Cashin didn't fancy the idea. 'If we have to. Can't see her presenting here.'

'Well, it's your business,' Hopgood said. 'Don't call us.'

'I need to talk to the Aboriginal liaison bloke.'

'Ask the desk where he's currently doing fuck all.'

A phone rang. Dove picked up one, wrong, tried another. 'Dove,' he said. 'Good, boss, yeah. Went off okay, yeah. I'll put him on.'

He offered Cashin the phone. 'Inspector Villani,' he said, impassive.

Cashin reached up. 'Supreme commander,' he said.

'Joe, we are talking a cooling-off period,' said Villani.

'Meaning?'

'Let things settle down. I saw your court crowd today, our television friends showed us their pictures for the evening news. The word is no more turbulence like that is wanted.'

'Who said that?'

'I can tell you I don't quote the bloke at the servo.'

'The kid's been charged on close to zero. Now you're saying you don't want us to find any actual evidence or try to get a plea out of him?'

'Nothing is to be done to inflame this situation.'

'That's a political order, is it?'

Villani expelled breath as a whistle. 'Joe, can't you see the sense?' he said.

Cashin felt Dove and Hopgood looking at him, a man lying on the floor, talking on a phone, his calves on a chair.

'I'd like to say, boss,' he said, 'that we have a short time here when we might shake something loose. We let that pass, we will need jackhammers.'

Silence.

Cashin focused on the ceiling, yellow, creased and spotted like the back of an elderly hand. 'That is my common sense,' he said. 'For what it's worth.'

Silence.

'For what it's worth, Joe,' said Villani, 'taking Shane Diab parking outside Rai Sarris's place was your idea of common sense.'

Cashin felt the cold knife inside him, turning. 'Moving on,' he said. 'How long is a cooling-off period? For example.'

'I don't know, Joe, a week, ten days, more.' Villani spoke slowly, like someone talking to an obtuse child. 'We'll need to use our judgment.'

'Right. Some of us will use our judgment.' Cashin was looking at Dove. 'In the meantime, what's Paul Dove do?'

'I need him back here for a while. I want you to take some time off. Handle that?'

'Is that suspension again, boss?'

'Don't be a prick, Joe. I'll call you later. Put Dove on.'

Cashin handed up the handset to Dove.

'What's he say?' said Hopgood.

'He says there's a cooling-off period over Donny.'

'Is that right?' said Hopgood, something like a smirk in his voice, on his lips. 'You won't be needing this comfortable office then.'

In light rain, Dove and Cashin walked up to the Regent, got beers in the bar and sat in the dim cooking-fat-scented bistro, the only customers.

Dove read the laminated menu, ran his index finger down the list.

'Twelve main courses,' he said. 'You need at least three people in the kitchen to do that.'

'In the city,' said Cashin. 'Three bludgers. Here we do it with a work-experience girl.'

'A steak sandwich,' said Dove. 'What can they do to that? How badly can they fuck that up?'

'They meet any challenge.'

A worn woman in a green coverall came out of a back door and stood over them with a notepad, sucked her teeth, sounds like the last dishwater going down a blocked drain.

'Two steak sandwiches, please,' said Cashin.

'Only in the bar,' she said, her gaze on the wall. 'No sangers here. The bistro menu here.'

'Cops,' said Cashin. 'Need a bit of privacy.'

She looked down, smiled at him, crooked teeth. 'Right, well, that's okay. Know all the cops. You here for the Bourgoyne thing then?'

'Can't talk about work.'

'Black bastards,' she said. 'Two down, why don't you nail the bloody lot of them? Bomb the place. Like that Baghdad.'

'Could you cut the fat off?' said Dove. 'I'd appreciate that.'

'Don't like fat? No worries.'

'And some tomato?'

'On a steak sandwich?'

'It's a boong thing,' said Dove.

At the kitchen door, she glanced back at Dove. Cashin saw the uncertainty in her eyes. Across the gloomy space, he saw it.

'An attractive woman,' said Dove. 'So many attractive people around here, it must be something in the white gene pool.' He looked around. 'Stuff like the other night bother you? Still bother you? Ever bother you?'

'What do you think?'

'Well, you're fairly hard to read, if I may say so. Except for the lying on the floor stuff, that's a real window into the soul.'

Cashin considered telling him about the dreams. 'It bothers me.'

'Shooting the kid.'

'Somebody shoots at you, what do you do?'

'What I'm getting at,' said Dove, 'is whether the kid fired first. Did you tell them that?'

Cashin didn't want to answer the question, didn't want to consider the question. 'You'll know what I told them when we get to the coroner.'

'Cross your mind we were set up? Hopgood puts us together in a dud car, claims he can't hear the radio.'

'Why would he do that?'

'Leave himself and his boys a bit of slack if anything went wrong.'

'That may be too far-sighted for Hopgood. You missing the feds?'

Dove shook his head in pity. They talked about nothing, the sandwiches came, the woman fussed over Cashin.

'Could this be whale steak?' said Dove after a bout of chewing. 'I don't suppose they honour the whaling treaty here.'

Walking back in drizzle and wind, Dove said, 'Cooling-off period my arse. This thing's in the freezer and it's staying there. Still, I escape the fucking Whaleboners' Tavern.'

'Whalers' Inn.'

'That too.'

On the station steps, Dove offered a long hand. 'Strong feeling I won't be back. I'll miss the place so much.'

'So good, the whale steak, Miss Piggy's coffee.'

'Aunty Jemimah's.'

'You feds are trained observers,' said Cashin. 'See you soon.'

DEBBIE DOOGUE was sitting at the kitchen table, school books spread, mug of milky tea, biscuits, cartoon show on television. The room was warm, a wood heater glowing in the corner.

'This's the place to be,' said Cashin.

'Want tea?' she said.

She was a pale gingerhead, ghosts of freckles, her hair pulled back. She looked older than fourteen.

'No, thanks,' Cashin said. 'Full of tea. How's school?' It was a pointless question to ask a teenager.

'Okay. Fine. Too much homework.' She moved her bottom on the chair. 'Dad's in the shed.'

Cashin went to the sink, wiped a hole in the fogged window. He could see rain speckling the puddles in the rutted mud between the house and the shed. Bern was loading something onto the truck, pushing it with both hands. He had a cigarette in his mouth.

'He's worried about the stuff your mum found,' said Cashin, turning, leaning against the sink.

Debbie had her head down, pretending to be reading. 'Well, had to dob me, didn't he?' she said.

'What's to dob? I thought it wasn't yours?'

She looked up, light blue Doogue eyes. 'Didn't even know what it was. She just gave me this box, said, hang on to this for me. That's all.'

'You thought it was what?'

'Didn't think about it.'

'Come on, Debbie, I'm not that old.'

She shrugged. 'I'm not into drugs, don't want to know about them.'

'But your friends are? Is that right?'

'You want me to dob in my friends? No way.'

Cashin stepped across, pulled out a chair and sat at the table. 'Debbie, I don't give a bugger if your friends use drugs, wouldn't cross the road to pinch them. But I don't want to see you dead in an alley in the city.'

Her cheeks coloured slightly, she looked down at her notepad. 'Yeah, well, I'm not …'

'Debbie, can I tell you a secret?'

Uneasy, side to side movements of her head.

'I wouldn't tell you if you weren't family.'

'Um, sure, yeah.'

'Keep it to yourself?'

'Yeah.'

'Promise?'

'Yeah.'

The inside door opened violently and two small boys appeared, abreast, fighting to be first in. Debbie turned her head. 'Geddout, you maggots!'

Eyes wide in their round boy faces, mouths open, little teeth showing. 'We're hungry,' said the one on the left.

'Out! Out! Out!'

The boys went backwards as if pulled by a cord, closed the door in their own faces.

Debbie said, 'I promise.'

Cashin leaned across the table, spoke softly. 'Some of the people selling stuff to your friends are undercovers.'

'Yeah?'

'Understand what that means?'

'Like secret agents.'

'That's right. So the drug cops know all the names. If your friend bought that stuff, his name's on the list.'

'Not my friend, her friend, I don't even know him.'

'That's good. You don't want to know him.'

'What would they do with the names?'

'They could tell the school, tell the parents. They could raid the houses. If you were on the list, they could knock on the door any time.'

Cashin rose. 'Anyway, got to go. I wanted to tell you because you're family and I don't want to see anything bad happen to you. Or to your mum and dad.'

At the door, he heard her chair scrape.

'Joe.'

He looked back.

Debbie was standing, hugging herself, now looking about six years old. 'Scared, Joe.'

'Why's that?'

'I bought the stuff. For my friend.'

'The girl friend?'

Reluctant. 'No. A boy.'

'From a Piggot?'

'Yeah.'

'Which one?'

'Do I have to say?'

'I won't do anything. Not my line.'

'Billy.'

'You tabbing?'

'No. Well, just the one, didn't like it.'

He looked down, looked into her eyes, waited.

'Smoking?'

'No. Don't like it either.'

A chainsaw started outside, the roar, bit into something hard, a savage-toothed whine.

'They won't, will they?' she said. 'Tell on me? Come here?'

'Out of my control,' Cashin said. 'I can talk to them, I suppose. What do you reckon I could say?'

She gave him some hints about what he could say.

Cashin went out to the shed, mud attaching itself to him. At the back, in the gloom, Bern was on his haunches, applying a blowtorch to an old kitchen dresser. Layers of paint were blackening and blistering under the blue flame. The smell was of charring wood and something metallic.

'I smell lead,' Cashin said. 'That's lead paint you're burning.'

Bern turned off the torch, stood up. Paint flakes were stuck to his beard stubble. 'So?' he said.

'It's toxic. It can kill you.'

He put the torch on the dresser. 'Yeah, yeah, everythin can kill you. How'd you pricks manage to kill those kids?'

'Accident,' Cashin said. 'No harm intended.'

'That Corey Pascoe. He was in Sam's class. Bound for shit from primary.'

'Bit like Sam then.'

'No harm in Sam. Led astray. You talked to Debbie?'

'Gave her a message, yeah.'

'What's she say?'

'Seemed to get it.'

Bern nodded. 'Well, you can only fuckin hope. I'd say thanks except I give you that wood. Dropped it off today. There's a bloke there, helpful.'

'Dave Rebb. Going to help me with the house.'

'Yeah? Where'd you find him?'

'In a shed over at Beckett. Mrs Haig. A swaggie.'

Bern shook his head, rubbed his chin stubble, found the paint flakes and looked at them. 'Point about swaggies,' he said, 'is they're not real strong on work.'

'We'll see. He's giving Den Millane a hand, no complaints so far.'

'Seen him somewhere, I reckon. Long time ago.'

They walked to the vehicle. Cashin got in, lowered the window. Bern put dirty hands on the sill, gave him a look.

'I hear someone punched out that cunt Derry Callahan,' he said. 'Stole a can of dog food too. You blokes investigatin that?'

Cashin frowned. 'That right? No complaint that I know of. When it happens, we'll pull out all the stops. Door-to-door. Manhunt.'

'Let's see your hand.'

'Let's see your dick.'

'C'mon. Hiding somethin?'

'Fuck off.'

Bern laughed, delighted, punched Cashin's upper arm. 'You fuckin violent bastard.'

On the way home, the last light a slice of lemon curd, Cashin reflected that his lies to Debbie would probably keep her straight for about six months, tops.

Still, six months was a long time. His lies generally had a much shorter shelf life.

FOR REASONS Cashin didn't understand, Kendall Rogers wanted him to be in charge of policing the march.

'I'm on leave,' he said.

'Just be an hour or so.'

'Nothing's going to happen. This is Port Monro.'

It was the wrong thing to say.

'I'd just appreciate it,' she said, not quite looking at him. 'It would be a favour to me.'

'Favour, now you're talking. The favour bank.'

The demonstrators assembled at the post office in the main street. Kendall was at Cashin's end, Moorhouse Street. Carl Wexler was handling traffic at the Wallace Street intersection, not a taxing job at 11 am, winter, Port Monro. He was making a big thing of it, studied movements, like an air hostess pointing out the exits. Cashin thought it was easy to pick the blow-ins, those who had bought into Port at a high price and now wanted the drawbridge up. They had good haircuts and wore expensive outdoor clothes and leather shoes.

At the march's advertised starting time, the fat photographer from the Cromarty *Herald* was looking with sadness at the crowd, about thirty people, more than half women. The primary school came around the corner, all in rain gear, a multicoloured crocodile led by the principal, a thin balding man holding the hands of a girl and boy. The children carried signs written on white cardboard and tacked to lengths of dowel, no doubt a full morning's work in the art class:

KEEP AWAY FROM OUR MOUTH
DONT SPOIL OUR BEACHES
NATURE'S FOR EVERYONE NOT JUST THE RICH

Three shire councillors Cashin knew arrived. The *Herald* reporter got out of his car and signalled to the photographer, who went into sluggish action. Then two small buses banked up at Carl's end of the street. He directed them on with flourishes. A minute or two later, the occupants came back, walking in a group – about thirty people, all ages from about fifteen. To one side was Helen Castleman, talking on a mobile. She put it away, came past Cashin, gave him a nod.

'Good day, Detective Cashin.'

'Good day, Ms Castleman.'

Cashin watched her talking to the organiser, Sue Kinnock, a doctor's wife. She'd come to the station to show the shire permit for the march. 'We'll assemble at the post office, march down Moorhouse Street, cross Wallace, turn right into Enright, left into the park,' she'd said.

The sunlight had caught the pale yellow down on her cheeks. She had big teeth and a clipped way of speaking. Cashin put her down as the Pommy nurse who got the Aussie doctor, to the envy of her better-looking colleagues.

She came over with Helen Castleman. 'I gather you know each other, detective. Helen's WildCoast Australia president in Cromarty.'

'A person of many parts, Ms Castleman,' said Cashin.

'And you, detective. One minute, you're homicide, the next you're crowd control.'

'Multiskilling. These days we turn our hands to anything. How's Donny?'

'Not good. His mum's worried about him. How's your investigation?'

'Moving along. The way this parade should be.'

'The Channel 9 chopper's on the way, they're giving Bobby Walshe a lift. If you don't mind, we'll wait for them.'

'A reasonable wait I don't mind,' said Cashin. 'What's reasonable?'

'Fifteen minutes? They're landing on the rec reserve.'

'We can do that.'

Helen Castleman went over and helped a young man in a green WildCoast windcheater organise the marchers: children in front, the rest in ranks of five. She stood back and took a look, went over to the school principal. They talked. He didn't look happy but agreed to something. Helen chose six kids and eight of the oldest locals. They were arranged in two rows, four adults and three children in each, holding hands. Then came the school crocodile and the other marchers.

When he was finished, Helen went to Sue Kinnock. Sue raised her loud-hailer. 'We'll be off in a few minutes. Please be patient.'

A helicopter thrummed over, dropped below the line of pines. The occupants arrived soon after in one of the small buses. Carl waved them through. They parked outside the library. The door slid open and Bobby Walshe got out, followed by a young man in a dark suit. Cashin saw a woman in the front seat move the rearview mirrow to fine-tune her lipstick.

Bobby Walshe was in casual gear: light blue open-necked shirt, dark blue jacket. He kissed Helen Castleman, he knew her, you could see that by the way they laughed, the linger of his hands on her arms. Cashin felt envy, shook it away.

'Right everybody,' said Sue Kinnock, amplified. 'Sorry to keep you waiting. Banners up, please. Thank you. And ready, set, off we go.'

Cashin looked across the street. Cecily Addison was lecturing Leon, a hand raised. Leon caught Cashin's eye, nodded in a knowing way. The vinegary couple from the newsagency were in their shop doorway, mouths curving southwards. Triple-bypassed Bruce of the video shop was beside saturated-fat dealer Meryl, the fish and chip shop owner. At the kerbside bicycle rack, shivering in yellow teeshirts, three young women, the winter staff of Sandra's Café, had an argument going. The spiky-haired one with the nose rings was taking on the others.

Outside the Supa Valu supermarket stood seven or eight people in anoraks, tracksuits. An old man in a raincoat had a beanie pulled over his ears.

Cashin walked along the pavement. 'Didn't know we had so many cops,' said Darren from the sports shop. 'Out in force.'

It began to drizzle at the instant the marchers broke into thin and ragged song: '*All we are saaaying, is saaave our coast.*'

The children had gone by when two men came out of the bar of the Orion. Ronnie Barrett and his mate, a slighter shaven-headed figure in a yellow and brown striped tracksuit, small tuft of hair on his chin.

Barrett came to the pavement edge, made a megaphone with his hands: 'Fuck off wankers! Don't give a shit about jobs, do ya?'

The other man joined him, 'Rich bastards pissouta Port!' he shouted. He took a step backwards, then another, unbalanced, almost fell over.

Cashin saw Barrett gesture at someone in the march, step off the kerb, all drunken belligerence. His companion followed.

A man stepped out of the column, a black beret on the back of his head, said something to Barrett.

Cashin got moving. Carl Wexler was trotting down the street, a TV cameraman behind him. They weren't close when Barrett lunged at the marcher with his left hand, trying to hold him for a punch.

The marcher, loose-looking, took a step forward, allowed Barrett to touch him. Barrett swung with his right, the man was inside the fist, he blocked it casually with his left forearm, stood on Barrett's left foot and hit him under the chin with the heel of his right hand.

It wasn't a hard blow, there was contempt in it, but it knocked Barrett's head back, and the marcher's left hand punched him in the ribs, several quick, professional punches.

'Break it!' shouted Carl.

Barrett was down, making sounds, his friend backing off, no more interest in a fight.

The marcher turned his head, looked at Cashin, went back into the ranks, expressionless, adjusted his beret. An old man next to him patted him on the arm.

The march had stopped. Cashin turned his back on the camera, he didn't want to be on television again. 'Let's get moving here,' he said loudly. 'Move on, please.'

The crocodile moved.

'Arrest, boss?' said Carl.

'Who?'

'The greenie.'

Cashin stood over Barrett. 'Get up and fuck off,' he said, 'See you again today, mate, you're sleeping over.'

To Carl, he said, 'It's over. Back to work.'

At the park, Sue Kinnock stood on the bandstand and made a short speech about people despoiling the beauties of nature, not wanting Port Monro to end up like Surfers Paradise. Cashin looked at the storm clouds boiling in the south, saw the cold drizzle falling on umbrellas, on dozens of little raincoat hoods. Like Surfers Paradise? Please God, could the weather part of that be arranged?

Sue Kinnock introduced Helen Castleman.

'As you may know,' Helen said, 'WildCoast is dedicated to preserving what remains of Australia's unspoilt coastline and to keeping it open to everyone. We came here today to say: If you want to stop developers ruining everything that makes your place special, well, we'll stand with you. We'll fight this project. And we'll win!'

Loud applause. Helen waited for silence, nodding.

'And now I'd like to introduce someone who identifies with our concerns and who's made a huge effort to be with us today. Please welcome the leader of Australia's newest political party, someone who grew up in this area, Bobby Walshe of United Australia.'

Walshe stepped up. The crowd was pleased to see him. Sue Kinnock tried to hold a big golf umbrella over him. He motioned her away, said his thanks, paused.

'Silverwater Estuary. Wonderful name. Brings to mind a place where a clean river meets the sea.'

Walshe smiled. 'Well, the reality is that Silverwater Estuary will end up as a place where a landscape and an ecosystem have been wrecked in the name of profit.'

He held up a newspaper.

'The Cromarty *Herald* is pretty excited about the project. Two hundred and fifty new jobs. How can that be bad? Well, let me tell you that these people always get the local paper excited about creating jobs. New jobs. It's the magic phrase, isn't it? Justifies anything. But all over Australia there are once beautiful places now ugly. Hideous. Ruined by projects like Silverwater Estuary.'

Bobby Walshe paused. 'And the developers and the local papers sold every single one of these projects as a job creation scheme.'

He ran fingers through his wet, shiny hair. 'We also have to ask what jobs did they actually create? I'll tell you. Jobs for part-time cleaners and dish-washers and waiters. Jobs that pay the minimum wage and come and go with the seasons and airline strikes and events thousands of kilometres away.'

Applause.

'And while I'm at it, let's talk about so-called local papers. Local? No, they're not. Take this newspaper.'

He waved the Cromarty *Herald*.

'This local paper is owned by Australian Media. The head office of AM is in Brisbane. That's pretty local, isn't it? The editor of this local paper arrived three months ago from New South Wales, where he edited another AM local paper. Before that he was in Queensland, doing what he's been sent to Cromarty to do. And what's that?'

Bobby waited.

'To boost advertising revenue. Make more money. Because, like the people behind Silverwater Estuary, money is all that matters. And this environmentally dangerous project means large amounts of advertising money for the paper. As for the company behind this, well, they're just flak-catchers. It'll be sold to other people once they get planning permission.'

Walshe was wet now, rain was running down his face, his shirt was dark.

'The state government can shut the door on this project in a second,' he said. 'They show no sign of doing that. It's not in the coastal reserves, they say. It's a matter for the shire council, they say. Does that mean that areas outside the coastal reserve are fair game for any shonky developer who comes along? I'm here today to say to hell with that bureaucratic rubbish. United Australia will support you in this fight. In all the fights like this going on all over our country. And that includes the cities.'

Bobby brushed water from his hair, put his hands in the air. 'One last thing,' he said. 'Do you know what a project like this is? I'll tell you what it is. It's an insult to the future.'

Applause. Bobby Walshe shook his head and rain droplets flew.

Cashin thought that Walshe knew how this would look on television: a handsome politician standing in the rain for a cause more important than his comfort.

To long applause, Bobby stood down. There followed a bad speech by a man with a bad haircut and a bad beard, shire councillor Barry Doull. When the hard rain came, Sue shut him up, said the thanks, directed people to the Save the Mouth fighting fund booth.

The crowd broke up, people wanted to shake Bobby Walshe's hand and he shook every one offered, bent to talk to an old lady and she kissed him, the camera on them. The school crocodile re-formed, set off, taking the short route home.

Cashin walked back with Kendall. 'A spunk,' she said. 'He's got my vote. I didn't know he was local.'

'Make sure it's his policies you like,' Cashin said.

In the main street, Bobby Walshe did a short on-camera interview with the woman who'd arrived with him. Now Cashin recognised her from when he and Dove were leaving the Cromarty station to go to court. She had asked the question.

Bobby talked to Helen Castleman. They were animated. He looked over his shoulder, met Cashin's eyes, said something to Helen. They came over.

'I know you,' said Walshe. 'Joe Cashin. Bern Doogue's cousin. From primary school.'

'That's right.'

Walshe put out a hand, they shook.

'How's Bern?' he said.

'Fine. Good.'

'What's he do now?'

'Well, this and that.'

'I couldn't have survived primary school without Bern,' said Walshe. 'The best kid on your side in a fight.'

'Some aptitude there, yes,' said Cashin.

Walshe laughed. 'You see him?'

'No week goes by.'

'Luke and Corey,' said Walshe. 'You were there.'

'Unfortunately.'

'It's a pretty sad business.'

'Kids go around carrying shotguns, there's always the chance things will turn sad.'

Walshe shrugged. 'Well, the inquest will decide whether it was his weapon, who fired first. Give Bern my regards. Tell him I haven't forgotten.'

'I'll tell him.'

They shook hands again.

'Don't forget to vote United Australia,' said Walshe.

'Can you vote for a soccer team?'

Walshe laughed, Helen gave Cashin a downturned smile. They went back to the vehicle and the television woman spoke to Walshe again.

Walking back to the station, Kendall said. 'You didn't say you knew him.'

'He knows me. Listen, Billy Piggot. What's he mean to you?'

'Don't know a Billy. There's a Ray Piggot that's a piece of work.'

'What's he done?'

'Ripped off a rep staying at the motel. Five hundred-odd bucks. The bloke came in the next morning. Cromarty handled it.'

'Ripped off how?'

'He had a story, the rep, but it was probably ...' She made a sign with her right hand, the wiggle.

'Pillars of society, the Piggots,' said Cashin. 'Well, I'm off, two weeks to life, starting in five minutes.'

'And we're fully staffed. If you call a musclebound beach boy and a work-experience kid staff.'

'With your guidance, they'll grow,' said Cashin. 'Be fair but firm. Brunette but soft.'

She gave him a little nudge in the back with a fist, an act of disrespect given his rank, insubordination really.

LATE IN the day, a man in his seventies called Mick arrived from outside Kenmare and towed a mower around Tommy Cashin's wilderness, broke bottles, mangled metal, bumped over solid obstacles hidden in the grass.

'Should charge you bloody danger money,' he said when he'd loaded the tractor and the mower onto his truck. 'Can't, can I? Cause I'm doin this for nothin and you're givin me sixty bucks to pass on to the charity of my choosin.'

'I'm a cop,' said Cashin. 'Sworn to uphold the tax laws of our country.'

'Make it fifty,' said Mick.

Cashin gave him a note. He folded it and tucked it into the sweatband of his hat. People in this part of the world had an aversion to collecting the goods and services tax on behalf of the government.

While the dogs hunted the cleared area, much taken with the smells released by the mowing, Dave Rebb and Cashin walked around the ruined building, measuring it. Cashin held the end of the tape and Rebb wrote down the distances and drew on a pad of graph paper. At the end, they sat on a piece of wall and Rebb showed him what he had recorded.

'Big,' said Cashin. 'Never thought it was that big.'

'Rich bugger, was he?'

'He made money on the goldfields, blew it all on the house. Also breeding horses, I think.'

A wind had come up, flattening the grass beyond. They could smell the land it had run over, smell the cold sea.

'He must've gone nuts early,' said Rebb. 'Could've built it somewhere warm.'

'It's about showing off,' said Cashin. 'He had to do it here. The Cashins had bugger all before that. Bugger all after that too.'

Rebb finished making a smoke, lit it, spat tobacco strands off his bottom lip. 'So you want to do that again, more showing off?'

'I do. What now?'

'Asking me? What do I know?'

They sat for a while, stood, the wind stronger now, pushing at them. They watched the dogs. The animals sensed their eyes, looked around, ran over and visited briefly, went back to work. Cashin thought about the stupidity of the project. This was the moment to quit, no harm done.

'What about the picture?' said Rebb. 'There's a whole piece missing, blown to buggery. Also we need a shelter, keep stuff dry.'

They walked back, the dark ponding in the valley. Days ended quickly now, twenty minutes from full light to ink black. Cashin's body ached from the bending.

Near the shed, Rebb said, 'Old bloke give me a bunny. In the fridge. See that?'

'No.'

'Bin there two days. Better cook it tonight.'

Cashin didn't say anything. He didn't feel like cooking.

'I can do it,' said Rebb. 'A bunny stew.'

A moment of hesitation. A cop meets a swaggie, the swaggie goes to live on his property, cooks meals. The locals would take a keen interest in this. Poofs, mate. Detective Poof and his swaggie bumchum.

Cashin didn't care. 'Sounds good,' he said. 'Go for your life.'

He fed the dogs, made a fire, got out beers, sat down, some relief from the pain. Rebb cooked like someone who'd done it before, cutting up the rabbit, chopping the wilted vegetables, browning the meat.

'This wine?' said Rebb, pointing at a bottle on the shelf. 'Saving it for something?'

'There's a corkscrew hanging there.'

Rebb opened the wine, poured some into the pot, added water. 'That's done,' he said. 'Be back.'

He went to the side door and the dogs roused themselves and followed him out. Cashin read the newspaper, drowsed. Rebb came back, dogs in first, they came to greet Cashin as if they'd been to the North Pole, thinking of him all the way there and back.

Cashin thought it was a very good stew, piled on rice. He ate in front of the fire and the television. Dave ate at the table, reading the newspaper. The news came on. The Port Monro march was item number six:

United Australia leader Bobby Walshe was in the seaside town of Port Monro today to speak at a rally against a proposed resort development.

The rally had things television liked: kids holding hands with the elderly, singing, the brief fistfight.

'That bloke's lucky to escape an assault charge,' said Cashin without looking at Rebb.

'Self defence,' said Rebb. 'He didn't hurt him much.'

'You swaggies know how to handle yourselves.'

'Just a drunk,' said Rebb. 'No challenge there.'

They watched the snatches of Bobby Walshe's speech. He looked good wet, there was a close-up, raindrops running down his face. They saw the old lady kiss him, his kind smile, his hand on her elbow.

Walshe did a brief interview. Then the camera followed him and Helen Castleman going over to Cashin and Kendall and Wexler. The camera zoomed.

Cashin shuddered. He hadn't seen the lens pointing, he would have turned away. The woman with the freeze-dried hair said: 'Bobby Walshe also took the opportunity to speak to Detective Joe Cashin. Cashin was one of the police present at the death on Thursday of Walshe's nephew Corey Pascoe and another Aboriginal youth, Luke Ericsen, both from the Daunt Settlement outside Cromarty.'

Bobby Walshe again, running a hand through his damp hair: 'Just saying hello to the officer. I went to primary school with him. My hope is we'll find out exactly what happened that night and we'll get justice for the dead boys. I say I hope. Aboriginal people have lived in hope of justice for two hundred-odd years.'

Rebb got up, went to the sink, washed his plate, his knife and fork. 'You shoot that kid?' he said, neutral tone.

Cashin looked at him. 'No. But I would have if he'd pointed the shotgun at me.'

'I'll be off then.'

'You've got a touch with a dead bunny,' said Cashin. 'Bring one around any time.'

At the door, dogs trying to go out with him, Rebb said, 'When's the chainsaw coming?'

'Tomorrow. Bern reckons he'll drop it off with the water tanker first thing. That could be sparrow, could be midnight.'

'Also. We need stuff – cement, sand, timber, all that. I wrote it down by the sink there.'

'How much cement?'

Cashin thought he saw pity in Rebb's eyes. 'Make it six bags.'

'Need a cement-mixer?'

Rebb shook his head. 'Not unless you planning to bring in a few more innocent blokes you find on the road.'

'I'm always looking,' said Cashin.

He rang Bern and then, tired, hurting, sad, he went to bed early. Sleep came, a nightmare woke him, a new one. Dark and rain and garish light and screaming, people everywhere, confusion. He was trapped, held by something octopus-like, he fought it, it was crushing him, the space was shrinking, no air, he was suffocating, dying, terrified.

Awake in the big chamber, thin green light from the radio clock, feeling his heart in his chest and hearing the wind planing over the corrugations.

He got up. The dogs heard him and barked and he let them in. They ran for the bed, bumping, jumped, snuggled down. Cashin put on the standing lamp, threw wood into the stove, wrapped himself in a blanket and sat down with *Nostromo*.

Always an army chaplain – some unshaven, dirty man, girt with a sword and with a tiny cross embroidered in white cotton on the left breast of a lieutenant's uniform – would follow, cigarette in the corner of the mouth, wooden stool in hand, to hear the confession and give absolution; for the Citizen Saviour of the Country (Guzman Bento was called thus officially in petitions) was not averse from the exercise of rational clemency. The irregular report of the firing squad would be heard, followed sometimes by a single finishing shot; a little bluish cloud of smoke would float up above the green bushes ...

He fell asleep in the big shabby chair, woke in early light, two dogs nudging him, their tails crossing like furry metronomes. The phone on the counter rang when he was filling the kettle.

'Constable Martin, Cromarty, boss. I'm instructed to tell you that Donny Coulter's mother rang a few minutes ago to says he's missing. She doesn't know since when. She saw him in bed at 11 pm last night.'

Cashin put a hand over the mouthpiece and cleared his throat. 'He hasn't done anything till he doesn't clock in. Tell his mum to check his mates, see if anyone else's gone. Call me on the mobile.'

He went outside, had a piss, looking at the hillside. The scarlet maples came and went through the mist like spot fires. He moved his shoulders, trying to ease the stiffness.

Donny wasn't going to sign the bail book at 10 am. He knew that.

'DONNY DIDN'T show,' said Hopgood. 'The mother says the little prick's been weepy.'

In misty rain, Cashin and Rebb had just started clearing the path that led to the former front door, uncovering red fired tiles, the colour still bright.

'She's had a look around?' said Cashin.

'I gather.'

'What about his mates?'

'Sounds like they're accounted for. Fastafuckingsleep like the rest of the boongs.'

'Take anything? Bag, clothes?'

'I would've said.'

Cashin was watching Rebb digging into the deep layer of couch grass, weeds, earth. He swung the long-handled spade tirelessly, scooping, scraping the hidden tiles. It made Cashin feel feeble, his own excavations meagre things.

'You might be on holiday but you're still in charge,' said Hopgood. 'We await instructions.'

'Bail violation,' said Cashin. 'Matter for the uniforms. The liaison bloke can work with Donny's mum, get the locals to search the whole Daunt. Every garage, shed and shithouse.'

'The locals are going to find Donny? You off the medication?'

Cashin looked at the sky. 'Keep me posted,' he said.

Back to digging his side of the path, feeling hollow in the stomach, as if he hadn't eaten for a long time. He was four or five metres along, Rebb as far as that ahead of him, when the water trailer arrived, a battered tank towed by Bern's Dodge truck, equally dented and scarred. Bern got out, unshaven, greasy overalls, cigarette in mouth. He looked around, unpleased by what he saw.

'Jesus, you're nuts,' he said. 'Cash on delivery.'

'Half past eleven?' said Cashin. 'This's first thing?'

'First thing I'm deliverin to you today. One-twenty bucks for the chainie, all tools included, owned by an old lady cut flowers with it, twenty for the corrie iron, twenty a week for the tanker, four weeks minimum hire, ten for delivery. Water, free first time, that's generous, refills ten. Let's say two hundred, throw in the first top-up. Present to you since you're family and a fuckwit.'

Cashin walked around the water tanker. It had been crudely sprayed black with aerosol paint. But before that rust had set in where markings had been erased, probably with a steel brush on a grinder. The rust was bubbling the new paint.

'Where'd you get this?' he said.

Bern flicked his cigarette end. 'Listen,' he said, 'you go in the McDonald's drive-in, you ask the kid where'd you get the mince?'

Cashin did another circuit of the tanker. 'The army reserve complaint,' he said. 'They were down the other side of Livermore, in the gorge, buggering about, rooting under canvas, went into town for a few beers. The next day they couldn't find two water tankers and a big tent and some tarps and gas bottles. Missing in action.'

'In the army reserve,' said Bern, 'takes three to wipe one arse. Bloke brung this in the yard. Says he's coming back to talk money. Never seen him before, never see him again.' He spat. 'What more can I say?'

'Don't say anything that could be used against you in a court of law,' said Cashin. He got out his wallet, offered four fifties.

'What, no argument?'

'No.'

Bern took three fifties. 'Jesus, you bring out the Christian in me.'

'Be a small Christian. Like a garden gnome Christian. We need some building hardware here. The trowels and the spirit levels, that sort of thing.'

Bern looked at Rebb, leaning on his spade, gaze elsewhere. 'Hey, Dave,' he shouted. 'Know a bit more about buildin than this bloke?'

Rebb turned, shrugged. 'I wouldn't know what he knows.'

'Yeah, well, I suggest you blokes come around,' said Bern. 'I got some brickie's stuff. Not cheap, mind you, hard to find. Take their gear to the grave, brickies.'

'There was a burg at Cromarty Tech,' said Cashin. 'They got into the building department storeroom.'

'Well, whoopy fuckin doo. Another thing I never heard of. You make up this shit, don't you?'

'I don't want to buy anything on the list of items missing,' said Cashin.

'Where you get your ideas I dunno. Not a stain on me. Your mates come down on me, that fuckin Hopgood, him and a footy team of pricks. An hour of fuckin around, messin up my place, they go off empty-handed, not so much as a fuckin sorry.' Bern spat. 'Anyway, give us a hand with this iron,' he said. 'You got any good corrie iron stories?'

They unloaded the corrugated iron. Bern got into the truck. 'Dave, been meanin to ask,' he said. 'Don't I know you from somewhere?'

Rebb was examining the chainsaw. 'Well, I don't know you,' he said. 'But I know a buggered chainie when I see one.'

They got back to work. When Rebb reached the house, he turned and began digging on Cashin's side, coming towards him.

Cashin's mobile.

'For your information,' said Hopgood. 'No Donny. They checked every square inch of the place.'

Cashin was looking at the blisters on his left palm, one pale pregnant bump for each finger. 'Stage two,' he said. 'Probably should have done that in the first place.'

'Talking about us or you?'

'Just talking.'

'The alert's been out since before 9 am. We didn't wait for your say so. They tell you Bourgoyne's on the way out?'

'No.'

'Maybe you're out of the loop.'

When they were nearing each other on the path, casting the last sods into the green wildness, Rebb said, 'That Bern. He's your cousin?'

'Right.'

'Through your old man?'

'My mum. His dad's my mum's brother.'

Rebb gave Cashin a full stare and went back to work. After a while, he said, 'This was a serious garden. Got pictures of it too?'

'I'm going to Cromarty, I'll see,' said Cashin. He wasn't thinking about gardens, he was thinking about Donny and the dead boys and Hopgood.

HELEN CASTLEMAN was in court, said her firm. Cashin walked around the block, had just sat in the courtroom when she rose, all in black, silky hair.

'As your honour knows, the Bail Act of 1977 does not give us a definition of exceptional circumstances ...'

The magistrate stopped her with a raised finger. 'Ms Castleman, don't tell me what I know.'

'Thank you for your guidance, your honour. The defendant has no history of involvement with drugs. He has two convictions for minor offences involving second-hand goods. He has four children under twelve. The family's only income is the defendant's scrap–metal business. Mrs O'Halloran cannot care for the children and run the business without her husband.'

The magistrate was looking in the direction of the windows.

'Your honour,' Helen Castleman said, 'I'm told that my client's trial is at least three months away. I submit with respect that these factors do add up to the exceptional circumstances demanded by the Act and I ask for him to be granted bail.'

'In this community,' the magistrate said, 'heroin possession is regarded as an extremely serious offence.'

'Attempted possession, with respect, your honour.'

Cashin could see the magistrate's jaw muscles knot. 'Possession of heroin is regarded as an extremely serious offence in this community. Perhaps that wasn't the case in Sydney, Ms Castleman.'

The magistrate made a croaking noise and looked around for appreciation, showed yellow dog teeth. The prosecutor smiled, her eyes dead. The magistrate came back to Helen, teeth still showing.

'The points I wish to make, your honour,' said Helen, 'are that my client, if convicted, faces a penalty at the bottom of the scale, and that his circumstances make the prospect of bail violation remote.'

The magistrate stared at her.

'If your honour wishes,' said Helen, 'I will address the subject, including the recent judgment by Mr Justice Musgrove in the Supreme Court on an appeal against a magistrate's court's refusal of bail.'

He took out a tissue and blew his nose. 'I don't require any instruction from the depths of your inexperience, Ms Castleman. The conditions are as follows.'

The magistrate set bail conditions.

'Your honour,' said Helen. 'With respect, I submit that $20,000 is so far beyond the defendant's capacity as to constitute a denial of bail.'

'Oh really?'

'May I address the court on precedent?'

He heard her without interjection. Then, silver motes of spittle catching the light, he reduced bail to $5,000.

When Cashin came out, a criminal investigation unit cop he knew called Greg Law was leaning against the balustrade, smoking a cigarette in fingers the colour of the magistrate's teeth.

'Jesus, that woman's cheeky,' Law said. 'You're supposed to lick his arse, not threaten to ram an appeal judgment up it.'

'When to lick and when to kick,' said Cashin. 'The central problem of life in the criminal courts.'

Law's eyes were on the street. Cashin followed them to a rusting orange Datsun with one blue door. The driver was slumped like a fat crash–dummy, her beefy right arm hanging out of the window, a cigarette in fat fingers. She lifted it to mouth. Cashin could see three big rings, knuckledusters.

'Gabby Trevena,' said Law. 'The lord knows, she's overdue. Broke a woman's jaw outside the Gecko Lounge, she's pregnant like a balloon. When she's down, Gabby puts in the slipper, cracks four ribs. What a piece of fucking work.'

A man in middle age and a youth came down the street, came up the steps, looking at Greg Law. The man was thin faced, faded ginger hair, mildewy suit from long ago, looser on him now than when he wore it to the wedding. The youth looked like his father, with longer ginger hair, bright with life, and a gold ring in an earlobe.

'Straight on, with you in a moment,' said Law, twinkling fingers at them. 'The story is the woman pinched these plants Gabs had growing in the roof. At crop time.'

'A roof garden,' said Cashin. 'Up in the ceiling of the fibro, a few deckchairs, plants in pots, Gabs sunbathing. I can see it.'

'Today the fat bitch walks. Complainant can't be found. Might need an excavator to find her.'

Law levered himself away from the railing. 'Talking licking and kicking, I hear Hopgood's your best mate.'

'Yeah?'

Law shot his cigarette into the street. 'Gabby Trevena's not the most dangerous person in this town. Almost but not quite.'

'What's that mean?'

'What do you think? Got to go.'

Helen Castleman came down the stairs. Cashin stepped forward. 'Good day,' he said. 'Can I have a word?'

'If you want to walk with me. I'm late for a client.'

They went down the steps, turned left.

'Get my complaint about Donny being harassed?' she said.

'No. I'm on leave. Harassed how?'

'I complained to your Mr Hopgood. Patrol cars driving by the house, shining spotlights. What kind of shit is that? Are you surprised he's taken off? That was the aim, wasn't it?'

'I don't know about this.'

'You simply don't have a case, that's your problem.'

'We've got a case,' Cashin said. It was a lie.

Two skateboarders were coming, in line, the front one too old to be having fun. Cashin moved left, the pair rolled between them.

'Tell that to the two dead kids,' said Helen.

'No sane cop wants to shoot kids, shoot anyone actually. But normal kids don't get out of a wreck with a shotgun.'

'Well, that's your story, that's not a matter of fact. What do you want from me?'

Cashin didn't want her to dislike him. 'It would help if we knew he'd done a runner.'

Helen shook her head in a musing way. 'Do you think I'd tell you if I knew?'

'What would it hurt to tell me?'

'If I knew, it would be knowledge gained in representing him. How could I pass that on to you? I cross here.'

They stood at the corner, waiting for the lights, not looking at each other. Cashin wanted to look at her, looked. She was looking at him.

'I don't remember you as being so tall and thin,' she said.

'Late growth spurt. But you're probably thinking of someone else.'

Green light. They crossed.

'No,' she said, 'I remember you.'

Cashin felt a blush. 'Returning to the present,' he said. 'You're an officer of the court. There's no ethical problem.'

No reply. They walked in silence, stopped at her office, a bluestone building.

'I'm told you were city homicide,' she said.

'Been there, yes.'

He saw the shift of her head, readied himself.

'So it's your experience that lawyers tell you things about their clients?'

'I don't generally ask lawyers things about their clients. But your client's violated his bail. All I'm asking you is that if you know he's left the area, you save us the trouble of looking for him here. It's not a big ask.'

'I'm prepared to say that I don't know any more than you do.'

'Thank you, Ms Castleman.'

'My pleasure, Detective Cashin. Any time. By the way, I found out yesterday that we're to be neighbours.'

'How's that?'

'I've bought the place next door. The one with the old house. Mrs Corrigan's property.'

'Welcome to the shire,' said Cashin. Today we fence that boundary, he thought.

He walked back to the station. Hopgood wasn't there, out on the matter of a body in the ashes of a house in Cromarty West.

Cashin left a short message, drove to the library for the photograph. Closed, the librarians' day off. On the way home, he thought about the night in his last year at school, the final days. Tony Cressy drove out to pick him up in a Merc, a car from Cressy's Prestige Motors on the highway. Tony was the full back in the Cromarty High team, he had no pace, could hardly get his body off the ground, but he was big and he intimidated the opposition.

The four of them in the car, driving to the Kettle, to the Dangar Steps, two males and Helen Castleman and Susan Walls, he had not spoken more than a few words to either of the girls before that night.

The steps had long been fenced off, warning signs put up, but that only encouraged people. He helped Helen climb the wire, made a stirrup with his hands. She had no trouble with stirrups, she was a show jumper, people said she could go to the Olympics. They walked across the rock, along the worn path, in the footsteps of Mad Percy Hamilton Dangar, who spent twelve years cutting the narrow steps that began close to the entrance and ran around the walls, going down to the high-tide waterline. Everyone knew the story. Perhaps a hundred steps remained, unsafe lower down, gnawed by sea and spray and wind.

That night, they didn't descend far. They sat with backs against the cliff, the boys smoking, passing a bottle of Jim Beam, taking burning sips, not really drinkers, any of them. It was just for show. You had to do it. Cashin and Helen sat on the step below Tony Cressy and Susan. Tony kept them laughing, he could make anyone laugh, even the stern teachers.

Cashin remembered the feel of a breast touching his bare arm when Helen laughed, rocked sideways.

She wasn't wearing a bra.

He remembered the huge waves breaking against the entrance, the thunder, the white spray rising, the heart-stopping moments when the water exploded into the round chamber beneath them, surged up the limestone sides. There was no certainty it would stop – it came up and up and you thought that this one would pluck you from your perch, take you down into the hole, falling, falling into the boiling Kettle.

But it didn't.

It climbed the cliff to within five or six metres, fell back, tongues of water spat from the rock caves. The Kettle frothed and surged, then the big hole drained and it was calm.

He remembered the jokes, the next-time-it's-us-mate jokes.

They dropped Susan first, parked half a block from Helen's house. Joe walked her to the gate. She kissed him quickly, unexpectedly, looked at him, then she kissed him again, a long kiss, her hands in his hair.

'You're nice,' she said, went in her gate.

He walked back to the car, heart pumping. 'Now that,' said Tony Cressy, 'now that is class. And you're a lucky boy.'

IT WAS almost dark, the wind up, when they finished digging the rotten timber out of the last posthole. Cashin ached everywhere, it hurt to stand upright.

'Get it done by night tomorrow,' said Rebb. 'Given we got the materials.'

'Bern'll bring everything in the morning,' said Cashin. 'He's got a better understanding now of what's meant by first thing.'

They shouldered the tools, began to climb the hill for home. Cashin whistled and black heads appeared at the creek, together, looking up.

The house roof was in sight when his mobile rang, a feeble sound in the soughing wind. He stopped, put down the spade, found the phone. Rebb kept going.

'Cashin.'

Static. No reply. He killed it.

Cashin followed Rebb up the slope, every step an effort. On the flat, the phone rang again.

'Cashin.'

'Joe?' His mother.

'Yes, Syb.'

'You're faint, can you hear me?'

'I can hear you.'

'Joe, Michael tried to commit suicide, they don't know ...'

'Where?' A feeling of cold, of nausea.

'In Melbourne, in his unit, someone rang him and they realised there ...'

'What hospital?'

'The Alfred.'

'I'll go now. Want to come?'

'I'm scared, Joe. Did you ring him? I asked you to ring him.'

'Syb, I'm leaving now. Want to come?'

'I'm too scared, Joe. I can't face ...'

'That's fine. I'll call you when I've seen him.'

'Joe.'

'Yes.'

'You should have spoken to him. I told you, I asked you twice, Joe. Twice.'

Cashin was looking at Rebb and the dogs. They were almost at the house, dogs criss-crossing in front, noses down. They had the air of point men, at the sharp end of a dangerous mission. At the gate, they would look back, each raise a paw, give those watching the all-clear.

'I'll ring, Syb,' he said. 'Call me if you hear anything.'

It was full dark when he came to the Branxholme junction and turned for the highway and the city. The headlights swept across a peeling house, a car on its axles, lit up devil-green dog eyes beside a bleeding rainwater tank.

CASHIN FELT a near-panic as the doctor led him down the long room, between the curtained cubicles. He knew the smell, of disinfectant and scented cleaning fluids, the computer-pale colour of everything and the humming, the incessant electronic humming. It came to him that a nuclear submarine would be like this, lying in a freezing ocean trench, hushed, run by electronics.

As they passed the stalls, Cashin saw bodies attached to tubes, wires. Tiny lights glowed, some pulsed.

'Here,' said the doctor.

Michael's eyes were closed. His face, what showed of it around the oxygen mask, was white. Strands of hair, black as liquorice, were drawn on the pillow. Cashin remembered his hair as short, neat – salesman's hair.

'He'll be okay,' said the doctor. 'The guy who rang him called emergency. Lucky. Also, the paras weren't far away, coming from a false alarm. So we had a small window of time.'

He was young, Asian, skin of a baby, a private-school voice.

'Took what?' said Cashin. He wanted to be gone, into the open, breathe cleansing traffic fumes.

'Sleeping pills. Benzodiazepine. Alcohol. Lots of both, a lethal amount.'

The doctor felt his jaw with a small hand. He was very tired. 'He's just come off the dialysis. Feel like hell when he wakes up.'

'When will that be?'

'Tomorrow.' He looked at his watch. 'It's arrived already. Come around noon, he should be talking then.'

Cashin left the building and rang his mother, kept it short. Then he drove to Villani's house in Brunswick, parked in the street and walked down the driveway. He'd rung on the way. 'Tony's room's open, next to the garage,' Villani had said. 'I think it's been disinfected recently.'

The room was papered with posters of football players, kick-boxers, muscle cars, a music stand stood in a corner, sheet music on it. A cello case leant against the wall. Cashin looked at the photographs pinned to the corkboard above the desk. He saw his own face in one, long before Rai Sarris, a younger Cashin, looking at the camera, in the pool at someone's house, holding up a small Tony Villani. The boy was the adult Villani shrunken, retouched to take away the frown lines, to restore some hair at the temples.

That's how old my boy is now, Cashin thought, and sadness rose in him, to his throat. He sat on the bed, took off his shoes and socks, slumped, elbows on knees, head in hands, tired and hurting. After a while, he looked at his watch: 2.25 am.

A car in the driveway. A few minutes later, a tap on the door.

'Come in,' Cashin said.

Villani, in a suit, tie loosened, bottle in one hand, wine glasses in the other. 'The news?'

'He's going to be okay. They got him in time.'

'That's worth a drink.'

'Just the one bottle?'

'You're supposed to be fucking frail. Although, personally, I think it's all been wanking.'

Villani sat in his son's desk chair, gave Cashin a glass, poured red wine. 'Serious attempt?' he said.

'The doctor says so.'

'That's a worry. Know the why?'

'He rang my mum a few times, feeling down. She asked me to talk to him. I didn't.'

'That's like a summary of a short story.'

'What the fuck would you know about short stories?'

Villani looked around the room. 'Been reading a bit. Can't sleep.' He ran wine around his mouth, eyes on the posters. 'This isn't just any grog,' he said. 'But wasted on some. Smoke?'

'Yes, please.'

'I'm giving up tomorrow. Because you've given up.'

The nicotine hit Cashin the way it used to after a surf – raw, eye-blinking. He drank some wine.

'Definitely not your 2.30 am cask piss,' he said. 'Somehow I can tell that.'

'Bloke gave it to me, I couldn't say no.'

'Work needed on that before you front up to ethical standards. Is this early rising or late to bed?'

'Remember Vic Zable?'

'Amnesia is not the problem.'

'Yeah, well, Vic got it tonight, carpark at the arts centre, can you believe that? The guy doesn't know an art from a fart. In his ribs, couldn't get closer range unless you stick it up his arse. The shooter was sitting next to him, the silver Merc Kompressor, quadraphonic radio on, heater's going, he gives Vic the whole magazine. One little fucker bounces around inside Vic, comes out behind his collarbone, hits the roof.'

Cashin took a sip. 'How many left-handed friends has Vic got?'

'You're like a cop in a movie. Two we know so far. One's in Sydney, the other one's not home. I've just been there. There was a moment when I thought we'd get lucky.'

'Gangland hit arrest. Cop hailed.'

'In my dreams.'

'How's Laurie?'

'Good. The same. Pissed off at me. Well, we're mutually pissed.'

'What's wrong?'

Villani took a drag, his cheeks hollowed, pulsed out three, four smoke rings, perfect circles rolling in the dead air. 'Both of us having … affairs.'

'I thought you just looked?'

'Yeah, well, not much joy at home, if I'm not knackered, Laurie is. She's got all these night functions, the races, corporate catering, sometimes we don't see each other for days. We don't talk anymore, haven't talked for years. Just business, the bills, the kids. Anyway, I met this woman and the next day I actually wanted to see her again.'

'And Laurie?'

'I found out about her little adventure. Don't leave your mobile account lying around.'

'Cancel out then, don't they? Two little adventures?'

'It's a question of who went first, cause and effect. I'm said to be the cause of her rooting this cameraman dickhead. She's with him now, in Cairns, catering for some moron television shit. Probably on the beach, fucking under a tropical moon.'

'Grown poetic,' said Cashin. He didn't want to hear any more, he liked Laurie, he had lusted after her. 'Is that what being the boss does?'

Villani poured wine. 'I just pedal. I've got this pommy cunt Wicken on my back, he's cut out Bell, report directly to him. Don't understand the politics, don't fucking want to. I want Singo back, I was happy then.'

He sighed.

'We were both happy then,' said Cashin. 'Happier. I'll drop in on him in the morning.'

'Shit, I've got to get out there, there's never a fucking minute in the day. Well, what's with Donny?'

'The lawyer says there's been harassment, cars keeping the family awake. Why didn't you tell me about Hopgood?'

'Thought you knew the history of bloody Cromarty. Still, Donny might turn up.'

'Or not,' said Cashin. 'And we never had a fucking thing on him. Nothing.'

Villani shrugged. 'Yeah, well, we'll see. Forward, what do you do about your brother?'

It had been on Cashin's mind. 'Failed suicides. I know bugger all about it.'

'Wayne's alive, failed suicide. Needs to put in more effort. Bruce's dead. Well done, Bruce. Your brother's the family success, is he?'

'No,' Cashin said. 'He's just clever and educated. Plus the money.'

Villani filled the glasses. 'And the happiness, in spades. Not married?'

'No.'

'Someone?'

'No idea. The last time I saw him was when I was in hospital. He didn't sit down, took a few calls. I don't blame him, we don't know each other. Just doing his duty.'

'Sounds like Laurie on me and the family. If he wants a shrink, there's this bloke Bertrand saw when he went sad after that Croat cunt stabbed him. Not a cop shrink.'

'The Croat's the one needed the shrink. Bertrand needed a panelbeater.'

They had shared a life, they talked, smoked, Villani went into the night and came back with another bottle, open. He poured. 'You think about the job? A person of leisure. Time to think.'

'What else was I good for?' Cashin was feeling the long drive, the hospital, the drink.

'Anything. You've got the brain.'

'Don't know about that. Anyway, I never thought, I didn't know what to do, stuffed around, surfed, then I just joined. Lots of fuckwits but ... I don't know. It didn't feel like a job.' Cashin drank. 'Getting introspective, are we?'

Villani scratched his head. 'I never felt the worth of it till I got to homicide. The robbers, well, that was full-on excitement, us against the crooks, like a game for big kids. But homicide, that was different. Singo made me feel that. Justice for the dead. He say that to you?'

Cashin nodded.

'Singo could pick the right people for the squad. He just knew. Birkerts was bloody hopeless at everything but Singo picked him. Bloke's a star. Now I pick people like Dove. University degree, all chip and no shoulder. Doesn't want to be black, doesn't want to be white.'

'He'll be okay,' Cashin said. 'He's smart.'

'And now,' said Villani, 'I'm trying to get justice for drug scumbags got knocked before they could knock some other arseholes. Plus I get lectures on politics and fucking dress sense and applying the right spin. I now know why Singo blew a brain fuse.'

They drank most of the bottle before Villani said, 'You're more knackered than I am. Set the alarm if you want to. I'd have a fucking decent sleep myself.'

Before bed, Cashin slid open the window, got under the duvet on the narrow bed. The smell of cigarette smoke lingered. He thought of being seventeen, in the room he shared with Bern, lying on their backs in the dark, passing a smoke between the single beds before sleep.

When he woke, the clock said 8.17 am. He rose, dizzy for a moment. He had slept as if clubbed, felt clubbed now.

An envelope under the door.

Joe: Back door key. Eggs and bacon in the fridge.

Cashin ate breakfast at a small place on Sydney Road. It was either Turkish or Greek. The eggs were served by a wide man with eyes the colour of milk stout.

'I know you,' he said. 'You come after they shoot Alex Katsourides next door. You and a small one.'

'That's a long time ago,' said Cashin.

'You never catch them.'

'No. Maybe one day.'

A big sniff. 'One day. You never catch them. Gangland killers. That bloke on the radio, he says police useless.'

Cashin felt the blood coming to his face, the heat in his eyes. 'I'm eating,' he said. 'You want to talk to a cop, go down to the station. Where's the pepper?'

MICHAEL WAS out of intensive care, in a single room on the floor above. He was awake, pale, darkly stubbled.

Cashin went to the bed and touched his brother's shoulder, awkward. 'Gave us a scare, mate,' he said.

'Sorry.' Hoarse, breathless voice.

'Feeling okay?'

Michael didn't quite look at him. 'Terrible,' he said. 'I feel like such a creep, wasting people's time. There are sick people here.'

Cashin didn't know where to go. 'Serious decision you took,' he said.

'Not actually a decision. It just happened, sort of. I was pretty pissed.'

'You hadn't been thinking about it?'

'Thinking about it, yes.' He closed his eyes. 'I've been pretty low.'

Time went by. Michael seemed to go to sleep. It allowed Cashin to study him, he had never done that. You didn't usually look at people closely, you looked into their eyes. Animals didn't stare at each other's noses or chins, foreheads, hairlines. They looked at the things that gave signals – the eyes, the mouth.

He was looking when Michael said, eyes closed, 'Sacked three weeks ago. I was running a big takeover and someone leaked information and the whole thing went pear-shaped. They blamed me.'

'Why?'

Eyes closed. 'Photographs of me with someone from the other side. The other firm.'

'What kind?'

'Nothing sordid. Just a kiss. On the steps outside my place.'

'Yes?'

Michael opened his black eyes, blinked a few times, he had long lashes, turned his head enough to look at Cashin.

'It was a he,' he said.

Cashin wanted a smoke, the craving came from nowhere, full strength. It had never entered his mind that Michael was queer. Michael had been engaged to a doctor at one time. Syb had showed him a photograph taken at an engagement party, a thin blonde woman, snub nose. She was holding a champagne flute. She had short nails.

'A kiss?' he said.

'We were in a meeting late, eleven, we met again in the carpark, he came back to my place for a drink.'

'Sex?'

'Yes.'

'Did you tell him stuff?'

'No.'

'Well,' said Cashin, 'I've heard of worse shit.'

His brother had closed his eyes again, there were deep furrows between his eyebrows. 'He killed himself,' he said. 'The day after his wife left him, took the three kids. Her father's a judge, he went to law school with my head of firm.'

Cashin shut his eyes too, put his head back and listened to the sounds – low electronic humming, the sawing of traffic below, a far-away helicopter whupping the air. He stayed that way for a long time. When he opened his eyes, Michael was looking at him.

'You all right?' he said.

'Fine,' said Cashin. 'That is serious shit.'

'Yes. They told me you were here in the small hours. Thanks, Joe.'

'Not a matter for thanks.'

'I haven't been much of a brother.'

'Two of us then. Want to talk to someone? A shrink?'

'No. I've been to shrinks, I've made shrinks rich, I've helped shrinks buy places in Byron Bay, there's nothing they can do. I'm a depressive. Plain and simple. It's in me. It's a brain disorder, it's probably genetic.'

Cashin felt an unease. 'Drugs,' he said. 'They've presumably got the drugs.'

'Turn the world into porridge. If you're on anti-depressants, you can't work sixteen-hour days, plough through mountains of documents, see the holes, produce answers. My kind of depression, well, it's not like the tent collapses on you. It's just there. I can work, that's the thing that keeps it at bay, you don't want an idle moment. But there's no joy. You could be, I don't know, washing dishes.'

Michael was crying silently, tears running down his cheeks, crystal streams on each side.

Cashin put a hand on his brother's forearm, he did not squeeze. He did not know what to do, he had no physical language for comforting a man.

Michael said, 'They told me about the photograph and Kim's death at the same time. I walked out, got on a plane, drank and slept and drank, and it got worse and then I took the pills.'

He tried to smile. 'I think that's more than I've said to you at one time in our whole lives.'

A nurse was in the doorway. 'Keeping up the fluids?' she said, stern. 'Important, you know.'

'I'm drinking,' said Michael. He swallowed. 'Is it too early for a gin and tonic?'

She shook her head at his flippancy. Cashin could see she liked the look of Michael. She went away.

'Who took the picture?' he said.

A shrug. 'I don't know. There was a whole sequence, five or six shots. From across the street, I think.'

'Someone watching you or him. Who'd do that?'

Another shrug.

'When was the leak? Before or after?'

Michael put a hand to his hair. 'You're a cop. I forgot that for a while. After. In the next day or so. They knew what happened at a meeting our team had the morning after. Anyway, it doesn't matter now. Kim's dead, I don't have a career, everything's gone, twenty years of grind wasted.'

'Dangerous occupation you chose.'

Michael remembered. He smiled, a sad smile.

'You'd better come down and stay with Sybil for a while,' said Cashin. 'Help the husband napalm the roses.'

'No, I'll be all right. I'll stay with a friend, she's got lots of room. Get back on the medication. Avoid the drink. Exercise, take some exercise. I'll be okay.'

Silence.

'I'll be fine, Joe. Really.'

'What can I do?' said Cashin.

'Nothing.' Michael put out his left hand. Cashin took it, they held hands awkwardly.

'Don't get depressed, do you?' said Michael.

'No.' It was a lie.

'Good, that's good. You've escaped the curse of the Cashins.'

'The what?'

'Dad, me. Probably a long line before us. Tommy Cashin for sure. Mum says you're rebuilding his house. We're all the same, he was just at the extreme edge. Wanted to take his house with him.'

'What about Dad?'

Michael took his hand away. 'Mum's told you?'

'What?'

'She said she'd tell you when you were older.'

'What?'

'About Dad.'

'What?'

'That he committed suicide.'

'Oh,' said Cashin. 'That. Yeah, I know about that.'

'Okay. Listen, tell Mum I'm fine, Joe. Tell her it was all a silly mistake. Accidental overdose. Do that?'

'Sure.'

'Give her my love. Tell her I'll ring her tomorrow. Don't feel up to it today.'

Cashin said goodbye, kissed his brother on the forehead, a taste of salt, caught the lift with a family of four, near-adult children, everyone sombre. On the ground floor, he found the toilets, went into a booth and sat down, slumped, hands between his thighs. It was peaceful. From time to time, the urinal cleansed itself, a wash of water.

He saw himself in the Holden, a boy sitting next to his mother, on the way to strange places, for a reason unknown.

His father. No one ever told him. They all knew and no one ever told him.

THE NURSING home was a yellow brick veneer island in a sea of bitumen and concrete, not a blade of grass. A nurse in a dark blue skirt and spotted white shirt showed him to the room.

Singo was wearing a checked dressing-gown, sitting in a wheelchair in front of a glass door. The view was of a concrete strip and a high metal fence the colour of dried blood.

'Someone to see you, Dave,' she said. 'You've got a visitor.'

Singo didn't react.

'I'll leave you,' said the nurse.

Cashin moved the chair in the room, sat facing Singo's profile, moved the chair closer. 'G'day, boss,' he said. 'It's Joe.'

Singo turned his head. Cashin thought he'd aged since he'd last seen him, the paralysed side of his face now younger than the other.

Singo made a sound. It could have been 'Joe', it was a short sibilant sound.

'Looking much better, boss,' said Cashin. 'You're on the mend. Villani says to please come back. He'll tell you himself, he'll be out to see you soon. Snowed under. You'll know about that.'

Singo's lips worked, he made another sound, spitty, but Joe thought he was amused, something in his eyes. He raised his left arm, the working arm, stretched his fingers. He seemed to be offering his hand to be held.

Not shaken. Held.

You could not hold Singo's hand, no. Singo could not possibly want that. He wasn't brain damaged, not that way, he was hindered, bits of him didn't work. Singo was in there, the hard man was there under the slack muscle, the disobedient tendons.

Cashin didn't know what to do, the second time in two hours.

Perhaps the hard man wasn't there anymore. Perhaps there was just a helpless and hopeless man reaching out.

Cashin thought about his father and he put out his right hand and touched Singo's.

Singo knocked his hand away.

Not reaching out. A mistake.

'Sorry, boss,' said Cashin. 'Water? Want some water? Anything?'

Singo blinked his left eyelid repeatedly. His eyes were saying something. He released another moist splutter of sound.

'Watching the TV, boss?' There was a television on the wall, no sign of a remote control. They would decide what he saw and for how long.

A nod, it could be a nod.

'Villani's got his hands full, see that?' said Cashin.

Singo raised his hand again, the fingers stretched.

Oh shit, thought Cashin, he's pointing.

He looked. There was a pad on the bedside cabinet and a pen, a fat pen. He fetched them, put the pad on Singo's tray, offered the pen to the left hand. Singo took it, clumsily, shakily, moved it in his big fingers.

'Why didn't she tell me you could write, boss? The nurse?'

Singo was trying to write on the pad, he was concentrating, the pen would not obey him, the pad shifted, veins stood out on his forehead,

Cashin reached out and moored the pad. Singo made scratch marks on it, possibly a C, possibly an R, a scribble of lines. His strength seemed to leave him, the hand slumped, his eyes closed.

Cashin waited.

Singo was asleep.

Cashin stood up and went to the door. He turned and said, not loud, 'Be back, boss. We're on your case. Get you out of here.'

He could see Singo reflected in the glass door and he thought he saw his eyes looking at him. He went back. Singo's eyes were closed. He moved the pad from under the big hand, long hairs on the fingers, and tore off the page.

'See you, boss,' he said, took his life in his hands and said, 'Love you.'

He sat in the vehicle for a while before he switched on, trying to make sense of Singo's marks. Then he put on music, shut his mind against the hours ahead, drove. Near home, exhausted, pains down both legs, the mobile rang.

'Found someone,' said Hopgood. 'Want to be there?'

CASHIN WALKED down the pier in the last light, stood behind the half-dozen watchers, cold salt westerly gale in his face. He saw the cat heel around the breakwater, stern down, twin engines howling. A man in yellow was at the wheel, two figures behind him, standing, dark wetsuits.

Hopgood, in a black leather jacket, turned his head, edged back through the group.

'Bloke in a plane saw a body outside the Kettle,' he said. 'In the Rip.'

For a moment Cashin thought that he would be sick, that he would spew over Hopgood.

'You're looking ratshit,' said Hopgood. 'Even more ratshit.'

'Bad pie.'

'What's the other kind?'

Cashin had heard of bodies being pushed into the sea caves by the powerful surges. Sometimes it was days, weeks, before they were sucked out of the holes, out of the Kettle and into the Rip.

Close in, the helmsman throttled back, the craft died in the water, rose and fell in a trough, motored to the pier and snarled to turn broadside at the pontoon. Two men were waiting, casual toss of a line, the boat was secured bow and stern.

They carried the body up wrapped in an orange nylon sheet, a man at each corner, the bottom ones fearful. On the pier, they put the burden down on the rough planks, gently, stood back, unwrapped it. Hopgood leaned over.

Cashin caught a glimpse of a bloated face, a bare foot, jeans torn to shreds. He didn't want to see any more, he'd seen enough of dead people, crossed to the shore-side railing and looked at the lights of the town above, not bright in the gloom. Cars flicked by at the two roundabouts on Marine Parade, people going home. People with families waiting. Children.

He wished he had a cigarette.

'In his pocket,' said Hopgood, behind him. 'In the jacket.'

Cashin turned. Hopgood offered him a grey nylon wallet, zipped. 'Torch here,' he said.

A torch came on, crossed the pier. Hopgood took it, shone it on Cashin's hands.

Cashin unzipped the wallet, found a card, a photograph in the corner. He strained to look at it, put it back.

Then a grey booklet, a prancing unicorn on the cover, inside it a plastic envelope.

Daunt Credit Union.

It was almost dry, water-stained only along the edges.

Perhaps twenty entries on two pages, smudged printer type, small sums in and out.

Donny Coulter drowned in the Kettle with $11.45 in his account.

Cashin put the passbook back in the wallet, zipped it, gave it to Hopgood.

'That's probably the full stop,' he said. 'I'm going home now. I'm supposed to be on leave.'

'Time to smarten up,' said Hopgood. 'Here it comes.'

A television crew was on the pier, coming towards them, already filming.

'Tip them off yourself?' said Cashin. 'Or have you got some suckhole does it for you?'

'Transparency, mate. That's the way it is now.'

'Bullshit. Told Donny's mum?'

'Told her what? She'll have to ID him.'

'Is that before she sees this on television?'

'This still your investigation? Your wog friend hasn't told me.'

'This has got nothing to do with the investigation,' said Cashin. 'And there never was any fucking investigation.'

He walked, straight at the television crew. The frozen-haired woman recognised him and said something to the sound recordist. Then she blocked his way.

'Detective Cashin, can we have a word, please?'

Cashin walked, he didn't reply, went around her. His shoulder knocked aside a furred microphone, the holder said, 'Steady on.'

'Fuck off,' said Cashin.

He drove the last stretch with Callas full blast on the player, roared down the dark and jolting roads with her beautiful voice filling the cab. The Kettle. A body floating outside the Kettle. In the big, foaming, shifting Rip.

They went to see it for the first time when he was six or seven, everyone had to see the Kettle and the Dangar Steps. Even standing well back from the crumbling edge of the keyhole, the scene scared him, the huge sea, the grey-green water skeined with foam, sliding, falling, surging, full of little peaks and breaks, hollows and rolls, the sense of unimaginable power beneath the surface, terrible forces that could lift you up and suck you down and spin you and you would breathe in icy salt water, swallow it, choke, the power of the surge would push you through the gap in the cliff and then it would slam you against the pocked walls in the Kettle, slam you and slam you until your clothes were threads and you were just tenderised meat.

It was called the Broken Shore, that piece of the coast. When Cashin was little, he had heard it as one word – the Brokenshaw. At some point, someone told him the first sailors to see the coast called it that because of the massive pieces of the limestone cliff that had broken away and fallen into the sea. Perhaps the sailors saw it happen. Perhaps they were close in and they saw the edge of the earth collapse, join the sea.

Home, thank god, the headlights passing across Rebb's shed.

He parked close to the building and sat, the pains in him, all over. Lights off. Reluctant to move. It would not be a hardship to sleep where he was. A little sleep.

Knocking, he heard knocking, came upright, full of alarm.

Two dog heads at the window, the wash of light from a torch. He wound down the glass.

'You okay?' said Rebb.

'Yeah, just tired.'

'Brother okay?'

'He's okay.'

'That's good. Dogs had their tucker. Finish the fence tomorrow.'

Rebb walked away. Cashin and the dogs went inside. He rang his mother. She wanted more than he had to give. He cut her off, washed down codeine tablets with a beer, poured a big whisky. He sat in the upright chair and sipped and waited for the relief.

It came. He drank more whisky. Before he went to bed, he watched the local news.

Police will not comment on speculation that the body found in the sea outside Cromarty's notorious Kettle, scene of many suicides over the years, is that of eighteen-year-old Donny Coulter, charged with the attempted murder of local identity Charles Bourgoyne. Detective Senior Sergeant Joe Cashin left Long Pier without comment after the body was brought to shore.

He saw himself coming down the pier – slit-eyed, shoulders set, hair being whipped around a stone face. Hopgood was next, pious-looking. There was something of the priest about his face, the mask of sadness and sincerity assumed for an occasion. 'Always bad to find a body,' Hopgood said. 'We have no other comment at this time.'

The reporter said: 'Donny Coulter's mother, Mrs Lorraine Coulter, spoke out tonight about police treatment of her son, missing since Tuesday.'

Donny's mother standing in front of a brown brick veneer house with a threadbare lawn, concrete wheel strips running to a carport. 'They hound him. Ever since the bail. They come by every night, put the spotlight on the house, right on Donny's window, they sit out there. He went to sleep in the back, he couldn't stand it no more. Drivin us all mad, Donny had enough to worry about, the boys the cops killed, all that ...'

Cashin went to bed without eating and fell asleep instantly, did not wake until the dogs complained and the cold world was fully lit, no cloud in the sky.

REBB HAD the square redgum corner posts in, buttressed with diagonals notched into the strainers. Star posts were lying along the line of the new fence. In the middle was another strainer post.

'Bern give you a hand?' said Cashin.

'Didn't need a hand. Not much of a fence.'

'By my standards, it's much of a fence. What now?'

'Get the stars in. Line em up.'

'We'll need string.'

'Don't need string. Eye's good enough.'

'My eye?'

'Any prick's eye.'

Cashin squinted over the corner post, moving Rebb back and forth until he held each star post in line with the three strainer posts. Rebb used a sledgehammer to tap in the posts, held it in one hand as if it had no weight. Then he marked a pole with the height of the strainers and sent Cashin down the line to chalk the height on the lower part of each star post. Rebb came behind him, hammering the posts until they reached the mark. He swung with a fluid grace, a full overhead swing, no sign of effort, hit the small target cleanly, never a mishit. The sound was a dull ring and it went across the valley and came back, sad somehow.

After that they strung wire, four strands, bottom strand first, working from the middle strainer post, using a wire strainer, a dangerous-looking device. Rebb showed Cashin the knot used to tie off the bowstring-taut wire around the post.

'What's that called?'

'What?'

'The knot, the wire knot.'

'What's it matter?'

'Well,' said Cashin, 'no names, the world's all grunts and sign language.'

Rebb gave him a long sidelong look. 'Called a strainer hitch, you've got no use for that name. Have a look for mine?'

Cashin hesitated. You didn't talk about things like this. 'Your name? Had a look, yeah. That's my job.'

'Find anything?'

'Not yet. Covered your tracks well.'

Rebb laughed. It was the first time.

They worked. The dogs came, interested, bored, left, other things to do. When they were finished, it was almost mid-afternoon, no food eaten. Cashin and Rebb stood at the high point and looked down the line. It ran true, the posts straight, the low light singing silver off the new wire.

'Pretty good fence,' said Cashin.

He felt pride, it had not often been given to him to feel pride in work. He was tired and hurting in the pelvis and up his back but he felt happy, a kind of happy.

'It's a fence,' said Rebb. He was looking away. 'This the new neighbour?'

Cashin didn't recognise the woman coming down the grassy slope. Her hair was loose and she was in jeans and a leather jacket. She lost her footing a few times, narrowly avoided falling on her backside.

'I'll take the stuff up,' said Rebb. 'Milking time.'

Helen Castleman.

Cashin walked down the fence to meet her.

'What's this?' she said, out of breath. She looked scrubbed. It made him aware of how sweaty he was.

'Just fixing the fence,' said Cashin. 'Replacing the fence. I'm not asking you to pay half.'

'Generous of you. I understand the creek to be the boundary.'

'The creek?'

'Yes.'

'That's not so. Who told you that?'

'The agent.'

'The agent? A lawyer relied on the agent?'

Helen's cheekbones coloured, an autumn shade.

'Of all the people you might rely on,' said Cashin, 'the real estate agent ...'

'That'll do, thank you. Having a good run, aren't you, Mr Cashin? Feeling pretty smart. You drive the poor frightened kid to suicide, now you don't have to make any case, he's made the case for you. And everyone else's dead, all suspects dead. Because you and your fucking mates killed them.'

She turned and began the climb, slipping.

All day, seeing a boy on the Dangar Steps, a brown boy in cheap jeans, nylon anorak, broken runners, standing on a crumbling limestone ledge, the salt spray rising like a mist to bathe him, looking down at the churning water.

'Listen,' he said, 'give me a break, it's ...'

Her head came around, her hair swung. 'You don't deserve a break and I'll have a survey done, we'll see about this fucking boundary.'

Cashin watched her climb the slope. She had a few slips, a few slides. Half-way, she turned and looked down at him.

'What are you looking at?' she shouted. 'Why don't you just fuck off?'

In the shower, thinking about what he should have said, the phone rang. No towel. He went, dripping.

'Draw a line under this then,' said Villani. 'They switched off Bourgoyne. We're never going to know exactly what happened that night.'

'Exactly?' said Cashin. He was shivering, the place was a giant fridge. 'We never had the vaguest fucking idea.'

'The watch, Joe, the watch. Not found in a lucky dip at the church fete. Someone took it off an old bloke … anyway, what the fuck, it's over.'

Cashin wanted to say more but he caught himself, his gaze fell on his shrivelled penis, lying in the wet crinkly hair like something in a tidal pool.

'The harassment stuff,' he said, 'there's something about that …'

'Cromarty should have been purged long ago,' said Villani. 'They had the chance after the deaths in custody. But no, they moved the boss and put in a cleanskin, made his name in traffic, traffic dynamo. And presto, six months later Hopgood and his cocksucker offsiders were running the show again.'

'I'm not happy,' said Cashin.

'Nor am I,' said Villani. 'I'm at home. They say I'm never here. That's right, that's the way it is. So I make an effort tonight to eat with my kids and there's no one here. How's that?'

'I have no sympathy. Go back to gangland. I'm always home alone.'

In the night Cashin woke, tried to hypnotise himself with the measured breathing, the words to stifle thought. He was falling when he saw the Kettle, the clouds parting, a full moon lighting the world silver-grey, huge waves coming in, fretting at the top, exploding through the keyhole, pure untrammelled murderous power.

CASHIN ROSE early, unease in him like a stomach ache, took the dogs on the long route. They crossed the creek high up and walked back on the path below the shining new fence, on Cashin land, now demarcated.

After they had all breakfasted, he loaded the dogs and set off for his mother's house. Near the coast, he took the road that ran between the two volcanic hills, their caldera lakes home to swans, ducks, swamp hens, wicked-eyed bickering gulls by the hundreds. The lakes were never known to dry up. Cashin thought about the swims in them when he was living with the Doogues. They rode out on bicycles, five or six boys. They waded out in the black water, cold mud oozing through their toes, shivering on the hottest days. They walked around the dead tree trunks, avoided the branches that lay almost submerged like big snakes, green with moss and slime, streaked with birdshit.

At a shout, they would all throw themselves in and swim. In the middle, they crowded together, treading water, feeling the black and sucking deep beneath them. The idea was to dive and come up with a handful of grey mud. But no one wanted to be the first. Eventually, the boldest duck-dived. They would wait for him to come up before anyone else went down. Once Bern dived and swam away under water, rose silently behind a dead tree.

They waited for him to appear. They looked at one another. Then they panicked. Cashin remembered that, no signal given, they all made for the shore, swam for their lives, abandoned Bern.

When they were standing in the shallows, Bern shouted: 'Cowardly bastards. How'd you know I wasn't stuck down there?'

The news came on.

Four people, including a policewoman, are in hospital after what Cromarty police claim was an attack on a patrol car in the Daunt Settlement outside the city last night. Police said a car on routine patrol was stoned shortly after 10 pm. Two other cars went to the scene. They found the first car on fire and a hostile crowd blocking the street.

The officers attempted to drive through the crowd to reach their colleagues, a police spokesperson said. However, they were forced to leave their vehicles and shots were fired before order was restored.

Police Minister Kim Bourke today defended the police actions.

'Of course this will be fully investigated but it's clear that it was an

*extremely dangerous situation. The officers' lives were in danger and they
feared for the lives of their colleagues. They took what action was necessary.'*

*A forty-six-year-old man, a young woman and a youth from the Daunt
Settlement were admitted to Cromarty Base Hospital with injuries. They are
in a stable condition. A policewoman with head injuries is also said to be off
the danger list. Two other people were treated and discharged.*

A routine patrol? Through the Daunt on the night they found Donny
Coulter? What kind of station commander didn't tell them to keep out of
the Daunt?

*You drive the poor frightened kid to suicide, now you don't have to make any
case, he's made the case for you. And everyone else's dead, all suspects dead.
Because you and your fucking mates killed them.*

His mother and Harry were having breakfast in the kitchen, muesli and
fruit, eating out of lopsided purple bowls.

'Had breakfast?' said his mother.

'Not yet.'

'Probably nothing to eat in that ruin.' Sybil got up and filled another
bowl with muesli from a glass jar, poured the remains of the tin of mixed
fruit into it.

Cashin sat down. She put the bowl in front of him, brought the milk jug
closer. He poured and ate. It was surprisingly edible.

'Michael rang,' she said. 'He's fine, very chipper.'

Harry nodded. 'Very chipper.' He was a repeater, it was his role in the
marriage.

'Good,' said Cashin.

'An accident,' said Sybil. 'All that stress he's under in the job. So high-
powered, it's not a good life.'

Cashin's eyes were on the bowl. What were the black bits? Pips?

'He's coming down soon to have a bit of a rest.'

'Bit of a rest,' said Harry.

'Chance for you to spend some time together,' said his mother. 'He was
very warm about you, very appreciative.'

'I love being appreciated,' said Cashin. 'It's so rare in my life.'

Harry laughed but he caught Sybil's eye and he choked it, gazed into his
bowl.

'Probably been over-appreciated,' said Sybil. 'The love and care that's
been bestowed on you.'

Cashin thought about drunk Sybil in the caravan, the nights of waiting
for her to come back. He ate a piece of peach and a piece of something else,
pinkish. The same taste.

'Disgraceful business in the Daunt last night,' said Sybil. 'It's turning into Israel, police provoking the dispossessed into violence. Manufacture of deviance.'

'Manufacture of what?'

'Of deviance,' said Sybil. 'You're part of that. You produce the justification for your existence.'

'Me?'

'The machinery of control. You're an unselfconscious part of it.'

'You get this from uni?'

'I've always felt it. Uni gives you the intellectual back-up.'

'I think I could use some intellectual back-up. What's this course called?'

'Finish your food, I don't want that muesli wasted. It's organic, cost the earth, I bought it at the farmers' market.'

'The farmers' market,' said Harry, and smiled, he had the smile of a mother's boy.

Sybil came with him to the vehicle. The dogs went berserk. 'They don't like me,' she said.

'Barking's not a judgment on you. It's just barking.'

Sybil kissed him on the chin. 'Keep in touch with Michael, will you, dear,' she said. 'Ring him. Promise?'

'Why didn't you tell me Dad killed himself?'

She took a pace back, clutched herself. 'He didn't. He fell. He slipped and fell.'

'Where?'

He saw water in her eyes.

'Fishing,' she said.

'Where?'

'Where?'

'Yes. Where?'

'At the Kettle.'

Cashin didn't say anything. He got into the vehicle and drove, didn't wave goodbye.

JUST AFTER noon, on his way back from Cromarty, the photographs of Tommy Cashin's house finally copied, Cashin registered that he was near the turnoff that led to the Bourgoyne place.

He slowed, turned, went up the hill. There was no thought behind it. He could turn left at the top, take the road around the hill, go through Kenmare, say hello to Bern.

He turned right, went around the bends and through the gates of The Heights.

He had no idea why he was doing this except that it seemed the way to close the business, where it began. He parked and walked around the house, clockwise. At least a dozen cops would have walked the south side, in a line, moving in slow-motion, studying the ground, picking up twigs, looking under leaves.

Today, there were few leaves. Everything was trim, the local football legend and his son were obviously still employed, had been on the job recently, plucking weeds, mowing grass, raking gravel. He went by the kitchen entrance, through an arbour, leafless but with branches so intricately twined as to deny the light.

Single-storeyed redbrick outbuildings to the left, a paved courtyard, old pink bricks in a herringbone pattern, sagging in places, depressions holding saucers of water.

Cashin walked between two buildings, looked through an ornate cast-iron gate into a drying yard, washing lines strung between wooden crosses, enough to dry the washing of an army. He went on, to where mown grass ran to a rustic post-and-rail fence, fifty metres away. Beyond that was a big paddock, its boundary a line of tall pines. The road lay beyond them.

He went back, around the south-west corner of the house. This was a clean space, a long empty rectangle bordered with lemon trees in big terracotta pots. Many of them looked unhappy, leaves yellow.

They'd had four lemon trees at the old house, out the back. You needed to piss on lemon trees, around the trunk. His father had often taken him out to do that after tea. They went from tree to tree, Mick Cashin had enough for all four, the last one got a little less. Joe ran out early but he carried on, stood with his father, aiming his small empty hose at the ground.

'Some places, it's all they get,' said his father. 'Dry countries. Nothin wrong with piss. Filtered by the body. Mind's the same. Hangs onto the bad stuff.'

Across the courtyard was a long double-storeyed brick building, doors and windows on the ground floor, sash-hung windows above. Cashin crossed and tried the big double door in the middle. It opened onto a corridor running the width of the building.

A door on the right was ajar. He went in a short way.

It was a big room, well lit from windows on two sides, a pottery studio – two big wheels, a smaller one, trestle tables, several steel trolleys lined up, bags stacked against the far wall, shelving holding small bags and tins of all sizes, implements of various kinds laid out. There were no pots to be seen. The place was neat and clean, like a classroom swept and tidied after the students each day.

Cashin went down the corridor to the door on the left. It opened on darkness. He felt for a light switch, found several, clicked them.

Spotlights came on, three rows in the roof. It was a gallery, windowless, the floor of stone, dull-grey, smooth, the bare walls a pale colour.

A narrow black table ran almost the width of the room. On it, at regular intervals, stood – Cashin counted them – nine vessels. They were big, more than half a metre high, the shape of eggs with their tops cut off, tiny lips. Cashin thought it was a beautiful shape, the shape pots might want to be if potters would let them.

He went closer, looked at them from both sides. Now he saw small differences in shape, in bulge and taper. And the colours. The pots were streaked and lined and blotched and speckled in blacks that seemed to absorb light, in reds that looked like fresh blood leaking through tiny fissures, in the sad and lovely blues and browns and greys and greens of the earth seen from space.

Cashin ran a hand down a pot. There were smooth parts and then rough, like moving from a woman's cheekbone to a late afternoon stubble. And ice cold, as if the hellish passage through fire had conferred a permanent immunity to warmth.

Was this Bourgoyne's entire output as a potter? All that he kept? There were no pots in the house. Cashin picked one up carefully, turned it upside down: the letters C B and a date, 11/6/88.

He replaced the pot and went to the doorway. He stood looking at the pots. He did not want to kill the lights and leave them in the dark, their colours meaningless, wasted.

He killed the lights.

The rest of the building was an anticlimax. Upstairs, there were empty rooms on one side, living quarters on the other comfortably furnished, perhaps in the 1970s, a sitting room, a bathroom, a kitchen. He opened a door: a small bedroom, a stripped double bed, a bedside table, a wardrobe. The view from the window was across the paddocks, nothing for kilometres.

At the door to the corridor, he looked back into the sitting room. There was a bolt on the bedroom door. He went downstairs, out the back door onto a stone-paved terrace, looked at mown lawn, old elms, an oak wood beyond a picket fence. Straight ahead was the horse barn and the paddock where the helicopter landed.

A concrete path led off from a ramp at the left edge of the terrace. Cashin followed it, went through a gate in the fence and into the dense wood. The oaks were huge, no doubt planted by a Bourgoyne ancestor, trees to climb into, branches arranged in ladders. They were still heavy with brown leaves in spite of the thick new layer on the ground.

The land sloped up gently, the path twisted through the trees, its route dictated by the plantings. He was thirty or so metres along it when he caught himself enjoying the walk, a stroll in a wood on an early winter day, and was about to turn back.

A sound. He stopped. It was hollow, mournful, someone blowing into a cowrie shell.

He went on, the sound growing louder. The oaks stopped, a firebreak and then old eucalypts, towering. They thinned and there was a clearing on a gentle slope. The path veered left around a pile of split wood under a tin roof.

There was the smell of a hardwood fire, long dead.

Cashin stopped, uneasy. He went on, rounded the wood stack.

In the clearing stood a tunnel-like structure of cement-coloured bricks. It tapered in both dimensions, the narrower and lower end pointed at an opening in the trees, at the sea a few kilometres away. At the back was a square chimney.

He went closer. The earth at the base of the walls had a crust like bread. Low along the flank were square steel-shuttered openings, the bricks around them blackened. The chimney had a steel plate sticking out of it, a damper, Cashin thought, it could be moved in and out to regulate the flow of hot air. On the other side were more shuttered windows.

The front was open. On his neck, Cashin felt the westerly blowing straight into the mouth of the chamber, making the hollow sound. This was Bourgoyne's kiln, the furnace from which the pots emerged.

Blackened bricks were neatly stacked around the mouth. He stooped to look: beyond the scorched entrance were three tiers, like a short hierarchy of broad altars. There was a strong smell of things heated, vaguely chemical.

The wind off the sea would blow into the burning kiln like breath into a trumpet. Was it alight at night? The kiln would hum, the fire holes would glow white. It would have to be fed at intervals to maintain the heat.

Suddenly Cashin wanted to leave the clearing with its sad sound and smell of dead fires. He became conscious that the wind was cold, rain in the air. He went back through the trees, down to the buildings, continued his walk around the house, looking, thinking about what it would be like to approach the buildings at night, where the place would be to break in.

A few metres down the the north-western side of the house was a door, half glass, four panes. He looked in: a small room, tiled floor, benches on either side, coats and hats on pegs.

He turned. The severely tended garden ran for at least two hundred metres to a picket fence, then there were paddocks fenced with hedges, stands of trees, glints of water.

Perhaps a whim, half-pissed kids driving by, one of them given an idea by the big gates and the headlights catching the brass plate. It would have sent a message, as if in neon lights: RICH PEOPLE LIVE HERE.

Driving by? Going where? Heading back to the Daunt after fishing and drinking on the beach, you might take this route. It would be less risky than the main road.

Did the boys park a vehicle somewhere along the road, climb a fence, walk to the house? A kilometre in the dark, crossing paddocks, opening gates? No, they hadn't done that.

They would have parked near the gates and walked up the driveway, a dark passage, no lights in the grounds, the massive poplars, still in leaf, blocking the moonlight.

The boys, standing in the dark at the end of the drive, looking at the house. Were there lights on? Bourgoyne's bedroom was at the back of the house. He wasn't in bed. Where was he? In the study? Did they walk around, see the study and bedroom lights? If so, they would have broken in as far away as possible.

Thieves didn't break into occupied houses where there were lights on. The householder might have a gun.

What did they use to beat Bourgoyne? Did they bring it with them, take it away? There would be a post-mortem on him now, the pathologists would have an opinion, but it might be no more useful than ruling out faceted instruments or round ones bigger than a golf club shaft.

There was a noise. A door from the sunroom opened and Erica Bourgoyne came out. She was in soft-looking clothes, shades of grey, younger looking today, she could have passed for thirty.

'What's this about?' she said.

'Just having another look,' said Cashin. 'I'm sorry about your step-father.'

'Thank you,' said Erica. 'What's the point of looking around now?'

'The matter isn't closed.'

A man came out behind her, prematurely grey curly hair. He was just taller than short, tanned, dark suit, pale shirt and blue tie. 'What's happening?' he said.

'This is Detective Cashin,' said Erica.

He came around Erica, held out a hand. 'Adrian Fyfe.'

When Cashin felt the hard grip, the real man's grip, he gave Fyfe the dead fish, took his hand away. This was Adrian Fyfe the solicitor-developer who wanted to build a resort at the Stone's Creek mouth. Cashin remembered Cecily Addison's outrage that morning in the newsagency. *What this rag doesn't say is buying Stone's Creek mouth's no use unless you can get to it. And the only way's through the nature reserve or through the camp.*

'He would have been convicted, wouldn't he?' said Erica. 'Donny Coulter.'

'That's not certain,' said Cashin.

'What about the watch?'

'We have someone who says two of the suspects tried to sell it to him. We don't know how they got it.'

'Don't know?' said Adrian Fyfe. 'Pretty bloody obvious, isn't it?'

'There's no obvious in these things,' said Cashin.

'Anyway, it's over,' said Fyfe. 'The whole thing. Some justice done.'

'So pointless,' said Erica, listless now. 'To kill an old man for a watch and a few dollars, whatever it is they took. What kind of people do that?'

Cashin didn't try to answer. 'We'd like access to the buildings if you don't mind.'

A moment's pause. 'No, I don't mind,' she said. 'I won't be coming again. The place will be sold at some point. There's a big bunch of keys in the kitchen. Dozens of keys. Give them to Addison when you're finished.'

She followed him around the house. They shook hands.

The same security man was leaning against the Saab, smoking. 'That gravel stunt,' he said to Cashin. 'One day I'll rip your head off, stick it up your arse.'

'You threatening a police officer?' said Cashin. 'Above the law, are you?'

The man turned his head away in contempt, spat on the gravel. Cashin looked back. Erica hadn't moved. He returned, climbed the steps.

'By the way,' he said. 'Who inherits?'

Erica looked at him, blinked twice. 'I do. What's left after the bequests.'

REBB WAS laying bricks, rebuilding the fallen north-east corner of the house. Cashin watched him for a while – the slicing pick-up of the mortar, the icing of the brick, the casual placement, the tapping with the trowel handle, the removal of the excess.

'Supervising?' said Rebb, eyes on the job. 'Boss.'

Cashin wanted to say it but he couldn't. 'What do I do?' he said.

'Mix. Three cement, nine sand, careful with the water.'

Cashin was full of care. Then he ruined the mixture by flooding it.

'Same again,' said Rebb. 'Half spades now.' He came over and put in the water, a slop at a time, took the spade, cut and shuffled the mortar. 'That's the pudding,' he said.

The dogs arrived from a mission in the valley, greeted Cashin with noses and tongues, then left, summoned to some emergency – a rabbit rescue perhaps, the poor creature trapped in a thicket.

Cashin carried bricks, watched Rebb, got the mixture more or less right the next time. The trick was extreme caution. The work moved to the opposite corner, a string was strung, tight enough to ping.

'Ever laid a brick?' said Rebb.

'No.'

'Have a go. I need a leak.' He left.

Cashin laid three bricks. It took a long time and they looked terrible. Rebb came back and, saying nothing, undid the work, cleaned the bricks. 'Watch,' he said.

Cashin watched. Rebb relaid the bricks in a minute. 'Got to keep the perps the same width,' he said. 'Otherwise it looks bad.'

'Want to eat?' said Cashin. 'Then I'll work on my perps. Whatever the fuck a perp is.'

It was after 3 pm. He had bought pies from the less bad bakery in Cromarty. Beef and onion. They ate them sitting in the lee of the brick pile, in the diluting sunlight.

'Not bad,' said Rebb. 'There's some meat.' He chewed. 'The problem here is the doors and windows,' he said. 'We don't know where they are.'

'We do. I've got the pictures. I forgot.'

When Cashin got back with the photographs, Rebb had made a cigarette. He looked at the pictures. 'Jesus, there's bits missing here all right. This is a serious proposition.'

'Yes,' said Cashin. 'It's not a proposition at all. I should have said.'

He had known the moment he looked at the old photographs. In one, Thomas Cashin and six men, builders, stood in front of the house. Thomas could have been Michael in an old-fashioned suit.

They sat in silence. In the valley, one dog gave the high-pitched hunting bark, then the other. An ibis rose, another, they flapped away like prehistoric creatures. Rebb got up, walked beyond the brick pile and held up the picture. He looked at his newly repaired piece of building, looked at the picture. He came back and sat.

'Bit like putting in twenty mile of fence, I suppose,' he said. 'You just think about the bit to the next tree.'

'No,' said Cashin. 'It's a stupid idea.'

He was relieved that the lunacy was over. It was as if a fever had peaked, leaving him sweaty but lucid. 'House's fucked, it should stay that way.'

Rebb scuffed the earth with a boot heel. 'Well, I dunno. You could do worse. Least you're building something.'

'I don't need to. There's no point.'

'What's got a point?'

'It's a stupid idea. I admit it, let's leave it at that.'

'Well, got all this stuff here. Bit of a waste to stop now.'

'I'm making a judgment.'

'You can be too quick making judgments.'

Cashin felt the flash. 'I've had a bit more practice making judgments than your average swaggie,' he said and regretted his policeman's voice.

'I'm an itinerant labourer,' said Rebb, not looking at him. 'People pay me to do jobs they don't want to do themselves. Like the state pays you to keep property safe for the rich. The rich call, you come with the siren going. The poor call, well hang on, there's a waiting list, we'll get around to it some time.'

'Bullshit,' said Cashin. 'Bullshit. You've got no fucking idea what you're talking about …'

'Those dead boys,' said Rebb. 'That the judgment you talking about?'

Cashin felt his anger drain, the taste of tin in his mouth.

'The difference between us,' said Rebb, 'the difference is I don't have to stay on the job. I can just walk.'

In the silence, the dogs came with licks and nudges, as if, in the valley probing the undergrowth, they had heard the violence in the voices of their friends and had come in haste to calm them.

'Anyway, it's not as if I have a right to speak my opinion to you,' said Rebb. 'Being a swaggie.'

Cashin had no idea what to say, the ease that had grown between them over the days was gone and they had no history of arguments – won, lost, drawn, abandoned – to fall back on.

'Milking time,' said Rebb.

He rose and walked, left the spade stuck in the mound of sand, his brick-laying implements in the bucket, handles sticking out of silver water.

The dogs went with him, down the slope, even blacker against the sere grass. They trotted along happily. Then they stopped, turned, dark eyes on Cashin sitting on the bricks.

Rebb marched on, hands in his pockets, head down, shoulders sloped.

The dogs were torn.

Cashin wanted to tell them to go with Rebb, to say to them, you faithless things, I took you in, I saved you, you'd be in a concrete backyard now, knee-deep in your own droppings, you would not know a rabbit from a take-away barbecue chicken. But I was only ever a meal-ticket and a soft bed, legs to lie on.

So go. Fuck off. Go.

The dogs bounded back to him, the lovely bouncing run, the ears afloat. They jumped up, put their paws on him and spoke to him.

He shouted, 'Dave.'

No response. 'DAVE.'

Rebb turned his head, didn't stop walking.

'OKAY, WE'LL FIX THE FUCKING THING!'

Rebb walked on, but he raised his right arm and gave a thumbs-up.

THE PHONE rang when he was making toast.

'Joe, time to leave this,' said Villani. 'It's over.'

'How did we get to over?' said Cashin. 'Because Donny tops himself? That's not a confession, that's an indictment of these local deadshits.'

'Did you see Bobby Walshe last night?'

Cashin sat down at the table. 'No.'

'Stay in touch with the world, son. We have apparently crucified three innocent black children. It's Jesus and no thieves, everyone's clean.'

'Can I say …'

'And another matter,' said Villani. 'Someone spoke to someone who spoke to the deputy who spoke directly to me. It concerns your visit to the Bourgoyne house yesterday.'

'Yes?'

'I'm asked why we are still hanging around The Heights.'

'Just doing the job. That's a complaint from Erica, is it?'

'The place's been X-rayed. What the fuck were you doing there?'

'Having a sniff. Remember having a sniff? Remember Singo?'

'It's too late for sniffing. Let it rest, will you?'

'There's no certainty the boys did it,' said Cashin. He had not planned to say that.

Villani whistled, rueful. 'Well, Joe, I've got a lot on the plate, it's a full plate. Every day. And night. What say we talk about this insight of yours later? I'll give you a call. First free moment. Okay?'

'Okay. Sure.'

'Joe?'

'Yes.'

'A cop, Joe, don't forget that. You don't obsess. You do your best and then you move on.'

Cashin could hear the voice of Singo.

'No one's done their best about this,' he said. 'No one's done a fucking thing.'

'Have a relaxing day,' said Villani. 'Did I say your holiday's been extended? The deputy wants you to take the full five weeks you're owed. He's worried about your health and wellbeing. He's like that. Caring. I'll get back to you.'

You don't obsess. Words chosen to remind, to caution. To hurt.

Cashin felt the nausea rising and the pain in his shoulders that would move up his neck into his head. In the worst times, these symptoms had signalled the coming of the frozen images, the ghostly negatives that lingered on the retina after he looked away from things. It had seemed clear to him then that he was going mad.

He took three tablets, sat in the big chair, head back, eyes closed, concentrating on his breathing, waiting. The pain did not reach its former heights, the nausea receded. But it was almost an hour before he could get up. He washed his face and hands, brushed his teeth and gargled, drove down empty roads to Port Monro. The cattle were indifferent to his passing.

He parked outside the post office. Four letters in the mailbox, nothing personal. No one wrote to him. Who would write to him? Not a single soul in the world. He walked around the corner to the station.

Kendall was on the desk. 'Can't live with it, can't et cetera,' she said. 'Boss.'

'Keeping the sovereign's peace?'

'Yes, sir. Spread the word to the locals that in the event of bad behaviour you'd come back.'

Cashin went to his desk, read the log, the official notices, sat looking at the backyard.

'While you're here, can I do some personal business, boss?' said Kendall.

'On your way,' said Cashin.

She had been gone a minute when a whippet-thin young man came in the door, looked around like a first-time bank robber. Cashin went to the counter. 'Help you?'

'They reckon I should talk to youse.' He pulled down on the rounded visor of his cap.

'Yes? Your name?'

'Gary Witts.'

'What can we do for you, Mr Witts?'

'Problem with the girlfriend. Yeah.'

Cashin gave him the compassionate nod. 'The girlfriend.'

'Yeah. Don't want to get her in no trouble. She's me girlfriend.'

'And the problem?'

'Well, it's me ute.'

'The girlfriend and your ute?'

'It's not like I wanna lay a charge.'

'Your girlfriend? No, you wouldn't.'

'Don't mean I'm not pissed off. I'm no fuckin rug, mat, whatever. Not me.'

'What's she done?'

'Went to Queensland in me ute. With this mate of hers from Cromarty, they're hairdressers, apprentices. You know that place WowHair? That's where.'

'So she took your ute without your permission?'

'Nah. Gave her a lend of it. Now she reckons she's not comin back. Met this Surfers Paradise bloke, Carlo, Mario, some wog name, he's got three saloons, offered her a job. Now she reckons I owe her the ute.'

'Why's that?'

Gary tugged at his visor again until Cashin couldn't see his eyes. 'She loaned me the deposit.'

Cashin knew. 'And she's been making the payments?'

'Just tempory. Pay her back. Got a job now.'

'How long did she make the payments?'

'Jeez, I dunno. A while. Year, bit more. Could be two. Yeah.'

'So what do you want?' Cashin said.

'I thought, like, you could get the cops up there, they could tell her to bring it back. Lean on her a bit. Y'know?'

Cashin put his forearms on the counter, laced his fingers, looked under Gary's visor. 'Gary, we don't do that kind of thing. She hasn't committed a crime. You lent her the ute. You owe her lots of money. Best thing you can do is go up there, pay her what you owe her, drive the ute home.'

'Well, fuck,' Gary said, 'can't do that.'

'Then you'll have to see a lawyer. Take some kind of civil action against her.'

'Civil?'

'A lawyer'll explain it to you. Basically, they write her a letter, tell her to hand over the ute or else.'

Gary nodded, scratched an ear. 'She's pretty scared of cops. Wouldn't take much to scare her, I can tell you.'

'We're not in the scare business, Gary.'

Gary went to the door, disappointment in his shoulders. He hesitated, came back, sniffed. 'Nother thing,' he said. 'How come you blokes don't do nothin about the fuckin Piggots?'

'What should we do something about?'

'Getting fuckin rich on drugs.'

'What's the point here, Gary?'

'Well, the mate she went with. She's fuckin thick with the Piggots. I reckon they dropped off a bag on the way, who's gonna check two chicks, right?'

'You know this, do you?'

Gary looked away. 'Won't say I do, won't say I don't.'

'What's her name? The friend?'

'Lukie Tingle.'

'An address and a phone number for you, Gary.'

'Nah. Don't wanna be involved. See you.'

'Gary, don't be dumb. I'll find you in five minutes, park outside your house, come in for a cup of tea, how's that?'

'Shit, gissus a break, will you?'

He gave an address and a phone number, left without another word, passed Kendall at the door.

On the way home, a man on the radio said:

'The state government's problem is that if it's seen as soft on law and order in Cromarty, it risks losing the white vote and the seat at the next election. And it needs every seat. So there's a real quandary. For the federal government, Janice, the mileage Bobby Walshe has got out of Cromarty is a nightmare. But of course a huge plus for United Australia.'

'Exactly how much mileage, Malcolm?'

'Bobby's performance last night was amazing, the passion, his sadness. He got on every TV news in the country, huge radio airplay. Bobby's given Cromarty a kind of symbolic status, and this is very important, Janice. The bit about the three crucified black boys, it had so much power, I can tell you it spoke to all kinds of people. Biblical. The talkback today has been amazing. People crying, even from the redneck belts. Those words struck a major chord, they resonated.'

'But will that translate nationally, I mean...?'

'These are interesting times, Janice. The government's fear isn't just about losing Cromarty. The government can live without Cromarty. No, now it's a real fear that United Australia will split the vote all over the place. Become a genuine coalition of the disaffected. And the big shiver is that Bobby Walshe will roll the Treasurer in his own seat. It used to be rusted on. Now it'll take nine per cent and Bobby might be able to do that, Janice.'

'Thank you Malcolm. Malcolm Lewis, our political editor on the big issues driving political life today. Did I say life? Excuse me. My next guest knows about life, he almost lost his in a ...'

Cashin found the classical station. Piano. He was coming around to the classical piano – the quick-fingered tinkling, the dramas, the final notes that floated like the perfume of women you'd lusted after. Most of all, he liked the silences, the gaps between what had been and what was to come.

THEY WORKED on the building again. By milking time, they had laid bricks to the first doorway to windowsill height.

'Stone sills in the picture,' said Rebb. 'Be stone lintels too, probably. Huge bloody door here.'

'I'll talk to Bern,' said Cashin. 'He may well have stolen them in the first place.'

Rebb left. Cashin worked on the garden for an hour, took the dogs for a short walk in the cold dusk. Tonight, he had only twinges of pain. He was tired but not hurting. Feed dogs, shower, make the fire, open a beer, water on for pasta.

Rebb knocked, came in, the dogs were on him.

'Surveyors down there,' he said, he was half in shadow, menacing. 'At the fence. Two blokes. When I went to milking.'

'She's unhappy,' said Cashin. 'Wasting her money. The agent is the snake, she should survey him. There's pasta on the way here.'

'Ate with the old bloke, he gets a bit lonely, doesn't want you to go. Not that he'd admit it. Wouldn't admit a croc's hanging off his leg.' He paused. 'About the house.'

'What?'

'We can get it up till you can see your way to going on yourself,' said Rebb.

Cashin felt the pang of loss anticipated. 'Listen,' he said, 'this's about that swaggie thing? I'm sorry. I'll say sorry.'

'No,' said Rebb. 'I'm a swaggie, swaggie's got to keep moving. We're like sharks. Tuna, we're more like tuna.'

'The old bloke'll miss you.'

Cashin knew that he was speaking for himself.

Rebb was looking down, fondling dog heads. 'Yeah, well, everything passes. He'll find someone else. Night then.'

Cashin ate in front of the television, the dogs on the couch, limp as cheetahs, a head at each end. He refuelled the fire, made a big whisky, sat thinking.

Michael the fag. Did his mother know Michael was queer? Bisexual, he was bisexual. She knew. Women always knew. What did it matter what Michael was? Vincentia Lewis the nurse who gave him her father's CDs was a lesbian. Given the chance, he'd have married her, lived in hope.

What hope? What did men have to offer? They died calling out for their mothers.

Mick Cashin drowned in the Kettle. *Took his life.* There was something terrible about that expression.

To take your life. That was the ultimate assertion of ownership – to choose to go into the silence, to choose sleep with no prospect of the dawn, of birdsong, of the smell of the sea on the wind.

Mick Cashin and Michael both made the choice.

This was not something to think about.

His father was always laughing. Even after he'd said something serious, scolding, he would say something funny and laugh.

Why did his mother still say it was an accident? She told Michael she would tell him his father had killed himself. And she couldn't, after all this time. She had probably changed her mind about what happened. Sybil had mastered reality. No need to tolerate the uncomfortable bits.

But why had no one else told him? He had come back and lived in the Doogue house, they all knew, they never said a word, never mentioned his father. The children must have been told not to speak about Mick Cashin. No one ever said the word *suicide*.

In the hospital, in the early days, when he had no idea of time, Vincentia had sat with him, held his hand, run fingers up his arm to the elbow. She had long fingers and short nails.

The Cashin suicide gene. How many Cashins had killed themselves? After they'd reproduced, created the next generation of depressives.

Michael hadn't done that. He was a full stop.

So am I, Cashin thought, I'm another dead end.

But he wasn't. The day he saw the boy walking from the school gate he knew he was his own beyond question – his long face, the long nose, the midnight hair, the hollow in his chin.

His son carried the gene. He should tell Vickie. She should know.

Rubbish. He wasn't a depressive. He felt low sometimes, that was all. It passed, as the nausea passed and the pain and the ghostly frozen images passed. He'd been fine before Rai Sarris. Now he was someone recovering from an accident, an assault. A murderous attack by a fucking madman.

Rai Sarris. Afterwards, in the hospital, he began to see how obsessed he'd become with him. Sarris wasn't an ordinary killer. Sarris had burnt two men to death in a lock-up near the airport. Croatian drug mules. He tortured them and then he burnt them alive. It took five years to get to the point when there was enough evidence to charge him.

And then Sarris vanished.

Where was Rai at this moment? What was he doing? Pouring a drink in some gated canal estate in Queensland, the boat outside, the whole place owned by drug dealers and white-collar criminals and slave-brothel owners and property crooks?

Had Rai been prepared to die the day he drove his vehicle into them? He was mad. Dying had probably never entered his mind.

Cashin remembered sitting with Shane Diab in the battered red Sigma from surveillance, looking at the grainy little monitor showing the two-metre-high gates down the street.

When they began to slide apart, he felt no alarm.

He remembered seeing bullbars, the nose of a big four-wheel-drive.

He didn't see the station wagon coming down the street, the chidren in the back, strapped into their seats.

The driver of the tank didn't care about station wagons with children in them.

Watching the monitor, Cashin saw the tank gun out of the gate and swing right.

There was a moment when he knew what was going to happen. It was when he saw the face of Rai Sarris. He knew Rai Sarris, he had spent seven hours in a small room with Rai Sarris.

But by then the Nissan Patrol was metres away.

Forensic estimated the Nissan was doing more than sixty when it hit the red car, rolled it, half-mounted it, rode it through a low garden wall, across a small garden, into the bay window of a house, into a sitting room with a piano, photographs in silver frames on it, a sentimental painting of a gum tree on the wall behind it.

The vehicles demolished that wall too, and, load-bearing structures having been removed, the roof fell on them.

Slowly.

The driver of the station wagon said the four-wheel-drive reversed out of the ruins, out of the suburban front garden, and drove away. It was found six kilometres away, in a shopping centre carpark.

Shane Diab died in the crushed little car. Rai Sarris was never found. Rai was gone.

Cashin got up and made another big whisky, he was feeling the drink. Music, he needed music.

He put on a Callas CD, settled in the chair. The diva's voice went to the high ceiling and came back, disturbed the dogs. They raised their heads, slumped back to sleep. They knew opera, possibly even liked it.

He closed his eyes, time to think about something else.

How many people like Dave Rebb were there out there, people who chose to be ghosts? One day they were solid people with identities, the next they were invisible, floating over the country, passing through the state's walls. Tax file numbers, Medicare numbers, drivers' licences, bank accounts, they had no use for them in their own names. Ghosts worked for cash. They kept their money in their pockets or in other people's accounts.

Did Dave ever have an earthly identity? He was more like an alien than a ghost, landed from a spaceship on some dirt-brown cattle station where the stars seemed closer than the nearest town.

An imperfect world. Don't obsess. Move on.

Sensible advice from Villani. Villani was the best friend he'd had. Something not to be forgotten. Best friend in a small field. Of how many? Relations excluded, relations didn't qualify as friends. Not many.

Cashin had never sought friends, never tried to keep friendships in good repair. What was a friend? Someone who'd help you move house? Go to the pub with you, to the football? Woody did that, they'd drunk together, gone to the races, the cricket. On the day before Rai Sarris, they'd eaten at the Thai place in Elwood. Woody's new ambition, Sandra, the high-cheek-boned computer woman, was looking at Woody and laughing and she ran her bare stockinged foot up Cashin's shinbone.

Instant erection. That was the last time he'd felt anything like that.

Woody came to the hospital a few times but, afterwards, Cashin didn't see him, they couldn't do the same things as before. No, that wasn't it. Shane Diab lay between them. People thought he was responsible for Shane's death.

They were right.

Shane was dead because Cashin had taken him along to see if his hunch was right that Sarris would come back to the house of his drug-trader partner. Shane had asked to come. But that didn't exonerate Cashin. He was a senior officer. He had no right to involve a naïve kid in his obsession with finding Sarris.

Singo never blamed him. Singo came to see him once a week after he was out of danger. On the first visit, he put his head close and said: 'Listen, you prick, you were right. The bastard came back.'

More drink. Think about the present, he told himself. People wanted Donny and Luke to be Bourgoyne's killers. If they were, it justified the deaths of Luke and Corey. And Donny's suicide, it explained that – the act of a guilty person.

Innocent boys branded as the killers of a good man, a decent, generous man. Two injustices. And whoever did it was out there, like Rai Sarris – free, laughing, sneering. Cashin closed his eyes and he saw the boys, unlined faces, one barely breathing, chest crushed, one gasping, spraying a dark mist, dying in the drenched night, the lights gleaming off the puddles of rain, of blood.

He had another drink, another, fell asleep in the chair and woke in alarm, freezing, fire low, rain heavy on the roof. The microwave clock said 3:57. He took two tablets with half a litre of water, put out the lights and went to bed fully clothed.

The dogs joined him, one on each side, happy to have been spared the middle passage of exile to their quarters.

THE LIGHT came back to a freezing world, wind from the west, bursts of rain, hail spits the size of pomegranate pips.

Cashin didn't care about the weather. He was beyond weather, felt terrible, in need of punishment. He took the dogs to the sea, walked to the mouth in a whipping wind, no sand blowing, the dunes soaked, the beach tightly muscled.

Today, Stone's Creek was strong, the inlet wide, the sandbars erased. On the other side, a man in an old raincoat, a baseball cap, was fishing with a light rod, casting to the line where the creek flow met the salt, reeling. A small brown dog at his feet saw the poodles and rushed to the creek's edge, barking, levitating on stiff legs with each hoarse expulsion.

The poodles stood together, silent, front paws in the water, studying the incensed animal. Their tails moved in slow, interested scientific wags.

Cashin waved to the man, who took a hand off his rod. There was little of him to see – a nose, a chin – but Cashin knew him from Port, he was an odd-job man for the elderly, the infirm, the inept, replaced tap washers, fuses, patched gutters, unblocked drains. How is it, he thought, that you can recognise people from a great distance, sense the presence of someone in a crowd, know their absence in the instant of opening a door?

On impulse, he turned left, walked along the creek, threading his way through the dune scrub. The dogs approved, brushed past him, went ahead and found a path worn by human feet over a long time. The land rose, the creek was soon a few metres below the path, glass-clear, shoals of tiny fish flashing light. They walked for about ten minutes, the path diverging from the creek, entering a region of dunes like big ocean swells. At the top of the highest one, the coastal plain was revealed. Cashin could see the creek winding away to the right, a truck on the distant highway, and, beyond it, the dark thread that was the road climbing the hill to The Heights.

Below, the path ran in a gentle curve to a clearing of several hectares, cut from bushland now coming back. It led to a roofless building, to the remains of other structures, one a tapering chimney standing amid ruins, a brick finger sticking out of a black fist.

The dogs reached the scene well ahead of Cashin, stopped, eyed the place, tails down. They looked back at him, got the signal, kicked off, running for a pile of bricks and rubble. Rabbits unfroze, scattered, bewildered the dogs for choice.

Cashin walked to the edge of the settlement, stood in the spattering rain. The flat area to the left had been a sports field. Three football posts remained, sunk in long grass, paint gone, wood bleached white. He became aware of the sounds the wind was making as it passed through the ruins – a tapping noise, a creaking like a nail being pulled from shrunken hardwood, a variety of low moans.

He went to the roofless timber structure, four rooms, a passage between them, looked in a window socket, saw a vandalised, pillaged space where fires had been made and people had defecated on bare earth once covered by floorboards. Fifty metres beyond it stood the chimney. He crossed to it, went around to the highway side. Once the brickwork had housed two stoves in big recesses, between them an oven. The cast-iron door lay rusting on the brick hearth, broken from its hinges.

The dogs were running around frantically, demented by rabbit scents everywhere. But the rabbits were gone, safe beneath the broken bricks and rusted sheets of corrugated iron. Behind the kitchen, in the grass on the other side of an expanse of cracked concrete, Cashin found the brick footings of a long building, two rooms wide. The top bricks were blackened and, inside the footings, he stumbled over a charred floor joist.

That's history, been nothing there since the fire. Companions are history too. Cecily Addison's words.

Cashin whistled, a chirpy sound in the forlorn place. The dogs appeared, joined at the mouths by something, tugging at it. He made them sit and release the object.

It was a leather belt, stiff and cracked – a boy's belt, a size to span a waist no bigger than a football. Cashin picked it up. On the rusted buckle, he could make out a fleur-de-lis and parts of words: B Prepa .

Be Prepared. It was a boy scout buckle.

He raised his arm to cast it away and then he could not. He walked across the overgrown playing field and bent the small hard belt around a goalpost, buckled it, let it slide into the grass.

On the highest dune, Cashin looked back. The wind was moving the goalposts, waving the grass. From the highway came the sound of a truck's airhorn, lonely somehow, nocturnal. He called the dogs and walked.

They drove home on empty roads, past houses sunk in their hollows, greenwood smoke being snatched from chimneys. The age of cheap dry wood from a million ringbarked trees was over.

He thought about Bourgoyne. Short of a startling piece of luck, it would never be known who bashed him, killed him. But it would always be stuck on the boys, their families, stuck on the whole Daunt, and even on people like Bern and his kids. Bourgoyne's killing was ammunition for all the casual haters everywhere.

Takin out those two Daunt coons. Pity it wasn't a whole fuckin busload. Most of Derry Callahan's customers would have said Fuckin A to that.

Don't obsess, he thought. Listen to Villani, leave the business alone.

Rebb was waiting, out of the wind, he had heard the vehicle. He walked across, flat cigarette in mouth. Cashin got out, released the dogs. Rebb held his hands low, palms up, the dogs went to them and didn't jump, waggled their whole bodies.

'Listen,' he said, 'you going to town today?'

'I am,' said Cashin, deciding in the instant. 'You eaten?'

'No, just come from the cows.'

'We can eat somewhere. Give me ten, I need to shower.'

THEY ORDERED bacon and eggs at the truckstop on the edge of Cromarty. An anorexic girl with a moustache and a pink-caked pimple between her eyebrows brought the food. The eggs lay on tissue-paper bread, the yokes small and pasta-coloured. Narrow pink steaks of meat could be seen in the grey pig fat.

Rebb ate some egg. 'Not from chooks living out the back,' he said. 'You in a position to pay wages?'

Cashin closed his eyes. He hadn't paid Rebb anything for the work done at the house, the fence. It had not entered his mind. 'Jesus, sorry,' he said. 'I just forgot.'

Rebb carried on eating, wiped his mouth with a paper napkin. He reached inside his coat and produced a folded sheet of paper torn from a notebook. 'I reckon it's twenty-six hours. Ten an hour okay?'

'Don't you get the minimum rate?'

'No rent, eating your food.'

'Yeah, well, let's say fifteen.'

'If you like.'

'I'll need your tax file number.'

Rebb smiled. 'Do me a favour. Use Bern's number. Know that by heart, wouldn't you, your cousin, all the transacting you do? Paying the tax on it all.'

Hopelessly compromised, thought Cashin. Just as guilty as any woman with two kids caught shoplifting.

He parked two blocks from the bank. He could have parked behind the police station but something said that wasn't a good idea. He took money out of the machine and paid Rebb.

'I'll be half an hour,' he said. 'Enough for you?'

'Plenty.'

He walked down wet streets to the station. Hopgood was in, writing in a file, a neat stack to his left awaiting his attention.

'Paperless office,' said Cashin from the door.

Hopgood looked up, expressionless eyes. 'What can I do for you?'

'I'd like to know who ordered the spotlight on Donny's house.'

'That's the Coulter bitch's story, lies, they all fucking lie. It's a way of life. Just a routine patrol.'

'I thought the Daunt was Indian territory? What happened to the *Blackhawk Down* stuff?'

Bright spots on Hopgood's cheekbones. 'Yeah, well, time to show the fucking flag in the pigsty. Anyway, where do you get off? I don't answer to you. Worry about your own fucking pisspot station.'

Cashin felt the heat in his own face, the urge to hit Hopgood in the middle of his face, to break nose and lips, to see the look he'd seen in Derry Callahan's eyes.

'I'd like to see the Bourgoyne stuff,' he said.

'Why? It's over.'

'I don't think it's over.'

Hopgood tapped a nostril with a finger. He had fat fingers. 'The watch? How does that feel?'

'I'd like to have a look anyway.'

'I'm busy here. Take it up with the station commander when he gets back from leave.'

Their eyes were locked. 'I'll do that,' Cashin said. 'There's something we haven't discussed.'

'Yeah?'

'That dud Falcon. You knew it couldn't keep up, didn't you?'

'Didn't know you couldn't drive, mate. Didn't know you were a gutless fucking wonder.'

'And the calls. You heard them.'

'Is that right? There's nothing on tape. You two boongs making up stories now? Like Donny's fucking mother? You related? All fucking related, aren't you? How's that happen, you reckon? All in the one bed fucking in the dark when they've cut the power cause you spent all the money on grog?'

Cashin's vision was blurred. He wanted to kill.

'Let me tell you something else, you fucking smartarse,' said Hopgood. 'You think you can shack up with a swaggie out there and nobody knows? You can let your arsefucker punch out innocent citizens and you look the other way? Is that a thrill for you? You like that kind of thing? Come in your panties, do you?'

Cashin turned and walked. A uniform cop was in the door. The man moved away quickly.

CASHIN WENT down to the esplanade and stood at the wall, the salt wind in his face. There were whitecaps across the bay, a fishing boat was coming in, cresting the grey swells, sinking into the troughs. He did his deep breathing, trying to take control of his nervous system, feeling his heartbeat slow.

After ten minutes, he went back, the only people on foot a group of kids coming down the hill in a rolling maul. He turned right halfway up, went the way he'd walked with Helen Castleman from the court, climbed the steps to her office. The receptionist was a teenager, too much makeup, looking at her nails.

He asked. She spoke on the telephone.

'Down the passage,' she said, a big smile, lots of gum. 'At the end.'

The door was open, her desk was to the right. Helen was waiting for him, looking up, unsmiling. He stood in the doorway.

'Two things,' he said. 'In order of importance.'

'Yes?'

'Donny,' he said. 'I've raised the harassment. They deny it. I'll take it as far as I can.'

'Donny's dead,' she said. 'He shouldn't be. He was a boy who wasn't very bright and who was very scared.'

'We didn't want that. We wanted a trial.'

'We? Is that you and Hopgood? You were fishing. You had nothing.'

'The watch.'

'Being with someone trying to sell a watch is evidence of nothing. Even having the watch means nothing.'

'I'll move on to the fence,' said Cashin.

'You've taken more than a metre from my property,' she said. 'Have your own survey done if you don't accept mine.'

'That's not what bothers you. You thought the property went to the creek.'

'Quite another matter. What I want you to do, Detective Cashin, is to take down the fence you so hastily ...'

'I'll sell you the strip to the creek.'

He had not planned to say this.

Helen's head went back. 'Is that what this is about? Are you a friend of the agent?'

Cashin felt the flush. 'Offer withdrawn,' he said. 'Goodbye.'

He was in the doorway when she said, 'Joe, don't go. Please.'

He turned, conscious of the blood in his cheeks, did not want to meet her eyes.

She had a hand up. 'I'm sorry. I retract that. And my outburst on the evening, I apologise for that too. Unlawyerly behaviour.'

The disdain, then the surrender. He didn't know what to do.

'Accept?' she said.

'Okay. Yeah.'

'Good. Sit down, Joe. Let's start again, we know each other in a way, don't we?'

Cashin sat.

'I want to ask you something about Donny.'

'Yes?'

'There's something, it came up, it bothers me.'

'Yes?'

'The pursuit, roadblock, whatever it was, that was because of a watch someone tried to sell in Sydney. Is that right?'

Cashin was going to say yes when Bobby Walshe came into his mind. This was about politics, the three crucified black boys. Bobby wasn't going to let it rest, there was mileage left, miles and miles. She wanted to use him.

'There's the coroner to come,' he said. 'How's Bobby Walshe?'

Helen Castleman bit her lip, looked away, he admired her profile.

'This's not about politics, Joe,' she said. 'It's about the boys, the families. The whole Daunt. It's about justice.'

He said nothing, he could not trust himself.

'Do cops think about things like justice, Joe? Truth? Or is it like your football team, it can do no wrong and winning is everything?'

'Cops think much like lawyers,' said Cashin. 'Only they don't get rich and people try to kill them. What's the point here?'

'Donny's mother says that Corey Pascoe's sister told her mother Corey had a watch, an expensive-looking watch.'

'When was that?'

'About a year ago.'

'Well, who knows what Corey had?' Cashin heard the roughness in his voice. 'Watches and what else?'

'Will you do anything about this?'

'It's not in my hands.'

She said nothing, unblinking. He wanted to look away but he couldn't.

'So you're not interested?'

Cashin was going to repeat himself but Hopgood came into his mind. 'If it makes you happy, I'll talk to the sister,' he said.

'I can get her to come here. You can use the spare office.'

'Not here, no.' That was not a good idea.

'She's scared of cops. I wonder why?'

There had been a Pascoe in his class at primary school. 'Ask them if they know Bern Doogue,' he said. 'Tell them the cop is Bern's cousin.'

Cashin bought the Cromarty *Herald* at the newsagent. He didn't look at it until the lights, waiting to cross.

MOUTH RESORT GO-AHEAD
Council approves $350m plan

He read as he walked. Smooth and tanned Adrian Fyfe was going to get his development, subject to an environmental impact assessment. Nothing about access, about buying the Companions camp from the Bourgoyne estate.

CASHIN SAW them as he rounded the old wool store – two big men and a woman near the end of the jetty. He parked, got out, put his hands in the pockets of his bluey and walked into a wind that smelled of salt and fish, with hints of burnt diesel.

The jetty planks were old and deeply furrowed, the gaps between them wide enough to lose a fishing knife to the sea, see it flash as it hit the water. Only three other people were out in the weather, a man and a small boy sitting side by side, arms touching, fishing with handlines, and an old man layered with clothing, holding a rod over the railing. His beanie was pulled down to his eyebrows, a red nose poking out of grey stubble.

The men watched him coming, the woman standing between them had her eyes down. Closer, Cashin could see that she was a tall girl, fifteen or sixteen, snub nose, bad skin.

'Joe Cashin,' he said when he reached them. He didn't offer to shake hands.

'Chris Pascoe,' said the man closest, the bigger of the two. He had a broken nose. 'This's Susie. Don't remember you from the school.'

'Yeah, well, if you remember Bern Doogue, I was there.'

'Tough little shit that Bern. All the Doogues. Seen him around, not so little now, he don't know me. Gone white, I reckon.'

The other man stared into the distance, chin up, like a figurehead. He had dreadlocks pushed back, a trimmed beard and a gold ring in the visible earlobe.

'The lawyer says there's something I should know,' said Cashin.

'Tell him, Suse,' said Pascoe to the girl.

Susie blinked rapidly, didn't look at Cashin. 'Corey had a watch,' she said. 'Before he went to Sydney.'

'What kind of watch?'

'Leather strap, it had all these little clock things.' She made tiny circles on her wrist. 'Expensive.'

'Did he say where he'd got it?'

'Didn't know I'd seen it. I was just lookin for my CDs, he pinched my CDs all the time.'

'Why didn't you ask him?'

She looked at Cashin, eyebrows up, big brown eyes. 'So he'd know I looked in his room? Shit, not that fuckin brave.'

'Watch your language,' said her father.

'If I showed you a picture of the watch, would you recognise it?' said Cashin.

Susie shrugged inside the anorak, it barely moved. 'Dunno.'

'You had a good look at it?'

'Yeah.'

Cashin thought about the band of pale skin on Bourgoyne's wrist. 'How come you're not sure you'd recognise it?'

'Dunno. I might.'

'The name of the watch?' he said. 'Notice that?'

'Yeah.'

Cashin looked at the men. It gained him nothing. The dreadlocked one was rolling a cigarette.

'You remember the name?'

'Yeah. Bretling. Something like that.'

'Can you spell that?'

'What's this spell shit?' said Chris Pascoe. 'She seen the watch.'

'Can you spell it?'

She hesitated. 'Dunno. Like B-R-E-T-L-I-N-G.'

If they'd schooled her, she would have got it right. Unless they'd schooled her not to.

'When was this?' said Cashin.

'Long time ago. A year, I spose.'

'Tell me something,' said Cashin. 'Why'd you only talk about the watch now?'

'Told me mum the day after.'

'After what?'

'After you shot Corey and Luke.'

He absorbed that. 'What did she say?'

The girl looked, not at her father but at the dreadlocked man. He opened his mouth and the wind took smoke from it. Cashin couldn't read his eyes.

'She said don't talk about it.'

'Why?'

'Dunno. That's what she said.'

'Got to go,' said Chris Pascoe. 'So she's told you, right? Can't say you don't know now, right?'

'No,' said Cashin. 'Can't say that. Didn't catch your friend's name.'

'Stevo,' said Pascoe. 'He's Stevo. That right, Stevo?'

Stevo sucked on his cigarette, his cheeks hollowed. He flicked the stub, the wind floated it across the jetty. A gull swooped and took it. Stevo's face came alive. 'See that? Fuckin bird smokes.'

'Thanks for your time,' said Cashin. 'Got a number I can ring you on?'

The men looked at each other. Stevo shrugged.

'Give you my mobile,' said Pascoe.

He found the mobile in his jacket and read out the number written on the cover.

Cashin wrote it in his book. 'You'll hear from me or the lawyer,' he said. 'Thank you, Susie.'

'He wasn't a bad kid, Corey,' said Pascoe. 'Could've played AFL footy. Just full of shit, thought he saw a fuckin career in dope. You a mate of Hopgood and that lot?'

'No.'

'But you'll stick with the bastards, won't you? All in together.'

'I do my job. I don't stick with anyone.'

Walking down the uneven planks, looking at the fishermen, at the shifting sea, Cashin felt the eyes on him. At the wool store, he turned his head.

The men hadn't moved. They were watching him, backs against the rail. Susie was looking down at the sodden planks.

'IT'S DIFFICULT,' said Dove, his voice even hoarser on the telephone. 'I'm not a free agent here.'

'This thing's a worry to me,' said Cashin.

'Yeah, well, you have worries and then you have other worries.'

'Like what?'

'I told you about the freezer. The election's coming on. You go on worrying and then you're in charge at Bringalbert North. And your mate Villani can't save you.'

'Where's Bringalbert?'

'Exactly. I have no fucking idea.'

'The difference is that then we thought the boys had done it and you thought someone'd gone soft-cock on Donny, he was going to walk.'

'Yeah, well. Then. Talked to Villani?'

'He told me to get on with my holiday,' said Cashin.

'That'll be coming from on high. The local pols don't want to turn the sexy white hotel staff of Cromarty against them and the federal government doesn't want to give Bobby Walshe any more oxygen than he's getting now.'

It was late morning, a fire going. Cashin was on the floor in the Z-formation, trying to hollow his back, lower legs on an unstable kitchen chair. Silent rain on the roof, drops ghosting down the big window. No working on Tommy Cashin's ruin today.

'If this thing is left,' he said, 'it dies. The inquest will say very unfortunate set of events, no one to blame, it'll pass into history, never be picked up again. Everyone's dead. And then the kids and the families and the whole Daunt have it stuck on them. They murdered Charles Bourgoyne, a local saint. A stain forever.'

'Tragic,' said Dove. 'Stains are tragic. I used to like those stain commercials on TV. Joe, do you get television where you are?'

'And see what?'

'Bobby Walshe and the dead black boys.'

'I may be stuck out here in the arse,' said Cashin, 'but the brain's still functioning. If you don't want to do this, just say it.'

'So touchy. What do you want?'

'Bourgoyne's watch. Did anyone bother to find out where he bought it? It's fancy, I think they have numbers, like car engines.'

'I'll see. That doesn't run to risking the Bumbadgery transfer.'

'I thought it was Bringalbert North?'

'I'm told they're the twin stars in the one-cop constellation. Still doing that lying on the floor business?'

'No.'

'Pity. An interesting practice, a conversation starter. I'll call you.'

Cashin disconnected, stared at the ceiling. He saw Dove's serious face, the doubting eyes behind the little round glasses. After a while, he went into a near-sleep, hearing the rain coursing in the gutters and downpipes. It sounded like the creek in flood. He thought of going down to it after rain when he was a boy, the grass wetting him almost to the armpits, hearing the rushing sound, seeing the water brushing aside the overhanging branches, swamping mossy islands he'd fished from, foaming around and over the big rocks. In places there were whitewater races, small waterfalls. Once he saw a huge piece of the opposite bank break off. It fell slowly into the stream, exposing startled earthworms.

The money Cecily Addison paid out on behalf of Bourgoyne. Cecily's payment records, he had them.

Cashin lifted his legs off the chair, rolled onto his right side, got up with difficulty and went to the table. The thick yellow folder was under layers of old newspapers.

He made a mug of tea, brought it to the table. The first payment sheet was dated January 1993. He flipped through them. Most months were a page, single-spaced.

Start at the beginning and work back? He looked at the top page. Names – shops, tradesmen, rates, power, water, telephones, insurance premiums. Others gave only dates, cheque numbers and amounts. He'd given up the first time he looked at the statements and then things happened and he never went back.

Cashin read, circled, tried to group the items. After an hour, he rang. Cecily Addison was not available, said Mrs McKendrick.

Taking her nap, thought Cashin. 'This is the police,' he said. 'We're terribly polite but we'll come around and wake Mrs Addison if that's necessary.'

'Please hold on,' she said. 'I'll see if she'll speak to you.'

It was several minutes before Cecily Addison came on. 'Yeees?'

'Joe Cashin, Mrs Addison.'

'Joe.' Groggy voice. 'Saw you on television, being rude. Won't get promoted that way, my boy.'

'Mrs Addison, the payments you made for Bourgoyne. Some don't have names. You can't tell who's being paid.'

Cecily began clearing her throat. Cashin held the telephone away from his ear. After a while, Cecily said, 'That's the regulars, the wages, that sort of thing.'

'There's two grand every month to someone, going back to the beginning of these payments. What's that?'

'No idea. Charles provided an account number, the money was transferred.'

'I need the numbers and the banks.'

'Confidential, I'm afraid.'

Cashin sighed as loudly as he could. 'Been through that with you, Mrs Addison. This is about a murder. I'll come around with the warrant, we'll take away all your files.'

A counter-sigh. 'Not at my fingertips this information. Mrs McKendrick will ring.'

'Inside ten minutes, please, Mrs Addison.'

'Oh, right. Galvanised now, are we? It took the third dead boy and Bobby Walshe.'

'I look forward to hearing from Mrs McKendrick. Very soon. Who was Mr McKendrick?'

'She lost him in Malaya in the fifties. Tailgunner in a Lincoln.'

'A man going forward while looking back,' said Cashin. 'I know that feeling.'

'In this case, falling forward. Off a hotel balcony. Pissed as a parrot, excuse the expression.'

'I'm shocked.'

Inside ten minutes, Mrs McKendrick provided the information, speaking as if to a blackmailer. Then Cashin had to ask Dove to make the inquiries. He rang when Cashin was bringing in firewood.

'I had to suggest, tell half-lies,' Dove said. 'I hardly know you. From now on, I want you to tell your own half-lies.'

'Truth Lite, everyone does it. The name?' The day was almost done, embers behind the western hills.

'A. Pollard. 128A Collet Street, North Melbourne. All withdrawals through local ATMs.'

'Who's A. Pollard?'

'An Arthur Pollard.'

The dogs were nudging him. It was time. 'We have a mystery bloke on the payroll for umpteen years,' he said. 'Needs a bit of work, don't you think?'

Cashin heard a sound. Dove was tapping on his desk.

'Yes, well,' Dove said, 'there's no shortage of things need work around here. And this little inquiry took fucking hours.'

'The extra mile. Force'll be proud of you.'

Three slow knuckle taps. 'I have to say this. I'm unsuited to homicide. It was a mistake. The death of a rich old cunt doesn't move me. I don't care if the guilty walk free. I don't even care if possibly innocent people now dead get the blame.'

Cashin rubbed dog heads in turn, the ridges of bone. 'Bourgoyne's watch?' he said. 'What about that?'

'May I say fuck off, pretty please?'

Time. Cashin put on his father's Drizabone, the short coat, dark brown, wrinkled like the skin of a peatbog man. One day about a year after he came to stay with the Doogues, Bern's father had offered it to him when they were going out with the ferrets.

'Your dad's. Hung onto it for you. Bit big. Mick wasn't small.'

Man and dogs in the rain, going downhill, escaping the worst of the wind. The long dry was over, the creek was filling. The dogs looked at it with amazement, affronted. They tested it with sensitive toes.

Cashin put his hands in the big pleated pockets. Was he wearing this that day? Was it night? Did he take it off and put it on a stone step before he jumped into the Kettle?

Was it the step I sat on with Helen?

He felt cold, whistled for the dogs. They looked around in unison.

RAIN SUITED Cromarty. In the old town, it turned the cobbled gutters to silver streams, darkened the bricks and stones and tiles, gave the leaves of the evergreen oaks a deep lustre.

Cashin parked outside the co-op and sat, wiped the side window to look at the street: a fat damp man pushing a supermarket trolley four blocks from the shop, two skateboarding kids wagging school, two women in shapeless cotton garments arguing as they walked, heads jerking. He didn't understand Cromarty, Cashin thought, he didn't know who had the Grip.

Singo had introduced him to the Grip.

It's the power to hurt, son. And the power to stop anyone hurting you. That's the Grip. There's blokes with millions got it and there's blokes with bugger all. There's blokes with three degrees and blokes can't read the Macca's menu.

The Bourgoynes would have had the Grip when the engine factory employed half the town. Did Charles keep the Grip after it was sold? Did he have any need for it?

Cashin got out. The rain soaked his hair, overran his eyebrows. He bought two big bags of dry dog food, drove to the supermarket and filled two trolleys, bulk buying. Never again could he enter Derry Callahan's shop. No more was there a milk, bread or dog food lifeline. Then he bought some whiting fillets at the fish shop and drove to Kenmare.

The street was empty, a windless moment, straight lines of rain. He went into the butcher. A new person stood behind the counter, a pudgy young man, spotted face, dark hair. They said good day.

'Couple of metres of dog sausage to begin,' Cashin said. 'Where's Kurt?'

'Cromarty. Dentist.'

'Helping out?'

'Permanent. Bit short on the dog, mate.'

'What you've got then.'

The youth weighed the sausage, wrapped it in paper, put it in a plastic bag.

'Plus three kilos of rump,' said Cashin. 'The stuff he hangs.'

He fetched the meat, cut, weighed. 'Take three-thirty?'

'That's fine. Mincer clean?'

'Yeah.'

'Run three kilos of topside, will you? Not too much fat.'

'Need some warning, mate. Come back tomorrow?'

'Too busy, are you?'

'Now, yeah.'

'Tell Kurt Joe Cashin's looking for another butcher, will you?'

The youth thought for a moment. 'Spose I can do the mince,' he said.

Cashin went out, sat in the vehicle, looked at the rain, placed the youth. He was wrapping the mince when Cashin opened the door.

'Local, aren't you?' said Cashin. 'What's the name?'

'Lee Piggot.' Lee was a bad wrapper, his fingers were too big. 'You the Doogues' cousin?'

'That's right. Know the Doogues?'

'Some. When I was at school.'

'Lee Piggot. Hear your name around the Cromarty drug squad?'

Flush, pink turning red. 'No.'

'Must be a name like yours. Butcher's a good job, a career. Honest work. People like their butcher. They even trust their butcher.'

Your police force, Cashin thought. Working with the community to create a better society. Using methods of fear and intimidation.

Last stop, Port Monro. The station was unattended. He let himself in and checked his desk: an envelope of pages faxed by Dove.

Heading home, a man on holiday, five weeks to go. The rain had stopped, the clouds dispersed, the world was clean and light. How much clearing and building could you do in five weeks?

Rebb was at work in the garden. He had found a low drystone wall.

'Jesus,' said Cashin. 'The elves been working here? In the rain?'

'Work's work. Can't let rain stop you.'

'Stops me.'

'You're a cop. You don't know about work. Pulling down the zip, that's work for cops.'

'You'd get on really well with Bern. Soulmates.'

They put in two hours, exposed twenty metres of stacked fieldstone and the remains of a wrought-iron gate.

'Made something to eat,' said Rebb. They walked back to the house and he produced four sandwiches neatly tied with cotton and toasted them under the grill.

'Not bad,' said Cashin. 'Old bushie recipe?'

'Tomato and onion's not a recipe.'

They went back and worked for another hour and then Rebb went to milking. 'Old bloke's taking me for a feed,' he said. 'At the Kenmare pub.'

Cashin carried on for half an hour, then he walked around and looked at the work they'd done in the garden and on the house. He realised that it gave him pleasure to see the progress, that he was proud of his part. It also came to him that he'd laboured for almost four hours without much pain.

Inside, straightening from giving the dogs their bowls, the current went through him. He moved slowly to a kitchen chair, sat bolt upright, eyes closed. It was a long time before he felt safe to rise. Then, tentative movements, he made a fire, opened a beer, sat at the table with the papers from Dove.

There were three medical reports on Bourgoyne. One was on his condition on arrival at the hospital. The second was from a forensic pathologist, who, at the request of the police, examined him as far as was possible in intensive care the next day. The third was the autopsy after his death. Bourgoyne's death was caused by his head striking the stone hearth.

The experts found that the marks on his knees and palms and feet were consistent with walking on hands and knees on rough carpeting. His facial bruises indicated being slapped repeatedly by someone standing above him, slapping with both sides of a hand about nine centimetres wide. The strokes across his back had almost certainly been administered with a bamboo stick of the kind sold by nurseries to support plants.

Cashin opened another beer. He stood at the counter, bottle in hand, pictures in his mind.

An old man roused from his bed, made to crawl down a long passage over a rough carpet.

A half-naked old man on his knees, someone slapping him, jerking his head from side to side, slapping him with fingers and palm, then backhand with the knuckles.

Then someone caning him across his back. Ten strokes.

Finally, he fell forward, hit his head on the stone hearth.

Cashin opened a can of tomato soup and shook the contents into a pot, added milk. Soup eaten with bread and butter. It had been a standard winter evening meal at the Doogues, home-made soup though, full of solid bits, they emptied their bowls.

He should make some proper soup. How hard could it be?

He thought about catching the bus to Cromarty every school day with Bern and Joannie and Craig and Frank, six of them spread across the back seat, their seat. On the way there, Bern and Barry and Pat mucked around, he finished his homework, Joannie and Craig, the twins, whispered and bickered. On the way home, they were all in high spirits. Then, one by one, Barry, Pat and Bern dropped out and it was just the three of them.

Cashin took the beer back to the chair, wished he had a smoke. How long did the craving last? It would last forever if he kept chipping every chance he got.

He thought about that morning at The Heights – the old man on the floor, the blood, the sour smell. What was the smell? It wasn't one of the smells of homicide. Blood and piss and shit and alcohol and vomit, they were the smells of homicide.

Why was the painting slashed? What was that about? Why would you bother?

He got up, found Carol Gehrig's number in his notebook. It rang for no more than three seconds.

'Hi, Alice here.'

A girl, a teenager, bright voice. She was hoping for a call, hanging out.

'Is Carol Gehrig in?'

A disappointed silence. 'Yeah. Mum! Phone.'

There were sounds and then Carol said hello.

'Joe Cashin. Sorry to bother you again.'

'No bother.'

'Carol, the painting at Bourgoyne's, the cut painting.'

'Yeah?' Another disappointed person.

'Is it still on the wall?'

'No. I got Starkey to take it down.'

'Where is it?'

'I told him to put it in the storeroom.'

'Where's that?'

'Next to the old stables. You go through the studio.'

'Did they ask you about the painting?'

'The cops? No. I don't think so.'

'Why would anyone cut that painting?'

'Beats me. Pretty awful picture. Sad, sort of.'

MRS MCKENDRICK was in her seventies, gaunt, long-nosed, with grey hair scraped back. On her desk stood a computer. To her left, at eye level, was an easel holding her shorthand notebook. To the right, on the desk in two rows, were containers holding paper clips, split pins, pencils, a stapler, a hole punch, sealing wax.

'If she hasn't got anyone with her,' said Cashin, 'it'll only take a few minutes.'

'This firm asks visitors to make appointments,' she said, stroking the keyboard.

Cashin looked around the dark room, the prints of stags at bay, lonely waterfalls and hairy highland cattle grazing in the glens, and he found no patience.

'I'm not a visitor,' he said. 'I'm the police. Would you mind leaving the decision to Mrs Addison?'

The tapping stopped. Grey eyes turned on Cashin. 'I beg your pardon?'

Cecily Addison appeared behind Mrs McKendrick. 'What's all this?' she said. 'Come in, Joe.'

Cashin followed Cecily into her office. She crossed to the fireplace wall and leaned against the small bookcase, moved around, not much flesh to cushion her weight but no great weight to cushion. 'Sit down,' she said. 'What's the problem?'

He handed her the payments statement. 'The ones I've ringed.'

Cecily's gaze went down the list. She frowned. 'Wages, most of these. This I think is the turf club membership. The Melbourne Club this, goes up every year. Credit card bill. Small these days, used to be huge. This is ... oh, yes, rates for the North Melbourne property. Wood Street. They go up every year too, don't know why he hangs onto it. The Companions used the place. I did the conveyance for that.'

'What kind of place?'

'It's a hall. They had concerts there in the beginning, I gather. Music. Plays. It was Companions headquarters.'

Cecily began the search for her cigarettes. Today, a quick find, in a handbag. She plucked one, found the Ronson, it fired at the first click. A deep draw, a grey expulsion, a bout of coughing.

'Tell me a bit about the Companions,' said Cashin.

'Well, the money came from Andrew Beecham. Mean anything?'

'No.'

'Andrew's grandfather owned half of St Kilda at one point. Lords of the city, the Beechams. And the country, a huge property other side of Hamilton. It's broken up now, cut into four, five. They had royals there. The English aristocracy. Sirs and the Honourables. Playing polo.'

Cecily looked at her cigarette, turned her palm upwards, reversed it.

'Educated in England, the Beechams,' she said. 'Nothing else good enough. Not Melbourne Grammar, not Melbourne Uni. Andrew never did a day's work in his life. Mind you, he won an MC in the war. Then he married a McCutcheon girl, nearly as rich as he was, half his age. She hanged herself in the mansion in Hawthorn and Beecham had a stroke the same day. Paralysed down one side, gimpy leg, gimpy arm. Ended up marrying a nurse from the hospital. After a decent interval, of course.'

Cashin thought that he could understand marrying the nurse from the hospital.

Cecily was looking out of the window. 'They come to you like angels, nurses,' she said. 'I remember my op, waking up, could've been on Mars, first thing I saw was this apparition in white ...'

Silence.

'Mrs Addison, the Companions,' said Cashin.

'Yes. Raphael Morrison. Heard of him?'

'No.'

'He was a bomber pilot, bombed the Germans, Dresden, Hamburg, you know, fried them like ants, women and kids and the old, not many soldiers there. He came home and he had a vision. Teach the young not to make the same mistakes, new world, that kind of thing. Moral improvement. So he started the Companions.'

Cecily covered a yawn with fingertips. 'Anyhow, Andrew Beecham heard about the Companions from Jock Cameron, they were in the war together. Jock introduced Andrew and Morrison to old man Bourgoyne and he got the bug because of his dead older boys, and that's why the camp's where it is. On Bourgoyne land. In the late fifties, I was in the firm then.'

'Bit lost here. Who's Jock Cameron?'

'Pillar of this firm for forty years. Jock got wounded crossing the Rhine. Came out here for his health.'

Cecily stared at Cashin. 'You look a bit like Charles Bourgoyne,' she said.

'So, the Companions.'

'Lovely family, Jock's,' she said. 'Met them in '67, we went to England on the *Dunedin Star*. Never forget those stewards, pillowbiters to a man. They'd come along these narrow passages and rub against my Harry. He didn't take kindly, I can tell you.'

Cashin looked away, embarrassed. 'Something else. Jamie Bourgoyne apparently drowned in Tasmania.'

'Another family tragedy,' she said, not much breath. 'First his mother's death so young.'

'What happened to her?'

'She fell down the stairs. The doctor said she was affected by sleeping pills. Tranquillisers, it might have been tranquillisers, I can't recall. Same night as the Companions fire. Double tragedy.'

'So Bourgoyne brought up the step-kids?'

'Well, brought up's not quite the term. Erica was at school in Melbourne then. Jamie had his own teacher till he was about twelve, I think.'

'And then?'

'School in Melbourne. I suppose they came home in the holidays, I don't know.'

Cashin said his thanks, went out into the day. Ice rain was slanting in under the deep verandahs, almost reaching the shopfronts, soaking the shoes of the few wall-hugging pedestrians. He drove around to the station. Dove's faxes were on his desk and he started reading.

The phone rang. He heard Wexler being polite.

'Look after business for ten or so, boss?' said Wexler, behind him. 'Shoplift at the super.'

'I need the union,' said Cashin. 'On leave, I can't come in here without being exploited.'

He was on the sixth page when Wexler returned, looking pleased.

'Took a while, boss,' he said. 'This woman, she's got no idea the two little kiddies in the cart got stuff up their anoraks, chockies and that. The owners, they jump on her like she's some ...'

'Sores?' said Cashin. He couldn't remember her name. He touched the corners of his mouth.

Wexler blinked. 'Yeah. Like little blisters, yeah.'

The first name came. 'Jadeen something?'

Eyes widened. 'Jadeen Reed.'

'Jadeen's just run out of supermarkets in this town. Shopping's in Cromarty from now on.'

Wexler kept blinking. 'Get it wrong, did I, boss?'

'Well,' said Cashin, 'Jadeen might have enough problems without a shoplifting charge.'

He left the station, bought the papers at the newsagent, avoided conversation, walked down to the Dublin. Two short-haired elderly women were at the counter, paying. They nodded and smiled at him. Either they were on the march or they'd seen him on television or both.

Leon thanked them for their patronage. When the door closed, he said, 'So, now retired due to post-traumatic stress caused by the march of toddlers and the aged? Looking forward to a life on the disability pension?'

'Long black, please. Long and strong.'

At the machine, Leon said, 'On that note, I see you and Bobby Walshe are school chums.'

'Kenmare Primary. Survivors.'

'And on to Cromarty High, you two boys?'

'Bobby left. Went to Sydney.'

'So you'll be voting for your other spunky school chum. Helen of Troilism.'

'Of what?'

'Troilism. Threesomes.' Leon was admiring the crema on his creation. 'Try under T in the cop manual. It's probably a crime in Queensland. She's standing in Cromarty for Bobby's all-purpose party.'

'You see that where?'

'The local rag. I've got it here.'

Leon found a copy of the newspaper, opened it to the page. There was a small photograph of Helen Castleman. It did not flatter. The headline said:

SOLICITOR TO STAND FOR NEW PARTY

'Did it cross your mind,' Leon said, leaning on the counter, 'that our lives are just like stories kids tell you? They get the and-then-and-then right, and then they run out of steam and just stop.'

'You've got kids?' It had not occurred to Cashin.

'Two,' said Leon.

Cashin felt a sense of unfairness. 'Maybe you shouldn't think about your life that way. Maybe you shouldn't think about your life at all. Just make the coffee.'

'I can't help thinking about it,' said Leon. 'When I was growing up I was going to be a doctor, do good things, save lives. A life with a purpose. I wasn't going to be like my father.'

'What was wrong with him?'

'He was an accountant. Dudded his clients, the little old ladies, the pensioners. One day he didn't come home. I was nine, he didn't come back till I was fourteen. Not a single word from him. I used to hope he'd come on my birthday. Then he arrived … anyway, forget it, I get maudlin in winter. Vitamin D deficiency, drink too much.'

'Why can't dentists have a purpose?'

Leon shook his head. 'Ever heard anyone appeal for a dentist to come forward?'

'My feeling,' said Cashin, 'is that you're being a bit hard on yourself.'

CASHIN WAS looking into the fridge, thinking about what to cook for supper when the phone on the counter rang.

'Get anywhere with the matter we discussed?' said Helen Castleman.

'I had the chat with them, yes,' said Cashin.

'So?'

'It's worth thinking about.'

'Just thinking?'

'A manner of speaking.'

Silence.

'I don't know how to take you, detective,' she said.

'Why's that?'

'I don't know whether you want the right result.'

'What's the right result?'

'The truth's the right result.'

Cashin looked at the dogs, splendid before the fire. They felt his gaze, raised heads, looked at him, sighed and sagged.

'You'd be good in parliament,' said Cashin. 'Raise all the standards. The looks, the average IQ.'

'Blind Freddy's dog's got a better chance of getting into parliament,' she said. 'I'm standing to give some choice in this redneck town. Moving on. What are you doing then?'

'Working on the matter.'

'Is that you or the homicide squad?'

'I can't speak for the homicide squad. There's no great ...'

'Great what?'

'I forget. Interrupting me does that. I'm on leave. Out of touch.'

'And you've no doubt worn a path between your mansion and the illegal fence on my property.'

'There's a pre-existing path. Historical path to the historical boundary.'

'Well, I'm coming up it,' Helen said. 'I want to see your eyes when you talk this vague bullshit.'

'That's also a manner of speaking, is it?' said Cashin.

'It is not. I'll be there in ... in however long it takes. I'll be inspecting my boundary on the way.'

'What, now?'

'Setting out this very minute.'

'Dark soon.'

'Not that soon. And I've got a torch.'

'Snakes are a problem.'

'I'm not scared of snakes. Mate.'

'Rats. Big water rats. And land rats.'

'Well, eek, eek, bloody eek. Four-legged rats don't scare me. I'm on my way.'

IN THE FADING afternoon, he saw the red jacket a long way off, a match-flare in the gathering gloom. Then the dogs sniffed her on the wind and took off, ran dead straight. They monstered her but she kept her hands in her pockets, no more scared of dogs than of snakes or rats.

When they met, Helen offered a hand in a formal way. She looked scrubbed, fresh out of the shower, colour on her cheekbones. 'I suppose you could charge me with trespass,' she said.

'I'll keep that in reserve,' said Cashin. 'Let me walk in front, lots of holes. I don't want to be sued.'

He turned and walked.

'Very legalistic meeting this,' said Helen.

'I don't know about a meeting. More like an interview.'

They walked up the slope in silence. At the gate, Cashin whistled the dogs in and they appeared from different directions.

'Highly trained animals,' she said.

'Hungry animals. It's supper time.'

At the back door, he said, 'I'm not apologising for the place. It's a ruin. I live in a ruin.'

They went in, down the passage to the big room.

'Jesus,' she said. 'What room is this?'

'The ballroom. I have the balls in here.'

Cashin shunted the dogs into the kitchen, led the way to the rooms he lived in, cringed at the half-stripped wallpaper, the cracked plaster, the piles of newspapers.

'This is where you go after the balls,' said Helen. 'The less formal room. It's warm.'

'This is where we withdraw to,' he said. 'The withdrawing room.' He had read the term somewhere, hadn't known it before Rai Sarris, that was certain.

Helen looked at him, nodding in an appraising way, biting her lower lip. 'My embarrassment about this visit has been growing,' she said. 'I get so angry.'

Cashin cleared newspapers from a chair, dropped them on the floor. 'Now that you're here,' he said, 'have a seat.'

She sat down.

He didn't know what to do next. He said, awkward, 'Time to feed the dogs. Tea, coffee? A drink?'

'Is that the choice for the dogs? Do I get to choose? Give them tea. And a bickie.'

'Right. What about you?'

'A drink like what?' She was taking off her coat, looking around the room, at the sound equipment, the CD racks, the bookshelf.

'Well, beer. Red wine. Rum, there's Bundy. Coffee with Bundy is good on a cold day, that's every day. With a small shot. A big shot, that's good too.'

'A medium shot. Do you do that?'

'We can try. Tend to extremes here. It's coffee made in a plunger. Warmed up.'

The light caught her hair, shiny. 'Very good. That's a big advance on what I usually drink.'

By the time he'd fed the dogs, the coffee was hot. He poured big hits of rum into mugs and filled up with coffee, picked the mugs up in one hand, sugar in the other, went back.

Helen was looking at the CDs. 'This is heavy stuff,' she said.

'For a cop, you mean?'

'I was speaking for myself. My father played opera all the time. I hated it. Never listened properly, I suppose. I'm a bad listener.'

He gave her a mug. 'A bit of sugar takes the edge off it,' he said.

'I'll be guided by you.'

He spooned sugar into her mug, stirred, did his mug. 'Cheers.'

She shuddered. 'Wow,' she said. 'I like this.'

They sat.

'It's been a sad business,' she said, eyes on the fire.

'No question.'

'I'm feeling bad about this because I think you think I'm trying to use you in some way.'

Barks.

'Mind the dogs?' he said. 'They won't bother you.'

'Let slip the dogs.'

Cashin took her mug, let them in. They charged Helen. She wasn't alarmed. He spoke sternly and they went to the firebox and sank, heads on paws.

'It's not an interview, Joe,' she said. 'I want to talk about what's going on, it's not like I'm wearing a wire. To say what I think, I think the government's happy to see Bourgoyne pinned on these boys if it helps politically.'

'No politics about homicide.'

'No?'

'No one's talked politics to me.'

'There should be a taskforce on this. Instead, there's you and Dove, you go on leave, not suspended, on leave. Dove's back in Melbourne. And you tell me you haven't been told this thing's filed under Forget It?'

Cashin didn't want to lie to her.

'I understand the idea is to let things cool down,' he said. 'The man's dead, the boys are dead, we're not pressed for time. It's hard to investigate when you've got people full of rage. Who's going to talk to you?'

'That's the Daunt you're talking about?'

'The Daunt.'

She drank. 'Joe,' she said, 'do you accept that it's possible that the boys didn't attack Bourgoyne?'

The firebox didn't need stoking. He got up and stoked it. Then he put on Björling. The balance had drifted slighty. He fiddled with the controls. 'Yes,' he said, 'that's possible.'

'Well, if it wasn't the boys, you don't have to worry about the Daunt cooling off. You don't have to clear the boys before you look elsewhere, do you?'

'Helen, I'm seconded from homicide to Port Monro. They were stretched and they drafted me. Then things happened.'

'Did Hopgood have any say?'

Cashin sat down. 'Why would he?'

'Because he runs Cromarty. I'm told the station commander doesn't go to the toilet without Hopgood's nod.'

'Well, I'm in Port Monro. Maybe you hear things I don't hear.'

They looked at each other over their mugs. She did a slow blink.

'Joe, people say he's a killer.'

'A killer? Who says that?'

'Daunt people.'

Cashin thought he would believe anything about Hopgood. He looked away. 'People say anything about cops, it's the job.'

'You've got Aboriginal family, haven't they told you?'

'The people I'm related to see me as just another white maggot cop,' he said. 'But you wouldn't understand that. Let's talk about rich white kids who want to run the world.'

Helen closed her eyes. 'Not called for. I'll start again. People say Corey Pascoe was executed that night. You were there. What do you say?'

'I'll say what I have to say to the coroner.'

'You tried to call it off.'

'Did I?'

'Yes, you did.'

'You get that from where?'

'It doesn't matter for present purposes.'

'For present purposes? There aren't any present purposes. Anyway, the coroner will decide what people did and didn't do.'

'Jesus,' she said, 'I can't seem to get this right. Can you relax for a single fucking second?'

He felt the flare, the flush.

'I think you're just spoilt,' he said. 'You come over with all this passion but you're just a rich smart brat. If you can't get what you want, you stamp your little shoe. Well, go to the media. Get the girl to tell them the watch story. You can be on television. It'll help your campaign. Yours and Bobby's both.'

Helen got up, put her mug on the wonky table, picked up her coat. 'Well, thanks for seeing me. And for the fortified coffee.'

'Any time.'

Cashin got up and walked ahead, through the huge room with its sprung floorboards that uttered faint mouse-like complaints. Outside, a three-quarter moon, high clouds, dispersed and running. He said, 'I'll walk with you.'

'No thanks,' she said, pushing an arm into her coat. 'I can find my way.'

'I'll walk to my fence,' said Cashin. 'I want to be a witness to any alleged slips and falls.'

He took the big torch from the peg and went ahead. She followed in silence, down the path, out the gate, across the grassland, into the rabbit lands. Near her fence, he moved the torch and eyes gleamed – four, no, more.

He stopped.

Hares. Transfixed, immobilised hares. The dogs would love this, he thought.

'Dogs would like this,' she said behind him.

He half-turned. She was close behind him, they were centimetres apart.

'No, can't take the dogs out with a light. Hares don't stand a chance.'

She took a small step, put a hand on the back of his head and kissed him on the mouth, pulled back and then kissed him again.

'Sorry,' she said. 'Just an impulse.'

She went around him, switched on her torch. He didn't move, astonished, half-erect, light on her, watched her stoop through the wires of the sagging side fence that met his new corner post, start to climb the slope, fade into the dark, become a moving, rising light. She didn't look back.

Cashin stood there for a time, fingers on his lips, thinking about the night at the Kettle, the other long-ago kisses, two kisses. He shivered, just the cold night.

Why did she do it?

WOOD STREET in North Melbourne was a short dead-end, narrow, blank factory walls on one side facing five thin weatherboard houses. At the end of the street stood a brick building modelled on a Greek temple, no windows, four pillars and a triangular gable. It was a hall of some kind, like a Masonic hall, but the gable was blank.

Cashin drove slowly, angle-parked in front of unmarked roller doors. He didn't get out, thought about driving all the way for no good reason, about how he could agonise about some things for days and weeks and months but do others with no consideration at all.

Vickie had spotted it early, when he'd come home one day driving a second-hand Audi. 'You work it all out intelligently, don't you?' she said. 'Think it through. Then you just do something, anything. You might as well be a total fuckwit, what's the difference in outcomes?'

She was right. That was why Shane Diab was dead, that was why the blood ran out of his mouth and his nose and his eyes and he made terrible sounds and died.

Cashin got out, walked around the vehicle. The floor of the narrow portico of the temple was hidden beneath mouldy dog turds, dumped junk mail returning to pulp, syringes, beer stubbies, cans, bourbon bottles, condoms, pieces of clothing, bits of styrofoam, a rigid beach towel, a length of exhaust pipe.

He went up the two steps, walked over the rubbish to the huge metal-studded double doors. They bore the scars of many attacks. A bell button had been gouged out but the cast-iron knocker had survived. He bashed it against its buffer – once, twice, thrice. He waited, did it again. Again. Again. Then he knelt and pushed back the letterbox flap. Dark inside. He felt eyes on him, stood and turned.

A woman was on the front doorstep of the nearest weatherboard, tortoise head peeping from a shell of garments, the top one a huge floral apron.

'Whaddayadoin?' she said.

Cashin went down the steps, approached her. 'Police.'

'Yeah? Show me.'

He showed her. 'Who looks after this place?'

'Hey?'

'This building.' He pointed at it. 'Who looks after it?'

'Ah. Used to be a bloke. Never come out the front. Never seed him open that door.' She sniffed, wiped a finger under her nose, studied Cashin in silence, unblinking.

'So how did you know he was in there?' he said.

'Merv's got a garage there, he seed him.'

'A garage where?'

She looked at him as if he were slow. 'In the lane. I said that.'

'Right. How do you get to the lane?'

'Next to Wolf's.'

'Where's Wolf's?'

'Well it's in Tilbrook Street. Where'd ya think it would be?'

'Thanks for your help.'

She watched him three-point turn, drive off. He waved. She didn't respond. In Tilbrook Street, he found the sunken lane, just wide enough for a vehicle. He parked in the entrance and walked along the bluestone gutter running down the middle, looking on the left for the entrance to the back of the temple.

It had to be the plank door with the rotten bottom beside the rusted steel garage doors. Yale lock, no door handle. He put both hands on the door and pushed tentatively. It didn't yield. He tested the right-hand gatepost, it gave a little.

Knocking was required. He knocked, called the name, did it again. Then he looked up and down the lane, stepped into the gateway, braced his back against a gatepost, put a foot on the opposite post, pushed against it and leant on the door.

The door squeaked open and he almost fell in.

Forcible entry, no warrant.

An alley four or five metres long, brick walls on either side, a rubbish bin. Cashin walked to the end. A concreted yard, a rectangle behind a high wall broken only by three small windows and a door. At the left were washing lines, empty.

He went to the door in the building, stood on the top step and knocked, three times, harder each time, hurting his knuckles.

He tried the doorknob. Locked. Another Yale lock, a newer one.

The lane door was one thing, that could be explained away. Forcing entry into a building was another matter. He should ring Villani, tell him what he wanted, what he was doing here.

He examined the door. It had shrunk over the hundred-odd years of its life, no longer fitted snugly into its frame. When you fitted a new lock to an old door, you needed to compensate for the years. That hadn't been done. He bent to look. He glimpsed the lock's tongue.

Go away, said the voice of sense. Leave. Ring Villani. Get a warrant.

That would take forever. Villani would take his guide from Singo, he would cite Singo. He would want a proper case made for the intrusion.

Cashin thought that he wanted to go home, walk the dogs in the clean wind, lie on the floor for a while, sit by the fire and listen to Callas, roll red wine around his mouth while he read some Conrad.

He took out his wallet and found the thin, narrow piece of plastic. For a moment, he held it between thumbs and forefingers, bending it. It was strong, just enough flex.

Oh, well, what the hell, come this far.

The lozenge went in easily, slid around the tongue, pushed it back just enough. He put pressure on the door.

The tongue slipped its lodging.

The door opened.

Light fell on a wide passage, linoleum on the floor, black and white squares, he could see the lines of the boards beneath the covering. He took a step inside. The air was cold and stale, scrabbling noises from above. Birds. They would be starlings, no roof could keep them out. In a few weeks, they could insulate a ceiling with crap.

'Anyone home?' he shouted.

He took a few more steps down the passage, shouted again. No sound, the starlings paused for a few seconds.

Cashin opened the first door on the left. It was a bathroom and toilet, a shower head above the old claw-footed bath. A cabinet above the basin was empty except for a dry cake of soap.

The next door along was open: a kitchen, ancient gas stove, bare pine table, an empty vegetable rack.

Cashin crossed the passage. The room on the other side was a bedroom – a single bed, made with white sheets, a bedside table, a lamp. Two folded blankets stood on a pine chest of drawers. Nothing in the drawers. Cashin opened a narrow wardrobe. It was empty except for wire coathangers.

The next room was the same, a single bed with a striped coir mattress and a table. Across the way, the door opened reluctantly. Clicking the light switch on the right showed an office with a desk and a chair and a grey three-drawer filing cabinet and a wall of wooden shelves holding grey lever-arch files. Cashin touched the bare desk. His fingers came away coated with dust.

He went to the shelves. There were labelled, handwritten cards in brass holders tacked to each shelf: General Correspondence, Correspondence Q'land, Correspondence WA, Correspondence SA, Correspondence Vic. The Vic shelf was bare. Other shelves were labelled Invoices. Nothing on the Invoices Vic shelf. He chose a file from Correspondence WA, flicked through it. Originals and carbon copies and photostats of letters to and from the Companions Camp, Caves Road, Busselton, Western Australia.

Cashin replaced the file, opened a desk drawer.

Used cheque books, in bundles held together with rubber bands, some of which had perished. He took out a book, looked at a few stubs. All the Moral Companions' bills appeared to have been paid from this place.

He closed the drawer, left the room, opened the door at the end of the passage. Darkness. He groped, found the switch, three fluorescent tubes took their time flickering into life. Another passage, transverse, three doors off it. Cashin opened the first one, found switches, one, two, three, flicked them all. On the wall opposite, a few lightbulbs lit up around mirrors.

It was a theatre dressing room. He had been in one before, the woman's body was in the toilet. It had been there for sixteen hours. She appeared to have fallen and struck her head against the bowl some time after the last performance of a play by an amateur group. There had been a party. What set the bells ringing was a bruise on the back of her head. The play was written by a doctor. Singo wanted him and they flame-grilled him but in the end there was nothing except an admission that he'd screwed another cast member.

Cashin checked the other rooms. Also small dressing rooms. Two bulbs popped in the second one as he flicked the switches. He walked back, opened a door, went down a long flight of stairs, another door.

A big room, dimly lit by dusty windows high on the walls. He took a few steps.

It was a theatre from another time, longer than it was wide, slightly raked, about thirty rows of seats, all uptilted. To his left, a short flight of steps went up to the stage.

One more time. 'Anyone here?' he shouted. 'Police.'

Starlings up above here too and, from the street, the sound of a car revving, the test-revving of mechanics.

A smell over the dust and the faint odour of damp coming up from beneath the floor. Cashin sniffed, could not identify it. He had smelled it somewhere before and he felt a tightening of the skin on his face and neck.

He walked to the back of the room and pushed open one of a pair of doors. Beyond was a small marble-floored foyer and the front doors. He went back, climbed the stairs to the stage, pushed aside heavy purple velvet curtains. He was in the wings, a dark space, the bare-boarded stage glimpsed through gaps in tall pieces of scenery.

Cashin went to an opening.

Sand had been dumped on the stage, clean building sand, in heaps and splashes.

Sand?

He saw the buckets at the back of the space, three red buckets with FIRE stencilled on them. Someone had emptied the fire buckets onto the stage, thrown the sand around.

Hoons? Hoons wouldn't limit themselves to throwing sand around, they'd trash the whole place, pull down the curtains, shit on the stage, piss off it, jump on the seats till they broke, rip them from their moorings, light fires.

Not hoons, no. This wasn't hooning.

Something else had happened here.

He walked out onto the stage, could not avoid treading on sand, it crunched beneath his feet, a startlingly loud sound. At centre stage, he looked around. Dust motes hung in their millions in the pale yellow glow from the windows.

There would be stage lighting. Where?

In the wings, he looked around, found a panel near the stairs with switches – four old-fashioned round porcelain switches, brass toggles. He tipped them all, solid clicks, the stage was illuminated.

He walked back onto the stage. A spotlight above the arch now lit a painted backdrop and perhaps a dozen footlight bulbs were alight. As he watched, two died, a moment, then a third was gone. He looked at the backdrop. It was of a soft rolling landscape, farm buildings here and there, white dots of grazing sheep, a yellow road snaking over the plain and up a hill, a green, softly rounded hill. On its peak stood three crosses, two small ones flanking a cross twice their size.

Cashin went closer. Crucified figures hung from the smaller crosses. But the big cross was empty. It was waiting for someone. He looked at the sand on the floor in front of the backdrop.

Why would anyone throw sand on the stage? To put out a fire? Perhaps someone had started a fire, poured an inflammable fluid on the floorboards, lit it, then panicked, grabbed a fire bucket, smothered the flames.

That was the obvious explanation.

Hoons lit fires.

But they didn't put them out.

He moved sand with a shoe, scraped at it. The bottom grains were dark, stuck together, they came away in clumps. He scraped some more, revealed the boards.

A black stain. He felt a twinge of nausea, the cold in his neck, the back of his head, his ears.

Something bad had happened here.

Time to ring the squad, wait in the vehicle.

He squatted and put out an index finger, touched the floor, looked at his fingertip.

Blood.

He knew blood.

How old? The sand had trapped the moisture.

He stood up, back aching, flexed his shoulders, he was facing the auditorium, the spotlight on, the footlights in his eyes, he could not see the hall clearly.

He saw it.

ALL THE seats in the hall were turned up.

Except for one seat. Six rows back, in the middle of the sixth row.

One seat was down. In the whole auditorium only one seat was down.

Someone had sat on that seat. Someone had chosen that seat. It was the best seat in the house to see something.

To see what?

Nonsense. The seat had probably fallen down, seats did that, everything did that, falling down was a law of nature. You lined up a dozen things that could fall over, at least one did.

Cashin left the stage, went down the stairs, walked down the aisle until he was at the sixth row, took out his mobile and rang homicide.

'Joe Cashin. Is Inspector Villani in?'

'He's on the phone. No, he's off. Putting you through.'

Villani barked his surname. He sounded more like Singo every day.

'It's Joe. Listen, I'm in this hall place in North Melbourne, something's happened here needs looking at.'

Villani coughed. 'Is this Joe from Port Monro? Calling from North Melbourne? On a trip to the big city, Joe? Go ahead, tell us what's on your mind.'

'Here's the address,' said Cashin.

'What the fuck's this?'

'There's blood here, not old.'

'What's this about?'

'Bourgoyne.'

'Bourgoyne?'

'I think so. Yes.'

'In North Melbourne?'

'It's complicated, okay? I'm just reporting this, I'll ring CrimeStoppers if you like. You like?'

'Well that sounds so fucking urgent and imperative I'll drop everything and come myself. What's the address?'

Cashin told him, ended the call. He stood looking at the stage, at the backdrop of an idealised Calvary. Then he walked down the row of seats and up the hall to the stairs on the other side of the stage, climbed them, stood in the dark space beside the stage.

The smell, he knew it. Stronger here. The cold came back to his neck and shoulders and he shivered.

It was the smell in Bourgoyne's sitting room that morning.

He sniffed, looked around, realised he was clenching his teeth. To his left, against the wall, he made out a cast-iron wheel with two handles at right angles. He stepped closer. A cable ran up from behind the wheel, into the darkness. The cable was wrapped around a drum and behind that was a ratchet-wheel with a steel pawl engaged.

It took a moment to work out.

The cable raised and lowered the scenery, the painted backdrops. The ratchet-wheel controlled the process. It ensured that the scenery couldn't come crashing down.

There was something behind the cable, between the cable and the wall. Cashin put out a hand, tugged at it.

A piece of cloth, wadded, stiff but still damp.

The smell. He did not need to sniff the towel. Vinegar. It was a kitchen towel soaked in vinegar.

He held it to the light from the stage. It was dark.

Blood.

The questions came without thought. Why was the ratchet-wheel locked? Why was the cable taut?

He pulled back on the iron wheel and the pawl on the ratchet-wheel disengaged. He let the wheel run, the pawl click-clicked, the cable was paying out.

Metallic creaks. A piece of scenery was coming down.

He looked out between the slats, at the piece of stage he could see.

Oh, Jesus.

Bare feet, dark, swollen legs, rivulets of dried blood running down them, striping them, matted pubic hair, a torso dark, the arms upraised, a black hole beneath the ribs, in the side ...

Cashin let go the wheel. The pawl engaged, the cable stopped paying out.

The thin, naked, blood-caked body moved gently.

Cashin walked down the hall, into the foyer, unlocked the front door, went out into the cold toxic city air, stood on the top step and breathed it deeply.

A silver car turned into the street, drove down the middle, straight at him, stopped two metres away with front wheels touching the kerb, no concern for angle parking.

The front doors opened. Villani and Finucane got out, pale and black as undertakers, eyes on him.

'What?' said Villani. 'What?'

'Inside,' said Cashin.

THE THREE of them sat in the big untidy room on the seventh floor, desks pushed together, files on every surface, a concert of phone sounds – trings, warbles, silly little tunes.

'Like old times,' said Birkerts. 'Us sitting here. Any minute Singo comes through the door.'

'I fucking wish,' said Villani. He sighed, ran fingers through his hair. 'Jesus, got to get out to see him. Guilt building up on all fronts. The things left undone.'

Cashin thought Villani looked even more tired than the last time, when they drank wine beyond midnight in his son's room.

'Talking undone,' said Birkerts. 'Did I tell you this Fenton bloke's got form for flashing? Out there in the sticks in Clunes, near Ballarat. At Wesley girls.'

'Wesley girls? In Clunes?'

'The school's got something there. Outreach program, the rich kids help the rural poor, give them hints on cooking the cheaper cuts.'

'Freezing place,' said Cashin. 'Check his dick for frostbite.'

'One sick, pathetic case at a time,' said Villani. 'Dr Colley says this bloke on the stage had his hands tied. No clothes on, he's been jacked up on the winch thing and he's been tortured, cut all over, front and back, stabbed, blood everywhere. Gag in the mouth, like a bit, it's a handkerchief, there's another one in his mouth. Then he's been winched right up into the roof. At some point, he died, possibly choked to death. We'll know in the morning.'

'He sat there and watched him hanging,' said Birkerts. 'Bleeding.'

Finucane came in with Dove, who nodded at Cashin. The seated men all looked at Finucane.

'Found the bloke's clothes,' he said. 'In a plastic bag in a rubbish bin. Keys in the pocket.'

'ID?' said Villani.

Finucane showed his palms. 'Nothing,' he said. 'No prints either. No one around there saw anything. Been through the missing reports, no one like him there, not in the last month. We'll hear about his prints soonest.' He looked at his watch. 'His picture's on the news in five minutes, may help.'

Villani turned his head to Cashin. 'So tell everyone.'

'The hall was the headquarters of something called the Moral

Companions,' said Cashin. 'A charity. Once they ran camps for poor kids, orphans, state wards. Camps in Queensland and Western Australia. Bourgoyne was a supporter. He owned the land they built a camp on outside Port Monro and he owned the hall.'

'What happened to them?' said Finucane.

'There was a fire at the Port Monro camp in 1983. Three dead. They packed it in.'

'So what's the connection between Bourgoyne and this bloke?' said Birkerts.

'I don't know,' said Cashin. 'But I smelled vinegar that morning at Bourgoyne's.'

'No cloth found there,' said Villani.

'Took it with him,' said Cashin.

'Why'd he leave it this time?'

Cashin shrugged. He was tired, a girdle of pain around his hips, hours spent waiting for forensic to finish.

'Vinegar,' said Birkerts. 'What's with vinegar?'

'They gave me gall to eat: and when I was thirsty they gave me vinegar to drink,' said Dove.

'What?' said Villani. 'What's that?'

'It's from the Book of Common Prayer. A psalm, I forget which one.'

No one said anything. Dove coughed, embarrassed. Cashin registered the ringing phones, the electronic humming, the sound of a television next door, the traffic noises from below.

Villani got up, stretched his arms above his head, palms to the ceiling, eyes closed. 'Joe, this Moral shit,' he said. 'That's religious, is it?'

'Sort of. Started by an ex-priest called Raphael something. Morris. Morrison. After World War II. He had a life-changing experience.'

'I need that,' said Villani.

'Got some nice new suits,' said Cashin. 'Ties too. That's a start.'

'Purely cosmetic,' said Villani. 'I'm unchanged, believe me. The telly, Fin.'

It was the third item on the news. The media hadn't been given much: just a dead man found in a hall in North Melbourne, nothing about him being gagged and tortured, hung naked above a stage.

The man's face was on the screen, clean, almost alive, lights in his eyes. He had been handsome once, longish straight hair combed back, bags under his eyes, deep lines from nose to thin-lipped mouth.

The man is aged in his sixties. His hair is dyed dark brown. Anyone knowing his identity or who has any information about him is asked to call CrimeStoppers on 990 897 897.

'He scrubbed up well,' said Finucane.

'Purely cosmetic,' said Birkerts. 'He's still dead.'

They watched the rest of the news, saw Villani make an appearance to say nothing on the subject of another gangland killing, touch the corner of an eye, his mouth.

'Bit of Al Pacino, bit of Clint Eastwood,' said Cashin. 'Dynamite cocktail, may I say?'

'You may fuck off,' said Villani. 'Just fuck off.'

'Boss?'

Tracy Wallace, the analyst, a thin worried face.

'A woman, boss, transferred from CrimeStoppers. The dead bloke.'

Villani looked at Cashin. 'You take it, skipper,' he said. 'You seem to know what's going on.'

Cashin went to the telephone.

'Mrs Roberta Condi,' said Tracy. 'She lives in North Melbourne.'

He didn't have to write, Tracy had the headphones on.

'Hello, Mrs Condi,' said Cashin. 'Thanks for calling. Can you help us?'

'That's Mr Pollard. The bloke on the telly. I know him.'

'Tell me about it,' said Cashin, his eyes closed.

CASHIN PUT the green key in the lock, turned.

'The home of the late Arthur Pollard,' he said and opened the door.

The terrace house was dark, cold. It took him a while to find a light switch.

An overhead lamp came on, two globes lit a sitting room, furniture that was modern in the 1970s. A newspaper was on the coffee table. Cashin went over and looked at the date. 'Four days ago,' he said.

Off the sitting room was a bedroom – a double bed tightly made, no bedspread, a wardrobe with two mirrors, a chest of drawers, shoes in a wire rack. A passage led to another room with a single bed, a desk, a chair and a bookcase.

Cashin looked at the book spines. All paperbacks. Crime novels, disaster novels, novels with golden titles on the spines. Bought from second-hand shops, he thought.

'Neat kitchen,' said Dove from the door.

Cashin followed him down the passage to a 1950s kitchen: a single bare light bulb with a green shade, an enamelled gas stove, an Electrolux fridge with round shoulders and a portable radio on a formica-topped metal table. On the sink stood a blue-and-white striped mug, upside down.

'Like a monk,' Cashin said. He went to the sink and tried to look out of the window but all he could see was the reflection of the sad room.

Dove clicked switches beside the back door and a powerful floodlight lit the straight rain falling on a concrete yard. It ran to a brick wall with a steel door. Beside the party wall, a single washline held soaked washing: three shirts and three pairs of underpants.

'There's a lane at the back,' said Dove. 'That must be the garage door.'

They went outside, Cashin first, he felt the wet, slippery concrete under-foot. No key on Pollard's ring would unlock the steel door.

'I'll try the door in the lane,' said Dove. He took the keys.

Cashin waited in the house, looked around. In the desk drawers, he found folders with bank statements, power, gas, telephone and rates bills. There was nothing personal – no letters, photographs, no tapes or CDs. Nothing spoke of Arthur Pollard as a human being with a history, with likes and dislikes, except the four cans of baked beans in tomato sauce and a half-empty bottle of whisky and an empty one in the bin.

Dove came in. 'Not a garage anymore,' he said. 'Door's bricked up.'

Dove's mobile rang. He exchanged a few words, phrases, and gave the phone to Cashin. 'The boss,' he said.

'We need the big key here,' said Cashin. 'Sesame. And not tomorrow.'

'How come you give all the orders and you are on long-term secondment from homicide?' said Villani.

'Someone's got to be in charge.'

They waited in the car, streetlights streaming down the windscreen. Cashin found the classical station. His thoughts drifted to home, to the dark ruined house under the wet hill, to the dogs. Rebb would have fed them by now, he didn't have to be asked. They would all be in the shed, the dogs sacked out, drying, the three of them around the old potbelly stove, the rusty shearers' stove not fired for at least thirty years before Rebb, the warmth moving through the building, awakening old smells – lanolin, bacon fat, the rank sweat of tired men now dead.

'This could be coincidence,' said Dove.

'Maybe you should've stayed with the feds,' said Cashin.

A van's lights came around the corner. The driver nosed along, looking. Cashin got out and raised a hand.

The two men in overalls followed them through Pollard's arid house. It was quick.

One man opened a builder's bag and took out an angular piece of metal with a mushroom head. He held it to the garage door jamb, level with the lock. The locksmith tapped it with a sledgehammer, brisk taps, getting harder. When the chisel was wedged, he stood back, flexed his wrists.

'Open Sesame,' he said, swung the hammer like an axe, administered a clean blow to the mushroom, made a sound like a gunshot.

The steel door burst open, hell-dark within.

CASHIN FOUND the switches.

A white-painted room, carpeted floor, windowless. Stale air. Against one wall stood a trestle table with a computer tower, a flat-screen monitor, a printer and a scanner. Next to it were a grey metal filing cabinet and three metal shelf units, four shelves each, the kind sold in hardware shops. The shelves were neat: four for video tapes, four for CDs and DVDs, the others for folders, books, magazines.

Against the door wall was a double bed with a purple sateen quilt and big shiny red pillows. A big-screen television was on a table at the foot, a video player and a DVD player stacked beside it. Beside it stood a tripod. On all the walls were posters – pictures of muscular half-naked men: athletes, bodybuilders, kickboxers, swimmers.

Dove opened the filing cabinet. 'Digital still camera,' he said. 'Digital video camera.'

He closed the drawer, went to the computer, sat down, pressed a button on the tower. 'Give you a feeling, this?' he said.

Cashin didn't say anything. He found a remote control and fiddled with it, switched on the television, got fuzz, pressed buttons.

Vision.

Something filling the screen. It looked like a smooth-skinned vegetable, an eggplant perhaps, the camera moved. An opening, a hole. It was not a vegetable.

The camera drew back.

A face, a young face, a boy. His mouth was open, top teeth showing. There was fear in his eyes.

Cashin pressed the OFF button.

'Look at this shit,' said Dove.

Cashin looked for a minute or two.

'Can't be more than twelve,' said Dove. 'Tops.'

'I'm going home now,' said Cashin. They were at the door when he noticed the two white mugs with yellow spots on the table beside the computer. The tag of a teabag hung over the side of one.

'Had a cup of tea,' he said.

Dove looked back. 'One liked it strong.'

In the car, Cashin spoke to Villani.

'Not surprised,' said Villani. 'Pollard's got form. Sex offences against minors. One gig suspended, done one. Six months. What's there apart from the kiddy-porn chamber?'

'Bank statements, phone bills.'

'Why didn't you stay at home? Stir up all this shit, nobody to do the work.'

'The thought occurred to me.'

'Anyway, I've got a whole house for you to crash in. No one there except me from time to time. You sleep, do you? At some point?'

'Don't project your problems onto me, mate. Any more of that bribe wine?'

'Maybe.'

Before he fell asleep, Cashin saw the vile room, saw on the table the two cheerful spotted mugs, and he put his head beneath the pillow and concentrated on his breathing.

DOVE WAS waiting, reading the *Herald*. He folded it, put it on the back seat. 'Nice to be your driver. I've got something on Bourgoyne's watch.'

'Presumably came in a cleft stick, the runners went via Broome,' said Cashin.

Dove's expression didn't change. 'Bourgoyne bought a Breitling watch from a shop called Cozzen's in Collins Street in 1984. Then six years ago he bought another one.'

Carol Gehrig had described the watch. The girl on the pier, Susie, she had only given the name. Bretling, she said. Why hadn't he asked her to describe the watch? Singo would have closed his eyes, shaken his head: 'You didn't ask? Would you like that engraved on your tombstone? *I didn't ask.*'

Had the pawnbroker in Sydney described the watch the boys offered him that day? Had a cop taken it down? Pawnbrokers had the eye, they knew value, it was their miserable job. 'The shop can describe the watches?' Cashin said.

'Well, I suppose so. I didn't ask.'

'You want that inscribed ...' He stopped.

'What?'

'Nothing. Get Ms Bourgoyne?'

'She'll see you in the art gallery at 10.30. The café upstairs. She's on the gallery board. An arts powerbroker.'

'A what?'

'Read it in the *Financial Review* today.'

'I missed that. Just read the Toasty Sugarflakes box. Law, art, politics, the woman's got it covered.'

They drove in silence. In Lygon Street, Cashin retrieved the newspaper from the back seat. Pollard's face was on page five, the story had no more detail than the television news.

'The Pollard calls,' said Dove. 'There's about thirty. Parents, victims. The guy was a very active ped. Sounds like people would have queued to string him up. One bloke says he knows him from a long time ago. Raved on, then he clammed up.'

'I'm going home after this,' said Cashin. 'Handpass the matter to the experts.'

They crossed the city, nothing said until Dove pulled up on the service road across from the gallery. 'You sulking?' he said.

'That's cheeky,' said Cashin.

'What's cheeky mean in homicide?'

'If I was still homicide, it means I outrank you. And that a reject from the Canberra dregs and a proven slackarse should show respect. That's part of what cheeky means.'

'I see. I'll get a description of the watches.'

'You never ran the name Pollard when you checked those Addison payments?'

Dove sucked in his nostrils. 'I was doing you a favour. Anyway, it was three days ago. Pollard was dead.'

Cashin looked at the traffic.

'You're allowed to fuck up,' said Dove. 'Let Hopgood run it that night and kill the boys and you're still okay. The mates look after you.'

'Get the watch descriptions,' Cashin said. 'And see if Sydney got a description from the pawnbroker, whatever he calls himself. Either way, we want it now and that is this very day.'

'Yes, sir.'

Cashin crossed the road to the gallery, dodging traffic and a tram. In the foyer, he looked up and, in the way of it, met the eyes of Erica Bourgoyne. She was leaning on the rail. He went upstairs, found her seated.

'Sorry I'm late,' he said. 'Is this private enough for you?'

'If you don't shout.' She was in dark grey, drinking black coffee, didn't offer. 'What line of investigation is this?'

'Just a chat.'

A downturned mouth. 'I'm not available for chats. What's the point? My step-father's dead, the suspects are dead.'

Cashin thought of Singo, the grey eyes under eyebrows like stick insects. 'Our obligation is to the dead,' he said. 'Your step-father paid money every month to a man called Arthur Pollard.'

'Did he?'

'You don't know Pollard?'

'Never heard of him.'

A group of Japanese tourists were trying to leave the gallery through the entrance. The attendant was redirecting them and they either didn't understand or thought he was an idiot.

'He was murdered a few days ago. In a building owned by your step-father.'

'Christ. What building?'

'A hall in North Melbourne. It used to be a theatre. Did you know he owned it?'

'No. I don't know what he owns. Owned. What has this to do with Charles?'

'There are similarities.'

'Meaning?'

Cashin saw the man, black turtleneck, three tables away, turning a page of a newspaper, a tabloid. 'We're still working on it,' he said. 'Do you know anything about the Moral Companions? The camp at Port Monro?'

'I remember the camp, yes. There was a fire there. Why?'

'This hall was the Companions' headquarters.'

'To be clear here,' said Erica. 'You're saying the Daunt boys didn't bash Charles?'

Cashin looked away, at the water running down the huge plateglass window. Two blurred figures outside were running fingertips across the stream, making wavy transient lines. 'That's possible,' he said.

'What about the watch?'

'Never conclusive.'

'Just because Charles gave this man money doesn't link the attacks,' said Erica. 'Who knows how many people Charles gave money to?'

'I do.'

She sat back, hands on the table, linked them, parted them. 'So you know everything and you say nothing. What can I possibly tell you that you don't know?'

'I thought you might think of something to tell me.'

Erica looked at him, a steady gaze, blue-grey eyes. She touched the slim silver choker around her neck, ran a finger behind it. 'I have nothing else to tell you and I have a meeting to go to.'

Cashin did not know why he had waited to say it. 'Pollard was a paedophile,' he said. 'Fucked boys. Children.'

She shook her head as if mystified. Colour came to her cheekbones, she could not stop that. 'Well,' she said, 'I'm sure that information is useful to you, but ...'

'It's not useful to you?'

'Why should it be? Are you scratching around because it's going to be embarrassing if the Daunt boys are innocent?'

'We'll wear that.' He looked away and, at the edge of his vision, he saw the man in the black turtleneck flexing his right hand. 'What are you scared of, Ms Bourgoyne?'

For an instant, he thought she was going to tell him. 'What do you mean?'

'The bodyguard.'

'If I was scared of anything that fell in your area of concern, detective, I'd tell you. Now I have my meeting.'

'Thank you for your time.'

Cashin watched her go. She had good legs. At the escalator, she looked back and caught his eyes, held them a moment longer than necessary. Then the bodyguard blocked his view.

'THE FIRST watch Bourgoyne bought from Cozzen's,' said Dove, 'is this model.' He pointed to a picture in a brochure. 'The receipt is 14 September 1986.'

'Very nice. Time yourself going down the Cresta Run.' It was a technical-looking watch, black face, three white dials, three bevelled winders, recessed, a crocodile strap.

'It's called the Maritimer, still in production.' Dove's speech was clipped, he radiated antagonism. 'Here's the second one he bought, another Maritimer, 14 March 2000.'

It had a plain white face, three small dials, also on a crocodile leather strap.

Cashin thought about the morning at The Heights. A smart watch, Carol Gehrig said. A crocodile skin strap. 'What's the pawnbroker say?'

'He made a statement at the time,' said Dove. 'Sydney sent it but in the excitement it seems to have fallen into a hole.'

Cashin felt as if he had missed a night's sleep somewhere. 'What did he say at the time then?'

'He said, I quote: "It was a Breitling. A Maritimer. It's a collectable. Very expensive. The one with three small dials, black face, crocodile strap."'

Cashin got up, full of pain, went to the window and looked at the school grounds, the public gardens, all soft in the misty rain. He found Helen Castleman's direct number.

'Helen Castleman.'

'Joe Cashin.'

A moment.

'I've tried to call you,' she said. 'Your home phone just rings, your mobile number appears to be off.'

'I'm using another one. I'm in the city.'

'I don't know what I should say. You were so insulting. Arrogant. Dismissive.'

'Got the right person? Listen, I need a description of the watch Susie saw. She gave me the name but I need a description from her. Can you get that?'

'This is because the case is still under investigation?'

'It always has been. Can you get that soonest?'

'I'll see. Give me your number.'

Cashin sat down, looked at Dove. Dove didn't want to look at him.

'Hopgood says there's no record of the messages to him that night,' said Cashin.

Now Dove looked. 'The cunts,' he said. 'They've wiped them. They've wiped the fucking record.'

'It could be at our end, a technical thing.'

Dove shook his head, the overhead light blinked in his round lenses. 'Well, then you can blame me at the inquest,' he said. 'Didn't press the right buttons. Just fucked it up. As a boong does.'

Cashin rose, sitting was worse than standing, went back to the window. He said, 'Hopgood said, and I quote him, "You two boongs making up stories now?"'

'What?'

'He said, you two boongs making up stories now.'

'That's us?'

'I took him to mean that, yes.'

Dove laughed, real pleasure. 'Welcome to Boongland,' he said. 'Listen, bro, want to get some lunch round the corner? Grub sandwich?'

'Had it with round the corner,' said Cashin. 'Had it for six years and I've had it.'

'There's a Brunetti's at the arts centre,' said Dove. 'Know Brunetti's in Carlton?'

'You fucking blow-in, you don't know Brunetti's from Donetti's.'

Finucane joined them in the lift, gave them a ride down St Kilda Road.

'Fin, looking at you,' said Cashin, 'I'm giving you a nine point six on the over-worked, under-slept, generally-fucked-over scale.'

Finucane smiled the small modest smile of a man whose efforts had been recognised. 'Thanks, boss,' he said.

'Want a transfer to Port Monro?' said Cashin. 'Just pub fights and sheep-shagging, the odd cunt nicks his neighbour's hydroponic gear officially used to grow vine-ripened tomatoes. It's a nice place to bring up kids.'

'Too exciting,' said Finucane. 'I've got six blokes to see on Pollard. This one in Footscray, he says he goes back a long way. Probably turn out he rang from his deaf and dumb auntie's house where he isn't and doesn't live.'

At Brunetti's, they queued behind black-clad office workers and back-packers and four women from the country who were overwhelmed by the choices. Cashin bought a calzone, Dove had a roll with duck and olives and capsicum relish and five kinds of leaves. They were drinking coffee when Cashin's mobile rang. He went outside.

'I hear traffic,' said Helen. 'Makes me nostalgic. Where are you?'

'Near the arts centre.'

'So cultured – opera, art galleries.'

'Get hold of Susie?' Cashin was watching a man coming down the pavement on a unicycle, a small white dog perched on each shoulder. The dogs had the resigned air of passengers on a long-distance bus.

'She says the watch had a big black face and two or three little white dials.'

Cashin closed his eyes. He thought that he should say thanks for your help and goodbye. That was what he should do. That was what the police minister and the chief commissioner and the assistant crime commissioner and very possibly Villani would want him to do.

It wasn't the right thing to do. He should tell her that the watch the boys tried to sell in Sydney wasn't the watch Bourgoyne was wearing on the night he was attacked.

'Still there?' said Helen.

'Thanks for your help,' he said.

'That's it?'

'That's it.'

'Well, goodbye.'

They finished their coffee and walked back. Cashin had to wait twenty minutes to see Villani. 'Bourgoyne wasn't wearing the watch the boys tried to sell in Sydney,' he said.

'How do you know?'

Cashin told him.

'Could've pinched that one from the house too. Pinched both watches.'

'No. Corey Pascoe's sister saw the fancy watch about a year ago. Corey had it before he went to Sydney. I've spoken to her.'

'Well that could be bullshit.'

'I believe her.'

'Yeah?'

'She knew the name. She's described the watch.'

'Fuck,' said Villani. 'Fuck. This is not looking good.'

'No. What's showing on Pollard?'

'A woman down the street from the hall's ID'd him. Seen in the vicinity a few times. Once with a kid. About twenty victims to interview. The computer stuff will take forever. Thousands of images. I don't fancy our chances. Just be happy he's dead. Like these drug scumbags we're trying to get justice for.'

'Anyway, I'm off,' said Cashin. 'Going home. I'm on enforced holiday. Over and out.'

'Just when you were settling in again. Want to end this secondment shit? There's fuck all wrong with you.'

'I'm over homicide,' said Cashin. 'I don't want to see any more dead people. Except for Rai Sarris. I want to see the dead Rai Sarris. And Hopgood. I'll make an exception for Hopgood too.'

'Unprofessional attitude. The vinegar smell. You sure about that?'

'Yes.'

Villani walked with him to the lifts. 'I should say,' he said, he looked down the corridor. 'I want to say I've been squeezed on this. I'm not happy with my conduct. Not proud. I am considering my position.'

Cashin didn't know what to say. The lift doors opened. He touched Villani's sleeve. 'Take it easy,' he said. 'Don't obsess.'

LONG BEFORE he'd cleared the city, the mobile rang. Cashin pulled over.

'Boss, Fin. This bloke rang in …'

'Yes. Footscray.'

'You should talk to him, boss.'

'Out of this, Fin, I'm on my way home.'

The traffic was picking up, the early leavers, commuters to the satellite towns, lots of four-wheel-drives, trade utes, trucks.

'Yeah, well, the boss says to ask you, boss.'

'Tell me.'

'Well, this one's pretty fucked up. He drifts off the station, know what I mean?'

'What's the station?'

'He knows Pollard. He hates Pollard. Hates everyone, everything, actually, spit going everywhere, you need a riot shield.'

'How old?'

'Not old old. It's hard to say, shaven head, buggered teeth, maybe forties. Yeah. Major drug problem, no doubt.'

'Get a statement?'

'Boss, this is not statement territory. This is door-punching territory.'

'Door-punching?'

'I was trying to get through to him, he went quiet and then he came out of the fucking chair and he ran across the room, punched the door, two shots. The second one, his hand's stuck in the door, blood everywhere.'

'His name?' said Cashin.

'David Vincent.'

Cashin expelled breath. 'What's the address? I'm close.'

Finucane was waiting for him, parked in a street of rotting weatherboards, dumped cars and thin front yards silting up with junk mail. Cashin walked over, stood at the car window, hands in his pockets.

'He'll be happy to see you again?'

Finucane scratched his head. 'No. He told me to fuck off. But he's not aggro about me. It's the world that's the problem.'

'Live alone?'

'There's no one else there now.'

'Let's go.'

It took several bouts of knocking before the door opened. Cashin could see a veined eye.

'Mr Vincent,' said Finucane, 'a senior police officer would like a little chat about the things worrying you.'

The door opened enough to show both eyes and a discoloured nose broken more than once, broken and shifted sideways. The eyes were the colour of washing powder. 'Nothing's fuckin worrying me,' Vincent said. 'Where'd you get that crap?'

'Can we come in, Mr Vincent?' said Cashin.

'Fuck off. Said what I wanted.'

'I understand you know Arthur Pollard?'

'That's what I fuckin said. CrimeStoppers. Told the fuckin idiot. Give him the name.'

Cashin smiled at him. 'We're very grateful for that, Mr Vincent. Thank you. Just a few other things we'd like to know.'

'Nah. I'm busy. Got a lot on.'

'Right,' said Cashin. 'Well, we'd really appreciate your help. There's a man murdered, an innocent man ...'

Vincent pulled the door open, smashed it against the passage wall, jarred the whole building. 'Innocent? You fuckin mad? The fuckin bastard, shoulda killed the fuckin cunt myself ...'

Cashin looked away. He hadn't meant Pollard, he'd been thinking of Bourgoyne.

A woman had come out of the house next door. She was of unguessable age, wearing a pink turban and wrapped in what looked like an ancient embossed velvet curtain, faded and moulting.

'Dint I tell you to bugger off last time?' she shouted. 'Comin around with yer bloody Yank religion, yer bloody tower of Pisa, leanin bloody watchtower, whatbloodyever.'

'Police,' said Finucane.

She went backwards at speed. Cashin looked at Vincent. The rage had left his face as if the outburst had drained some poison from him. He was a big man but stooped and gone to fat, rolls at his neck.

'Woman's mad,' said Vincent in a calm voice. 'Completely out of her tree. Come in.'

They followed him into a dim passage and a small room with a collapsed sofa, two moulded plastic restroom chairs and a metal-legged coffee table with five beer cans on it. A television set stood on two stacked milk crates. Vincent sat on the sofa and lit a cigarette, holding the lighter in both hands, shaking badly. Blood was caked on the fingers and knuckles of his right hand.

Cashin and Finucane sat on the plastic chairs.

'So you know Arthur Pollard, Mr Vincent?' said Cashin.

Vincent picked up a beer can, shook it, tested another one, found one with liquid in it. 'Many fuckin times you want me to say it? Know the cunt, know the cunt, know the …'

Cashin held up a hand. 'Sorry. Where do you know him from, Mr Vincent?'

Vincent drank, looked down at the floor, drew on the cigarette. His left shoulder was jerking. 'From the fuckin holidays.'

'What holidays, Mr Vincent?'

'The fuckin holidays, you know, the holidays.' He raised his head, fixed his gaze on Cashin. 'Tried to tell em, y'know. It wasn't just me. Oh no. Nearly, poor little bugger, saw em. Saw em.'

'Tell them what, Mr Vincent?'

'Don't believe me, do you?'

'What holidays are you talking about?'

'Givin me that fuckin look, I know that fuckin look, HATE THAT FUCKIN LOOK.'

'Steady on,' said Cashin.

'Piss off. Piss off. Got nothing to say to you cunts, all the same, you're all fuckin in it, bastards kill a kid, you, you … you can just fuck off.'

'Spare a smoke?' said Cashin.

'What?'

Cashin mimed smoking. 'Give us a smoke?'

Vincent's eyes flicked from Cashin to Finucane and back. He put a hand into his dirty cotton top and took out a packet of Leisure Lights, opened it with a black-rimmed thumbnail, offered it, shaking. Cashin took. Vincent offered the box to Finucane.

'No thanks,' said Finucane. 'Trying to give up.'

'Yeah. Me too.' Vincent gave the plastic lighter to Cashin.

Cashin lit up, returned the lighter. 'Thanks, mate,' he said. 'So they wouldn't listen?'

'Wouldn't listen,' said Vincent. 'Copped a thrashin from the bastard Kerno. Thrashed me all the time. Thin as a stick, I was. Broke me ribs, three ribs. Made me tell school I fell off me bike.'

A long silence. Vincent emptied the beer can, put it on the table. His shaven, scarred head went down, almost touched his knees, the cigarette was going to burn his fingers. Cashin and Finucane read each other's eyes.

'Didn't have a bike,' said Vincent, a sad little boy's voice. 'Never ever had a bike. Wanted a bike.'

Cashin smoked. The cigarette tasted terrible, made him glad he didn't smoke. Smoke much. Vincent didn't look up, dropped his butt on the carpet, aimed a foot at it, missed. The smell of burning nylon fibres rose, acrid and strangely sweet.

'I'd like to hear about when you were a kid,' said Cashin. 'I'll listen. You talk, I'll listen.'

Another long silence. Vincent raised his head, startled, looked at them as if they'd just appeared in the room. 'Got to go,' he said breathlessly. 'A lot on, blokes.'

He rose unsteadily and left the room, bumped against the door jamb. They heard him muttering as he went down the passage. A door slammed.

'That's probably it,' said Finucane. He stood on Vincent's cigarette.

Outside, in the rain, Cashin said to Finucane, 'The holidays. He's talking about a Moral Companions camp, Fin. His whole life, we need his whole life. That's ASAP. Tell Villani I said that.'

'Not staying then, boss?'

'No. Also the files at the hall. Someone needs to pull out everything that refers to Port Monro. Call me with what you get. Ring me, okay?'

'Okay. First to know, boss.'

'And for fuck's sake get some sleep, Fin. You're a worry to me.'

'Right. They stay dead, don't they?'

'You're learning. It's slow but you're learning.'

It was long dark by the time he switched off and saw the torch beam coming down the side of the house, saw the running dogs side by side, heads up, big ears swinging. They were at the vehicle before he could get out. He had to fight their weight to open the door. A spoke of pain ran down his right thigh as he swung his legs out.

'Thought we'd lost you,' said Rebb, a hulk behind the light.

Cashin was returning the dogs' affection, head down, allowing them to lick his hands, his hair, his ears. 'Got stuck in the city,' he said. 'I reckoned you might do the right thing by these brutes.'

'No brute food left,' said Rebb. 'I took the little peashooter of yours for a walk. Okay?'

'Good thinking.'

'The other bunny's in the oven. Used the olives in the fridge. Also a tin of tomatoes.'

'What do you know about olives?' said Cashin.

'Picked them in South Australia, worked in a place they pickled them. Ate olives till they came out of my ears. Swaggies eat anything. Roadkill, caviar.'

'I need a drink,' said Cashin. 'You left anything to drink?'

'I'm leaving in the morning.'

Cashin felt tiredness and pain expand within him, fill him. 'Can we talk about that?'

'I'll drop in if I come this way again.'

'Come in and have a drink anyway. Farewell drink.'

'Had a drink. Knackered. I'll shake your hand now.'

He put out a hand. Cashin didn't want to take it. He took it.

'I owe you money,' he said. 'Fix it up tomorrow. Promise.'

'Leave it on the step,' said Rebb. 'Haven't got it, I'll pick it up next time. Trust you, you're a cop. Who else can you trust?'

He turned and walked. Cashin felt a loss for which he was not prepared. 'Mate,' he said. 'Mate, fucking sleep on it, will you?'

No reply.

'For the sake of the dogs.'

'Good dogs,' said Rebb. 'Miss the dogs.'

A DARK DAY, the vehicle climbing a rainslicked road towards a hilltop lost in mist. In the gate of The Heights, up the driveway, the poplars dripping.

Cashin took the left turn, the road that wound around the house at a distance, ended at the redbrick double-storey building. He parked on the paving in front of the wooden garage doors, switched off, wound down his window. The cold and wet blew in. He sat in the quiet, engine clicks the only sounds, thinking about why this was a pointless thing to do.

He thought about Shane Diab's parents coming to see him in hospital, when he was out of danger. They didn't sit, they were awkward, their English wasn't good. He didn't know what to say to them, he knew their son was dead because of him. After a while, Vincentia saved him and they said goodbye. Shane's mother touched him on the cheek, then, quickly, she kissed him on the forehead. They left a white cardboard box on the cabinet beside the bed.

Vincentia opened the box, held it up, tilted it to Cashin. It was a square cake, white icing, a cross in red. It took him a while to see that names formed the bar of the cross: Joe+Shane.

He gave the cake to Vincentia. Later she told him the nurses on the shift shared it, a fruit cake, very good.

Cashin got out, walked around the building to the double doors in the centre. The mist was turning to rain.

There were about a dozen keys on the ring Erica Bourgoyne had given him. The seventh one worked. He unlocked the door, went down the corridor. The pottery room was dark, the shutters closed. He found the light switches and high up tubes flickered, lit the room. The door was directly opposite.

The lights showed a swept brick floor, gardening tools pinned on a pegboard, arranged on shelves like exhibits. A ride-on mower, a small tractor and a trailer stood in a line, showroom clean. A prim room, it spoke of organisation and discipline.

To Cashin's right, the painting leant against the wall, face averted, its slashed V held in place with masking tape. It was bigger than he remembered.

He went to it, gripped the frame and awkwardly lifted it, turned and settled it back against the wall. He could not see the painting properly before he had taken several steps back.

It was a painting of a moonlit landscape, a pale path running through sand dunes covered with coastal scrub towards a group of buildings in the distance, hints of lights in windows. Most of the canvas was of a huge sky of wind-driven grey-black clouds lit by a near-full moon.

Cashin knew the place. He had stood where the painter stood, on the top of the last big dune, looking towards the now-ruined buildings and the highway and the road that snaked up from the highway, went up the hill to the Kenmare road and driveway to The Heights.

He went closer. In the path were what appeared to be figures, a short column of people, three abreast, walking towards the buildings. Children, they were children, two taller figures.

The painting was unsigned. He turned it around. In the bottom left corner was a small sticker. On it was written in red ink:

Companions Camp, Port Monro, 1977.

'THE COMPANIONS camp,' said Cashin. 'At the mouth.'

There was a long silence. Cecily Addison, standing at the mantelpiece, staring at him. He never knew how long to meet Cecily's gaze because it was possible that she was not seeing him.

'You seem like a good person to ask,' said Cashin.

Cecily's head tilted, her eyelids fluttered. She took on the look of someone having her feet massaged. 'May I ask what this is about?'

'Charles Bourgoyne.'

'I thought that was over.'

'No.'

A last long draw on her cigarette, a raised eyebrow. 'Well, what do you want to know, my dear?'

'What kind of camp was it?' Cashin said.

'For boys. Orphans and the like. Boys in homes. Foster children. The Moral Companions gave them a holiday, a bit of fun. Lots of Cromarty people helped out, including my Harry. It was a good cause.'

'And it burned down.'

'In 1983. Tragic. Mind you, it could've been worse. Just three boys there on the night. And the man in charge. The Companion, that's what they called themselves. He couldn't save them. Overcome by fumes, that was the coroner's verdict.'

'Where were the other kids?'

'On some cultural jaunt.' She stretched an arm, dropped her cigarette into the vase on the mantelpiece. 'They used to take them to Cromarty. Music, plays, that sort of thing. Still a lot of that then. People didn't sit at home in front of the television watching American rubbish.'

'What caused the fire?'

'I think they said it was the boiler in the dormitory building, the double-storey. A timber building. The boys were sleeping upstairs.'

Cashin thought about the blackened brick foundations, the charred floor joist. He had stood where the boys had died.

'Apart from owning the land, did Bourgoyne have anything to do with the camp?'

Cecily frowned, deep lines. 'Well, I don't know. He took an interest, of course. Following on from his dad. Lots of people took an interest. Public-spirited place then, Cromarty. People did good works, didn't do it to get their names in the paper either. Virtue is its own reward. Are you familiar with that expression, detective?'

'My reward is the award wage, Mrs Addison.'

She narrow-eyed him. 'You are a cut above the dull boys couldn't find another job, aren't you?'

'So that was the end of the camp?' said Cashin.

'The camp, the Companions too. It was all over the papers. I think they just packed it in. It was the last Companions camp left. Charles gave the manager bloke a job. Percy Crake. A cold fish, Percy Crake.'

There was a knock on the half-open door.

'Yes,' said Cecily.

Mrs McKendrick. 'Your appointment will be twenty minutes late, Mrs Addison,' she said. 'Car trouble is the excuse they offer.'

'Thank you, my dear.'

Mrs McKendrick turned like a teenage ballerina, reaching behind her to close the door she had found open. It was a message.

'She was in love with Jock Cameron,' said Cecily. 'All those years. Sad, really. He never noticed. Often wondered if he'd taken a bit of shrapnel in the tackle.'

'I'm told there are no Companions' records for Port Monro at the hall in Melbourne.'

Fin had rung while he was driving from The Heights.

'All the other camps' records are there,' said Cashin. 'Could they be somewhere else?'

'No idea. Why would they keep them somewhere else?'

On the mantelpiece, the vase was emitting smoke like a fumarole. Cashin got up and took it to the window, pushed up the bottom sash and shook the container, sent the smouldering contents to float on the sea wind.

'Thank you, Joe.'

'I'll go then. Thank you for your time, Mrs Addison.'

'My pleasure.'

It was cold outside, no one loitering. Cashin felt the need to walk, went down the street, past the empty clothing boutiques, the aromatherapist, the properties in the window of the estate agent. He crossed Crozier Street and passed the pub lounge, saw three people watching a greyhound race on the television, the old man coughing as if he could die there, on his feet. Beyond the pub were houses, mostly holiday rentals, curtains drawn.

As Cashin walked, the singing from the bluestone church on the rise became louder. He turned the corner on the faltering and cracking last lines of a hymn.

Heaven's morning breaks, and earth's vain shadows flee;
In life, in death, O Lord, abide with me.

There was a time of silence, then an attenuated Amen that stood in the cold air, hung in the branches of the pines.

Cashin felt the sudden withering ache of loss and mortality and he turned and went back the way he had come, into the wind.

HE WAS CROSSING a rope bridge in a gale, water far below. The bridge was swaying and creaking and groaning and slats were missing. He looked down and it was the Kettle, a huge wave coming in, he was fighting to hold his footing, clinging to the side ropes, he couldn't hold on, he was losing his grip, he was going into the Kettle.

In his sweat, Cashin lay wide awake, heart like a speedball, relief coming over him. He knew what the sounds were: the television aerial was loose again, being pushed around by the wind, chafing against the strapping. The sounds had triggered the Kettle dream. How did dreams work?

He turned the clock around: 6.46 am. Seven-hour sleep, the longest unbroken sleep he could remember. Just twinges of pain in getting up, a good morning, let in the dogs, fed them, drank juice, showered.

It was a grey day, no wind to speak of. When the dogs came back from looking for Rebb, he chose the circular route, up the hill. The European trees were bare now, standing in their damp leaves, a hundred and more generations of leaves. They went down the slope and across the big clearing, no hares today. Cashin stepped from rock to rock to cross the creek, still turbulent. Then, no sign of the dogs, he turned westwards, towards Helen's property, the painting on his mind – the moonlit plain, the little procession of boys going towards the buildings, the lights in the windows. The Companions camp. He thought about Pollard hanging in the Companions hall, crucified, dying while someone sat as if watching a play or a concert, something to enjoy, to applaud.

When did Pollard lose consciousness? Did the watcher listen with pleasure to his sounds, to his agony? Did he ask for mercy? Was that what the watcher wanted?

Bourgoyne's payments to Pollard. Bourgoyne the patron of the Companions.

The Companions kept records for the camps in Western Australia, Queensland and South Australia, camps closed before Port Monro. What happened to the Port Monro records?

The belt the dogs found that day.

Be Prepared.

No bigger than a dog collar, adult hands could span a waist that small.

Work was in progress on the Castleman house. New corrugated iron on the roof, what looked like a weatherboard extension, pink primed boards, big windows, a platform sticking out, a deck when finished. It would be a place to loll, looking down at the creek, up at the hill. Looking at his property.

Why did he offer to sell her the creek strip? Because she was cross with him and she was the rich and beautiful and sophisticated girl who kissed him when he was a shy, gangling boy whose aunt cut his hair?

Offer permanently withdrawn.

It was a good fence, taut. Rebb's fence. How far could you walk in a day? Rebb wouldn't ask for lifts, people would have to ask him. Every tool Rebb had used was lined up inside the shearing shed, cleaned and oiled. His mattress was leaning against the wall, the blankets were on the bed springs, folded square, the pillow on them and the washed pillowslip on top.

Cashin was chewing porridge cooked in the microwave when the phone rang.

'Tuesday arrived down there yet?' said Dove.

'Of what week?'

'I should've said the year. Done the full sweep on this David Vincent.'

'Yes?'

'It's a brick high.'

'The summary. You've done that, of course.'

'Of course. Born Melbourne 1968, taken into care 1973, lived somewhere called Colville House 1973 to 1976. Then foster family number one until 1978, number two until 1979, ran away, found, number three until 1980, ran away. Still with me?'

'Keep going.'

'Next record is an arrest in Perth in 1983 for theft of a handbag. Age fifteen. After that it's a list of petty stuff, sent to juvenile in '84 for six months, again in '86, nine months. That's it for form.'

'The rest?'

'It's a sad story. Institutions. It says here, on this one report, clinical depression compounded by multiple addictions. Four years in Lakeside, Ballarat. That sounds nice. By the lake. I read the problem as smack, amphetamines, methadone, dope, booze, gets in fights and sustains injuries to many parts of the body.'

Cashin had not noticed the cloth of sunlight unroll across the old room's boards. 'Thank you,' he said. 'Listen, I need the number Dave Vincent called CrimeStoppers from. Tracy's got it.'

'I thought talking to Vincent was a problem?'

'Sometimes it's people looking at you that's the problem.'

An observation from Singo. Early in the piece, in the first year, the Geelong man who wouldn't say anything, his hands clenched, his neck a fence of tendons. Singo wrote his extension number on a pad and gave it to the man. They left and waited in Singo's office. The phone rang inside a minute and Singo talked to him for almost an hour.

'Well, I'm glad you can look at yourself so objectively,' said Dove. 'Over the phone, that is. For my education, may I ask what you want from Vincent?'

'I think he was at the Companions camp at Port Monro.'

'Yes? Where does that get you?'

'Just having a sniff.'

'Ah, the sniff. I keep hearing about it. A trade secret. Hang on.'

Dove was back with the number inside two minutes.

'Back to work then,' said Cashin. 'Go around to whatever the drug squad is now called and arrest the first prick you see.'

'So old-fashioned, so out of touch with modern policing.'

David Vincent's number rang out. Too early for him, Cashin thought. His day would probably begin when most people were thinking about lunch.

'UNEMPLOYED,' said Carol Gehrig, shifted on the chair, pulled at the crotch of her tracksuit. 'Sixteen weeks pay, how's that for twenty-six years on the job?'

The cheap timber house stood in the teeth of the wind on a low hill looking over Kenmare. Behind it was a big shed, open in front, a truck shed with just an old yellow Mazda in it.

'Who sacked you?' said Cashin.

'The lawyer. Addison. Place's going on the market some time. She wants me to clean up when the time comes.'

She sucked on her stub, ground it out among the five or six already in the abalone shell on the table. She offered Cashin the packet. He shook his head.

'Coffee?' she said. 'Tea? I should've asked. Caught me without my face too. Not used to being here at this time of the morning.'

He'd had to wait minutes, didn't knock again after he heard movements inside.

'No thanks. Ever heard of someone called Arthur Pollard?'

'Pollard? No.'

The sagging foam chair made his back hurt. Cashin sat up straight, tried to extend his spine. He took out the doctored, sanitised photograph of Pollard. 'Know this man?'

She looked at it, held it away. 'Something familiar ... don't know. Local?'

'No. Tell me about Percy Crake.'

'Well, he came after the fire at the camp. Little moustache. His sister arrived, a bitch. Face like an axe, moustache too. Bigger than Crake's. Called herself Mrs Lowell. Christ knows how she got Mr Lowell. She used to come behind me with a tissue looking for dust.'

'What did Crake do?'

'Took over, marched around like a dork. He used to make us stand outside his office for our wages, keep us waiting like he was busy inside. Then he'd open the door and he'd say: Now then, line up in alphabetical order.'

The voice she imitated wasn't loud and commanding. It was thin and grating. 'Five people. In alphabetical order, I ask you? Pommy shit. Fucking scoutmaster.'

Be Prepared.

Cashin saw the stiff and cracked little belt, the round rusted buckle. 'That was in 1980,' he said.

'Year I started, full-time in 1978. Mrs B was there with the kids. She was nice, gave him about twenty years. Real tragedy that, falling down the stairs.'

'How did they take it, the kids?'

'The boy never said a word. Erica followed Mr B around like he was a pop star. She was in love with him. Girls can be like that.'

An intake of smoke, a blowing, a tapping into the abalone shell. 'They used to have parties. Garden parties, cocktail parties, dinner parties, all the Cromarty money, people from Melbourne. For the autumn races, there'd be people staying. I got help. There was a cook and a waiter come from Melbourne.'

Carol sucked her cheeks hollow. 'Anyway, old times. History. What's this about?'

Cashin shrugged. 'Just curious.'

'Thought the black kids did it?'

'What do you think?'

'No surprise to me. Daunt's a fucking curse on this town.'

'You must know a lot about the Bourgoynes.'

'Not that much. Cleaning up behind people, that's the job. Washing, ironing. Twenty hours a week the last ten years or so. That's it.' More smoking. 'Head down, bum up around there, mate,' she said. 'Unless you're Bruce Starkey.'

'He got special treatment?'

'Well, in the old days, Crake was always checking. He caught you havin a smoko, he'd dock your pay quarter of an hour. Can you believe that? Bloody Starkey, he never went near him, didn't have to line up for his pay, the big prick.'

'How'd Bourgoyne and Crake get on?'

'Pretty good. Only time I ever heard Crake laugh was when Mr B was in his office. Crake helped him with the pots, the kiln. They used to do it at weekends. Burn it all weekend.'

'You saw that?'

'No. Mrs Lowell told me. Burn through the night. Starkey used to be chainsawing and chopping for a week before.'

'How often was this?'

'Jeez, it's been a long time. I suppose twice a year. Yeah.'

'Those pots in the gallery room. Nine pots. That's all he kept?'

'He used to smash em up. Starkey took the bits to the tip. Half a ute load at a time.'

Cashin looked at the barren green view, thought about how nice it would be if this had never begun, if he had never received the call that morning.

'Sure you don't want coffee? I'm going ...'

'No thanks,' said Cashin. 'Erica says she knows almost nothing about her step-father's affairs. What do you think?'

Carol frowned, aged ten years. 'Well, wouldn't surprise me. I can count on one hand the times I've seen her there since she was about fourteen. Fell out of love with her step-dad.'

She came with him to the vehicle, hugging herself against the cold. The dogs liked the look of her and she had no fear of them, scratched their chins.

'Twin buggers,' she said. 'What kind's this?'

'Poodles.'

'Nah. Poodles are sooky litle things. Rough buggers, these.'

'Neglected,' said Cashin. 'Short of haircuts and brushing.'

'Bit like me.' She was fondling big dog ears, not looking at him. 'You married?'

'Not anymore.'

'Kids?'

He hesitated. 'No.'

'Kids are good, it's bloody jobs that's the problem. My ex went to Darwin, don't blame him. Fisherman. I couldn't hack it, never saw him, he just slept here.'

'Thanks for the help,' said Cashin.

'Any time. Come again. Have a beer.'

'That'd be good. Starkey get the boot too?'

'Dunno. Place'll need some keeping up if it's on the market.'

Cashin was in the vehicle when he thought to ask. 'The Companions camp. Know anything about it?'

Carol shook her head. 'Not much. Starkey used to work there before the fire.'

THE CROMARTY *Herald*'s editorial office was in an ugly yellow-brick 1950s building on the edge of the business area.

Cashin went through glass doors into an area with a long counter staffed by two young women. A glass wall cut them off from a big office, half a dozen desks, five women and a man, all with heads down. He had to wait for three people to pay bills, one to lodge a classified advertisement.

'I'd like to see back copies of the paper, please,' he said.

'Through that door,' the woman said. 'There's about six months.'

'For 1983.'

'Jeez. Don't think you can do that.' She wasn't interested, looking at the person behind him.

'Is there a library?'

'Library?'

'Where you keep your files.'

Puzzled brow. 'Better ask editorial,' she said. 'In there.'

Another reception room, an older woman behind a desk. He asked the same question. This time, he said police. She spoke on the phone. In seconds, a door opened and a man in his fifties, bald, florid, big belly, came in. Cashin introduced himself, showed the badge.

'Alec Clarke,' the man said. 'Assistant editor. Come through.'

It was a big room, six or seven people at desks, looking at computers, three men doing the same at a cluttered table in the centre. It was not unlike a squad room. Clarke led Cashin to the first office in a row of four cubicles. They sat.

'How can I help?'

Cashin told him.

'That far back? Looking for something in particular?'

'A fire. At the Moral Companions camp near Port.'

'Right, yes. Big news that, the boys. Very sad. What's the interest now?'

'Idle curiosity.'

Clarke laughed, held up his hands, palms out. 'Message received. I'll have a check, back in a minute.'

He went out, turned right. Cashin looked at the workers. They were all young women except for the three at the middle table, seedy older men, pale, moulting and flaking. The ginger one who appeared to be in charge was methodically fossicking in his nostrils, from time to time studying the finds. A painfully thin young woman came in and went to the prospector, spoke in a respectful manner. He pulled a face, waved his right hand dismissively. She nodded and she went to a seat at the back of the room. Cashin saw her shoulders slump, her chin go down.

'Sorry to be so long, detective,' said Clarke. He sat behind the desk.

'Always a pleasure to watch a well-oiled machine,' said Cashin.

A tight smile. 'Now there's a problem here,' said Clarke. 'We went modern in '84, put everything on microfiche. You're probably too young to remember microfiche.'

'I know microfiche.'

'Yes. Well, we had a fire in '86, a cigarette someone dropped in a bin, but we lost the fiche for about ten years from 1976.'

'What about the actual papers?'

'Destroyed in '84, unfortunately. No concern for heritage then. In retrospect, we should never ...'

'The State Library would have them?'

'Worth a try. Certainly.'

Outside, Cashin walked to the vehicle in a cold morning, looked up at a sky deep as heaven, pale as memory. The dogs beat each other with their tails at the sight of him.

THE STATE Library did not hold the Cromarty *Herald*. Cashin put down the phone and thought about Corey Pascoe and Bourgoyne's watch. Did it matter now?

He closed his eyes, put his head back. The boys were dead because of a Bourgoyne watch. The whole terrible business turned on the watch.

How did Corey come to have a watch belonging to Bourgoyne? Chris Pascoe said something that day on the pier, it hadn't registered as important. *He wasn't a bad kid, Corey. Could've played AFL footy. Just full of shit, thought he saw a fuckin career in dope. You a mate of Hopgood and that lot?*

A career in dope. Was he talking about Corey smoking dope? That wouldn't be remarkable on the Daunt, it wouldn't be remarkable anywhere in the country. Dope was like beer in the 1960s. People then didn't say the beer kept them from playing professional footy.

No, Pascoe didn't mean smoking. He meant growing, dealing.

He watched the dogs patrolling the backyard, complaining to each other of sensory deprivation. They didn't like the place, they wanted to be somewhere with Rebb. What kind of memory did dogs have? Did they miss Rebb?

The Piggots were drug people. Billy Piggot was dealing to schoolkids. Debbie Doogue had been a customer.

Kendall behind him. 'Am I allowed to say I'd like you back in that chair permanently ASAbloodyP? I am so bored by these boy wonders I could face a charge any time now.'

'I'm back soon,' said Cashin. 'Never heard of anyone missing me.'

'Staging for compliments, that's not allowed,' she said. 'What I appreciate is that you don't go on about reality crap on television and how many slow curls for the maximum upper-body benefit.'

'Actually, I've been thinking about curls. This kid came in about the hairdresser girlfriend took his ute to Queensland. He says the Piggots are getting rich. Been busted to your knowledge, the Pigs?'

'In my time, no.'

'Why's that?'

'Don't know. It's Cromarty's business.'

'Yes, but someone has to tell Cromarty.'

'I don't think they need telling. I think they know.'

'This come up before I arrived? When Sadler was in charge?'

'We had complaints.' Kendall looked away. 'Sadler said he'd talk to Cromarty. Anyway, work to do.'

'Just hold a sec, Ken. The day of the march, I asked you about Billy Piggot, you said something about a Ray Piggot. What was it again?'

'Ripped five hundred bucks off a rep staying at the Wavecrest. He said he gave Ray a lift from outside Cromarty, invited him to his room for a beer. Later the money was gone. Just two thirsty blokes, you understand, one's about fifty, the other one looks like he's fourteen.'

'He had Ray's full name?'

'Yes. Sadler rang Cromarty. Hopgood and that Steggles arrived. Parked in the back. Ray Piggot was in the car. Must've picked him up on the way. They left him there, talked to the rep in the interview room. He left, they left. Never heard any more.'

'Piggot not charged?'

'Nope. He got off a charge in Melbourne too. Stole a stereo and a laptop from a bloke he met in the park. Streetkid then.'

'What does all this say to you?'

Kendall smiled her small sad, comprehending smile, eyes down. 'I'm just happy to have my job,' she said. 'When I was physically stuffed, people didn't push me away, get me out of sight, pension me off. They were family to me. You'd know about that. Not so?'

She left. Cashin put his head back, heard the messages from his tired places. The morning at the court, Greg Law had given him a message about Hopgood. Head-kicking, grass-growing Gaby Trevena wasn't the most dangerous person in town, he said. Had Law been delivering a threat from Hopgood? Or had he been saying he wasn't a Hopgood man?

You a mate of Hopgood and that lot?

Hopgood and Lloyd. And Steggles, presumably.

Steggles vomited that night. In the pouring rain, face down, his gun pointed at the sky, a tube of vomit sprang from his mouth. The hamburger he had been eating at the briefing, the greasy yellow chips with sauce-red tips, they exited his body after he shot the boy.

Didn't have the stomach for it, Steggie.

Cashin rang Helen Castleman.

'I want to talk to that Pascoe again,' he said.

'Your bedside manner needs some work. Has anyone told you that?'

'I'll talk to him in your office. You can be there.'

'This is official, is it? An official interview?'

'No. Just a chat.'

'Well, I don't represent Pascoe, so I have no standing when it comes to chats. Also I have no desire to assist the police in their chatting work.'

'I'll start again. I'm trying to clear the boys. Clear your client.'

'My late client.'

She was silent. Cashin waited.

'I'll get back to you,' she said. 'Where are you?'

Cashin went outside, walked around the block in the wind, only a few people in the main street, moving between vehicles and shops. Leon's place was empty.

'Police,' said Cashin loudly. 'This business open?'

'Open to bloody suggestions,' said Leon, coming out of the kitchen. 'Open to offers of any kind. Limited menu today. Soup, that's all I'm offering, a proper minestrone made with a ham bone.'

'To take away?'

'Seven-fifty eaten on premises. For removal, I'll accept four-fifty. Three-fifty because you're the police.'

'You can keep the bone.'

'Three-fifty. I'll chuck in a slice of bread. Proper bread. Buttered. With butter.'

'Two slices.'

'Stood over. I'm being stood over. What kind of music do you like?'

Cashin was eating the soup at his desk when the phone rang.

'He doesn't want to come here,' said Helen. 'He's a very uninterested person, he's not interested in chatting.'

'That's it?'

'He says if you want to chat, you can come to his house tonight. He would like to point out that he owes the police nothing. I'm paraphrasing and editing here so as not to offend your tender sensibilities.'

So smart. Cashin thought he could read books for another ten years and it wouldn't help. 'I'll do that then,' he said. 'Thank you and goodbye.'

'I have to drive you, come with you. He doesn't want the squad car outside his place. And so, since you're trying to do something about a major injustice, I'm willing to do that.'

He looked at the dogs in the yard and he thought about her mouth, the kisses. Kisses from nowhere. Separated by twenty years.

CASHIN AND Helen sat at a kitchen table in what had been the garage of a house. Now it was like a small pub with a bar and a full-size snooker table and an assortment of chairs. A television set was mounted on a side wall.

Chris Pascoe brought a six-pack of beer from behind the bar and put it on the table. He sat down, took one and popped it. 'Help yourself,' he said. 'So what's this about?'

'The watch Corey had,' said Cashin.

'Suse told you.'

'I'm keen to know how he got it.'

'Thinkin of chargin him with theft? Well, he's had the fuckin death penalty. Slipped your mind?'

'No. What we want is to find out who bashed Bourgoyne. It wasn't the boys, I'm pretty sure about that.'

'Since when?'

'Since I decided to believe Susie about when she saw the watch.'

Pascoe drank, wiped his lips, found a cigarette. 'Yeah, well, Suse don't know where he got it, his mum don't know.'

'His mates might know though.'

'Mates mostly dead.'

Helen coughed. 'Chris, I said on the phone, I'm here because of Donny. I want his name cleared, the names of all the boys. And the Daunt. The Daunt shouldn't have to wear this.'

Pascoe laughed, a smoker's ragged laugh-cough. 'Don't worry about the Daunt. Wearin the blame's nothin new for the Daunt. Anyway, how's it help to find where he got the watch? Bloody thing must've been pinched some time.'

'If it turns out Corey pinched it, that's it,' said Cashin. 'We'll just leave it there, call it quits.'

'I hear Hopgood doesn't like you,' said Pascoe.

'How would you hear that?'

Pascoe shrugged, smoked, little smile. 'Walls got ears, mate. You'd be sleepin under the bed these days, right?'

The side door opened violently, banged the wall. The other man from the pier, the gaunt-faced man with dreadlocks. Cashin thought he looked bigger indoors.

'So what's the fuckin party?' he said.

Pascoe held up a hand. 'Havin a talk, Stevo.'

'Talk? Beer with the cops? Things fuckin changin around here, mate. Havin the fuckin trivia nights with the cops next.'

'Gettin the Corey watch stuff sorted,' said Pascoe. 'That's all.'

'Yeah, well,' said Stevo. 'It's sorted. Who's the lady?'

'The lawyer,' said Pascoe. 'Donny's lawyer.'

Stevo stepped across, stood behind Pascoe, reached over and picked up the six-pack, ripped out a can, looking at Cashin, at Helen, back at Cashin, blood in his eyes. 'Not drinkin?' he said. 'Don't drink with boongs?'

Pub fight shit, thought Cashin, no answer would defuse it. He looked at Pascoe. 'Listen, if your mate here's in charge, I'm gone.'

'So piss off,' said Stevo.

Pascoe didn't look around. 'Settle down, Stevo,' he said, a briskness to his tone.

'Settle down? Don't you fuckin tell me to settle down, where the fuck you …'

Pascoe shoved his chair back, took Stevo by surprise, knocked him off balance. He was upright in one quick movement and walking Stevo backwards, barrel chest bumping, three steps, pinned him against the bar. In his face, their chins touching, Pascoe said something to Stevo, Cashin couldn't catch it.

Stevo raised his hands. Pascoe stepped back, gestured. Stevo went behind the bar, leaned on it, didn't look at them. Pascoe went back to his chair, drank some beer.

'What I'll say is this,' he said as if nothing had happened. 'What I'll say is Corey coulda got the watch in a trade like, y'know.'

'For what?' said Cashin.

'Jeez, how'd I know? What do you reckon?'

'So who'd be on the other side?'

'Big ask, mate.'

'That's useful. Got any other stuff you'd like to tell me? Other people don't like me? How about Steggles? Wall ears hear anything about Steggie?'

'Dead man walkin. The fuckin prick.'

'Do it myself,' said Stevo, slurring. 'Fuckin tonight. Blow the cunt away.'

'Shut up, Stevo,' said Pascoe. 'Just fuckin shut up.'

Cashin took a can, ripped the top. He glanced at Helen. She had the air of someone watching a blood sport, lips parted, smears of colour on her cheekbones.

'Listen,' said Cashin. 'You want something, tell me quick, I'm thinking about food now. I eat around this time of the day, the night.'

'Corey done some stupid stuff, will of his own,' said Pascoe. 'Couldn't tell him a fuckin thing, just go his own way.'

Cashin said, 'This's dope you're talkin about?'

Pascoe waved a big hand. 'People grow a bit of weed, make a few bucks. No work around here.'

'So what did he do?'

'Well, y'know, there's ways of doin business. I'm not talkin fuckin truckloads, you understand, just beer money. Anyway, I hear Corey did these private deals, him and Luke, he's another kid wouldn't listen, bugger all respect.'

Pascoe offered the cigarettes. Cashin took one, the lighter, lit up, blew smoke at the roof, his instinct told him to make the leap. 'Piggots,' he said. 'This is Piggots?'

Pascoe looked at Helen, looked at Cashin. 'Not all asleep in Port, are you? Yeah, Piggots. They got ambitions, the fuckin Piggots, such dickheads but they reckon they're headin for the big time, they're gonna be players.'

'Fuckin Piggots,' said Stevo. He had a Jim Beam bottle in his hand now. 'Blow the cunts away. White fuckin maggots.'

'Stevo,' said Pascoe. 'Shut the fuck up. Watch TV. Find the fuckin cartoons.'

Helen said, 'Chris, correct me, you're saying Corey traded for the watch with the Piggots?'

'That's, that's possible, yeah.'

'Tell me how the Piggots got the watch,' said Helen.

Pascoe was looking at Cashin. 'Can you imagine?' he said. 'These Pigs got the idea this shit's easier than poachin abalone. Don't even want to grow it themselves, don't want to move it. All reward and no risk.'

'That's very ambitious,' said Cashin.

'My fuckin oath. And I hear they got someone to do a cook for em, too. This bloke, he's like a travellin speed cook.'

'Is that right?'

'Shouldn't be allowed, should it?'

'No.'

Pascoe leaned forward, put his face as close to Cashin's as he could. 'Can't expect fuckin Hopgood and the local boys to do anythin, can you? Be unreasonable since Hoppy's got a share in the horse. Whole leg, I hear.'

'Something'll have to be done about that,' said Cashin.

'Fuckin right.' He sat back. 'Hearin me.'

Cashin nodded. 'Hearing you.'

Helen coughed. 'About how the Piggots got the watch,' she said. 'Can we get on to that?'

Cashin thought that he knew the answer, delivered to him by some process in the brain that endlessly sifted, sorted and shuffled things heard and read, seen and felt, bits and pieces with no obvious use, just clutter, litter, until the moment when two of them touched, spun and found each other, fitted like hands locking.

'Ray Piggot,' he said.

'You're so fuckin quick,' said Pascoe. 'Yeah, the bumboy. That's what I hear.'

The complaint against Ray Piggot. Hopgood and Steggles at the station, Ray in the car outside. Ray who looked all of fourteen.

'Ray Piggot stole the watch from Bourgoyne?' said Helen, uncertainly.

'Well, wouldn't have been a present.'

'I don't understand what's going on here,' said Helen. 'Who's Ray Piggot? Am I just …'

Cashin said, 'So to clear this up, we're not talking about Ray and a burg?'

Pascoe laughed. 'Hopgood woulda dropped him off up there for old Charlie Bourgoyne. This cunt Ray knew what he was in for but he's not the first kid been fed to Charlie and his mates. That's one of Hoppy's jobs. That's the way it's always been.'

THEY DROVE in silence to the forecourt of the service station where Cashin had parked. 'Thank you,' he said, made to go.

'Wait.'

There were no cars at the pumps. The windows of the small cashier's cabin were steamed up by breath.

'I need some things explained to me,' said Helen. 'What the hell was going on there?'

Cashin thought about what to say to her. She had no further part to play in this shit, she didn't have a client. 'Pascoe's growing,' he said. 'Also, he delivers, he does the tightarse run. The Piggots get other people to grow, make tablets, deliver. Pascoe says Hopgood and the mates are in it, building up their super.'

'Why's Pascoe telling you?'

'He wants me to take care of the Piggots. For telling me how the boys got the watch.'

'This is another watch, an earlier one?'

'That's right. Different model.'

'So it was a stuff-up from the beginning?'

'It was.'

'And you believe the story about this Ray Piggot?'

Cashin looked at her. A car turned in and the headlights splashed her face and he felt again the full sad stupidity of teenage lust for someone beyond reach. 'Ray's a quickpick,' he said. 'Rips off the punters if he can.'

'A quickpick?'

'Drivethrough, a hitchhiker. One size fits all.'

'Joe, I was in corporate law until a year ago.'

'It doesn't matter,' he said. 'There's nothing left for you to do. Just a mess for us to clean up. Of our own making.'

'Joe.'

'What?'

'Give me a break. You wouldn't know what you know if I hadn't pushed you to see Pascoe. Pascoe says Hopgood delivered Ray Piggot to Bourgoyne. And other boys. Nobody's ever said this about Bourgoyne.'

'In your circle.'

'What's that mean? In my circle?'

'Maybe you Bayview Drive people don't talk about stuff like that. Too vulgar.'

Helen tapped second knuckles of both hands on the steering wheel. 'Not rising to that bait,' she said, a pause between each word.

'Got to go,' said Cashin. 'I'll get back to you.'

It was cold and damp outside, a sea mist. He ducked his head to say thanks.

'Are you often in pain?' said Helen.

'No.'

'Well, you fooled me. Anyway, I'm in the house, we're neighbours. Care to stop off for a drink? I can microwave some party pies. I gather people in your circle enjoy them.'

He was going to say, no thank you, I'll give that a miss, but he looked into her eyes. 'I'll follow you,' he said.

'No,' she said, 'you go first. You know the road better.'

The driveway to the Corrigan house ran between old elms, many dead. It was newly graded, the earth white in the headlights. Cashin parked to the left of the homestead gate and switched off. Helen parked beside him. He got out, uneasy. The moving sky opened and a full moon appeared in the wedge, lit the world pale grey. They went down the long path in silence, climbed new timber steps to the front door.

'I'm still a bit spooked out here,' she said. 'The dark. The silence. It may be a mistake.'

'Get a dog,' said Cashin. 'And a gun.'

They went down a passage. She clicked lights, revealed a big empty room, two or three of the old house's rooms knocked into one, a new floor laid. There were two chairs and a low table.

'I haven't got around to furniture yet,' said Helen. 'Or unpacked the books.'

He followed her into a kitchen.

'Stove, fridge, microwave,' she said. 'It's your basic bed-and-breakfast establishment. No personality.'

'Party pies are just right then,' said Cashin. 'Very little personality in a party pie.'

Helen hooked her thumbs in her coat pockets. She lifted her chin. Cashin saw the tendons in her throat. He could feel his heartbeat.

'Hungry?' she said.

'Your eyes,' said Cashin. 'Did you inherit that?'

'My grandmother had different coloured eyes.' She half-turned from him. 'You were a person of interest at school. I like that term. Person of interest.'

'That's a lie. You never noticed me.'

'You looked so hostile. Glowering. You still glower. Something sexy about a glower.'

'How do you glower?'

'Don't question your gift.' Helen crossed the space and took his head in her hands, kissed him, drew back. 'Not too responsive,' she said. 'Are cops intimate on the first date?'

Cashin put his hands inside her coat, held her, inhaled her smell, felt her ribs. She was thinner than he expected. He shivered. 'Cops generally don't have second dates.'

There was a long moment.

Helen took Cashin's right hand, kissed it, kissed his lips, led him.

In the night, he awoke, sensed that she was awake.

'Do you still ride?' he said.

'No. I had a bad fall, lost my nerve.'

'I thought the idea was to get on again.'

She touched him. 'Is that a suggestion?'

THE HOUSE could be seen from a long way, the front door dead centre at the end of a drive of pencil pines. As Cashin drove, the weak western sunlight flicked unnervingly through the trees.

A thin, lined woman wearing a dark tracksuit answered his knocks. Cashin said the words, offered the ID.

'Round the back,' she said. 'In the shed.'

He walked on the concrete apron. The place had the air of a low-security prison – the fence around the compound, the building freshly painted, the watermelon scent of newly mown grass in the air. No trees, no flowers, no weeds.

The shed, big enough for a few light aircraft, had an open sliding door on the north side. A man appeared in it when Cashin was ten metres away.

'Mr Starkey?' said Cashin.

'Yeah?'

He was wearing clean blue overalls over a checked shirt, a huge man, fat but hard looking, head the shape and colour of a scrubbed potato.

'Detective Senior Sergeant Cashin. Can we talk?'

'Yeah.' He turned and went inside.

Cashin followed him. Mrs Starkey's kitchen would be this clean and neat, he thought. Power tools in racks. Two long benches with galvanised iron tops shone under the fluorescent light. Behind them pegboards held tools – spanners, wrenches, pliers, metal snips, hacksaws, steel rulers, clamps, calipers – arranged by size in laser-straight rows. There was a big metal lathe and a tiny one, a drill stand, two bench grinders, a power hacksaw, a stand with slots and holes for files and punches and other things.

In the centre of the space, under chain hoists, four old engines in stages of disassembly stood on square steel tables.

A tall thin youth, dressed like Starkey, was at a vice, filing at something. He glanced at Cashin, looked down at the work, a lock of hair falling.

'Go talk to yer mum, Tay,' said Starkey.

Tay had an oily cloth in his back pocket. He took it out and carefully wiped the bench, went over to a stand, wiped his file and put it in its place.

He went without looking at Cashin again. Cashin watched him go. He held one shoulder lower than the other, walked with it leading in a crab-like way.

'Working on these engines,' said Cashin.

'Yeah,' said Starkey. His eyes were slits. 'Bourgoyne & Cromie engines. What can I do for you?'

'You fix them?'

'Restore em. Best ever made. What?'

Cashin realised there was nowhere to sit. 'The watch Mr Bourgoyne was wearing,' he said. 'Can you identify it?'

'Yeah, I reckon.'

Cashin took out a colour copy of the brochure, folded to show only the watch with the plain white face, three small dials.

'Yeah, that's it,' Starkey said.

'He was wearing that watch that day?'

'Wore it every day.'

'Thanks. Just a few other questions.'

'What's the problem? Daunt coons bashed him.' Impassive face, grey marble eyes.

'We're not sure of that.'

'Yeah? That fuckin little Coulter took the Kettle dive to have a swim? Guilty as shit.'

Starkey walked to the door and spat, wiped his lips, came back, planted himself, questioning head angle.

'At home that night?' said Cashin. 'You and Tay?'

Starkey's eyes narrowed, full of threat. 'Answered that question already. What's your fuckin problem?'

'Come down to the station,' said Cashin. 'The two of you. Bring the toothbrushes, just in case.'

Starkey exercised his jaw, up and down, back and forth.

'Know a cop called Hopgood?' he said. 'I know him. Mate.'

Cashin took out his mobile, held it out. 'Ring him,' he said.

'In my own fuckin time.'

'Want me to ring him? I'll ring him for you.'

Starkey put his hands in his pockets. 'We was at home, ask her. Don't go out at night much. Just footy stuff.'

'Still working at The Heights?'

'Till it's sold, yeah.'

'Well-paid job, The Heights.'

'That right?'

'About four times what your gardener gets around here. Five, maybe.'

'Two of us.'

'Twice as much then.'

'Twice as much fuckin work as anywhere else.'

'You drove him around too.'

Starkey put a huge hand to his neck. 'Didn't drive him around. Took him to the bank, to the city. He didn't like to drive anymore.'

'Know someone called Arthur Pollard?'

'No.'

'Know this man?' He showed him the full-face mugshot of Pollard, watched his eyes.

'No.'

Cashin considered where to go, took the soft route. 'Mr Starkey, I'll tell you we don't think the Daunt boys attacked Mr Bourgoyne. So if you can tell me anything you saw or heard, any feeling you might have …'

'You don't think?'

'No.'

'Why?'

'Some things don't add up.'

'Charged that Coulter, didn't ya?'

'We thought he was involved, it was a holding action.'

'What's that mean?'

'What did you think when you heard about it?'

There was an instant, something in Starkey's muddy eyes. 'Well, shock, that's it, yeah.'

'That's all?'

'What else? Don't happen around here that kind of thing, does it?'

'Did you like him?'

'He was all right. Yeah. Not likely to be mates, were we, him and me?'

'Who could want to harm him?'

'Apart from thievin scum?'

'Yes.'

'No idea.'

'Had any visitors recently, Mr Bourgoyne? Apart from the step-daughter?'

'Nah. Not that I saw.'

'What about burglaries at The Heights before this happened?'

'Not in my time. Had some horses pinched once. They cut the wire, pinched three horses from the bottom paddock. You'd have the records, wouldn't ya?'

'If it was reported.'

'Why wouldn't it be reported?'

'Crake. How'd you get on with him?'

Starkey shrugged. 'Okay. Had his ways he wanted things done. I did em that way.'

'He helped Bourgoyne with the kiln, didn't he?'

'Can't remember that well.'

'You worked at the Companions camp.'

Starkey scratched his head again, an uncertain look, averted his eyes. 'Long time ago,' he said.

'So you knew Crake from the camp?'

'Yeah. He was the boss.'

'What was your job?'

'Maintenance. Bit of footy coaching. Showed the kids the ropes.'

'There on the night of the fire?'

The big hands were expressive now. 'Nah. At the pub in Port.'

'Tell me about driving him to the city. Where'd you go?'

'The flat in Relly Street. He took taxis from there.'

'Stay over?'

'Hotel in St Kilda. Gedding's Hotel.'

Cashin went over to the engines. 'This one a generator?' he said.

'Made in '56. Better than anything you can buy today.'

'How much ground you got here?'

'Thirty acres.'

'Farm it?'

'Nah. Put the house in the middle of the block. Didn't wanna hear neighbours. Now the one bastard's complaining about the engines.'

'Well,' said Cashin, 'tell him you'll connect him up if the power fails. I could use a generator. Sell them?'

'Don't sell, not a business,' said Starkey. 'Only restore ones my granddad and my dad finished off. They punched their initials under the number.'

'How do you find them?'

'Advertise, Queensland, WA, Northern Territory. I got auctioneers keep a lookout at clearing sales, that kind of thing. Found one in Fiji, rusted to buggery. Cost a bit to bring it home.'

'And you've found four?'

'Thirteen. Got another shed for em.'

'Where do you stop?'

'Stop?'

'Collecting them.'

'Don't have to stop.'

There was no point in asking why. It was a pretty useless question most of the time. The answer was either obvious or too complicated to understand. Cashin looked for the engine number. 'Ever drive Bourgoyne to a house in North Melbourne?'

'North ... no. Only took him to Relly Street.'

The fortress had a crack, a hairline fracture. He didn't look at Starkey. 'A hall in North Melbourne, you drove him there.'

'A hall? Just Relly Street.'

'The Companions hall. You know it, don't bullshit me, Mr Starkey.'

'No, don't know it.'

Cashin went to another engine. They were simple machines, he could probably learn to fix one. Easier than making a decent soup. 'Your dad, he'd have been pretty pissed off when they sold the factory.'

Silence. Starkey coughed, off balance. 'Never said a word. Mum told me that.'

'What'd he do afterwards?'

'Nothin. Died before the payout. Some serious brain thing.'

'That's sad.' Cashin didn't look at him. 'I'll tell you what's a serious brain thing, Mr Starkey. Bullshitting me. That's a seriously bad brain thing. Tell me about the hall.'

'Don't know no hall.'

'I'll need to talk to Tay,' said Cashin. 'By himself.'

'Why?'

'He might have seen something. Heard something.'

Starkey stared at Cashin. 'He wouldn't know nothin, mate. Always with me.'

Cashin shrugged. 'We'll see.'

'Listen,' said Starkey, a different voice. 'Boy's not the brightest. She dropped him on the lid when he was tiny. Short-circuited the little bugger. No use at school.'

'Get him in here.'

Starkey scratched his scalp, slowly, urgently. 'Do me a favour, mate,' he said. 'Let him alone. Gets nightmares. Screams.'

The felt moment of power. Cashin could see Starkey's fear. 'That's really tough. Get him.'

'Mate, please.'

'Just get him.'

'I'm gonna ring Hopgood.'

'Listen, Starkey,' said Cashin. 'Hopgood can't protect you. This is a city matter. And now, because you're so fucking obstructive, I'm not going to talk to Tay here, not going to talk to him at the station. I'm taking him to Melbourne. Pack his toothbrush and his jarmies and a couple of biscuits. What kind of bickies does he like?'

He saw hate in Starkey's eyes, and he saw pure shining fear, fear and panic.

'Can't do that, mate. I ask you, please, I ask you …'

'North Melbourne. The house in Collett Street. You drove him there?'

'No, I didn't, you gotta …'

'Wasting my time. Got a trip ahead of me. Tell me the truth or get Tay. Now.'

Starkey looked around the shed as if the answer might be written on a wall, he could read it out. 'Okay. Took him there.'

'When last?'

'Five, six years, I dunno.'

'How many times?'

'Few.'

'Every time you went to Melbourne?'

'I suppose.'

'How often was that?'

Starkey swallowed. 'Four, five times a year.'

'And the hall?'

'Don't know the hall.'

Cashin caught the tinny sound in the big man's voice.

He took out the mugshot of Pollard, didn't show it. 'I'm asking you again. Do you know this man?'

'I know him.'

'What's his name?'

'Arthur Pollard. He used to come to the camp.'

'Where else do you know him from?'

'Collett Street. I seen him there.'

Cashin walked to the work bench, ran a finger over the piece of metal Tay had been filing. It was a part of some sort. 'Pollard's a perv,' he said. 'Know that? He likes boys. Small boys. Fucks them. And the rest. Lots of the rest, I can tell you. Know about that do you, Mr Starkey?'

Silence. Cashin didn't look at Starkey. 'Didn't drop your boy off in Collett Street, did you, Mr Starkey? Feed him to Pollard?'

'I'll kill you,' Starkey said slowly, voice thick. 'Say that again, I'll fuckin kill you.'

Cashin turned. 'Tell me about Bourgoyne.'

Starkey had a hand on his chest. His face was orange, he was trying to control his breathing. 'Never saw anything. Nothin. So help me, I never saw anythin.'

'What about the hall?'

'Just the once. Picked up a lot of stuff, files and that. He said to burn it.'

'Bourgoyne?'

'Yeah.'

'So where'd you burn it?'

'Nowhere to burn there. Brought the stuff back here to burn.'

'Dad.'

Tay was in the door, chin near his chest, looking through a comb of pale hair that touched the bridge of his nose.

'What?'

'Mum says spaggy bol okay for tea?'

'Tell her to go for it, son.'

Tay went. Cashin walked to the door, turned. 'Don't go anywhere,' he said. 'There's plenty more we want to know. And don't mention this little talk to anyone. You go running to fucking Hopgood, running anywhere, I'm coming back for you and Tay, you'll both rot in remand in Melbourne. Not together either. He'll be in with blokes fuck dogs. And so will you.'

'Didn't burn the stuff,' said Starkey quietly.

CASHIN SAT at the table and sifted through the contents of Starkey's cardboard boxes. It was half an hour before he came upon the clipping of a photograph from the Cromarty *Herald*. The date at the top of the page was 12 August 1977.

A strapline above the picture said:

CLEAN AIR IS A KICK FOR CITY BOYS

The caption read:

Coach Rob Starkey, North Cromarty star half-forward, fires up the Companions Camp under-15 side at half-time in their game against St Stephen's on Saturday morning. The city boys, having a much-needed holiday at the Port Monro camp thanks to the Moral Companions, went down 167–43. But the score didn't matter. The point was to have a good run around in the bracing air.

The black-and-white photograph showed boys in muddy white shorts and dark football jumpers facing a big man. He was holding the ball horizontally and he was saying something. The boys, hair close-cut back and sides, were eating orange quarters – sour oranges, said the nearest boy's puckered face, his closed eyes.

In the background were spectators, all but two of them men, rugged up against the cold. To the right were two men in overcoats and, in front of them, a small boy. The men were smoking cigarettes.

Cashin got up from the table and took the clipping to the window, held it to the dying light. He recognised the man in the centre wearing a camel overcoat from the photographs at The Heights: Charles Bourgoyne. He had long fingers. The man on his right could be Percy Crake – he had a small moustache.

Cashin looked at the other spectators: middle-aged men, a sharp-nosed woman wearing a headscarf, a laughing woman of indeterminate age. The face behind Bourgoyne was turned away, a young man, short hair combed back, something about him.

Was the boy with Bourgoyne and Crake? He was frowning. He seemed to be looking at the camera. Something in the small face nagged at Cashin. He closed his eyes and he saw Erica Bourgoyne across the table from him at the gallery.

James Bourgoyne. The boy with the sad face might be the drowned Jamie, Erica's brother, Bourgoyne's step-son.

Cashin went back to the papers and looked for other photographs. In a folder, he found more than a dozen 8x10 prints. They were all same: boys lined up in three rows of nine or ten, tallest at the back, the front row on one knee. They wore singlets and dark shorts, tennis shoes with short socks. The man with the moustache was in all of them, dressed like the boys, standing to the right, apart. His arms were folded, fists beneath his biceps, bulging them. He had hairy legs, big thighs and muscular calves. At the left stood two other men in tracksuits. One of them, a stocky dark man wearing glasses, was in all the photographs. The other one – tall, thin, long-nosed – was in five or six.

He turned a photograph over: *Companions Camp 1979.*

The names were written in pencil in a loose hand: back row, middle row, front row. *At left: Mr Percy Crake. At right: Mr Robin Bonney, Mr Duncan Vallins.*

Vallins was the tall man, Bonney the dark, solid one.

Cashin looked for the name and he found it in 1977.

David Vincent was in the middle row, a skinny, pale boy, long-necked, his adam's apple and the bumps on his shoulders visible. His head was turned away slightly, apprehensively, as if he feared some physical harm from the photographer.

Cashin read the other names, looked at the faces, looked away and thought. He fetched the telephone and dialled, listened, eyes closed. David Vincent was out or out of it. He rang Melbourne, had to wait for Tracy.

'Two names,' he said. 'Robin Bonney. Duncan Vallins. Appreciate and so on.'

'You are Singo's clones,' she said. 'You and the boss. Have people told you that?'

'They've told me young Clint Eastwood. Does that square with you?'

'And so on. You going to actually speak to me the next time you come in here? As opposed to acknowledging my existence?'

A dog rose on the sofa and, in an indolent manner, put its paws on the floor and did a stretch, backside high above its head. The other dog followed suit, an offended look.

'Preoccupied then,' said Cashin. 'I'm sorry. Still married to that bloke in moving?'

'No. Divorced.'

'Right. Moved on. Well, next time I'm in we can exchange some more personal information. Blood types, that kind of thing.'

'I'm holding my breath. Got a Robin Gray Bonney here. Age fifty-seven. Possibility?'

'About right.'

'Former social worker. Form is child sex offender. Suspended sentence on two charges. Then he did four years of a six.'

'More and more right.'

'Well, he's dead. Multiple stab wounds, castrated, mutilated and strangled. In Sydney. Marrickville. That's, that's two days ago. No arrest.'

Cashin tried to do the front stretch exercise, the opening of the shoulder-blades, felt all the muscles resist.

'Here we go,' said Tracy. 'Vallins, Duncan Grant, age fifty-three. Anglican priest, address in Brisbane, Fortitude Valley but that's 1994. Child sex form, suspended sentence 1987. Did a year in 1994–95. I presume he's a former priest now.'

'Why would you presume that? Trace, three things. All the details on Bonney. The mutilation. Two, on Vallins, beg Brisbane to check that address and stress we don't want him spooked. Three, tell Dove we need the coroner's report on a fire at the Companions camp, Port Monro, in 1983.'

He was at the window. Ragged-edged ribbons of pink ran down the sky, died on the black hill.

Same night as the fire. Double tragedy.

Cecily Addison's words. Bourgoyne's wife fell down the stairs on the night of the fire. Tranquillisers blamed.

'Now that I think about it,' he said, 'I might come to town. Pass that on to the boss, will you?'

'I'll pass it on to all the lovesick in this building. Dove's here, want to talk to him?'

'No, but put him on anyway.'

Clicks.

'Good day,' said Dove. 'The CrimeStoppers log on Bourgoyne. You looked at it?'

'How the fuck would I have looked at it?'

'I don't think anyone's looked at it. On the night it was on television, a woman rang. She saw it, rang straight away. Mrs Moira Laidlaw. Her words are, I suggest you investigate Jamie Bourgoyne.'

'That's it?'

'That's it.'

'Well, Jamie's dead. Drowned in Tasmania.'

'You don't have to drown to be dead in Tasmania, but I thought this was worth a sniff. Is that it? Sniff? Snuff?'

'You've talked to her?'

'This is ten minutes old. I rang but you were busy.'

'Get the full sweep on the dead Jamie. Tracy'll tell you what else. I'll see you tomorrow.'

Cashin knew he should go immediately, tell Villani, get in the vehicle and go. He knew he wouldn't. What did it matter now?

'I SAW HIM quite clearly,' said the old woman in a dry and precise voice. 'I was waiting at the lights in Toorak Road and they changed and a car stopped. For some reason, I looked and Jamie was in the passenger seat.'

'You knew him well, Mrs Laidlaw?' said Cashin.

'Of course. He's my nephew, my sister's child. He lived with us for a time.'

'Right. And you saw him when?'

'About six weeks ago. On a Friday. I go shopping and have lunch with friends on Fridays.'

It was just past 4 pm but Cashin thought that it felt much later in the sitting room, the light dim outside, a row of raindrops waiting to fall from a thin branch framed in the French doors. 'And you know that Jamie is said to have drowned in Tasmania in 1993?' he said.

'Yes. Well, obviously he didn't because I saw him in Toorak Road.'

Cashin looked at Dove, passed to him that there was no point in questioning the identification.

'May I ask why you thought we should investigate Jamie over the assault on his step-father?' said Dove.

'Because he's alive and he's capable of it. He hates Charles Bourgoyne.'

'Why's that?'

'I have no idea. Ask Erica.' She turned her head and the light made her short hair gleam.

'When last did you see Jamie?' said Dove. 'Before Toorak Road, I mean.'

'He came to my husband's funeral. Turned up at the church. God knows how he knew. Didn't talk to anyone except Erica. Not a word to his step-father.'

'He liked your husband?' said Cashin.

She picked at nothing on her cardigan. 'No. And my husband certainly wasn't fond of him.'

'Why was that?'

'He didn't like him.'

Cashin waited but nothing came. 'Why didn't he like him, Mrs Laidlaw?'

She looked down. A dove-grey cat had come into the room and was leaning against her right leg. It was staring at Cashin, eyes the colour of ash. 'My husband never forgot his nephew's death. Mark drowned in the pool when he was ten. Jamie was here. No one else.'

'Was there a suspicion that Jamie was involved?'

'No one said anything.'

'But your husband thought he was?'

She blinked at Cashin. 'Jamie was three years older than Mark, you see.'

Cashin felt the silken ankle-winding of the cat. 'Was that important?'

'He was supposed to be looking after Mark. We loved Mark very much. He'd been with us since he was six. He was like a son to us.'

'I see. And Jamie came to your husband's funeral?'

'Yes. Out of the blue and dressed like some sort of hippy musician.'

'When was that?'

'In 1996. The twelfth of May 1996. He came here the next day.'

'Why?'

'He wanted a photograph of Mark. He asked if he could have one. He knew where the photographs were too, where we kept Mark's things. He said he'd thought of Mark as a brother. Quite unbelievable, frankly.'

'And you never saw him again?'

'No. Not until Toorak Road. A cup of tea? I could make tea.'

'No thank you, Mrs Laidlaw,' said Dove. 'How long did Jamie live with you?'

She took off her glasses, touched the corner of an eye carefully, replaced them. 'Not very long. Less than two years. He came after he stopped boarding at the college. His step-father asked us.'

'And that was here?'

'Here?'

'You lived in this house then?' said Cashin.

Mrs Laidlaw looked at him as if he were not the full quid. 'We've always lived here. I grew up here, my grandparents built this house.'

'And after Jamie finished school…?'

'He didn't finish school. He left.'

'He left school?'

'Yes. And he left here. He was in year eleven and one day he just left.'

'Where did he go?'

'I don't know. Erica told me he was in Queensland at one point.'

A telephone rang in the passage.

'Excuse me.'

Cashin and Dove stood up with her. She walked slowly to the door and Cashin went to the French doors and looked at the garden, at the big bare trees – an oak, an elm, a tree he couldn't identify. Their leaves had not been raked and they lay in soggy drifts. A stone retaining wall was leaning, blocks loose. Soon it would collapse, the worms would be revealed.

'These charity calls,' said Mrs Laidlaw. 'I don't really know what to say to the people. They sound so nice.'

She sat down in her chair. The cat elevated itself into her lap. Cashin and Dove sat.

'Mrs Laidlaw, why did Jamie stop boarding at the school?' said Cashin.

'I didn't hear the details. The school could tell you, I suppose.'

'And the reason he left here?'

'You might ask the school about that too. I'd be lying if I said his departure wasn't a great relief.'

She stroked the cat, looking at it. 'Jamie was a strange boy. He was very attached to his mother and I don't think he got over her death. But there was something else about him …'

'Yes?'

'Silent, always watching, and somehow scared. As if you might hurt him. Then he'd do these horrible things. Once when he was here for the weekend from school he made a bow and arrow and shot the cat next door. Through the eye. He said it was an accident. But there was a dog set on fire down the road. We knew it was Jamie. And he drowned Mark's budgies in the pool. In their cage.'

She looked from Cashin to Dove. 'He used to read my husband's medical books. He'd sit on the floor in the study and look at anatomy texts for hours.'

'Do you know anyone he might be in contact with?' said Cashin.

She was stroking the cat, her head down. 'No. He had a friend at school, another problem boy. They expelled him, I gather.'

'What school did he go to, Mrs Laidlaw?'

'St Paul's. The Bourgoynes all went to St Paul's. Gave it a lot of money.'

'You said he hated Charles Bourgoyne.'

'Yes. I didn't realise how much until I suggested he might like to spend a holiday with Charles. He'd been spending them here. He ran into the front door with his head. Deliberately. And he sat there on the floor screaming no, no, no, over and over. Sixteen stitches in his scalp, that's what it took.'

'Thank you for your help, Mrs Laidlaw.'

'You're not what I expected.' She was looking at Dove.

'We come in all types,' Cashin said.

She smiled at Dove, an affectionate smile, as if she knew him and thought well of him.

They went down the passage to the front door. Cashin said, 'Mrs Laidlaw, I have to ask you. Is there even the slightest doubt in your mind over the man you saw in Toorak Road? Is it possible that it wasn't Jamie?'

'No doubt at all. I'm perfectly sane, I had my glasses on and it was Jamie.'

'You told Erica you'd seen him?'

'Yes. I rang her as soon as I got home.'

'What did she say?'

'Nothing really. Yes, dear, that sort of thing.'

A thin but steady rain fell on the men as they walked down the balding gravel path and along the pavement to the vehicle. The gutters were running, carrying leaves and twigs and acorns. In some dark tunnel, they would meet the sordid human litter of the city and go together to the cold slate bay.

It came to Cashin as they reached the car. 'Be back in a sec,' he said.

Mrs Laidlaw opened the door as if she'd been waiting behind it. He asked her.

'Mark Kingston Denby,' she said. 'Why?'

'Just for the record.'

In the car, Cashin said, 'The school. The expelled friend.'

THE DEPUTY headmaster was in his fifties, grey-suited, tanned and fit-looking like a cross-country skier. 'School policy is that we do not disclose information about students or staff, past or present,' he said. He smiled, snowy teeth.

'Mr Waterson,' said Cashin, 'we'll ruin your evening. We'll be back inside an hour with a warrant and a truck to take away all your files. And who knows, the media might show up too. Can't keep anything secret these days. So St Paul's will be all over the television news tonight. The parents will like that, I'm sure.'

Waterson scratched his cheek, a pink square-cut nail. He wore a copper bracelet. 'I'll need to consult,' he said. 'Please excuse me a moment.'

Dove went to the office window. 'Dusk on the playing fields,' he said. 'Like England.'

Cashin was looking at the deputy headmaster's books. They all seemed to be about business management. 'We fucked this thing up,' he said. 'So badly. I'm glad Singo's not around to see it.'

'Thank god it's we,' said Dove. 'Imagine what it would be like to have fucked it up all by yourself. Even mostly.'

The door opened. 'Follow me please, gentlemen,' said Waterson. 'I caught our legal adviser on her way home. She works here two days a week.'

They went down the corridor and into a big wood-panelled room. A dark-haired woman in a pinstriped suit was at the head of a table that could seat at least twenty.

'Louise Carter,' said Waterson. 'Detective Cashin and Detective Dove. Please sit down, gentlemen.'

They sat. Carter looked at them in turn.

'This school jealously guards the privacy of its community,' she said. She was about fifty, a long face, taut skin around her eyes, a slightly startled look. 'We don't accede to requests for information unless requested to do so by the community family or the community family member concerned, if that person is in a position to make such a request. And, even then, we reserve the right to exercise our own judgment on acceding to any requests.'

'You've got that written in your hand,' said Dove. 'I saw you look down.'

She was not amused.

'The community family I'm talking about is in serious shit,' said Cashin. 'Just yes or no, we're in a hurry.'

Carter moved her mouth. 'You can't bully St Paul's, detective. Perhaps you don't realise the position it occupies in this city.'

'I don't give a bugger either. We'll crawl all over the place. Inside an hour. Believe me.'

She didn't blink. 'What is it you want to know about these students?'

'Why Jamie Bourgoyne was kicked out as a boarder, the name of the friend he had here who was expelled and why.'

A head movement of refusal. 'Not possible. Please understand that the Bourgoyne family has a long and close association with the school. I'm afraid we can't …'

'Don't loosen your seatbelt,' said Cashin. 'We'll be back soon. You might want to check the lippy, you're going to be on television.'

Cashin and Dove stood.

'Wait,' said Waterson, getting up. 'I think we can meet this request.'

He left the room and the woman followed him, heels clicking. There was a brief exchange outside and she came back and stood at a window. Then she sat down and there was silence until she coughed and said, 'Have I seen you two on television?'

Cashin had his eyes on the big painting opposite, vertical bars of grey and brown. It reminded him of a jumper Bern wore, knitted by some old relative, a person with self-respect would compost it.

Once he would have wanted this woman to think well of him.

'You may have seen me,' said Dove. 'I'm the undercover cop. Sometimes I have a beard.'

Waterson came in. He put two yellow folders on the table and sat. 'I'll deal with all your inquiries in a narrative,' he said, businesslike. 'Feel free to interrupt.'

The woman said, 'David, can we …'

'James Bourgoyne and a boy called Justin Fischer were in the same class and in the boarding house together,' said Waterson.

He looked at the woman, at Cashin. 'I feel compelled to say that I considered James to be a seriously disturbed young man. And Justin Fischer is the most dangerous boy I've encountered in my thirty-six years in education.'

The lawyer leaned forward. 'David, there's absolutely no call for this kind of candour. May I …'

'What happened?' said Cashin.

'Among other things, they were suspected of lighting two fires. One burnt down a sports equipment store, the other was lit in the boarding house.'

'David, please.'

'Police matters,' said Cashin.

'The police were called in, of course,' said Waterson, 'but we didn't pass on our suspicions and they could find nothing. Instead, we asked James's step-father to remove him from the boarding establishment. This was an attempt to separate the pair.'

The lawyer held up her hands. 'This may be the moment ...'

'In retrospect,' said Waterson, 'we should have told the police everything and expelled both students. In that order.'

The woman said, quickly, 'David, before you say another word, I must insist that the headmaster be consulted.'

Waterson didn't look at her, kept his eyes on Cashin. 'Louise,' he said, 'the headmaster has the moral sense of Pol Pot. Let's not now compound our earlier atrocious judgments.'

Cashin saw in the tanned man's eyes the relief he had seen in people who were confessing to murder. 'Go on,' he said. He had the feeling now, the cough tickle in the mind.

'After Bourgoyne left the boarding establishment,' said Waterson, 'there were hedge-burnings locally. Three or four, I can't remember. Then in Prahran a boy, he was seven or eight, was taken to a quiet spot by two teenage boys and tortured. There's no other word for it. It was brief and he wasn't badly hurt but it was torture, sadism. One of our students came to us, he was a boarder, and he said he'd seen Bourgoyne and Fischer near the scene around the time.'

'You told the police?'

'To our eternal discredit, we did not.'

'The student wasn't told to go to the police?'

'David,' said the woman, 'I must now advise you to ...'

'He was discouraged from doing so,' said Waterson. 'On instructions from the headmaster, I discouraged him.'

'Is that the same as telling him not to?' said Dove. 'Discouraged?'

'Pretty close,' said Waterson. 'We then expelled Bourgoyne and Fischer. That day. It was the only right and proper thing we did in all our dealings with the pair.'

'I'd like copies of the files, please,' said Cashin.

'These are copies,' said Waterson. He pushed them across the table.

'Thank you,' said Cashin. He got up and shook hands with Waterson. He didn't look at the lawyer. 'There won't be any reason that I can see for us to mention the school.'

Going down the stone stairs, Cashin opened a file. 'Get Tracy,' he said to Dove. In the entrance hall, Dove handed him the mobile.

'Tracy, Joe. This is top of the list, front burner. Everything on a Justin David Fischer. That's an S-C-H-E-R. The last address is for an aunt, Mrs K. L. Fischer, 19 Hendon Street, Albert Park. Ask Birk to see if someone can chase that.'

'We've got the Jamie Bourgoyne sweep and the inquest on the Companions fire. Fin's looking at them.'

'Ask him to ring me, will you?'

'And Brisbane checked that Duncan Grant Vallins address. He left there two years ago. They don't have anything more recent.'

'Bugger.'

'The neighbour says a bloke was asking for him last week. Long hair, beard. Another one in the car.'

In the twilight, they crunched softly down the gravel driveway. Boys in green blazers and grey flannels were coming along a path to their right. The pale one in front was eating chips out of a box. A boy behind him put a headlock on him, pulled his head back. Another boy walked by and casually took the chip box, kept walking, put one in his mouth.

'Year ten mugging class,' said Dove. 'Been out on a prac.'

'WHAT'S HE SHOW?' said Cashin. They were at lights in Toorak Road. Three blonde women were crossing, damp combed hair, no makeup, flushed from an after-work gym class.

'My oath,' said Dove. 'These things are sent to try us.'

'Never on the electoral roll,' said Finucane. 'Never registered for Medicare, the dole, anything. A driver's licence issued Darwin 1989, you get that in a show bag. Then he's on the move. Minor drug stuff in Cairns, arrest for assaulting a kid age twelve in Coffs Harbour. Not proceeded with. Suspended sentences for assault in Sydney in 1986. In a park, victim age sixteen. Possession of heroin in Sydney in 1987. Two years for aggravated burglary in Melbourne in 1990.'

The lights turned green. Without a glance either way, an old woman, small and hunched, head down, wearing a transparent plastic raincoat, pushed a pram-like homemade trolley into the crossing.

'Like Columbus,' said Dove. 'She has no idea.'

The car behind them hooted, two long blasts.

Dove waited until the woman had crossed to safety before he pulled away slowly, held the speed, an act of provocation.

'Go on,' said Cashin.

'That's it. Jamie came out in '92 and he's presumed drowned in Tassie in '93.'

Cashin said, 'Fin, Tracy's on this Fischer bloke. Get whatever and ring me, okay? Also she's got a Duncan Grant Vallins. He's a ped, former Anglican sky pilot, address unknown, see if he's in our system, see if the church knows anything about him. Tell the choirboy who does the church's spin to co-operate or they'll turn in the fucking wind. On *The 7.30 Report* tonight.'

'Boss.'

'And one other thing. Try the name Mark Kingston Denby. Ring Dove if you get anything.'

'Boss.'

Cashin closed his eyes and thought about Helen Castleman naked. So smooth. Nakedness and sex changed everything. No bacon and onion and tomato sandwich would ever taste like that again.

'Where to?' said Dove.

'Queen Street. Know that?'

'Memorised the map, that's the first thing I did.'

'Then there'll always be a job for you driving cabs. Probably sooner than later.'

In Queen Street, Dove said, 'Accepting that I might have come on a bit like ...'

'Here,' said Cashin. 'Park in there. I want to talk to Erica Bourgoyne.'

'Bit late in the day, isn't it?'

'She's a lawyer. They don't go home.'

Cashin had the door open when Dove's mobile rang. He waited while Dove answered, held up a finger. 'Putting him on,' said Dove, offered the phone.

'Boss, I got through to this church bloke, he gave me Duncan Grant Vallins straight off,' said Finucane. 'Living in a place in Essendon, St Aidan's Home for Boys. It's shut down but this bloke says church people in need sometimes stay there.'

'In need of what?' said Cashin. 'The address?'

The night was upon them now, rain blurring the lights, dripping from the street trees, the pavement a parade of pale faces above dark garments.

'Also Mark Kingston Denby, found him. Came out of jail nine weeks ago. Six years for armed robberies. There's a co-accused here.'

'Yes?'

'A Justin Fischer,' said Finucane. 'He got the same.'

Cashin thought of calling Villani, changed his mind, told Dove where to go.

THE HEADLIGHTS lit the pillars and the double gates: cast-iron, ornate, fully two metres high, once painted, now an autumn colour and flaking. Beyond them was a driveway, and the lights threw the gates' shadows onto dark, uncontrolled vegetation.

'If the prick's at home, we're taking him into protective custody,' said Cashin. His whole torso was aching now and the pain slivers were going down his thighs.

Dove switched off, cut the lights. The street was dark here, the nearest lamp on the other side, fifty metres down. They got out, into the cold evening, the rain holding off for a while.

'What do we do?' said Dove.

'Knock on the front door,' said Cashin. 'What else is there to do?'

He tried the gate, put his hand through an opening and found a lever, raised it with difficulty, a screech of metal. The right-hand gate resisted his push, then swung easily. 'Leave it open,' he said.

They walked up the drive side by side, trying not to brush the wet bushes. 'You armed?' said Dove.

'Relax,' said Cashin, 'it's one old ex-priest ped, not party night at the Hell's Angels.' He knew he should be carrying. He'd got out of the habit, lost the instinct.

The building came into sight, double-storeyed, brick, arched windows, steps up to a long porch and a front door with leadlight windows on either side. A slit of light showed in a window to the left, a curtain not fully drawn.

'Someone home,' said Cashin. 'Someone in need.'

They climbed the stairs, he pulled back a solid ring of brass, pounded a few times, waited, hammered again.

The leadlight on the left glowed dimly – red and white and green and violet, a biblical scene, a group of men, one haloed.

'Who's there?' A firm male voice.

'Police,' said Cashin.

'Put your identification through the letter slot.'

Cashin gestured to Dove, who took out his ID card, pushed it through the slot. It was taken. They heard two bolts slide. The door opened.

'What is it?' A tall unshaven man in black, many-chinned, round glasses, thin grey hair combed back, oily, curling at the tips.

'Duncan Grant Vallins?'

'Yes.'

'Detective Senior Sergeant Cashin, homicide. Detective Dove.'

'What do you want?'

'Can we come in?'

Vallins hesitated, stood back. They went into a marble-floored entrance hall with a staircase rising in the centre, branching left and right to a gallery. Six metres up hung a many-tiered crystal chandelier.

'This way,' said Vallins.

They followed his pear shape into a room to the left. It was a big sitting room, one dim unshaded bulb above, one standing lamp near a fireplace. The furniture was old, shabby, unmatched chairs, a sagging chintz sofa. The smell was of damp and mouse droppings and ancient cigarette smoke trapped in curtains and carpet and coverings.

Vallins sat in the chair next to the lamp, crossed his legs, adjusted them. His thighs were fat. Next to a white cup, a filter cigarette was burning in a brass ashtray and he picked it up and drew deeply, long thin fingers stained the colour of cinnamon sticks. 'What do you want?' he said.

'Do you know an Arthur Pollard?' said Cashin, looking at the room, at the high ceiling, at the group of bottles on a side table, whisky bottles, seven or eight, empty except for two.

'Vaguely. Years ago.'

'Robin Gray Bonney. Know him?'

Vallins sucked on the cigarette, spat smoke, waved a hand. 'Also a long time ago. Donkeys' years. Why?'

'Charles Bourgoyne,' said Cashin. 'You probably know Charles. Vaguely. From a long time ago. And Mr Crake of course.'

Vallins didn't say anything, found a cigarette in a packet, lit it from his stub, had trouble docking, a shake in both hands. He ground the donor in the ashtray. 'What is this nonsense?' he said, high, proper voice. 'Why have you come here to bother me?'

'You may want to be in protective custody,' said Cashin. 'You may want to sit around and tell us about the Companions camps, those golden days. You looked really fit in the photographs. Took a lot of exercise then, did you, Mr Vallins? With the boys?'

'There's nothing I want to tell you,' said Vallins. 'Not a single thing. You can go now.'

'Bit of a hermit here, are you, Mr Vallins? All alone in this place for Anglicans in need?'

'None of your business. You know the way out.'

Cashin looked at Dove. Dove didn't seem happy, he was scratching his skull. Did scalps still itch without hair? Why was that?

'Fine,' said Cashin. 'On our way then. We'll leave you to think about how your friends Arthur and Robin were tortured. Robin's was nasty. Had something hot shoved up him. The knife sharpener. Know that thing? The steel? They think it was heated over the gas ring. Red hot. Came out the front.'

Vallins' face screwed up. 'What?'

'Tortured and killed,' said Cashin. 'Bourgoyne, Bonney, Pollard. We'll find our own way out then, Mr Vallins. Good night.'

Cashin walked. He was at the door when Vallins said, 'Please wait, detective, I'm sorry, I didn't know …'

'Just stopped by to keep you informed of the mortality rate among people like you,' said Cashin. 'Offer extended and refused. That's on record. Good luck and sleep tight, Mr Vallins.'

They were in the entrance hall, Cashin in front, then Dove, Vallins a pace behind.

'I think you might be right, detective,' said Vallins, high voice. 'Do I need …'

'I know what you need, Duncan,' said a voice from above, from the gallery. 'You need to repent your filthy life and die at peace with the Lord.'

CASHIN COULDN'T see the man. The light from the sitting room was too feeble.

'Who is it?' he said.

He knew.

Someone laughed, not the speaker. 'Cops,' he said. 'I can smell cops, filthy stinking, rotten cops.'

Cashin looked at Dove. His eyes were on the gallery, he was pushing back his overcoat with his right hand, Cashin saw the spring-clip holster, the butt, Dove's reaching fingers.

Bangs, bright red muzzle-flash.

Dove went backwards, spun around to face Cashin, Cashin saw his glasses glint, saw Dove's open mouth, his hands coming up to his chest, he was falling sideways.

'ONE DOWN!'

Cashin saw the fusebox on the wall beside the stained glass window. He went for it, two paces, dived, clawed at it with his left hand, off-balance, going down, saw the flash at the edge of his vision, felt a knife slice across his back below the shoulderblades.

'TWO DOWN!'

Coal dark. He was on his knees, his whole back seemed to be on fire.

Shit, he thought, I've taken one.

'Please!' shouted Vallins. 'I'll give you money, I've got money!'

Cashin put out a hand and found Dove's shoulder, the feel of cloth, touched his face. He was breathing. He crawled across, heard Dove's small snoring noise. He felt for Dove's holster, slid his hand down his body.

Empty.

Jesus, he got the gun out, dropped it. Where?

'COMING FOR YOU, BOYS!'

The squeaking voice.

Cashin was groping frantically, the marble floor was ice-cold.

'Please!' shouted Vallins. 'Pleeease!'

'First you must repent, Duncan,' said the deeper, calmer voice.

Cashin was crawling fast, there was a door to the right of the stairs, he needed to get there before they switched on the mains, they'd seen him switch off, they'd find it, you never went unarmed, you never needed the fucking thing until you needed it so badly that your teeth ached.

He crawled into a wall, stood up, went left, groping, knocked over something, a table, an object hit the floor, smashed.

Bang, gun-flash. From half-way down the stairs.

Cashin found a deep recess, found the door, found the doorknob, twisted, the door opened, he was inside.

A scent. A faint, sickly perfume.

Don't close the door, they'll hear the click.

He was feeling light-headed. He walked into something solid, thigh-high, turned right, felt his way, it was the back of something, it went on, it ended, a post, carved, he put out a hand and touched a wall.

A pew. This is a church. A chapel. That's the smell.

Right hand on the wall, he took a step, felt something, knocked it off its mounting. It hit the floor, a loud noise, he stopped.

'Over there,' said the first voice. 'He's over there. He doesn't have a gun.'

'Blow this cop away,' said the high voice. 'Blow his head off.'

'No, get the other cop, Justin. We'll let this one bleed out. He's a lamb of God. I'll pray for him.'

Cashin heard a whimpering, a terrible sound, fear and pain combined.

He was trying to become accustomed to the dark, he was blinking, trying to blink quickly, but he couldn't, his eyelids were too heavy. Loss of blood? He put his right hand under the overcoat, felt his back.

Wet. Warm.

He felt the need to sit. He put out his hand, found the back of a pew, leaned against it, urgency gone, it didn't matter. He was going to die here, in this ice-cold and sickly-sweet room.

No. A way out of here. Find the door. Follow the wall.

His eyes weren't working. He was underwater, black water, not water, something thicker. Blood. Trying to move in blood. Water and blood. Diab and Dove, he'd killed them both. He couldn't feel his toes move. Couldn't feel his legs. Couldn't breathe. He took his hand off the pew and he felt himself falling, saw something, a pole, tried to grab it.

It was loose, fell with him. Something hit his head. Terrible pain, then nothing.

HE WAS IN the hospital, something cold on his face, they wiped your face with wet towels, it was someone speaking loudly. Not to him. It wasn't close, it was the radio, the television …

Cashin didn't open his eyes. He knew he wasn't in hospital, he was lying on something stone hard. A floor. An icy marble floor. Everything came back.

'Do you remember what you did to me, Duncan?' said the voice. 'How I cried out in pain? How I asked for mercy? Do you remember that, Duncan?'

A silence.

I'm alive, Cashin thought. I'm lying on the floor and I'm alive.

'I was so happy when I found out you'd become a priest, Duncan,' said the voice.

Jamie Bourgoyne. Except he was now his dead cousin, Mark Kingston Denby.

'We've both given ourself to the Lord, Duncan,' said Jamie. 'It changes everything, doesn't it? I was a sinner. I've done bad things, Duncan. I've caused terrible suffering to some of God's creatures. You'll understand that, won't you? Of course, you will. You didn't come to the Lord with a pure heart either.'

A sound of agony.

'The little children, Duncan. Do you think about what our Saviour said? Answer me, Duncan.'

Words, a burbling of words.

'Duncan, our Lord said, Suffer the little children to come unto me. What a wonderful thing to say, wasn't it, Duncan? Suffer the little children to come unto me, and forbid them not, for of such is the kingdom of God.'

The scream filled the chapel, filled Cashin's head, seemed to enter his ear from the marble floor.

'Can I?' said the high voice. 'Give me a chance, Jamie.'

'Soon, soon. I must prepare Duncan. Duncan, the word suffer, what an important word it is. The word *suffer*. In both its meanings. Speak to me, Duncan. Say *Suffer the little children to come unto me*. Say that, Duncan.'

Cashin realised that his eyes were working, there was light. It was candle-light, it moved, flickered, shadows on the wall, they hadn't bothered to switch on the lights, they had lit candles, Dove was dead, they thought he was dead too, or dying quickly. Bleeding out.

Bleeding out.

Vallins was croaking something, trying to form the sentence.

'A child,' said Jamie. 'Duncan, a little boy. Did you ever feel any regret? Any remorse? I don't think so. You and Robin and Crake. I was so sad to hear Crake died while I was in jail. The Lord wanted me to minister to Crake too.'

'Give me a go,' said Justin. 'C'mon Jame.'

Cashin tried to raise himself, he had no strength in his body, he could not move, he should lie here, they would kill Vallins, then they would go. He could hold his breath. Jamie didn't care about him, didn't hate him.

'And in those days shall men seek death,' said Jamie, 'and shall not find it, and shall desire to die, and death shall flee from them. I had to go to prison and live with bad people before I understood those words. Do you understand them now, Duncan?'

'Please, please, please ...' Groans, wretched and terrible sounds.

'I often wanted to die and I couldn't, Duncan. Now I know that the Lord wanted me to live with my torment because he had a purpose for me.'

'Let me, Jame, let me,' said Justin.

'I am he that liveth, and was dead, and behold, I am alive for evermore, Amen, and have the keys of hell and of death. Do you know those words, Duncan? St John the Divine. *The keys of hell and death.* The Lord has given them to me. Is this hell for you, Duncan? Is this?'

I just lie here, thought Cashin. I've killed Dove, they're torturing a man to death. If I live, what'll I say to Singo? Never mind Singo. To Villani. Fin. Birkerts. I'm a policeman, for Christsakes.

'The Lord wants you to know the meaning of pain, of pain and fear, Duncan,' said Jamie. 'He wanted Charles to know that too because of what Charles did to me. And your friend Robin. Do you know, I never forgot your faces, you and Robin? They say children don't remember people. Some do, Duncan, some do, they see them in their nightmares.'

A shriek, a pure scarlet spear of pain.

'Courage, Duncan. Robin didn't have any courage, he was lucky we were so rushed. And Arthur Pollard. I didn't know about Arthur, but in prison the Lord brought me together with a man, a very sad person, and he told me about Arthur.'

'Please, Jesus, ah, ah ...'

'I looked for some to have pity on me but there was no man, neither found I any to comfort me,' said Jamie. 'They gave me gall to eat, and when I was thirsty, they gave me vinegar to drink. Duncan's thirsty, Justin, give him a drink.'

A sound, a gurgling sound, coughing, choking.

'There, that's better, isn't it?'

Silence.

'All done, Duncan, you can't make any more noise now, can you? You look like a pig, Duncan. Are you saying a prayer in your mind? To the beast? You can only pray to the beast, can't you? Here Justin, the Lord wants you to send Duncan to meet his king the beast.'

Cashin pushed himself to his knees, lifted his head, heavy.

Flickering yellow light. A thing was on a bare stone altar, a pink fleshy thing tied with rope, trussed like a piece of meat for roasting. It was bleeding everywhere, blood was running down it in streams.

Two men were standing at the altar. The short one on the right was holding up a knife, the candlelight played on the blade. The other man, taller, was holding the thing, Vallins, holding his head, Cashin could see it was his head, the man, Jamie, was holding Vallins' head by the ears, the hair and the ears, he seemed to be kissing Vallins' head …

No.

Cashin shook his head, he didn't ask his system to shake his head, it shook his head. He tried to stand up. There was something on the floor, a pole, no … yes, a pole with a cross at the top, a brass cross with pointed tips, not arrowheads.

No. Not arrowheads.

Diamonds, yes, diamonds.

He put his hand on it, tried to grasp it, he had no grip, he could not quite feel it.

He grasped it and he stood up, he surprised himself, he was upright and he had the pole with the cross in his right hand.

He was looking at them.

They weren't looking at him. They hadn't heard him.

'Go to the eternal fires, Duncan,' said Jamie. 'Send him, Justin.'

'No,' said Cashin.

They turned their heads.

Cashin threw the pole with the brass cross. It hung in the air. Justin turned, the long knife in his right hand.

The diamond-shaped tip entered his throat, in the hollow, between the clavicle bones. It stuck there, fell back. He raised his hands to his throat, embraced the holy spear, took a step, uncertain step, his left leg abandoned him, he fell, his feet slid on the cold hard floor.

'Under arrest,' said Cashin, thick tongue.

Jamie was holding the head of Vallins, looking down at Justin. 'Justie,' he said. 'Justie.'

He let go of the pig-tied Vallins, went to his knees.

Cashin could see only the top of his head.

'Justie, no,' he said. 'Justie, no, Justie, no, no. Justie no, my darling no, Justie, no, no, nooo …'

Cashin walked back the way he had come. It seemed to take a long time to reach the chapel door. He crossed the entrance hall to the switchboard, found the mains switch.

The sitting room light came on.

Dove's pistol was lying almost at his feet. He bent to pick it up, fell over, got up, tried again, reached the weapon. He didn't look at Dove, walked back to the chapel, through the door, found a light switch, walked down the central aisle, stopped three or four metres from the altar.

Jamie was hunched over Justin. There was blood everywhere. He looked at Cashin, stood up, the knife in his hand.

'Under arrest,' said Cashin.

Jamie shook his head. 'No,' he said. 'I have to kill you now.'

Cashin raised Dove's pistol, aimed at Jamie's chest, you aimed for the broadest part, he pulled the trigger.

Jamie cocked his head like a bird. Smiled.

Missed him, Cashin thought. How did I do that? He couldn't see Jamie properly, the gun was too heavy, he couldn't hold it up.

'The Lord doesn't want me to die,' said Jamie. 'He wants you to die because you took Justin from me.'

He took a pace towards Cashin, held out the knife. Cashin saw the light on it, saw the blood. His legs were going, he couldn't stand any longer, he was going down ...

The knife, Jamie's eyes above it, so close.

'Now you must pray to your father who art in heaven,' said Jamie.

'Our father,' said Cashin.

'SURE YOU don't need a hand with that?' said Michael.

'No,' said Cashin. The small bag was almost weightless – toothbrush, razor, pyjamas, the things his brother had brought to the hospital. They stood waiting for the lift, awkward, shoulder to shoulder.

'I've got a new job,' said Michael. 'In Melbourne. A small firm.'

'That's good,' said Cashin. He had dreamed about Dove, walking down a street with Dove, and then Dove's face had become Shane Diab's.

'Start in a fortnight. I thought I might come down for a week or so. I could help you build. Not that I've ever built anything. I've got some gym muscles though.'

'No experience necessary. Just brute strength.'

The lift came, empty. Inside, they faced the door.

'Joe, I want to ask,' said Michael, eyes on the floor indicator panel. 'It's been on my mind ...'

'What?'

'Going there unarmed. That wasn't a self-destruction thing, was it? I mean ...'

'It was a colossal stupidity and arrogance thing,' said Cashin. 'That's my speciality.'

'There's something else,' said Michael. 'I talked to Vickie, Mum put her on to me.'

'Talked about what?'

'She says to tell you you can see the boy. She's told her partner he's your child.'

Short of breath, Cashin said, 'She's told the boy?'

'Yes.'

The lift stopped, the door opened, Villani was there.

He shook hands with Michael. They went through the sliding doors, down the ramp and along the side of the building. It was between showers, big jagged holes blown in the clouds, a sky to eternity.

'See you in a few days,' said Michael.

'Buy some gloves,' said Cashin. 'Work gloves.'

Finucane had parked the vehicle behind Villani's. He came to meet them.

'G'day, boss,' he said. 'Feelin okay?'

'Fine,' said Cashin.

'Get in for a minute,' said Villani. 'And you, Fin.'

Cashin got in the passenger side. The cop car smell.

'You look like death,' said Villani. 'Are you telling me they don't have those tanning machines?'

'I was shocked too.'

'Anyway, pale or not, you and Dove, you're a charmed fucking pair,' said Villani. 'That's charmed, not charming. He's coming out next week. Clotting power of a lobster, the doc says.'

'A lobster?' said Finucane from the back. 'A lobster?'

'That's what he said. Listen, Joe, stuff to tell you. First, Fin's got some sense out of that loony Dave Vincent. On the phone, mark you. Fin's got his notebook. Speak Fin.'

Finucane coughed. 'He was at the camp the night of the fire,' he said. 'Called Dave Curnow then, the name of his foster family. He says he was supposed to go to some concert thing but he was planning to run away and he hid. Then two men arrived and they took a body out of the back of the car. Small body, he says.'

Cashin was looking at the road, not seeing the traffic.

'They took it into the building where the boys slept. Then they left and he says he saw flames inside the building. He ran away and he slept on the beach and the next day he hitched a lift and he was gone. Ended up in WA, a boy age twelve.'

'What did the autopsies on the dead boys show?' said Cashin.

'Local doctor did them,' said Finucane. 'I gather that's the way it was then. Smoke inhalation killed them.'

'All three.'

'That's right.'

'No mention of anything else?'

'Nothing, boss.'

Cashin regretted eating breakfast, a sick feeling rising in him. 'Remember the doctor's name?'

'I've got it here. Castleman, Dr Rodney Castleman. Signed Bourgoyne's wife's death certificate too. A busy GP.'

Helen's father. Cecily Addison said:

Lots of people took an interest. Public-spirited place then, Cromarty. People did good works, didn't do it to get their names in the paper either. Virtue is its own reward.

'Here's something weird,' said Villani. 'Dave Vincent remembers the car that night.'

'Got a thing about cars, Dave,' said Finucane. 'He says it was a Merc station wagon. He knows that because it was the first wagon Mercedes made. 1979.'

'Was that useful?' said Cashin.

'I tracked it.'

'Let me guess. Bourgoyne.'

'Company car. Charles Bourgoyne and someone called J. A. Cameron were directors.'

'Jock Cameron. Local solicitor. Who was the Companion there that night?'

'Vallins,' said Villani.

'Got a smoke?' said Cashin.

Villani took out a packet and pushed in the lighter. They waited in silence, lit up.

The nicotine hit Cashin like a headbutt, he couldn't speak for a while, then he said, 'Jesus, how did they get away with it? Ran the camp as a brothel, murdered at least three boys, not a murmur. What kind of fucking investigation was there?'

Villani ran down the front windows, a smell of exhaust fumes, of newly spread bitumen. 'Something else to tell you. Singo died two days ago. Another stroke. Big time.'

'Shit,' said Cashin. 'Well. Shit.' He felt tears coming, turned his head away from Villani, blinked rapidly.

'Singo did the Companions fire,' said Villani. 'He was number two then.'

Cashin saw Singo in his exhausted riven raincoat, saw the burnt ruins in that place, the goalposts in the grass, the little belt. Singo had never mentioned Cromarty. Late at night, drink taken, he talked about jobs in Stawell and Mildura and Geelong and Sale and Shepparton, about the travelling prostitute murders in Bendigo, the man who killed his uncle and aunt on the tobacco farm near Bright, planned to turn them into silage and feed them to the pigs.

Singo never spoke of Cromarty.

'I got a bad feeling,' said Villani. He shifted, uncomfortable. 'We pulled his bank records. I never thought that day would come, not if I lived to … anyway, nothing. Just his pay and dividends from some Foster's shares.'

'He wouldn't drink their beer,' said Cashin. 'He hated their beer.'

Villani looked at him in a hopeless way, opened his window and flicked his butt, almost hit a seagull, caused it to hop. Cashin thought about the meeting on the pier, the gull catching the stub in mid-air.

'Three years ago,' said Villani, 'Singo inherited a million bucks from his brother. Derek. Derek left the whole family rich. About fourteen million in the estate.'

'Yes?' said Cashin.

'Singo's like a fuckin parrot on my shoulder, I'm where I am because of him. Think the job's done, son? Well, go the extra yard. Ninety-nine times, it's a waste. But then there's the one. So I went the yard, we went the yard.'

Fat raindrops on the windscreen. Cashin thought that he wanted to be home now, in the buggered old house, in the buggered old chair, he wanted the dogs burrowing their noses into the cushions beneath his thighs, the fire going, the music. He wanted Björling. It would be Björling first. Björling and then Callas.

'Someone paid two hundred thousand dollars into brother Derek's three bank accounts in 1983,' said Villani. 'Three days after the Cromarty fire. Then, after the inquest, Derek got another two hundred grand. He bought land on the Gold Coast. No cunt, Derek.'

Cashin looked at Villani. Villani held his gaze, deep lines between his eyebrows, nodded, small nods, drew on his cigarette, tried to blow smoke out of the window. It came back.

'Singo took money from Bourgoyne?'

'Paid from a company bank account. You have to go back through three other companies to find it's a Bourgoyne outfit.'

Cashin thought that there was no firm ground in life. Just crusts of different thicknesses over the ooze. They sat in silence, watching three nurses going off duty, level as cricket stumps, the one in the middle moving her hands as if conducting an orchestra.

'It's like two deaths to me,' said Villani. 'I woke today, something's missing, something's gone.'

'Anything else?' said Cashin. 'Any other bits and pieces I should be aware of? No? I'll be on my way home then, thank you for coming.'

'Fin's driving,' said Villani. 'Birkerts's down there, he's finished, he'll bring him back. Don't like that, you can take a cab, take a fucking walk.'

Cashin wanted to argue but he had no strength.

'There is something else,' said Villani. 'Singo's lawyer rang. We're in the will, you and me and Birk.'

'Last untainted place in the force, homicide,' said Cashin. 'The Salvos can have my share.'

When they were on the road, Cashin said, 'Fin, I need to go to Queen Street. Won't take long.'

ERICA BOURGOYNE, handsome and severe in black, was standing behind a glass-topped desk. 'I really don't have time today,' she said. 'So can we keep this as brief as possible?'

'We can,' said Cashin.

He took his time, looked around the big wood-panelled office, at the glass-fronted bookshelves, the leather client chairs, the fresh violets in a cut-glass vase on the windowsill, the bare plane branches outside.

'Very nice office,' he said.

'Please get on with it.' Head on one side, the voice and face of a schoolteacher with a dim pupil.

'I thought I might put a few things to you. Propositions.'

She looked at her watch. 'I can give you five minutes. To the second.'

'Your brother was sexually abused by your step-father and you know that.'

Erica sat down, blinking as if something had lodged in her eyes.

'Jamie and Justin Fischer tortured and killed Arthur Pollard and I think you know that. Jamie and Justin murdered a man called Robin Gray Bonney in Sydney and you may or may not know that.'

Erica held up her hands. 'Detective, this is absolutely ...'

'Why didn't you tell me, tell anyone, that Mrs Laidlaw had seen Jamie?'

A vague gesture. 'Moira's getting on, she can't be relied upon ...'

'Mrs Laidlaw appeared to me to be in complete command of her faculties. She had no doubt that she saw Jamie. And you believed her, didn't you? That's when you hired the security. It was before Charles was bashed.'

'Detective Cashin, you've overstepped the mark. I can see no point in going on with this.'

'We can do it in a formal interview,' said Cashin. 'Put the day on hold and come down to St Kilda Road. It's probably better that way. You're the one who's overstepped a mark. You're looking at conspiracy.'

Silence. She held his gaze but he saw the sign.

'You spoke to Jamie, didn't you?' said Cashin.

'No.'

Erica closed her eyes. He could see the tracery of veins. Cashin said what had been on his mind for a long time. 'Just the two of you after your mother's accident. All alone at night in that big house with Charles. What happened at night, Erica?'

'Joe, please, no.' Her chin was on her chest, a piece of hair fell across her brow. 'Please, Joe.'

'What happened to you in that house, Erica?'

Silence.

'Did you become Charles's little wife? Was it before or after your mother's death? You followed him around. You worshipped him. Did you know those men were fucking Jamie? Did you know Charles was?'

She had begun to shake. 'No, no, no ...' It was not a denial. It was a plea for him to stop.

'Still believe your mother's death was an accident, do you, Erica? The same night as the fire at the Companions camp, remember that? Three boys died that night. Charles killed one of them with his own hands at The Heights. Did your mother see something? Hear something?'

'Joe, no, please, I can't ...'

Cashin looked at her bowed head, saw the pale skin of her scalp, her hands clenched at her throat.

Erica did not raise her head, she was saying something inaudible, saying it to herself, again and again and again, saying a mantra.

Cashin knew about mantras. He had said a million mantras, against pain, against thought, against memory, against the night that would not surrender its dark.

She straightened in her chair, she was trying to regain her composure.

Cashin waited.

'What does it matter now, Joe?' she said, voice drained of life, an old voice. 'Why do you want to drag this from me? Do you get pleasure from this?'

'The bodyguard,' said Cashin. 'What was that about?'

'A client threatened me.'

'I don't believe you. I think you always knew Jamie was alive. You were protective of him but you were also scared of him. That's right, isn't it?'

No reply.

'You watched them torture Pollard, didn't you? There was one seat down in the hall. Just one. You sat there, Erica.'

She was crying silently, tears gouging her makeup.

'Did Charles hand you on to Pollard, Erica? Pollard liked young girls too. We found the pictures in his computer. You wanted Jamie to kill Charles and Pollard, didn't you? You couldn't be there for Charles but you weren't going to miss Pollard. That's right, isn't it.'

Erica began to sob, louder and louder, her head down, her upper body shaking.

'Did you stay to the end, Erica? Did you clap when they raised him? Did it cleanse you?'

A woman crying, her whole body crying, her whole being crying.

Cashin stood.

'You're a sick person, Ms Bourgoyne,' he said. 'Sickness has bred sickness. Thanks for your time.'

Solid rain was falling on Queen Street. Fin was double-parked, obstructing the traffic, reading the paper.

'How was that, boss?' he said.

'Pretty ordinary,' said Cashin. 'Take me home, son.'

THE DOGS were unrecognisable.

'What have you done to them?' said Cashin. 'Look at those ears.'

'They've been properly clipped and groomed for the first time in their lives,' said his mother. 'They loved it.'

'They're in shock. They need counselling.'

'I think they should stay here. They're happy here. I don't think they want to go back to that ruin.'

Cashin walked to the vehicle and opened a back door. The dogs looked, didn't move.

'See, Joseph,' said his mother. 'See.'

Cashin whistled, one clear whistle, and jerked his thumb at the door. The dogs raced for the vehicle, managed to get through the doorway abreast, sat bolt upright, looking straight ahead.

Cashin closed the door. 'I'll bring them to visit,' he said.

'Often,' said his mother. 'Bonzo loves them. They're his best dog friends.'

Cashin thought he saw a tear. 'I'll drop them off to see Bonzo when I go to town,' he said. 'Provided there's no dioxin spraying going on.' He went over and kissed her.

'You should think about counselling, Joseph,' she said, holding his head. 'Your life is the most awful litany of horrors.'

'Just a run of bad luck.' He got in.

She came to the window. 'They like chicken, have you got chicken?'

'They like fillet steak too. They get dead animals I find by the roadside. Bye, Syb.'

Driving home with the last pink in the west, the night taking the land ditch by ditch, hollow by hollow. At the crossroads, he switched on the lights and, five minutes later, they panned across the dark house and a man leaning against the wall, smoking a cigarette, holding a torch.

Rebb came to the vehicle, opened the back door for the dogs. 'Sweet Jesus,' he said, 'you traded the dogs?'

They leapt on him, ecstatic.

'Don't blame me,' said Cashin. 'My mother did it. I thought you'd gone?'

'Went, nothin there, come back this way,' Rebb said. 'Old bloke not walking too good. So I thought I might as well give him a hand, do a bit of work on the cathedral in between.'

They walked around, looked by torchlight at what Rebb had done.

'Bit,' said Cashin. 'Call that a bit?'

'Bern come around, give me a hand. Bad mouth on him, Bern, but he works.'

'The works part is news to me. He's got a good memory, that I know.'

'Yeah?' Rebb shone the light on a new wall, walked over and ran a finger along the pointing.

'The day he brought the water tank. He remembered you from all those years ago, when you were kids. Played footy against you. Against the Companions camp.'

Rebb said, 'Well, that's news to me. Never heard of the Companions camp.' He turned the torch on the dogs.

'I've got a picture of you,' said Cashin. 'Eating an orange slice. Age about twelve.'

'Never been twelve,' said Rebb. 'I could make a bunny pie. Took the popgun again.'

'Anything happen to you there?'

Cashin thought Rebb smiled.

'Just stayed the one day,' Rebb said. 'Didn't like the food.'

'I've got steak,' said Cashin. 'How's that?'

'That'll do. The neighbour was here. Left something for you. Wrapped like a present.'

'I need a present,' said Cashin. 'Long time since anyone gave me a present.'

'Being alive's a present,' said Rebb. 'Every minute of every hour of every day.'

IN THE late afternoon, Cashin took the dogs. They put up the first hares close to the house, the creatures grown bold in their absence. Then, in the meadow, they interrupted a communion of rabbits. The dogs ran themselves to exhaustion, put not a tooth on fur.

At the creek, the dogs strode in, got wet to the shoulder, stood in holes, scrambled, alarmed. Cashin got wet too, up to the knees, water inside his boots. He didn't care, slopped up the hill, thinking about what he should do. In the end, he didn't have to make a decision, he saw her coming down the slope from her house.

They met at the corner post, Rebb's corner post, said hello. She looked thinner, better looking than he remembered.

'They're tired,' she said. 'What've you done to them?'

He summoned up saliva to speak. 'Unfit,' said Cashin. 'Too fat, too slow. Spoilt. That's going to change.'

'How are you, Joe?'

'Fine. I'm fine. Flesh wound. Plus I'm really brave and I never complain.'

Helen shook her head. 'I wanted to come and see you but I thought … well, I don't know what I thought. I thought you'd be surrounded by your family and your cop friends.'

The dogs took off, talk was boring, they wanted action.

'Good thinking,' said Cashin. 'That's the way it was, night and day. They worked shifts, family, cop friends, family.'

'You prick. See Bobby Walshe on television?'

'No.'

'He said you and Dove deserved medals.'

'For stupidity? I don't think they've got that.'

Helen shook her head. 'And the news about the resort?'

'No.'

'Erica Bourgoyne decided not to sell the Companions camp to Fyfe. She's giving it to the state to be part of the coastal reserve. So there's no access to the mouth and the whole resort project collapses.'

Cashin thought about the seat in the Companions hall, Erica in her office, the marks of tears on her cream silk shirt, the sobbing.

'That's good,' he said. 'Leaves you free to concentrate on winning the election.'

'I'm counting on getting at least one cop vote.'

'Depends on a number of things falling into place. But we cops aren't allowed to talk politics.'

'Allowed to drink?'

'My liver is in near-new condition. Nothing to do for weeks.'

They looked at each other, he broke away, saw the dusk in the creek hollow, the treetops moving on the hill. 'I always meant to ask. When did your dad die?'

'In 1988. He didn't take a bend on the coast road. The year after we finished school. Why?'

'Nothing. He signed Bourgoyne's wife's death certificate.'

'Signed hundreds, I imagine.'

'Yes.'

'So. Come up for a drink? I could feed you.'

'Is that party pies?'

'We didn't get around to them last time.'

'Feed these beasts first,' he said. 'I'll be back.'

'Don't get waylaid,' she said.

'Waylaid. I've never heard anyone say that word.'

'You're a work in progress,' she said. 'There are words to come.'

He set off up the rise, legs like logs, whistled the dogs, and he looked back and she had not moved, she was watching him.

'Go home,' he shouted. 'Why don't you just go home and put on the party pies.'

He woke lying on his side. Above the window blind was a line of daylight, the colour of smoke. He could feel her warmth against him and then she stirred and he felt her breath on the skin between his shoulderblades and then her lips moved against his spine, and then she pressed them to him and she kissed. The world opened, the day began, he felt that he was alive again, forgiven.

'JOE?'

'Yes.'

'Carol Gehrig. Early for you?'

'No.'

'Joe, this is rubbish but last night, had a few wines, it came into me head.'

'What?'

'There was chockie wrappers in the bin a few times. Twice.'

'Yes?'

'Well, he didn't eat em,' Carol said. 'Nothin sweet in the place. Didn't even have sugar in his tea.'

'You saw chocolate wrappers in the kitchen bin?'

'Not the kitchen bin. The big one outside. Saw em when I put the stuff in. Mars bars and that shit.'

'Well, someone staying?'

'No. Not then.'

'Twice?'

'Well, I remember twice. Wastin your time with rubbish?'

Rebb came into sight, coming home from Den's cows, a dog on each flank, looking around like bodyguards, alert for assassins hiding in the grass.

'Never,' he said. 'Any idea when?'

'I know the one, it was Kirstie's birthday the day before and I'd had this ... anyhow, the day. A Monday, twenty-three seven and it's 1988. That's for sure. Yes.'

23.07.88.

'Interesting,' said Cashin. 'Think about the other time. A month would help, a year. Even winter or summer.'

'I'll think.'

They said goodbye and he stayed where he was, in his mind the image of Bourgoyne's nine pots, all the pieces the perfectionist had thought worth keeping. Into the base of one was scratched a date: 11/6/88.

Was that the day it was made? Could you upturn a newly-thrown pot that size and scratch a date on the bottom? Or did that come later?

He went to the telephone, looked at it for a while, thinking about being upstairs in the old brick building at The Heights, looking back and registering the bolt on the bedroom door.

If you walked up the hill on a night when the kiln was burning, you would hear it before you saw it – it would be a powerful sound, a vibrating, a thrumming. And when you rounded the woodpile, you would see the fire holes glowing white hot, they would light the clearing, and you would feel on your face the force of the sea wind that was blowing into the kiln's mouth.

He dialled the direct number. It rang and rang and then Tracy answered, more reprimand than greeting.

'It's Joe,' he said. 'Do me a favour, Trace. Kids missing in June, July, 1988. Boys.'

'No end to it,' she said.

'Not on this earth.'

A morning of sunlight on the round winter hill, above it cloud strands fleeing inland, and the wind on the long grass, annoying it, strumming it.

A bark at the door, another, more urgent, the dogs taking turns. He let them in and they surrounded him and he was glad to have them and to be there.

IN THE EVIL DAY

For Horst and for Dorle
with gratitude for friendship, hospitality and kindness,
for laughter, good times and stimulating conversation

1

JOHANNESBURG …

NIEMAND CAME in at 2 pm, stripped, put on shorts, went to the empty room, did the weights routine, ran on the treadmill for an hour. He hated the treadmill, had to steel his mind to endure it, blank out. Running was something you did outdoors. But outdoors had become trouble, like being attacked by three men, one with a nail-studded piece of wood. The trouble had cut both ways: several of his attackers he had kissed off quickly.

Still, you could not pass into the trance-like state when you had to break off from running to fight and kill people. So, resentfully, he had given up running outside.

Niemand didn't get any pleasure from killing. Some people did. In the Zambesi Valley in the early days, and then in Mozambique and Angola and Sierra Leone and other places, he had seen men in killing frenzies, shooting anyone – young, old, female, male, shooting chickens and dogs and cows and pigs and goats.

In command, he had dealt with soldiers for this kind of behaviour. The first was Barends, the white corporal the men had called *Pielstyf* because he liked to display his erection when drunk. Niemand had executed him with two shots, upwards into the base of his skull, come up behind him when he was firing his LMG into a crowded bus. The military court found the action justified in that Barends had twice failed to obey a lawful command and posed a threat to discipline in a combat situation.

The second man was a black soldier, a Zulu trained by white instructors, a veteran killer of African National Congress supporters in Natal, in love with blood and the hammer of automatic fire. In Sierra Leone, on patrol in the late afternoon, the Zulu had shot a child, a girl, and then shot the old woman with her, the child's grandmother perhaps, but it could have been her mother, the women aged so quickly. Niemand had him tied to a tree, a poor specimen of a tree, had the villagers gathered. He told the interpreter to apologise for what had happened, then he dispatched the Zulu with a handgun, one shot, close range, there was no other sensible way. The man looked him in the eyes, didn't blink, didn't plead, even when the muzzle was almost touching his left eye. There was no military court to face this time. Niemand had become a mercenary by then, saving the sum of things for pay, and his employers didn't give a shit about a man killed unless you wanted him replaced: one less pay packet.

The third time was at a roadblock. A fellow-mercenary called Powell, a redheaded Englishman, a Yorkshireman, a deserter from two armies, had for no good reason opened fire on three men in a car, two white journalists and their black driver. He killed the driver outright and wounded one of the white men. When Niemand arrived, Powell told him he was going to execute the survivors, blame it on rebels. Niemand argued with him while the unhurt journalist tried to stop his friend's bleeding. Powell wouldn't listen, high as a kite, pupils like saucers, put his pistol to the man's head. Niemand stood back, took one swing with his rifle, held by the barrel, broke Powell's freckled neck. He drove the journalists to the hospital.

Niemand showered under the hosepipe he had run from the rainwater tank on the roof when the water was cut off. Then he lay down on the hard bed, fell asleep thinking about all the other killings, the ones that were the means to the ends. Other people's ends.

The alarm was set for 5.30 pm but he woke before it sounded, showered again, dressed in his uniform of denims, T-shirt, gun rig, loose cotton jacket, left the building by the stairs. The lift didn't work but even when it did, no one used it except as a lavatory or to shoot up. He walked with his right hand inside his coat, the .38 shrouded-hammer Colt out of its clip above his left hip. He stayed close to the inside wall. That way, you bumped head-on into dangerous men coming up. They always hugged the inside wall. And if you encountered one of them, then the quickest man won.

Niemand didn't doubt for one instant that he would be the quickest.

The car was waiting at the kerb, engine running, an old Mercedes, dents everywhere, rust at the bottom of the doors, no hubcaps. The driver was smoking a cigarette, looking around at the street. It was crowded, a third-world street full of shouting hawkers, idlers, street boys, garishly made-up prostitutes, black illegal immigrants from all over Africa the locals called *maKwerekwere*, interlopers who eyed their surroundings warily. This was the fringe of the old business district of Johannesburg, Hillbrow, a suburb long abandoned by all the whites who could afford to move to more secure areas. Not secure areas, only less dangerous areas. Nowhere was secure, not even buildings with dogs and razor wire and four kinds of alarms and round-the-clock security.

It had never occurred to Niemand to move. He had no possessions he valued, had been looking after himself since he was fifteen, didn't care where he lived. He couldn't sleep for more than a few hours unless he was physically exhausted, what did it matter where he slept?

Zeke saw him coming, reached across and unlocked the door. Niemand got in.

'Rosebank,' he said.

'You always look so fucken clean,' said Zeke. He took the vehicle into the street. No one driving the car would mistake it for an old Mercedes. Which it wasn't, except for the body. The driver's full name was Ezekiel Mkane.

His father had been a policeman, a servant of the apartheid state, and Zeke had grown up in a police compound, a member of a client class, no respect from whites, utter loathing and contempt from blacks. A smart boy, good at languages, a reader, Zeke had nowhere to go. He joined the army, put in sixteen years, took in three bullets, two exited, one extracted, and shrapnel, some bits still there.

'That's because I'm white,' said Niemand. He had known Zeke for a long time.

'You're not all that white,' said Mkane. 'Bit of ancestral tan.'

'That's the Greek part of me. The Afrikaner part's pure white. You kaffirs get cheekier every day.'

'Ja, baas. But we're in charge now.'

'We? Forget it. Money's in charge. Took me a long time to understand that. Money's always in charge.'

Niemand's mobile rang. It was Christa, who ran the office. 'After Mrs Shawn,' she said, 'Jan Smuts, flight 701, arriving 8.45 pm, a Mr Delamotte and his personal assistant, whatever that fucken means.'

'His travelling screw, that's what it means,' Niemand said.

'Ja, well, at the British Airways desk. To the Plaza, Sandton. He had a bad experience in a taxi last time he was here.'

Niemand repeated the details.

'Right,' said Christa. 'Then it's two restaurant pick-ups, both late. They've got your number. Zeke's due to knock off at 11. Can he stay on? Coupla hours.'

They were out of the inner city, in dense traffic heading for the northern suburbs. 'In a hurry tonight?' Niemand said to Zeke. 'Couple of hours, probably.'

'Some people have plans, you know.'

'What about you?'

'Double time?'

'Double time.'

Zeke raised a thumb. He saw a gap and put his foot down. The Mercedes responded like a Porsche.

Mrs Shawn was waiting with a shopping centre security guard. She was about forty, pretty, too much sun on her skin, slightly tipsy, a flush on the prominent cheekbones. She'd had a long lunch, gone shopping. Probably had a swim before lunch, Niemand thought, a swim and a lie in the sun. The guard put her purchases into the boot, four bags, and she gave him several notes.

'This *smells* like a new car,' she said as they queued to get into the early evening traffic on Corlett Drive. She was English, Yorkshire. Niemand knew the accent from the old days, the Rhodesia days. Lots of people from Yorkshire in Rhodesia.

'It is a new car,' said Niemand. 'In an old body.'

'God,' she said, 'that's how I feel.'

Niemand smiled, didn't say anything. He could feel that she wanted to flirt. They often did, these rich women, but it was bad for business. He'd screwed a few in the beginning but no good came of it. One took to phoning six times a day, then for some reason confessed to her husband when Niemand wouldn't take the calls. They'd lost the company's business, at least twenty thousand rand a year, and he'd narrowly escaped being fired. That was too much to pay for a fuck you couldn't even remember.

'People down the street got hit two weeks ago,' she said. 'The car got in behind them before the security gate could close. Three men. Fortunately, they settled for money. He had a few thousand in his safe.'

'Lucky,' said Niemand. 'Mostly it's your money and your life.' He switched on the thin fibre-optic rear-view screen in the roof of the car, looked up. It was providing a 120-degree view of the road behind but it could cover 160 degrees.

'Wow,' said Mrs Shawn. 'That's technology. My husband'd crave that.'

'When we get there,' said Niemand, 'we want to be inside quickly. How does it open?'

'Remote,' she said. 'You punch in the code.'

'How far away?'

'You have to be at the gates.'

'Put in the code now.'

Mrs Shawn searched in her bag, found a device. 'I can't see,' she said. She was too vain to put on her reading glasses, held the control close to her face and tentatively pressed soft buttons.

'I *think* I've done it,' she said.

Zeke turned his head to Niemand, who kept his eyes on the rear-view screen.

The house was in a leafy street in Saxonwold, a rich part of the city. It was one of four large mock-Georgian houses built on land carved from the grounds of a mansion. The perimeter walls were three metres high, topped with razor wire. As Zeke drew up in front of the steel gates, Niemand opened his door.

'Open them,' said Niemand. 'Close as soon as you're in, Mrs Shawn.'

'It's very fast,' she said.

'Me too.'

Niemand was out, on the edge of the kerb, looking around. Early summer Highveld dusk, fresh-smelling, hint of jacaranda blossom in a broad street, no traffic, a calm street, a stockbrokers' street, a place to come home to, have a swim, pour a big scotch, shed the cares of the day. There was a sharp sound, the gates unmated, and Zeke drove into the driveway, a walled corridor leading to the doors of a three-car garage.

Niemand, walking backwards, got inside just before the gates met.

On the driver's side, a 14-inch security monitor was mounted against the wall under a small roof. Mrs Shawn handed Zeke another remote control. With Niemand leaning against the car, they went on a video tour of the house, room by room, two-camera vision. It was furnished in a stark style, steel louvre internal shutters instead of curtains, not many places to hide. Beside the monitor a green light glowed. It meant that no window and no door, internal or external, had been opened or closed since the alarm was activated.

'Looks okay,' said Niemand. 'Let's see the garage.'

There was one vehicle in it, a black Jeep four-wheel drive. A camera at floor level showed no one hiding underneath it.

Niemand gestured.

Mrs Shawn used the remote.

The left-hand door rose. Pistol out, held at waist level in front of his body, Niemand went in, looked into the Jeep, waved to Zeke. He parked behind the Jeep, and the garage door descended. Zeke took the short-barrel, pistol-handled automatic shotgun out of its clips under the driver's seat.

Mrs Shawn unlocked the steel door into the house with a card and a key. Niemand went first, Zeke behind him.

They were in a hallway painted in tones of grey, mulberry carpet, a single painting under a downlight, a print, Cezanne. Niemand liked paintings, even paintings he didn't understand. He bought art books sometimes, threw them out after a while.

Mrs Shawn disarmed the alarm system.

'Wait here,' said Niemand.

She shook her head vigorously. 'No, I don't want to be on my own.'

Niemand in front, they went into a passage, then into every room. He opened every cupboard, every wardrobe, Zeke covering him. The beds were all box, no way to hide under them.

In the sitting room, for the second time, Niemand said, 'You can relax, Mrs Shawn.'

He holstered the pistol, didn't feel relaxed.

She went into the kitchen and came back holding a bottle of champagne, Veuve Clicquot, and a flute, a crystal flute. 'I'm having a glass of bubbly,' she said. 'This all makes me so tense. There's everything else. Beer, scotch, whatever.'

The men shook their heads. 'You're expecting Mr Shawn when?' said Niemand.

She brought her watch up to her face. 'Any time now, any time. Can you get the top of this off for me?' She held out the bottle to Niemand. He took it and offered it to Zeke, who put the shotgun on a chair.

'He does champagne,' Niemand said. 'I do beer bottles. With my teeth.'

Mrs Shawn smiled, a wary smile, uncertain of Niemand's drift, whether she'd been wrong in automatically asking the white man. Zeke stripped off the foil, removed the cage, wriggled the cork out slowly, no bang, just a whimper of gas, poured.

'Thank you,' said Mrs Shawn. 'You are an expert.'

Zeke smiled and took the bottle into the kitchen.

Mrs Shawn drank half the glass. 'Jesus, that's better,' she said. 'Let's sit.'

They sat on the leather chairs. Zeke came out of the kitchen. 'Calls to make,' he said. He left the room, closed the door. Mrs Shawn knocked back the rest of her glass, went into the kitchen. Niemand heard a cupboard open, close. Silence. She came back with a full glass and the bottle.

'Well,' said Mrs Shawn, sitting, smiling the smile, crossing her legs. Niemand knew the coke smile. He looked at her legs. They were brown legs, filling out in the thighs, the feet in soft-looking shoes. 'Home at last,' she said. 'You're very professional ... what do I call you?'

'Mike,' said Niemand. He held her eyes, smiled, looked at his watch. He had a bad feeling about this house, the kind of feeling that had sometimes come over him on patrol, brought on by nothing in particular. 'The houses next door, you know the people?'

She drank. 'Well, we're the longest survivors in the row here. What, two months, just under. Can you believe that?' She closed her eyes, stubby eyelashes. 'I was so naive when we came. I mean, I thought it'd be like Malaysia. I lived there with my first husband, we had this lovely house in KL – the poor don't bother you there. Jesus, what a shock I got. I hate this fucking country, I'd be back in the UK tomorrow ...'

Niemand was already tired of listening to her. He was forced to listen to people like her every day. To some people, he called his business Parasite Protection.

'... Bloody Brett told me it was going to be for two or three weeks. Then people are buggering him around, the deal falls through, next thing ...'

'Don't know the neighbours?' Niemand said.

She blinked, had trouble adjusting. 'Well, I see the people on that side every now and then.' She gestured with a thumb to the left. 'To wave to. They're Americans. With live-in security. An Israeli. He used to be one of the Prime Minister's bodyguards. Christ knows what that costs.'

'The other side?'

'Empty. They left a few weeks ago. Only here for a few months. Lucky them.' A phone rang, in two places. She drained her glass, went to the kitchen.

There was something wrong here.

Niemand went into the passage, looked up and down, went into the dining room, a formal dining room with a big blond table and ten chairs. Zeke was on his mobile, half-sitting on the table. He looked at Niemand, raised an eyebrow. Niemand shrugged, went back to the sitting room.

Mrs Shawn was coming out of the kitchen, glass refilled.

'My husband,' she said. 'He'll be here in a minute. He's going to London tomorrow. Won't take me. Sometimes I think he'd like to see me murdered.'

Niemand felt some of his feeling go away, went out to escort the husband in. The driveway and street outside were floodlit, bright as day, and as the man drove the Audi past him, he saw a chubby face.

In the garage, the man got out, briefcase in his left hand, looked at his watch. He was short and paunchy and even an expensive suit didn't improve that.

'Just you?' he said.

Niemand shook his head. 'My partner's inside.'

The man looked at him. He'd been drinking, face flushed. 'What colour's he?'

'Black.'

'No blacks in the house. Don't trust any black.' He pointed at the floor. 'Next time, he waits here.'

This man should be allowed to die violently, thought Niemand. He didn't say anything, walked to the door into the house and waited.

The man came over and opened the door. Niemand went in first, went through the hall, into the sitting room. The woman was standing in the kitchen doorway, champagne flute in hand. Zeke was sitting in a leather chair, the shotgun on his thighs.

Brett Shawn dropped the briefcase on a chair, was taking off his jacket, didn't look at his wife, eyes on Zeke, threw the expensive garment sideways, careless of where it fell, walked to the middle of the room, made a stand-up sign to Zeke, palm upwards, short fingers held together, flicking urgently.

'Up,' he said. 'On your bike. Don't pay a bloody fortune to have people sit on my bloody furniture.'

Zeke's expression didn't change. He stood, weapon at the end of a slack arm, looked at Niemand. Niemand nodded at Mrs Shawn.

'Thank you,' she said. 'Thank you both.'

Brett Shawn went into the passage first, Zeke behind him. Shawn was at the door to the hall, had his hand on the door handle, when the hair on the back of Niemand's skull pricked. He looked up, saw something on the ceiling behind him, something at the edge of his vision, a dark line not there before, shouted Zeke's name, spinning around, finding the pistol at his waist, throwing himself away from the line of sight, hitting the floor, rolling into position.

The man in the ceiling pushed open the inspection hatch, fired a pumpgun, hit Shawn in the side of his belly as he turned around, in the pinstriped shirt distended over the sagging gut, almost cut him in half, fired again. Zeke raised his shotgun and fired at the ceiling without turning, just his head tilted backwards, deafening noise in the corridor. Then Zeke's head blew apart, a balloon of blood and bone and pink and grey material exploding.

Niemand had the .38 out, was about to fire into the roof behind the inspection hatch, didn't.

Waited.

Silence.

A noise overhead, a bumping sound.

Waited.

A shortened shotgun dropped into the passage. Then a bare arm and a shoulder in a T-shirt fell through the hatch. A dark hand dangled.

Niemand registered the voice of Mrs Shawn screaming. He paid no attention, reached forward, got Zeke's shotgun, ran his hand over his friend's head, smeared his own throat and chest with Zeke's blood, lay back and looked at the hatch.

Mrs Shawn stopped screaming.

Behind him, the door to the sitting room opened. Niemand closed his eyes.

Mrs Shawn screamed again, slammed the door.

Niemand lay on the mulberry carpet, shotgun at his side, eyes closed, looking through his lashes at the hatch.

Nothing. Just blood running down the bare arm, down the fingers, dripping.

Mrs Shawn was shouting. She was on the telephone. She'd got through to someone. Niemand couldn't make out the words.

They'd been in the ceiling all the time. They'd come via the empty house next door, probably bridged the gap between the roofs with a ladder.

Niemand waited. His sight was going fuzzy. No sound from above.

Dead or gone, he thought.

He tensed his shoulder muscles, readied himself to get up.

A scraping noise.

The gunman's body fell through the hatch, landed in front of him, just missed his feet, blood going everywhere.

He'd been pushed.

Niemand didn't move, didn't breathe.

The other person in the ceiling didn't have a firearm, his instinct told him that. And the person was running out of time: the rest of the team would be close now, waiting to have the gates opened for them. If it didn't happen soon, they would probably desert him.

Seen through his lashes, the hatch was just a black square.

Nothing happened.

Niemand heard the door to the sitting room open.

Mrs Shawn didn't scream this time, she said, in a small voice, a child's voice, 'Oh, Jesus, God, are you all dead?'

Niemand was looking at the hatch through his lashes.

Nothing.

Feet first.

The black man came out of the hole feet first, just stepped into air, dropped from the roof like an acrobat, long butcher's knife held to his chest.

Mrs Shawn screamed, high-pitched, the scream of steel meeting steel at great speed.

The man landed feet astride his partner's body, a slightly built man, perfectly balanced, as if he'd jumped from a chair, knife hand down, the blade pointed at Mrs Shawn.

'Shut up, bitch,' he said.

He looked at Niemand lying on the floor, didn't change his grip on the knife, took a step forward, bent at the waist, took his arm back to put the blade into Niemand's groin, sever the femoral artery.

'No!' Mrs Shawn, the abrading metal shriek.

Niemand opened his eyes, raised the shotgun, pulled the trigger, heard the hammer fall.

Nothing. Shell malfunction, one in five thousand chance.

The man lunged.

Niemand brought his right leg up, kicked as hard as he could, his shin just below the knee made contact with the man's crotch, a shout of pain, he saw the knife hand move away, sat up, braced himself on his left hand, hooked his left knee around the man's right calf, rolled savagely to the left, right knee pressing in the man's upper thigh.

He felt the joint give, tendons, cartilage tearing, saw the man hit the wall with his shoulder, head turning sideways, mouth open and twisted in pain and surprise, saw the teeth and the furred tongue, the knife hand coming around, the knife huge, shining. Pain in his shoulder. He grabbed for the man's wrist with his left hand, clubbed at his head with the shotgun, laid the short barrel across his jaw and his ear, pulled the weapon back ...

The shotgun went off, a shocking concussion. Niemand hadn't realised he'd pulled the trigger.

For a second, they were frozen, two men, one black, one white, legs twisted and locked together, faces close, looking into each other's eyes.

He's strong, Niemand thought.

The man got his right hand on the shotgun barrel, had the advantage of pushing. Niemand felt the strength leaving his left arm, he was going to lose this, he wasn't the quickest this time, he could see the knife blade, see his blood on it.

No. He couldn't die here, in this bastard's house, in the service of this English prick.

He let his right arm go slack, caught the black man by surprise, pushed the shotgun barrel at him, pulled the trigger.

It worked. Eyes closed against the muzzle flash, he saw its furnace flame through his lids, felt it burn his face, felt the man go limp, felt hot liquid in his mouth and his eyes and up his nostrils.

After a time, ears ringing, he pushed the body away and raised his shoulders from the darkening mulberry carpet.

'Mrs Shawn?'

No reply.

He got to his knees.

She was on her back, one leg folded under her, one outstretched. He looked at her and knew she was dead. He didn't need to feel for a pulse. He did.

She was dead. He'd shot her in the chest. When the man was on him and he'd pulled the trigger he'd shot Mrs Shawn.

She would have been trying to help him. He remembered her shout. She'd shouted and then she would have been trying to help him.

He got up, went into the kitchen, wiped Zeke's shotgun, went back and put it into his friend's hands. He had to bend them, rearrange him. He wanted to kiss Zeke goodbye, kiss him on what remained of his face, but he didn't. Zeke wouldn't have wanted that.

Then, quickly, he kissed Zeke's throat. It was still warm.

He rang Christa, had a look around, found the coke stash, opened Brett Shawn's big briefcase, a small suitcase.

A large yellow envelope holding three stacks of American $100 bills, perhaps $20,000. Three yellow envelopes, papers, two telephone books of papers. A video cassette with a piece of paper taped to it, letters, numbers written in a slanty hand.

Niemand took the envelopes and the cassette and went out to the Mercedes, Colt in his hand. No sign of the intruders' friends or the Israeli next door. He put the stolen goods in the safe box under the floor. Then he went back inside and did a line of coke while he waited, two lines. He thought it was a weakness to use drugs, could take them or leave them, but he couldn't bear the idea of wasting coke on the police.

He was flushing the rest down the sink when the telephone rang.

He let it ring, dried his hands, then he couldn't bear it and picked it up. Long-distance call.

'Shawn?'

'Mr Shawn's had an accident. He's dead.'

A silence.

'And you are?' An accent. German?

Niemand gave it some thought. 'An employee,' he said.

'Shawn had some papers. And a tape. You have them?'

'Yes.'

'I assume you'll be bringing them out?'

More thought. 'What's it worth?' Niemand said.

'For the London delivery, the agreed sum. Ten thousand pounds. And expenses. Return airfares and so on. Say another five thousand.'

'Twenty thousand,' said Niemand. 'And expenses.'
'Done. When you get to London, this is what you do ...'
He should have asked for more.

2

... HAMBURG ...

TILDERS RANG just before four. Anselm was on the balcony, smoking, looking at the choppy lake, the Aussen-Alster, massaging the lifeless fingers of his left hand, thinking about his brother and money, about how short the summers were becoming, shorter every year. Beate tapped on the glass door, offered the cordless telephone.

Anselm flicked the cigarette, went to the door and took the phone.

'Got him,' said Tilders.

'Yes?' said Anselm. Tilders was talking about a man called Serrano. 'Where?'

'*Hauptbahnhof*, 7.10. On the *Schnellzug* from Cologne.'

'Train? This boy?'

'Yes. Three of them now.'

'How's that?'

'There's a woman. Otto says the muscle went out and bought a case and she's carrying it.'

Serrano's bodyguard was a Hungarian called Zander, also known as Sanders, Sweetman, Kendall. These were just the names they knew.

'Call back in five,' said Anselm. 'I've got to consult the client.'

He went to his desk and rang O'Malley in England. O'Malley wasn't in, would be contacted and told to ring immediately. Anselm went back to the balcony, lit another Camel, watched the ferry docking. The day was darkening now and rain was in the air. Above the sturdy craft, a mob of gulls hovered, jostling black-eyed predators eyeing the boat as if it contained edible things, which it did. He had a dim memory of being taken on his first ferry ride on the Alster, on the day the *schwanenvater* brought out the swans from their winter refuge. The man chugged out of a canal in his little boat towing a boom. Behind it were hundreds of swans and, in the open water, pairs began to peel off to seek out their canals. For years, Anselm thought this happened every day, every day a man brought the swans out, the Pied Piper of swans.

He heard the door open behind him.

'Herr Anselm?'

The pale bookkeeper. Could an approach be more obsequious? What made some people so timid? History, Anselm thought, history. He turned. 'Herr Brinkman.'

'May I raise a matter, Herr Anselm?' Brinkman bit his lower lip. Some colour came into it.

'Raise it to the skies.'

Brinkman looked around for eavesdroppers, spoke in an even lower voice. 'I don't like to bring this up, Herr Anselm, but you are the senior person here. Herr Baader does not seem to grasp the urgency. The landlord is making serious threats about the arrears. And there are other problems.'

'He'll be back soon. I'll impress the urgency of this on him,' said Anselm.

Baader owned the business. He was in the West Indies on honeymoon. Honeymoon number four, was it five?

'There is more,' said Brinkman.

'Yes?'

Brinkman moved his head from side to side, bit his lower lip.

'What is it?'

'Herr Baader wants me to charge certain expenses to the firm which we cannot justify as business expenditure. I could go to jail.'

Anselm wasn't in the least surprised. 'Have you mentioned your concerns to him?'

Brinkman nodded. 'He doesn't hear me.'

'I'll talk to him.'

'Herr Anselm, Herr Baader interferes in the payments.'

'How?'

'He signs some cheques. Others don't come back to me.'

'I'll talk to him. I promise.'

Duty done, fearful, Brinkman nodded. Anselm turned back to the window and thought about Baader and his lusts, his juggling of the accounts.

The tap on the glass. Beate with the cordless, again.

It was O'Malley. He whistled when Anselm told him about Serrano.

'You're sure it's his case she's carrying, boyo?'

'Yes,' said Anselm. Tilders didn't say yes when he meant, I think so. He had trained Otto and Baader had trained him and Baader had been properly trained at everything except probity in accounting.

'Not socks and shirts and the dirty underpants?' said O'Malley.

'Could be hand-carved dildos and old copies of *Vatican News* for all we know.'

'Shit,' said O'Malley. 'John, I'm desperate on this bastard. We need a look, just a quick look. Minutes.'

'Take a look,' said Anselm. 'Feel free. You have the time and place. Our work is done.'

'John, John.'

'Not our usual line of work,' said Anselm. 'You know that.'

'Nonsense, I know Baader would do it.'

He would too, thought Anselm. 'I don't know that. Ring him on his mobile.'

'Listen, you can find someone to do it, John.'

'Even if I could, these things come home to you.'

'Ten grand.'

'What do you want for ten grand?'

He told Anselm, who sighed. 'That's all? Take on a bodyguard for ten grand? The prick may take his job seriously. I am of the absolutely not opinion.'

'Twelve.'

Anselm thought about it. He knew they shouldn't get involved in things like this. But there were salaries to be paid, including his. He knew someone who might be able to arrange it for a thousand, fifteen hundred dollars. 'No,' he said.

'Twelve, that's it.'

'Fifteen, win or lose.'

O'Malley's turn to sigh. 'Jesus, you're hard.'

Anselm pulled a face. He could have got twenty, more. He disconnected and rang Tilders. 'There's something we have to do.'

'Yes,' said Tilders. 'What?'

'What kind of case did Zander buy?'

'Aluminium photographer's case.'

Anselm was silent for so long that Tilders thought the line had died. 'John?'

'Tell Otto to buy one. The same. Exactly.'

It took a call to the locksmith and four more calls, twenty minutes on the phone.

3

... HAMBURG ...

THE *SCHNELLZUG* slid into the huge vaulted station, punctual to the second by the *Hauptbahnhof*'s great clock. Zander, the bodyguard, appeared first, blocked the doorway of his sleek carriage and didn't give a damn, looked around, took his time. He was slight for someone in his line of work, blond and elegant in a dark suit, jacket unbuttoned. When he was satisfied, he moved to his left and Serrano stepped onto the platform. He too was in a dark suit but there was nothing elegant about him. He was short and podgy, a sheen on his face, hair that looked lacquered, and a roll of fat over his collar. A laptop computer case was slung over his shoulder.

Next off was a middle-aged businessman, a man with a pinched and unhappy face who raised his head and sniffed the stale station air. After him came an elderly woman, an embalmed face, every detail of her attire perfect, then a family of four, the parents first. Once *Gastarbeiter* from Anatolia, Anselm thought, now wealthy. Their teenage boy and girl followed, citizens of nowhere and everywhere. The pair were listening to music on headphones, moving their heads like sufferers from some exotic ailment.

A woman was in the doorway. She was thirty, perhaps, in black, pants, sensible heels, dark hair scraped back, charcoal lipstick. Her face was severe, sharp planes, not unattractive.

'The woman,' said Tilders. He had a mobile to his face, a long, earnest philosopher's face, a face made for pondering.

Anselm half turned, sipped some *Apfelkorn* from the small bottle, swilled it around his mouth, felt the soft burn of the alcohol. He was on his second one. He was scared of a panic attack and drink seemed to help keep them away. He drank too much anyway, didn't care except in the pre-dawn hours, the badlands of the night. The woman was carrying an aluminium case in her left hand, carrying it easily.

'From the East,' said Tilders.

'Sure it's just three?'

'Don't blame me,' said Tilders. 'This is not our kind of work. Is it on?'

Anselm drained the tiny bottle. 'Yes,' he said. 'Blame's all mine.'

Tilders spoke into his mobile. They followed the woman and Serrano and his bodyguard down the platform towards the escalator that led to the concourse. The woman kept a steady distance behind the men, people between them. On the crowded escalator, Zander looked back once, just a

293

casual glance. Serrano had his head down, a man not interested in his surroundings, standing in the lee of his hired shield.

When they reached the concourse, Zander paused, looked around again, then went right, towards the Kirchenallee exit. The woman didn't hesitate when she reached the concourse, turned right too, walking briskly.

The concourse was crowded, workers and shoppers, travellers, youths on skates, buskers, beggars, petty criminals, pimps, whores, hustlers.

Zander and Serrano were almost at the exit. Zander looked around again. The woman had been blocked by a group of schoolchildren on an excursion. She was ten metres behind them.

'Getting late,' said Anselm. This wasn't going to work, he was sure of it.

'*Scheisse*,' said Tilders.

From nowhere came the gypsy boy, moving through the crowd at a half-run, twisting around people, a wiry child in a drab anorak, tousled black hair, ran straight into the woman, bumped her in the ribcage with his shoulder, hard, bumped her again as she went back. She fell down, hit the ground heavily, but held onto the case.

Without hesitation, the boy stomped on her hand with a heavy Doc Martens boot, thick-soled. She screamed in pain, opened her hand. He grabbed the aluminium case with his left hand but she hooked an arm around his left leg.

The boy kicked her in the neck, stooped and punched her in the mouth, between the breasts, one, two, his right hand, a fist like a small bag of marbles. The woman fell back, no heart for hanging on. He was off, running for the exit.

No one did anything. People didn't want to get involved in these things. They happened all the time and it was dangerous to tackle the thieves. Even young children sometimes produced knives, slashed wildly. Recently, a man had been stabbed in the groin, twice, died in the ambulance. A father of three.

But Zander was suddenly there, running smoothly, going around people like a fish. The boy's start wasn't big enough, the woman had been too close to Zander, it had taken too long to get the case away from her.

'*Scheisse*,' said Tilders again.

Then someone in the crowd seemed to stumble, bumping a long-haired man into Zander's path. The man went to one knee. Zander tried to avoid him but he couldn't. His left leg made contact with the man. He lost his balance, fell sideways, bounced off the ground, came to his feet like a marionette pulled up by strings.

It was too late. The boy was gone, the crowd closed behind him. Zander paused, uncertain, looked back. Serrano had joined the woman, outrage and desperation on his face, both arms in the air. Zander got the message, turned to take off after the boy again, realised it was hopeless, stopped and walked back to Serrano. Serrano was enraged. Anselm could see spit leave his mouth, see Zander recoil. Neither of them looked at the woman, she'd failed them.

Two policemen arrived, one talking into his throat mike. The woman was on her feet, nose bleeding a little, blood black in the artificial light, her right hand massaging her breastbone. Her hair had come loose and she had to brush it back with her left hand. She looked much younger, like a teenager.

A third policeman appeared, told the crowd to get moving, the excitement was over.

The woman was telling her story to the two cops. They were shaking their heads.

Anselm looked at Tilders, who was looking at his watch. Anselm felt the inner trembling, a bad sign. He went over to the newspaper kiosk, bought an *Abendblatt*. The economy was slowing, the metalworkers' union was making threats, another political bribery scandal in the making. He went back, stood behind Tilders.

'How long?'

'Five minutes.'

Serrano and Zander were arguing, the short man's hands moving, Zander tossing his head, arms slack at his sides. Serrano made a dismissive gesture, final.

Anselm said, 'I think we're at the limit here.'

A tall man was coming through the crowd, a man wearing a cap, a blue-collar worker by his appearance. The throng parted for him. In one hand, he had the gypsy boy by the scruff of the neck, in the other, he had the photographer's case, held up as if weightless.

The woman and the policemen went towards them. When they were a few metres away, the boy squirmed like a cat, turned towards his captor, stamped on his left instep, punched him in the stomach. The man's face contorted, he lost his grip on his captive and the boy was gone, flying back the way he had first fled.

'What can you do?' said the man to the woman. 'The scum are taking over the whole world. Is this yours?'

Serrano came up behind the woman. He was flushed, had money in his hand, notes, a wad, offered it. The man in the cap shrugged, uncertain. 'It's not necessary,' he said. 'It's a citizen's duty.'

'Many thanks,' said Serrano, taking the case. 'Take the money. You deserve it.'

The man took the money, looked at it, put it in his hip pocket. 'I'll buy the children something,' he said. He turned and walked back the way he'd come, limping a little from the stomp.

Tilders went on his way. Anselm forced himself to take his time leaving, found the car parked in a no-standing zone, engine running. In Mittelweg, Fat Otto, the man who had bumped the innocent commuter into Zander's path, said, 'Kid's something, isn't he? Deserves a bonus.'

'Deserves to be jailed now before he's even more dangerous,' said Anselm.

His mobile rang. Tilders, the expressionless tone. 'They got about fifty pages. Out of two hundred, they guess.'

'That's good. Get it printed.'

'The reason it took three to transport the case,' said Tilders, 'is probably the diamonds.'

'Ah.'

Anselm took out his mobile and rang Bowden International. O'Malley was in this time. 'About fifty pages. Out of perhaps two hundred.'

'Good on you. As much as could be expected. I'll send someone.'

This is the moment, Anselm thought. 'We'll need the account settled in full on delivery,' he said. 'Including bonus.'

'What's this? We don't pay our bills?'

Anselm closed his eyes. He'd never wanted anything to do with the money side. 'No offence. Things are a little tight. You know how it goes.'

A pause. 'Give our man the invoice. He'll give you a cheque.' Pause. 'Accept our cheque, *compadre*?'

'With deep and grovelling gratitude.'

Anselm put the phone away, relieved. They were sitting in the traffic. 'Any takers for a drink?' he said. Fat Otto looked at him, eye flick.

'I'm offering to buy you lot a drink,' Anselm said. He knew what the man was thinking. 'Grasp the idea, can you?'

They went to the place on Sierichstrasse. He'd been there alone a few times, sat in the dark corner, fighting his fear of being in public, his paranoia about people, about the knowingness he saw in the eyes of strangers.

4

… HAMBURG …

IN THE closing deep–purple light of the day, Anselm turned the corner and saw the Audi parked across the narrow street from his front gate. He registered someone in the driver's seat and the jangle of alarm went through him, tightened the muscles of his face, his scalp, retracted his testicles.

He kept walking, feeling his heart drumming, the tightness in his chest. Not twice, not in a quiet street, not in a peaceful country. It wouldn't happen to him again. To him, no. Not here, not to him. No.

Just one person in the car, a man, there was another car further down, a BMW, empty.

The driver of the Audi got out. Not a man, a woman in a raincoat, shoulder–length hair, rimless glasses she was taking off.

'John Anselm?'

He didn't answer, eyes going to the BMW, back to her car.

'Alex Koenig,' she said. 'I've been writing to you.' She closed the car door, opened it again, slammed it, came around the front. 'Damn door,' she said. 'It's a new car. I was about to drive off.'

A shudder passed through him, an aftershock. He remembered the letters. Doctor Alex Koenig from Hamburg University had written to him twice asking for a meeting. He had not replied, thrown the letters away. People wanted to ask him questions about Beirut and he didn't want to answer them.

'I thought you were a man,' he said.

'A man?'

'Your first name.'

She smiled, a big mouth, too big for her face. 'That's a problem? If I were a man?'

'No,' said Anselm. 'The problem at the moment is how you got this address.'

'David Riccardi gave it to me.'

'He shouldn't have done that,' Anselm said. 'You stalk people, is that what you do?'

She had a long face and a long nose and she had assumed a chastised look, eyelids at half-mast, a sinner in a third–rate Italian religious painting. 'I'm sorry, I didn't mean to give you that impression.'

'Well, goodbye,' Anselm said.

'I'd really like to talk to you.'

'No. There's nothing I want to talk about.'

'I'd appreciate it very much,' she said quietly, head on one side.

He was going to say no again, but for some reason – drink, loneliness, perversity – he turned, unbalanced by liquor, and held the gate open for her.

In the house, standing in the empty panelled hall, taking off her raincoat, she looked around and said, 'This is impressive.'

'I'm glad you're impressed.' He led the way into the sitting room, put on lights. He rarely used the large room, with its doors onto the terrace. He lived in the kitchen and the upstairs study. 'A drink? I'm drinking whisky.'

'Thank you. With water, please.'

He poured the drinks in the kitchen, gave himself three fingers. When he returned with the tray, she was looking at the family photographs hung between the deep windows. She was tall, almost his height, carried herself upright.

'How many generations in this picture?' she said, turning her head to him.

Anselm didn't need to look. He knew the photograph. 'A few,' he said, sitting down. He was already regretting letting her in, offering the drink. What had come over him? He didn't want to answer questions, didn't want her prying. 'What can I do for you?'

She sat opposite him, in the ornately carved wooden chair. 'As I said in the letters …'

'I didn't read your letters. Unsolicited mail. How did you know where to send them? Riccardi?'

'No. I only met him a few days ago. I asked the news agency to forward the letters.'

'Kind of them.'

He hadn't worked for the agency since before Beirut, hadn't spoken to anyone there in a long time, five or six years, had never received anything in the mail from them. How would the agency know his address?

'Why would they do that?' he said.

She shifted in her chair, recrossed her legs, long legs. She was wearing grey flannels and low-heeled shoes. 'I'm a psychiatrist. I told them I was doing research.'

'That's a good reason is it?' He drank half his whisky and couldn't taste it, wished he'd made it stronger, the bad sign. 'Psychiatrist. Is that a special licence to invade people's privacy?'

Alex Koenig smiled, shrugged. 'I spoke to a man, I told him I was researching post-traumatic stress disorder suffered by hostages and that I very much wanted to talk to you. It was just a request. I would write to you. You could say no.'

'I didn't respond. That's no.'

'Well, I thought they hadn't forwarded the letters.'

'So you extracted my address from Riccardi.'

She laughed, not a confident laugh. 'I have to say I didn't do that. He offered the address, he said he'd ring you.'

'Well I have to say I don't have any disorder so you're wasting your time.'

She nodded. 'As you know, the symptoms can take a long time ...'

'When it happens, I'll let you know. Until then there's nothing I can tell you.'

They sat in silence. Anselm felt another bad sign, the urge to disconcert, didn't care and looked at her breasts, looked into her eyes, looked down again. She was wearing a white shirt, fresh, well ironed, creases down the arms.

Alex Koenig looked down at herself, looked up at him.

'They're not very big,' said Anselm. 'Size means everything to tit men.'

He could see her slow inhalation, the slow expulsion.

'Well,' she said, 'my body aside, my research is into the relationship between post-traumatic stress disorder and the life history and personality of victims.'

Anselm felt the dangerous light-headedness coming over him, the sense of trembling inside, knew he should end this encounter. He drained his glass, went to the kitchen and half filled it, no water, came back and sat down. The light from the table lamp lit one side of her face, emphasised her nose, the fullness of her lips.

'Life history? That's what you're interested in?'

'Yes.'

'And personality?'

'Yes.'

'I've got those. Both. Two out of three. Missing only the disorder.'

Silence.

'Would you like to see my scrapbook? Stories from foreign wars? Pictures of dead people? Mutilated bodies?'

'If you'd like to show it to me,' she said.

'The shrink answer. If you'd *like* to. What would *you* like, Frau Koenig? It that Frau? Frau Doctor Koenig?'

'Alex is fine.'

'Alex is too informal for me, Doctor.' He felt himself speeding up. 'I think we need to keep a professional German distance here. Are you German? You don't look German. Some kind of *Auslander*, perhaps? A member of a lesser race? That's not quite an Aryan nose, not that I mind it, of course.'

'My father is Austrian.'

Anselm drank, a swig. 'Austrian? Of course. A psychiatrist, where else would your father be? The land of Freud, Jung and Adler. Adler never quite made it did he? A lesser light. I can't quite remember where Adler went wrong. You'd know, wouldn't you? Sorry, that might offend. Not an Adlerian are you, Doctor?'

'No.'

'Right. What about Jung? A Jungian. He was a big prick, wasn't he? Saw this huge one as a child as I remember it. This massive phallus. In a dream. Is that right, Doctor Professor?'

'I'm not a Jungian.'

Anselm couldn't stop himself. He leaned forward. 'Dream about massive phalluses too, do you? Monsters? Huge pricks with men attached?'

'I'm not an analyst.' Her smile was tight.

'No? You'd be into drugs then. Terrific. I'm with you. The best approach is drugs. Just give the crazies drugs. For fuck's sake, they're deranged, shoot them full of drugs, that'll keep the nuts quiet.'

Alex Koenig hadn't taken her eyes off him.

'Unfortunately I didn't keep a scrapbook,' said Anselm. 'And I don't remember much about my illustrious career. That's got nothing to do with post-traumatic stress. That's the result of being struck on the head with a rifle butt. But I do remember that trouble spots are all the same. Only the colours of the people change. Outside. Inside they're all the same colours. Red and pink and white. The intestines, they're a sort of blue, purply blue, the colour of baby birds, seen baby birds? Only they're wet and slimy, like big worms. Big earthworms or the worms in swordfish. People worms.'

He sat back and smiled at her. 'Well, so much for my life history. That leaves personality, doesn't it? Is that in the ordinary meaning? Or is it *persona* we're talking about? The mask, the actor's mask? Your Jung was keen on that, wasn't he? Stupid phallic fart that he was.'

He waited. The way she was looking at him, her silence, her neutrality, brought back the American military psychiatrist.

'What kind of shrink are you?' he said. 'Are you a couch-type? Plenty of couches in this house. We could talk on a couch, how's that? Both on it. Prone and supine. Which would you be?'

There was a long silence. Then Alex Koenig stood up, eyes on his, glass held in both hands, licked her lower lip, a slither of pink tongue. 'I like both,' she said. 'I like to alternate. I like to fuck and be fucked. But you wouldn't be much good either way, Herr Anselm. Your prick's useless. Even if you wanted to fuck me, you couldn't. You're not a performer. You're impotent.'

He sat in the armchair and heard the heavy front door close behind her. He stayed there, head back, massaging the fingers that wouldn't work, and after a time he fell asleep, waking beyond midnight, stumbling to his cold unmade bed in the room where his grandfather had died.

5

… HAMBURG …

ANSELM ALWAYS woke early, no matter how much he'd drunk, got up immediately, couldn't bear the thoughts that lying awake in bed brought. Showered, dressed, some toast eaten, he wandered the house, watched television for a few minutes at a time, too early to go to work. There was always something to look at. Anselms had lived in the house since before World War One. It had been built by his great-grandfather, Gustav. Bits of family history were everywhere – paintings, photographs, books with inscriptions, letters stuck in them to mark pages, three volumes of hand-written recipes, an ivory-handled walking stick, diaries in High German, collections of invitation cards, wooden jigsaws, mechanical toys, there was no end to the Anselm relics. In the empty, cobwebbed wine cellar, he had found a single bottle stuck too deep into a rack, 1937 Lafite. He'd opened it: corked, undrinkable.

Today, he took the tape recorder to the kitchen, sat at the table. In the damp hole in Beirut, Anselm's thoughts had often turned to his great-aunt Pauline. His first memories of her were when he was eight or nine. She was always very old in his mind, thin, wiry, always in grey, a shade of grey, high collars, strong grey hair, straight hair, severely cut. She smoked cigarillos in a holder. He had no memory of making the recordings. They had come from San Francisco, four tapes in a box with other tapes.

He pressed the Play button. Hissing, then the voice of great-aunt Pauline.

Of course this house has seen terrible arguments.

Then his young voice.

What about?

Oh, business, how to run the business. Times were difficult before the war. And about the Nazis, Hitler.

Who argued about Hitler?

Your grandfather and your great-grandfather. With Moritz.

I don't know anything about Moritz.

There was a long silence before Pauline spoke again.

Moritz was so foolish. But he looked like an angel, lovely hair, so blond, he had the face of Count Haubold von Einsiedel, you know the portrait?

No, I don't know it.

The von Rayski portrait? Of course you do, everyone does. I remember one particularly awful evening. We were having a sherry before dinner, we always did, I was fourteen when I was included, just a thimbleful of an old manzanilla fino. Hold it to the light, my father said. See pleasure in a glass. I did. I went to that window, it was summer. They seemed to last much longer then, summers, we had better summers. Much better, much longer.

Another silence.

When was that?

When?

The awful evening.

Oh, I suppose it would have been in '35 or '36. Soon after Stuart's death. Stuart never wanted to be in commerce but he had no choice. Eldest sons were expected to go into the firm. I don't know what he wanted to do. Except paint and ski. But his family, well, they were like ours. Two weeks in Garmisch, they thought that was quite enough relaxation for a year. Anselms had dealt with Armitages for many years, more than a hundred, I suppose. Many, many years. My father used to say we were married to the Armitages long before I married Stuart. He was at Oxford with Stuart's father. They all did law. That was what you did. Of course, the families had almost been joined before. My aunt Cecile was engaged to an Armitage, I forget his name, Henry, yes. Henry, he was killed in the Great War.

The awful evening.

What?

The evening of the terrible argument.

What did I say about that?

Nothing.

Yes. Let's talk about something else.

She talked about her childhood, about rowing on the Alster, birthdays, grand parties, dinners.

We always went to the New Year's Eve ball at the Atlantic. So glamorous. Everyone was there. They had kangaroo tail soup on the menu on New Year's Eve in 1940. That was the first time I went after Stuart's death. Also the last year we went. I went with Frans Erdmann, he was a doctor. Much younger than I was. He died at Stalingrad.

After eight, he left for work, closed the massive front door behind him. The temple of memory, he said to himself. The only memory missing is mine.

6

… HAMBURG …

ANSELM WALKED along the misty lake shore carrying his running gear in a sports bag. His knees were getting worse and his right hip hurt, but he ran home on most days. The long route on good ones, the slightly shorter one on others. The number of others was increasing.

Today, Baader was coming from the opposite direction, every inch a member of the *Hanseaten*: perfect hair, navy-blue suit, white shirt, grey silk tie, black shoes with toecaps. They all dressed like that, the commercial and professional elite of the *Hansastadt*. They met at the gates to the old mansion on Schöne Aussicht.

'Christ,' said Baader, 'I was hoping that thing was an aberration.'

Anselm looked down at his windbreaker, a nylon garment, padded, quilted, red. 'What's wrong with it?'

'It's football hooligan wear, that's what's wrong with it,' said Baader.

'I aspire to be a football hooligan,' said Anselm. 'Engage in acts of senseless violence.'

'Join the police,' said Baader. 'That way you get a uniform and they pay you.'

They walked up the driveway.

'What's this walking?' said Anselm. Baader drove a Porsche, a new one every year, sometimes more often.

'Being serviced.'

'I didn't know you did that. I thought you bought a new one when the oil got dirty.'

'Lease,' said Baader. He had a long thin face, long nose, and a near-continuous eyebrow, just a thinning in the middle. 'Lease, not buy. Deductible business expense.'

'A joke, Stefan,' said Anselm. 'A very old joke. But on the subject, Brinkman's in a state of panic. He says the kitty's empty.'

Baader stopped, eyed Anselm. 'Brinkman is an old woman,' he said. 'An old woman and a bean counter.'

'Well, he says there aren't many beans to count and some of your expenses aren't deductible. He's worried about illegality. He doesn't want to go to jail.'

Baader shook his head, started walking again. Anselm thought that he knew what was going through the man's mind: I gave this sad, drunken, amnesiac, neurotic prick a job when he was unemployable, too fucked-up even to commit suicide properly. I've put up with behaviour no sane employer would countenance. Now he's the voice of conscience.

'How was the honeymoon?' said Anselm. He should have asked earlier.

'I've had better.'

At the front door, finger on the button, not looking at Anselm, Baader said, 'When there were just three people and I did the books, I made money. Now we have to have fucking super-computers that cost as much as blocks of apartments. Maybe I should go back to three.'

'It's worth a try,' said Anselm. 'Of course, you had fewer ex-wives then and it was pre-Porsches and apartments in Gstadt.'

Baader pressed the button, waved at the camera. From his cubicle, Wolfgang, the day security, unlocked the door.

They went upstairs to the big rooms on the second floor of the grand old building that housed the firm of Weidermann & Kloster. There was no Weidermann, no Kloster and the firm was no longer the publishing house the two men founded after World War Two. Now W&K's business was looking for people, checking on people.

The biggest room was lit by a dim blue light. It held six computer work-stations clustered around a bank of servers, a 1000-CPU super-computer, state-of-the-art equipment. Two tired, stale-mouthed, gritty-eyed end-of-shift people were in residence.

Anselm's office led off the room. On the way to it, he passed a shaven-headed man in black sitting on his spine, his head back, eyes closed. He was chewing in a bovine, cud-shifting way.

'You're eating in your sleep, Inskip,' Anselm said. 'Wake up and go home.'

'Home,' said Inskip, not opening his eyes, 'is where they have to take you in. That is not the situation at my lodgings.'

Inskip was new in the job, six months, but he was suited to it, not a normal person. He'd been recommended to Baader by someone who knew his father, once a lieutenant in the Army of the Rhine, now something in the British Foreign Office, probably an MI6 employee. Inskip's mother was a German doctor's daughter and he'd learned German at her knee.

Inskip had a degree in mathematics from Cambridge and his only real job had been six months as a junior lecturer at an English provincial university.

'Kicked out for GMT,' Inskip had told Anselm one night. They were standing on the balcony, smoking, snowflakes dancing in the cold light from the windows.

'GMT?'

'Gross moral turpitude. I committed an unspeakable act.'

'What was it?'

'Search me. No one would speak of it. I was off my face, drink and drugs, so I had no recollection. Anyway, I couldn't be bothered to ask, told them to fuck off. Loathed the place, all ghastly grey concrete, stuck out in these fields, students thick as sheep.'

Now Inskip opened his eyes. 'The Indonesian's on the radar. Two minutes ago.'

'Where?'

The man's name was Sudrajad. He had not been sighted in Europe since stealing four million dollars from a French construction company trying to swing a contract in Indonesia. The French wouldn't have felt so bitter if they'd got it, but it went to Americans who made a member of the Soeharto family a partner in their firm.

'Swissair 207 into Zurich from New York, 11.20.'

A list of names, dates and numbers appeared on his computer screen. Inskip began to scroll it.

'What name?'

'Hamid. The Malaysian passport.'

'Told them?'

'I'm looking for a hotel ... here it is. Schweitzerhof. One night. There's a limo booked.'

'Tell them. He may go somewhere of interest on his way to the hotel.'

The clients chasing the Indonesian were a Paris firm of commercial investigators, good clients.

Anselm went into his office and read the night reports. The Serrano watchers said the woman appeared to be paid off at the station. Serrano and the bodyguard went to the Hansa Bank, where the case went into a safe-deposit box. The bodyguard left and Serrano took a cab to the Hotel Abtei in Harvesthude and had not left the premises. This information had been passed on to O'Malley in London.

In the tray was a long complaint about payment from Gerda Broeksma, the firm's representative in Amsterdam. They couldn't afford to lose her. If Anselm understood the figures, she had brought in almost 5 per cent of the firm's turnover in the past year. Holland was good for business. The Dutch were a suspicious lot. They knew that people who left their sitting room curtains open at night were not necessarily without anything to hide.

Anselm went down the short passage to Baader's office. The door was open. He was on the phone, beckoned, pointed to the Marcel Breuer chairs at the window. Anselm sat down. Baader stopped grunting into the phone and came over.

'What?'

'Gerda. She says we're three months behind. She wants to quit.'

Baader put his chin on his hands, closed his eyes. He had long lashes. 'Why does everyone go to you? The caring fucking ear. You running a complaints booth?'

'I don't encourage it, Stefan,' said Anselm. 'Believe me.'

Baader didn't open his eyes. 'No,' he said. 'Sorry. I know you don't. I'm in shit, John. Uschi's skinned me, her fucking lawyer.'

Anselm didn't feel much compassion. He'd rather liked Uschi, a failed singer. Baader had met her through someone who worked for Bertelsmann in the music business. Despite dressing like an old-school *Hanseaten*, Baader frequented the haunts of the Hamburg media types, places like Fusion and Nil and Rive that Anselm read about in *Morgenpost*.

'Then my cousin tips me off, this bio-tech company, get in big and get rich,' said Baader. 'But he didn't tell me to get out even quicker, the whole thing's just gas, a fucking Zeppelin. The prick, I'm going to kill him.'

Pause. 'I may have to sell some of the business,' he said. 'A big piece.'

'Hell of a business to sell,' said Anselm. 'Eighty per cent clearly illegal, the rest lineball.'

Baader opened his eyes. They were dark brown, something of the intelligent dog in them. Alsatian dog. 'But there's a buyer.'

For years, Anselm had been waiting for this. 'Yes?'

'An English company.'

'Yes?'

'Mitchell Harvester. Corporate risk management, that sort of thing. Take 51 per cent, give us all their work.'

'Mitchell Harvester? Is that so? They approached you?'

'Well, indirectly, sounded out, yes. They'll do it through a nominee company, no direct involvement.' Baader looked at him, didn't blink. Nothing.

Anselm stared back for a long time, waited for a sign. He got up, knee pains, left knee worse, found a cigarette and lit it with the old Zippo, disregarding the policy on smoking.

'Stefan,' he said, 'I want you to consider whether fucking teenagers hasn't destroyed important parts of your brain.'

Baader frowned, the single eyebrow dipping in the middle. 'What's wrong, don't want to work for them?'

'For that arm of the United States government, no.'

The frown disappeared. Baader smiled. He looked even more vulpine. 'John,' he said, 'I understand your position. But relax, it's not a problem.'

'No?'

'No. They want you sacked before we do the deal.'

'Fuck you.' Anselm sat down. 'Can we talk about business? I pulled fifteen grand yesterday. Against my better judgment.'

'That's my man,' said Baader, the little smile. 'Already I feel more able to resist a takeover.'

7

… JOHANNESBURG …

NIEMAND PARKED near the Chinese wholesaler's barred premises in a filthy side street near the market square. Two street boys appeared, danced around him, offered all manner of services. He gave them several notes to guard the car, opened his jacket to show them the gun and threatened them with certain death. To get to the door, he had to step around papers, car bits, cartons, bottles, food containers, pieces of styrofoam, a new pile of human excrement with a filter cigarette stubbed out in it.

The guard, a huge man, knew him.

'Where's the Chinaman?' said Niemand in Zulu. He called the Chinaman *uChina*.

'Deliveries,' said the Zulu. He was behind a steel gate. A shotgun was leaning against the wall, an old Remington, grip polished with hand sweat.

The Chinaman supplied Soweto hawkers, met them on the fringe to hand over goods, payment in cash, not one cent of credit. Niemand and Zeke had ridden shotgun for him for a few months before the escort service job came up. They had been held up four times: Chinaman 4, hijackers 0.

The guard opened the gate. Niemand crossed the storeroom, walked down the aisles of packaged goods that reached to the ceiling. Substandard, damaged, dangerous, mislabelled, overcooked, undercooked, production mistakes, very old, the Chinaman's stock came mostly from Eastern Europe and Asia.

At the doorway of the back room, Niemand pushed aside the curtain. The Chinaman's new wife was sitting in an armchair covered in tigerskin plush velvet, one of four arranged in a row in front of the television set. She heard the sound of the curtain rings, looked over her shoulder, barked his name and went back to watching an advertisement for miracle kitchen knives. A man with a bad hair transplant was sawing slices off a broom handle. Then he went to work on a piece of cheese, processed cheese, sliced off squares of yellow rubber.

'Try that with your favourite knife and see how far you get,' said the salesman.

The camera showed the audience clapping. Many of the people did not look like kitchen-knife buyers. They looked like people recruited from the street to applaud men with irregular hair. The camera showed the set of knives on offer. Eight knives. One of them looked like the weapon in the hand of the man who'd dropped from the ceiling.

'Cutting, chopping, slicing, dicing, they'll never be the same again,' said the salesman.

'Jackie,' said Niemand. 'I've got a video I need to watch.'

The Chinaman had told Niemand that he imported Jackie through an agency in Macau and that his resentful son, sent to take delivery of her at the airport, was screwing his father's new companion within days.

'She says she was a model,' the Chinaman had said. 'I think she model without her clothes on, know what I mean?'

Jackie used the remote to kill the knife man, went to an empty channel, just electronic fizz. 'Put it in,' she said.

Niemand went to the set. There was a video in the slot, something called *The Wedding Singer*. He plugged in Mr Shawn's cassette.

Jackie got up, her nylon dressing gown slid like water, showing a length of thin thigh. She handed over the remote and went to the back door. 'Come and have drink when you finish,' she said, staccato. 'No one to talk to here. Boring.'

Niemand sat on the edge of a chair and found the Play button. Static. It became an aerial view of wooded sub-tropical country, late in the day, shadows. Taken from a helicopter, Niemand thought, probably from the co-pilot's seat, the colour the result of filming through darkened glass.

Then the photographer was descending and Niemand wasn't sure what he was looking at, a fire, fires, an African village burning, thatched huts on fire, perhaps two or three dozen, cultivated ground around them ...

The camera went left and another helicopter could be seen, a Puma, no markings visible. Now they were on the ground and the filming was being done through the open door of the helicopter, a dark edge visible.

There were bodies everywhere, dozens and dozens of bodies. Black people.

The camera zoomed in on a group, at least a dozen people near what looked like a water trough made of steel drums sliced vertically and welded together. Black people, poorly dressed, most of them women and children, a baby, lying on the ground, hands held to their faces, some face down as if trying to kiss the packed dirt.

Men in uniform came into view, white men in combat gear carrying automatic weapons. Niemand recognised the firearms, American weapons. The soldiers were Americans. Niemand knew that because of their boots, American Special Forces boots, he'd once owned a pair.

The soldiers were standing around, five or six of them, they weren't alert, weapons cradled. The camera moved, three people in coveralls, probably civilians, talking to a tall soldier, the only one without headgear. The camera zoomed in on the group, the soldier was talking to one of the civilians, a man with a moustache. The soldier took off his dark glasses, wiped his eyes with the knuckle of his index finger. The man with the moustache said something to the person next to him, a man, short hair, a mole on his cheek. He shook his head, gestured, palms inward. The group broke up, the soldier was turning towards the camera, the screen went dark.

When the picture came back, the tall soldier was standing at the bodies lying around the water trough.

He moved a man's head with his boot.

The man was alive, he lifted his arm, his fingers moved.

The soldier shot him in the head, gestured to the other soldiers in the background.

Niemand watched the rest of the film, another two minutes, rewound it and watched it again. He retrieved the cassette and left without seeing Jackie, drove to his place and packed his one bag.

Two hours later, he was in a British Airways business class seat. Johannesburg fell away beneath him, the flat, featureless townships smoking as if bombed, smoking like the village on the film.

Could be Mozambique, he thought. Could be Angola, could be further north.

8

… HAMBURG …

INSKIP LOOMED in Anselm's open doorway. 'Your friend called,' he said. 'The one who won't give his name.'

David Riccardi was his name. Presumably it was the call to tell him about Alex Koenig. Many hours too late. Anselm closed his eyes at the thought of her visit.

He had known Riccardi for ten years before they were taken hostage. They'd worked together a few times, run into each other in odd places. Then they spent thirteen months together, close together. Manacled, chained to walls and beams, in the dark or half-dark, the last four months in a damp cavity beneath a cold-storage plant where they could not fully extend their legs. That was where his knee trouble had started. His knee trouble and his hip trouble.

'When?' said Anselm.

'Oh, two–fifteen, two–thirty.'

The wrong side of the night. But Riccardi's circadian rhythms were permanently disturbed, so was much else of David.

'Why doesn't he ring you at home?' said Inskip, stretching, reaching up, hands embracing, his ribs showing against his T-shirt. He was about two metres tall and thin.

'He doesn't want to wake me.'

'I see. So he rings you where you aren't.'

'Not everyone who phones you wants to talk to you.'

'I'll ponder that,' said Inskip. 'The Frogs are happy about the Indonesian, happy as Frogs can be. May I ask you a question?'

'You may *ask*.'

'What exactly *is* Bowden's business?'

'Debt collection.'

'Debt collection?'

'Say the Ukrainian government owes you five million dollars, they won't pay, you're desperate. You go to Bowden. They offer ten, twenty cents in the dollar for the debt, it depends. For you, that's better than nothing, cut your losses. Now Bowden's the creditor.'

'That impresses the Ukrainians, does it?'

'Bowdens wait until they find a Ukrainian government asset to target somewhere, maybe a Ukrainian Airways plane in Oslo, something like that.

Something valuable. They bring up the legal artillery, get a court order impounding the asset. Now the Ukrainians have to fight a legal action in a foreign country to get their plane back. That or pay up the million. Bowden's bet is that they'll want to talk a settlement. Say sixty cents in the dollar. And they usually do.'

'I see. What a sheltered life I've lived.'

'All that is changing.'

Anselm went back to reviewing the logbooks. Every file had one, all checks, results, speculations, actions, all recorded in writing. As behoved parasites who lived off other people's computer systems, professional prowlers of the cyber world, W&K kept no electronic records of their own, worked only through proxy computers, and otherwise sought tirelessly to erase the traces of their electronic trespasses. If W&K was interested in you, the safest thing was to ensure that your name or names and the names of anyone near you did not appear on the electronic record: no bank accounts, no vehicle registrations, no passport or visa applications, no customs records, no credit-card transactions, no plane tickets, no car hire, no hotel bookings, no bills from public utilities or department stores, no electronic commerce, no emails, no accidents, no hospital admissions, no court appearances, no nothing.

It was safe only to have your death recorded.

W&K was not the only company providing this kind of service. What set W&K apart was that, when their own efforts bogged down, Baader could ring some faceless secret servant in Munich or Moscow or Madrid or Montevideo. Then there was a chance they would get moving again. That came from fourteen years with German intelligence, the BND, the *Bundesnachtrichtendienst* – ten years in Department One, Operations, and four in Department Three, Evaluation.

Most of W&K's work was commercial, companies spying on each other, on themselves, trying to find out where executives went, who they saw, who visited companies, what people said, what they wrote. But the firm took on missing persons, anything it could handle.

Just before ten, Carla Klinger knocked and came in. She used a rubber-tipped aluminium stick to walk. She was in her late thirties, thin and angular, a scar on her nose where it had been broken. The BND had sacked her because she was found to have had an affair with another female, possibly once a STASI person, Baader had been vague about the details. Then she had a car accident, broke one side of her body, arm, ribs, hip, leg. Someone told Baader about an expensively trained talent going to waste and he offered Carla a job.

'Serrano,' she said, taking the logbook out from under her left arm and offering it. 'He rang this man and they're meeting tomorrow. At the Alsterarkaden.' She always spoke to Anselm in English.

Anselm looked at the log. The man's name was Werner Kael. He lived nearby, off Sierichstrasse, in the millionaire belt, a wide belt.

'What shows on him?' said Anselm. Carla wasn't much for volunteering information, a trait she shared with Baader. Possibly something nurtured in the BND.

'Calls himself an investment consultant, holiday house in France, four weeks in the Virgin Islands in winter. He used to travel a lot, short trips. Not for a few years. Four tax investigations in the past twelve years, no action taken.'

'Tell O'Malley,' said Anselm. 'It may have meaning for him.'

She nodded, put the logbook under her arm and left.

Anselm waited, then he went down the passage. Baader was staring at his big monitor, figures.

'Werner Kael,' said Anselm from the doorway.

Baader didn't look at him. 'What's he done?'

'Arranged to meet O'Malley's man, the money man.'

Baader touched his chin with a long index finger. 'Arms, drugs, slaves, body parts. Israel, Palestinians, Iranians, Iraqis, Süd-Afs, Tamil Tigers, everyone. Sold the IRA half a container of Semtex. Then there's a fucking shipload of ethyl ether to Colombia out of Hamburg. Five thousand per cent profit.'

'What's his secret?'

'Party donor. Learned the trade from one of Goebbels' cocksuckers. Dieter Kuhn. Dieter only died last year, the year before, about ninety, the old cunt. Fascism is good for health. Hitler would still be alive. Plus Kael's got American friends, a big help in life.'

Baader swivelled. 'O'Malley's chasing money?'

'As far as I can tell,' said Anselm.

'Well, there's no knowing. Kael's got to put his dirty money somewhere, could be this man does it for him, what's ...?'

'Serrano. You don't know the name?'

'No. Tell O'Malley that as far as I know Kael doesn't talk to his clients. He's got cut-outs for that. So Serrano isn't buying or selling. Which probably means he's doing something for Kael.'

Anselm went back to his office, tried to concentrate on the task, focus on the logbook. He had to work at concentration. His mind wandered, wanted to go back to dark places, drawn as a dog was to old buried bones, rotten things, just a layer of earth on them.

The mobile on the desk rang. It was said to be secure. But nothing was secure or W&K wouldn't have a business.

9

… LONDON …

NIEMAND HAD a long wait at Heathrow customs. When his turn came, the dark pockmarked man looked at him for a time and said, 'Central African Republic. Don't see a lot of these. No. Quite unusual. What's the population?'

'Going down all the time,' Niemand said. 'Volcanic eruptions, human sacrifice, cannibal feasts.'

The official didn't smile, kept looking at him while he photocopied the passport page. Then he said, 'Enjoy your stay in the United Kingdom, sir. Mind the motorised vehicles now.'

Niemand changed a thousand dollars into sterling, rang a hotel, bought a pre-paid mobile phone, and took the underground to Earls Court. He didn't trust taxis, the drivers cheated you and then things became unpleasant.

It wasn't until he came up from the tube station that he felt he was in England: a cold late-autumn day, soiled sky, an icy wind probing his collar, chasing litter down filthy Trebovir Road. The hotel was close by. He had stayed there before, on his way back from his uncle's deathbed in Greece. That was a long time ago and they wouldn't remember him. Besides, he had a different name now.

The woman at the desk was somewhere out beyond sixty, crimson lips drawn on her face, high Chinese collar hiding chins, slackness.

'I rang,' he said. 'Martin Powell.'

'Did you? Just the night, dear?'

'Three.'

'Forty pounds twenty a night,' she said. 'In advance.'

'I'll pay cash.'

She smiled. 'Always happy to accept real money.'

He waited, looking at her, not producing it. He didn't care about the money but he liked to see how people behaved when off-the-record money was offered. 'What does that come to then?'

'One hundred pounds exactly,' she said. 'Dear.'

Niemand registered and carried his pilot's flight bag up the stairs covered with balding carpet. In his room on the third floor, he went through his no-weights exercise routine, twenty minutes. Then he showered in a scratched fibreglass cubicle. The water never went above warm, gurgled, died, spat into life again.

Towelling himself, he thought: A gun, do I need a gun?

He considered it as he dressed, put on clean black jeans, a black T-shirt, the weightless nylon harness that carried his valuables, a black poloneck sweater, his loose-fitting leather jacket. He didn't know who he'd be dealing with. Guns were for showing. Guns were like offering cash. People understood, you didn't have to spell it out.

Downstairs, unconsciously hugging the inside wall like a blind man, around the corner to a pub, a mock-old place with fake timbers, hungover staff, just a dozen or so customers, one sad man with a pencil moustache drinking a pink liquid, possibly a Pimm's, the last Pimm's drinker. At a corner table, he ate a slice of pizza, tasteless, just fodder, rubber fodder, he was hungry, couldn't eat much on planes, someone sitting so close to him he could hear their teeth crush the food, the drain sound of swallowing. When he was finished, he moved his plate to an empty table. He couldn't bear smeared plates, dirty cutlery, mouth prints on glasses, the cold, congealing bits of leftover food.

From under his sweater he brought out his nylon wallet and found the number. He looked around, dialled.

'Kennex Import. How may I help you?'

'Michael Hollis, please,' Niemand said in his Yorkshire accent. He had always been able to mimic accents. He heard them in his head like music, the stresses and timbres, the inflections.

'Who may I say is calling?'

'Tell him it's in connection with a package.'

'Please hold.'

Not for long.

'Hollis.' The faint German accent.

Niemand waited a few seconds. 'I have a package from Johannesburg.'

'Oh yes. The package.'

Two women came in, girls, shrieking, spiky hair, faces violated by rings, full of push and bump and finger-point.

'I'm sorry, I can't do it for less than fifty thousand, US.'

A pause. A sniff, an intake, just audible.

'What?'

'You heard.'

A pause, the sniff, another sound, a click-click. 'I'm not sure we can do that. Can I call you back? Give me your number.'

'No,' said Niemand. 'I'll give you an hour to decide. Then you can say yes or no. If it's no, the package goes somewhere else. I'll ring. Goodbye.'

Niemand went for a walk as far as Kensington Gardens, sat on a bench and watched the people. He had been there before, on his second visit to London. He was supposed to be on his way to Papua New Guinea to fight headhunters, that came to nothing, some political fuck-up. For ten days, he'd been stuck in a hotel near Heathrow with half a dozen other mercenaries – the stupid, the brain-dead, and the merely kill-crazy. Every day, early, he'd take the underground somewhere and run back, long routes plotted with a map. He got to know London as far away as Hampstead and Wimbledon and Bermondsey. Then they were paid off and given plane tickets home.

He always felt strange in England, hearing English everywhere. His father had hated the English, *rooinekke*, anyone who spoke English, Jews in particular, said it was in his blood: Niemands had fought against the British in the Boer War, been put in concentration camps, sent to Ceylon, a *koelie eiland*, a coolie island. But then his father had also hated Greeks and Portuguese, called them *see kaffirs*, sea-kaffirs. For Greeks he reserved a special loathing, having married a Greek girl and lost her because of his drinking and violence. When Niemand and his mother came back from five years on Crete, he found that his father came home drunk from the mine every day, drove the loose old Chev V8 into the dirt yard at speed, stopped in a dust cloud inches from the tacked-on verandah. One day, he braked too late, took out a pillar, half the roof fell on the Chev. He just stayed where he was, opened the bottle of cheap brandy. Niemand found him when he came home, carried him to bed, surprised at how light he was, just bones and sinew.

Niemand looked at his watch. Five minutes to go. Two young women behind three-wheeled pushchairs came from opposite directions, saw each other, cried out. Stopping abreast, they walked around and inspected each other's cargoes beneath the plastic covers, made delighted scrunched-up faces.

He dialled.

'Kennex Import. How may I help you?'

'Mr Hollis. About the package.'

No further questions.

Niemand watched the mothers talking, hands moving, talking babies, faces alive with interest.

'Ah, the package.' Hollis. 'Yes, I'm having trouble getting authorisation for the deal you suggest without seeing that the goods are as described.'

'No,' Niemand said. 'You give me the money. In cash. I give you the package.'

'It's not that simple.'

'I think it is. Yes or no.'

'We have to see the goods. You can understand that.'

Niemand didn't like the way this was going. He didn't have contingency plans. 'Now the price is sixty thousand,' he said. 'Inflation.'

'I'm sure we can agree on price when we know what we're getting. I'll give you an address to bring the package to. You do that soonest, say in an hour, thereabouts, soonest. Then we look at it, we authorise payment. How's that?'

'Forget it. You're not the only buyer. How's that?'

'That's quite persuasive. Can you give me time to discuss this with my colleagues? I'll recommend that we do it your way. I'm sure they'll agree. Call me at ten tomorrow morning?'

Niemand didn't reply for a moment. He needed to think. 'Okay,' he said.

'Good. Excellent. There's no need to look elsewhere, I assure you.'

Niemand sat for a while, not easy in his mind.

10

... HAMBURG ...

ANSELM TOOK the firm's BMW and drove to Winterhude. He found a parking space in Barmbeker Strasse, went to the *Konditorei* and bought a small black chocolate cake, walked to the apartment in Maria-Louisen-Steig to see Fräulein Einspenner, whose service to the Anselm family began in 1935.

She came to the door in seconds. She was just bone covered with finely lined tissue paper but her eyes were bright. She seated him in the stiff sitting room on a striped chair, took the cake to the kitchen and came back with it, sliced, on a delicate plate, on a tray with cake plates and silver cake forks.

They talked about the affairs of the day. She knew about everything, watched the news and current affairs on television, her eyes not up to reading the paper.

'How is Lucas?' she said.

'Well. He's well.'

'When is he coming to live in his house?'

'I don't know. He has a house in London.'

'Then he should give the house to you.'

'Perhaps his son will live in it one day.'

Fräulein Einspenner thought about that for a while, nodding. Then she said, 'Your German is very good.'

She always said that to him at some point. She had said it to him for thirty years.

Fräulein Einspenner separated a tiny piece of chocolate cake with her fork, put it to her mouth slowly. There was no perceptible chewing movement. She was ingesting it.

Anselm waited until he thought she had swallowed.

'Moritz,' he said. 'Do you remember much about him?'

She was looking at her plate, making another incision in her thin slice of cake with the side of her fork.

'Moritz?'

'My great-uncle.'

'I was a servant,' she said.

'You do remember him?'

She finished the cut, didn't impale the fragment, didn't look up, began another separation.

'I saw him, yes. He came to the house.'
'What became of him? Do you know?'
More work on the cake.
'Became of him?'
'What happened to him?'
She rested the fork on the plate.
'The war,' she said, looking up.
'He was killed in the war?'
'A lovely cake. When will you come again? I so look forward to seeing you. I see your father and your grandfather when I look at you.'

This meant she was tired. She walked to the front door of the building with Anselm, holding his hand, two fingers of his hand, and there he stooped to kiss her papyrus cheek.

She smelled as she had thirty years before, when she had stooped to hug him, kiss his cheek.

'Remember when we used to go to Stadtpark together?' she said. 'The birds. You loved them so much.'

He walked back to the car, stopped to buy cigarettes, drove down Dorotheen Strasse and into choked Hofweg. Turning down to Schöne Aussicht, he saw the last light of day on the silver lake. Three small boats were tacking towards the Pöseldorf shore, on their sails a colour the palest rose.

In the building, Baader was gone, returned to his child bride, and the shifts had changed. Inskip was back.

'There may be life outside this place,' he said in his languid English voice, not looking at Anselm. 'Have you considered that?'

'Movement, yes,' Anselm said. 'Life is another matter.'

'I'll settle for movement,' said Inskip. 'Up and down. You may or may not be pleased by some initiative I've shown. A Ms Christina Owens came up on the Continental database. The Campo woman checked in as C. Owens at a hotel in Vancouver six years ago. Someone in Canada found that out for the client.'

'Yes?'

'Christina Owens is staying at a hotel in Barcelona. The security man's given me some pictures.'

'Let's see.'

Inskip tapped, they waited, the screen began running a jerky hotel lobby surveillance film, four cameras: entrance, reception desk, seating area, lifts.

A couple came in the door, a woman with shoulder-length hair and a man walking just behind her. They saw him at the desk collecting a key. At the lifts, waiting, she turned her head to him, a younger man, said something, curt, impatient. He shrugged, raised a hand. The lift doors opened and they entered.

'Again.'

The couple came into view walking through the doors from the street. Anselm raised a finger.

Inskip froze the film. She was head-on to the camera.

Anselm made the enlarge sign.

It was a taut-skinned face, perky nose, eyebrows pencilled in, full lower lip.

'Save it.'

The box file was at Inskip's elbow. Anselm opened it, took out the top photograph: a woman, mid-twenties perhaps, hair pulled back, long nose, glasses. She had the face to play a librarian in a Hollywood film and she bore no resemblance to the woman in the Barcelona hotel surveillance video.

Anselm looked at the name and date pencilled on the back: Lisa Campo, October 1990.

'What's the nature of her malfeasance?' said Inskip.

'She's an accountant. Worked for Charlie Campo, a Midwest pizza prince. She became Mrs Campo, stashed around six million dollars offshore for Charlie. Skimmed money. Then she took off. Our client says there's five million moved, vanished. And all Charlie's got is this old driver's licence shot.'

'Sad, really.'

'Send the pic and the whole video to the Jocks, marked Rush. They may still be upright, capable of responding today.'

The firm sometimes used people in Glasgow, experts in facial recognition, academics making a buck on the side, putting taxpayer-funded research to good use.

Inskip said, 'You're suggesting that these totally different women might be the same person?'

'I'm just running up the bill.'

He nodded. 'How uncommercial of me. What do the Jocks do? Apply haggis-fuelled intuition?'

In spite of his considerable hacking skills, Inskip pretended to technological bewilderment, an upper-class English attitude of puzzlement and disdain.

'This'll be over your head, old fruit,' Anselm said, 'but they use something called PCA, principal component analysis. You establish a person's eigenface, then you compare any other face's eigenvectors, beginning with eyes, nose and mouth. It's well established but the Jocks have come up with a few tricks of their own.'

Inskip rolled his chair back, ran fingers through his hair. 'Eigenface? Why do the English think a German word is more serious than an English one? I mean, really, what has *Doppelgänger* actually got going for it?'

'Didn't register anything except the one word, did you? Send the pics.'

Anselm was reading the logs when Inskip loomed in the doorway.

'John. The sporran-swingers say 100 per cent positive.' He wrinkled his brow. 'I cannot believe that.'

Anselm looked at him for a while. 'Her eigenface. Plastic surgery couldn't hide it. Nothing they can do about the distance between her pupils. Her eye sockets. Booked in for how long?'

'Didn't notice.'

'Notice, James. Check it.'

Inskip sniffed, disappeared. Anselm signed a logbook, went back to the big room.

'It's three nights, two to go,' said Inskip.

'The man to ring is called Jonas. Campo's lawyer. The emergency number's in the file. If I remember, Charlie Campo offers twenty-five grand if he gets to confront her. Half for us.'

'My God.' Inskip was looking for the number. 'Who gets it?'

'Our policy,' said Anselm, 'is to give half of our cut to the finder.'

'The other half?' He was dialling, tapping on his keyboard.

'Distributed to the needy. For example, to someone who needs a new wife or a new Porsche.'

'Vulgar vehicle,' said Inskip. 'Do you want to speak?'

Anselm shook his head. You didn't want to deny people the pleasure of bearing good news. Inskip put on his headset. Anselm listened to the crackling from space, the crisp sound of a phone being picked up.

'Jonas.' Vague voice.

'Weidermann & Kloster in Hamburg, Mr Jonas. Sorry about the time. It's the Campo file.'

'What?' A cough, cigarette cough.

'The airline's found your client's luggage.'

'What, you found the name?'

'No, we've identified the actual luggage.'

'You're kidding?'

'No.'

A cough. 'Listen, fuck this spy shit, it's Lisa?'

Inskip looked at Anselm. 'We believe a hundred per cent positive,' he said.

'The face?'

He looked at Anselm again. Anselm nodded.

'The face. One hundred per cent.'

'Christ. Where?'

'Barcelona. Last night. Booked in for two more nights.'

'Barcelona, Spain?'

'Yes.'

'That's a hundred per cent?'

Inskip raised an eyebrow. Anselm nodded again. The Scots were never wrong. Eigenfaces didn't lie.

'Yes.'

'Ten years,' Jonas said, 'Charlie'll come in his pyjamas. Listen, Barcelona, some cover there, local knowledge, you can get that?'

Inskip looked at Anselm, opened his hands. Anselm took the headset off him, put it on. 'Mr Jonas, John Anselm. We can arrange that but it's expensive.'

Jonas cleared his throat, not a sound to wake up to. 'Fuck expense, John,' he said. 'Lose this fuckin fish, I'll die. Do it now.'

'Can you transfer fifteen thousand US immediately?'

'Check your balance in thirty.'

Anselm said, 'Give us your flight details when you have them and you'll be met.'

'Tonight,' said Jonas. 'We fly tonight. Barcelona, Spain. Some place quiet, we need that, you with me?'

'The person who meets you will have arranged that.'

Jonas made a sound like a snore. 'This works, I'm comin around, drinks, dinner. Fucking breakfast. For days.'

'And lunch?'

Jonas laughed. 'For wimps, man. Remember that movie?'

Anselm reminded him about the bonus and said goodbye. Inskip was looking at him, mouth open a little, teeth showing. He was more than interested, a little excited. 'Cover?' he said, no sign of languor now. 'What's that mean?'

'Make sure she doesn't vanish again.'

'We can do that?'

'We can do anything. Record this in the log.'

Anselm sat down at the workstation next to Inskip and rang Alvarez in Barcelona, exchanged pleasantries in Spanish, told him what was needed.

'Expensive,' said Alvarez.

'Within reason, Geraldo.'

'In advance, a thousand? Perhaps.'

'Because this is short notice, yes. I'll send it tonight.'

Anselm was heading for the door when Inskip said, 'What'll happen to the woman? Lisa?'

Anselm looked over his shoulder. 'What do you think? Charlie gets his money back, they fall in love again, go on a second honeymoon. Eat pizza.'

Inskip nodded a few times, licked his lips, turned back to his screen.

11

... LONDON ...

NIEMAND OPENED his eyes, out of sleep instantly, disturbed by some-thing, some irregularity, some change in the background noise he'd listened to as he drifted away on the too-soft bed.

Listening. Just the night–city sounds: wails, growls, whines, grates, squeals.

It had been a sound from inside the hotel. Close by.

Listening. Thinking: a hard sound, metallic, like a hammer strike. What could make a harsh metal-on-metal sound?

He knew, threw the sheet and blanket aside, was out of bed, wearing just his watch and running shorts.

Someone had opened the fire–escape door.

He was at the back of the building, last room in the corridor, a door away from the short passage that led to the fire–escape exit. Someone had pushed on the lever of the steel fire–escape door, found it reluctant to come out of the latch, applied more force, too much. It had come out, hit the restraining pin above it hard. That was the sound, a ringing, metallic sound.

Someone inside the hotel had opened the fire–escape door to let someone else in.

More than one?

He looked at his watch. 1.15 am.

If they're coming for me about the tape, he thought, there'll be a big one to break open the door, then they'll want to be finished in seconds, down the fire escape inside a minute.

He pulled the bed covers straight, they'd look there, that might give him a second, they were hardly rumpled by his few hours of sleep. He looked around for anything useful – the chair, a flimsy thing, better than nothing.

Stand behind the door? His instinct said: No, see what I'm up against, don't get slammed against the wall by a door shoulder-charged by a gorilla.

He stepped across the worn carpet and stood to the left of the door, back against the wall, holding the chair by a leg in his left hand.

Waiting in the dark room, wall icy against his shoulderblades, listening, all the city sounds amplified now. Calm, he said to himself, breathe deeply, icy calm.

No sound came to his ears from the passage.

Wrong. He was wrong. Too jumpy, the fire–escape latch just an invention of a mind looking to explain something, something in a dream probably. They couldn't have found him. How could they find him, they didn't even have a name? He dropped his head, felt tension leave his neck and shoulders.

The door came off its hinges.

A huge man, shaven-headed, came with it, went three steps across the room with the door on his right shoulder, his back to Niemand.

Close behind him was a tall, slim man with a silenced pistol in both hands, arms outstretched, combat style. He saw Niemand out of the corner of his eye, started to swing his arms and his body.

Niemand hit him in the head and chest with the chair before he had half swung, broke the chair back to pieces, hit him again with the back of the seat, more solid, caught him under the nose, knocked his head back.

The man stepped two paces back, his knees bending, one hand coming off the pistol.

The big man had turned, stood frozen, hands up, hands the size of tennis racquets.

Niemand threw the remains of the chair at him, stepped over, grabbed the gunman's right hand as he sank to the floor, blood running down his face, got the pistol, pulled it away, pointed it at the big man.

'Fuck, no,' said the big man, he didn't want to die.

Maori, maybe, thought Niemand, Samoan. He shot him in each thigh, no more sound than two claps with cupped hands.

'Fuck,' said the man. He didn't fall down, just looked down at his legs in the black tracksuit pants. Then he sat on the bed, slowly, sat awkwardly, he was fat around the middle. 'Fuck,' he said again. 'Didn't have to do that.'

The gunman was on his knees, lower face black with blood. He had long hair and it had fallen forward, hung over his eyes, strands came down to his lips. Niemand walked around him, pushed him to the carpet with his bare foot. There was no resistance. He knelt on the base of the man's spine, put the fat silencer muzzle into the nape of his neck.

'Don't even twitch,' Niemand said. He found a wallet, a slim nylon thing, in the right side pocket of the leather jacket. Took the mobile phone too. In the left pocket were car keys and a full magazine, fifteen rounds. That's excessive for taking out one man, Niemand thought. He stood up.

'Scare, mate,' the gunman said. 'That's all, mate, scare.'

It was hard to pick the accent through the blood and the carpet but Niemand thought it was Australian. An all-Pacific team.

'How'd you find me?'

The man turned his head. He had a strong profile. 'Just the messenger here, mate. Bloke gave me the room number.'

'What's your car?'

'What?'

Niemand ran the pistol over the man's scalp. 'Car. Where?'

'Impreza, the Subaru, at the lane.'

'Don't move.'

Niemand went to the doorway, now a hole in the wall, looked down the dim corridor. Nothing, no sounds. The room next door was empty, he'd seen the whiteboard in the reception office.

He went back. 'Unlucky room number,' he said to the man on the floor and, from close range, shot him in the backs of his knees. Clap, clap.

While the man keened, thin sounds, demanding, Niemand dressed, stuffed his things in his bag. The big man was lying back on the bed now, feet on the ground, making small grunting noises. If he wanted to, Niemand thought, he could have a go at me, just flesh wounds, like cutting your finger with a kitchen knife. But he doesn't want to, why should he? He's just the battering ram, the paid muscle.

Like me, all I've ever been, just the paid muscle. And always stupid enough to have a go.

'Give me your mobile,' he said to the big man.

The man shook his head. 'No mobile.'

Niemand went down the fire escape, not hurrying, walked down the alley, saw the car, pressed the button to unlock the driver's door. He drove to Notting Hill, light traffic, rain misting the windscreen, feeling the nausea, the tiredness, not too bad this time. He'd never driven in London but he knew the inner city from his runs, from the map. Near the Notting Hill Gate underground, he parked illegally, left the car unlocked with the keys in it, Three youths were nearby, laughing, one pissing against a car, he saw the joint change hands. With luck, they'd steal the Subaru.

On the underground platform, just him, two drunks and a woman who was probably a transvestite, he took out the gunman's mobile, flipped it open, pressed the numbers.

'Yes.' Hollis.

'Not a complete success to report,' Niemand said. 'Those boys you sent, one's too fat, one's too slow. I had to punish them. And I'm going to have to punish you too, Mr Hollis.'

'Hold on,' said Hollis. 'There's some ...'

'Goodbye.'

Niemand put the mobile away. One of the drunks was approaching, silly slack-jawed smile.

'Smoke, mate?' he said.

Glasgow. Niemand knew what people from Glasgow sounded like, he'd spent time with men from Glasgow. He turned side-on to the man, moved his shoulders. 'Fuckoff, throw you under the fucking train,' he said in his Scottish accent.

The man put up his hands placatingly, walked backwards for several steps, turned and went back to his companion.

12

... HAMBURG ...

'WHAT'S SERRANO'S business in Hamburg?' said Anselm. He was uneasy, his scalp itched. The other people in the restaurant seemed too close, he felt that they were looking at him.

They were in Blankenese, finishing lunch at a table in the window. Below them flowed the Elbe, wide, grey, unhealthy. Two container ships attended by screeching flocks of gulls were passing each other. The huge vessels – clumsy, charmless things bleeding rust at the rivets and oozing yellowish liquids from their pores – sent small waves to the banks.

'Moving money, papers,' said O'Malley. 'He shifts stuff all the time. Can't keep any computer records. No paperless office for Mr Serrano.'

'The pages any use?'

'The ones we can understand don't help us. We sold them to a firm in Dublin, so we'll get a bit of our money back. In due course. We don't demand cash on delivery. Unlike some.'

'Cash flow problems. The boss's been away on honeymoon.'

'Why does he have to marry them?'

'Some Lutheran thing. What's Serrano want with Kael?'

'We'd like to know.'

'You came over to tell me that?'

'No. I've got other business here. Mention this matter to Baader?'

'Yes. He says Kael's a man of parts.' Every time Anselm looked around, he thought he caught people staring at him.

O'Malley looked pensive, chewing the last of his *Zanderfilet*. He was big and pale, a long patrician nose between sharp cheekbones. He looked like an academic, a teacher of literature or history. But then you looked into his bleached blue eyes, and you knew he was something very different.

In the disordered and looted album of Anselm's memories, Manila was untouched. Manila, in the Taproom at the Manila Hotel. The group came in laughing, O'Malley with a short, bald Filipino man, two elated young women who looked like Rotary exchange students from Minnesota, and dark and brooding Paul Kaskis. O'Malley was wearing a *barong tagalog*, the Filipino shirt worn over trousers. The Filipino was in a lightweight cream suit, and Kaskis was in chinos and a rumpled white shirt.

The Filipino ordered margaritas. Anselm heard him say to the blondes that he'd started drinking them at college in California. At Stanford. They shrieked. They shrieked at the men's every utterance. It struck Anselm that if they were on an exchange, it was an arrangement between Rotary cathouses, an international exchange of Rotary harlots.

There was a moment when the shrieking women had gone to the powder room and the Filipino was talking softly to Kaskis and O'Malley was standing next to Anselm, paying for cigars.

'I think I know you,' said O'Malley. 'You're a journalist.' He was Australian.

'No and yes,' said Anselm.

'Don't tell me, you're with ...'

'I'm a freelance, not with anyone in particular.'

O'Malley's washed-out blue eyes, remarkable in his sallow face, flicked around the room. Then he smiled, a smile full of rue. 'Not CIA then?'

'No. I don't think they'd have me.'

'Fuck it,' O'Malley said. 'Met two today, I was hoping for a trifecta. Well, have a drink with us anyway.'

Anselm ended up having dinner with them. At one point, shrieking Carol, the taller and bigger of the American women, put an accomplished hand on him under the table, seemed to look to O'Malley for guidance.

Now O'Malley asked for guidance. 'What's Baader say about him?'

'Arms, drugs, possibly slaves, human organs. Untouchable. He has friends.'

'Just another Hamburg businessman then.'

'I suppose,' said Anselm. He had a cautious look at their fellow-lunchers, members of Hamburg's haute bourgeoisie, serious people noted for being cold, tight-lipped and very careful with a mark. Most of them were in middle age and beyond, the men sleek-haired and hard-eyed, just on the plump side, the women lightly tanned and harder eyed but carrying no excess weight, taut surgically contoured faces many of them, bowstring tendons in the neck.

'Baader says Kael doesn't talk directly to his own clients,' said Anselm, 'so he may be a client of Serrano's. Kael's money's all dirty and Serrano may be helping him with it.'

'This meeting tomorrow,' said O'Malley. 'Can that be covered?'

'Outdoors, it's a put-and-pluck on Serrano,' Anselm said. 'With possibilities of disaster. Want to wear that?'

'I'll have to.' O'Malley ran a hand over his tightly curled greying black hair, touched the collar of his lightweight tweed suit, the knot of the red silk tie. 'The world used to be a much simpler place, didn't it? There were things you could do, things you couldn't. Now you can do anything if you can pay for it.'

'Nostalgia,' Anselm said. 'I was thinking the other night. I've never asked. What happened to Angelica?'

'She doesn't work any more. She paints. She married an Englishman and now there's an American.'

'People you know?'

'The Pom, yes. I liked him. Eton and kicked out of the Guards. Rooting the CO's batman probably, much worse than rooting the CO's wife, he doesn't fuck his wife. The American's rich, inherited. I had dinner with them in Paris, in their apartment, the Marais can you believe? They have a cook, a chef. But there's hope, she's really distant with the hubby. Not surprising, he's an Egyptologist, the place's like a tomb and he could bore Mormons stiff.'

O'Malley drank the last of his wine. 'Still interested?'

'Just curious.'

'I could bring you together. Accidental meeting.'

'We only actually kissed once. While very drunk.'

'I remember. The Angel didn't kiss casually, though. Not a serial kisser.'

'I may be too late for accidental meetings. I may have had my ration of accidental meetings.'

'No, there's always one left.'

A youth in white had appeared to take away the plates. Close behind him came another young man, dark, Italianate, long-fingered. He fawned over O'Malley, suggesting the dessert trolley or something from the kitchen, anything, any whim. O'Malley ordered cognacs. He had the accent identified with Cologne, somehow frivolous in the intonation. North Germans found it annoying.

The waiter gone, O'Malley sighed. 'Well, a business lunch. What's a put-and-pluck cost?'

'As an estimate, plenty.'

O'Malley was looking away, watching three sailors on a Japanese container ship taking photographs of the shore. He said nothing for a while, drank some riesling, nodded in answer to some inner question. 'Yes,' he said, 'I thought it would be in that vicinity.'

They sat in silence until the cognacs came, more fawning. O'Malley rotated his fat-bellied glass and sniffed the small collar. 'If angels peed,' he said, and sipped.

Anselm felt the unease returning, wanted to be out of the place, away from people. He saw O'Malley's mouth rolling the liquid, his upward gaze, the calibrating.

'Nice lunch,' said Anselm. 'Thank you.'

O'Malley landed his glass on the heavy white linen. 'My pleasure. You eat quickly, not so much a diner as an eater.'

'I usually eat in the street,' Anselm said. 'Vendor food. You get into habits like that.' The unease was growing. He steadied himself. 'I have to go.'

On their way out, O'Malley stopped and bent over a handsome woman in dark business clothes, alone. 'Are you stalking me, Lucy?' he said. 'How did you know I'd be here?'

Anselm kept going, he wanted to be outside. A flunky was waiting to open the door. He went out onto the pavement, closed his eyes, breathed deeply, said his mantra.

In the taxi, O'Malley said, 'That woman, she's English, a very smart maritime lawyer based here. Froze a Polish ship for us in Rotterdam. I hope she's going to do the trick again.'

'I'm sure the courts look kindly upon her.'

'She's persuasive. They say she blew a judge when she was starting out in England. That's the gossip. Judgment overturned on appeal. Black mark for a judge.'

'At least he's got his memories,' Anselm said. 'Keep her wig on?'

O'Malley shook his head. 'How can you be so ignorant of legal decorum?'

13

… LONDON …

HALLIGAN, THE deputy editor, presided over the news conference. Caroline Wishart was nine minutes late, just behind skeletal Alan Sindall, the chief crime reporter.

'Welcome,' said Halligan. 'I'm thinking of making this meeting's time more flexible. We'll just run the fucking thing from 2 p.m. to whenever, open-ended, pop in whenever it suits you.'

'Sorry,' said Sindall, eyes down.

Caroline said nothing, eyes on the styrofoam cup of coffee she was carrying.

'Came together did you!' shrieked Benton, the small, fat deputy news editor, clapping his hands in front of his glasses. 'Came together!'

'Shut up, Benton,' Halligan said, 'we don't have to be *like* our readers. We *purvey* smut. That does not require that we ourselves be amused by childish double entendres.'

'Just a joke, Geoff,' said Benton, eyes down.

'Pathetic. Since by the grace of something or other the chief criminal reporter and the stand-in to the power of three for the editor of Frisson or Pissoir or whatever it's called are now here, let's hear it. About Brechan, Marcia?'

'Where's Colley?' said Marcia Connors, the news editor, a sharp-faced woman in her late thirties. 'Does he still work here? Does anyone know?'

Colley ran the paper's Probe team.

'He's accounted for his absence,' said Halligan. 'What's happening?'

'Nothing,' said Simon Knight, the chief political correspondent, slumped, looking over his glasses, chins rolling into a loosened collar already dirty. 'Brechan apparently doesn't have a care in the world.'

'The question was addressed to me,' said Marcia.

'Oh,' said Knight. 'Well, go for it, old dear.'

Marcia eyed him briefly, touched a canine with a short-nailed fingertip. 'Brechan gave us the slip last night.'

'And the catamite?' Halligan was looking at her hopefully.

She shook her head.

'Can't find him?'

'No.'

'Marcia, someone is going to find out about this and find the prick. We heard it first. You're saying it's not going to be us?'

'We can't find him.' She ran a hand over her hacked-short hair. 'Simple as that. If someone else can, good fucking luck to them. Gary vanished on Tuesday, thereabouts. His ex-boyfriend, this little poof is more vegetable than animal, into very serious substance abuse, he *thinks* Gary rang at some time around Tuesday to say he was going into a private clinic somewhere. He *thinks*. And he's never heard of Brechan.'

'Somewhere?' said Halligan.

'Somewhere. We've tried, believe me, we've tried. Could be in fucking Montevideo.'

'Have you tried Montevideo?' said Simon Knight.

Marcia didn't look at him. 'Oh fuck off, you fat ponce,' she said.

Halligan waved his hands placatingly, swivelled his chair to face the window. 'How did we come to stuff this thing up so comprehensively? Handed to us on a plate.'

'Don't know about handed anything,' said Marcia. 'It was only a tip-off.'

'Perhaps it *is* a pack of lies,' Simon Knight said. 'The man's got more enemies than Thatcher at her peak. And he's only the Defence Minister in waiting.'

Halligan came back to face the room, deep lines across his forehead. 'Bugger it,' he said. 'I told the boss we'd get the story. He was beside himself with joy. His favourite position.' He shook his head. 'Well, what is there for the front then?'

'Public schoolboys selling drugs,' said Marcia.

'That's news?' said Merton, the industrial affairs editor. 'What about pubs selling beer?'

'And fuck you too,' said Marcia.

Caroline put up a hand.

'Yes?' said Halligan.

'I've got pictures,' she said.

Silence in the room.

'What?' said Marcia.

'What?' said Halligan.

'Pictures.'

Marcia showed teeth, both top and bottom. 'I think it's too early in the day for you, darling. Up all night with the braying coke snorters. Tell us about your shitty little shots when we get to the rubbish end of the paper.'

'I've got pictures of Brechan and Gary,' Caroline said to Halligan.

A silence lay on the room, a religious silence. Halligan clicked his nails on the table. Nails too long for a man, Caroline thought. Her father would have thought so, anyway.

'Brechan and Gary?'

'Yes. And Gary's story.'

Marcia leant towards her. 'What kind of pictures? Doing what exactly?'

Caroline looked pointedly at the woman's bleached moustache, savoured the moment. She'd heard that Marcia had once had an affair with Halligan. 'I'm talking to Geoff,' she said. 'When I want to talk to you, I'll give you a sign. I'll indicate.'

'Doing what?' said Halligan.

Caroline took the lid off her coffee cup, had a tentative sip. 'Christ, the coffee's terrible around here,' she said. She wanted to make them wait. Since her first day on a free suburban rag in sodden Birmingham, all her life really, she had wanted a moment like this.

'Well?' said Halligan. His mouth was open and, with his pendulous jowls, he looked like a dog about to drool. 'Well? Doing what?'

Caroline had another sip of coffee. 'We should probably talk in private,' she said.

'Meeting adjourned for ten minutes,' Halligan said. 'Don't stray too far.'

Everyone got up and filed out except Marcia, who was lighting a cigarette.

Caroline waited until the door closed behind the last person before she looked at Marcia. 'You too,' she said. 'Out.'

Marcia was about to draw on the cigarette. She took her hand away, her mouth frozen and fish-like. 'Who the fuck do you ...'

Halligan raised both hands to her, palms outward. 'This won't take a moment, dear ...'

'Don't you fucking call me dear you spineless shit.' She got up. At the door, she said, 'This is going to be a defining moment in both your lives. I'll make fucking sure of that.'

She slammed the door.

Halligan pulled at his nose with thumb and forefinger. 'Now,' he said. 'The pictures.'

'Gary and Brechan fucking.'

'Fucking,' he said. 'Each other? Is that right?'

'Yes.'

'Taken by?'

'I don't know. It could be a remote thing.'

'You've got the pictures in your hands?'

'Yes. And Gary's story on tape. The full story. I've promised him thirty thousand pounds.'

Halligan looked at the table, tapped his pink forehead with his knuckles. 'Chickenfeed,' he said. 'Wait till the boss hears. Unbelievable. This is terrific. Terrific. You are terrific.'

Caroline took the folded sheet of paper out of her inside pocket, gave it to him.

He read it, looked up at her. 'Yes, you can leave the Frisson section immediately. Yes, you can be off–diary. Yes, you can have an office. But as for the rest of this, Caroline, it's ridiculous …'

She stood up and started for the door. 'Read the story in the *Sun*.'

'Caroline my dear, sit down, let's talk,' he said.

14

... HAMBURG ...

LIGHT DRAINING from the world, the coming winter on his skin, knee joints pleading, Anselm ran home, not stopping till he stood at his gate in the silent street, slumped in the shoulders, seeing his ragged breath in the air.

He was in the kitchen, about to drink bottled water, weak, unshowered, when the knocks sounded on the huge front door. He froze. There was a bell, it worked, someone chose to knock. Pause – again the hollow knocking.

He spoke to himself, calmed himself, and went down the cavernous passage into the hall, switched on the outside light. A shadow lay on the front door's stained-glass window.

'Who is it?' he said.

'Alex Koenig.'

Anselm opened the door. She was formally dressed, a pinstriped suit, dark, a white shirt with a high collar, dark stockings. She looked severe and striking.

'I came to apologise,' she said. 'I was wrong to come here uninvited and what I said was unforgivable.'

Anselm shook his head. 'You don't have to apologise. No one who deals with me ever has to apologise.'

'You will accept my apology?'

'Of course, but ...'

'I won't bother you again.'

She turned and went quickly down the path. He wanted to call after her, ask her to come back, come inside, show her that he was not the savage and unpleasant person he had presented to her.

But he did not. He was scared of her. Of what she knew about him.

Alex Koenig didn't look back, the gate clicked behind her. A wait, then a car drove away, its sound lost in the murmuring city.

Anselm went back to the kitchen, down the flagstone passage so wide he could not touch the walls with outstretched arms. He put the bottle of water away, opened a beer and downed it in two long-throated drinks, the clean tawny smell filling his nasal cavities. He poured a glass of white wine, sat at the pine table. Just to sit there comforted him. The great, worn table in the kitchen always comforted him.

In Beirut, fighting against claustrophobia and pain and panic, his memories of the house on the canal, of the kitchen and the garden saved him. He had forced himself to think about the house and his childhood, his family: being woken by his brother in the middle of the night and seeing adults in the garden throwing snowballs; walking by the canal with his grandfather, autumn leaves underfoot; in the kitchen helping Fräulein Einspenner to shell peas, peel potatoes, knead dough. The kneading he had remembered most clearly: the feel of the dough, the life in it, the resistance building beneath his hands, the sensual, silky, breast-like resilience.

And he remembered the roses one summer – the ones the colour of burnt cream in the big pots on the terrace, the three or four shades of pink around the front gate, the dark satiny reds that smothered the boundary wall.

Later, after he had been beaten, after the panic when he began to discover the holes in his mind, the blank spaces, the lacunae, it began to gnaw at him that he didn't know the names of so many things. For a long time, he could not distinguish between what he had never known and what he had forgotten. And when he thought he could, he was filled with an aching despair that he would die without knowing the names. In that hopeless space, always dark, the world was gone, the whole world of sky and earth and trees moving in a cold wind. Gone.

And with it the names.

Now, sitting at the table in the flagstoned room, he remembered clearly the ache to know the names, to be able to say them to himself.

The need to know names.

The names of so many things.

'Do you know the names of any roses?' he had asked.

'What?' Riccardi, a whisper.

'Roses.'

'Roses?'

'Yes. Roses. Their names.'

And so it began. In that foetid hole, black, a shallow grave, two men lying so close together they could not be sure whose breath they smelled, whose body sounds they heard, whose heartbeat they felt – they began to name things. In three languages. Roses. Trees. Give me ten trees. Dogs, name twelve dogs. Fifteen saints. Twenty mountains. Flowers, stars, saints, rivers, seas, singers, capitals, wars, battles, writers, songs, generals, paintings, poets, poems, actors, kinds of pasta, ocean currents, deserts, books, trees, flowers, desserts, architectural periods, cars, American presidents, parts of speech, characters in books, prime ministers, volcanoes, hurricanes, bands, waterfalls, sculptors, American states, meat dishes, actors, breads, wines, winds, women's names from A to Z, men's, towns, villages, statues, operas, kings, queens, the seven dwarves, engine parts, films, directors, diseases, biblical figures, boxers, names for the penis, for breasts, the vagina, for eating and shitting and pissing and kissing and fucking and pregnancy and telling lies.

But not words for dying.

No, not words for dying. They didn't need words for dying. They were going to die.

The tape recorder was on the table. He went to the study and fetched the box of tapes. He went back and forth on the one with 2 written on it, circled.

You were talking about Kate yesterday.

Oh. Yes. Kate was a Jew.

Who's Kate?

Our cousin's wife. I'll show you her photograph. Beautiful girl, lovely. A Jew. Nominally. Her family. Not in a religious sense. I don't think they had any religion to speak of. We, of course, we thought of ourselves as Christians. But all we did was observe the traditions. We only went to church on Christmas day, to the Landeskirche, just a family tradition. And of course we had the most wonderful Christmas Eves, the Feuerzangbohle, *the presents, my dear, the wonderful presents.*

What about Kate?

Moritz was abominable. Isn't that a lovely word? Abominable. English is a lovely language. Stuart used to call all kinds of things abominable. Do you know about the creature of the snows? In the Himalayas? Where do you place the stress in that? I've never been comfortable with the word.

About Kate? Moritz?

Moritz said we should put the Stürmer *sign on the entrances to the family businesses. Such a stupid and dreadful thing to say ...*

What sign?

Oh, you know, Juden sind hier nicht erwünscht. *He was talking about how Germany needed to be cleansed of Jews, it was a matter of hygiene, nonsense like that, he had obviously been drinking.*

Kate heard that?

Your great-grandfather didn't like that kind of talk. We dealt with many Jews. He was an old-fashioned person. Well, he was old. Not that old, I suppose ... as old as I am now, I suppose. Good heavens. I would need to work that out. How old he was. One forgets.

This was just before the war?

You looked like Moritz when you were a boy, do you know that? A little bigger, he was thin. But your eyes and the hair and the chin.

No. Did many people you knew feel the way Moritz did?

About Jews? People said things. But the Nazis, we had contempt for their rubbish. We all did. The people we mixed with. The old merchant families. We had all travelled, you see, we were ... worldly, I suppose that's the word. 'That Man', that's what we called Hitler. That Man. A vulgar person. They were all vulgar, the women were all ... well, I shouldn't. He was Austrian too, not German.

Moritz. What happened to him?

I remember when you came to this house the first time. Lucas was quiet, he didn't move from your mother and you just ran around madly and Einspenner was so taken with you, she took you into the kitchen and showed you the cellar ...

Before he went to bed, Anselm made a cheese omelette, ate it with toasted five-day-old bread. He wasn't hungry, just a duty the mind owed the body. In the study, he saw the American Defense Secretary on television. He was behind a desk, Michael Denoon, a hard-faced man, boxer's scars on his jaw and right cheekbone. Through the pancake, the lights caught them, thin lines where skin and flesh had been jammed against bone and split open. But his nose was straight, no one had got through to his nose.

A CNN woman came on, lots of hair, eyes wide open, and a big cone-shaped mouth. She said:

Pressure on US Defense Secretary Michael Denoon to enter the presidential race intensified today when Newsweek *reported that an informal poll showed 155 of 222 Republican members of the House of Representatives would support Denoon's candidacy.*

Republican Senator Robert Gurner is thought to be unelectable since the disclosure three days ago of his two-year homosexual relationship with New York actor Lawrence Wellman.

Denoon again. He put his head to one side, ran a hand across his hair, modest, straightened, looked at the camera.

Of course I'm deeply honoured by this expression of confidence by people who speak for millions of ordinary Americans. I'm humbled too. This nation bears deep wounds from the great sacrifices it has made in faraway places to fight evil and promote freedom and democracy. Now we need calm, peace and prosperity. We need to renew ourselves, to put America first, to see clearly our place in the world. But whether I am fit to take up this great challenge is a matter for long and careful thought.

Anselm went to bed and thought about America. He tried to remember what it had been like to feel wholly American, to look at the world as an American. He knew he had once but he could not recapture it. Over the years, moving from war to war, horror to horror, his nationality had been bled from him. The more he saw of the world's conflicts, of people dead, wounded, mutilated, raped, dispossessed of what little they had, the more unreal America seemed, the more the cruel naiveté of America embarrassed him. That was partly why he was drawn to Kaskis. Kaskis didn't expect America to behave sensibly and so he wasn't disappointed when it didn't. He remembered sitting in a dark bar in San Francisco with Kaskis. It was the mid-1980s. He was about to go to Pakistan and Afghanistan, Kaskis had just come back.

'The CIA wants to fight this one to the last dead Afghan,' Kaskis said. 'More CIA in Islamabad than in fucking Langley. Bill Casey's got this hick from Texas, he's the point in Congress. The prick's been up in the hills hanging out with the mojahedin. He thinks we give them the right stuff we can do a reverse Vietnam. And for nickels and dimes. This time we stay at home and our proxies kill Russians. Lots of Russians. Fifty-eight thousand would be a nice number.'

Kaskis had stubbed out his cigarette, fished for another. 'I weep for my fucking country,' he said. 'Everywhere we go we sow dragon's teeth.'

On the long slope towards sleep, he saw Kaskis, saw his face as he was taken away, the look back, the lift of his dark-stubbled chin, the wink. Anselm tried to shake the image away, dislodge it, but it clung, tenacious.

The dark eyes of Kaskis, the flash of his teeth. In all of it, Kaskis had never shown a sign of fear.

Before dawn, Anselm woke in a foetal clutch, straightened his body and lay on his back, stretched his arms and legs. I haven't woken myself by crying out loud for a while, he thought. I haven't woken wet with sweat to find tears on my face.

15

... LONDON ...

THE MAN on the front page of the newspaper was overweight, middle-aged, naked. He was looking at the camera, standing, flabby. Sagging teats, hairy belly out, engaged in a sexual act with someone lying face down. The detail had been obscured. A big headline said:

**WELL, I'LL BE
BUGGERED,
MR BRECHAN!**

Niemand took the newspaper from the next table when he sat down with his breakfast on a styrofoam tray. The story was about a politician called Brechan, filmed having sex with someone called Gary. Gary was quoted as saying: 'Look about fifteen, don't I? That's why they like me. I'm twenty-two. Believe that? Anyway, Angus passed me on to this other bloke. Not a clue till I saw him on telly. Oh my God, I said to ...'

Niemand ate the scrambled eggs, powdered eggs, and the small tasteless meat patty and the piece of extruded bacon. He didn't mind food like this. It was assembly-line cooking, reasonably clean. They couldn't risk people getting ill. Counter-productive. Easier to be hygienic. Just like the military.

He turned the page. The story went on. Three politicians were involved but the others weren't named. The writer said they would be: tomorrow.

The writer's name was Caroline Wishart. There was a picture of her above her byline. She had long hair and her nostrils were pinched as if she were drawing a big breath, sucking in air. He sat and thought, eyes on the street. London was much dirtier than he remembered, more poor people, more junkies.

A face. Inches away, beyond the glass, bulging hyperthyroid eyes stared at him, a woman in a knitted hat, dirt marks on her face, ash smears, darker marks. She tapped on the glass, a hand in a cotton gardening glove with its fingers cut off at the second joint.

Niemand looked away. The woman tapped again, angrily, then gave up. He watched her go. Her crammed plastic bag was splitting. Soon her possessions would begin to fall out, just more rubbish on the street.

He couldn't deal with Kennex Imports. They wouldn't send a fat and a slow the next time. He was well ahead, he had Shawn's money. He should cut his losses, take a ferry to France, Holland, Belgium, anywhere, post the tape to a newspaper or a television station.

But he didn't like being thought of as something they could simply squash, a capsule of blood, like a tick. They had tried to get the tape for nothing. Next to nothing. The price of hiring a fat and a slow.

What was the tape worth?

He found the newspaper's telephone number in the middle of the paper, on the opinion page. They kept him on hold for a long time. He had to listen to a news radio station. Then she came on.

'Caroline Wishart,' she said, a voice like the women on English television, the newsreaders who could talk without moving their lips.

He used his Glasgow accent again. 'I've got something that will interest you,' he said. 'A film. Much more important than that article today.'

'Really,' she said, dry. 'I get a lot of calls like this.'

'A massacre in Africa.'

'A lot of that goes on.'

'Soldiers killing civilians.'

'What, the Congo? Burundi?'

'No. White soldiers. Americans.'

'American soldiers killing civilians in Africa? Somalia?'

'No. This is … it's like an execution.'

'You've got a film?'

'Yes.'

'What's your name?'

'Doesn't matter. Just give me five minutes of your time.'

He heard her sigh. 'You'll have to come here. Not today, today's impossible.'

'Has to be today.'

'Are you, ah, offering this film for sale?'

'Twenty thousand pounds.'

Caroline Harris laughed. 'I don't think you've come to the right place.'

'See it and decide,' said Niemand.

She laughed again. 'Are you a crank? No, don't answer that. Let me see, ah … twelve noon.'

She gave him the address. 'Tell reception you've got an appointment. Give me a name.'

'Mackie,' he said, seeing in his mind's eye the little redheaded killer, the empty blue eyes, the big freckles. 'Bob Mackie.'

16

... HAMBURG ...

ANSELM SAT in the driver's seat of the Mercedes and watched the ferry heading for the landing. It was a windy day, tiny whitecaps on the water, windsurfers out, three of them, insouciant, skidding over the cold lake on a broad reach.

'Noisy,' Tilders said. 'May not work.' He had a scope suspended from roof brackets trained on the boat. It was an English instrument made for military use with an image-stabilised lens, 80x magnification. A small LCD colour monitor sat on the console. He fiddled with the plug in his ear. Its cord ran to a black box on his lap.

They had nailed Serrano inside the hotel. He was alone, bodyguard no longer needed. In the lobby, a frail-looking old man crossed his path, stumbled and fell. For a moment, it looked as if Serrano was going to walk around him, then he bent down, put out a helping hand. The old man got up shakily, leaned on Serrano for a few seconds, thanked him profusely. Serrano continued on his way to the restaurant for breakfast.

Outside, in the car, they waited. Tilders was looking upwards, pensive. Then he closed his eyes, nodded.

'Working,' he said. 'Orange juice, eggs Florentine.'

Serrano was now wearing a micro-transmitter.

'Working,' said Tilders.

In the BMW, watching the ferry, Anselm raised his right hand, the hand that worked fully, mimed. Tilders raised the volume.

Serrano, speaking German: ... *this ferry. What's the problem?*

Kael: *Nothing's safe any more.*

Serrano: *I can get seasick just looking at boats. In a harbour.*

Kael: *Tell me.*

Serrano: *Werner, I just heard from Hollis, they fucked the business up.*

The transmission went fuzzy, fragmented for about five seconds, abrasive sounds.

Serrano: ... *contact him.*

Kael: *He fucking hopes. Why should he do that? This is the most hopeless ...*

Serrano, a laugh: *Well, Lourens is dead, that's ...*

Sound lost again, for seconds the rough abrasive sounds.

Kael: ... *Can you grasp that? If this prick's got the papers and the film, whatever the fucking film is ... How did Lourens die?*

340

Serrano: *In a fire. Chemical fire. Not even teeth left.*

Kael: *Well, that's something. Shawn?*

Serrano: *Shot by blacks. So it appears. The business is strange. Werner, the question is what do we do now?*

Kael: *You ask me, you idiot? We'll have to tell the Jews. They'll blame us.*

Serrano: *You're the one who went to the Jews. You're the one who did what they said. I thought we weren't going near them again? I thought you took a holy vow?*

Silence. Sounds, bumping sounds, the ferry hitting the chop as it passed another vessel.

Kael: *You should wear a hat in Provence in summer.*

Silence. A noise. Anselm thought it was Serrano clearing his throat.

Serrano: *Well, fuck you. Maybe you need a smarter person. Have you got one?*

Silence, the bumping sounds, a cough.

Kael: *Don't be so sensitive. Hollis? What does the cunt say?*

Serrano: *He's shitting himself. He thought he was doing the right thing.*

Kael: *He should. He should shit himself. I'm going to kill him personally. Tell Richler.*

Serrano: *What?*

Kael: *What do you fucking think? Just tell him. They're up to their balls in this. If the Ashken stuff is in the papers, well …*

The ferry was docking, they could hear the sounds of movement, the voices of passengers.

Kael: *I walk from here. Thomas will take you.*

'Good bug,' said Anselm. Tilders nodded.

Kael's Mercedes, dark blue, was waiting about fifty metres from the landing, the driver standing at the rear passenger door. He was a big man in a dark suit, feet wide apart, hands at the buttons of his jacket. Tilders got him on the monitor. The shutter release was silent.

Serrano and Kael were the first passengers off the ferry. Anselm looked at the monitor. The two men were on it, Tilders was looking at the screen and taking pictures.

Silence until the men were at the car. Anselm saw Kael give Serrano something.

Serrano: *What's this?*

Kael: *Ring the number and leave a time, five minutes before the ferry I've marked leaves.*

Serrano: *Extreme, this is extreme.*

Serrano got into the Mercedes and was driven away. Kael walked off in the direction of his house. The last passenger off the ferry was a fat man in a suit carrying a briefcase. Anselm watched him come in their direction. When he was near you could see that he was a dispirited man, in him no

341

satisfaction at the end of the working day, no expectation of ease to come. He walked past them with his head down.

'Otto will go to Hofweg,' said Tilders. 'I don't know if all this is worth it.'

'They pay for a full record,' said Anselm. 'We don't have to ask whether it's worth it.'

17

... HAMBURG ...

ON THE outer fringe of Barmbek, once a working-class suburb, O'Malley was waiting for him, beer on the counter.

Anselm looked at the brown walls, brown carpet, brown curtains, the dead-faced barman.

'Impressive venue,' he said.

'Well, you're not Bavarian,' said O'Malley. 'This is a Bavarian hangout. Beer fresh from the cask. Stick around, you'll be singing old Bavarian songs.'

'Songs wildly popular in the 1930s, no doubt,' said Anselm. He was rubbing his dead fingers, bending them, turning his hand. He wanted to be outside.

The barman brought another beer without being asked.

O'Malley paid.

'I thought the Marriott was more your speed,' Anselm said, casual voice, he could do that, he got better at it every day. 'Full of rich and dubious people. Still, I can see they know you here.'

O'Malley drank, ran an index finger along his lower lip. 'I'm the customer,' he said, 'with all the rich meaning the word holds. And I like the beer. Also I'm staying nearby. How'd it go?'

'Well.'

'Listen?'

'Part of the service.'

'So?'

'Serrano told Kael about someone that's gone wrong. They talked about people now dead. Kael told him to tell a person called Richler. He could be an Israeli. Serrano's coming back tomorrow.'

'Dead people?'

'Shawn. Lourens. Something like that.'

A card game in the corner detonated, exclamations of disbelief.

Anselm went rigid, every muscle, tendon.

Four players. War babies, in their fifties, leather-faced men in leather jackets. Brown leather jackets.

Anselm drank. The beer had the feral-yeast taste. That and the men playing cards brought a hotel on the Ammersee into his mind. Had he forgotten it? He hadn't remembered it for a long time. The woman's name

343

was Paula, an artist, he'd lived with her in Amsterdam for a while. They'd gone on holiday, had an argument that night about another woman. Seated in the hotel's dining area, the locals looking on, she'd punched him in the mouth, a full swing across a table. Her little walnut fist drew his blood but a bone broke in it. Worth it, she said to him later, in pain, unrepentant.

'We may have to go on,' O'Malley said.

Anselm found a cigarette, put it on the table, let it lie. Any delay in lighting up was good. Some tension left him. 'I would warn of expense. If that's of consequence.'

O'Malley raised his hands, not high, big and pale strangler's hands. 'Discount for repeat business?'

'Second time's much harder.'

'Yes, women have said that to me,' said O'Malley. His eyes went to the door.

Anselm looked, tight muscles in the stomach, shoulders, thighs.

Two young men came in from the street, one tall, one average, short hair-cuts, soft and expensive leather jackets, not brown. They were not at their ease, eyes going around, over O'Malley and him.

The barman didn't care for them, just a small and telling shift of hips and shoulders.

O'Malley drank his final centimetres, leaned closer. His expression was amused. 'Well, got to go, a dinner date,' he said. 'These boyos ...'

Anselm didn't look at the two men. 'Is there an anxiety you haven't told me about?' He held O'Malley's eyes, smoked, sipped beer.

'You never know,' said O'Malley. 'Serrano's a dangerous man. Give me something else.'

Anselm felt in the inside pocket of his jacket. Condoms, a packet of condoms, old, some forgotten optimism in the purchase. 'I'm going to give you something worth much more than any tape,' he said.

O'Malley nodded, smiling, teeth showing, the O'Malley smile that meant nothing, not pleasure, not fear. 'I'm parked about twenty metres down, left.'

'Cowbarn beer, Bavarian nostalgics, now it's intrigue. Anything else?'

'Give it to me, mate.'

Anselm slid his hand out of his coat, put it palm down on the table. O'Malley smiled, covered his hand, gave him a pat, a gesture of friendship from a large hand, scar tissue on all the knuckles.

'*Compadre*,' said O'Malley.

Anselm removed his hand and O'Malley pocketed the condom packet.

'I liked Manila,' said Anselm. 'Can we go back?'

O'Malley shook his head. '*Ein ruheloser Marsch war unser Leben.* All the fun people are gone, Ferdie's gone, Imelda's gone, Bong-Bong's gone.' He paused. 'Angel's gone too. So am I. Anyway, you can't go back, anywhere.'

Anselm saw Angelica for a moment, the tiny tip of pink tongue, the swing of dark-red hair half curtaining an eye. 'That theory,' he said, 'has it been properly tested? Scientifically, I mean.'

O'Malley shook his head in wonder, got up, left. The inner door closed loudly on its spring. Anselm put the glass to his lips and looked around. The two newcomers were in mid-glance at each other. The taller one shrugged, looked at the barman, raised a hand to get attention.

'*Zwei Biere, bitte*,' he said in an irritated tone, not a Bavarian accent. '*Ist das tatsächlich möglich?*'

Anselm got up. At the door, he turned his head. The two men had no interest in him. He went outside, into a cold early winter evening perfumed with vehicle fumes and cooking smells, walked to where O'Malley stood beside an Audi.

'My condoms for this tape.'

'I don't know,' said O'Malley, 'I could use these frangers. The night is young.'

'Unlike you and the condoms. Will she wear her wig? It excites me, the thought.'

O'Malley smiled. 'Really, John, that's pathetic. You need more exoticism in your life. I like women in full surgical gear, green smock, rubber boots, the cap, the face mask.'

'You're sick.'

'The exact point, my good man.'

18

… HAMBURG …

ANSELM TOOK the car back to the office. He was looking at the logbooks when the phone rang.

'We go on,' said O'Malley.

'So be it.'

He finished his reading, signed, changed and set off for home, running in the cold dark, hearing the city humming like a single organism. There was no wind. The lake was still and the lights of the far shore all came to him in silver lines, followed him as he moved: he was the focus, the point of intersection.

As he ran, he thought about coming back to the house that day, after Beirut. It had been spring, late evening, the house empty and shuttered, almost everyone who had lived there dead. He was mostly dead too, and he had begun to cry when he opened the gate, saw the roses in bloom. He was half drunk, and he wept, sitting on the steps, his head in his hands, tears pooling in his palms. He knew that he was home, as close to home as he would ever be.

Inside the house, the power was off, the heating had not been on for years, the air smelled of dust and ancient lavender furniture polish and, somehow, faintly, of cigar smoke, of the Cuban cigars smoked by his grand-father – his great-grandfather, for all he knew. He had walked through the ground-floor rooms, opened the curtains, heavy as wet canvas, pulled the shrouds off the furniture.

That day he took the whisky out of his bag, chose a glass from dozens in the pantry, rinsed it in one of the porcelain sinks in the scullery, the water running dark for a good while. He sat on a huge, deep embossed-velvet sofa looking out at the terrace, the overgrown darkening garden, took the tablets and drank himself to sleep. At some point, he drew up his legs, becoming as small as he could.

The next day, he was woken by the pounding of the knocker on the front door. His brother, Lucas, fresh, pink-cheeked. They embraced, awkwardly, they had no easy way to touch each other, there was no fit of body, arm or hand. Anselm had felt his stubble scrape the smooth cheek of Lucas, pulled back. They drew apart.

'This is stupid,' said Lucas. 'For God's sake, we were worried, this is not a good idea, John, you're coming to stay with us, you can't stay here. Lucy's adamant, I'm adamant, for God's sake …'

'Just for a while,' Anselm heard himself say. 'Get myself sorted out.'

They went inside. Anselm followed Lucas, his older brother grown small, as he walked around inspecting things. Lucas owned the house. It had been left to him.

In the kitchen, Lucas said, 'Are you sure? About staying here?'

'Yes.'

'I'll say it again, you're more than welcome in London. There's also the cottage in …'

'No. Thank you. Thank Lucy. I want to be here.'

The relief in Lucas showed in his eyes, in a movement of his mouth. He took out his telephone. 'We'll need some German efficiency. Yes. Get things liveable here. I'll talk to a man I have dealings with. Deutsche Bank.'

By late afternoon, lunch had been delivered, the power was on, the phone connected, a new refrigerator was cooling in the pantry, a plumber had been, a new water-heater installed, six people had cleaned the house, cartons of food and drink delivered by a small van had been stored.

At the gate, the taxi's diesel engine thumping, Lucas said, 'Listen, I'd like to stay but I've got to be in New York tomorrow, we're in a shitfight with Murdoch's people.'

Anselm said, 'Thanks, I appreciate … all this.'

'I'll have your stuff from San Francisco sent. It's in storage, I did that, I thought … well, need anything, just call the number. It's on the pad. Next to the phone? I wrote it down. They'll get me. Any time, it doesn't matter.'

Anselm nodded.

'The time doesn't matter. Okay?'

His brother put out his right hand and touched Anselm's cheek, found himself doing it, crumpled his hand, tapped Anselm's face with a loose fist.

'You will,' he said. 'John, you'll call me, won't you?'

Anselm said, 'Yes. Thanks. For everything. Give my love to Lucy. And the boy.'

He'd forgotten the boy's name.

'Hugo, it's Hugo.'

'I know that. You don't always name things. You don't always have to say the name.'

He saw wariness in Lucas's eyes.

'No,' said Lucas. 'Of course. I know you know Hugo's name. I wasn't suggesting otherwise.'

They tried to hug again, failed miserably, and Lucas was driven away, a hand at the window.

Tonight, as he ran, Anselm remembered going inside and walking around, standing in the kitchen. He had been close to Riccardi for so long, so close. He had dreamed of being alone, of walking on an empty beach, no one near, and now he was alone and it frightened him. He had sat down at the table and rested his forehead on the lined scrubbed wood, cool, and he had begun to cry again.

Now, in his street, almost walking, sweat cooling on him, that day seemed close. He thought that he was only marginally different now. In some ways, he was worse now.

He went inside, showered, drank, watched television. He hoped the phone would ring. It didn't. He went to the kitchen, sped across tape number 3, sampling, looking for a mention of Moritz, his own teenage voice strange to him. He caught the word:

Moritz. What happened to him?

It's a lovely day. We could go for a walk. Are you bored here? With an old woman? Two old women.

I'm not bored. I like being here. I want to know about the family, my dad doesn't say much so it's …

It was the summer he was seventeen, the five weeks he had spent with his great-aunt, the two of them and Fräulein Einspenner in the huge house. Next door, a girl lived, Ulrike, a year younger. She wore a big straw hat when she was out in the long garden that ran to the canal, and she was pale in a way no American girl was pale. He lusted after her. Once, after they were introduced, they sat side by side on the terrace. She leant forward and he looked into the big, loose armhole of her summer blouse and saw that she was not wearing a bra. He saw the full hanging curve of her right breast. Even paler than her face. Pale and veined like graveyard marble. His blood changed course. He made an excuse, went upstairs to his bedroom and stood looking down at her, penis in hand.

Einspenner has always been besotted by you. From the day you came here, a little American boy who spoke German.

What happened to Moritz?

He didn't come back from the war.

He was killed?

Well, the war.

A silence.

Afterwards, we tried to forget the war, you know. It was so unfortunate. Such a mistake. Your great-grandfather went into a decline. The business was ruined. All those years, the tradition. Destroyed. Gone. Your grandfather tried to pretend it wasn't happening. He would not accept it. For him, London was closer than Berlin or Munich, he went to England five or six times a year. He talked about going to London as we would talk about going to, going to Mönckebergstrasse. He had old friends from Oxford. And the people we dealt with of course. He knew Chamberlain, do you know that?

No.

And there was his mistress in London.

Chamberlain's mistress?

No, your grandfather's mistress, that drew him to London. Of course. She lived on Cheyne Walk.

You knew about his mistress?

It was no secret. We all knew. I met her after the war. A woman of great charm. And dignity. She was not a kept woman, she had her own money. He was a very attractive man, my brother. He hadn't been close to your grandmother for a long time. They were friends, but they weren't close. You know what I mean. She had her own interests.

Didn't the war ... I mean, what did his mistress feel about Germans then?
Silence.

She understood that Hitler didn't speak for all Germans. But lots of English people admired Hitler. It made your grandfather so angry. That Mitford girl who hung around Hitler. Her father was an English lord.

About Moritz, didn't you ...

What do they teach you at school? Do you read the great works?

Well, we have to read a lot of ...

My father loved English poets. Milton and Wordsworth. They were his favourites. And Blake, he liked Blake. He used to read them to us. Thackeray and Dickens he liked too. And Gibbon, he used to take Gibbon on holiday to the sea.

So was Moritz ...

And Shakespeare, he loved Shakespeare, the tragedies. He used to say that Shakespeare didn't write the tragedies, a German must have written them and had his work stolen because no one except a German could be so ...

Sitting at the kitchen table, Anselm listened until the end of the tape, lulled by Pauline's quiet voice talking about people whose blood ran in his veins and who were now just faces in faded photographs. He heard himself ask about Moritz again and receive no answer.

19

... HAMBURG ...

IN THE morning, Anselm spread out the family tree his great-aunt had drawn up on pieces of paper, taping pages together as the record widened and lengthened. He had found it, carefully folded, in a desk drawer in the small sitting room. Unfolded, it was half the size of a single-bed sheet.

Pauline had traced the family back into the German primeval forest. The Hamburg branch had come to the city in 1680. From then on, she had recorded in her minute script the occupation of every member who achieved some distinction. Here a senator, here a consul, aldermen, physicians, a writer, a judge, attorneys, scholars, a composer. The rest were presumably just merchants. There was a French connection too, Anselm noticed. Pauline had written *Huguenot* in parentheses after the French names of people two Anselms married in the late 1600s.

Anselm found his grandfather, Lucas, and siblings Gunther, Pauline and Moritz. The birth dates, marriages and offspring of the first three were recorded, as were Lucas's death in 1974 and Gunther's in 1971. For Moritz, there was only his date of birth: 1908.

What became of Moritz, who looked like Count Haubold von Einsiedel? Did he marry? Were there children? When did he die?

Anselm remembered his father talking about Gunther. In 1940, the three children had been sent to live with Gunther and his American wife in Baltimore and they never really went home to Hamburg. But his father had never mentioned Moritz.

Time to go to work. Beginning to run in the morning was like starting an old machine, like pulling the cord of a lawnmower never oiled, the moving pieces reluctant, grating.

When he was warm, moving without pain, Manila came to his mind: Angelica Muir, the side-on look of her, the small nose, her teeth, the taste of her.

After the first lunch, he had many meals – lunches, dinners, late breakfasts, early breakfasts – with O'Malley, Angelica and Kaskis. They went to all kinds of gatherings and parties, everything seemed to turn into a party. O'Malley floated in the culture, spoke fluent Tagalog, knew everyone from millionaire Marcos cronies to penniless hardline Communists. He never stopped paying, no one else was allowed to pay. And, when things were moving at some party, he broke into song – country & western songs, Irish songs, operatic arias, songs from the War of Independence against the Spanish, Neil Diamond's greatest hits, Cuban revolutionary songs.

O'Malley had called himself a financial adviser. His firm was Matcham, Suchard, Loewe, two secretaries and an elegant crew-cut Filipino with an American accent and a wardrobe of Zegna suits.

After he had filed his last story from the Philippines, Anselm had dinner with O'Malley and Angelica and Kaskis. She was wearing a green silk dress that touched her only on the shoulders, her nipples, her sharp hipbones. By midnight, fifteen people were in the party. At 4 am, they were in a garden, smoking the weed from the mountains, drinking out of the bottle, San Miguel, vodka, anything, fifty or sixty people, talking politics, breaking off to join O'Malley in songs about heartbreak, revenge, and dying for freedom. Around 5 am, under a tree in the heady night, he told Angelica that he was in love with her, it had come to him suddenly, no, a lie, from the moment he met her.

In the shadows, she kissed him, his head in her hands, her tongue in his mouth, touched his teeth with her perfect teeth, moved them, a silken abrasion felt in the bones of his face. It went on for a long time.

That kiss was in Anselm's mind as he ran down the home stretch, a cold wind coming over the Alster, his eyes watering. He remembered the soft, damp night, the feel of the tropical tree against his back, against his spine, Angelica's hipbones, her pubic bone on his, that he wanted to kiss her forever. If necessary, they could be fed intravenously while they kissed.

And then, at 5.30 am, he had to leave, the day already opening, a sky streaked from edge to edge with pale trails as if some silent armada of jets had passed in the darkness. Angelica put her hands into the taxi, ran them over his face like a blind person, said, 'You should have spoken.'

She put her head in, one last kiss, their lips bruised, puffy, like boxers' lips.

O'Malley appeared. 'The right thing now, boyo,' he said. 'Go home and tell them to pull the plug on the miserable old cunt.'

Taking off, looking down at the hopeless tilting shanties, children, dogs, his numb fingers trying to direct the nozzle's airstream onto his face, his eyes, it came to Anselm.

On the first night in the Tap Room, the Rotary harlot with the hand that lay on him like a big spider, O'Malley had believed that he was CIA and he had never changed his mind.

Years later, on that morning in Cyprus, two clean men, soaked, scrubbed, shampooed, cleaner than they would ever be again, after the doctors took off their gloves and left, Riccardi said something.

'Why me?' Riccardi said, not looking at Anselm. 'Why am I the one they didn't hurt?'

A hundred metres to go to the gates, no wind left, aching.

He couldn't run it out, stopped, stood with his hands on his hips, feeling sick. Walked the rest of the way, trying to regain composure.

Eyes on him. He felt them and he looked.

Inskip was on the balcony, black T-shirt, shaking his head. He drew on a cigarette. A second, then smoke came out of him like his spirit escaping.

20

... LONDON ...

SECURITY RANG and she went to the bare, functional room and looked at the man downstairs. The equipment was good quality, big colour monitor, and there were two angles, full frontal, close up, and full length, left profile.

He was tall, dark hair flat on his head, cut short. He looked French, Mediterranean, a long nose, broken, no twitches or quick eye movements, that was a good sign, coat with a leather collar.

'Bag?' said Caroline Wishart.

'All okay metalwise,' said the security man.

'Send him up.'

He was standing when she came into the interview room, nodded at her, eyes grey-green, the colour of the underside of poplar leaves, the poplars at the bottom of her grandmother's garden.

'Caroline Wishart,' she said. 'I've only got a couple of minutes.'

He took a video cassette out of a side pocket.

'Sit down,' she said.

She took the tape. A slip of paper was taped to the side with numbers written on it in a strong vertical hand: 1170. Slotted it into the machine, and found the remote control. She switched the set on, pressed the Play button. Just static. She pressed again, pressed anything. Numbers appeared at the bottom of the screen.

'Fuck this,' she said. She looked at him. He was sitting with his hands on his stomach. Most men would have been twitching to intervene. Either he was different or he was even more technologically incompetent that she was.

He said nothing. He didn't look at her.

'Can you do this?' she said, hating to have to say it.

He held out his hand. She gave him the remote. He switched off the set, switched on, pressed a button, pressed another.

The film began.

The sub-tropical plain, dark.

When she saw the bodies, Caroline felt sweat start in her hair and she began to feel sick, a small wave of nausea, a ripple. She glanced at the man, Mackie. He had laced his fingers.

At a certain point, Caroline closed her eyes. She turned her head slightly so that Mackie couldn't see.

'That's it,' he said.

She opened her eyes and watched him retrieve the tape. He didn't sit down again, stood looking at her. She didn't know what you did with something like this. This wasn't politicians fucking rent boys. That was simple, just an extension of the story that got her to London, her breakthrough story: *Mayor Denies Brothel Payoff.* She should get Halligan in … no, he'd simply take over, it wouldn't be her story any more.

'They tried to kill me,' he said.

'Who?'

He shrugged. 'Sent people to my hotel.'

'And?'

Another shrug. 'I'm here.'

She realised. 'You offered it to someone else?'

'And now I'm offering it to you.'

'Could be faked,' she said because she couldn't think of any other response. Distrust, suspicion – they were always sound responses in journalism. 'I'd have to show it to other people here, they'd check it out … then we could talk about money.'

He said nothing, just picked up his bag and walked. She hadn't expected that, he was going. She felt something slipping out of her hands, got up, went after him, touched his sleeve, grabbed his arm.

'Settle down, hold it,' she said. 'Just hold on for one second, will you, I'm not …'

Mackie stopped, turned his head. 'What?'

'I don't have the authority to buy something like this.' She stood close to him, still holding his sleeve, looked into his eyes, it often worked. 'I'm sorry I said that about, about being faked. I'm sorry. Will you leave the tape with me? A copy? I promise I'll give you an answer today.'

He moved away from her, just a small distance. 'No,' he said, 'this was a mistake.'

Caroline knew she should plead. There was a time for pleading. It was any time you saw the shimmer of a story that would go on the front page without argument, would require no exercise of editorial judgment by any drink-befuddled executive prat, would speak for itself in short headline words an eight–year–old could understand.

'Listen,' she said, holding on to his arm. 'I don't need a copy, an hour, two hours, that's it, two hours, that's all I need, I'll talk to people. An answer in two hours. No bullshit. Give me a number.'

He looked at her for so long that she let go his arm and blinked.

'Please,' she said. 'Trust me.'

'One o'clock,' he said. 'I'll ring you at one. Just say yes or no.'

His accent wasn't Scottish now. It was South African.

'Mr Mackie, we might need a contract, a legal document, you know, we could do this through lawyers, you'd be protected and we'd …'

'Just say yes or no. Twenty thousand. I'll tell you where to send it.'

When he was gone, she went to her tiny cubicle, her first day in it. She rang security and asked for prints of Mackie, sat back and thought for a long time about what she should do. This was her story: the man had come to her because of her byline on the Brechan story. But it was too big for her. He wanted cash for something that might be worthless.

It wasn't. She felt it in her marrow. Her instinct said this was a big story. And her instinct was good. It had taken her to three big stories in Birmingham.

But Halligan would take it away from her. The story would disappear into the inner sanctum without her.

She had to deliver it personally, the way she'd delivered Brechan. Brechan had been the most wonderful luck. She would be writing lifestyle crap now, ten hottest pick-up bars in the City, if someone hadn't decided to give her Brechan's rent boy.

'We know your work from Birmingham,' the gaunt man in the pub in Highgate said. 'We think you're the person to expose this.'

Luck, just pure luck.

It didn't happen twice.

Who to go to now? Who to trust? Who could get the money?

Colley. He was the only one. She'd been introduced to him in the pub and he'd bought her drinks and made lewd suggestions. Her boss in the permanent catfight that was the Frisson section had told her that Colley ran his own mini-empire. He kept his own hours, only came to conferences when he felt like it.

She went to his office, not a cubicle, a proper office with floor-to-ceiling walls, and knocked.

'Enter,' shouted Colley.

He was sitting at a large desk covered with files and newspapers looking at a laptop, a cigarette burning in an old saucer. She thought he looked like someone who had lost a large amount of weight quickly.

'Caroline Wishart,' she said. 'We met in the pub?'

'I remember. Some things I remember.'

'I need help.'

Colley looked at her. His eyes were heavy-lidded and he was squinting as if caught in a spotlight. 'First you pinch the Brechan story from under my nose,' he said, 'now you come crawling for help.' He pointed downwards. 'Under the desk, you upper-class slut. Unzip me with your teeth.'

Caroline sat down. She had to tough this out. 'I thought your generation still had button-ups,' she said. 'Button-up flies are hard on teeth. All I need is the benefit of your experience.'

He smiled, thin lips, yellow teeth. 'All? Took me thirty years to get where I am. Cost me my liver and my hair, most of my brain. You ruling-class gels walk in, you pout and shake your little tits and they make you editor of some new fucking rubbish section. Grovel to me.'

'I've just seen a film. Soldiers killing civilians. White soldiers killing blacks. A man wants to sell it.'

She told him about Mackie, about the tape labelled 1170.

'Well,' he said, 'probably South Africans, won't surprise anybody. Killed blacks like flies. That's not news any more.'

'He says the soldiers are American. They're shooting people lying on the ground. Seems like a whole village. It's like an execution. Kids too.'

Colley moved his head around, light catching his dirty glasses. 'What was the name again?'

'Mackie.'

'What's he want?'

'Twenty grand.'

'That's it? Comes in, shows you the film, says he wants twenty grand?'

'Yes.'

'Generally, there's a bit more mystery and foreplay. What's your feeling about the film?'

'Real. And awful. Some of the people might be identifiable.'

'Soldiers?'

'There's a group near helicopters. Might be two civilians. He says someone who wanted to buy the film tried to kill him. When I said I needed time, he walked.'

'Bluff.'

'He was walking,' said Caroline. 'He was going. No doubt in my mind.'

'Well, the walk. I've had walkers. Let them piss off, get to the lift. Where'd you let him get to?'

'Okay, I'm learning,' Caroline said. 'He's ringing at one, he wants a yes or no. Should I take it to Halligan?'

She watched Colley scratch his head, a delicate operation. He'd had two kinds of hair transplants and a surgical procedure involving strips of his scalp being moved around, with strange results.

'Yes,' he said. 'My view is that the proper thing to do is take this to Halligan immediately.'

'Well,' she said, 'if that's your advice.'

'No,' he said. 'It's not. Twenty grand's nothing. Is this a joint venture then?'

'It is.'

'Give me an hour. We can deliver this without Halligan and the fucking lawyers.'

21

… LONDON …

NIEMAND FOUND a car hire firm in Clerkenwell, used his passport, the international licence, paid for seven days in cash, a ridiculous sum. He would be gone much sooner, but his instinct said to leave a margin. Hired killers had come for him in the night and he didn't know how they found him.

He drove around for a few hours, places he knew from his runs. He wanted to be gone, London was full of rich people, he didn't care about that one way or another, but the poor and the desperate were shamefaced, hiding in alleys and under bridges when they should be in the open, shaming the rich.

He parked and waited for 1 p.m., mobile on the passenger's seat. He would go to Crete and stay with his cousin. Dimitri was like him, they looked alike, all the relatives said that when they'd come to look at him and his mother after their arrival from Africa. It had been late afternoon when they reached the village in the hills. The taxi dropped them in the square. His mother went somewhere and came back with two men, who took their suitcases. They'd all walked down some narrow broken streets and then it was all old women in black, men with moustaches, staring children, everyone seemed to pay more attention to him than they did to his mother. They didn't look at her in the way they looked at him. He knew now they were looking at the other blood in him, they didn't see a lot of strange blood.

Dimi became his friend quickly, in hours, no one ever wanted to be his friend before. Dimi had to be dragged away that evening, was at the door the next morning to take him away, show him things. Dimi taught him how to fish, taught him the Greek swearwords, how to deal with the bigger boys at school, and how you could see the woman undressing if you crept out late, went over the roofs, dead quiet, like cats, and leaned dangerously over a parapet, holding on to a television aerial. He remembered the wait, the agony, the way she came and went, and the final delirious moments when she stood in their full sight, the pull of her petticoat over her head, the slither, the release of her big breasts, their lift and sag, the long dark nipples and the loaded bottom-heavy swing as she turned, tossed her hair, black hair, coffin–black and shiny.

Did she know they were watching?

He looked at his watch, his mind still on Crete, a boy leaning over a parapet in the warm barking night, engorged, pulse beating in his head, erection pressed against the rough surface like a spring – painful, pleasurable.

It was just on 1 p.m. He considered his plan. Careful was seldom wrong, everything he'd been through told him that. He found the piece of paper with the number, switched on the phone, and dialled.

'Yes.' The woman, Caroline Wishart.

'It's Mackie,' he said. 'Yes or no.'

'Yes.'

'Cash. I'll need cash. Today.'

'That's very difficult,' she said.

His didn't like the sound of that, his hand needed something to do, opened the glove compartment. A McDonald's packet, scrunched up, greasy. They had rented him an uncleaned car. He would buy a roll of shit-paper and block the air intake before he gave it back.

'I'm going. Yes or no?'

'Mr Mackie, the answer is yes but you must give me until tomorrow to get the money. I will get it, I promise you but I can't until tomorrow. It's very difficult to get a sum like that quickly in cash. But I will. I will. Please bear with me. Will you?'

Niemand hesitated but he believed her. 'Okay, I'll ring you tomorrow at twelve, at noon. Have it in a bag, a sports bag. In fifties. Give me your cell-phone number.'

She gave it to him.

'Mr Mackie, how can we be sure ...'

He told her where to be.

22

... WASHINGTON ...

ABOVE THE tree line, the mountain was a cone of purest white and the sky behind it was grey, grey with darker streaks, the colour of the puffs of smoke that issued from the trees – a ragged line of puffs, one, two, three, four, five. When the sound of the incoming shells came to the ears of the men and boys watching in the village, they took shelter, casually, it wasn't done to hurry, show any anxiety, not in front of the cameras, the journalists.

Scott Palmer looked at his empty whisky glass, didn't resist the temptation. He went to the drinks table and poured two fingers of whisky and one of mineral water. There was no sleep without whisky, precious little with it. Sleep had gone with Lana. Before, really, he hadn't been sleeping much for a long time.

The television camera was moving around trying to find artillery shells landing on the village, it found a hole in a roof, possibly an old hole, went to two men with cigarettes under their moustaches.

'Don't stay up all night.'

His son was in the doorway, head on one side, hair falling over an eye. Palmer looked at him and he felt the pulse of love in his throat. The boy was hopeless, twenty-four and still taking useless college courses, talking eco-nonsense, playing his guitar, surfing.

'Finishing up, son,' he said, showing the glass. 'Long day.'

Andy came over and put his hands on Palmer's shoulders.

'Don't work so hard,' he said. 'Where's it get you? We ever going to play golf again? Feels like years.'

'Soon,' said Palmer. 'Soon. We'll take a decent break, go to the Virgins, play golf, sail.'

'Count me in,' said Andy. He ran a quick hand over his father's hair. 'Just that one, right? Then you go to bed.'

Palmer nodded. When he looked around, Andy was at the door, looking back at him.

'I used to say that to you,' Palmer said.

Andy nodded, didn't smile, a sadness in his look.

'Goodnight, Dad.'

'Goodnight, boy. Sleep tight.'

He put his head back, held whisky in his mouth, thought about Andy, about the day Lana drove the Mustang under a car transporter on Highway

401 outside Raeford, North Carolina, 2.45 in the afternoon. She was alone, leaving a motel, lots of drink taken.

Everyone knew who. Two years later, drinking with Ziller, they were old buddies, they'd been through shit together, Ziller said, 'That day. Who was it?'

'Seligson. But you know that.'

'Never thought of killin him?'

'Wife and a kid, a girl. What's the point of two dead? And me doing life. Who'd look after Andy?'

The phone on the side table rang.

Palmer looked at his watch. He muted the television sound, let the phone ring for a while, cleared his throat.

'Yes.'

'General, I'm sorry if I've woken you. It's Steve Casca.'

'One forty-five? Asleep? Who does that?'

'Sir, may I ask you to ring me back?'

Palmer put the phone down and dialled the number showing on the display. Casca answered after the first beep.

'Thank you, sir. Sir, a minor Langley asset in London has contacted their resident. The asset's been offered a film. US military personnel in action. Said to be filmed in Africa, some kind of massacre. That's the asset's term.'

'Taken when?'

'Not known, sir.'

'What else?'

'The tape has the numbers One, One, Seven, Zero. Eleven seventy, that is. On a label.'

Palmer closed his eyes. Eleven Seventy. No.

'We can find nothing on that,' said Casca. 'We thought to ask if this might have meaning for you.'

The television was now showing a building with a third-floor balcony hanging away from the wall, hanging from one support. The double doors leading out to it had blown off. In the street, a crowd had gathered, policemen in *kepis*. It was a French city, possibly Paris.

'Probably best not to take it any further,' said Palmer. 'Leave it with me. I'll talk to some people.'

'If you say so, sir.'

'I'll need the names, the asset and so forth.'

'I can give you that now, sir.'

Palmer listened and wrote on the pad. 'That's fine,' he said. 'Steve, I don't think you need to log this call.'

'What call was that, sir? Apologies about the time.'

'Sound instincts.'

'Goodnight, sir.'

'Goodnight, Steve.'

He'd always thought well of Casca, even after the serial fuck-ups in Mogadishu. He'd behaved well in Iran, he'd showed his worth. Palmer put the television sound on again. The building was the Turkish embassy in Paris. Mortared, four rounds, possibly five. Mortared? An embassy in Paris? The whole world was turning into Iraq.

He muted the set again and dialled a number. Eleven Seventy. Would it never go away?

'Yes?'

It was the boyfriend.

'I need to speak to Charlie.'

'I'm afraid …'

'Palmer.'

'Please hold, Mr Palmer.'

It took a while. People had worried about Charlie being a fag. But no one was going to blackmail Charlie. Anyway, faggotry had an honourable history in the service. British fags were another matter altogether.

'Sir.'

'Serious situation, Charlie,' said Palmer. 'Some things have to happen. I want you to arrange it now and I want you to go tonight and make sure everything's neat. Neatness is important.'

'Yes, sir.'

23

... HAMBURG ...

BAADER RAISED his eyebrows and puffed his cheeks. After a while, he expelled air and said, 'You're asking me?'

'No,' said Anselm. 'I'm just going around exposing my personal life to anyone who's breathing.'

'When did you last ask anyone for advice?'

'I had the idea I should change,' Anselm said. 'Clearly a very stupid idea.' It was. He was already full of regret.

Baader looked unhappy. 'Well, change, you're almost normal these days. Except for the fingers. Just hung over. Christ knows how you run with a hangover. I can't walk with a hangover.'

'It's my way of punishing myself,' said Anselm. 'You get women to cane you. I run. Should I talk to her?'

'I should cane myself. No, that doesn't work. Like massage, can't massage yourself. Can you buy a caning machine? Do they have that?'

'Everything. They have everything. Are you hearing me?'

'Jesus, John, talk to her. What does she look like?'

Anselm hesitated. 'Not like Freud,' he said.

A smile from Baader, the sly-fox look. 'Attractive, that's what you're saying, is it?'

'The academic look, not necessarily my taste. The scholar. A certain primness.' He used the word *geziertheit*.

'Glasses?' Baader was interested.

'No. Well, yes.'

'I like glasses. Black frames?'

'Me, we're talking about me. Less about you.'

Baader looked away, bent his head, scratched an ear. 'To be serious,' he said, 'what the fuck would I know? The things that happened to you, I can't begin to ... Well, are you feeling okay?'

'I'm feeling fine.'

'The memory?'

'Bits come back. It doesn't bother me as much as it used to.'

'Well, talking can't hurt. You've never talked to me. Who did you talk to?'

'I'm sorry I mentioned this. Paid Gerda? If not, I'm looking for another job.'

A hand in the air, a stop sign, gentle. 'John, relax. Gerda's paid, the land–

lord's been paid, everyone's been paid. We're up to date on payments. I'm personally skinned but everyone's been paid.'

Anselm went back to his office. Talked to anyone? What was there to say? How did you talk about fear, about cringing like a whipped child, about pissing in your pants, other things, sobbing uncontrollably, other things?

Carla Klinger knocked. 'The new file,' she said. 'The chemist. He flew to London. Now I've got him on a flight to Los Angeles from Glasgow, took off an hour ago.'

It was a second before he placed the chemist. Yes. The chemist's company in Munich thought he was planning to defect to the competition. Five years he'd been on a research project, they were close.

'That's good work, Carla. Tell the client.'

She smiled her cursory smile, nodded, turned on the stick.

Good work? Thieves, contract thieves, spying, stealing to order, stealing anything for anyone. Anselm thought about the woman they'd found in Barcelona, Lisa Campo. He remembered his reply to Inskip's question.

What do you think? Charlie gets his money back, they fall in love again, go on a second honeymoon. Eat pizza.

For all they knew, Charlie Campo wanted to find his wife so that he could torture her and kill her. For all they cared. Just a job with a success bonus. Good work? He'd enjoyed it at the start, four of them using Baader's purloined software, learning how to search the waters for a single rare fish, the net ever expanding, dropping deeper. Sitting in a quiet room, in the gloom, watching the radar, waiting for the blip, waiting for the coelacanth. He'd felt removed from himself, a relief from the running introspection, the endless, pointless internal dialogue. Just the quiet lulling of the electronic turbines, the hard drives spinning, spinning, spinning. But now ...

Anselm went down the passage to Beate's office. She wasn't there. He was grateful not to have to endure her remarks about health as he went onto the balcony to smoke.

A cold day but dry, patches of blue coming and going in the high, wispy cloud. In line with Pöseldorf, a ferry with a ragged tail of gulls was cutting through the chop. Kael and Serrano would be off their ferry by now.

Alex Koenig.

He could ring her to say he would talk to her about what had happened to him. Within limits. He could set limits, things he wouldn't talk about, the parameters of their talk.

What was the point of that? How could he set limits? What would they be?

Beate tapped on the glass. Anselm flicked his cigarette end into the garden below – not a garden, just balding lawn and unpruned leaf-spotted roses, no one cared.

This would be Tilders. He went inside. Beate smiled her beatific smile.

'I'd have brought the phone but I saw you were almost finished with that vile thing.'

'You're never finished with vile things,' said Anselm.

24

... LONDON ...

THE STORE was warm and fragrant, like a palace in a dream. As Niemand wandered around, the expensive scents of the women shoppers brushed his face, clung to him. On an escalator, he stood behind three youngish Japanese women in grey, sleek as pigeons, eyes rounded by the knife. They appeared to be crying.

When he'd finished looking, riding the escalators, he left by a back exit and walked around the block. He found a spot to watch the front doors and dialled. Caroline Wishart answered on the third ring.

He told her where he was, where to go.

He didn't see her go into the store, there were two entrances, the pavement was crowded. After a while, he crossed the street, went into the store through the right-hand doors, turned right and climbed the stairs to the third floor. He went through jewellery and handbags, around four Asian women talking in undertones, rings on their fingers flashing like lights. At the escalator, he dialled again.

'Yes,' she said.

'I got bored,' he said. 'I'm on the fourth floor looking at the toys. Come up the escalator next to the stationery, in the corner, know where that ...'

'Yes,' she said. 'I know.'

He waited, saw her pass. Waited, watched the people, dialled her again.

'Sorry,' he said, 'you'll have to come down again. To the second floor.'

'Don't mess me around,' she said. 'This isn't a spy film.'

He looked at his watch, stepped onto the up escalator.

Caroline Wishart didn't see him until the last second, when he was offering the package. She opened her mouth to speak, closed it, held out the bag with one hand, took the package in the other.

Niemand took the bag.

'Goodbye,' he said.

He walked up the escalator, three people ahead of him, bag in his left hand, three steps at a time, glanced back. She was off the escalator, half hidden by a man in a dark suit. Another man was in front of her, facing her, close.

When he turned his head, looked up, he saw a woman at the top of the escalator, back to him, a young woman in black, dark hair on her shoulders, talking on a cellphone held in her right hand, her head back.

PETER TEMPLE

Niemand thought: Who do these people phone? Who phones them? What do they have to say to each other? He looked down, watched the metal belt slide beneath the shiny steel plate, he'd always felt some unease at the moment; in his life he had been on escalators no more than a few dozen times.

He was taking the step to solid ground, to safety, when the woman on the cellphone raised her left hand, fingers spread, her hand moving, her fingers speaking.

She had hair on her knuckles, dark hair.

She turned, less than two metres from him, smiling, a nice smile, big mouth, dark lipstick, brought the cellphone away from her head, looking at it, chest-high.

Niemand took a pace and dived at the man in drag.

He was in the air when he saw the two short black barrels protruding from the top of the phone.

He heard nothing. Saw only a lick of flame.

The blow was high in his chest, no great pain.

Fuck, he thought, why didn't I expect this?

Then he had his left hand on the weapon, brought his right hand down the man's face, clawed his face, nails just long enough to gouge flesh from forehead, eyebrows, eyelids, cheekbones. He made a screeching noise, then Niemand had his fingers hooked behind the man's lower lip, nails beneath the teeth, wrenching.

The man in drag was not prepared for this kind of attack, this kind of ferocity, this kind of pain. Blood running into his eyes, blind, he let Niemand drag him to his knees. Niemand got the weapon away from him, no resistance, let go the jaw, kneed him in the head twice, three times, the man fell sideways, head hit the carpet, the wig was half off, near-shaven skull revealed, pale, shocking.

Niemand jumped on his head, kicked it, looked around, grabbed the sports bag, suddenly aware of the people, shouting.

Go down, said his instincts.

He went up, ran up the escalator, hurting a little in the chest now, not much, people getting out of his way on the moving steel ramp. On the next floor, he told himself, Walk, be calm, no one here saw anything, no one heard anything. Seconds, it lasted seconds.

Walk, just walk.

He walked through games and dolls, toys, saw a stairway, no, not that one, a section full of plump women, maternity wear, shoes, children's shoes, children standing around looking bored, rich children buying school uniforms, veer right, through a doorway, stairs. Yes.

He went down, as fast as he could go without causing people to look, not many people coming up the stairs, he was bleeding a lot, he could feel the warmth of his own blood on his skin now, but the pain was bearable.

Bearable, he said to himself, you're not dying, this is not a terminal wound, not a lung shot. No, definitely not a lung shot. He'd seen enough lung shots, he knew lung shots. The sound, the strange bubbling sound. Nothing like that. He was breathing fine, just pain and blood, that was nothing.

Sonny, you die when I fucken tell you to and not a fucken second before.

They were the words mad Sergeant Toll shouted at him when he lay in an erosion gully, bruised all over, arm broken, at the School of Infantry obstacle course. Niemand used the same words to the curly-haired boy, Jacobs, whose blood was lying like red mercury on the ancient dust of Angola. But Jacobs hadn't obeyed. He'd coughed blood and he'd died.

Floors, he'd lost track of floors, surely this was the ground floor. No, one to go, shit no, more than one. He wasn't feeling well. Not a good idea this, he should have left Mr Fucking Shawn's cassette where he found it.

More stairs. Another floor? No, he remembered this section, the smell, perfume, somehow not women's perfume, too much lemon and bay, this was the ground floor, carry on down, he'd be in the basement.

An exit, right there, to his right, he hadn't noticed it. He walked towards the doors. Upright, don't hunch, the tendency was to hunch when hurt, why was that? It didn't help, didn't take away any pain.

He looked around, not feeling alert. Where were they? They hadn't sent one man to kill him. One man in a dress and a wig. They'd sent two men to the hotel, that hadn't worked. Second try, this place would be crawling with killers, a full fucking platoon of them.

He went past the doorman, who stared at him, then onto the pavement, lots of people, they were hard to avoid, all carrying bags. He bumped into a woman, said sorry. Daylight fading. Cold day, cold on his face, he felt warm inside, that was a good sign, they always talked about feeling cold when you were hit badly. The old hands. He was an old hand now. But he'd never taken a bad hit. Just the piece out of his side, the flesh wound in the bum and the grenade slivers in his arm and his chest.

He knew where he was. The underground was just around the corner. Catch the tube as planned.

The pain was in his jaw now, why was that?

He crossed the side street, walked to the corner, turned into the busy street. No, he shouldn't catch the tube, he'd be trapped down there. He walked past the station entrance, halfway down the block. Cross, better to cross, he thought. Crossing the street, traffic stalled, walking between the cars. This was a silly thing to have done, you didn't want to die for this kind of shit.

Too late to think about that. Anyway you didn't want to die protecting parasites in Joburg, that would be a really seriously stupid way to go.

'You all right?'

Someone was speaking to him. Someone on a motorbike, sitting in the traffic, a yellow helmet, waiting for the lights.

'Need a lift,' said Niemand. 'I'm hurt.'

'Get on,' said yellow helmet.

Niemand got on, bag on his lap, held the sides of the rider's leather jacket. He looked back. Two men in dark suits were on the corner outside the store, looking around.

Then, through the cars, he saw another man in a dark suit coming, running around cars.

Coming to get him. Make sure this time.

He couldn't move, couldn't get off the bike.

What was the point? He couldn't run.

The man was fifteen metres away, a pale face, dark hair, coming quickly.

Fuck, he thought. Stupid.

With a roar, the bike pulled away, went between a car and delivery vehicle. Niemand's head went back and when it came forward he couldn't stop it, it came to rest between the rider's shoulder blades, wanted to stay there.

This wasn't good. How much blood had he lost? He took a hand off the rider's jacket and felt his shirt. It was wet, soaked.

Too much blood.

25

… LONDON …

'YOU TELL me what's going on,' said Caroline Wishart. 'Two bastards sandwich me, take the package. Stolen goods, the one says. Then someone attacks Mackie.'

'Close the door, will you?'

Colley was holding a plain cigarette in long ochre fingers, tapping it on his desktop, tapping one end, turning it over, tapping the other. 'I'm buggered,' he said. 'Who knows how many people he's swindled.'

'Where'd you get the money?'

'The money?'

'Yes, the money.'

He lit the cigarette with an old gas lighter, many clicks before the flame and the deep draw, belched smoke, did some coughing. 'Chalk this one up to character building,' he said. 'Some you win, some are fuck-ups. That's life.'

'Who'd you tell?'

'Tell? Who'd you tell?' He put on a high-pitched and squeaky voice, his idea of an upper-class girl's voice.

Caroline wanted to strangle Colley, go over to him and slap his face and put her hands around his mottled neck.

'Leaving aside the pathetic quality of your imitations,' she said, 'where'd the money come from?'

He smiled, a pleased expression. 'It wasn't actually real money.'

'What?'

'The top and the bottom ones, yes. The middle ones … shall we say Middle Eastern?'

It was dawning on Caroline that she was missing something. 'Well, shall "we" tell me what the fuck's going on here?'

Colley formed his lips into an anus and blew tiny, perfect smoke rings. She saw the pale, vile tip of his tongue. The grey circles met the thermal from the ground-level heating duct, rose, dissolved.

'You came to me for help, remember,' Colley said. 'You could've gone to Halligan, but no, you thought he'd pinch your story, make you sorry you screwed him with your non-negotiable demands.'

She could not contain herself. 'Well, not doing that, that was probably a big mistake.'

Carefully, Colley rested his cigarette in a saucer, finger-shaped nicotine stains around the edges, looked up at her. 'Listen, sweetheart,' he said, 'your big scoop, it happened to you, you didn't happen to it. Now you've got to produce another one. And you gels, you can't actually do that, you can't actually do anything, and once you stop giving the working-class old farts cockstands, once the next little upper-class tart comes along, well then you're back to writing your lifestyle crap.'

He was telling her something but she couldn't quite grasp what it was.

'Still,' said Colley, 'you can always get daddy to set you up as an interior decorator, can't you?'

'So what do I do?' she said.

'Nothing. Move on, this never got off the ground, no harm done, we just forget it. We don't put it in the CV and we don't entertain the pub with the story.'

'That's it?'

Colley took off his glasses, looked for something to clean them with, found a crumpled tissue and breathed on the filthy lenses. 'Well,' he said, not looking at her, rubbing glass, 'some good can come out of a cockup. You never know.'

She waited. He didn't look up, started on the other smeared lens. He wasn't going to say any more, she was dismissed.

She left, feeling the tightness in her chest, the sick feeling.

One day she would kill Colley. Tie him to a tree in a forest, torture him and kill him. No, torture him and bury him alive, shovel damp soil alive with worms onto his head, into his mouth, watch his eyes.

But she knew that what she hated most was not Colley.

No, she hated herself for being so stupid as to go to him, to trust him.

26

… HAMBURG …

HE FOUND her on the university website.

Dr Alexandra Koenig, Dr. med., Dr. phil., Dipl.-Psych. Clinical psychologist. Research: Empirical validation of psychoanalytical concepts; psychophysiology; post-traumatic stress disorder.

A homepage carried a photograph, properly severe. He went to her curriculum vitae. It listed at least two dozen articles. She had been a visiting fellow at the Harvard Medical School. She was on the editorial board of the *Journal for Trauma Studies*.

There was an email address. Anselm stared at the screen for a while, then he opened the mailer, typed in her address. Under Subject, he put: Rudeness, contrition.

In the message box, he typed: We could meet, for a walk perhaps. John Anselm.

He felt relieved after sending the message and went back to the logbooks. The phone rang.

'It's done,' said Tilders. 'Some luck too. Two for the price of one.'

'Not a concept known to this firm,' said Anselm. He didn't know what Tilders was talking about. They must have got the bug on Serrano earlier than expected.

His email warning was blinking. He clicked. Alex Koenig.

The message was: A walk would be nice. Does today suit you? I am free from 3 pm.

Anselm felt flushed. He couldn't think of anywhere to meet her, and then he thought of his childhood walks with Fräulein Einspenner in Stadtpark. He hadn't been there in thirty years.

She was waiting in front of the planetarium, formally dressed again, wearing her rimless glasses. There weren't many people around, a few mothers with prams or pushers, lovers, older people walking briskly.

She saw him from a distance, didn't look away, watched him approach.

'Herr Anselm,' she said, long and serious face. She held out her right hand. 'Perhaps we start again?'

'John,' said Anselm.

'Alex.'

They shook hands.

'Shall we walk?' she said.

They walked on the grass, away from the building. There wasn't much left in the day. A wind had come up, serrated edge of winter, hunting brown and grey and russet leaves across a lawn worn shabby by the summer crowds.

'Well,' she said, not at ease. 'You know what I do for my living. You are not still a journalist.'

'No,' he said. 'I'm in the information business.'

'Yes?'

'We gather it and sell it.' That was true, that was what they did. He didn't want to tell this woman the sordid truth but he didn't want to lie to her, he'd told a lot of lies, most of them to women.

They were at the road. She stopped and turned. He turned too and they looked back at the planetarium: it was big, solid, domed, towering over the parkland, a faintly sinister presence, alien in its setting.

'That's an Albert Speer kind of building,' Alex said. 'Hitler must have liked it. It says, look at me, I'm huge.'

'Well, I don't want to stand up for Adolf's taste in architecture but if you have to have water towers, it's not too bad.'

'Water tower? I thought it was a planetarium.'

'Now it is. It think it was built as a water tower. We could have coffee, something.'

He needed a drink, he hadn't had anything to drink all day, nothing at lunch time, he usually drank beer from the machine in the basement.

'Yes, good. Do you know where?'

'I think so. It's been thirty years, almost that.'

They set off again, crossed the road. She took big strides, he'd always had to shorten his stride with women, the women he remembered walking with. That was not many. He remembered one. He remembered walking in Maine with Helen Duval, she complained constantly about being bitten by midges, then she tripped over a root and claimed to have sprained her ankle. They were within sight of the cabin he'd hired. That was as far as they ventured.

'You're a medical doctor,' he said. 'As well.'

'In theory,' she said. 'In practice, I can't even diagnose myself. I get flu and I think I'm dying. You came to the park when you were young?'

'I was brought to see the birds. They used to have wonderful exotic birds and all kinds of fowls, these huge fluffy things, golden pheasants, I remember. May still be here somewhere. Do you enjoy what you do?'

She had taken off her glasses. He hadn't noticed her do that.

'I suppose so.' She looked at him, looked away. 'Yes. Well, I do what I do and I don't give much thought to whether I enjoy it. It's not that ... it's not a question that arises. It's my work.'

She was not used to being asked questions. *She* asked the questions.

They walked in silence for a time, gravel hissing underfoot, the wind tugging at them, lifting their hair. Then they saw a sign and went down a path and found the café. There were more people in it than in the park, people rewarding themselves for taking exercise.

'Hot chocolate with rum,' said Anselm. 'That's what we should have.'

'Right.'

'The woman who brought me here always had one. She used to give me a teaspoonful. That's where it all began. My decline.'

A waitress in black with a white apron came and he ordered two, stopped himself ordering a drink as well, asking her whether she wanted a drink.

'What brought you to hostages?' said Anselm.

He wasn't looking at her, he was looking at the people. He had been doing that since they entered, doing an inventory of the people in the big room. Then he realised she would notice that and he looked at her. She's pretending she hasn't noticed, he thought, she's wary. She thinks I'm capable of repeating last time's performance.

I am.

'Well, most of the post-trauma research in this area has been on large groups,' said Alex. 'I'm interested in the dynamics of survival in small groups.'

'What about personality and life history?'

She smiled. 'You didn't take well to that. May I say that?'

Anselm nodded. 'Certainly. To my shame. Did it come under the heading of an extreme reaction?'

'Mild, I'd class it as mild.'

'On the extreme scale.'

Alex laughed. Some of the wariness was leaving her, he felt that.

The drinks arrived. She sipped.

'Wonderful. I haven't had one of these in years. Not since Vienna.'

'Does research like this have a use?' said Anselm.

'That's a journalist's question,' she said. 'Academics hate questions like that. It might have a use one day. Everything has a use one day, doesn't it?'

'That's not a very academic answer,' said Anselm. 'I thought the idea was to present your research as vital to the survival of the universe?'

She held up her hands, the long fingers, no rings. 'I know, I should say that. Vital to the survival of my career would be more like it. Let's say my project is part of the giant mosaic of research, we can't quite see the pattern in it yet. But ...'

'You're not very German,' he said. 'You don't take yourself seriously enough.'

'If I'm not very German it's because I'm Austrian-Italian. A quarter Italian. My mother is half Italian. Her family is Italian-Jewish. Jewish-Italian. Atheists until they think they're dying. How do you describe yourself?'

'Once I thought I was American. American–German. But I don't know now. My mother was American but her father was British.'

There was silence. She looked away.

'Not being sure about what you are, that wouldn't be a trauma symptom, would it?'

Alex looked at him impassively, she had a judge's face, and then she smiled. 'Everything's a symptom of something,' she said.

She finished her drink, a pale collar of froth left around the glass. Anselm drained his.

'I could drink many of these,' she said. 'But I have to see a doctoral student, a frighteningly earnest young man. How did you travel here?'

He told her he was parked off Ohlsdorferstrasse.

'I'm near there. We can walk together.'

He paid and they walked back, light failing fast, shadow pools around the trees, streams of shadow under the hedges, the planetarium brooding, like a monument to something. He sometimes thought that everything old in Germany was a monument. The past had suckers, it attached itself to everything. There was no need to visit the sites or the *denkmäler*. Places spoke, whispered, smoked of what had been. The old railway lines held in their steel the weight of death trains, the city streets knew black boots, the songs, the slogans, the jeering and the tears. And lost hamlets and dripping cowpatted country lanes held voices, not always the voices of murderers and haters but of simple men and boys dead for the Führer in frozen land-scapes far away, the tanks bogged in mud set like concrete, the soldiers' last thin intakes of air not reaching their lungs, going back into the huge grey world, then the rattle and then nothing. Just snow and ice and useless metal and human innards cooling, cooling, freezing. And over it all the sky of lead.

'It's a little menacing,' she said.

'Yes.'

They talked, it was easier now, leaves playing about their feet, they talked about the city, the traffic, the weather, the coming of winter, of *Winterangst*, of the need for sunlight, for Vitamin D, about where she lived. She lived in Eppendorf. She volunteered that she had been married. Her ex-husband was in America.

At their parting, she ran a hand over her hair and he thought he heard the sound it made.

'So,' she said. 'Will you talk to me?'

He put his hands in his pockets. He was reluctant to part from her. 'If you think it'll help you get better. Come to terms with your life.'

She bit her bottom lip, looked down, smiling, shook her head.

'It might,' she said. 'There is the possibility also that it could save the universe.'

'Just added value, a bonus.'

Anselm drove back to Schöne Aussicht, met Baader on the stairs.

'I saw you smile,' said Baader, pointing at the lobby below. 'Down there. At the door. Feeling okay?'

'Facial tic,' said Anselm. 'That's what you saw.'

27

… LONDON …

'HEAR ME?' the voice asked.

Niemand opened his eyes, raised his head, didn't know where he was.

He was still on the motorcycle, leaning against the rider, who was talking to him, head turned, mouth close, inside the helmet.

He looked around. Rubbish bins, cardboard boxes, walls close.

'Yes,' said Niemand. 'I hear.'

He straightened up, lost his balance and fell sideways and backwards off the motorcycle. It didn't hurt when he hit the ground, it was like being very drunk, nothing hurt.

Where was the bag?

'The bag?' said Niemand.

The yellow helmet was standing over him, holding the bag. 'Got it. You need a doctor, I'm ringing for an ambulance, okay?'

'No,' said Niemand. He was trying to concentrate, it was difficult, he didn't want to go to a hospital, they would find him there, they had no trouble finding him anywhere.

'No, hold on,' he said. 'Just a sec …'

He put his hand into his jacket and found the harness, found the nylon wallet in his armpit. There was a card in it with numbers, five numbers, Tandy's number was there, Tandy was a pethidine addict but he was a good doctor, for a mercenary he was a good doctor, he knew a gunshot wound when he saw one.

He wasn't going to be able to unzip the wallet, find the card, his fingers were too fat, he'd developed fat fingers, no feeling in them.

'Listen,' he said to the yellow helmet. 'Inquiries. Ring and ask for a Doctor Colin David Tandy, T-A-N-D-Y, Colin, that's the one. Tandy. Tell him Con from Chevron Two … needs a favour.'

'Tandy? Chevron Two?'

'Colin Tandy. Tell him Con from Chevron Two. A favour. I've got a phone here in my pocket, you can …'

'Just lie there,' said the helmet. 'I'll ring from inside. I live here.'

'Listen,' Niemand said. 'Tell him … tell him Con says blood's a … a bit short. Might need some blood.'

'Jesus,' said the helmet. 'Don't die.'

He lay there. It wasn't uncomfortable. A bit cold, but not uncomfortable. He knew what uncomfortable felt like. This was easy. His neck was cold and his hands and feet but it wasn't bad. He thought about getting up. The car was in the parking garage, wasting money. Money. Shit, the bag? Where's the bag?

He felt for it, both hands, both sides, but his fingers were too fat and his arms were fat too, heavy, fat arms and fat fingers, it was very difficult to …

When he woke, he was on a bed and someone was standing over him, doing something to his arm, two people there, he wanted to speak but his lips felt numb.

'… fucking lucky prick …' said a voice, he knew the voice. Tandy. Tandy had taken shrapnel out of him.

He woke again and he was alone, on a bed, naked, tape on his chest. He raised his head, and he could see a railing, like a railing on a ship. He was on some kind of platform, it wasn't daytime, there was light coming from below, white light, artificial light. Banging, he heard bangs, not loud, chopping?

The bag, where was the bag? But he was too tired to keep his head up and he went back to sleep.

The third time he woke, he was clearer in the mind. He was on a big bed, a sheet over his legs, a black sheet. The bed was on a platform, a platform at one end of a huge room. He could see the tops of windows to his right, five windows, he counted them. Steel-framed windows. Big.

'Awake?'

He looked left and saw half of a woman, cropped white hair, spiky, a black T-shirt. More of her came into view, she came up the stairs, she was all in black.

'The guy on the bike,' said Niemand. His mouth was dry. The words sounded funny, not like his voice. 'What happened to him?'

'I'm the guy on the bike,' she said. 'I have to give you an injection. Your friend left it. You have really useful friends.'

'Are you Greek?' She looked Greek, she looked like one of his cousins.

'Greek? No, Welsh. I'm Welsh.'

Niemand knew a Welshman, David Jago. He was dead.

'Thanks very much,' he said. 'Picking me up, everything. Tandy. I'm feeling a bit strange.' He was feeling sleepy again.

'He told me to say the bullet seems to have chipped your collarbone and gone out your back. You've missed paraplegia by a centimetre. He's says he's given you a battlefield clean-up, he takes no responsibility, don't mention his name to anyone and don't call him again. Ever.'

She came closer. 'I've got to inject you,' she said.

Niemand focused on her. Welsh. She had a Greek look. The mouth. The nose.

'What's the chance of a fuck?' he said. 'In case I'm dying.'

She shook her head and smiled. It was a Greek smile. 'Jesus, men,' she said. She held up the syringe. 'Listen, I'm the one with the prick. Do you need to pee?'

28

... HAMBURG ...

VOICES IN the background, scuffling noises, other sounds. Tilders was watching a display on the small silver titanium-shelled machine.

'Alsterarkaden,' he said. 'Having coffee. The first bit's just small talk, ordering.'

Anselm was looking at the photographs of Serrano and a dark-haired man. They were sitting at a table in one of the colonnade's arches on the bank of the Binnenalster. In one picture, the man had a hand raised.

'What's his name?'

'Registered in the name Spence,' said Tilders.

'Looks like joints missing on his right hand,' said Anselm, showing the picture.

Tilders nodded. He was moving the tape back and forth.

Serrano's voice, speaking English: ... *anxious, you can imagine.*

Spence: *It's very unfortunate.*

Serrano: *You would be able to get some help locally.*

Spence: *Things aren't what they used to be, you understand.*

Serrano: *Surely you've still got ...*

Spence: *We don't enjoy the same relationship, there's a lot of animosity.*

Serrano: *So?*

Spence: *The other party may have to be told.*

Serrano: *You understand, it was a long time ago, we feel exposed, we're just the sub-contractors.*

Spence: *You were his agents, not so?*

Serrano: *Agents? Absolutely not. Just in-betweens, you should know that.*

Spence: *I only know what filters down. I'm a bottom-feeder.*

Serrano: *His agents never. A dangerous man. Unstable.*

Spence: *You're worried?*

Serrano: *You're not? You should be worried. The Belgian's one of yours.*

Spence: *I don't know about that. I don't work in the worry department. That's a separate department. So I don't have that burden.*

Serrano: *This isn't helping, I hoped ...*

Spence: *You lost him. If you'd come to us this needn't have happened.*

Serrano: *Well, it's happened, there's no point ...*

Spence: *His assets, you know about them.*

Serrano: *We gave some financial advice but beyond ...*

Spence: *Beyond bullshit, that's where we should be going. I'll say one word. Falcontor. Don't say anything. It's better we clean this up without the principal party being involved. They make more mess than they take away.*

Serrano: *So?*

Spence: *The person can be found. Marginalised. But we need all the financial details. The Belgian's too. We would want control of everything now.*

Serrano: *I'm sorry, you don't know who you're dealing with. We don't disclose things like that.*

Spence: *You came to us. I'm saying it's the only way to guarantee your safety.*

Serrano: *Well, perhaps we'll let this take its course, see what happens. See whose safety we're talking about.*

Spence: *That's an option for you. A very dangerous option, but, you want to be brave boys …*

Serrano: *A threat? Are you …*

Spence: *Don't worry about money, worry about life. Know that saying? We need to know your position quickly.*

Tilders pressed a button, opened his hands. 'That's it. Spence goes, doesn't wait for the coffee.'

'The service is bad everywhere,' said Anselm.

'Same place in two days.'

'Kael's all paranoia,' said Anselm, 'but Serrano doesn't seem to give a shit.'

Tilders nodded, flicked back a piece of pale hair that fell down his forehead, separated into clean strands. 'It appears like that.'

Anselm took the photograph of the man with the missing finger joints down the corridor, knocked. Baader swivelled from his monitor.

Anselm held out the photograph. 'Calls himself Spence.'

Baader glanced. 'Jesus, now you're playing with the *katsas*?'

'*Katsas*?'

'His name's Avi Richler. He's a Mossad case officer.'

'Thank you.'

Anselm went back to his office. Tilders put another tape in the machine, watched the digital display, pressed a button.

Serrano: *Richler wants the details. He knows about Falcontor. Bruynzeel too.*

Kael: *The cunts, the fucking cunts.*

Serrano: *I said that to him. He says it's about our personal safety.*

Kael: *They must have holes in their fucking heads if … Jesus.*

Serrano: *Well, who brought in the Jews? This boat is making me sick.*

Kael: *Don't be such a child. What could be in the papers?*

Serrano: *Lourens said to me at the Baur au Lac in '92 when we were meeting the fucking Croatians, he was snorting coke, he said people who betrayed him would have a bomb go off in their faces. He was paranoid you understand …*

Kael: *In the papers? What?*

Serrano: *I don't know. I told Shawn to take anything he could find. There could be instructions. Notes maybe, things he wrote down. There's nothing on paper from us. Not directly.*

Kael: *What do you mean not directly?*

Serrano: *Well, obviously he would have had proof of some deposits I made.*

Kael: *Your name would be on them?*

Serrano: *Are you mad? The names of the accounts the deposits came from.*

Kael: *How secure is that?*

Serrano: *As it can be.*

Kael: *And this film?*

Serrano: *I told you. He said he'd found a film, someone came to him with a film, it was dynamite. He said, tell them it's Eleven Seventy, they'll fucking understand. That was when he wanted us to go to the Americans to solve his problem.*

Kael: *Eleven seventy? And you didn't ask what it meant?*

Serrano: *He was shouting at me, you couldn't ask him anything. And he was on a mobile, it kept dropping out. I couldn't catch half of what he said.*

Kael: *You set this up, you're the fucking expert who's left us turning in the wind, you should fucking know better than ...*

Serrano: *Christ, Werner, he was your pigeon. You brought him to me. You're the one who said the Süd–Afs were like cows waiting to be milked, stupid cows, you're ...*

Kael: *You should shut up, you're just a ...*

Serrano: *Calm down.*

Kael: *Don't tell me to calm down.*

A long silence, the sounds of the ferry, something that sounded like a series of snorts, followed by laboured breathing.

Silence, sounds of movement, a cough.

Kael: *Paul, I'm sorry, I get a bit too excited, this is a worrying ...*

Serrano: *Okay, that's okay, it's a problem, we have to think. Richler wants an answer today.*

Kael: *You know what they want to do, don't you?*

Serrano: *Maybe.*

Kael: *They want to tidy up. And they want the assets.*

Serrano: *These boats, I'm not getting ...*

Kael: *Tell him we agree but it'll take time. Seventy-two hours at least.*

Serrano: *Where does that get us?*

Kael: *They'll have this prick by then. If what he's got is bad for us, we're possibly in trouble. If not, we haven't handed them our hard work on a plate.*

Serrano: *You don't actually think he'll believe me?*

Kael: *Of course he won't. But they won't take a chance.*

Tilders switched off. 'That's it,' he said.

'Good bug,' said Anselm. 'You're doing good work.'

'Another put and take ...' Tilders shook his head.

'If you can't, you can't. We don't want to spook anyone.'

Tilders nodded. His pale eyes never left Anselm's, spoke of nothing.

29

... LONDON ...

'THERE'S MONEY in my account I know nothing about,' said Caroline. 'Ten thousand pounds.'

Colley was looking at her over the *Telegraph,* narrow red eyes, cigarette smoke rising. 'Wonderful, darling,' he said. 'I'm surprised you noticed. Perhaps mummy popped it in.'

'The bank says it's a transfer from the Bank of Vanuatu. An electronic transfer.'

'Electronic money. Floats in cyberspace, falls anywhere, at random. Like old satellites. Finders keepers. Congratulations.'

'I'm declaring it to Halligan, I'm handing it over.'

He lowered the paper. 'Are you? Yes, well, that's probably a sound thing to do. In theory.'

'In theory?'

'Well, it may be a bit late to develop principles. After you've played the bagwoman.'

Caroline wasn't sure what he was saying. She had no anger left, it had taken too long to get the bank to tell her where the money had come from. The blood drained from her face. She was no longer certain that she knew what had happened. But she had a strong feeling about what was happening now and she felt cold.

'I've been set up,' she said. 'You know about this, don't you?'

Colley shook his head. He had an amused expression. His strange hairs had been combed with oil and his scalp had a damp pubic look.

'No,' he said. 'But if you're unhappy, that probably stems from something unconnected with the present situation. It could come from realising that you're just a pretty vehicle, a conduit. Something people ride on. Or something stuff flows through.'

She had no idea what he was talking about. 'I've been set up.'

'You've said that, sweetheart. Remember? Not too much nose-munchies with the public schoolboys last night? All I know is you came to me with a proposition involving paying someone for something that we could make a lot of money out of. I told you that the right thing to do was to go to Halligan. I said I wanted nothing to do with your proposal.'

He opened a drawer, took out a flat device. 'You're out of your depth here. Like to hear the tape?'

Caroline felt the skin on her face tighten, her lips draw back from her teeth of their own accord. She turned and left the room without saying anything, went down the corridor, through the newsroom. In her cubicle, door shut, she sat at the desk with her eyes closed, clenched hands in her lap.

Out of your depth.

Her father had said those words, those words were in her heart. The image came to her of her toes trying to find the bottom of the pool, toes outstretched, nothing there, the water in her mouth and nose, smell of chlorine. She could still smell chlorine anywhere, everywhere, smell it in the street, anywhere, any hint of it made her feel sick. Her father had used the phrase that day when she was a little girl wan from vomiting and he had repeated it every time she failed at anything.

She shut the memory out, stayed motionless for a long time. Then she opened her eyes, pulled her chair closer to the desk, and began to write on the pad.

Out of her depth? Go to Halligan and tell him the whole story? Who was going to be believed? Colley had a doctored tape. She had no hope.

Out of your depth.

No. Death before that.

The phone rang.

'Marcia Collins. You probably don't remember me. I'm the features editor now. Does your personal arrangement with the executive branch permit me to ask what the hell you're doing? Am I allowed to ask that?'

'No, you aren't,' said Caroline. 'Don't call me, I'll call you.'

A silence.

'I suppose you've heard they found your little Gary. Dead of an overdose. Been dead for days.'

30

... HAMBURG ...

WHEN TILDERS had gone, Anselm went out on the balcony and smoked a cigarette, watched him drive away. He looked down at the unloved roses and thought about his first days in the family house.

On his second morning, he had woken in fright from a drunken sleep and did not know where he was. He had been fighting the top sheet, twisting, it was tight around him. He'd lain back and felt his hair. It was wet with sweat. He got up. The pillowslip was dark. He stripped it from the pillow. It gave off a chemical smell, the smell of the pink fluid the doctor gave him to drink before he left the hospital.

In the huge tiled bathroom, pissing into the rusty water in the toilet bowl, the same smell had risen, richer now, it sickened him.

He showered, standing uncertainly in the huge bath. Water fell on him, a warm torrent, he was inside a rushing tube of warm water. He did not want to leave it. Ever. But eventually he went downstairs. There was bread and butter and tea, tea in bags, a box of leaf tea. He made toast and tea, that was an ordinary thing to do.

An ordinary thing on an ordinary morning.

Tea brewed in a china pot. In a kitchen. Toast with butter.

He had thought it gone forever.

He'd made two slices of toast, put them on a plate, and put the pot of tea and the toast and butter and a bowl of sugar on a tray and gone out onto the terrace. There was an old, dangerous chair to sit on and a rusty garden table. He'd gone back and forth to the kitchen and, in all, eaten seven slices of toast, toast with butter, just butter. He drank three cups of tea from the English china cup, roses on it.

Just eating toast and drinking tea, sitting in the sunshine in the wobbly chair, massaging the two fingers on his left hand, he could not remember more peace in his life.

Then he was sick, he could not reach the bathroom.

He had not left the house for two weeks. There was enough food and drink for ten weeks, more. He did nothing, existed. The milk ran out, he drank black tea. He sat in the spring sun, dozed, tried to read *Henry Esmond*, found on his great-aunt's bedside table, drank gin and tonic from before midday, ate something from a tin, slept in an armchair smelling faintly of long-dead dog, he had a memory of the dog, a spaniel, one eye opaque. He'd woken dry-mouthed, empty-headed, drunk water, poured wine, watched television in the study, not very much of anything, often went to sleep in the chair, woke cold in the small hours.

His brother had rung every second day. Fine, said Anselm, I'm fine. I'm pulling myself together. He had no idea what together would look like. There were terrifying blanks in his memory of the years before the kidnap – big blanks and small blanks, with no pattern to them. They seemed to go back to his teens. It was hard to know where they began.

He'd exhausted his clean clothes. Where was the laundry? He'd remembered a passage off the kitchen leading to a courtyard. The washing machine was unused for a long time, the hose disintegrated, water everywhere. He washed his clothes with old yellow soap in the porcelain sink, found a pleasure in it, in hanging the washing in the laundry courtyard.

And every day, he'd walked around the garden, looking at the roses, smelling them. One morning, when he woke, he'd known what he was going to do. Before noon, he left the house for the first time.

He knew where the bookshop was. He had been there on his last visit to his great-aunt, on his way to Yugoslavia. He had bought her a book.

He walked a long route, up Leinpfad to Benedictstrasse and down Heilwigstrasse and through Eichenpark and on to Harvesterhuder Weg and through Alsterpark. He walked all the way to the Frensche bookshop in the Landesbank building. In the crowded shop, he was assaulted by fear bordering on panic but he found the book. It was waiting for him, twelve years old, never opened, an encyclopaedia of roses. He paid and left, sweating with relief.

He walked down to the Binnenalster, bought a sausage on a roll from a street vendor, sat on a bench in the sun and opened the book. His was the hand that cracked its spine. He looked at the pictures, read the descriptions, while he ate. Then he walked all the way home, too scared to catch a bus, and, exhausted, went around the garden trying to identify the roses. It was more difficult than he had imagined. He was sure about Zephirine Drouhin at the front gate, *Gruss an Aachen* on the terrace, Madame Gregoire Staechelin on the wall, and three or four others.

But that wasn't enough. He wanted to know the name of every rose in the garden, and there were so many he couldn't be sure of – the pictures were fuzzy, the descriptions too imprecise.

Like his memory.

Beate knocked on the glass. Anselm finished the cigarette and went in.

31

… HAMBURG …

BAADER CAME into Anselm's office and slumped in a chair. He put a new case cover sheet on the desk.

'I gave this to Carla,' he said. 'You were busy with Tilders.'

Anselm looked at the form. The subject was someone called Con Niemand aka Eric Constantine, South African, occupation security guard, last seen London.

'Lafarge Partners?' he said.

Baader was looking down, fingers steepled. 'Credit check's okay. Corporate security. How many corporate security consultants does the world need?'

'Demand and supply. Ever think about what happens to these people after we find them?'

Baader closed his eyes, shook his head. 'John, please.'

'Do you?'

'This is a business.' He still didn't look up.

Anselm went ahead, knew how stupid he was being. 'These people, they can pay. That's all we care?'

Baader lifted his fox head. 'Care? Care about what? Lafarge. Probably run by Catholics. If you like, we could ask the Pope to give them a moral clearance. On the other hand, the Pope cleared Hitler.'

He looked away, not at anything. 'John, either we provide this service for anyone who can pay or we don't provide it at all. You're unhappy with that, I'll give you a very good reference. Today if you like.'

Silence, just the sounds from the big room, the hum of the internal fans cooling sixty or seventy electronic devices, the air-conditioning, noise from a dozen monitors, a phone ringing, another one, people laughing.

'I'm really tired,' said Baader. 'I've sold the shares, the car, the apartment. I'm moving to this shitty little apartment, two rooms, all night the trains run past, eye level, ten metres away, the noise, people look at you like you're in Hagenbeck's fucking zoo.'

He got up. 'So I'm not receptive to ethical questions right now. Next year perhaps.'

'I'm sorry,' said Anselm. He was.

'Yes, well, when you're in trouble, you too can sell your dwelling. Then you can buy your own island, buy Australia, it should get you enough to buy Australia, world's biggest island, live happily ever after.'

'My brother owns the house,' said Anselm. Baader knew that, he just didn't want to believe it.

Baader was at the door, he stopped, turned his head, said, 'War criminals from three wars, Pinochet's number two executioner, a Russian who leaves five people to die in a meat fridge, a man who swindles widows and orphans out of sixty million dollars, a woman who drowns two children so that she can marry an Italian beachboy. And the fucking rest.'

They looked at each other.

'Count for something? Yes? Yes?'

'Yes,' said Anselm. 'I'm a prick, Stefan. I'm a self-confessed prick and contrite.'

'Yes,' said Baader. 'Anyway, it's too late to change. We can't. You can't. I can't. The fucking world can't.'

Anselm stared out of the window for a long time, just a sliver of lake view, a slice of trees and water and sky, endless sky, the water fractionally darker than the sky. He still had the dreams, dreams about sky, about lying on his back, he was on a hilltop looking at a huge blue heaven, birds passing high above, twittering flocks so large their shadows fell on him like the shadows of clouds, and then the real clouds came, the mountains of cloud, darkening the day, chilling the air.

After a while, his thoughts went to Alex Koenig. It was not a good idea. She wanted something from him. A paper in a learned journal. He was a scalp. No one else had interviewed him. On the other hand ...

He started at the knock.

Carla Klinger.

'Cut your hair, I see,' said Anselm. 'I like it.'

She blinked twice, moved her mouth. 'Two weeks since then but thank you. The new British file, Eric Constantine, Seychelles passport, he hired a car from a Centurion Hire in London.'

'When?'

'Yesterday. Seven days hire. Paid cash. To be returned to the place of hire.'

'Centurion Hire? How big are they?'

'One site.'

'And they're online?'

'No. I looked at the big hire companies, nothing, so I thought about what all the small car-hire businesses would have to do. One thing is insure, they have to insure the cars, and I asked an insurance person. In the UK, three insurance companies get most of the hire car insurance. They don't just insure all of a company's vehicles, blanket cover. Every hire, they want a record of who the hirer is. Inskip and I opened them up and we found the name.'

She licked her lower lip. 'Not a great problem,' she said.

Anselm shook his head. 'Not for you maybe. For people like me, a great problem. Why didn't anyone think of it before? Can we run all the British currents through it, see what happens?'

'Inskip's doing that now. Then we'll see what we can do in the States. I don't know the insurance position there.'

'You should be in charge here.'

'Then who would do my work?'

She left. Walking with a stick didn't make her any less attractive from behind. From any angle.

He went back to looking out of the window. He had said it. He wasn't necessary. Carla could do her job without him and probably do Inskip's too.

Baader could save a lot of money by showing him the door. It would cross the mind of someone who'd had to sell his shares, his Blankenese apartment, the Porsche, now lie awake in a two-room post-war walk-up listening to the trains' electric screech vibrate his window.

Baader could have got rid of him a long time ago.

Baader was his friend, that's why he hadn't done it.

It was thirty minutes before his meeting with O'Malley. Anselm got up and put on his good overcoat.

32

… HAMBURG …

A FERRY was on its way to the Fährdamm landing. Anselm paced himself to get there to meet it. The lake was choppy, north wind raising whitecaps. He got off at the Fährhaus landing and walked back along the shore towards Pöseldorf, along the gravel path through Alsterpark, not many people around, some old people and women with prams, two junkies on a bench, workers sucking up leaves, the devices held at the groin, big yellow whining demanding organs.

A high sky, a cold day slipping away. Anselm thought about how his father had told him that Alsterpark was only as big as it was because so many Jewish families had lived on the west side of the lake and had been dispossessed. They were gone, gone to horrible death or exile, when the Allied bombers came in the high summer of July 1944. Then people walked into the lake to escape the unbearable heat of a city set on fire by teenage boys dropping high explosive bombs, incendiary bombs, napalm and phosphorus bombs. Aunt Pauline talked about it early on the first tape.

I went to the coffee factory that day. Otto, our driver, took me. We had two coffee factories. I used to do the accounts, I couldn't bear to do nothing. I hated sitting around the house, I begged to be allowed to do something, it was difficult for women to do anything in families like ours, you understand. Marriage, children, the domestic world, that was the domain of women, my mother never questioned that for one second, she could not understand that women might want something else. I didn't have children, of course, so I think she made an exception for me, not a full exception, she always hoped I'd marry again. I tried to tell her … what was I saying?

The bombing.

Oh. Yes. I was at the factory in Hammerbrook, in Bankstrasse. I used to work until late, after 9 pm, it was summer, it had been terribly hot for weeks. We were driving back when we heard the sirens and then the bombs started to fall. And we stopped and got out and we ran to some trees, I don't know why. After that, you can't imagine. The whole world was alight. Buildings fell down. The flames went up forever, the sky was burning, it looked as if the clouds were on fire. Burning clouds, like a vision of Armageddon. The heat. There was no air to breathe. The flames burnt up all the air. And the people ran out of the buildings, the screams of the children. The tar melted, people stuck in the tar. The car windows melted. Things just burst into flame. We were lying down against a wall trying to get air from the cobblestones. I was absolutely sure that I was going to die, that we were all going to die. And then the Feuersturm *began, it was like animals howling, the wind, so strong it pulled me away from the wall and Otto grabbed my leg and hung onto me.*

Operation Gomorrah, it was called. How did they choose the name? Whose idea was that? Gomorrah, one of the cities of the plain. The Hamburg fires burnt for nine days. Forty thousand people died, most of them women and children. Nine days of hell, the dead lying everywhere, rotting in the heat, black swarms of flies over everything, and then the rats, thousands of rats eating the bodies. Anselm remembered reading the planner of the raids' words:

In spite of all that happened in Hamburg, bombing proved a relatively humane method.

Air Vice-Marshall Harris.

Relatively. What was the Air Vice-Marshall thinking of? Relative to what? Auschwitz? Were there relatively humane ways of killing children? Relatively speaking, where did Bomber Harris's raids rank on the table of twentieth-century horrors that had at its head the cold-blooded annihilation of Jews and Gypsies and homosexuals and the mentally infirm?

Not a cheerful line of inquiry, Anselm thought. Turn to other things. What would Alex want to know? What would he tell her? He didn't want to tell her anything. This was a mistake, the product of loneliness. His life was full of lies, he could lie to her. But she was trained in lie-detection, she would know. Did that matter? Wasn't lying the point? You were supposed to lie. The truth was revealed in your lies, by what you tried to conceal. Telling the truth ruined the whole exercise. There was nothing under truth, beyond truth. Truth was a dry well, a dead end. You couldn't learn any more after you knew the truth.

Anselm walked down Milchstrasse, feeling dated, dowdy. Pöseldorf was as smart as it got in Hamburg. The *Zwischenzeiten* was over now, the people were in winter gear. Shades of grey this year, grey flannel, grey checks, grey leather, soft grey shirts, grey scarves. Grey lipstick even.

Eric Constantine, wanted man, he'd bring the hire car back in a week; people would be waiting. What would happen to him?

Too late. Baader was right.

In the café, O'Malley was at a corner table, in a grey tweed suit, in front of him a small glass and a Chinese bowl holding cashew nuts.

'More to your taste than Barmbek?' he said.

It was a French sort of place, darkish, panelled, a zinc bar, dull brass fittings, freckled mirrors, paintings that impoverished artists might have traded for a few drinks, new-shabby furnishings.

'It's marginal,' said Anselm. 'It's better than all brown. What's that you're drinking?'

'Sherry. A nice little amontillado fino. Want one?'

'Please.' He'd only had two beers and an *Apfelkorn* all day. He looked around. The man behind the counter was talking on the phone. He had a cleft in his chin and highlights in his blonde hair.

Without moving his head, O'Malley caught the man's eye. He pointed at his glass, signed for two.

'So, what are these blokes talking about?'

'We got an earlier conversation. With the Israeli. The *katsa*. Want it?'

O'Malley finished his sherry. 'That's extra, is it?'

'Well, yes. Five hundred, that's in the basement. We'll throw in the pictures.'

'And steak knives?'

The barman arrived with the sherries. He said to O'Malley in English, Irish in his English, 'You must try the dry oloroso, it's exceptional, very nutty.'

'I have no doubt I will,' said O'Malley. 'Again and again. Thank you, Karl.'

When the man had gone, Anselm said, 'You're a stranger here, then.'

'He's a computer bloke, made a few quid in Ireland, now he's realised his dream, come home, opened this little bistro.'

'German?'

'Certainly. From Lübeck.'

'Ireland. Isn't there something wrong with that story?'

O'Malley shook his head. 'Change, John, the world's changed. Narratives don't run the same way any more. All the narratives are at risk.' He drank some sherry. 'Of course, you're in the cyberworld most of the time, that's not real. How are my blokes?'

'They're worried. This Spence who is actually Richler is threatening them. The deceased Lourens in Johannesburg apparently left something dangerous behind. Kael is agitated. May I ask what you actually want from these people?'

O'Malley looked at him for a while, rolling sherry around his mouth, his cheeks moving. He swallowed. 'No,' he said, 'you may not. But since you take secrets to the grave, I'll tell you. My clients are looking for assets, thirty, forty million US Serrano and Kael handled in the early nineties. Falcontor. Did they say that name?'

'Yes. Richler.'

O'Malley looked interested. 'Richler?'

Anselm tried the sherry, drank half the small flute. He remembered the British embassy in Argentina when the Falklands business was beginning, his first war, standing in a high-ceilinged room in Buenos Aires, drinking sherry with the press attache. She had narrow teeth and she talked about the international brotherhood of polo. 'It's so unfortunate because of course we're both polo-playing nations so there's always been a real affinity …'

Later she made a pass at him. He took the pass. Her husband was an art dealer, that was all he remembered. That and the bites on his chest, tiny toothmarks like the attack of a crazed ferret.

'Whose money?' Anselm said.

O'Malley smiled, the canines showing. 'Well, that's an awkward one, boyo. This is money without provenance, without parentage. Conceived in sin, sent out to make its own way in the world. It doesn't belong to Serrano, that much is certain.'

He chewed a cashew nut, picked up the bowl, turned it in a big hand. 'They found bowls like these in a Chinese galleon lying on the bottom of the sea, hundreds of years old, I forget how many. Amazing, no?'

'I'm not sure,' said Anselm. 'Amazing's not what it used to be. I presume these people are all lying to each other.'

'It's a way of life for these blokes. Their relationships are based on porkies. Darling, promise me you'll never tell me the truth.'

Four people came in, three young women, tall, anorexic, bulemic too probably, and a small man, plump, no trouble keeping food down. It was all shrill laughter, hair moving, hands moving, waving, shrieks, going over to the owner and kissing him on both cheeks. Anselm felt the need to be outside. Not an urgent need, just a strong wish to be in the open.

He put the small tape case on the table. 'I suppose we can skip the condom routine here. If you want to go on, tell me tonight. This isn't getting easier. It may have to be on Kael and he's hypochondriac.'

'I'll ring,' said O'Malley. 'I'll have a little listen and ring. And since when do you know who's a *katsa* and who isn't?'

'Everyone knows.'

Anselm walked to Fährdamm and the luck was his again, the ferry was coming in, nosing in to the jetty, a bump, two bumps. He sat on deck and smoked, cold wind wiping the smoke from his lips. The dark came suddenly and the shore lights came through the trees and lay on the water like strips of silver foil, bending, turning.

33

… LONDON …

THE MAN opened the door within seconds. She knew he had heard the gate's small noise, not so much a screech as a scratch. It was not a timid opening. He opened the door wide.

'Yes?'

'Good evening. Sorry to bother you,' said Caroline.

'Well then don't.'

Nothing of the courtly doorman about him, not a smiling doorman this. Just a big bald man in shirtsleeves, a wide man, downturned mouth, pig-bristle grey eyebrows.

Caroline had her card ready. She offered it to him. He looked at it, held it up to his face, looked at her, no change in expression.

'Yes?'

'It's Mr Hird?'

'It is.'

'Could we talk? It won't take long.'

'About what?'

'Something that happened at the store yesterday.'

'Don't talk about what happens at work. That's company policy. Goodbye.' Hird didn't move.

Caroline took the chance. 'Can I bribe you?'

He touched his nose with a finger, pushed it sideways, sniffed. 'No.'

'Is that a no or a maybe?'

'It's a no. Come inside.'

They went down a cold short passage into a cold room that looked unchanged for fifty, sixty years, a sitting room from around World War Two. The armchairs and the sofa had antimacassars and broad wooden arms. Two polished artillery shells flanked the fireplace. Above the mantelpiece was a colour photograph of the Royal Family – King, Queen and the two little princesses. A collection of plates and small glass objects stood on mirror-backed glass shelves in a display cabinet with ball-and-claw feet.

'Havin a glass of beer,' he said. 'Want one?'

'Yes, please.'

'Sit down.' He left and came back with two big glasses of beer, tumblers that bulged at the top.

'Well, what?' he said, sitting down.

Caroline sat and drank a decent mouthful. She moved to put the glass down, didn't for fear of marking the chair arm.

'Put it down,' Hird said. 'Not a museum. Looks bloody like it but it's not.'

She put the glass down, opened her bag. 'A man was shot in the store yesterday. On the third floor.'

Hird looked at her, drank beer. It left a white line on his upper lip and he didn't remove it. 'Entirely possible,' he said, 'I'm down on the ground, noddin and smilin.'

A black cat came in, fat, gleaming, silent as a snake, glided around the room, around chair legs, around Hird's legs, brushed Caroline's ankles. She failed some feline test and it left.

Caroline took out the security camera photographs of Mackie, held them out. 'He might have left through your door,' she said, she didn't know that. 'Can you remember seeing him?'

Hird put down his glass, took the pictures, held them on his stomach. He looked at them, gave them back to her, said nothing, drank some beer.

'Recognise him?'

'Busy store. How many people d'ya reckon go through my door every day?'

'He's on camera going through your door. The question is whether you remember him.'

'They send you around here?'

'No. Only my mole knows I know.'

She was lying. She had no mole. Store security denied all knowledge of the incident.

Hird kept his eyes on her. He had a big drink of beer. Caroline matched him. Their glasses were down to the same level.

'A mole in security?'

'Yes.'

'He'd tell you what's on the street cameras.'

'There's some problem there.'

'So how'd you know where to come?'

'It's my business to find out.'

'Right,' he said. 'Right. Saw your name in the paper. That Brechan. Shafted the bastard, din you. Shafter shafted.' He laughed, he enjoyed his joke. 'Bloody rag, your paper.'

Caroline shrugged, said, 'I gather the Prime Minister reads it.'

He laughed again. 'Bloody would, wouldn't he? See which Tory prick's been up a kid's bum last night. Course the lovin wife'll give the bastard an alibi, won't she?' His voice turned to purest Home Counties. 'We were at home all evening, officer, just the two of us, a quiet dinner, watched some television, had an early night.'

'So you saw this man,' said Caroline as a matter of fact.

Hird nodded. 'This an interview? Read me name in the paper?'

'No. Just background. No name. Nothing that can identify you. I promise.'

He studied her, drank some beer. 'Just looked odd,' he said. 'Then I saw his hand up to the chest, blood comin out between the fingers.'

In her heart, she felt the spring of pleasure uncoil at her cleverness.

'Did security see him?'

'Nah, been called away.'

'You didn't tell them?'

Hird studied her. 'What's your mole say?'

'He says he's not aware of any report.'

'Well, there you have it.'

'So the man went out the door and …'

'I went out, just to the corner to have a look-see. Deserted me post. Sackable offence. Still, had a customer's welfare at heart, din I?'

'And?'

'Well, he was pretty normal, not wobbly, but he wasn't walkin too straight. Bit of bumpin. Went into Brompton, thought he might be heading for the tube. Then these two fellas come along, they were lookin for him, that's for sure.'

'And?'

'Well, he keeps goin up the street, then he crosses and he gets on the back of this motorbike.'

'Waiting for him? The motorbike?'

Hird shook his head. 'In the bloody traffic, couldna been. He just stood there, then he got on the back of the bike. Another fella come from somewhere, he was runnin at them, then off the thing went like a rocket. Yellow helmet, one of them big helmets, spaceship helmet. Know what I mean?'

'And the men?'

'Buggered off.'

'Didn't get the number of the bike, did you?'

'Too far.'

Caroline nodded, finished her beer, got up. 'Thanks, that's a big help.'

Hird stood up, not easily. 'Can't see how.'

'You'd be surprised,' said Caroline.

They left the room. He went first. On the way down the passage she found a fifty, rolled it up. He opened the front door. She went out, turned.

'Well,' she said. She tapped the side of her nose with the rolled note, offered the roll. 'We were at home all evening, officer, we watched television …'

Hird laughed, gave her the nod, nod, wink, wink, took the note and put it in his shirt pocket.

'Keep insertin it up the bastards,' he said.

34

… HAMBURG …

INSKIP WAS watching the vision from some pale anonymous formica-walled airport terminal, views of queues, of passengers, close-ups of faces when their turns came at the counter. He jumped from queue to queue, face to face.

'Real time in Belgrade,' he said. 'It's a feed to the people who sold them the system. Quality control purposes.'

'Very nice,' said Anselm. 'What's our interest?'

'Intellectual, for the moment. Another breakthrough in techniques of invasion. I thought that earned praise.'

'It does. You're a promising person.'

Inskip sniffed. 'That's a theatrical sniff,' he said.

'Don't get to the theatre much.'

'Moving on, I have the new London subject's hire car in a parking garage near Green Park. Bills mounting, they've run a check on it.'

Eric Constantine. The name stuck in his mind.

'Probably a dead end then,' said Anselm. 'I'm going home.'

'Do you do that?' said Inskip.

Anselm was packing up when the phone rang.

'It's yes,' said O'Malley.

Anselm rang Tilders.

'Yes,' said Tilders. 'They understand this is going to be difficult?'

'Yes.'

'Wish us luck.'

'I do. Luck.'

Anselm had no urge to run home, walk home. He went out into the cold, misty night and, for the first time, took the sagging BMW car home. Outside the house, he got out and opened the wooden gates. It was a fight. Bolts and rusted hinges contested his wishes. He parked in front of the garage. No car had stood there for a long time, on those brick pavers.

Standing on the dark threshold, looking for the key, and inside, when he was sitting in the kitchen, glass in hand, he thought again about his Moritz: pro-Nazi. An anti-Semite. He looked like some count painted by von Rayski. And I look like him.

Anselm went to the photographs on the wall, the photographs Alex had looked at on the first night. There were dozens, going back more than a century – formal portraits, groups, weddings, dinners, sailing pictures, pictures taken at balls, in the garden, on the beach at Sylt, pictures of children, children with dogs, him with his parents and Lucas, Gunther and his wife, him with his grandfather in the garden, both with forks, big and small. No photograph of anyone who could be Moritz.

Surely Moritz could not have missed every single photographic occasion?

He went back to the kitchen, sat down. Alex. He should telephone her and say that he had changed his mind, apologise for wasting her time in Stadtpark. He had enjoyed talking to her, he could say that, but he didn't want to talk about the past.

The telephone rang and Anselm knew. He let it ring for a while and then, suddenly fearful that the ringing might stop, he went to answer it.

Alex's apartment was the size of a house, on the third floor of an old building in Winterhude, built between the wars, an *Altbauwohnung*.

Anselm said, 'May I lie on a couch? Or have I suggested that before?'

Alex Koenig smiled. 'You have and you may not. I've got coffee. Or brandy and whisky. Some gin left. I like to drink gin in summer.'

She was all in black, a turtleneck sweater and corduroy. Her hair was pulled back. Anselm thought she looked beautiful and it made him even more uneasy.

'You can't drink gin after sunset,' he said.

'Yes? Is that a British rule? It sounds British.'

'I suppose so.'

'But you're not British.'

'My mother's family are English.'

'Ah, mothers. They like rules. Impose order on the world, that's a mother's primary function. There is also beer and white wine.'

'White wine, thank you.'

She left the room and he went to the window. The curtains were open and he looked out at the winter Hamburg night, moist, headlights, tail lights reflected on the shiny black tarmac skin. The streetlamps made the last wet leaves on the trees opposite glint like thousands of tiny mirrors. He turned, noticed the upright piano, an old Bechstein, went across and opened it, he could not resist. His right hand played. The piano was badly in need of tuning. So was his hand, he thought.

'You're musical,' she said.

Anselm turned around. 'Playing "Night and Day" doesn't make you musical.'

'It makes you more musical than I am.'

He took a glass from her. 'Thank you. Interesting furniture.'

'The chairs?'

'A passage lined with chairs. About twenty chairs in this room. Yes, the chairs.'

'Kai's obsession. My ex-husband. Did I say his name? He likes things people sit on. Very much. He seeks out chairs.'

'Would you say he craved chairs?'

She tilted her head. 'Chairs he doesn't have, yes. There is an element of craving.'

'He must miss them.'

'I don't think he cares about them after he's got them. It's the thrill of getting them. He wants them but I don't think he cares about them.'

'Napoleon was like that,' Anselm said. 'So were the Romans, I suppose. Whole nations they didn't care about and wouldn't part with. Did this chair thing bother you?'

'Very much. It kept me awake. And then again, not at all. Are you sure you've eaten?'

'Is this going to be taxing? Do I need to be in shape?'

'Let's sit down.'

They sat, a narrow coffee table of dark wood between them, a modern piece. On it was a tape recorder, a sleek device.

'May I record this?'

'My instinct is to say no,' said Anselm. 'But why not?'

'Thank you.' She touched a square button. 'To begin,' she said. She wet her lips with wine. 'Can I ask you about your memory of the events? Is it clear?'

'It's fine. It's earlier and after that's the problem.'

'After your injury?'

'Yes. I don't remember anything for about a month.'

'And earlier?'

'There are holes. Missing bits. But I don't always know what's missing. There are things you don't think about.'

'Yes. So, the beginning. Your experience in trouble spots, that would have prepared you to some extent?'

'Well, by '93 Beirut wasn't really a trouble spot. Southern Lebanon, yes. Anyway, I thought we were dealing with GPs.'

'GPs?'

'Gun pricks. Paul Kaskis coined the term. Long before. A prick with a gun.'

'Ah. You would fear them surely? Gun pricks.'

Gun pricks. She said the words with a certain relish.

'There's a survival rule,' said Anselm. 'Paul invented that too. DPGP. Don't Provoke Gun Pricks. He didn't but they killed him anyway.'

'So you were scared?'

'I was scared. I thought you were interested in personal history?'

'I am. But I need to know about the specific circumstances too. Does it bother you to talk about them?'

He had come in trepidation and had been right to. He didn't want to talk about Beirut, it was stupid to have agreed to. She wasn't that interesting, appealing, she wasn't going to be the answer, an academic, they bled most of them of personality before they gave them the PhD. But he wanted to behave well, he had a bad history with her, he didn't want her to think he was disturbed.

'Well,' said Anselm, 'you should always be scared around GPs. The first few minutes, there's usually a lot of shouting, all kinds of crap, you just hope it dawns on them killing you might not be smart. Or that someone more intelligent or less drugged will come along, tell them to back off.'

'So you thought it would soon end?'

'I hoped. It's new every time. You hope. You pray. Even the godless pray. You shut up. Keep still, try to breathe deeply.'

'When did it change?'

Now was the moment to go. He felt the pulse beating in his throat, he knew that pulse, that sign, the blood drum.

She said, 'Your glass is empty. Can I?'

He nodded, relieved. She went out and came back in seconds with the bottle, filled his glass.

She'd known, she'd felt his pulse.

Anselm drank, lowered the level by an inch. 'They taped us,' he said. Then, quickly, 'Wrists and ankles, across the eyes, put hoods on, I couldn't breathe.'

He had said it. *I couldn't breathe.*

'And that scared you even more?' she asked, voice soft.

There was no turning back. 'Yes.'

Silence. He didn't look at her, wanted a cigarette badly. There was an ashtray on a side table. After a while, he looked at her and said, 'What did Riccardi tell you?'

'He was ... a little emotional.'

'What did he tell you?'

'He said you were silent in the beginning.'

'I had tape over my mouth.'

'After that, in the first place they kept you.'

'Riccardi is a vocal person. It's like having the radio on. I'm surprised he noticed.'

'He says he talked because you were both silent.'

'Riccardi doesn't need an excuse to talk. He talks in all circumstances. He'd talk over the sermon on the mount, the Gettysburg address. What else did he say?'

'He says he never thought it was political.'

'Everything's political. Anyway, you wouldn't want to make Riccardi your judge of what's political. He's a photographer. Born to take snaps. I was with him in Sri Lanka for a month and in the plane on the way back he said, "So what was all that about, anyway?" '

'He says it was never clear to him what you and Paul Kaskis were doing in the Lebanon.'

'Kaskis wanted to talk to someone. He asked me to go with him, I had nothing better to do.'

'Talk to someone? About what?'

'I don't know. Paul never told you anything. How does this line of inquiry further post-trauma research?'

She frowned. 'I'm sorry, I'm just curious. You have to be in my work.'

'Riccardi might have asked me before he opened his heart to you.'

As he said the words, Anselm heard the whine in them. He sounded like a betrayed lover.

'He didn't think he was doing any harm,' Alex said. 'He's your friend. He admires you very much. And he finds relief in talking about a painful experience. Most people do. Is it that you don't?'

'Can I smoke?'

'Of course, I should have said. This place was full of smoke when Kai was here. Pipe smoke. I rather liked it. It reminded me of my father.'

He fetched the ashtray and lit a cigarette, blew smoke at the distant ceiling. 'I was more than scared when they put the tape over my mouth, the hood,' he said quickly. 'I panicked. I lost control of myself.'

'Your body?'

'Yes.'

There was relief. Why had the thought of that moment of helpless indignity been so clenched in him? He knew. Because, at that moment, John Anselm reporter, John Anselm detached observer, was no more. He had become a victim. He wasn't the storyteller any more. He was in the story. He had joined it. He was a foul-smelling minor figure in an ancient story, no different from any civilian casualty of war, from any red-eyed, black-garbed crone pushing a barrow of sad possessions down a rutted road on the way from precious little to much, much less.

He remembered too that, in the aftermath of that moment, it had come to him with complete certainty that there would be no return to safety and a shower, to drinks and a meal, more drinks, reminiscences, laughter, to a long sleep in a bed with sheets.

'I think I have to go,' said Anselm. 'I think I've changed my mind about talking. I'm sorry.'

Alex shook her head. 'It's not to be sorry about. This is painful for you, I understand that. We can talk about something else.'

'I have to go.'

At her front door, he turned, awkward. 'Goodbye. I've wasted your time.'

She put out a hand, seemed to hesitate, then she touched his arm, just above the elbow. 'No. Not at all. Can I ask you one more thing? A personal thing.'

'Yes.'

'Would you like to see me again? Not professionally?'

35

... HAMBURG ...

TILDERS LOOKED tired. His eyes half closed, he talked more than usual. Anselm listened but his mind was elsewhere, on Alex Koenig.

'This is the end,' says Tilders. 'We had to put it inside his raincoat sleeve. We had no choice. It's a bad place, desperation. Dangerous. You will hear. He kept pulling at his cuff, he crosses his arms.'

'Yes,' said Anselm. 'Let's hear it.'

Serrano: ... *didn't get excited. He's very reasonable.*

Kael: *That's a bad sign. They're looking for this ...*

Serrano: *He says they've called in a few favours ... Shawn had been ... the British possibly.*

Kael: *Well, the prick ... anything for ...*

Serrano: *... ever mentioned the film.*

Kael: *Did he?*

Serrano: *I can't recall. I used to turn off ... say ... when he was like that, on drugs, drinking. He said ... Bill Casey when he was ... the CIA, that kind of thing. Knew everyone. North. Sharon ... when he was a soldier. Fucking Gaddafi even ...*

Kael: *What else does Richler say?*

Serrano: *The worrying thing, he says he hopes fucking Shawn did a good clear out ... this special office, the Süd-Afs, they're looking for assets ... target now.*

Kael: *Shit. Still, he could be lying. Second nature to them.*

Serrano: *Also fucking Bruynzeel, he says that's a priority. They want to know what we have.*

Kael: *He can wait.*

Serrano: *I was thinking last ...*

Kael: *Glad to hear there is thinking.*

Serrano: *I'm getting really annoyed ...*

Kael: *Thinking what?*

Serrano: *He talked about buying property, a house in England I think, other places ... there might be something there.*

Bumping and scratching noises.

'We thought the thing had fallen out,' said Tilders.

The sounds went on for at least fifteen seconds. Then Serrano was heard.

Serrano: *Possibly.*

Kael: *This is your business, you understand. I'm too old to have to deal with shit …*

Serrano: *My business? Excuse me, Werner, excuse me, who benefited most from this? I'll tell you. I'll tell you …*

Kael: *… down. We're expendable, do you fully understand that?*

Serrano: *What about your friends? Your friends won't …*

Kael: *The world changes. Your friends get old, they forget, they die.*

Anselm made the gesture, Tilders touched the button. Anselm gave him the slip of paper. 'Put it in his hands. I'll ring him now.'

Tilders rose, gathered up his possessions.

'You're tired,' said Anselm. 'How many jobs do you have?'

Tilders smiled, a wan thing without humour or pleasure. 'Only as many as it takes,' he said.

36

... LONDON ...

CAROLINE WISHART knew what to do. Charcoal-suited Dennis McClatchie had taught her, sixty-five years old, pinstriped cotton shirts with frayed collars, full head of slicked-back hair, breath of whisky and cigarette smoke and antacid tablets. She should have thought more about Dennis before going to Colley.

Early on, someone told her McClatchie had been a famous reporter, sacked from every Fleet Street paper.

'What happened, Dennis?' she asked him one day, shivering in the cold, shabby office, grey northern light coming through the bird-crapped window panes.

'Bad habits, darling. For one, the horses, bless 'em, blameless creatures, innocent, with these ruthless, terrible blood-sucking humans around them.'

He drew on his cigarette, pulled in his cheeks, let the smoke dragon out of his nostrils. 'Punching editors, that was of little career assistance. But. No regrets there. Well, perhaps. One or two I should have nailed more thoroughly. Just laziness really. And I didn't like hurting my hands. I had nice hands once.'

He'd lit a new cigarette from his stub, stifled a cough.

'Married a lot too,' he said. 'Can't recall some of 'em. Women I hope. Damn lawyers sent me demands from people I'd never heard of. Had to get a death certificate forged in the end.'

He looked at her, turned the head, the skull, she thought she heard his spine creak. 'All of it drink-related, I should say in my defence,' he said. 'All my crimes have been drink-related. All my life has for that matter. I'll call my autobiography *A Drink-Related Offence.*'

One day in her first week, she felt the eyes of Dennis on her when she was sitting frozen with anxiety. She had been expelled from school, sacked from Sotheby's, asked to leave Leith's cooking school, told lies to get this job. Now the slovenly Carmody, class-hate written all over him, had given her an assignment, spat a few words from the side of his mottled mouth.

'What's the cheerless cretin want, darling?' said McClatchie.

'A story on community services. I'm not quite sure where to start.'

McClatchie looked at her, looked at his hands for a while, the nails, the palms. A plain cigarette burned between two long fingers the colour of old bananas. She knew that he knew that she'd lied about her experience.

'I always start with a proposition,' he said. 'A headline. Gets you going. Pope Hid Nazi War Criminals. Moon Landing Fake.'

She hadn't grasped the point. Her eyes showed it.

'Community Leaders Slam Burnley Services,' said McClatchie.

'Do they?'

'No idea. Probably. There's no gratitude in the world. Get on the blower and ask 'em.'

'Who?'

'Start with that Tory prat. He'd like to cull the poor but he'll give you the compassionate bullshit. Tell him you're hearing a lot of complaints about services. Baby clinic, that sort of thing?'

'Is there one?'

'Not the foggiest. The phone book, darling. Peek at that. Under Council. Something sexy like that.'

Start with a proposition. She sat in her cubicle office far away from Birmingham, McClatchie mouldering in the wet ground now, thought about what she'd seen and what Mackie had said in their first conversation.

A massacre in Africa.

A lot of that goes on.

'Soldiers killing civilians.'

'What, the Congo? Burundi?'

'No. White soldiers. Americans.'

'American soldiers killing civilians in Africa? Somalia?'

'No. This is … it's like an execution.'

So, the proposition, the headline:

US troops in Africa massacre.

That would do to go on with. It would help explain why Mackie thought the film was worth twenty grand and why other people thought it was worth killing him. She knew that for a fact.

Just looked odd. Then I saw his hand up to the chest, blood comin out between the fingers.

She thought about Colley, how she was tricked. She wanted to kill him.

Colley's time would come, that wasn't important for now.

Africa. Where in Africa?

Southern Africa? Mackie was South African.

American troops in Southern Africa?

Had there ever been? Where? When?

She logged on, put the words *US troops southern africa* into the search engine. Hundreds of references came up, fifty at a time. She rejected, read, printed, the morning went by, she ate a sandwich, the afternoon advanced, her eyes hurt.

The phone. Halligan.

'Marcia's upset. She's got some right to know what you're working on. In her new position.'

Caroline tried to compose the right response. She was tired.

'I'm sorry she's upset. Such a nice person. I simply explained to her the terms of my contract.'

'Yes. Entered into under the gun. Leaving fucking Marcia aside, what the hell are you doing? You report to me, remember? So please report. ASAP.'

Caroline took her career in her hands. 'Bigger than Brechan,' she said. 'Just an estimate, mark you.'

She thought she heard Halligan swallowing, his throat's slimy clutch. Just imagination.

'I'll calm the woman down,' he said. Decisive. 'Report to me soonest.' Pause. 'When would that be?'

'Soonest.'

Silence. She heard the silent sound of his chagrin and his regret.

'Yes, well,' he said. 'Posted. Keep me.'

'Of course. Geoff.'

She went back to the screen. She now knew more about American involvement in Africa since the 1950s than anyone needed to know. And she knew very little of any use to her in understanding Mackie's film.

What would McClatchie do? She saw McClatchie in the eye of her mind. She saw his burial, the half dozen of them around the pit, the soil that had come out of it under pegged plastic, half a dozen people standing in the drizzle at the edge of the flat, wet necropolis.

Get on the blower and ask 'em.

Who?

She went back to the screen.

37

… LONDON …

'WHAT'S HE say?'

'He says congratulations on the good work, love you. What do you think? He says find him or die. We're going to carry this like nail holes in our fucking palms, you know that? Ten to the woman, twenty to the fink, six hundred in the bag. Plus we have to pay these idiots. And for what? *Caddyshack*. We get an ex-rental video starring Chevy fucking Chase. I hate the cunt. Is he still alive?'

'He's alive. It's his hair that's dead. The biker, I don't understand. That doesn't make sense.'

'Now this boy knows he's dealing with incompetents. Be comforting, wouldn't it? To know you're dealing with pricks? Two of them run out after him and they don't get the bike number. I still cannot believe that.'

'Hire for a week, next day you park in a garage, your intention is not to come back, you're going to be picked up by a bike. No.'

'The hospitals?'

'Nothing local. They're going wider. On a bike, could have gone anywhere.'

'He won't stick around. If he's alive, he's running. Just make sure these fucking Germans don't miss some fucking ferry, charter flight to Ibiza, balloon, something.'

'We could ask for help. Ask Carrick. They'll find him.'

'Find him, they find the fucking film. The bike, that's what we need. Find the bike, we nail the cunt. Ring of steel, now that would have helped.'

'Just around the City, no use. Although …'

'What? What?'

'I read they were trying out cameras in other parts for when Bush was here …'

'Who would know? Who would know?'

'I don't know, how would I …'

'Ask the fucking Germans, ring the fucking Krauts, they're supposed to know everything.'

'How much can you tell them?'

'Just tell them everything we know. Okay? We're hanging out here. Time, the bike, the place, two people, the fucking direction, anything you can think of. Now. Please?'

38

... LONDON ...

NIEMAND WOKE, an instant of bewilderment. Then he knew where he was. It was night, there was light coming from downstairs.

He needed to piss, urgently. He sat up, put his feet on the floor. His shoulder felt stiff but there was little pain.

He stood up, went to the bathroom naked. There was a mirror above the toilet and his face looked pale. He went back to the bed, wrapped the sheet around his waist and went to the top of the staircase. Looking down made him feel dizzy. Below was a big room with a long trestle table at one end under a row of windows. On the table stood several models of buildings and what looked like a model of a town, a village with a church in a square.

She was not in view. He didn't know her name.

Niemand started down the steep stairs. The woman appeared, a knife in her hand.

'Not you too,' said Niemand.

She frowned, then she realised. 'I'm cooking,' she said. 'I'm chopping vegetables.'

'How long has it been?'

She looked at her wristwatch, a man's watch. 'Nearly twenty-four hours.'

There was no point in hurrying. They'd have found him before this if they could.

'My clothes,' Niemand said. 'I have to go.'

'You can't wear what you came in. Except for the jacket, that's okay.' She pointed to her right. 'In there, there's a cupboard. You might find something to fit you.'

He was at the bedroom door, when she said, 'Or you could just carry on wearing that sheet. Won't raise an eyebrow around here.'

He liked the way she spoke. It was a musical sound, it had tones. In the bedroom, a wall of cupboards was full of men's clothes, one man's clothes, jackets, suits, shirts, shoes. He found underpants, a pair of jeans, they looked a bit short in the leg for him, too big in the waist. They would do. He took a grey T-shirt, too big, that didn't matter, found socks.

He went back upstairs and showered in the big cubicle, wetting the bandage. When he went to soap his side, he felt a sharp pain at the collarbone, in his back.

The clothes didn't look too bad. His shoes were under the bed. He put

them on and went to his bag on the dressing table. The money was in
bundles held with rubber bands. He opened one, saw the fakes immediately,
only the top notes looked real.

'Bastards,' he said without venom. It didn't surprise him. It had been
nothing but betrayals since the beginning. Plus he had been stupid.

He examined all the bundles. Probably five hundred pounds in real
notes. His jacket and his nylon holster were hanging over the back of a chair.
Blood had dried on the jacket lining. He put the real money in the holster,
took the bag and went downstairs.

The kitchen was a counter along one wall. She had her back to him,
doing something with a pot.

'Did I say thank you?' he said. 'Thank you.'

She turned, not surprised, she had heard him on the stairs. She was a
good-looking woman, a strong face, dark eyes.

'Quite all right,' she said. 'I often pick up wounded men. It's a service I
provide to the community. Are you hungry?'

Niemand thought for a moment. He should leave. 'Yes,' he said. 'Please.'

'It's a kind of stir fry. Chicken. Sit down.'

She put out two plates, cutlery, napkins, two wine glasses, a bottle of red
wine, not full. She poured wine without asking.

The food was good. She wasn't bad to eat with either. No noises, she kept
her mouth closed when she was chewing, she didn't talk with food in her
mouth.

'Your name's Con,' she said. 'I'm Jess.'

He waited until he'd swallowed. 'Jess. Where are we?'

'Battersea.'

He knew where it was. He pointed at the trestle table to his left. 'Is that
your hobby?'

'I'm a model maker. I do it for a living. A very bad living.'

'Make models?' It had never occurred to him that there could be such an
occupation.

'For architects. Usually. The village there, that's a development in
Ireland. A typical Irish village for millionaires. Americans.'

They carried on eating. Then she said, direct gaze, 'Who shot you?'

Niemand finished chewing, swallowed, wiped his mouth with the
napkin. He drank wine. He liked red wine, it was the only alcohol he liked.
'A man dressed as a woman,' he said.

Jess drank. 'I'll put that again. Why did you get shot?'

She had probably saved his life. She had a right to ask.

'I was stupid,' he said. 'I was selling something to people I didn't know.'

'Drugs?'

'No.'

'They shot a dealer around the corner the other day. In his car. Two men.
One from each side.'

'I'm not a drug dealer.' He didn't have strong feelings about dealers in drugs, the whole world was built on addictions, but he didn't want her to think he was one. 'I'm not a drug dealer,' he said again.

'Point made.' She finished her wine and stood up. 'I have to go out,' she said. 'I'll be back around ten, ten–thirty.'

He stood up too. 'I'll be gone. Thanks. I'll wash up.'

There was a moment of awkwardness.

'You should stay quiet for a few days, the doctor said,' she said. 'He doesn't really have a bedside manner, your doctor.'

He heard the sound upstairs. Pivoted.

Christ, no, not again.

'It's the cat,' she said. 'Climbs up the pipes, gets into the bathroom. Always knocks something over. Deliberately. It's not even my cat, thinks it owns the place.'

'Just the night,' said Con. 'Would that be okay?'

There was a pad and pen beside the phone. She wrote.

'My cellphone number. Ring if you come over weak.'

He nodded. 'What floor are we on?'

'Third. There's another one. It's empty.'

'How'd you get me up here?'

'In the lift. This was a factory. The fire–escape door's in the corner over there. They made radio parts, valves and condensers, stuff like that.'

'How do you know about old radios?'

'My dad,' she said. 'He wanted a boy, so he taught me how to fish and shoot and change a fuse and hotwire a car.'

Niemand sat down. 'I wish I'd met you earlier in my life,' he said.

39

... HAMBURG ...

THEY RAN on the river path, saw the backs of the houses across the water, here and there a rowboat pulled onto the bank, fowls strutting and pecking, a man hanging washing. There were few runners, many people on bicycles. The sun came and went, gave no heat.

Anselm had not run with anyone since college, since his runs with his room-mate Sinclair Hollway, who went on to become a Wall Street legend for putting twenty-six million dollars on a nickel play. The unauthorised money lost, Sinclair was found dead in his house on Cape Cod a week later.

'Anselms have been in Hamburg for a long time,' she said.

He looked at her. Her hair was pulled back and she was wearing anti-glare glasses, the kind target shooters wore, yellow. She looked different.

'What do you know about Anselms?'

'I looked them up. I suppose you know all the family history.'

'Some.'

'Pioneers of the Hanseatic trade with America, it said.'

'That's quite possible. How old are you?'

The yellow eyes. 'Thirty-seven next month. Why?'

'No reason.'

'You simply wanted to know?'

'Yes. Simply wanted to know. Innocent inquiry. Or isn't it?'

'I have no opinion.'

'No innocent inquiries. Is that it? Nothing is innocent.'

'A question about age, that could certainly be innocent, yes.'

'But you don't think this is?'

'I didn't think you had any curiosity about me. This is really a conversational cul-de-sac. What kind of books do you enjoy? Do you read novels?'

'I read novels.'

Once he had read two or three a week, on planes, while eating, waiting for something, someone, somewhere. He never went anywhere without at least two, usually three, buying five or six at a time and leaving them where he finished them. He had donated books to planes, airports, trains, railway stations, left them in parks and bars and hotels and coffee shops, government offices and embassies, taxis and buses and hire cars. Once he left a book in a brothel, the woman had seen it in his coat pocket, asked for it.

They ran. He looked down and saw how shabby his running shoes were, bits were peeling. No German would run in such shoes.

A family on bicycles was coming at them, two abreast. He dropped behind Alex. The plump mother said thank you, three children each said thank you, the father said another thank you.

Running behind her, he admired her backside. He also admired her action. No show to it, no big knee lift or arm action. She just ran, everything straight. When he went up to join her, they touched, just a brush of upper arms, a sibilant friction.

'DeLillo,' she said. 'Do you like him?'

'I read the earlier books, the Oswald book, that was the last one I read.'

'You liked that?'

'I don't know. I must have, I finished it.'

'You give up on books easily?'

'Yes. It's an American thing. Gratify me or be gone.'

'You don't want to live in America again?'

In the beginning, in the early days in the old house on the canal, he had sometimes thought about going back to America. But the idea disturbed him, made him weepy. Go back where? He had no home, the people he had loved were gone, father, mother gone, he was alone. Lucas was all he had, if he had Lucas, they could not even touch properly and Lucas lived in London, he was English now. Go home to the place he left to go to Beirut? To Kaskis's tiny apartment on the hill? It would belong to Kaskis's family since Beirut. And later he came to think that Hamburg suited the way he felt, his condition. He was of it and not of it. He belonged and he didn't. The Germans had partial memory loss and so did he. They had chosen what pieces to forget, but then perhaps so had he.

'America overwhelms me,' he said. 'There's too much of too little. Why would you think I don't have any curiosity about you?'

The yellow eyes looked at him, away. 'I should not have said that. A silly thing to say. What else do you read?'

'Mostly, I get drunk and go to sleep in front of the television with the cable news on.'

It was true. He sat with a book in his lap, a glass in his hand and on the television an endless loop of death, destruction, pain, fear, famine and misery. Often he came back and watched again when he woke far out on the wrong side of the night, wet with sweat from his dreams.

They ran.

'I also listen to music while I'm getting drunk watching the news,' he said. 'A multi-media experience.'

They ran. Anselm's knee was beginning to hurt, the pain that started as dull, like a memory of a pain, gradually turned to fire in the joint.

'You're not interested in the music I listen to?' he said.

They ran. He thought that this would probably be the only run they

413

would ever take together and he did not know how to prevent that from being so.

'People like you probably listen to Wagner,' she said. She did not turn her head.

'Wagner?'

He had no idea what she meant, he had no view on Wagner, his father had hated Wagner, the Wagners as a whole. But he also disliked her tone, it sent a current of annoyance through him and, for an instant, he wanted to bump her into the canal – it would be easy, hip and shoulder. Splash. There would be no coming back from that and it would be over. He would go home. Resume his life without shrinks. She could crawl home, wet, have her own post-traumatic stress.

'People like me?'

She said nothing, didn't look at him.

They ran and he kept looking at her. 'What kind of person am I?'

She still didn't look at him. 'You're an adrenalin addict,' she said. 'You like percussion. You're a seeker after percussion.'

'I was a hostage, that's all you know about me. Where do you get all these other opinions from?'

'Just intuition. Professional intuition. You say you were often scared but you never stopped looking for chances to be scared.'

Anselm heard bicycles coming up behind them. He fell back to let them pass, thin androgynous people in latex outfits, helmets, thin dark glasses. Alex slowed for him.

'That's not a terribly clever thing to say,' he said. 'That was my job. That was what I did. I didn't go to these places on holiday.'

'Did you take holidays?'

The sun went. His knee was getting worse, soon he would be showing it, favouring it, he would be pathetic. This was why you didn't run with other people.

'Time to turn,' he said. 'I've got to be at work in an hour.'

They turned. He tried to slow the pace but she wouldn't be slowed. She wanted to push him, he felt that.

'Holidays,' she said. 'Did you take holidays?'

He didn't want to answer. He couldn't remember. He remembered the artist who hit him, that was all. It was possible that he hadn't taken other holidays. Then he remembered sailing with Kaskis in the Bahamas. That wasn't really a holiday. Kaskis was doing something there, some story on money laundering and corruption. He rang, said come over and we'll have a sail, I'll hire a boat. They took the boat out the morning Anselm arrived. There was a strong wind to begin with. It got a lot stronger and it changed direction. His experience was on smaller boats and this one was a pig. They should have expected that, it was a cruising boat, not meant for heavy conditions. Kaskis didn't want to make for harbour. He also didn't want to take down the mainsail. He agreed only after they dug in and, for a few seconds, it seemed as if they would pitchpole. Taking down the mainsail, Anselm was almost knocked overboard, cut his head. Under power with just the jib up, the boat threatened to breach in the troughs. Getting home took a long time. Kaskis loved it, he lit up with pleasure. You could see how he'd made Special Forces in the army.

'I took some holidays,' said Anselm.

The knee was not good. It was sending signals up and down. He looked at her. She was looking at him.

'What kind of holidays do you shrinks take?' he said. 'Or do you just stay at home and introspect? Keep in touch with your inner selves. Do some mental scoping.'

'Scoping?'

'You could scope your anima. Do an animascope. An animoscopy. That's got a nice medical sound to it.'

'So you didn't take holidays?'

'What is this about holidays? Since when were holidays the measure of people? Did Marie Curie take a lot of holidays?'

'I don't know. Do you?'

'I don't care.'

'Your memory loss. Has that been permanent?'

'How did we get on to that? What's permanent? Permanent is a retrospective term. I'm still alive. Just.'

More cyclists, no leanness or androgyny here, a group of overweight women, bikes wobbling, breasts alive, jostling inside tracksuits.

'Precision,' said Alex. 'It is important. Do you still experience the loss of memory? Correction. The absence of some memory.'

'Some. Yes. I've lost all the good bits, the holidays. I'm left with the crap.'

Both knees were hurting now. He would have to stop, walk the rest of the way. He did not want to do that.

They ran for another hundred metres.

'I'm tiring,' she said. 'Can we slow?'

He felt relief, he'd outlasted her, he didn't have to be humiliated. 'It's just a kilometre,' he said. 'I was thinking we should pick it up.'

The yellow glance, a shrug. 'If you like.'

She went away from him without effort, no sign whatsoever of fatigue. He watched her backside and could make no effort to go after her. The path turned and she was gone.

Anselm stopped, walked. She had tried to be kind to him, to spare him embarrassment. She had pretended to a weakness she didn't have. His response, wired into his brain, was to go for her throat.

She was waiting at her car, grey tracksuit on, yellow glasses off, breathing normally.

'I found a reserve of energy,' she said.

'I noticed.'

They didn't speak until she stopped outside the office gates. She didn't look at him.

'Perhaps that is not a thing we should do together,' she said. 'It might not bring out our best natures.'

Anselm took his bag from the back seat. 'I don't have a best nature,' he said. 'Least worst, that's my best.'

40

... HAMBURG ...

THE REQUEST from Lafarge to find a motorcycle was on his desk. He was tired, not just his knees hurt now, his left hip sent splinters of pain up and down. He summoned Inskip and explained.

'It's Mission Hopeless,' he said, 'but they're paying. Carry on, Number Two. Or is that Number One? No, I would be Number One, surely?'

'Number two,' said Inskip, 'is a crap in toddler talk.'

Anselm nodded. 'I shouldn't distrust my instinct for the language. Carry on, Number Two.'

In mid-morning, Inskip stood in the door, his egg head to one side. Anselm thought he saw a faint flush of blood in the pale skin. Also, Inskip was wearing a red T-shirt. He hadn't noticed that earlier. Had fashion changed? Was red in the ascendant?

Inskip said, 'Would you like to listen to something, Number One? Number One being a piss.'

Anselm nodded, rose and went to Inskip's workstation, sat beside him.

'I've found this person,' said Inskip. 'In a company that's doing closed-circuit TV trials in London. Roads, stations, shopping malls. The football. A minion of the coming total surveillance state. I haven't been entirely straightforward with him. Forgivable, is that?'

Anselm looked into the black eyes, looked away.

Inskip touched the key.

Asked and we could've fucking looked, couldn't we?

They didn't know. Inskip's voice.

Asking's how you find out what you don't fucking know.

They didn't know to ask.

What? Is this fucking philosophy? This what I fucking missed by not going to fucking Oxford?

George, what could you have told them?

What? Every fucking pushbike and Porsche and cunt on a skateboard that went through the check, that's what.

Can we get that now? It's a small window, five, ten minutes.

I'm waiting. We serve you lot, don't we. Only to ask. Say again?

Four-fifty on. The passenger might be leaning on the rider. He might have a

417

bag, a sports bag, that would probably be on his lap, hard to see. No helmet, the passenger …

No helmet. That's where you start, sunshine. Hang on.

I've got an offender here, five-three, that's a nice bike, he looks like he's gone to sleep, the bumboy, not at all alert, no helmet, shocking disregard for the law.

Plate? Can you run that?

Running, my lord … Yes, this is your person … I can give you an address, see how fucking easy it is when you simply ask?

Point taken. A salutary lesson, George. Name and address?

'He thinks you are?' said Anselm.

Inskip put a hand to his naked scalp, lay fingers on it. 'MI6,' he said.

'You may go far in this line of work.'

'And owe it all to my teachers.'

'Give it to Lafarge.'

41

... LONDON ...

SHE FOUND a person to start with, at the London School of Economics, in the School of Oriental and African Studies.

They sat in a small study that smelled of cigarette smoke. He was an overweight man in his fifties, head shaven, black polo-necked shirt. He looked like a Buddhist monk gone bad, in thrall to things of the flesh, the ascetic life a memory. His eyes were red, he smoked Camels in a hand that trembled a little, and he jiggled his right foot without cease.

'Well,' he said, 'Americans are not strangers to the region.'

'But massacres?'

'Massacres? A difficult term. Massacre. Imprecise. Like genocide. Used very loosely.'

'Killing civilians. Lots of them.'

He started to laugh, coughed, kept at it for a while, produced an unclean red handkerchief, crumpled like a tissue, tore it open and covered his mouth.

She looked away. He recovered.

'Sorry. Terrible tickle in the throat. Dust. Place never gets cleaned. So, yes. Killing of civilians? Common practice in the region. For about three hundred years.'

'But not by Americans.'

'Depends. Depends on what you think is the causal chain, I suppose. In Angola, for example.'

'For example?'

'You're not connected with television, are you?'

'No.'

'I do quite a lot of television. You may have seen me?'

'I thought your face was familiar.'

'Really?' He ran a hand over his scalp, a pass, quick. 'Yes. Well, I've been too busy recently, books and whatnot, can't drop everything because some television producer calls. They expect that, you know, incredible arrogance.'

'About Angola, you said ...'

'Lots of atrocity rumours about Angola in the eighties. One a month. What you'd expect from a superpower war-by-proxy, I suppose.'

He studied her, scratching an eyebrow. 'Wishart. Are you the person who wrote that Brechan story?'

He had assumed a prim expression. He looked like a Pope now, some Renaissance Pope whose portrait she'd seen somewhere.

'Not the headline,' she said. 'That was in poor taste.'

'Thoughts of Wilde crossed the mind. None so hypocritical about buggery as the unexposed buggers.'

'Yes. To get back to Angola ...'

She had to wait while he lit another cigarette. He had a big lower lip, red, and when he blew out smoke, it turned down and he showed paler flesh inside, the colour of tinned tuna.

'Angola,' he said. 'A resource war, one of the late-century resource wars. Many more to come. I'm considering a book on the subject ... working on it, actually. I've done a lot of work on it. I'm well beyond considering it.'

'Atrocities ...'

'Well, there's always talk. I remember a story about a village disappearing off the face of the map, in some American rag.'

'Would you know which one?'

'This is so long ago.'

'This is very important,' Caroline said. 'When you say American rag ...?'

He seemed to be galvanised, sat back in his chair, ready to speak to camera, chins up.

'Well, American rags. There've been a few. America's got this tiny left fringe. The right's a huge great heaving pit of snakes – but energetic. The left's always been quite pathetic, sad. No life and no theory at all. Well, a little, just the simpler bits they can half understand. Gramsci, they half understand bits of Gramsci. The hegemony stuff. But deep down the right loonies and the left share the same conspiracy mania, it's rooted in a small-town America paranoia. There's a plot out there to take things away from them, democracy, freedom of speech, a man's guns, a man's right to fuck his pig, there is no, I mean absolute zero, understanding of structural ...' He tailed off, seemed to have lost course, blinked at her with stubby eyelashes.

She said, 'A village in Angola disappeared off the map?'

He focused. 'Of course, you have to be *on* the map to disappear *off* it, don't you? The logical precondition. God knows how they could tell it had vanished.'

'And you say there were others? Atrocity stories?'

'Many. Both sides. Raped nuns are always good value. The atrocity story is a staple of modern conflict. It illustrates what utter monsters the other lot are. As in the ex-Yugoslavia. Take for example ...'

'So they said this Angolan village had been destroyed?'

'Something like that. Dimly recall, mark you. Dimly. It was a longish piece. Quite well done.'

He closed his eyes. 'Ah,' he said, 'got it. *Behind Enemy Lines*.'

'Yes?'

'California, I think. Published in some little place in California. *Behind Enemy Lines*. I liked the name.'

'No chance of you having the clipping?'

He shook his head. 'My dear, long gone, I've moved on. The thing didn't live beyond four or five issues, they never did. I subscribed to everything in those days. Remotely promising, I sent off my money. They probably owe me twenty quid. Do you get a penny back when these rags collapse with ten issues owing on your subscription? My arse. Try the library here. Hopeless though it is.'

The library had never held *Behind Enemy Lines*. But a librarian clicked keys at speed, interested frown. He found the complete *Behind Enemy Lines* for sale, a rarity, seven issues, good condition, twenty pounds, from an address in Portsmouth. Southpaw Books. Email, telephone, fax.

She went outside and rang. A man with a bad cold answered. She said fifty pounds if he would go through *Behind Enemy Lines* and fax all items involving American involvement in Africa.

'Go through them?' he said. 'Darling, basically, we sell the stuff. That's the business.'

'Sixty quid,' she said. 'How's that? And you keep the magazines. Inside an hour.'

'Time's money,' he said. 'I'm a slow reader.'

'A hundred. The contents pages too. I'm stopping there.'

'Credit card transaction, is this?'

'What else?'

'What's your fax number?'

42

… HAMBURG …

O'MALLEY RANG.

'I'm sitting here just down your very pleasant little road. Where the boats are. A word, perhaps?'

Anselm went out, didn't bother with a coat. It was much colder than when he had come to work. The sky was an army blanket, dirty grey, a shade lighter than O'Malley's BMW, which, in turn, was a lighter grey than O'Malley's suit.

'Flitting to and fro, you should open an office here,' said Anselm. It was warm in the car and there was the smell of leather and newness. 'Think of the fares you'd save.'

O'Malley shook his head. 'What would save some real money, mate, is buying your business. But I'm not flitting, I'm having a little stay, a sojourn. Did I not say that? No? Before the courts tomorrow, trying to get the attention of some naughty Poles. They have products we wish to render immobile. In a warehouse down by the river. Your beer, your ballbearings, your smoked hams, your binoculars, your pickled cucumbers, beetroot, artichokes. Even your Polish condoms, a container load. In packs of fifty, the weekend packs they're called.'

'For football teams, surely?'

'Aimed at the single male. These people are not called Poles for nothing. The brand is *Ne Plus Ultra*.'

Anselm put his head against the headrest. 'The old-fashioned Polish condom makers. I didn't know there were any left. Knew their Latin, history of the Peninsular Wars. Craftspeople in rubber.'

'Latex. Moving on, another task.'

A police car was coming towards them, slowly, no hurry, a shift to get through. Both occupants, men, gave them the lingering eye.

'Ceaselessly vigilant in the interests of the rich,' said O'Malley. 'Whereas out in the gloomy industrial hinterland, the lower orders have to beg and beseech the *Politzei* to come to their assistance.'

'I didn't realise you were familiar with the conditions of the German working class.'

'A lifelong interest. Like Engels in England.' He looked at Anselm's shirt. 'Winter's setting in. I could probably find an old coat to send you.'

'I'd be grateful. *Winterhilfe* usually toss a few warm garments my way. But not exactly Zegna.'

O'Malley was getting a slim notecase off the back seat. 'Mine wouldn't be Zegna. It would be hand sewn by my little man. Crouch is his name.' He opened the leather box, flipped through papers. 'Doesn't have the ring of Zegna, Crouch. Ermenegilda Crouch. No. This matter concerns something called Falcontor. Remember?'

Falcontor. Richler on the tape:

I'll say one word. Falcontor. Don't say anything.

O'Malley found an A4 envelope. 'From Serrano's case, at the station. Your excellent if expensive work. We can't make much sense of this stuff. The cross-trained bloodhounds you employ may have more luck.'

'I thought you said Serrano was still in the paper era?'

'He is. But the places he parks the ill-gotten stuff may not be.'

'What do you want?'

O'Malley scratched an eyebrow. 'Well, you know. Anything. The main interest is assets. But anything. Don't spook anyone, that's paramount. And speed. And the name Bruynzeel. Keep an eye out for that.'

'Flemish, I presume?'

'I would too. Sounds like a nasty symptom the nanny should report.'

A couple appeared on the jetty, began to take off the cover of a boat.

'I was like that once,' said O'Malley. 'Weather was no impediment. Serrano, the hotel, can you keep that running?'

'Yes.'

'Good on you. How many ways do I love a crisp affirmative? Concludes the business. Oh, and notice I've got a new number. The old one was boring me.'

Anselm put his hand on the door latch. 'You won't forget the coat?'

'No,' said O'Malley. 'Consider it in the mail. And this coincidence will amuse you. An email in my box from Angelica. The American bore. It's over. Taken his Egyptian artefacts, gone. She's holding on to the apartment in the Marais pending the legal nastiness. Sadly, the chef's been terminated.'

'I'm sure you can arrange food parcels. When you say speed?'

O'Malley looked at him. 'Yes. We'd be grateful. Things that are solid can melt into air.'

'I wouldn't be too hopeful.'

'In me, the hopeful genes. In all the O'Malleys. Globally. The O'Malley diaspora of optimistic genes.'

'Probably inherit the earth,' said Anselm. 'O'Malleys and cockroaches. Still, the evolutionary day has only just begun. Give us a few hours.'

'Hours, certainly. Not even units of time in the evolutionary day.'

Anselm felt the pressure fight the car door as he pushed it closed. It was even colder now. It felt like snow, the air still, the feeling of something pendant. Waiting for its time. But it was much too early in the year. Its time was nearer Christmas, when it would fall at night, the magic flakes hushing the discordant city.

In the blue gloom, Carla was at her workstation, text on her right-hand screen, green code on the black screens to her left. She saw Anselm coming and swivelled, her useless leg thrust out. He showed her the case folder.

'Some time?' he said. 'It's a priority.'

She nodded. He gave it to her. She read the cover sheet, opened it and looked at the pages inside, flipped them. Two columns to the page. Letters, numbers, names handwritten in ink.

'This has meaning?'

'Not to the client. Serrano, remember Serrano? These are his notes. The client is interested in something called Falcontor. Also the name Bruynzeel.'

He wrote them on her pad. 'Something might occur to you. I promised a preliminary report soon.'

She put the file down and laced her fingers, turned the palms outward. He heard her knuckles crack, a sound that always disturbed him, for no reason that he knew.

He went back to his office and the paperwork. Jonas was a happy agent. He had paid the bill, plus the $25,000 bonus. Pizza baron Charlie Campo and his runaway wife Lisa were reunited at last. In romantic Barcelona. All forgiven – a terrible, impulsive mistake. Sherry and tapas in a little bar off the Ramblas. Soft light, the bottles on the shelves glowing blood and oranges and rust. Glances. Touches.

Anselm thought of a woman with tape over her mouth, tied to a bed. Screaming through her eyes.

He went back to work, wrote an authorisation for Herr Brinkman to pay Inskip and Carla the equivalent of $6250 each.

Blood money. They were bounty hunters. The woman could be dead. He could find out, but he didn't want to.

Through his slice of vision, Anselm looked at the sky, the lake, both still. The day was darkening. Perhaps it would snow. An early snowfall. It wouldn't be a proper snowfall, though, just tiny flakes that turned into slush when they touched the ground. The earth wasn't cold enough yet. When he was about twelve, he had been in the garden helping his grandfather fork over the vegetable patch.

'Weather experts, they know nothing,' the old man said. His hair was the colour of the sky. 'The earth tells the clouds when it's time for snow.'

Thinking about his grandfather, about cold earth, a day came into his mind like a ghost. He remembered the hotel, the down mattress that buried you, folded over you. Rising early, long before first light, walking down the creaking corridor to the bathroom where the pipes shrieked and keened and moaned and hammered. Hours later, climbing, climbing in the elderly

Mercedes, first gear most of the way, they came around the side of a mountain. Suddenly they were above the mist. It lay below them, seething, stretching away, a savage sea, and, poking out of it, dark mountaintops like steep and inhospitable islands.

Where was that?

A cough from the doorway. Carla.

'You look ... distant,' she said.

'Visions from the past. Come in, sit down.'

Unusually, she did. She kept her bad leg straight when she sat down, took her weight on one arm, then the other. 'This is difficult,' she said. She did not quite meet his gaze.

Anselm nodded. 'Nothing easy from Bowden.'

'I can find a Luxembourg bank. That is it so far.'

Carla had the sad, lip-biting air of a child who thought she had disappointed. Bad marks, failed to win the race or didn't jump high enough, far enough.

'Well,' said Anselm, 'you'll find something sooner or later.'

Carla refolded her hands. He hoped she wouldn't crack her knuckles. They were hands too big for her thin frame, elegant, long fingers, the nails well kept, rounded for typing. Erotic hands.

'Kael,' she said.

'Kael?'

'Serrano is connected with Kael, not so?'

She didn't know about the bugging of Serrano and Kael.

'Yes.'

'The connection includes these papers?'

'Probably.'

'Kael isn't an investment consultant. You know that?'

'I know that.'

She shifted again. 'Kael. Herr Baader could possibly ... I don't know ...'

It hung. He knew what she was saying.

'Wait.'

Anselm went down the corridor to Baader's office. He was on the phone, a knee against his desk. His head movement said, come in. Anselm sat down. Baader was answering someone with yes and no. Then he said: '*Na klar. Die Sache is erledigt. C'est fini. Schönen Dank. Wiedersehen.*'

He looked at Anselm, shaking his head. 'My life is moving beyond intolerable. Into a new phase.'

'You can't go beyond intolerable.'

'You can. You're not German enough to understand that. What?'

'O'Malley's interested in dealings connected with Werner Kael. Carla's on it.'

'So?'

'She thinks you could help. She's embarrassed.'

Baader's head went to one side. He ran a finger back and forth over his upper lip, over the day's regrowth. Anselm could hear the faint sawing sound.

'I had dealings with Kael,' said Baader eventually.

'Dealings?'

'I knew him.'

'I thought you were an analyst?'

'I did other things first. You earn the right to become an analyst.'

'I'll file that. Carla's idea?'

'It's not a favour I want to ask.'

'Okay.' Anselm got up.

'Kael's file is sanitised. I told you, he's got friends.'

'Well, O'Malley's worth a lot to us. But ...'

'Find another direction. What have you got? Have you got banks? So-called banks?'

'One, I think. Luxembourg.'

Baader slid his chair back, pushed off the desk, spun around, feet off the ground, like a child on a roundabout. 'Give me the bank,' he said. He kept spinning. 'I'm more at ease approaching from that side.'

Anselm watched him going around. 'Stefan,' he said, 'if you ever feel the need to talk to someone, you know where to find me.'

'Damaged,' said Baader. 'Both of us, we're damaged goods. Return to sender.'

'Address unknown, no such number, no such phone.'

Baader smiled, a happier fox now. 'A man who knows his Elvis cannot be damaged beyond repair.'

Anselm went back to Carla. 'No,' he said. 'We'll see what we can do with the bank. Give me the details. And have a try at Bruynzeel.'

She nodded and left. Anselm rang O'Malley.

'This is not proving easy.'

'I was rather hoping your distinguished head of chambers might weave his magic.'

'He may yet.'

'Carry on, Hardy. Ring me tomorrow. In the pm. With luck, I'll be celebrating with my learned friend.'

'Eating your smoked ham with your pickles, beetroot, drinking your Krakow pils. And making use of your ...'

'Not another word.'

43

... LONDON ...

SHE HAD been gone for a while, perhaps half an hour, when the phone in the kitchen rang.

Niemand was watching television, the news, a dark-haired woman and a man with glasses taking turns reading it. The woman was finishing an item about illegal Kurdish immigrants found in Dagenham.

He let it ring. Her answering machine came on. Her calm voice saying, 'Thank you for calling Jess Thomas Architectural Models ...'

On television, the man was talking about calls for new crowd-control measures at football grounds, a teenager had died in Belgium, crushed.

Niemand pressed the mute button on the remote.

'... and leave a message,' said Jess's voice on the machine.

The tone.

'Get out now,' said Jess, quick, urgent. 'Just go. I don't know how long you've got.'

He was up, took his valuables holster, his jacket, stuffed them into the bag, went for the fire-escape door. He was there when he remembered and he went back and tore the page off the pad, her cellphone number.

The steel door's bar resisted, not opened for a long time, rusted, painted over, many times, he couldn't get it to move. He dropped the bag, put both hands to the lever, pushed down.

It wouldn't move. Did not give at all. Solid.

Take your time, said the inner voice. The voice of his first instructor, in time his own voice. The careless, languid voice: Take your time, chicken brain.

Jolt it free.

Hit it.

With what?

He looked around and he looked across the kitchen, across the big space of the sitting room and workroom to the far wall.

Three shadows.

He saw three shadows flit along the bottom of the big industrial window. Gone in an instant, just bits of grey behind the wire-impregnated security glass.

Tops of heads.

Three heads, quickly, stooping but not stooping low enough, the lights from outside throwing shadows upwards.

Niemand hit the lever with his clenched hands, brought them down, used them like a flesh hammer, the pain was instant. In his hands, his back, his shoulder.

The big lever jerked free, upwards. He grabbed the bag, swung the steel door inwards, went out into the cold, drizzling night. Closed the door. He looked for a way to bolt it from the outside. No bolt. Stupid. It was a fire escape.

They would know where he had gone.

Of course they would know. Where else could he go?

Third floor. He looked down. An alley, bins, wet cobblestones, a street-light at one end, a long way away. Straight lines of drizzle, a nimbus around each light. Where would they wait? At each end. That was what he would do. Someone at each end. Wait for him to come down, choose a direction.

He couldn't see the alley's end to the right. Dead end?

Suicide to go down.

What the hell. He went up. Treading lightly, wet metal stairs, keeping against the wall, looking down at the alley. The night was loud, sirens, music from somewhere nearby, two sources of music, vehicle noises.

The roof was flat. He could make out a tank and a square structure, probably the lift housing, three chimney-like things, ventilation intakes, vents, something like that.

Light from the alley below. Niemand went to the parapet, looked down with one eye.

Headlights at each end of the alley.

They didn't care. They knew they had him.

Six metres below him, a black figure was on the fire-escape landing, Jess's landing, a weapon upright in one hand – machine-pistol. He could see the fat silencer tube.

A gun. He should have bought a gun. You never needed one until you didn't have one.

He walked over the wet roof to the tank. It was on four legs. He ran a hand over it. Wet. Old. Rusty. He tapped the bottom, tapped the top. Full of something.

The legs were bolted to the concrete. A long time ago. One was bent under its burden. He kicked it and it gave without hesitation, the tank tilted.

He went around, stood clear, kicked another front leg. It didn't move. Just hurt his toes. He looked around, eyes adjusted now, he saw a piece of pipe: thick, not long, it lay in a pool of rainwater. Left when the building was converted, a shoddy conversion, the pipe sawn off from some old plumbing.

The burst of gunfire hit the tank, above him, well above his head.

He heard only the percussion, an ear-jangling thwang, saw sparks like fireworks in his brain.

He fell. And as he fell he reached for the length of pipe, got it – wet, slimy, hard to hold. Heavy. He lay, looking back, pain from his shoulder.

A penis-head above from the stairs. All black, head in a black balaclava, tight like a stocking mask, the man's eye sockets and eyelids blackened.

In the middle of London. Full fucking nightfighting shit.

'Don't move,' said the man, voice clear. 'You won't get hurt. We don't want to hurt you.'

This was better. They wanted him alive this time. For a while. Until they'd watched the film, made sure it wasn't Chevy Chase again, the holiday in Europe one.

Niemand rose to his knees. He held up his left hand in surrender, weakly, and he kept the pipe behind him. By its weight, it was cast-iron.

The man rose, he was on the roof, the weapon pointed at Niemand.

'Hands in the air, please,' he said.

'Don't point that fucking thing at me,' said Niemand.

The man bent his forearm, held the machine-pistol upright, pointed it at the heavens. He was confident. He knew that Niemand had nowhere to go, back-ups on the stairs.

Niemand threw the pipe.

Stood and threw in one movement.

He threw it with his arm below shoulder level, threw it as he would a grenade, he didn't want the weight to snap his elbow, he expected pain. And it came, from his chest, his neck, it seemed to come from his whole upper body.

The man saw what was happening, brought the barrel down. But he didn't want to fire.

The pipe changed its angle, side-on it hit him in the head. He went down, axed, the weapon in his hands slid away, across the wet concrete.

Niemand found the machine-pistol, picked up the cast-iron pipe, went over and struck the other front tank leg. At the third blow, it gave.

The tank fell gracefully, hit the roof with a dull sound, and released a thick liquid. Lots of liquid, and it flowed, flowed past the still man in black, the roof tilted towards the fire escape, and the liquid ran and spilled over the edge.

Niemand sniffed the fluid, found the matches in his holster.

The first match didn't strike.

The second one did, flared. He touched the fluid, the flame died.

A sound from the stairs, scratch on metal.

The back-up boys.

The third match wouldn't strike.

He would have to go now.

Go where?

He scraped another match. It flared, held, burnt bright.

He applied it to the liquid.

Nothing. He blew gently.

'HANDS IN THE AIR!'

Fire under his hand, jumping at him, burning the hairs in his nose.

Heating oil.

He saw the dark head at the fire escape, the weapon, saw the fire whipping down the stream, a blue-red flame reached the fire escape, went over the edge.

Liquid fire. A waterfall of fire.

One long agonised scream. Then screams, screaming.

The other back-ups on the stairs.

Niemand walked to the other side of the roof, he wasn't in a hurry now, looked down at the lane below. There was a car in it, blocking it, doors open, inside light on.

A big pipe ran down the side of the building, beginning three metres below. All the plumbing shared a pipe. He did not wait, put the machine-pistol in the bag, slung the bag around his neck so that it hung on his back.

He went over the side, face to the building, didn't hang, dropped blind to the pipe's first joint, hit it with his right knee, kept falling, caught the tight-angle bend with both hands, took his full weight with his hands and shoulders. The pain almost caused him to let go, it blotted out his sight for an instant. Then he went down the pipe without his feet seeking purchase, just hands holding, a controlled fall, hands slowing him, like going down a rope.

He hit the concrete hard, legs not ready for it, knees not bent, sat on his backside, jarred the bones. He got up, ran around the right side of the car, looked.

Keys in it.

Bag off, into the car, reach to close passenger door, a manual, thank Christ, turned the key.

A tortured sound. The motor was already on, running, they'd left it running, so quiet he hadn't heard it.

Reverse where it should be?

Shit no, forward. He hit the brakes, tried again.

Backwards down the lane, twenty metres, engine screaming. Into the street. Braked, looked, nothing coming, a tight left turn.

First gear. Missed it, got into second, pushed the pedal flat, it didn't bother the engine, the motor could handle second-gear take-offs. An old man in a raincoat looking at him. Down the rainslicked street, right at the first corner. Going anywhere, going away.

Slow down, chicken brain, said the inner voice. Take your time. Being picked up by the cops now would be silly. Stolen car.

Alive.
Jesus, alive.
Third-time lucky.
You didn't get more than three.

44

… LONDON …

THE FAX was there when she got back: three stories. Two were short, just a few paragraphs. The third spread over three pages. It was called: 'And Unquiet Lie the Civil Dead'.

The date was February 1993. The byline was Richard Monk.

She read quickly and she drew a line beside a section:

As for Namibia, the white South African regime regarded it as a fief. Soldiers killed with impunity. It was sport. One regiment was on horseback. They rode down running humans, teenagers many of them, just ill-nourished boys. The soldiers galloped alongside them and they shot them between the shoulderblades with automatic shotguns. And the riders laughed at what they saw. There were no consequences. Later, Mozambique was the same, a place to corral starving two-legged animals: blow them up with grenades, sizzle them with flame-throwers. But this had limited training value; it was too easy.

And then came Angola, sad, ravaged Angola, cursed with oil. At least 300,000 people – many of them civilians – have died in the civil war since Holden Roberto of the FNLA first took the CIA's coin in 1962. Together, Holden and the agency held a small war and the whole world came: the US, South Africa, China, the Soviet Union, Cuba. South Africa was invited in by the US and it came with alacrity. In August 1981, given the nod by a Reagan Administration foaming at the mouth over the Cuban presence in the country, it invaded southern Angola. The South African force of 11,000 men, supported by tanks and aircraft, laid waste to Cunene province. Some 80,000 Angolans fled their homes. How many died is unknown. The South African army settled down for a long and murderous stay.

From 1981, the US used both military power – South African troops (and their proxies) and Savimbi's UNITA forces – and economic pressure as it set out to destabilise countries in the region. As a result, some estimates put deaths by starvation at more than 100,000 in 1983 alone. Along the bloody way, there have been many chances to end the Angolan conflict. But, until last month, the US turned its face against any settlement that did not fully replace Soviet with American influence.

The CIA and the Defense Intelligence Agency will miss Angola and the nearby countries. They like the region a lot. It has been good to them, a wonderful place to train staff, hundreds of them (even black officers, although the South Africans didn't approve). It has also been a chance to provide extravagantly paid work for the agencies' loyal friends – the little 'civilian' airlines and the freelance specialists of all deadly and corrupt kinds.

As for the warm and loving community who live by selling arms, the misery of Angola has been a bonanza. Millions of dollars of US weapons have gone to the South Africans and their ally, Savimbi's UNITA.

And hasn't Angola been fun for America's so-called mercenaries, the live-action fringe of the gun-crazies. Almost every bar they infest has some thickneck who can tell you stories about high old times killing black people in Angola (with the odd rape thrown in). In Tucson recently, a man called Red showed me his photographs. In one, he was squatting, M16 in hand, butt on the ground.

Behind him was an obscene pile of black bodies, one headless.

'Soldiers?' I asked.

'Niggers,' he said. 'Commie niggers.'

Some of these men even claim to have fought Cubans, but that is highly unlikely. In Angola, the Cubans fired back.

Sick American porn-killers are bad enough but there is the possibility of much worse.

In early 1988, CIA and DIA propagandists began feeding the media stories about Cuban troops using nerve gas in Angola. (Angola was always 'Marxist Angola', the Cubans were always 'Soviet-sponsored', and Savimbi was always 'the US-backed freedom fighter'.) Highly dubious 'experts' were always cited. Of course, their South African and other connections were never mentioned.

Fragments of evidence now suggest that this campaign was in response to rumours in South Africa of a village in northern Angola being wiped out.

Wiped out by which side? How? We don't know. But should the rumours have spread outside South Africa and been investigated and confirmed, the CIA-DIA misinformation artists had done the groundwork for blaming the Cubans.

Richard Monk. Who was Richard Monk?

Caroline found the contents page. The Notes on Contributors said: 'Richard Monk is a freelance journalist who is no stranger to the world's trouble spots.' That wasn't going to help. She typed *richard monk* into the search engine.

An hour later she had nothing.

She circled the editor's name: Robert Blumenthal. Where would he be decades later?

Another search. Hundreds of Robert Blumenthal references came up. She went back and added *editor behind enemy lines*.

Half a dozen. The first one said:

... veteran radical editor Robert Blumenthal, 69, collapsed and died Saturday while giving the William J Cummings Memorial Lecture at the University of Montana's School of Journalism ... Behind Enemy Lines ...

She went to the source, *The Missoulian*, daily paper of Missoula, Montana. Robert Blumenthal was long gone. The Saturday he died at the podium was a Saturday in 1996. The story mentioned *Behind Enemy Lines* among seven or eight publications Blumenthal had edited. They had names like *The Social Fabric*, *To Bear Witness*, *Records of Capitalism*. It said he had lived in Missoula for ten years with his partner of twenty-two years, the photographer Paul Salinas.

Go home, lie in a bath with a big whisky, eat scrambled eggs for supper. Watch television.

Colley. The bastard. He'd treated her with contempt, casually used her. She didn't know why or how. But he had betrayed Mackie to someone who wanted to kill him, tried to kill him.

Mackie might be dead.

She might have killed him by going to Colley instead of going to Halligan.

Get on with it.

It took another hour to find a phone number for the right Paul Salinas. When she had the number, it rang but no one answered, no machine.

She waited. Tried again. Again. The fifth or sixth time, she was going to go home, it was after 8 pm, the receiver was picked up.

'Salinas.'

'Mr Salinas, my name is Carol Short. I'm ringing from Sydney, Australia. I'm a publisher's permissions person and I'm hoping you can help me.'

She carried on lying, told him a story about wanting to publish Richard Monk's piece in an anthology of political writing.

'Publisher? Sorry, did you say that?'

He was wobbly, she could tell. He might have been asleep, the phone ringing unheard.

'Yes. It's called The Conviction Press. It's new, no money, no track record. We're not acceptable politically.'

'Australia?'

'Yes. Sydney. I don't suppose you know, but there are radicals in Australia.'

Salinas laughed and she could hear that it took a lot out of him.

'We were in Australia in '75, late '75,' he said. 'Met a lot of people. Amazing people. Byron Bay, we went up there. That was really good stuff they were smoking. Big year for you Aussies, wasn't it, '75?'

She had no idea what he was talking about.

'People seem to have thought so at the time.'

Would that response pass?

Salinas laughed and he sounded stronger.

'That's what Bob loved about Australians. Give nothing away. *Not bad.* See something, read something, it's excellent, you love it. What do you say? *Not bad.* Bob adored that. He adopted that. It was our joke. Shakespeare? *Not bad.* Picasso? *Not bad.* You like this food, exotic ingredients, three hours in the making? *Not bad.* He had a time, any shit descended, he'd say, Paul, let's go live in Australia.'

Salinas had a deep voice. Each word had its space. She saw a big man with a beard, black hairs on the backs of his hands.

'We need to get Richard Monk's permission to publish,' she said. 'But I can't find a writer or journalist by that name on any database.'

'Doesn't surprise me,' said Salinas.

Silence.

'*Behind Enemy Lines* was Bob's last fling. Not that he knew it.'

'It doesn't surprise you that I can't trace Richard Monk?'

'Hell, no. Write for anything Bob published, brace yourself for wiretaps, mail intercepts, the short-haired men in the brown suits having a quiet word with your neighbours.'

'You're saying that wouldn't be the writer's real name?'

'Not if you can't find him.'

'Well, they say it's such an interesting piece. We'd be sad not to republish it. But if we can't, we can't. If I can't ask him, that's that.'

'Yeah, pretty much.'

Caroline sensed something. 'I feel like a failure,' she said. 'I am a failure. Can I ask you for advice?'

'Sure.'

'If you were some dumb publishing assistant and you wanted to find out who Richard Monk was so that you could ask him, what would you do?'

There was a moment of nothing, just a hollow sound on the line.

'I'd ask the person I was talking to.'

'Who is Richard Monk, Mr Salinas?'

'Hold on, I'll get Bob's secret ledgers.'

She held. The lonesome sound. This would all be worthless. Nothing would come of this. He came back inside two minutes.

'I'm sorry, I didn't retain your name?'

'Carol Short. The Conviction Press. Sydney. The number is 61 2 7741 5601.'

Please God, don't let him say, I'll ring you back.

'Doesn't seem to be here. I'll have to ring you back.'

Gone.

'At any time,' she said.

McClatchie wouldn't have fucked this up.

'Let me ring you back,' she said. 'There's no need for you to pay for the call.'

'No, wait. Here it is, this is it ... the last issue ... *And Unquiet Lie* ... here we are. Money order, address in San Francisco. Not much. Still, he would've been doing it for the cause.'

'There's a name?'

'John Anselm.'

45

... LONDON ...

WOULD THEY report the stolen car to the police? They'd tried to kill him three times. Tonight was just a delayed execution. They were not ordinary citizens who reported things to the police.

Three times in this huge city they'd found him. How had they done that? Once by the mobile, perhaps, he had worked that out, there was no other way.

But after that?

He had hurt three of them. Possibly badly. Possibly kissed them off.

Air. He needed air. He found the button, his window descended.

Cold London winter air. Exhaust fumes. A wet smell, like the smell in a cupboard where damp clothes had been hung.

Go where?

He was on a main street now, lots of traffic, bright shops, crowded pavements, no idea where he was. He saw a parking space, pulled in behind a Volvo. Sat, trying to think, too much adrenalin in the system to think straight.

'Lookin for me?'

Niemand jerked away, his right elbow coming up in defence.

'Relax, relax, mon. Need to calm down, chill out. Smell the roses. What can I get you? I'm your mon.'

A black man stooping, standing back from the open window. Not big. Shaven head, goatee beard. Tight leather jacket. Three strands of golden chains.

'I need a cellphone,' said Niemand. 'Quick.'

The man looked at the car, side to side, exaggerated movements of his head.

'Got any ID, officer?'

'Fuck you.'

The man looked at him, weighed him up.

'Sixty quid,' he said. 'Bargain. Today's special. Nokia, brand new. Okay for a week. Guaranteed. Well, say six days from today. Be safe not sorry, hey, mon?'

'Okay.'

'Wait.'

He was gone. Niemand looked around for something to identify the car's owner. Nothing in the glovebox, on the tray. He felt behind his seat, in the footwell.

Something.

A nylon jacket? No, too heavy.

It was a BB, a belly-and-balls bulletproof waistband, hips to solar plexus, fastened at the side with Velcro, tied between the legs. Niemand had owned one. Never mind the chest shot, what worried soldiers was the gut shot, groin shot, balls shot off – those were the major worries.

There was a pocket across the back, sideways. It held a Kevlar knife, like a piece of thin bone, a fighting knife. Weighed no more than a comb and you could carry it through a metal detector.

Niemand put the corset into his bag.

The man was coming back, weaving down the busy pavement. He came close, showed the device.

'State of the fuckin art, mon,' he said. 'The 6210. Internet. Voice diallin. Four hours talkin time to go.'

Niemand found a fifty and a ten. 'Where's the owner?'

'On holiday. Won't know till he comes back.'

They did the exchange.

'Where is this?' said Niemand.

'This?'

'Here. Where am I?'

The man shook his head. 'Battersea, mon. Thought it might be sunny fuckin Hawaii, did ya?'

Niemand watched him go down the crowded pavement, slick as a fish through kelp. He took his bag and got out, left the car unlocked, keys in the ignition. He walked in the opposite direction to the phone seller. Cold drizzle, smells of cooking oil in the air. It took a long time to find a cab.

'What is your desire?'

The driver was an Indian, a balding man with a moustache, a stern, worried face.

Jesus Christ, where to?

'Victoria Station.' It came to mind. What did it matter? At least he knew where Victoria Station was.

He leant back, felt his muscles let go, watched the world go by. Into a main road. Night traffic, heavy both ways. The driver said nothing. They crossed a bridge. Presumably Battersea Bridge. He must have come this way on the back of Jess's bike. On the other side of the bridge, the traffic was bad.

Who were these people trying to kill him? How did they find him? He should give them the film in exchange for letting him leave the country. Ring the woman who'd betrayed him. No. That wasn't the way it worked: they wanted the film and they wanted him dead. They knew he'd seen the film, he couldn't be left walking around.

Jess. They would kill her too.

They would think she was in this with him. Why shouldn't they think that? She'd picked him up on her bike. She'd taken him home. Of course, they'd think that.

'Pull up anywhere you can,' he said. 'I'll get out here.'

'Well, this is not hardly worth my while, you said explicitly you wanted ...'

Niemand found a twenty, showed it. 'Just pull up,' he said.

The driver didn't look impressed, pulled to the kerb. Niemand didn't say anything more, got out. It was the Kings Road, he recognised it, knew where he was. He leaned against a wall, got out the cellphone, found Jess's number.

It rang. And rang. The little electronic sound.

It wasn't going to be answered. He knew that.

He should have done this before. She had saved his life. Taken him onto her bike, into her house, organised his doctor.

And she had phoned him in time to save his life, save it for the second time.

There had been nothing in it for her. Nothing. She had simply done it for him. For another human being.

All I said was, Thanks very much. What kind of a person am I?

Ringing. Ringing.

The sound of being picked up. The button.

He closed his eyes for an instant. Thank God.

'Yes?'

'Jess?'

'Who's that?' A woman.

It wasn't Jess.

Jess was dead. He knew it.

'A friend. Is she there?'

Silence. He thought the line had gone.

'Con?'

Niemand let his breath go.

'Yes,' he said.

'Are you all right?'

'Fine,' he said. 'They tried to kill me again.'

'Where are you?'

He told her. He should have said thank you again and goodbye and sorry about your building, but he told her.

46

… HAMBURG …

THE PHONE.

'Mr Anselm?'

'Yes.'

'David Carrick from Lafarge in London. Does that mean anything?'

'It does.'

The man had the kind of English voice Anselm disliked. Eton and the Guards. He'd come across a few of them. The pinstriped suits with a white stripe. Not blue, not red. White. When had he come across them?

'Wonderful,' said the man. 'Good. We're secure here, are we?'

'What can be done has been done.'

'Of course. That's Latin, isn't it? Totally rotten at Latin. I wonder if I can ask you to run a credit check? Someone new to the UK.'

Customs.

'Name?'

'Martin Powell.' He spelled the surname. 'Recent arrival, we would think. And we'd also like a general search, anything that turns up in the name. May I say that this could not be more urgent.'

'You may. We'll give it priority.'

'Thank you. The numbers, you have them?'

In his segment of view, Anselm could see that the day was darkening.

'We do.'

'Immediate contact, please.'

They said goodbye.

47

... LONDON ...

'LET ME be clear. I'm tired, I don't want to be in this shithouse town. We have the place, the cunt is there alone. Now one man is dead and two are in hospital with burns and the cunt is gone.'

'Well, in essence.'

'In essence? That means?'

'Yes. Mr Price.'

'So keep your fucken Limey talk for your old private school pals. This's a fuck–up of some size, not so?'

'Yes. It is. But we had ...'

'Who hired these people?'

'We've used them before, Charlie, they've done ...'

'You hired them?'

'Well, ah, Dave ...'

'Don't be a prick. Don't fucken shift the blame. Who's the seller? In fucken essence?'

'We're not sure right now. We'll be ...'

'That's so fucken reassuring. You don't even know who the cunt is. We're trying to kill some cunt, we don't even know who he is.'

'Haven't had very long. This thing kind ...'

'*Very* long? *Very* long? You want *very* long? Oh, well, sorry to rush you. Listen to me. You now have *no* fucking long. You have absolutely *zero* long. You are in *negative* long.'

'We're doing everything we can.'

'I need to say to you, any more fucked up than this, you boys, you get skewered asshole to Adam's apple. Cooked like fucken barbecue pigs. All night long, meat falls off the bone. Only the pigs, they kill the fucken pigs first.'

'If I can say something, Mr Price ...'

'Say. Just say.'

'This is England, we can't just ...'

'Wow, you fucken Limeys are somethin. Dunkirk, fucken retreat, fucken disgrace, your finest hour.'

'It's the Battle of Britain actually.'

'What?'

'The Battle of Britain. That's England's finest hour.'

'That right? Excuse my fucken ignorance. Well, listen to me, goes for you both. Things don't get better quick your fucken worst hour's gonna happen real soon. Your fucken worst minute. Anyway. Now. Where the fuck are we?'

'Mr Price, someone shot two men in a hotel in Earls Court the night before last. In the legs. The room was in the name Martin Powell. No sign of him. The men have told a story – met a man in a pub, he invited them to his room to have a drink, he turned …'

'Just the fucken ending.'

'Mackie said people tried to kill him in a hotel, he told the woman that. Wishart. This Powell could be our man.'

'You heard this when?'

'An hour ago. We've got people on it.'

'So pleased to hear that. The motorbike rider? It's the one picked this Mackie up?'

'Yeah. The address we got for the bike, it's her old address. We sent someone, parcel to deliver, you know. Wrong address, this other woman, she gave the new address …'

'And your people went around there and shot themselves in the balls. Jesus, Martie, I cannot fucken believe …'

'They say they heard the phone ring inside. Hit the front door, he was already gone.'

'Who's carrying the can for this?'

'No problem. They're, ah, reliable. Good.'

'Are you fucken mad? One man. One solitary fucken individual. On a plate. First, your reliable cunts decide to take him out in the most public place they can find, make this brilliant fucken decision, you don't put them straight.'

'Can I say, I didn't …'

'Fuck that up, then they set a building alight, own casualties minor. Just one dead, two in hospital having emergency skin grafts …'

'Private clinic, it's …'

'Shut the fuck up.'

'Ah, there's no chance of any ID, not the vehicle either. It should be … okay. Yes. Safe.'

'Should be? Safe? Boy, who the hell trained you, you ask for your money back. Plus fucken interest. This Powell? When you gonna know?'

48

… HAMBURG …

'I'VE GOT a Martin Powell on entry.'

Anselm looked up.

Inskip, languid in the doorway.

'Yes?'

'Heathrow. Four days ago. Central African Republic passport. Age thirty-six, occupation sales representative. Flight from Johannesburg. Hand luggage only.'

He crossed the room and put a copy of the file note on the desk.

Anselm took the pad, got up and went to the filing cabinet, found the folder, the page. He wrote the key on the pad. 'Run this,' he said.

'Immediately, Minister. In my pigeonhole today I found a cheque.'

'Should keep you in black T-shirts for life. Or red.'

'You noticed. It crossed my mind to spend some of it on a decent dinner. Hamburg haute cuisine. Might invite you.'

'Very generous. Put most of it aside. When my anti-dining phase ends I'll take you up.'

Anselm thought he saw something, hurt perhaps, in Inskip's eyes.

'Take me up, take me down, just as long as you take me.'

Inskip left.

Anselm found the Lafarge file. The number rang twice.

'Lafarge International. How may I help you?'

'Mr Carrick, please.'

'Carrick.' The clipped tone.

'Weidermann and Kloster.'

'Right, yes. Hello.' Some anxiety in the voice.

'Is this a good line?'

'Go ahead.'

'The person entered from Johannesburg at Heathrow four days ago. Central African Republic passport. Age thirty-six, occupation sales representative.'

'Any background?'

'Not yet.'

They said goodbye. Anselm went to Inskip's station in the workroom.

'In,' said Inskip. 'Amazing. How can we do this?'

'They bought Israeli software.'

'Meaning?'

'Meaning it's got a rear entrance. Run Jackdaw.'

Shaking his head, Inskip clicked on an icon, a stylised bird with a D for *Dohle* superimposed on it. A box came up.

'The name?'

'The name,' said Anselm.

Inskip typed in *Martin Powell* and clicked.

Three sets of letters and figures appeared.

Anselm said, 'Select and click. And whatever you do, don't print anything. Take notes. Go back to Jackdaw when you're finished and erase.'

'Sir.'

Anselm went across to Carla, stood behind her. She had code on two monitors. Her eyes were on the screens, her fingertips were stroking the keyboard, not pressing keys, thoughtful, just running down, making small clicking sounds. He looked at her hands for a while before he spoke.

'Any luck?'

She swivelled slightly, put her head back, looked up at him. Her sleek hair touched his hip. 'Herr Baader's friends have not been very helpful. But now I think the bank's encryption, it may be out of date. I have someone in Canada testing it. A secure person.'

'Good.' Without thinking, he touched her shoulder, pulled his hand away. She showed no sign of taking offence. He thought he saw the embryo of a smile on her lips.

At his desk, Anselm worked through the files, made notes for operators, dictated instructions for Beate. Alex was always at the edge of his thoughts. She came to mind too often, he thought about what she might be doing, what her day-to-day life was like. The apartment full of chairs. The ex-husband in America. Alex when she was waiting for him at the car, flushed face and neck: pink, sexual pink. She had prominent collarbones and a deep hollow between them.

The internal phone rang.

Inskip.

'I've got something.'

Anselm went back to the blue room, to Inskip's station. He sat on the chair next to him. Inskip pointed at his main monitor. A column of names, one highlighted.

'Here's a Martin Powell on a list. The date on it's 1986.'

He scrolled down the column.

'It's alphabetical,' he said.

'I see that.'

'Here's the list that follows, dated a month later.'

The new column had names with figures beside them, amounts of money in rands, the South African currency. Inskip scrolled down it. R10,000 was the smallest sum. There was no Martin Powell.

'List number two,' said Inskip. 'Some kind of payroll. Notice that this list is *mostly* alphabetical. Five names from list number one have gone and in their places are five new ones.'

'Mostly alphabetical,' said Anselm. It took him a second to grasp the meaning. 'The new names are all in the alphabetical positions of the missing ones?'

'You're quick, Master. That's right. My assumption is that whoever made up list number two changed names but didn't bother to re-sort alphabetically. Just cut and pasted in the new names.'

'Payments,' said Anselm. 'Could be the five used false names on list number one, assumed names, but were then paid in their real names.'

'And Martin Powell is gone.'

Inskip selected a name. 'And in his place is this man.'

The name was: NIEMAND, CONSTANTINE.

Anselm was staring at the screen. 'What's the year?'

'1986.'

'Go to the top and scroll.'

Anselm looked at the names. He knew what the lists meant. He didn't know how he knew, but he knew. 'These people are mercenaries,' he said. 'This is the gang assembled for a coup in the Seychelles. Organised in England. The South African government backed it, then they betrayed it to the Seychelles government. Paid off the troops.'

Inskip turned his shaven head, blue in the light. He raised his eyebrows. 'How do you know that?'

Anselm got up. 'I know it because the world is too much with me. As for you, this is bonus-quality work. But there isn't a bonus.'

'Your approval, I'm content to bask in that.'

'While you're warm, run the Niemand name.'

Anselm went to his office and rang the number in London.

'Carrick.'

'W and K.'

'Hold on.'

Clicks.

'Go ahead.'

'We have something.'

Anselm told him.

'Your operator's very good,' said Carrick. 'We need that name checked. Soonest.'

Inskip, holding up a notepad. His eyes were bright.

'Hold on a moment, please,' said Anselm.

'Got him,' said Inskip softly. 'Got Niemand.'

Anselm said to Carrick, 'We have something on Niemand. I'm putting the operator on.'

Inskip came in, took the handset, cleared his throat. He looked at his notes. 'A man and his wife and a security guard were murdered by black burglars in a house in Johannesburg four days ago,' he said. 'Another security man killed the attackers. His name is given as Con Niemand. His firm says he's an ex-soldier.'

He listened. 'No. This is from the Johannesburg *Star*. British. The name is Shawn.'

Anselm was looking at his desk, sightless. He didn't register immediately.

'S-H-A-W-N,' said Inskip. 'Brett and Elizabeth Shawn. Ages forty-seven and forty-one.'

Sitting in the Mercedes with Tilders, Kael and Serrano on the ferry, the voices from the crackly bug:

Well, that's something. Shawn?

Shot by blacks. So it appears. The business is strange. Werner, the question is what do we do now?

49

… HAMBURG …

TOWARDS HOME in the cold night, late, Anselm walking, the far shore's lights lying broken in the lake.

Reading the names on Inskip's list, he had felt a sense of recognition and it had come to him: the farcical plot to stage a coup in the Seychelles, he had found out about it in late 1986. He remembered going to London from Paris, staying at the hotel in Russell Square. He'd stayed there often, he knew it well: the cramped bedroom, the tiny floral wallpaper pattern, the corner shower that steamed up the whole room, the small dining room where only breakfast was served, always eggs, bacon and sausage, pigeon-sized eggs cooked hard, bacon that was mainly fat, a single sausage like a pygmy's little finger.

He talked to the man in a pub, it was winter, December, near Christmas, the pub wasn't far away from the hotel, on a corner. They sat at a table in a corner of the saloon bar. The man wanted revenge on people, his superiors, he was sixtyish, bland-faced, a thin scar beneath his right eye. An accident in childhood, perhaps. Struck by a swing.

Anselm tried to remember whether he had written a story about the Seychelles business. The clipping would be in the cartons sent from San Francisco at Lucas's instructions. Some time in the first week, he had cut the tapes on one. Grey-blue document boxes, stacked neat as bricks. He remembered opening one and reading a clipping with his byline datelined BOGOTA, TUESDAY. It had meant nothing to him; something written by a stranger from a place he did not recall. He sat there for a long time, blinking away tears. He did not open the boxes again.

Two people were coming towards him: men, one medium, one shorter, they moved apart, he felt an alarm – they wanted him to pass between them. He moved to his right, the right-hand man shifted.

Guten Abend, and they were gone. The taller man was a tall woman. Her perfume brushed his face like a cobweb. He carried it a long way, he knew the scent, he knew it well. For a few moments, he wanted desperately to know who wore it, tried to will his mind to tell him.

The pulse in his throat quietened. He could not remember ever going to Bogota. He remembered his first trip to Beirut … since when did he remember that? Sleeping on the floor of the Dutch photographer's small apartment in Ashrafiyé near the Place Sassine. The bakery called Nazareth.

Henk introduced him to the crepes, the cheesy crepes. He remembered the impossible traffic, the insane driving, cocks crowing from gutted buildings, vegetable patches in the ruins, the feeling of people pressing upon you.

He could probably always have remembered his first time in Beirut. He simply hadn't thought about it. You didn't know what you remembered until you thought about it.

Nonsense.

Why were so many things coming back? Was everything going to be restored? An unbroken thread? A complete chronology? Would he remember his life again as one piece? Would he be whole again, remember people now unknown to him – people he had loved, people he had slept with? Were they all going to appear without warning, rise silently through the black mud and matted weed like peatbog men?

The thought made him uneasy. Perhaps it was better to be without the memories. What did it matter? What did holes, gaps, matter? Life didn't make any sense, it wasn't a story, it wasn't a journey. It was just short films by different directors. The only link was you. You were in all of them. You missed a plane and your life changed. You misheard a place name, went to the wrong bar and then you spent two years with a woman you met there. You were leaving for Europe and the agency rang and instead you went to Colombia. The difference was five minutes. Kaskis rang and then you almost drowned in the Caribbean. Kaskis rang again and if you'd been in Bogota you wouldn't have spent a year lying in holes in Beirut and you'd have missed the experience of a red-eyed teenager recircuiting your brain with the butt of a Kalashnikov.

Enough.

Shawn.

Waiting to cross Fernsicht, he thought about the man called Shawn murdered in Johannesburg. Kael and Serrano had some connection with him. And Lafarge in London were looking for a man called Martin Powell, whose real name was probably Constantine Niemand, and who was probably on the scene when Shawn died. Niemand, an ex-soldier who killed Shawn's killers.

Anselm thought that he was at the intersection of these things and he had no understanding of them. There was a film involved, Kael had talked about a film.

Kael: ... *Can you grasp that? If this prick's got the papers and the film, whatever the fucking film is ... How did Lourens die?*

Serrano: *In a fire. Chemical fire. Not even teeth left.*

Kael: *Well, at least that's neat. Shawn?*

Serrano: *Shot by blacks. So it appears. The business is strange. Werner, the question is what do we do now?*

His street was calm and wet, the traffic noise muted here, most of the leaves down now, the tree limbs silver in the light from streetlamps and front porches, their shadows on the ground like dark roadmaps of densely settled places.

The laundry had been delivered, neat packages on the porch. In the house, the answering machine's red beacon called to him as he passed the study. He poured a drink first, whisky and mineral water, not too strong. He was trying not to have three or four neat whiskies when he came home. It was a fight. He craved the quick hits.

He put on the heating and took the clean, ironed sheets upstairs and made the bed. Then he went down and made another drink, took it to the study, switched on the desk light, sat down in the leather armchair and pressed the machine's Play button.

John, Lucas. I've had a call from a woman, a journalist. She's been trying to find you. Says it's very urgent. Life and death. Her words. Persuasive woman. Something you wrote in, hold on … it's called Behind Enemy Lines. *One of your left-wing rags, no doubt. Her name's Caroline Wishart. W-I-S-H-A-R-T. I told her I'd pass on her number. It's a direct line, London …*

Anselm found a pen, played the message again and wrote down the number.

Life and death. A figure of speech.

Behind Enemy Lines? It meant nothing. Probably after 1989, that was where the major fault line seemed to run. There seemed to be bigger gaps after 1989. How could the brain be so arbitrary? He drank whisky and said the name over and over. Nothing.

Ring Caroline Wishart? About something he'd written. He hadn't written anything since Beirut.

Who would say the words 'life and death'? Journalists. Journalists would say them. Say or not say. They would say or not say anything. It was a trade of omission, implication, suggestion, allusion, half-lies, other fractions of lies. The challenge was to find a way to get people to tell you things. It was just technique – that was what he had said to himself then, in that life.

Lying even to himself.

The sound of water in the drainpipe outside. When the rain was steady, the house's drainpipes made special sounds, irregular, surging sounds. The gutters seemed to hold the water, then let it go. Silence, then a rush. You could count the time between flushes if you said *and* between each count. Three, sometimes four seconds. He had first noticed this when they came to Hamburg for his grandfather's funeral. Lying in the bedroom upstairs, in his father's childhood bedroom, in his father's childhood bed, Lucas asleep across the room – Lucas went to sleep instantly, anywhere – he had fallen asleep counting the pauses. How old? Ten or twelve.

The house had its own life, its own ways. When he came from Beirut, it was mute. He heard nothing, no sounds, a silent house. Then, gradually, it seemed to relax, accept him. One by one, sounds appeared. The house began to groan and creak, it moaned quietly in the wind. There were sounds of friction in the roof, strange rubbing sounds. Pipes began to choke and hammer, the heating whispered, the stair-treads released squeaks in descending or ascending order seconds after his passage.

Caroline Wishart.

He dialled W&K. Wolfgang answered.

'*Anselm. Herr Inskip, bitte.*'

'Inskip.'

'Anselm.'

'I thought you'd gone home.'

'I've done that. Now I'm bored. Run a Caroline Wishart, will you? A journalist. London. Nothing fancy.'

He spelled the name, waited. He heard keys clicking, the humming of the blue room. He finished the whisky. Only the second drink of the night. Remarkable.

'She's a hot new talent,' said Inskip. 'An exposé person. Exclusive. Minister Buggered Me Says Rentboy. Pictures.'

'Is that a complaint?' said Anselm. 'I thought rentboys understood what the job entailed.'

'He could be referring to the Minister's stamina. It could be a compliment.'

'Yes. Thank you and goodnight.'

Anselm fetched another whisky. He vacillated and then he dialled W&K again, Inskip.

'Put this through for me, would you?'

He would be giving her his number if he dialled direct. He put down the phone. It rang within seconds.

'Caroline Wishart.'

'John Anselm.'

He heard her sigh.

'Mr Anselm, I'm so pleased you've called. I'd almost given up hope.'

It was an upper-class voice.

'It's about what?'

'You wrote a piece for *Behind Enemy Lines* in 1993. Called "And Unquiet Lie the Civil Dead"? Under the name Richard Monk.'

Anselm didn't say anything. The title meant nothing to him. Nor did the name Richard Monk.

'I'm trying to follow up on something in it about a rumour that a village in Angola was wiped out.'

Blank.

'What makes you think I'm Richard Monk?'

'The person the publisher paid for the article was John Anselm. A cheque was sent to him to an address in San Francisco.'

San Francisco?

'What address?'

She told him.

Kaskis's apartment.

'Who told you that?'

'The publisher's friend told someone who told me. Robert Blumenthal's friend.'

He saw a man with hair like a dark, curly frame around his face, bright brown eyes. The look of an intellectual lumberjack. He remembered a voice, low, husky, quick speech.

That was all he remembered.

'I'm sorry,' said Anselm. 'I had an accident in 1993 and my memory's bad. I can't recall the piece. Not at all.'

She was silent. She doesn't believe me, he thought. Well, a person who seeks out rentboys who say they were fucked by a British Cabinet Minister, she'd probably be of a sceptical bent.

'Mr Anselm, it's terribly important,' she said. 'I wasn't being melodramatic when I said to your brother it was a life and death matter.'

He didn't say anything.

She made a small sound. Not a cough, a sound of embarrassment. 'I'd really like to say more,' she said, 'but I'm … I'm not comfortable speaking on the phone. You'll understand, I think.'

Anselm thought he heard something in her voice. Truth, you sometimes knew it when you heard it. Truth and fear and lies, they had their pitches and cadences and hesitancies.

'It's a long shot,' she said. 'I'm a bit desperate. Very. I've probably bothered you for nothing. Wasted your time.'

Anselm looked at his drink. Bob Blumenthal? How did he know him, know his face so well? What short film was that? Did he like or hate the Bob Blumenthal whose face he could see.

'I'll call you again,' he said. 'Give me some time.'

'Tonight?'

'I don't know. Possibly.'

'Please. I'd be … it's … well, it's not a story I'm chasing, it's something more. Anyway, I've said that. So …'

'Yes. Goodbye.'

Anselm sat for a while, smoked a cigarette. The room had warmed. He sipped the whisky, finished it, went to the kitchen and poured another one. People interested in his past, things he knew. Alex, this woman. Sniffing around him. He was a source. A repository of something. They thought he had something they could use.

But why did that make him uneasy? He knew about cultivating people, getting people to trust him, to tell him things.

Forget Caroline Wishart. She wanted something and there was no knowing what it was. It was unlikely to be what she said it was.

The life of question and answer. How had he fallen into it?

You've got an inquiring mind. Not many people have. Consider yourself blessed. His mother had said that to him. He couldn't recall anything else his mother said. So, from all the years together, all the nurturing, he came away with three sentences.

No.

He remembered something else. Her telling him, in this house, that she was leaving his father. He was seventeen. On the terrace of this house, sitting in the wicker chairs, losing their paint even then and never painted again.

The chairs were still on the terrace, the exposed surfaces bare of paint. His father had remembered them from before the war, before he was sent to America.

The last Anselm to sit in the chairs, look at the garden, at the canal. He would be that one.

The day she told him, it was autumn. He remembered the big drifts of leaves lying in the garden, in hollows, at trees. Leaves liked to cluster.

He had trouble recalling his mother's face. In Beirut, in the coffin for two, her smell had come to him in dreams, lingered in his nostrils when he woke as if it were actually in the air. Not a perfume exactly, cologne and something else, a talcum powder perhaps. The smell had filled him with a sadness and a longing so unbearable that he would gladly have died to extinguish it.

That day on the terrace, she said, she had a matter-of-fact way, she said: *Darling, your father and I are getting on each other's nerves. We're going to take a little break from each other. A sort of holiday, really. It'll be good for both of us. Don't look at me like that. It won't change anything. And you're both grown up now.*

She joined Médecins Sans Frontières. He went to college and she died in the Congo. His father said on the telephone that it was quick and painless, a fever, she lost consciousness. Some exotic viral infection, he couldn't remember what it was called.

What did people mean when they said *grown up?*

Anselm rubbed his eyes, finished the whisky. He went to the big stone-flagged room off the laundry, the boxroom, floor-to-ceiling shelves. In the corner, stairs went down to the cellar. Frau Einspenner had taken him down those steep stairs, a little of the exquisite apprehension came back to him.

The cartons from San Francisco stood on the floor, only one opened.

His life before Beirut lay in the boxes. He felt no attachment to that life, no curiosity about the missing pieces of it. He should leave the material remains alone.

He began with the open carton.

50

… LONDON …

'HIS NAME is Constantine Niemand. South African, an ex-soldier, a mercenary, worked as a security guard in Johannesburg. Two days before he arrived here, he was on the scene of an affair in Johannesburg, a burglary gone wrong, five people killed, three blacks, one a security guard, the other two …'

'Losin me, boy.'

'A white couple were killed. Brett and Elizabeth Shawn, British passports.'

'Your Krauts running that name?'

'Yes.'

'The woman, what'd you do there?'

'There's a watch on the place. She hasn't shown.'

'And the old address?'

'The old address?'

'Your reliable pricks heard the phone ring. Then he wasn't there. Who the living fuck do you think called him? And how the fuck did she know to call him? Hasn't crossed your brain has it? And don't say *in essence* to me again, I'll strangle you with my own hands.'

'With respect, Mr Price, I'm not prepared …'

'Sonny, deal with me or deal with the devil. There's much worse coming up behind me. I'm the good cop. You want to walk from this fucken Waco you created, get the fuck out. And wherever you go, get on your knees every morning, noon and fucken night and pray the Lord to take away the mark on your fucken forehead.'

'We'll cover this stuff, Charlie.'

'I truly hope so, Martie. I truly do. Or we're talking missing in action.'

51

... HAMBURG ...

IT WAS in the second carton. In the top box.

A flimsy magazine with a sombre cover of light grey type on a black background.

Behind Enemy Lines. A Journal of Argument.

February 1993.

Four articles were promoted on the cover. The top one was: 'And Unquiet Lie the Civil Dead'.

Anselm took the magazine to the study and sat behind the desk to read it.

From the first words, he knew that he had not written it. No matter how battered the brain, there was something in it that knew what it had created, and he had not created this. It was vaguely familiar but it wasn't his.

He found what the woman was talking about, the village in Angola.

Fragments of evidence now suggest that this campaign was in response to rumours in South Africa of a village in northern Angola being wiped out.

Wiped out by which side? How? We don't know. But just in case the rumours spread outside South Africa and were investigated and confirmed, the CIA–DIA misinformation artists had done the groundwork for blaming the Cubans.

Nothing. It meant nothing. Why had someone told Caroline Wishart that he had been paid for writing the article? And given her his San Francisco address as the place the cheque was sent to?

He paged through the rest of the magazine. On the last page was an offer for back issues of the magazine and three others:

The Social Fabric

Records of Capitalism

To Bear Witness

To Bear Witness: That was it, he knew the name, that was how he knew Bob Blumenthal. He pictured his face again. A café in San Francisco. In the afternoon. Long ago.

Anselm was looking for a cigarette when it came to him: he had written a piece for Blumenthal on the CIA and European intelligence services. That was what they talked about that day. In 1990. Blumenthal had rung him. Kaskis and Blumenthal went back a long way, Blumenthal had taught Kaskis at college after Kaskis left the army. Kaskis had written stuff for him.

454

Anselm thought about living in San Francisco, in Kaskis's tiny apartment on the hill. Kaskis knew the people who owned the building, Latvians, friends of his family. Kaskis never spent more than a few days at a time in San Francisco. Anselm remembered him staying for a week once, that was the longest. They went out at night, went to bars where journalists hung out, drank a lot. Kaskis always had somewhere to go later. Someone he had to see before the night was over.

Anselm remembered the piece. It was published in *To Bear Witness* and it was called 'American Spider: Global and Deadly'. It would be in the document boxes.

Why should he help this woman, this muckraker? Because he'd heard something in her voice. Perhaps it was a matter of someone's life and death. He rang Inskip again, got connected to the London number. She was close to the phone. Was it a work number?

'John Anselm,' he said. 'I found the article. A man called Paul Kaskis wrote it. He had the magazine pay me. He owed me money.'

A long sigh. 'Paul Kaskis, do you ...'

'He's dead.'

'Oh. Shit. The name, I think I remember it, he was kidnapped with you ...'

'He was murdered in the Lebanon.'

Another sigh. 'Well, thank you. I think I'm at the end of this road. As a matter of interest, what was he doing in the Lebanon?'

'He wanted to talk to an American soldier, an ex-soldier. A Lebanese-American.'

'You wouldn't remember his name?'

'Diab. Joseph Diab.'

He hadn't told Alex that. Why was he telling this woman?

'Did you know what it was about?'

'No. Paul never told you anything.' Anselm's eyes fell on the photograph albums on the bookshelf beside the door, three big leather-bound albums, he remembered looking at them when he was a child, Pauline pointing out people.

'Look,' she said, 'I'd really appreciate being able to ring you if I get any further with this. Is that possible?'

Anselm hesitated. Then he gave her the W&K number. 'Leave a message if I'm not there.'

He took the photograph albums from the study to the kitchen. He poured wine and opened an album. The pictures were in chronological order, little notes in ink under most of them identifying people by names and nicknames, giving places, dates, occasions. There was a photograph of Pauline and a young man sitting on the terrace. Fräulein Einspenner was standing behind them, the maid. She was young and beautiful. In the first album, the captions were in red ink. In the other two, they were in green, in Pauline's hand.

There were pictures missing, taken out of their corners. The captions were crossed out and cross-hatched in green ink until they were illegible.

The phone rang again.

'I feel I need company,' Alex said. 'I've had some news, I'm feeling a little ...'

'Come over,' he said. 'Can you do that?'

52

… VIRGINIA …

THEY WALKED in the day's cold ending and stopped beside a pond, silver, sat on a wooden bench bleached white as bone by sun and rain and snow.

'Got a smoke? I'm not allowed to.'

Palmer reached into his coat. 'Allowed? Fuck, who's running things here?'

They lit cigarettes, sat back. Smoke hung around them in the still air, reached the earth, curled. High on the wooded hill behind the pond a cluster of maples blazed amid the brown oaks, seemed to be sucking in the light.

'Pretty spot,' said the shorter man. 'The prick's hard to kill, is he?'

'He's quick.'

'And they're dead.'

'Yup. Messy. I sent Charlie Price to sort it out. They told him they'd use pros next time.'

Three ducks came around a small point in the pond, ducks keeping close together, missed the mass exodus to warmer places, just the three of them left.

'He's been in the trade,' said Palmer. 'Now he's riding shotgun. He drove this Shawn's wife home, the arrangement was that he stayed for the husband to get back. I think he just lucked onto this.'

'Shawn had the film?'

'Looks like it.'

'What about him?'

'Well. A known quantity. Courier mainly. They say Ollie North used him.'

'You wouldn't want that to be the high point of your career.'

Palmer shot his cigarette butt towards the water. It fell well short, lay on damp leaf mould. 'I gather he took Ollie. Like everyone else.'

Silence. The other man shot his butt. It almost made the water, died in a puddle.

'So who would be using him?'

'We're checking.'

'I was given to understand this history was history.'

Palmer put both hands to his head and scratched all over – back, top, sides. 'Burghman was in charge, we can't ask him. The film – well, that's something else. No one knew about a film then.'

'Not a huge cast of suspects.'

'No. Trilling says Burghman told him, he thinks it was in '93. Burghman said there'd been a problem but it was fixed and the slate was as clean as it needed to be.'

A deer had appeared from the thicket on the far shore of the lake. It looked around, advanced with delicate steps to the water's edge, lowered its head and drank.

'Never saw the point of killing animals like that.'

'No,' said Palmer.

'I might have another smoke.'

A breeze had come up, worrying the trees, worrying the water. Palmer lit a cigarette, handed it over, lit another.

'As it needed to be. That's not the same as clean.'

'No.'

'This guy's tried the media. Could try again.'

'We'll hear, we'll have some notice,' said Palmer.

'It's late to be caught in the rain, Scottie.'

They heard the sound of a jet on high, the booming hollow sound, filling the world, pressing on trees and water, on the throat. The deer started, was gone.

'Won't happen,' said Palmer. 'But we may have to go on with the Brits. I wanted to ask you.'

'Don't let Charlie near them. Subtle's a Mossberg up the arse.'

'I'll go myself.'

'Good. Time. Going back tonight.'

Out of the wind, on the path, deep in shadow, their heads down, feet disturbing the leaves. The other man looked at Palmer and Palmer looked at him, and they both looked away.

The man said, 'Well, judgment. Live or die by your judgment. Comes down to that.'

Palmer nodded.

'But you know that, Scottie.'

'I do. Sir.'

They walked, smoking, smoke hanging behind them like ragged chiffon scarves, the dark rising beneath them.

53

… WALES …

WHEN THEY were on the motorway, he told her to drop him somewhere, anywhere, a petrol station, but she said no, they were going somewhere safe, he could decide what to do then.

Niemand didn't argue. He tried to stay awake but the car was warm and quiet, the smell of leather, soft classical music on the player, and his head lolled and he fell asleep. He woke several times, registered nothing, and then they were entering a village on a narrow road with houses on both sides.

'Almost there,' said Jess.

He was asleep again before they were out of the village. He woke with the car going uphill on a stony dirt road, tight bends, their headlights reflecting off pools in the wheel ruts and turning stone walls silver.

They stopped.

An entrance, an old wooden gate.

'Here,' she said. 'This is it.'

She was looking at him.

'Where?' he said.

'Wales.'

'Right,' he said. 'Gate.'

He got out, shaky legs, no feeling in his feet. Wet air. Cold, a wind whipping. Dead black beyond the beam of the lights and the only sound the expensive hum of the Audi.

He expected resistance but the gate swung easily, old but maintained, no squeaks, grease in the hinges.

She drove through. Niemand closed the gate. He walked to the car, hurting in many places, the balls of his feet. He didn't mind. He was glad to be alive. There was a Greek saying for what he felt, for gratitude for life outweighing pain and suffering. He reached for it, the tone of it was in his head, the way it was said, but the words didn't come.

He got in. They went up a narrow, steep driveway, turned left. The headlights caught one end of a low building, a long cottage, small windows, and they went past it and lit up another building, a stone barn, a big building with brace-and-bar doors and a dormer window.

Jess stopped and got out, the engine running, the lights on. She stretched, arms to the sky, fingers outstretched, then she bent to touch her toes. She was smaller than he remembered her to be.

'Let's put it inside,' she said. 'I feel like I'm looking after someone's baby.'

'Me,' said Niemand. 'I'm the baby.' He said the words without thought but he didn't regret them, wanted to apologise more fully, thank her.

Jess didn't reply. She went to the doors, fiddled with keys and unlocked two padlocks. Niemand opened the doors, new doors. The Audi's lights lit a large space, new concrete floor. A vintage Morris Countryman was to the left, the one with a wooden frame. On a rack against the back wall were big tools: snipper, chainsaw, hedge-trimmer. In front of them stood a stack of bags of fertiliser. To the right, in a line, were an ordinary lawn mower, a ride-on mower, two trail bikes, a mulcher, all new-looking and clean.

Jess parked the Audi.

Lights off. Pitch dark.

The cabin light came on, she got out, opened the back door and removed their bags, closed the door. Dark again.

They didn't move for a moment, silence.

'Good gear,' said Niemand. 'And neat.'

'Doctors,' she said. 'They're rich. He's a slob but she loves order. She wants to come and live here for a few years, grow things.'

He took the bags, closed the doors, and she padlocked them. They walked around the house to the front door, crunching the gravel.

'No electricity,' said Jess.

Inside, she found a candlestick close to the door and lit the candle with a plastic lighter. They were in a small hallway, coats and hats above a bench. Three doors opened off the room. She went first, through the left-hand one into a big low-ceilinged room. He could make out armchairs, a sofa, an open hearth.

'There's a generator,' she said, 'but the lamps will do tonight.'

He followed her through a door into a kitchen. There were Coleman lamps on a shelf. She lit two, she knew what she was doing, how to pump them. The grey-white light brought back memories for him, other places far away and long ago.

'You need to eat,' she said.

'No,' Niemand shook his head. 'No thanks.'

In the car, he had woken each time with the nausea he always felt after fear, after firefights, any violence, the sick feeling, and with it the physical tiredness, as if some vital fluid in his body had been drained.

'Are you …?'

'Yeah, fine.'

His whole torso hurt, felt battered. It wasn't a new feeling. The first time was at the School of Infantry, he had boxed against men much bigger, much stronger, badly overmatched, taking heavy body punches, to the ribs, the shoulders, low blows too.

'Sure?'

'Sure.'

'Sleep then. It's late.' She pointed. 'Through there. A bedroom, down the passage there's a bathroom, I'll light the water heater.'

Niemand looked around the room. He didn't want to say it.

'Jess,' he said, 'this place, they can connect it with you?'

'Nice to hear you say my name,' she said. 'Con, who are they?'

'I don't know. The owners are your friends?'

'Yes. I was at school with her sister.'.

He was tired, he had trouble standing, legs weak, he had the feeling of not having feet. He put a hand on the back of a chair. 'Who would know you could get the car, come here, this house?'

Jess touched her hair, pushed it back, he could see the tiredness in her.

'I've been here with the owners,' she said. 'They're in America. I keep an eye on their house in London. I don't think anyone knows I've got these keys.'

Niemand tried to think about this but he gave up.

'Listen, Jess,' he said, 'tomorrow I'll go and you stay here and I'll make sure they know you're not with me, you're not involved.'

'Will you tell me what's going on?'

'Yes. In the morning. What I know.'

'Go to bed,' she said. 'We'll talk in the morning.'

For a moment, they stood looking at each other. Then he took a lamp and went to the bedroom, stripped. He walked down the narrow, short passage holding the lamp, almost bumped into her coming out of the bathroom, lowered the lamp to cover himself.

'It's too late for modesty,' she said, smiling. 'I've seen everything you've got.'

He showered, trying to keep the water off his bandage. Then he went back to the bedroom, dressed again and lay on the bed under the eiderdown, lay in the dark and listened.

Noise of the wind, hollow sound, lonely. He thought about the Swartberge, the survival course in the mountains, eyelashes frozen in the morning, lip cracks opening, the way human smells carried in the clean cold air.

They could find them here. There was no point in thinking otherwise. In the morning, he would ring the Wishart woman, tell her Jess knew nothing about the film, had never seen it, was only involved by accident. He would catch a bus, a train, go somewhere where he could work out how to get another passport.

The Irishman would help him. That was a possibility.

He drowsed, drifted away, not peaceful, exhausted.

54

… HAMBURG …

'I'M REGRETTING this,' said Alex. 'I was regretting it before I got into the car. It's stupid of me. An imposition.'

She was holding two bottles of red wine and she offered them to Anselm. 'To drink,' she said. 'Tonight.'

Even in the dim light, he could see that she was flushed. She had been crying and he thought she looked beautiful and desirable.

'Welcome to the house of remorse,' said Anselm. 'Here we regret almost everything we do.'

He took the bottles, showed her into the study and went to the kitchen. It was a choice between a 1987 Lafite and a 1989 Chateau Palmer. He drew the corks of both bottles and went to the pantry for good glasses. He'd broken many Anselm wine glasses, glasses his great-great grandfather might have drunk out of. But there were enough left to see him out.

In the study, Anselm said, 'This is kind of you but this wine's too good for me.'

'From my ex-husband's collection,' said Alex.

'It's nice of him to donate it.'

'He killed himself in Boston yesterday.'

Anselm poured the Lafite. They sat in silence, each in a cone of lamp-light, the wine dark as tar in their glasses.

'I don't know why I'm upset,' said Alex. 'For a long time I hated him. And then I came to terms with my feelings.'

'How did you find out?'

'A colleague of his rang an hour ago. I felt so … fuck, I can't express it.'

'Why would he do it?'

'Apparently the woman he lived with left him about a month ago. His colleague says he was depressed, he'd been drinking a lot, not going to the university, missing classes.'

More silence. She finished her wine and he refilled her glass. She leaned her head back, half her face in shadow. 'He rang me about two weeks ago,' she said. 'I didn't let him speak. I told him I had nothing to say to him.'

Anselm wanted to say that it wouldn't have made any difference but he could not bring himself to. 'Would you have taken him back?' he said.

'No. Never.'

'I wouldn't dwell on it then. How long were you married?'

'Six years. He left me for the American woman.'

Anselm rolled wine around his mouth, swallowed. 'You can keep coming around with this stuff,' he said.

'Kai wouldn't open a bottle except to impress. One day he brought his head of department home for a drink, a fat man, a medievalist, so self-important you wanted to kill him. But you would not be able to get your hands around that pig neck. And Kai opened a fifteen-year-old burgundy. The man couldn't believe it. *Life's too short to drink inferior wine*, Kai said. This is from a man who bought house wine from that little place next to the canal in Isestrasse, do you know it? You take your own bottles, he fills them with terrible Bulgarian liquids full of brake fluid. Whatever that is.'

She looked at him, she licked her lips, drank a lot of wine.

'I took the marriage seriously. That was the end of serious relationships for me.'

She drank. 'It had been going on for a long time before I found out. More than a year. He had all these trips, London, Copenhagen, seminars, that kind of rubbish. I believed him.'

All betrayals were the same, thought Anselm. The only tragedy was that, in the instant in which they became known, the life drained from everything that had gone before – like colour photographs turning into black-and-white.

Alex held out her glass. He half-filled it, added some wine to his. Her quick drinking made him nervous. He was the quick drinker, that was his escape.

She studied the wine against the light, took a big mouthful. 'He'd done it before,' she said, not looking at him, looking around the room.

'Done what?'

'Left one woman for another without any warning.'

He knew what she was going to tell him.

'He left his first wife for me,' she said. 'He sent her a telegram.'

Anselm went to the desk and found a cigarette. He could remember his grandfather sitting behind the desk smoking a cigar. The big brass cigar ashtray was still in position, to the right of the blotter in its embossed-leather frame.

He leaned against the desk. 'Well,' he said, 'he probably intended to tell her in person, never got around to it.'

'He was twelve years older,' she said. She swilled the last of her wine, looking at the scarlet whirlpool, drained it. 'More, please.'

Anselm poured the Lafite, left an inch in the bottle, there was sediment.

Alex drank. 'It tastes better and better,' she said.

'Twelve years,' said Anselm. 'An older man.'

'When he left me, I worked out that I was the same age his first wife was when he left her. He told me she was frigid, didn't like being touched, he thought she was a repressed lesbian, she was always kissing and hugging her women friends.'

'That could be a sign, yes.'

'No. I saw her with a man at an exhibition. He looked like a biker. She couldn't stop touching him, she rubbed herself against him like a cat.'

'What did that tell you? Clinically speaking? With hindsight?'

Alex finished her glass. She held it out and shifted in her chair, crossed her legs, a hint of languor in the movements.

It felt as if the atmospheric pressure had fallen. Anselm poured the Palmer into clean glasses.

'It told me, clinically speaking, that he'd lied to me from the start,' she said. She sat back. 'Talking about it makes me feel better. Have you betrayed many partners?'

'A few, I suppose.'

'You don't remember?'

'Some I remember. I remember the reverse too.'

'And how did you respond to that?'

There was something edging on the flirtatious in her voice, the way she was sitting, in the carriage of her head. It wasn't the manner of a bereaved person.

'I didn't bear grudges.'

'Would you say you were a forgiving person?'

'No. I think I just didn't care enough.'

Anselm looked away. He hadn't intended to say that, he hadn't wanted to admit his emotional callousness to anyone. He hadn't admitted it to himself. Much of his adult life had been spent in pursuit of things, including women, but in the moment of possession, they had lost some of their value. And, later, he had not felt any lasting pain at losing them.

'Are we talking about before or after Beirut?' she said. 'Or both?'

'Before. Things have been quiet in the partner business since.'

She tilted her head and her hair fell onto a shoulder. In the lamplight, her lipstick was almost black. 'Not enough big-breasted women around? For a tit man like you?'

'I was lying,' said Anselm. 'I'm really a leg man. Legs.'

Alex recrossed her legs, ran a hand over a thigh. 'I'm not quite sure what that expression means,' she said. 'Does it mean legs like dancers' legs?'

'Well, for some. We legmen are not all alike.'

'And you? Personally?'

'I like runners' legs.'

She smiled. 'I'm a runner.'

'Yes.'

'It's warm,' said Alex. She unbuttoned her waistcoat, leaned forward and took it off, threw it onto an empty chair. She turned her head to Anselm. 'Would you like me to keep going?'

Anselm's mouth was dry. He sipped wine. 'Yes,' he said.

She unbuttoned her shirt. She was wearing a white bra.

55

… HAMBURG …

'LAFARGE RANG,' said Inskip. 'They've added a name.'

Anselm took the file. He was feeling light-headed.

Jessica Thomas, born 1975, an address in Battersea, London. Inskip had filled in her electronic record.

'It's the woman on the motorbike,' said Inskip. 'The one who picked up Niemand. We could have been running her long ago.'

'Orders,' said Anselm. 'We await orders.'

'I thought initiative was what you liked?'

'After the orders, that's when I like it.'

'Tilders left this for you five minutes ago.'

A sealed pouch. A tape.

'May I know what Tilders does?'

'Outdoor work. Heavy lifting.'

'Thank you. Another veil lifted. Whatever he does, it gives him an air of sadness.'

'He comes across a lot of saddening things. Also he's tired. That can give you a sad air.'

Anselm went to Carla's workstation. She swivelled her chair and rested her hands on her thighs. 'We have had some luck,' she said.

Behind her two monitors had lines of green code on their black screens.

'Serrano's bank. Very careless for people who deal in secrets. Everything's outdated. I find on their log that four years ago they transmitted a large amount of data to a bank in Andorra. Gonzalez Gardemann.'

'Why would they do that?'

'Back-up, I suppose. I can't find any links but Gonzalez may be the same operation under another name.'

'Even so, you'd normally send information like that by hand from one stand-alone system to another.'

Carla shrugged. 'As I said, careless. Perhaps a salesperson convinced them the encryption was safe. Or someone inside the company wanted to compromise their data. There are other possibilities.'

There would be. Someone from the BND would know that. Deceit without end. Seamless deceit.

'The point is,' said Carla, 'Gonzalez are equally stupid. Instead of moving the data to a stand-alone, they have left it where we can reach it.

Their firewall is a joke, their encryption is hopeless. First generation. My Canadian cracked it like a walnut.'

She raised her arms above her head, entwined her fingers, stretched.

Anselm waited for her knuckles to crack. She was looking at him, she had a look about her lips. She knew he was waiting for the sound.

She smiled. Her fingers slid apart, her arms came down.

'The numbers on the documents you gave me,' she said.

The pages from the *Hauptbahnhof*, from Serrano's case.

'Yes?'

'One set worked. It must be the bank's code for Serrano.'

'And?'

'It's one big file, hundreds of transactions. Some small, some big. I need to put the figures we have through them.'

'How long?'

'An hour perhaps. This has taken time. You may wish to tell the client.'

'Yes. Your work is greatly valued. As always.'

She looked down, the glossy hair fell across her forehead like a dark comb sliding. 'Thank you. And may I say thank you for the bonus?'

'No, not me. It's the client's reward for your work.'

She turned her head to the monitors and she said, '*Nun, wir sollten uns eine Flasche Champagner teilen.*'

Anselm didn't register for a moment that she'd spoken to him in German. She had never spoken to him in German since the introductions on her first day.

She hadn't turned her body away from him, only her head.

She was asking him out. The words, the language of her body.

'*So bald wie möglich,*' he said.

Carla turned her head and looked into his eyes and nodded. No smile.

He went back to his office and opened Tilders's pouch. An audio-tape and a sticker with the logbook code DT/HH/361/02 and the words: *Bruynzeel & Speelman Chemicals*. It was Serrano at his hotel. A direct line.

Yes?

Serrano.

Yes?

This is worse than I thought. Our friend, have you got any anxiety there?

Me? Anxiety? What about?

Records he might have kept.

From me, nothing. Otherwise, how would I know?

Speaking in German, neither of them native speakers.

Would he keep his own records?

Well, he wasn't mad then.

He wouldn't?

I don't know. He might have. He was semi-government. Governments like records.

I must ask you again. This film, does it mean anything?
A silence.
I could guess but I don't want to.
What are we talking about?
Nothing.
You know what it could be?
What are you? The tax department? Forget it.
The Jews are putting pressure on us. They want our dealings with you too.
Silence. Then Serrano said:
Are you there?
They want what?
Records. Anything. Everything.
You have records?
No.
Well, just shut up. It's all bluff. These things pass. Just keep your mouth shut. Trilling's connections, there's no problem.
You can talk to him?
I'll see. Things in the past, no one wants to talk about the past.
This is in the present. Talk to him. About the Jews, I thought you were close to them?
Silence again, then the other man said:
Werner Kael gets close to his customers, does he? Who's spoken to you?
He's using the name Spence.
Yes, I know him. Kael would know him.
Kael says they want to rub us out and they want the assets.
Probably correct. If the Jews think something can damage them, they scorch the earth. But first they take the wheat. They must think you are hiding the wheat.
Nonsense. Talk to Trilling. I'll ring later.
Ring tonight. Don't worry so much. People are in deep here, it has to go away.
Serrano sighed.
We don't want to be put away.
The other man laughed.
You personally can relax. They never put the accountants away. They should but they don't.
Anselm rang O'Malley on the new number. In his view, he could see that the sun was out, the lake was strewn with glitter. A glass tourist boat caught the light.

56

... LONDON ...

THREE MEN kidnapped in Beirut in 1993. Paul Kaskis and John Anselm, American journalists, David Riccardi, Irish photographer.

Caroline read the clippings again. *The Times* described Kaskis as 'foreign correspondent and former military affairs correspondent for the Washington newsletter *Informed Sources*'. Anselm was a 'freelance veteran of news flashpoints from Somalia to Sri Lanka'. Riccardi was called an 'award-winning battle zone photographer'. The kidnappers were thought to be 'anti-American Hezbollah extremists'.

John Anselm said Kaskis was murdered. Caroline skimmed. There was no mention of the death of Kaskis. The last clipping, dated 17 July 1994, said Anselm and Riccardi had appeared at the US embassy in the early morning of the previous day.

So Anselm and Riccardi were never interviewed, never told their stories, didn't write about them.

Caroline closed her eyes. The time to stop this was now. She had fobbed off Halligan for the last time. Now she should tell him it had looked promising and then it had evaporated.

It would be humiliating. More humiliation, after being treated like a hooker – fucked over and given money.

She caught herself rubbing her hands, something she did without thinking when she was feeling stressed. Her cook's hands. Her father once said her brother had pianist's hands. Richard had no musical ability, couldn't whistle 'Happy Birthday'. After Sotheby's sacked her, her mother suggested cooking school. Her father was reading the paper, from behind it, he said, 'Good idea. The Digby women all have cook's hands.' The Digbys were her mother's family. After that, she took every chance to study the hands of the Digby women but she saw no sign of domestic-staff uniformity.

No more humiliations. She'd had her share. Think.

A man in drag had tried to kill Mackie. Only Colley knew about the meeting. She had set up the meeting and a man in drag had tried to kill Mackie.

And money appeared in her account. Colley could mock her because he had a doctored tape of their meeting. No one would believe her story.

The time to stop this thing? Colley arranged the money, arranged for the money in the briefcase the slight, dark woman gave her.

But Colley didn't arrange for Mackie to die at the head of the escalator. Colley was a slimy old hack who picked through celebrities' garbage and followed up-market call girls to see who their customers were, but he wasn't an arranger of killings.

No. For personal gain, he had told someone about the film and that someone had arranged to get it and kill Mackie and compromise her.

Who had Colley told?

There were no answers that way. The film, she'd seen the film, the whole thing was about the film. People would kill to get the film.

A village in Angola. Americans. That was still the way to go.

Anselm said Kaskis intended to interview Joseph Diab, an ex-soldier, Lebanese-American, in Beirut. In the Lebanon anyway, which was mostly Beirut as she understood it.

Did the paper have a correspondent in Beirut? She never read the foreign news pages.

It took five minutes to find out. They had a stringer called Tony Kourie who worked for a Beirut paper, a moonlighter. He answered the phone. A faint East End accent.

He said he knew her name, he'd seen the Brechan story. They compared weathers. Then she asked him and he whistled.

'No shortage of Joe Diabs here. Had a go from the American end, have you? US Army?'

'No. I will if I have to.'

'I'll have a try. Anything else might help?'

It came to her from nowhere.

'Okay,' he said. 'Get back to you.'

The phone. Halligan.

'Caroline, we're at the end of the road here, darling.'

'I need a little more time,' she said, confidence gone.

'Full account. Pronto. Today. In writing, in detail.'

'I think I've shown ...'

'Shown? You won't mind me saying turning up Brechan's bumboy, that's now looking less spectacular. A lot less clever of you. In the light of information received.'

The skin of her face felt tight. Information received?

'I'll get back to you,' she said.

'You will. Soonest. And the contract, well, study the fine print.'

Minutes passed. She realised she was rubbing her hands together. The phone again.

'Caroline, Tony Kourie. Listen, I've got a likely Joe Diab. Joseph Elias Diab, age thirty-six, born Los Angeles, parents both born in Beirut. Former US Army senior sergeant.'

'Yes?'

'And dead. Outside the house of his cousin, six shots to the body.'

'When?'

'Night of 5 October, 1993.'

'Thanks, Tony. Really, thanks. Repay you if I can.'

'Tell the bastards to run some more of my stuff.'

'I will.'

Caroline looked at the printouts, but she didn't pick them up for a while. She knew. Anselm, Kaskis and Riccardi had been kidnapped on the night of 5 October, 1993.

57

… HAMBURG …

SHE WOULD be full of regret.

Then again, she might not be.

He was going through the day before's logbooks, rendering them billable, thinking about Alex, thinking about what happened next.

The phone whispered. Beate.

'Herr Anselm, a Caroline Wishart. Yes?'

He thought to say no, he wanted to say no, but he had given her the number. She would try again.

'Yes. Thank you.'

Beate said, 'Mr Anselm will take your call.'

They said hello.

She said, 'Mr Anselm, I'm really sorry to bother you again.'

He waited, he didn't mind being rude to her, he didn't want to talk to her, let her feel that in his silence.

'It's about Paul Kaskis.'

He didn't want to talk about Kaskis or about Beirut, to this woman, to anyone.

'Ms Wishart, I don't know what you're working on, I know nothing about you except that you caught a politician with his pants down. And life and death is just a phrase. So, with regret, no.'

A pause.

'Mr Anselm, please, please just listen to me,' she said, rushing. 'It's not just a phrase. A man showed me a film of people being murdered. In Africa. By American soldiers. He wanted to sell the film. Then I saw someone try to kill him. I also want to ask you whether you know that Joseph Diab, the man Paul Kaskis was in Beirut to see …' She ran out of air. 'Joseph Elias Diab was murdered the same night you were kidnapped. He was executed.'

A film.

Anselm barely heard the rest.

A man called Shawn murdered in Johannesburg. And Lafarge in London looking for a man named Martin Powell, now thought to be Constantine Niemand, who was there when Shawn died and who killed Shawn's killers.

Kael had talked about a film.

If this prick's got the papers and the film, whatever the fucking film is … How did Lourens die?

'What's the man's name?' he said. 'The man with the film?'

'Mackie. He called himself Mackie. Bob Mackie.'

Not Powell or Niemand.

'I'll call you back in a few minutes,' said Anselm. 'Give me your number again.'

He went through to the workroom. Inskip wasn't at his station. The man next door, Jarl, the Scandinavian and Baltic specialist, pointed to the passage door and drew on an imaginary cigarette. A longing imitation.

Anselm followed Jarl's finger, braved Beate's eyes, and then it took muscle to open the glass door against the wind, then to prevent it slamming. Cold. It would be cold even with a coat. The north wind was running a rabble of clouds across a pale-blue sky. Across the road, the trees were stripped for winter now, shivering.

Inskip had his back to the view, to the lake, to the wind, lighting up. He handed over the cigarette and lit another. They hunched against the wind.

'A holiday,' said Inskip. 'I'm thinking, let's fly away to ten days of sun. Sun and naked skin.'

'Why waste money,' said Anselm. 'You can get the exposure here over two or three years. For naked skin, we have St Pauli.'

Inskip didn't look at him. He drew on the cigarette held high in his fingers, near the tips.

'My, you've thrown my thoughts into disarray,' he said. 'I had in mind a concentrated experience, two or three years of sun in ten days. And I was thinking of my own skin. My own etiolated skin.'

Anselm blew smoke. The wind's grab reminded him of a holiday in the Hamptons in winter when he was a teenager, smoking in the dunes, the wind-whipped grass, the stinging sand, grit on teeth.

'Those South African lists?' he said. 'Remember your piece of detection?'

'Indeed. The aborted coup gang.'

'Write them down?'

'In the file.'

'Of course.'

They smoked. Below them, on Schöne Aussicht, two police motor-cyclists appeared, riding abreast. A police car followed, then three dark-grey Mercedes Benz saloons. A second police car and two more motorcycles completed the convoy.

'Who's this?' said Inskip.

'Some nonentity. No mine detectors, no helicopters, no foot soldiers.'

Inskip rubbed his beard stubble. 'Pardon my inquisitive nature but I've wondered about something. Does this firm make enough to have premises a few spits from the Senate guesthouse?'

Anselm took a last draw, cartwheeled the butt into the sad garden below. 'It's complicated but the short answer is No. I need that file.'

They went inside, crossed the room, raked by the cold fire of Beate's disapproval. Anselm collected the file and took it to his office. He looked at the lists and then he went back to Inskip's station and gave him the name.

Ten minutes later, Inskip came in with a piece of paper.

'A charming woman in the newspaper's library,' he said. 'She looked it up for me. They still have actual paper clippings and file cards with names.'

'Quaint,' said Anselm.

He looked at the sheet of paper, then he put it in the file. He rang Caroline Wishart.

'I can't help you,' he said. 'The name Mackie means nothing. And Diab's death, that was just a coincidence. People got shot in Beirut all the time then.'

She was silent.

He didn't wait, said sorry and goodbye.

The file was open on the desk, the names of the brigands assembled to stage a coup in the Seychelles.

Just above POWELL, MARTIN on the first list.

Just above NIEMAND, CONSTANTINE on the amended list.

The name MACKIE, ROBERT ANGUS.

Robert Angus Mackie was a mercenary, killed in Sierra Leone in 1996 said the newspaper library in Johannesburg.

The man who showed Caroline Wishart the film, the man Lafarge were hunting, he wasn't Bob Mackie.

The man was Constantine Niemand.

58

... LONDON ...

CAROLINE LISTENED to her voicemail. It had gone unattended.

Listen you homophobic bitch, you think you can crucify this man because he ...

Next.

Hi, Caroline, my name's Guy and I think we should meet. I've been fucked by names, you would not believe, I'm talking about big names, I'm talking show business, I'm ...

Next.

Caroline, I'm Tobin Robinson's producer. Tobin would very much ...

Next.

Listen, sweetie, I really like your face, you have that kind of thin cocksucker...

Next.

We had a little chat, glass of beer, you came to see me. Remember?

It was Jim Hird, the doorman who saw Mackie.

I was talkin to a bloke today, he wrote down the number of that bike, know the one I mean? Some blokes come around askin but he didn't like the look of 'em, kept mum. I thought you might have a use for it.

He read out the number.

She was out of the door in seconds but she had to wait five minutes for Alan Sindall, the chief crime reporter, to get off the phone before she could ask him.

'You'll have to buy me a drink,' he said. 'I've got something urgent on at the mo. I'll send it around. Soonest.'

59

… LONDON …

THE MAN's name was Kirkby. He raised his wine glass to the light, studying the yellowish liquid like a pathologist with an unusual urine sample. 'We always try to help,' he said. 'Where possible.'

'It's finding someone,' said Palmer.

They were in a wine bar in the City, in a long room with tables under high windows. Casca had arranged it. Casca said MI6 suggested a meeting, and that meant something.

Kirkby put the glass to his beaky nose, sniffed deeply, sipped, took in air like a fish, closed his eyes, rolled wine around his mouth, swallowed. 'Helen Turley,' he said. 'A genius. One of yours.'

'What?'

'She made this drop. The proprietor here managed to get two cases. Exorbitant price. But.'

Palmer saw that Kirkby had caught the eye of the man behind the counter of the wine bar, a huge red-bearded, red-faced person wearing an apron. Kirkby toasted him wordlessly. The man nodded and raised his own glass.

Palmer drank. He liked wine. He'd come late to it. His father's view had been that wine was one of many European curses on America. For some reason, he regarded it as an Italian curse. Probably because his father disliked Italians even more than he disliked the Irish. 'The only good thing about the Irish is that they're not Italian,' he said when Palmer told him he planned to marry someone of Irish descent.

'We'd like to know if he leaves, of course,' said Palmer. 'But he's with a local. That's where we'd appreciate help.'

Kirkby looked at him, a neutral gaze, looked away, looked back. 'Yes?'

'She may be the easiest way to find him.'

'And she's not … helping?'

'Out of sight too.'

'Inquiries, who's been …?'

'A private firm. Lafarge.'

Palmer knew that Kirkby knew about Lafarge.

'Private. Yes.' Kirkby touched his oiled hair, smiled, raised his glass to his lips. He seemed to hold wine around his gums before swallowing.

'It's urgent,' said Palmer. 'We wouldn't ask otherwise.'

'No, of course you wouldn't. I'll, ah, I'll have a word with someone. Ask them to get a move on too.'

Palmer took out the card and held it edgeways on the table. Kirkby took it, delicately, at a corner, put it in his top pocket without a glance.

'We'd like to know where she might go, friends, that kind of thing,' Palmer said. 'Without alarming her.'

'Yes,' said Kirkby, 'that's more or less what I thought you'd like.'

He finished his wine, licked his lips, took a doubled envelope from an inside pocket and gave it to Palmer. It wasn't sealed.

Palmer took out his reading glasses. He hated having to do that.

Three pages. Phone-tap transcripts.

Palmer read, and he had to stop himself sighing.

'You can keep those,' said Kirkby.

'Thanks.'

'Well connected, unfortunately. The father.'

Palmer nodded. It was over and they got up and went to the counter. He paid. Exorbitant was about right for the wine, he thought. At the door, they shook hands.

'I'll make a call from here,' said Kirkby. 'Get things moving.'

60

... HAMBURG ...

ANSELM WENT to the basement and got a beer from the machine. Soon they'd take the machine away. The room was empty, the heating off, damp blistering the paint on a wall. No one used the place any more except to sneak a smoke, avoid going out into the chill. In the first years after his arrival, the room always had people in it, financial charlatans from the top floor, advertising people from the annexe, people drinking liquor and coffee, smoking, eating their packed lunches. Flirting. The truck had come to refill the beer machine every afternoon. He'd never lingered, nervous, hanging out, just got two beers, gone outside, drained them in minutes.

He sat on the formica-topped table, put his feet on a chair. The television in the corner was on, an old Grundig, the colour uncertain. Beyond midday and he was only on his first beer. What did this mean? He took a measured swig and lit a cigarette. Drink and smoke, the fatal, sweetest combination.

Constantine Niemand had a film of something terrible in Africa. He tried to sell it to Caroline Wishart and later she saw someone try to kill him.

Kael and Serrano sent Shawn to Johannesburg to look for papers, documents, anything that involved them. Shawn found a film too. Then he was murdered. Niemand was there, and then he had the film and the documents.

Lafarge were looking for Niemand and someone called Jessica Thomas.

Caroline Wishart wanted to connect Kaskis's one-paragraph reference to a rumour about an Angolan village to the film Niemand showed her.

Anselm thought about San Francisco, about Kaskis calling from somewhere, a message on the machine:

A few days in Beirut, it's on me, my grandpa's money's come through, to spend not on myself but in the interests of truth and justice. I need a witness, a reputable witness, but you'll have to do. And a photographer. Got one handy? Footloose and fancy-free?

On the plane two days later, Kaskis was just himself, giving away nothing, you didn't bother to question Kaskis, he told you what he wanted to tell you. It was a free trip to somewhere where there were always saleable stories to be found.

What had Kaskis said about Diab?

He's a bitter man, a wronged man, the army done him wrong ...

He couldn't remember when Kaskis had said that. At the hotel in Beirut perhaps. Riccardi arrived after them, the morning after. Kaskis and Riccardi went for coffee. How much did Riccardi know about the job? Who was he there to photograph? Stills or video? Black and white? Colour? So much photographic equipment hung off Riccardi that people in the street had been known to point and ask: How much for that?

But surely Riccardi already knew when he arrived in Beirut? Kaskis would have described the job when he rang him in Ireland. Told him who, why, the point of the exercise.

There was no certainty of that. Riccardi often forgot to ask the most basic questions. He simply didn't care. And Kaskis always had the *this-is-your-commanding-officer-and-I'll-tell-you-what-you-need-to-know* air. Presumably that came from the army. He joined at seventeen, became a Green Beret, ended up in Delta Force. He didn't talk about it much. Once he had said the army didn't want you to go beyond a certain stage of maturity:

'If you've got the brains to grasp that, then baby, it's time to saddle up and ride. The ones who don't, well, they're kids forever. Playing this fucking wonderful game with really dangerous stuff. And I'm not talking just the grunts, the cannon fodder. There are kids right at the top – the fucking Pentagon's full of them.'

Anselm stubbed his cigarette, tested the can for beer, wobbled it, drained it.

The television showed a heavily built man getting into a car, Secret Service protectors around him. The woman on television said:

In spite of strong rumours, American Defense Secretary Michael Denoon today continued to avoid declaring that he will next year seek the Republican Party nomination for the American presidency. Gerald McGowan reports from Washington.

A solemn-looking man came on, standing in front of the White House. He put his hands into the pockets of his black overcoat and said:

White House insiders are today saying that Secretary of Defense Michael Denoon is hours away from resigning his position to begin his late run for the presidency.

Since the collapse of the Gurney campaign, Denoon is said to have been urged to take the field by powerful interests. These include the US military, which he left twelve years ago as a much-decorated four-star general, and the Republican Party's most powerful business group, Republicans at Work.

Anselm was on the stairs when he thought about the flight to Beirut. Business class. Free drinks. He had been drowsing, cabin lights dimmed. Kaskis had taken a photograph out of his briefcase, adjusted the overhead spotlight to look at it. An 8 x 10 print, a group of men, perhaps a dozen, posing like a team, standing, some squatting or on one knee. Young men in casual clothes, jeans, T-shirts, some baseball caps. He remembered signatures

– they had signed across their chests with a broad-nibbed pen, a felt-tipped pen, not full names, first names. He remembered thinking some of the signatures were childlike, immature. He also remembered thinking they all looked like bodybuilders. The thick necks, the big, veined biceps.

Anselm went to his office and found a file. He took it into the humming workroom. Inskip was reading an airline passenger list.

'When you've got a moment,' said Anselm.

'This'll keep.'

Anselm sat down and wrote the name 'Joseph Elias Diab' on Inskip's pad. 'I need a US Army service record. National Archives and Records Admin database. They run something called CIPS, Centres Information Processing System. To get what's called a NARS-5 record, you need a user ID and a password. Users are federal agencies. And you can only access the record groups used by the agency you represent.'

'Naturally,' said Inskip. He looked at the ceiling and rubbed his chin stubble. 'Just sticks in the mind does it, this sort of stuff?'

'Veterans Affairs are easiest. They're allowed to see most things.'

'I'm going to need some handholding here.'

Anselm found what he was looking for in the file. He wrote it on the pad. 'The procedure's here. Carla did this one a couple of months ago.'

'Perhaps she could do it again?'

'She's busy. And you need to learn. The problem is the agency's password changes every ninety days. No indication when this one was issued. Could be outdated. Very likely. Then you start from scratch.'

'I love scratch. What's the US Government's view on such invasions?'

'On conviction, death or worse.'

'Ah, choice. The American way. With or without fries?'

Carla rolled into view, rolled from behind her partition on her chair. She was looking at Anselm, her head back, pale forehead free of hair, an unlined expanse of skin.

'Falcontor,' she said. 'When you're ready.'

He went over.

Carla had pages of notes in her clear, spiky handwriting.

'It's complicated,' she said. 'But what we seem to have is Serrano's business accounts going back to 1980. There are many, many transfers into the main one.'

'From?'

'What you would expect. Caymans, Panama, Hong Kong, Netherlands Antilles, Jersey, Liechtenstein, Andorra, Isle of Man, Vanuatu. The black money places.'

'Big money?'

'In total, yes, millions. But many are small, a few thousand. Lots of regular transfers. A possibility is that he has set up accounts for clients and pays himself fees from them. Then there are loan accounts.'

'Loans to Serrano?'

'Yes. One of them is called Falcontor. Big money – forty million dollars, thereabout, in big amounts. Six million dollars three times, one of seven million. All from a bank in the Antilles over two years. But others as small as 250,000 US. My experience says these will not be genuine loans.'

Anselm studied her. 'No?'

'No. The bank, well, to call these paper constructions banks is nonsense, the bank is owned by a blind trust in Hong Kong. It is very likely Serrano's own trust, his own bank. He pays interest on these loans – that would be strictly for tax purposes, a precaution. His place of permanent residence is Monaco, I doubt whether he has ever been audited anywhere. So. He lends himself money and pays himself interest. And he also makes loans.'

'Loans? From Falcontor?'

'No. There are transfers from Falcontor. Big sums. No details, just dates and amounts. I gave up on that and then I thought about it again and I thought these are probably internal bank transfers, so I looked for a password, tried a few dozen obvious ones, you can get lucky. And then I tried the name Bergerac.'

She looked at him, she was smiling a small, pleased smile, she wanted to be asked.

'Bergerac?'

'People like their names, they often look for ways to use them.'

Anselm got it. 'Cyrano de Bergerac.'

Carla laughed, he couldn't remember her laughing, it was a real laugh, deep. 'Correct,' she said. 'I tried it. It didn't work so I ran the anagrams. Raceberg opened the door. I got the account number. And the dates and amounts, they match.'

Anselm smiled and shook his head. He felt her delight, her pleasure lifted him. He knew the buoyancy of the moment when intuition intersected with luck. The lift-off. He wanted to put out a hand and touch her, complete a circuit.

He didn't.

'That's clever,' he said. 'That's very clever.'

'Amazing luck.'

'The clever are luckier.'

'In some things.'

She held his eyes, and then she said, 'It's called Credit Raceberg. It makes loans.'

'Not real loans either?'

'I would be surprised. Astonished.'

'The borrowers?'

She shrugged. 'Banks and account numbers. But some of the banks, well, if we can't open them we should be in another type of work.'

'I'll tell the client what we've got.'

'More in perhaps an hour.'

'I'll say that.'

Anselm went to his office and rang O'Malley. 'We're on our way with the inquiry,' he said. 'Another hour or two. We should meet.'

'I'll bring some Polish beer. Anything else you'd like? From Poland, I mean? I have your pickled ...'

O'Malley had his injunction.

'Like that, is it? Just some ballbearings. I'll call you.'

Forty-five minutes later, Carla was at his door, uneven on the sticks.

'I can come to you,' he said and he regretted it. He put fingers through his hair. 'That was not something I should have said, was it?'

She smiled. 'I'm not sensitive about being the way I am. Also, I like the exercise. Come and look.'

61

... LONDON ...

THE MAN on the phone ended the call and stood up.

'Mr Palmer,' he said, 'didn't expect you so soon.'

Palmer nodded to him, went to the corner window. Outside, the day was the colour of pack ice, low cloud, a wind tearing at two flags on a rooftop. He looked down at the river, slick and grey as wet seal fur. A feeble sun came out for a few seconds and caught the oil streaks.

'Where's Charlie?'

'Just stepped out. Get something to eat.'

'Call him.'

'Right away, yes.'

Palmer waited, eyes on the river, listened to Martie make the call.

'Charlie, Mr Palmer's here.'

He put the phone down. 'He'll be here pretty soon.'

Palmer turned, looked at Martie. Martie returned his gaze for seconds, then he looked down, touched the collar of his blue shirt.

'Not the best run of operations this, would you agree, Martie?'

'No, sir. Ah, yes, sir. Not the best, no, we've had some ...'

'Don't say bad luck, Martie.'

'No, sir.'

'These contractors.'

'Agincourt Solutions. Carrick knows the boss. Ex-army, ex-MI6.'

Palmer looked at him for a while. What to do with clowns? 'That's like saying ex-Mossad,' he said. 'There's only Mossad and dead. Why'd they shoot this guy?'

Martie stopped running his tongue over his teeth under his upper lip. 'Well, it's the back-up man, he's there if something goes wrong with the handover. He says the guy just got to the top of the escalator, looked at him, dived at him, he fired. Instinct.'

'Instinct of an arsehole,' said Palmer.

'Yes, sir.'

Palmer turned back to the window. In the building next door, on the third floor, he could see a man moving down a long white table. It was a restaurant. The man was putting out the cutlery, the implements flashed like fresh sardines. He had the precision and economy of a casino dealer.

He heard the door close. Martie coughed.

'Mr Palmer, this's David Carrick.'

Palmer turned. Carrick was medium-height, pale smooth hair, in a dark suit. He was going to fat but he held himself like a gasoline pump.

'Any other contractors you'd like to recommend, Mr Carrick?' said Palmer. 'Any other old friends?'

He noted Carrick's swallow, the bob in his short neck above the striped shirt.

Soldiers, dogs, kids. Kick 'em and forgive 'em. His father's dictum. That had been his father's ranking order too. Soldiers first. Dogs before children.

Palmer turned back to the window, to the river, stood rubbing his palms together, hands held vertical. His palms were dry and the sound was of water moving on sand, a tropical sound. Australia. Never mind the Virgins. The Great Barrier Reef. After this, with the boy. Golf, sailing. He hadn't sailed enough with the boy, they worked well together. You never had to tell him anything twice.

Kick 'em and forgive 'em.

The door.

'Scott.'

Charlie Price, in a dark-grey suit, grey shirt, no tie. From across the room, Palmer could see the blood in his eyes.

'I don't want to run this down the chain of command, Charlie,' said Palmer. 'I want you three to hear it from me. This business, it's maybe a bit more important than I've managed to get over to you. And it's getting more important and more fucked up by the minute. Now it isn't just this South African and the woman, now it's ...'

Carrick's mobile trilled. He looked at Palmer, who nodded.

'Carrick. Yes. Yes. A second, please.' He went to Martie's desk and wrote on a pad. 'Thank you. Well done. Stay on it.'

Carrick pocketed his phone.

'Progress,' he said. 'The woman used a card to buy petrol on the A44. We're back on track.'

62

... LONDON ...

'SHE DOESN'T live here any more and I don't know where she lives,' said the woman and slammed the door.

Caroline stood in the thin rain and thought about trying again. Then she went back to the car and got the phone book out of the boot. 'You can never find one when you need one,' McClatchie once said. 'I used to keep 'em in the boot. Whole of Britain. You never know.'

There were any number of J. Thomases and a Jess Thomas Architectural Models in Battersea. She tried that on the cellphone.

An answering machine message – a woman with a faint Welsh accent.

Caroline fetched the Yellow Pages. There weren't many architectural model makers. She rang the first one. A man answered.

'Hi, this is a really strange thing to ask but I'm trying to get hold of a model maker called Jess who rides a motorbike and ...'

'Jess Thomas,' he said. 'She's in the book.'

'Great, thanks, you wouldn't know anyone who could tell me something about her work, would you?'

'Her work? Why don't you ask her to nominate some clients?'

'I'd really prefer to do it before I approach her.'

'Well, she's pretty much in-house for Craig, Zampatti, you could ask them.'

'I will. Thanks very much.'

It took a long time to get to Battersea and it was wasted. No one answered the bell of Jess Thomas's place of work and dwelling. There was mail in the box. When she looked up, she saw a man watching her from the other side of the street. Something made her go over.

He was old, ancient, small, lifeless grey hair needing a cut, in a long rain-coat, pyjama pants showing above battered brown shoes.

She introduced herself, told the truth.

The man looked at her through glasses smudged and scratched. He dropped his top teeth and moved them sideways. She looked away.

'I'm looking for Jess Thomas. She lives in the building.'

'Hasn't come back since the fire,' he said. 'Up on roof. Run away, the boogers.'

'Who?'

More teeth movements. He looked around, took a hand out of a pocket and waved it vaguely. There were bits of sticking plaster on his hand, dirty strips.

'What?' he said.

'Who ran away?' Caroline prompted.

'Before fire brigade come,' he said. 'Burned uns. Two of 'em. I seed 'em, put 'em in the van. They come in a van. And a car. Burned. The two. I seed 'em.'

'And Jess, the one with the bike?'

'Bike?'

'The girl with the bike? Was she at home?'

'Home?'

'The girl on the motorbike.'

'Never in my day. Girls.'

Caroline bent over him. He had a sour dairy smell, like old spilt milk.

'Was she there, at home. Was the girl there when the fire happened?'

He shook his head with some vigour.

'Went off before, always hear the motorbike. Bloody racket. Nice girl. Never rode motorbikes, girls, no, never, not my day. On the back, mind you, now that ...'

'Has she come back?'

'Hey?'

'The girl?'

'Nah. Always hear the motorbike, never rode motorbikes in my day, girls ... one booger come down the pipe, seen him. Off he goes in the car. Like bloody lightning.'

'Whose car?'

'Car?'

'The one who came down the pipe? Whose car did he go off in?'

He shook his head, as if she'd said something stupid.

'Well, their bloody car, what else? Come in a van. And a car. Booger come down pipe, he's off. Bloody lightning. I can tell you. Down there, in that lane. The car.'

She thanked him, gave him a ten-pound note. He looked at her as if she were not quite right in the head.

Someone fleeing? Escaping? Mackie? Had Jess Thomas brought him here and people had tried to kill him again?

She sat in the sluggish traffic, sky leaking, windscreen fogging. She felt weak, tired, scared, a little, perhaps. This is not for me, the inner voice said, this is too serious for me. I'm not responsible for people trying to kill Mackie, villages in Africa, I'm involved by accident, he saw my byline, I owe him nothing. And there's nothing in this for me. There's no page one here.

There probably wouldn't be another page one.

... *turning up Brechan's bumboy, that's now looking less spectacular.*

The woman who rang her. The woman who said she had lived in

Birmingham and admired her for uncovering corruption and had a friend who was being harassed, he was really scared, he thought he was in danger, and he needed to talk to someone in the media. A person who could be trusted.

And then being run through the obstacle course. The no-shows, the phone calls, having to sweet-talk Gary's friend. Finally, finally, after two days, the meeting in the park, in the dark. And, before the handover of the film and the tape, Gary saying, quickly:

On this, there's just me talkin on this, right? Solo. Only it's like an interview, know what I mean? Tony asked me the questions, only he's not on the tape, that's wiped. Okay? So you can put in the questions. Say you did this interview with me. Anyone asks me, we had an interview, that's what I'll say. Cause I don't have the time to actually do that. So this is the same, know what I mean?

She had gone to the conference late, you had to be late on a day like that. She had waited, so high, so sure that she had it. She had sat there, the pulse felt in her throat, not really hearing what other people said, it didn't matter. She knew that she was going to be the star, they were just supporting acts before she came on.

Waiting to be the star. And for once she was. She remembered the silence. And Marcia's mouth frozen open.

The moment went a long way to balancing other memories. The one of running down a path towards her father, her brother behind her. Her father was coming home. They had been waiting all day. Her father held out his arms and she held out hers.

She remembered the feeling of complete delight. For the feeling, there was no adequate word. She ran to him and then her father's arms went over her head and took her brother, lifted him, tossed him into the air, caught him.

And she ran into her father's legs, was left clutching her father's legs, his long, thin, muscular legs.

That had come back to her soon after the wonderful moments, the screwing of Marcia, it had come in the midst of the euphoria, not in any distinct form, just a shiver. That night she woke dry-mouthed with the thought that she had done something terribly stupid when she thought she was being lucky because she was deserving. 'You earn your luck.' Her father's words. Things came to those who deserved them.

But why her? What had she done to deserve Gary? Halligan had said: *A lot less clever of you. In the light of information received.*

It was beginning to dawn on her what that meant. Colley had said something strange too:

… just a pretty vehicle, a conduit. Something people ride on. Or something stuff flows through.

Driving the small car in the electric city, the thought settled on her, dark fingers across a darkening day.

She had been a dupe.

She had been used to bring down Brechan. Someone had the tape and the film. Someone chose her to be the vehicle, the conduit. Not because she was smart. No, because she was dumb. Dumb and eager.

She should have come out with it: said that she never interviewed Gary, only Tony, the youth who said he was Gary's friend, was acting for him. She should have told Halligan the whole story about the woman whose telephone number suddenly ceased to exist. Along with dark-eyed, quick-talking Tony and his number.

I suppose you've heard they found your little Gary. Dead of an overdose. Been dead for days.

How many days? Was he alive when she got the film and tape from the man in the park who said he was Gary? They had been unable to determine the day of Gary's death, never mind the time.

She rested her forehead on the steering wheel for a second. She had to go on with this. Mackie. She had to find him before her role in the Brechan story was fully revealed.

63

... HAMBURG ...

'FALCONTOR. Forty million dollars in two years, 1983–1984. Six million dollars three times, one payment of seven million. All from a bank in the Antilles.'

O'Malley tapped the side of his nose with a long finger. The envelope with Carla's report lay on the table unopened. 'More,' he said, 'tell me much more.'

They were in the pub off Sierichstrasse, sitting in the corner. It was the post-lunch lull, only four or five other tables in use, young men in suits drinking the last of their wine. O'Malley was wearing a dark-grey suit and a blue shirt and a red tie dotted with tiny black castles.

'It's not simple,' said Anselm. 'Money in the Antilles bank goes into Falcontor. Money goes from there to the account of something called Raceberg Credit. Raceberg lends the money moved from Falcontor to five accounts. One is a Dr C.W. Lourens, one account in Johannesburg, one in Jersey.'

Anselm waited. O'Malley blinked, didn't comment.

'This is the Lourens of whom Serrano and Kael speak so warmly,' said Anselm. 'I presume that. Dangerous drug fiend. Now departed.'

O'Malley looked away, at the window, at the street beyond, at nothing. He had a half-smile, like someone hearing music he liked.

'Presume away,' he said.

'Then there's a South African company called Ashken Research, also a big receiver, Johannesburg bank account. And a Bruynzeel account in a Brussels bank. Plus a Swiss account, which could belong to anyone.'

Their drinks came, delivered by a dark woman, slim, swift, wearing a waistcoat over a white shirt. Beer from Dresden, pils. They drank.

'Cowbarn?' said O'Malley.

He forgot nothing.

Anselm shook his head in pity. 'This is civilised beer, northern beer.'

'These banks, they offer much resistance?'

'Only the Swiss. Total resistance.'

'Secretive bastards.'

O'Malley drank again, a good inch, and wiped his lips with a paper napkin. 'A little mannered for me, this drop. But otherwise you're cooking with gas.'

'Not all good news. The Johannesburg accounts, no electronic records before 1992. Jersey and Brussels, scanned all paper accounts still active. So we have those Lourens and Bruynzeel transactions.'

'Yes?'

'Lourens. Twelve million through the Jersey account. Most of it spent on properties. Four in England, one in France.'

O'Malley held up his right hand. 'In what name?'

'In the name of Johanna Lourens.'

O'Malley closed his eyes and smiled, a look of bliss. 'Go on,' he said.

'He has two English accounts, that's been shopping money. About a million, it's in the report.'

'The properties. Currently held?'

'Unless she's sold and parked the money somewhere else.'

'What's the detail?'

'Enough for you to drive by and see what the doctor's money bought.'

O'Malley put his head back and made a humming sound through his nose. He brought his chin down and said, 'No doubt this little tavern would run to a decent bottle of champagne.'

'Who paid Lourens this kind of money?'

'Ours not to wonder,' said O'Malley. 'I feel the lovely chill of frozen assets coming on. And I taste Krug. Krugish, I feel Krugish. Join me?'

Anselm wasn't sure how to go on. He looked out of the window, he could see a piece of sky, nicotine-tinted grey. Across the street, a silversmith's display window glowed like a square-cut jewel. There was a burst of sound and the street was full of brightly coloured children tethered to young women: a nearby kindergarten had released the inmates into the custody of their mothers.

'I'll pass for the moment,' said Anselm. 'The film Serrano and Kael talk about, the one Lourens found ...'

'Pass? I say again, Krug.'

'The man who's got the film, he's in England. People are trying to kill him.'

O'Malley tilted his head, his poet's head, ran a hand over the poodle curls. 'You learned this in your professional capacity, did you?'

He was saying: Do you tell other people about my business?

Anselm said, 'Do you know what Eleven Seventy means?'

'Eleven Seventy.' Not a question, just a repetition.

'Serrano said Lourens told him someone came to him with a film. Dynamite, he said. He said, tell them it's Eleven Seventy, they'll fucking understand. And then Serrano said, that was when he wanted us to go to the Americans.'

'I thought you had memory problems?' said O'Malley. He finished his beer, looked into the glass. 'Sure about the Krug?'

'A village in Angola. Wiped out. Does that have meaning?'

O'Malley looked up and sighed. 'Boyo, villages get the chop all the time.

Afghanistan, Burundi, Macedonia, Iraq, a man can't keep track. They go, villages, that is the historical fate of villages. Across the centuries, they go more than they come.'

'This particular one.'

'No. It has no meaning.'

Anselm looked into the pale blue eyes and he thought, I don't know what this answer means. I don't know what he thinks about anything. I've never seen beyond his eyes.

'I've got to get back,' Anselm said. 'Instructions?'

O'Malley tapped the envelope. 'When I've read it. Tell your crack team I'll be sending around a little something of appreciation if this bears fruit.'

Anselm was getting up.

'Sit for a moment.'

He sat.

'I say this *en passant*,' said O'Malley. He was inserting his car key into the envelope, concentrating.

'Yes?'

'Lourens is messy. Even after death.'

He didn't look up, ran the key through the yellow paper, slowly.

'These smart boys,' said O'Malley. 'They had a lot of money lying around doing nothing, this is pre-Mandela South Africa. So they lent some to Lourens. Well, not to him personally, to a company owned by his wife, it's registered in the UK. Lourens is a chemist by training and he promised them big returns. Some story about a breakthrough drug delivery system. Well, they got bugger all, then the big white dream-time ended. These boys waited till the new mob, bribed to the earlobes, let them shift their ill-gotten out of the country and they were gone. They're in Australia now, big in bio-tech, cutting edge in the fight against snoring, hot flushes, jock itch. Also manufacturing, they're applying the old South African talents to a new labour force, chaining the Asian poor to the wheel.'

'They sold you the debt.'

'A fully documented debt. My point is, the Süd-Afs were scared of Lourens. One of the charmers said, this is after we've done the deal, bought the debt, he says, good luck and sooner you than me, pal, they call you pal this lot, he says Lourens is poison himself and he's been in bed with even more dangerous people.'

O'Malley had the report out, looking at the first page. 'That's it,' he said.

'Thanks for the background.'

Without looking up, O'Malley said, 'You aren't a journalist any more, John. That part of your life is over.'

Anselm walked down fume-acrid Sierichstrasse, thinking about what had been. Once his trade had been going to sad and violent places and telling their stories, telling stories of death and barbarism, selling the stories.

The occupation seemed to have chosen him and it was without glamour or reward. Still, there was a certain dirty-faced dignity and pride in being the person who went where other people didn't want to go, asked questions they wouldn't ask, saw things they would rather not see.

But that was gone forever. He didn't need O'Malley to tell him what he wasn't.

Kaskis once said of a famous *New York Times* reporter, 'Covers wars from his hotel room. The dog's gun-shy.'

Gun-shy, that's what he was. He should leave Lourens and Niemand and films of Angolan villages alone.

As he walked down the howling street, he rubbed his useless fingers. My dead bits, he thought, the bits visibly and tangibly dead.

64

... HAMBURG ...

INSKIP SAW him coming in and raised an arm, the wrist cocked, a pale and bony index finger pointing. Anselm went to his side.

'I have entered the temple wherein all men's secrets are known,' said Inskip. 'It was a fucking doddle. But Joseph Elias Diab's file is marked "Out to Agency". Permanently removed.'

'What agency?'

'Defense Intelligence Agency.'

'There endeth the lesson,' said Anselm.

'Tilders wants you to call. Soonest. That's about ten minutes ago. Beate put him through to me, why I cannot think. Carla's here, she's the logical person to take your calls. The senior person.'

'Perhaps Beate favours you, dreams of the touch of your nicotine-scented fingers.'

He went to his office and rang Tilders. The line was strange, an echo, as if Tilders were in a tunnel.

Tilders said, 'The present matter, there is something ...'

'Yes?'

'Brussels?'

'Yes?'

'That person is dead, a suicide, in his office. A gun. Our party called him, they told him that.'

Bruynzeel dead. Anselm remembered the man's voice, his wry, weary tone.

'Thank you,' he said.

Bruynzeel, the account in Serrano's Credit Raceberg, recipient of large loans.

A suicide.

He got up and found Tilders's audiotape, DT/HH/31/02, put it in the machine.

Serrano at his hotel, talking to the Bruynzeel of Bruynzeel & Speelman Chemicals in Brussels.

Bruynzeel: *They want what?*

Serrano: *Records. Anything. Everything.*

Bruynzeel: *You have records?*

Serrano: *No.*

Bruynzeel: *Well, just shut up. It's all bluff. These things pass. Just keep your mouth shut. Trilling's connections, there's no problem.*

Serrano: *You can talk to him?*

Bruynzeel: *I'll see. Things in the past, no one wants to talk about the past.*

Anselm sat, touching the lost fingers, the Beirut fingers. Cold, they were always cold, like Fräulein Einspenner's fingers when he held them.

Trilling's connections.

Trilling. Who was Trilling?

Anselm called up the search engine and typed in *trilling.*

There was no shortage of Trillings. The search engine found 21,700 references.

Bruynzeel & Speelman Chemicals.

Lourens is a chemist by training ...

O'Malley said that. Perhaps Trilling was in the same line ...

A long shot. Anselm added *chemicals* to the search.

Too many.

Try *drugs.*

The first reference said:

Pharmentis Corporation president Donald Trilling tonight defended his company's record on the pricing of drugs sold to the third world.

The phone.

Beate, sandpaper voice. 'A Dr Koenig for you.'

'Thank you.'

Alex.

'Is this a bad time?'

'How can that be?'

'Can I say ... what can I say?'

'Say I could come around and see you. Or the reverse. Or anything.'

'Come around and see me, I'll say that?'

Anselm's heart lifted and he closed his eyes.

'That's fine,' he said, 'that's very good. About when would that be? The time doesn't matter much to me.'

'Whenever your work is, well, after work, whenever. I'm at home, I'm here. So. Any time. From now.'

'From now is fine. I'll see you soon.'

'Yes. That's good.'

'I'll just settle the bill here, get going. Bye.'

'Bye.'

A moment.

'I could pick you up,' she said.

'No, I'll get a cab, it's easy.'

'Fine. See you soon.'

'Soon.'

He put the phone down.

This elation was stupid, he knew that. He saw her face. The phone rang again. Tilders, the dry voice:

'Our friends are meeting again. The same place. In an hour.'

Kael and Serrano.

'I have something new,' Tilders said. 'Worth trying perhaps.'

'Two minutes,' said Anselm. He rang O'Malley.

'The person in Brussels is dead,' Anselm said. 'Apparent suicide by gunshot. Our friends here are meeting again. We can try.'

There was a pause. Anselm could hear background noises. Perhaps O'Malley was drinking Krug alone. A voice said, 'British Airways flight 643 to London ...'

'Sad news,' said O'Malley. 'But no thanks. I'm happy to stick with what I've got.'

Anselm said goodbye, sat for a moment. The light was going. He rang Tilders.

'Yes,' he said. 'Go ahead.'

'It is the same as the first time. I'll call you.'

'I'd rather not wait.'

'Otto will pick you up outside in twenty minutes.'

65

… HAMBURG …

THEY SAT in the Mercedes, parked at almost exactly the same place as the first time.

'When?' said Anselm.

'Four forty-five,' said Fat Otto. 'A few minutes.'

Otto liked to speak English. He had once worked in England, in restaurants.

Under the ashen, dying sky, the lake was still, pewter, mist on the far shore. A lone swan came into view, imperious in its bearing.

The words came to Anselm from his father and he said, 'And always I think of my friend who/amid the apparition of bombs/saw on the lyric lake/the single perfect swan.'

Fat Otto looked at him. 'What?'

'Edwin Rolfe. A poem.'

Fat Otto looked away, looked at his watch.

'He almost missed this appointment,' he said.

'Who?'

'Serrano. There was trouble about the hotel safe.'

Anselm's mind had turned to Alex, the Italianate face, the full lower lip she sometimes bit when she was listening.

'What kind of trouble?'

'Something about the keys.'

'What's that got to do with Serrano?'

Fat Otto's mobile rang. He listened.

'*Ja. Ja, alles okay.* Serrano's getting on,' he said.

'What have the keys got to do with Serrano?'

'His briefcase was in the safe. He couldn't get it while they were arguing about the keys.'

'Briefcase? The same one?'

'No, he has another.' Otto looked at his watch again. 'Paul has to get close with this new gadget.'

Anselm's mind had returned to Alex but something passed over his skin like a touch, like walking into a cobweb, cold.

Serrano's briefcase in the safe. Trouble over the safe keys.

Bruynzeel dead.

There was something wrong here.

'Ring Tilders,' he said. 'Tell him not to get on.'

Fat Otto opened his mouth.

'Do it,' said Anselm. 'Now.'

Fat Otto closed his mouth, tapped a number into his mobile.

Anselm watched Otto's face. Otto's eyes flashed at him, away.

Anselm's mouth was dry. Something very wrong.

'It's off,' said Otto. 'He's switched it off. Interference, he's scared of that.'

Anselm closed his eyes. He felt sweat on his forehead, his skin was prickling, the car felt intolerably hot.

'*Was ist los?*'

Otto was looking at him. Anselm shook his head. '*Eine Vorahnung. Nur einen Augenblick lang.*'

Otto shrugged. 'I get them too,' he said. 'Before plane trips, I always get them.' He turned his attention to the black box.

They sat and listened to crackling, to static. Anselm was rubbing his fingers, the premonition wouldn't go away, he felt panic coming.

Sit up straight. Put your hands in your lap, palms up, open. Breathe deeply, breathe regularly.

'From hearing-aid technology,' said Fat Otto. 'And the tuner you wear in your ear, like a hearing aid but tiny, invisible. Cordless. The mikes are in spectacles. Three mikes. You tune until you drop out everything you don't want. To six or seven metres, phenomenal, the clarity. I heard this couple in Spitalerstrasse talking dirty, whispers, whispering dirty, she said to him ...'

'This isn't phenomenal clarity,' said Anselm.

'We had no time to test transmitting.'

They sat for a long time listening to crackling and hissing, Fat Otto fiddled, Anselm tried to still his mind, slow the turning of the planet.

Serrano's briefcase in the safe. The keys to the safe. An argument about the keys to the safe.

Bruynzeel dead. Lourens dead. Falcontor. Credit Raceberg.

'The transmitter,' said Fat Otto. 'Still, we'll have it. Probably.'

The ferry came into view, sliding on glass, windows aglow, in the last moments of the day.

Anselm felt the panic recede. The beating in his chest was less insistent, his pulse rate was falling. He opened his mouth and his jaw muscles made a noise, relief from the clenching.

Kael's dark-blue Mercedes was in the same spot fifty metres from the landing, the driver leaning against it, looking at a hand, his nails, bored.

Calm. Anselm felt it come, his mouth was moist again, the salivary glands working.

All that troubled the lake was the ferry's wake, the chevron, corrugations expanding, dissipating.

The lyric lake.

Only the swan missing, alone and perfect. The swan had come along too early.

They would have to go somewhere to listen to Tilders's tape, ensure that there was something to listen to, that this hadn't been a complete fuck-up. Or they could listen in the car. This would have to be a separate bill, a private bill, this was not O'Malley work, O'Malley had his freezable assets, he had what he wanted. Not a bill, no, ask Tilders to name an amount for this evening's work, pay him in cash. Tilders would be impassive. But there would be something in his eyes.

In the distance, another Mercedes, black, parked illegally, there was no parking there. A wife, a driver, picking up the weary financial analyst, not parking, just waiting.

The day was dwindling, the far shore dark now.

Fat Otto switched off the noise, the crackling, the sibilance.

'We have to work on this,' he said.

Anselm ran hands up and down his cheeks, heard the sawing of the beard. He would ask Fat Otto for a lift to Alex's.

When they had heard the tape.

He thought about unbuttoning the shirt. She always wore shirts. Kissing the lower lip that she bit. Biting it for her.

He felt in his groin the possibility of an erection, perhaps more than a possibility. He moved his thighs apart, made room for possibility.

The ferry was about to dock, a handful of people waiting.

'An experiment,' said Fat Otto. 'Better next time.'

'Yes,' said Anselm.

Movement inside the ferry. Passengers getting up.

There was a sound, not loud.

The ferry lit up inside.

Light red as blood, dark streaks in it.

A hole appeared in the ferry roof, a huge scarlet spear through the roof.

The ferry lifted, not high, came down, settled on the water, listed, burning inside.

'*Um Gottes Willen,*' said Otto. '*Um Gottes Willen.*'

Anselm was out of the car and running for the landing when he looked for the black Mercedes.

It was gone.

66

… HAMBURG …

IT BEGAN to rain as Anselm neared home, cold sleet-like rain, but it didn't bother him. He had sent Tilders to his death. There would never be any escape from that fact.

On a whim. Not on business. Not on behalf of a client. On a personal whim. For that, Tilders was dead.

The house seemed colder than usual, the rooms darker. He rang Alex.

'I was wondering about you,' she said.

'I won't be coming,' he said. 'Someone's been killed. A friend.'

A silence.

'I'm sorry. That's terrible. Of course, you must … Whatever you have to do.'

'Nothing. There's nothing to do.'

'Where are you?'

'At home.'

'Well. I'll call you tomorrow.'

'Yes, I'll call you. I'm sorry.'

'No, please, don't be. These things, you need time.'

Anselm sat on the edge of the desk, looking at the carpet. He felt all his aches, no alcohol in the system to dull them.

A whim. Was it a whim?

No.

'You aren't a journalist any more, John,' O'Malley had said. 'That part of your life is over.'

It wasn't over. It had started again with the decision to put Tilders on the ferry. Sad-eyed Tilders, wry and icy-calm doer of the impossible, benchmark for reliability. It couldn't stop because he had been blown to pieces. The opposite. It had to go on because he was dead.

Dead. How many people in this unfathomable business were dead. Now Tilders by chance, Serrano and Kael murdered, Bruynzeel, probably murdered. Lourens, probably. Shawn.

And, long ago, Kaskis and Diab.

He thought about the Wishart woman. She connected Kaskis and Diab to the film shown to her by Mackie, who was Niemand, and that brought in Serrano and Kael and Shawn and Bruynzeel and Richler and Trilling, whoever he was.

Anselm went to the cold kitchen and poured half a glass of whisky, took the bottle back to the study, sat in the ancestral chair behind the desk. He found the number and dialled.

It rang and rang and cut out.

The other number, he dialled that, it was a mobile number.

It rang and rang.

She answered.

'John Anselm.'

'Hold on, I'm in the car, have to pull over, I don't have a hands-free.'

He waited.

'Hi, hello,' she said. 'Sorry, the traffic's terrible.'

He wasn't sure how to put it, then he said it. 'Mackie is a man called Constantine Niemand. He's a South African mercenary. The film comes from South Africa. He came upon it by chance, I think.'

A sound, a sigh, perhaps a passing vehicle, too close.

'Do you know what it's about?' Her tone was tentative, talking to a cat so as not to scare it away.

He didn't know what to say.

'No,' he said, 'but I think knowing about it is very dangerous.'

She said, 'Yes. I know that. They tried to kill him again. Last night.'

'Your paper knows what you're doing?'

'No. They don't. It's ... well, it's complicated.'

'I'll call you if anything else comes up.'

'Please. I'm feeling desperate.'

He put the phone down. It rang.

'Anselm.'

'I'm outside your house. Yes or no?'

'Yes.'

He waited for a while, drank some whisky, and then he went to the front door and opened it. Alex was there, hands in the pockets of a trenchcoat, face impassive, beautiful, rain on her hair.

'I want you to fuck me,' she said.

'I ordered a pizza.'

'We're out of pizza.'

'Well, this is most unsatisfactory.'

'We'll see about that.'

She came inside, closed the door, came up to him, close, he could smell her perfume. He put his hands on her waist and drew her to him.

They kissed, softly. Then harder and she pressed against him. He could feel her ribs under his hands. He slid his hands to her buttocks.

'Do you have a bed?' she said, not her usual voice, throatier.

'We never sleep.'

'I wasn't thinking about sleeping.'

She put a hand on him but it was already happening.

'I think you're recovering,' she said.

'Only clinical trials can confirm that.' His breath was short.

'I'm a doctor.' She unzipped him, put her hand in.

He was unbuttoning her red shirt. 'A red bra,' he said. 'That's provocative.'

'White didn't work last night.' She squeezed him. 'This is promising.'

'Upstairs,' said Anselm. 'Quickly, I don't know how long it will last.'

He was awake, lying on his back, still in the afterglow, and he caught the phone on the first ring.

'Haven't woken you?' Inskip.

'What?'

Anselm could make out Alex's pale shoulders, the curve of the shoulder-blades.

'I heard about Tilders. I'm really sorry.'

'Yes. Well.'

'This probably isn't of interest but that removed file, do you know ...'

'Yes.' He was talking about Diab's file.

'There was a number with the entry, a code. I didn't think anything at the time, but it nagged. I went back and fiddled, just curious, you understand, pure spirit of inquiry, and ...'

'What?'

'It was one of a group of files removed at the same time, a bulk buy. All gone for good. Same remover.'

Alex turned onto her back and he could see her left breast lolling, flat on the breastbone, the nipple prominent. She moved her head, disturbed, as if worried by a fly.

He said softly, 'How many?'

'Eight.'

He felt her hand on his thigh, the long fingers moving slowly. Slowly. It was happening again and he had no moisture in his mouth.

'Run the names,' he said. 'That's good work. And if you've got time, do a biog on a Donald Trilling, Pharmentis Corp, that's P-H-A-R.'

'Certainly, sir. Enjoy your rest.'

'Who said anything about rest?'

Her fingers were lying on him, doing nothing, he could feel each finger. Then they closed and she had him in her grip, a silken, strong grip. And there was something to grip.

'Calling for pizza again?' she said.

'A victim of night hunger.'

'Me too.'

He turned and she put her right hand to his head, he got his mouth on her breast, tried to engulf it, the whole breast, her, the whole of her.

67

… HAMBURG …

'THERE'S INSURANCE,' said Baader. 'Tilders's wife and children will be looked after, I'll make sure.'

Baader looked away, fleetingly touched his desk blotter, the computer mouse, pulled fingers away from them as if they were hot.

'I signed as a witness when they got married,' he said. 'He gave the boy my name. Well, he never said it was for me, but I always thought, well, you know …'

Anselm wanted to tell him that Tilders had not been on the firm's business. He wanted to confess. But he could not bring himself to.

Later. He would tell him later.

Baader shook his head, gathered himself. 'What does O'Malley say? This is his business. Fucking around with Kael.'

'I'll find out today.'

'We've never … This prick in Munich shot Fat Otto but that was a mistake …'

Baader looked away again. It was a tired face, the signs of too much and too little. 'On the doorstep, too. That's so fucking, I don't know. I can't …'

Baader shook his head. He made hand movements.

Anselm caught himself doing the same. Language has failed us, he thought. We have no way to express the ache. He went to his office.

The logs stood on his desk, high, two stacks, sixty or seventy files, the records of twenty-four hours, the doings of strangers, their comings and their goings, their gettings and their spendings. He sorted, found Inskip's pile, found the one he wanted.

The eight names.

Diab, Joseph Elias.
Fitzgerald, Wayne Arthur.
Gressor, Maurice Tennant.
Galuska, Benjamin Lincoln Garner.
Kaldor, Zoltan James.
Macken, Todd Garvey.
Rossi, Anthony Raimond.
Veldman, Elvis Aaron.

He felt something stir in a far corner of his mind, something in a crevice, stuck. He read the names again:

Diab, Joseph. Fitzgerald, Wayne. Gressor, Maurice. Galuska, Benjamin. Kaldor, Zoltan. Macken, Todd. Rossi, Anthony. Veldman, Elvis.

Nothing came to him. He turned to the next page.

Inskip's notes, in his sloppy hand, ballpoint, some letters upright, some slanting to the right.

Found five. With Diab, six.

Fitzgerald. Dead, suicide, gunshot, Toronto, Canada, 9 October 1993.

Gressor. Dead, drug overdose, Los Angeles, California, 7 October 1993.

Galuska. No trace.

Kaldor. Dead, apparent road-rage victim, Miami, Florida, 8 October 1993.

Macken. No trace.

Rossi. Dead, motor accident, Dallas, Texas, 14 July 1989.

Veldman. Dead, shot by intruder, Raleigh, North Carolina, 7 October 1993.

Early October 1993 was a really bad hair time for this bunch. Have some birth dates, could check horoscopes. Is this unusual mortality for a group of soldiers of average age forty? How would I know?

A good thing Baader didn't read the logs any more. He disliked frivolity. Except in its place. Anselm looked at his slice of view, not seeing it. Early October 1993 was certainly a bad time. They had been kidnapped on 5 October. Within a few days, Kaskis, Diab, and these five American soldiers, probably ex-soldiers, died violently.

There were two more pages from Inskip. The abbreviated biography of Donald Trilling, president of Pharmentis Corporation, fourth largest US pharmaceutical company.

Born Boston 1942, graduate of Stanford, PhD Cambridge, chemist, military service in Vietnam, founder of Trilling Research Associates of Alexandria, Virginia, developer of anti-depressants Tranquinol and Calmerion, consultant to the US Defense Department. Many more achievements. It was an impressive career, capped by the Pharmentis takeover of Trilling Research in 1988 and Trilling's rise to head of the corporation. There was a quote from *Time* magazine in 1996: '... scientist, corporate strategist, and, as convenor of Republicans at Work, one of the most influential men in America'.

At the bottom of the page, Inskip had written:

Not just consultant to US Defense Department. Congressional hearing in 1989 told Trilling Research received Defense contracts worth more than $60 million between 1976 and 1984. No details. Classified.

May be more about this elsewhere.

Was this the Trilling? The only connection was that Bruynzeel and this Trilling were in the same trade, roughly. Bruynzeel and Speelman sold chemicals. Lourens was a chemist, like Trilling.

Bruynzeel said to Serrano:

Trilling's connections, there's no problem.

If it was this Trilling, what connections was Bruynzeel referring to? With the US Defense Department?

And Serrano had said something to Spence/Richler about needing to worry because 'the Belgian's one of yours'.

Bruynzeel and the Israelis? Was this the Trilling? It was a thicket, hard to get in, easy to be trapped, no way out.

What exactly did Lourens do? He'd never bothered to find out. He swivelled to the machine.

There wasn't much about Dr Carl Lourens on the electronic record. The Johannesburg *Weekly Mail & Guardian* had a 1992 story that the Office for Serious Economic Offences, a branch of the Attorney-General's Department, was investigating his company, TechPharma Global, for currency and other offences under the apartheid regime.

The Johannesburg *Star* reported his death. It called him an importer of chemicals 'with links to the South African Defence Force'. The report said:

The body was burnt beyond recognition in a fire that destroyed the premises of TechPharma Global outside Pretoria. Police said gas cylinders and chemicals exploded, making it too dangerous to approach the blaze. It had been allowed to burn out.

It was rumoured in 1993 that Dr Lourens would be charged with serious offences relating to the apartheid era, but these never eventuated.

A spokesman for the Attorney-General's Department said yesterday that Dr Lourens had been questioned in recent weeks over allegations made by a former employee of TechPharma Global.

There was one more reference.

A man found dead of a gunshot wound to the head in a Sandton City car park yesterday has been identified as Dr Johan Scheepers, 56, a chemist of Craighall Park.

Dr Scheepers was found with a pistol. He was a former employee of TechPharma Global, whose director, Dr Carl Lourens, died in a fire two days ago. Dr Scheepers had been assisting the Attorney-General's Department with inquiries into the affairs of TechPharma.

Lourens, Shawn, this man, Serrano, Kael ... he didn't want to go through the list again. No end to the number of deaths. He was sick at heart and stomach and the twenty-four-hour logs were waiting.

Jessica Thomas, the name added to the Mackie file, had used a credit card to buy petrol at a stop on the A44.

TIME OF EVENT: *12.42 am, Thursday, 13/10.*

The CLIENT NOTIFIED box was ticked. TIME: *3.27 pm, Thursday, 13/10.*

In the COMMENTS box, Jarl had written: *Checked long delay in central transaction recording – Amex computer problems, system down.*

Lafarge looking for Niemand. Was Niemand with Jessica Thomas? Why not, she had picked him up on her bike. Lafarge looking for the film Niemand had. Dead soldiers. Dead Tilders.

Anselm's mind was sick of the puzzle, slid away to Alex. She had left the bed before dawn. He had woken but kept still, lying on his side, eyes closed, listening to her dressing, the fabric sounds, pulling, sheathing. She had come to the bedside, bent over, tried to place a soft kiss on his face, and he had taken her, caught her, pulled her down to him.

'This is over-compensation,' she said in his chest, breathless. 'You don't have to prove anything. It works.'

'It's not doing anything.'

'Are you sure? Let me check ...'

Riccardi. He should have spoken to him earlier. What did Riccardi know?

68

… LONDON …

'WE'RE PRETTY much in a holding pattern,' said Palmer. The small windowless room on the top floor of the embassy was overheated, and it made him feel tight in the chest.

'It's getting close for me, Scottie. I'd hoped things would be tidy by now.'

'I'm not taking this lightly.'

'No, I know you're not. What help have our friends given you?'

'Some. They're on the case. Could hear something any time.'

'Not a big country.'

'Big enough. Plus there's water around it.'

'Is that a thought?'

'We've got it covered, I hope.'

'There was something in Hamburg.'

'Yes. People did some housekeeping.'

'Simpler ways, surely?'

'They apparently thought it would be more surgical.'

'They think Hiroshima was surgical. Sorted out the clown problem?'

'An all-professional show next time.'

'Call me any time.'

'I will.'

'And not a loose thread, Scottie. Not a fucking thing.'

'Understood, sir. Goodnight.'

'Goodnight, Scottie.'

Palmer dialled the other number. There were two rediallings.

'Yes.' It was Casca.

'Palmer. Anything of interest?'

'The present matter, sir,' said Casca. 'We put together a bunch of stuff, bits and pieces, mostly from the one place. It adds up and it's not helpful. You might want to do something about it, sir.'

'Tell me.'

69

… HAMBURG …

RICCARDI SOUNDED groggy, as if woken from a deep sleep.

'What time's it?' he said.

'It's morning,' said Anselm. 'What sort of hours are you keeping there? Still up all night?'

'Yup but now I'm getting paid for it. Got a job. Night job.'

'What kind of job?'

'In a call centre. I answer customers' questions about software problems. From all over the world.'

'What do you know about software?'

'Fuck all. I've got an FAQ sheet, that won't do it, I say we'll get back to them.'

'Do you?'

'No. How you been?'

'Alive. Listen, there's something I want to ask you. Kaskis had a photograph.' Anselm described it.

'Yup. I saw it. The guy, he was in it.'

'Diab?'

'Yup. Diab. That woman get hold of you?'

'In every sense. Did Kaskis say anything about the picture?'

He could hear Riccardi yawn, a sound a bear might make in spring.

'She'd be an A1 fuck, I thought. Good legs. See her legs?'

'She appeared to have legs. She was walking. What did Kaskis say about the picture?'

'I turned it over and on the back was written SD and a date, I can't remember, 1980-something, early eighties.'

'SD?'

'I asked him and he said, "Special Deployment, Sudden Death, the funny guys."'

'Slowly, I'm slow. Say that again.'

'Special Deployment, Sudden Death. That's what he said. And he said, "There but for the grace." It stuck in my mind.'

'I'm amazed. Drugs are doing you good. You asked what he meant?'

'He said, just people who don't exist.'

'That's all?'

'Yup. Wildly talkative, Kaskis, notice that?'

'I did. He said, "But for the grace"?'

'That's what he said. Listen, you raking over all the shit again? Baby, it's history. Get on with life. Take drugs. Get a job in a call centre.'

'I'll pencil that in for tomorrow. Anything else about the picture?'

'The one musclehead was called Elvis – not a name you forget.'

Elvis.

'How do you know that?'

Riccardi said, 'Written on the picture. Guy next to Diab. Elvis. On his big fucking chest.'

Anselm had the log open, he found Inskip's list. *Elvis Aaron Veldman. Dead, shot by intruder, Raleigh, North Carolina, 7 October 1993.*

This was the something that had moved in a crevice of his mind. The names on the list were the men in Kaskis's photograph.

Most of them dead. Five of them killed in the space of a few days in October 1993.

When the picture was taken, in the early 1980s, they belonged to Special Deployment – Sudden Death.

SD, some kind of special unit. Unit of what?

Sudden Death.

Not the Peace Corps.

70

... WALES ...

THEY LAY in their sweat in the cold room, her head on his chest.

She had come to him in the early morning, light behind the curtains. He heard the door and he was moving, one leg off the bed.

'I dreamed you'd gone,' she said. 'I dreamed I came here and found you'd gone.'

He held out his arms. She came to him and he put his arms around her, put his head against the long white nightdress, against her stomach, smelled the clean cotton and her body, rubbed his face against her. She pushed him away gently, crossed her arms and lifted her garment over her head, revealed herself, lean, small breasts.

They made love slowly. He felt the hesitancy in her and he had it in himself, he did not deserve her, he was too crude a creature for her. But when he entered her, she became urgent, squeezed his flesh, made him roll, roll again, she bit him, scratched him, she groaned, and he could not maintain his silence.

Done, she was sleepy, languid, her body was aligned with him, her arm lay across him, a hand on his thigh.

Niemand spoke into her damp hair, softly, 'I want to say thank you. Better than I said it. I don't know why you did that for me.'

'I saw you coming,' she said. 'You had this look.'

He felt her words on his skin, the warm brush of her breath.

'I thought, shit, off his face, he shouldn't be in the traffic. And then I saw your eyes and I thought, no, not stoned, I didn't know what but I knew not stoned.'

He remembered the yellow helmet looking at him and the man coming from behind and the weak feeling.

'My brother died in Cardiff because no one would help him,' she said. 'They thought he was drunk but he was diabetic, he was having a hypo and people walked around him, walked away. So. No. Anyway, you looked so straight, your hair, the tan, and you looked hurt, there's a look you know, you see it in kids. And then I saw this guy coming, he was running. In a suit but not your suit person, like a bouncer, thug face, and I thought, fuck you, boyo, let's go, catch us if you can.'

She raised a hand, touched his lips, ran a finger along the thin ridge of cartilage on his broken nose.

'Do you have a job?' she said. 'Do something?'

How did you tell someone like this what you did, what you had done, without her rejecting you?

'A soldier,' he said. 'I used to be a soldier.'

71

… HAMBURG …

'TELL ME what the fuck you're doing,' said Baader. 'Just tell me.'

'What I'm doing?' The response of the guilty. Anselm turned his head to the window.

Baader looked down, tapped the edge of his desk with both sets of knuckles.

'I talked to O'Malley,' he said. 'Don't mess around with me, John. The boy's dead because of this. Paul's dead.'

Through the trees, Anselm could see a glass tourist boat going by, not so much a boat as a coach on water, light glinting on it.

How to tell this story to Baader? To anyone?

He tried. It took a while. Baader listened, head on hand, eyes closed.

When he'd finished, Anselm said, 'That's it. I'll take it to the grave. Sending Stefan.'

He felt relief. He had spoken of the weight on his heart.

There was a long silence. Baader didn't move, he didn't open his eyes, he could have died during the telling of the story.

'Say the word and I'm gone,' said Anselm. 'You are fully entitled.'

Baader opened his eyes, blinked several times. 'I should say it. But what if he'd been on O'Malley's business? He'd still be dead. And you'll be dead if you go on with this. I think you're fucking around with stuff you can't begin to understand. Leave it alone. It's got nothing to do with you.'

'It goes back to Beirut. That's got something to do with me.'

Baader shook his head. 'You can't bring back the dead. You can't change anything. Be grateful you're alive.'

'I'm grateful,' said Anselm. 'I'm grateful.'

'Go away,' said Baader. 'You worry me. Go away.'

Anselm was leaving, he stopped when Baader said, 'If they killed Kaskis for what he knew, you're alive because you knew fuck all. Then. Now you might just know something. Something you don't even know you know.'

'I'll reflect on that,' said Anselm.

'So composed. So fucking composed.'

Anselm stopped, didn't turn, the desire to be punished fully risen in him. 'Sack me,' he said. 'Why don't you sack me?'

Nothing. He turned. Baader was looking out of the window and the view gave him no peace. He had tramlines down his forehead, deep between the eyebrows. Anselm had never noticed them.

'Being sacked is too good for you,' said Baader. 'Sack yourself. Stand on your pride and your honour and your fucking dignity.'

Anselm went to his office. I'm like a small dog, he thought, only bark and snarl. The logs were waiting. He was grateful that he had something to do, working out how much to charge people he did not know for spying on other people for reasons he did not want to know.

72

... LONDON ...

FROM THE car park, Caroline rang Craig, Zampatti, the architects who employed Jess Thomas. She explained to the receptionist and was put through to a woman called Sandra Fox.

'I'm an old friend of Jess Thomas's, but I've been away, I've lost touch. I found her work address in the book but she's not there and someone told me she did a lot of work for you and ...'

'She lives there,' said Fox. 'Battersea. In that last little pocket of ... well, if she's not there, I really can't help. The people who could are in Nepal, climbing, I gather you have to, it's all uphill in Nepal. So that's not much use.'

'Who are they, the people in Nepal?'

'Mark and Natalie. They're the Craig and the Zampatti, the principals here. Look, leave your number, I'll ask around. Umm.'

A wait.

'There is someone you might try called David Nunn. They came to our Christmas party together. An item, I thought, more than just good friends. You could try him. He's with Musgrove & Wolters, I can give you a number, it's here somewhere ...'

Caroline left her number and rang Musgrove & Wolters. David Nunn was in Singapore. It took almost an hour to reach him, late afternoon there.

Too late to stop lying.

'Mr Nunn, Detective Sergeant Moody, Battersea police. I'm hoping you might be able to help me locate someone called Jessica Thomas. I understand you know her well.'

'What's happened?' He was alarmed.

'Possibly nothing. There was some sort of disturbance at her place the other night and she hasn't been seen since earlier that evening. We'd like to be certain she's unharmed.'

'Well, I don't know. I haven't seen her for a while, not since January or February.'

'Close family?'

'She doesn't have any.'

'Friends?'

'Anne Cerchi, she's a good friend.'

'Do you have an address?'

'Not a number, no, it's in Ladbroke Grove.'

The old address.

'We've tried her. Anyone else?'

'Umm, she's friends with Natalie Zampatti. Natalie and Mark Craig. They're architects, the firm's …'

'I know the firm.'

'Right. She goes back a long way with Natalie, with the family, I think.'

'They can't be contacted. They're in Nepal.'

'Shit.'

'Anywhere she might go? She might want to get away from everything?'

'Not that I know of, no.'

She said her thanks and sat for a long time with her eyes closed, slumped, an ache in her shoulders, in the back of her neck. Then, a man and a woman walked by, the woman laughed, a shrill birdlike sound.

What else to do, to try? Help me, McClatchie, she thought, wherever you are, help me.

73

... WALES ...

NIEMAND GOT up early, left Jess asleep, innocent-faced, and went for a look around. They were high here, the farm buildings on a terrace cut into the hillside. Behind it, the slope was dotted with scrubby wind-whipped trees and then there were conifers, solid, dark.

Below the farm, the road twisted down the hill and crossed a small stone bridge over a stream. He couldn't see water but the stream's course was marked by dense vegetation. Low drystone walls flanked the road and all around on the slopes other walls marked out fields, nothing in them, no farm animals, no signs of tillage.

He could see where the road ended at a gate. From behind the barn, a track, deep wheel ruts, went around the side of the hill. There were no other buildings in sight, no power lines.

He went into the dark house and took the map off the corkboard in the kitchen, went outside and sat on an old bench beside the front door. It was large-scale, British Ordnance Survey, a decent map. He knew about maps, he had had maps beaten into him – reading them, memorising them, summoning them up on moonless nights in swampy tropical lowlands and high, hard, broken country.

Someone had marked the position of the farm in ballpoint. He traced the road they'd come on, the village, some long name full of 'l's and 'm's, the other roads around them. There weren't many roads and most of them dead-ends. He studied the contours, the elevations, the beacons, the watercourses. A little peace began to fall on him. It would be hard for anyone to surprise them here.

'You sneaked away.'

Jess, still in her nightdress, arms folded against the cold, no make-up. She looked like a teenager, he thought. Beautiful. He looked away, shy.

'Nice country,' Niemand said. 'Looks like sheep country but no sheep.'

She came up behind the bench and kissed the back of his neck, put both hands on his forehead and pulled his head against her stomach. He felt the soft warmth of her and a lump rose in his throat.

Niemand made breakfast out of cans in the pantry: grilled tomatoes and pork sausages. There was mustard powder and he made some with water and a little dark fragrant vinegar.

'Useful around the house then,' she said when she came from the bath-room, shining clean, hair damp.

They ate.

'Good this,' she said. 'Who says you need fresh food? I could live out of cans.'

They were almost finished when he realised that he hadn't noticed her eating. His feeling about eating with other people seemed to have left him.

'There are clothes here,' she said. 'But you'll drown in them, he's big and overweight. Fat, actually.'

Niemand knew he should do what he had said he would do. Go. He had a chance of finding the Irishman and they could get him out of the country. But his fears had abated. How could they find them here, so far from London? He thought he knew how they'd found him at Jess's place. The motorbike. The registration. It was obvious. The man chasing him had got the number, they could bribe the owner's address out of some clerk.

But now these people had nothing to go on. Jess had brought him to a remote farm owned by a sister of a friend and the friend was somewhere far away, Nepal, and the sister was in America.

These people didn't have supernatural powers. They'd had luck, that was all. Just luck.

They washed up, she said, let me do it, she pushed him with a hip, he pushed back, they bumped and jostled, laughing, at the end she rested her head on his arm for a few seconds. He kissed her hair. She turned her head and he was kissing her lips, faintly salty.

He broke away. Something said, she'll think that's all you want.

'Could we stay for a while?' he said. As he said the word, he thought, *we*, who am I to say, *we*?

Jess nodded. 'I've got nothing urgent.'

He showered and found clothes that hung on him. They went outside, walked down the track around the side of the hill, shoulders touching, hips touching. He found her hand, long fingers.

'Tell me about your life,' she said. 'We're like people who meet because they crash into each other.'

They walked in the wind, a sky to eternity, torn-tissue clouds. He talked, he told her. He had never told anyone. He couldn't remember anyone ever asking, but he wouldn't have told them.

'When I was a kid, my dad wouldn't come home for days. An alcoholic. Once my mother was in hospital and he wasn't there and the welfare took me, put me in this place. The man there tried to make me ... do things. He beat me with a belt, I was bleeding. The belt buckle. I remember later I could see the buckle on my legs. Anyway, I ran away, to the railway yards. My pants and my shirt stuck to me, the blood. I was there for weeks, hiding in the old carriages, the black men gave me food, the workers, they had nothing, they owed white people bugger all, they were treated like dirt, but they looked after me. That, I've never forgotten that. No. You end up with these pricks, they'd waste any black. Well, this white guard saw me one day, he chased me, he couldn't catch me, and the police came with a dog and it sniffed me out. They took me home. My dad was sober and my mother came back, so that was okay for a while.' He stopped. 'You don't want to hear this stuff.'

Jess swung their arms, bounced her right temple against his upper arm. 'Yes. I want to hear it.'

They walked, the rutted track turning north-east, the land bare, never cultivated, small huddles of trees.

'Anyway, he started drinking again, hitting my mom ... next thing we were on Crete, me and my mom. I only had a bit of Greek but you learn quickly when you have to. I must've been ten, eleven. We were there for years, I kind of forgot about South Africa. When I thought about it, it was like something someone told me about, a story.'

The track ran out on the crest of the hill, just a circle where vehicles had turned, churned the thin topsoil, the far side in view, more of the same, farm buildings a long way away, perhaps five or six kilometres, it was difficult to judge, too much dead ground in between. Ahead was a low drystone wall. The farm boundary. They turned for home.

'Did you go back?'

'My mom had a fight with her family, I never worked it out, and my dad, he'd been writing to her about how he'd changed, how much money he had, that made her go back. So we went. It was all bullshit and we had no money to leave and she got sick again and she died.'

The landscape was spread before them – big fields, walls, far below the wandering, bushy line of the stream, the land rising again, another hill, this one bare and rocky.

'I really loved her, you know,' said Niemand. 'She was such a brave person. She wouldn't give up ...'

'What about school?' said Jess. 'Didn't you go to school?'

'Always. I finished school, on the automatic pilot. I liked reading, that helped, the other kids read nothing, just comics, junk, and I finished and I joined the army.'

He felt a lightness. He wanted to go on talking about himself, but he knew he should stop.

'I've never really talked about it, I've never met anyone ... well, that's my little story.'

'And the army?' she said.

'I was happy there. I came from this life, nothing was certain, then I had ... you knew what was expected of you. They tried to kill you, run you to death, weed out people, but they looked after you. If you could take it, you had value. I got into the parachute battalion. Then I found out what hard was like, the stuff before, that was nothing.'

'It's about killing people, isn't it?' she said, letting go his hand. 'Being a soldier?'

How many people had he killed? He didn't want to look at her, looked away, at the valley, the upland, there was cover up there, a fold in the hill, going up, you would go for that, jinking, east to west, back again, use the patches of vegetation.

'Have you killed people?'

On the opposite slope, a long and bare slope running up to a wainy edge and a dull silver sky, halfway up a tree spat black specks, birds, a scattergun spit of birds, disturbed by something.

'Have you?'

'Yes,' said Niemand.

They walked in silence. Apart. He looked at her quickly, he knew that he had lost her, she was a dream, he had never had her.

'No pleasure in it,' he said. 'I'm not like that.'

She was far, far too good for anyone like him.

They walked for a distance. He could not look at her but he knew how far she was from him. To a tenth of a millimetre. Then she took his sleeve, his hand, she moved against him, rubbed her shoulder against him.

'No,' she said, 'no, I don't think you're like that.'

74

… HAMBURG …

BAADER WAS right, he should do it, quit. He had no right to stay in the job. He had sent Tilders to his death.

No, he hadn't. It was the work Tilders did that killed him. Baader was also right about that. Clients often left open authorisations, do whatever you have to. O'Malley had talked him into the job at the *Hauptbahnhof* and he had agreed because they needed the money. If someone had been hurt, killed that day, would he feel as he did now?

Perhaps. Probably.

The job was all he had. If he quit, what would he do? He was gun-shy, there was nothing he could do that he knew anything about.

Think about something else. Think about Special Deployment. Sudden Death. What did these names mean? Deployed to do what?

Kaskis had said: 'There but for the grace.'

Kaskis had been in Delta Force. He had gone from the Green Berets. Was Special Deployment a unit of Delta Force? Did he mean that he was lucky not to have ended up in Special Deployment?

Kaskis had said something else in Beirut, on the way from the airport. Anselm remembered he had thought it odd, but that was all he remembered.

He stared at a log recording emails sent by a Swiss engineer from his home in Zurich to a company in Palo Alto.

Lourens in a hotel in Zurich with Serrano, snorting coke and meeting Croats. The Hotel Baur au Lac. Lourens burnt beyond recognition. His ex-employee dead in a car with a gun. What did Lourens have to do with all of this?

'That stuff from last night any use?' said Inskip from the doorway. 'The amazing disappearing soldiers and the drug czar?'

'Good stuff. You're early.'

'Can't stay away. I'm filling in for Kroger.'

'Any trace on the Lafarge file, bring it straight in. Don't send without having a word. And anything on Trilling and his Defense Department contracts.'

'As you wish, o masterful one.'

'Something else. In an idle minute, see if you can find a Dr Carl Lourens at the Hotel Baur au Lac in Zurich in 1992. Serrano should be there at the same time.'

'No minute shall be idle.'

The day went by. In mid-afternoon, Carla came in.

'Tilders,' she said. 'I'm sorry. I know you and Herr Baader were ...' She opened her hand on the stick for a moment.

'Thank you.'

'The English accounts of Dr Lourens, they were cleared yesterday. The money went to the Swiss account.'

'On whose authority?'

She shook her head, the swish of hair. 'There's no record, it must have been done on paper, personally.'

Mrs Johanna Lourens, probably. Had O'Malley got a court order on the properties?

It was almost dark when Alex rang. He had been on the point of ringing her several times.

'Are you going home on foot?'

'I am. Too little vertical exercise.'

She laughed. 'Does that mean too much horizontal? Would you like to stand up more?'

He had discovered that she was a laughing person, something her *Frau Doktor Koenig* persona tried to conceal.

'I suggest experimenting until a proper balance is found,' he said. 'I'm leaving in a few minutes.'

'Along the lake?'

'Yes.'

'I'll meet you. Look out for me. Don't let me pass in the dark.'

'No. I won't let you pass in the dark. Not if I can help it.'

75

… HAMBURG …

IT WAS cold outside but still. Just streaks of day left, lines of light running down the sky like the marks of raindrops down a dusty pane. His breath was mist as he did his rudimentary warm-up, his stretches.

The pain of the start, the complaints of the knees and ankles and hips, of ligaments and tendons and muscles. They did not want to do this any more.

Anselm got into his stride, no one on the path, a good time to be running, the day's traffic of walkers and runners and tourists and lovers and young mothers with high-speed babycarts and in-line skaters, all gone. Too cold, too dark.

You got used to running with a bag, passing it from hand to hand. It was heavier tonight, the bottle of Glen Morangie he'd bought from the super-market in Hofweg. He reached the ferry landing, no sign now of what had happened, he shook the thought from his mind. Just run. Try to run at a decent pace. Don't slop along. Run. You used to be a runner. You could run.

It was dark now. Alex was somewhere ahead, coming towards him. Was she running? I'll meet you, she said.

A runner coming towards him.

Alex?

No. A thin man. They both grunted, runners' greeting grunts.

The path turned right, following the lake. There was a moment when he heard the sound of the city, when his brain for some reason registered the noise. A loud hum, a soup of a thousand sounds, like living in the innards of a machine.

Go away, he thought. Would she go away with me? Somewhere quiet. We could read. And make love. Then eat and read.

She would be coming towards him, not far away.

To kill Serrano and Kael, they would trigger a bomb in a ferry. Kill anyone near the pair. Tilders had been close. He had managed to get within two metres, a few seats. Wearing glasses and an invisible hearing aid.

Two figures ahead, coming towards him, walking, heads together.

He felt the familiar alarm, the signs of panic.

There was nowhere to go here, no sideways escape.

He slowed. Heart beating much faster than it should from running. Dry mouth, the tightness of skin.

Relax. The pair from the other night? He picked up his pace. No, it wasn't, just two people out for a walk. One medium, one small, they parted to let him through. He was close, he started to say *Guten Abend*.

The bigger one on the left had his right hand in his coat, high up, at his chest.

A few paces away. The smaller man smiled at Anselm, white teeth. Polite.

The bigger one's hand came out of his coat, something caught the light, a blade, Anselm saw it clearly, the man's arm was back.

He tried to get out of the way, go to the left, but the blade came across him, it felt as if an ice cube had been passed over his flesh. He looked down. The old tracksuit had opened across his chest, parted.

He had stopped. He had not intended to stop. He stood there, bag in hand.

The knife man had the blade upright. Just a sliver of steel.

A thin expressionless face. Moustache and eyebrows of thatch. The man was in no hurry.

He's cut me and now he's going to knife me, Anselm thought. The traditional way of doing things. Not a German tradition but this is the new Europe. He had no feeling of panic or fear. It had happened. He was glad. All the waiting was over.

The man said, '*Tschüs.*'

The cheerful chirping goodbye.

Anselm swung his bag at the man. It knocked the knife hand back, the full weight of the whisky bottle caught him in the face. He went backwards, his knees bending.

Anselm hit him with the bag again, heard the bottle meet bone, felt it, turned, saw at the edge his vision something in the smaller man's right hand – a pistol, a pistol with a silencer.

Awkwardly, off balance, Anselm swung the bag at him.

Missed.

The man had stepped back, out of range.

He raised the pistol.

Anselm heard nothing but he felt an impact against his chest.

The smell of something.

Whisky.

He had raised the bag without thinking and a bullet had hit the bottle of whisky.

'*Leg den Beutel fallen,*' said the man. He had both hands on the pistol now, but not sighting, holding it at his chest. Unhurried, confident.

Anselm threw the bag at him, it missed, went into the dark.

'*Stupide,*' said the man.

'Shit,' said Anselm and it came into his mind that it wasn't an awful thing to die here, in the open, beside the lake. He could have died in a stinking hole in Beirut.

'*Nochmals Tschüs,*' said the man.

He raised the pistol, sighted.

Nothing to do, thought Anselm.

The man grunted and pitched forward, came towards Anselm, falling, the pistol pointing down, someone behind him.

Alex. She'd hit the man with her left shoulder, run into him at full stride.

As the man fell, met the ground, Anselm, the calm still upon him, stamped on the hand holding the pistol. He wished he wasn't wearing running shoes.

The pistol came free.

Anselm picked it up and pointed it at the man's head. '*Bewegen Sie sich nicht*,' he said.

Alex was standing behind the man, winded, bent at the waist, holding her shoulder, looking up at Anselm.

'*O mein Gott*,' she said.

Anselm held the gun on the smaller man and walked backwards to the knife man, bent to look at him. He was breathing. There were blood bubbles at his nostrils, foamy blood bubbles.

'*Was is los?*' said Alex.

Anselm said to the gunman: '*Steh auf. Zieh die Hose aus.*'

'*Was?*'

'*Ziehen sie Sich aus oder ich töte sie.*'

The man had to take off his shoes to remove his trousers. He stood awkwardly, pale legs ending in short black socks.

'*Machen Sie schon*,' said Anselm, showing him the direction with the pistol. '*Bewegen Sie sich.*'

The man took off at a half-run.

'Come,' he said to Alex.

'What about him?' she said, pointing at the man on the ground.

'His friend will be back for him,' said Anselm. He took the pistol by the barrel and threw it into the lake.

They walked back towards the office. Anselm put his hand to his chest and it came away black with blood.

He was beginning to feel nausea rise.

She took his arm and they walked back along the lake shore towards the cheerful lights.

'Where'd you learn to knock someone like that?' he said.

'Gridiron. I played in the States.'

'We didn't pass in the dark,' he said.

She leaned towards him and touched the side of his face with her lips.

'No,' she said. 'But it was close.'

... LONDON ...

CAROLINE FOUND the note on her desk:
See me soonest. Halligan.
End of the road. Goodbye Fleet Street, hello Leeds.
Family, McClatchie once said, you always start with the family. But Jess Thomas didn't have any family.
The architect in Singapore had said something.
She goes back a long way with Natalie, with the family, I think.
Natalie Zampatti had a family.
She rang Sandra Fox at Craig, Zampatti.
'Nat's got a sister somewhere, a doctor,' said Fox. 'Hang on I'll ask the secretary from whom no secrets are hidden.'
Caroline waited. The longest possible shot. The most fucking impossible shot.
'There? Try St Martin's Hospital. Apparently sister and husband are both doctors. Her sister's name's Virginia.'
It took a long time and she couldn't get hold of Virginia but she got the name of her mother. Finally she was speaking to Mrs Amanda Zampatti in Cardiff, a thin voice, uncertain.
Caroline gave her the Detective Sergeant Moody of Battersea police line.
'Oh my God, she's all right is she? Poor girl, she's got no one, you know.'
'We'd like to be sure. There's no actual cause for alarm at the moment. But we thought she might have gone somewhere to get away from everything.'
'Well, Virginia and David have a place, a farm sort of place. She's been there, I know that, Ginnie told me on the phone.'
'And where's that?'
'To tell you truth, I don't know. They wanted to take me but really I can't be ...'
'No idea where it is?'
'Well, Wales, but that's not much use is it? Up north, I think. She said it was away from anything, no phone or telly or anything. I can't think why you'd want to have a place ...'
'Thank you, Mrs Zampatti. I'll get back to you if we find out anything.'
Caroline slumped again. There was no quick way to do this.

… HAMBURG …

BAADER'S DOCTOR was in Mittelweg, a small, bald man, impassive. He looked at the wound under Anselm's pectorals and made clucking noises.

'*Das ist nicht übel,*' he said. '*Da können Sie von Glück reden.*'

Light-headed, Anselm watched as he cleaned the long cut, sprayed it with anaesthetic and stitched it up with the quick movements of a tailor. He wound a bandage around Anselm's body.

'Don't get it wet for forty-eight hours,' he said. 'Then change the bandage every day. Any sign of infection, come and see me straight away. Otherwise, in a week. Tell the receptionist you are Herr Baader's associate.'

He went to a cupboard and came back with two packets of tablets. 'This one twice a day. That's important. The others are for pain. If you have pain.'

Baader was waiting, sitting in an uncomfortable chair reading a fashion magazine. They walked to the car, drove in silence for a while.

'This is deep shit,' said Baader. 'Dieter says we've been opened. He doesn't know for how long.'

Anselm tried to focus on the meaning of this. 'What can they know?' he said.

'Where we go, what we want. Everything. Everything we know.'

'Won't make much sense.'

Baader turned into Schone Aussicht. 'In the end,' he said, 'everything makes sense if you've got enough of it.'

Not life, thought Anselm, not life. 'Who would they be?' he said.

For a second, the sad wolf face looked at him. 'People who are offended,' Baader said. 'People who don't mind blowing up a ferry full of people to kill two men. The people who want to kill you.'

Baader turned into the driveway, parked outside the annexe. He put his head back against the rest, looked at the roof, said, 'I think you should go away for a while. Tonight. Just go. Fat Otto will get you out of here, we can switch transport a few times. Do a few things like that. Go to Italy. Rome. I'll give you an address, you can collect cash there.'

Anselm didn't argue. He felt sick, weak, tingling in his veins, the taste in his mouth he remembered from Beirut.

He was part of someone's problem now. Whatever the problem was and whoever the people who had it were. He had joined Lourens and his ex-employee, joined Serrano and Kael and Bruynzeel. Yes. And Kaskis and

Diab and all the dead soldiers from Special Deployment. They had been a problem for someone and they had been killed for it. Tilders, he had been collateral damage. They hadn't cared whether they killed him or not.

And he was a target now. Two men sent to kill him. They would have killed Alex too, killed anyone who happened to be there, also collateral damage.

They would come for him again. Tonight. Tomorrow. He couldn't go home. He couldn't go anywhere.

At the annexe entrance, Baader rang the bell for Wolfgang to let them in. They were in Baader's office, both of them standing, when Inskip came to the door.

'Could I have a word?' he said to Anselm.

They went to Inskip's workstation. Inskip pointed at a screen.

'The Lafarge file. The woman, Thomas, she's used a card. Twice in the same place.'

'Where's that place?' Constantine Niemand and Jess Thomas. The film, Eleven Seventy.

'Some godforsaken Welsh hamlet.'

He needed to tell Caroline Wishart.

'There's something else,' said Inskip. He pressed a button on one of the recorders. A monitor came alive, a man in a military overcoat walking across tarmac. He wasn't smiling for the cameras.

The voiceover said:

General David Carbone, commander in chief of US Special Operations Command today denied the existence of a special unit of the US Special Forces' super-secret Delta Force called Sudden Death.

A woman was on screen, long grey hair, haggard, talking soundlessly, wiping her eyes with a tissue.

The voiceover said:

The mother of an ex-Delta Force soldier, Benjamin Galuska, found dead yesterday in Montana, has alleged that her son was haunted by things the Sudden Death unit had done but would never have taken his own life.

Soundbite from the woman:

Ben said they'd kill him, he said they'd killed the others. But we didn't believe him.

Cut to the man in the overcoat. He was shaking his head.

I'd like to say that I share Mrs Galuska's grief over the death of her son and I put out my hand to her. And I'd like to say that Benjamin Galuska served his country with courage and honour and pride. But I must also state categorically that the unit she speaks of did not and does not exist. Why Staff Sergeant Galuska invented this story we will never know. He seems to have been a troubled person. God rest his soul. Thank you.

'Galuska's one of the two I couldn't find,' said Inskip. 'Are we dealing with supernatural coincidence or what?'

'What,' said Anselm. 'Don't tell Lafarge anything. Even if they ask.'

He went to his office and rang Caroline Wishart's number. She picked up on the first ring.

'John Anselm. I've got something on Jessica Thomas.'

He heard her breathe in. 'Yes?'

He spelled out the name of the place, the business.

Breathe out, a sigh.

'Any use?'

'Yes. I think I know where she is.'

Anselm heard himself sigh in return. 'Listen,' he said. 'I'll come to England tonight. We might make sense of this if we find them.'

He went back to Baader's office and told him. Baader looked at him for a long time, a finger tracing the line of his upper lip.

'What the hell,' he said. 'Nothing to lose. Kill you here, kill you there. Not a fucking thing to lose.'

Anselm rang Alex.

'I wasn't pleased at being got off the premises as fast as possible,' she said. 'I have a small interest in whether you live or die.'

'He meant well. I have to go away for a day or two.'

'You're not going to tell me?'

'No. Would you like to go away for a while when I get back?'

'To do what?'

'Exercise in the morning, philosophise in the afternoon.'

'Leaving the nights free for ...?'

'Yes, that's what I thought.'

'I need to think about it. I've been behaving impulsively. It's a dangerous time.'

'I'm a dangerous man.'

'Much more than I thought. The answer is yes, call me.'

'I'll call you.'

'Be careful. Please.'

Baader made the arrangements. Anselm rang Caroline again. An hour later, tired, chest hurting, he walked across the tarmac at Fühlsbuttel to the executive jet.

… WALES …

NIEMAND SAT against the stone building in the last light, feeling the wall's warmth. He heard the car change gear to climb the hill, and he took the machine pistol and ran for the barn. He climbed the ladder into the loft and stood beside the dormer window looking down the hill at the twisting road. A hawk in the darkening sky rose and fell, planed sideways, watching for any small movement below.

The car came into view at the small stone bridge. It was the dark-green Audi. Jess coming back.

The gate was open. She drove up past the house and into the barn and he waited until she was out of the car and he was sure she was alone, no one crouching in the back, before he spoke.

She looked up, alarmed, then she smiled, the smile that changed her face. He climbed down and went to her and kissed her, took her head in his hands, ate her mouth, felt her hands on his back, on his buttocks, pressing him into her, pulling him.

When their mouths came apart, she said, thickly, 'Christ, is this allowed before lunch?'

They got as far as the sitting room. He had made a fire, the room was warm, and they fell on the sofa. He was underneath. They kissed, rolled, changed places. He found the button, the zip. She pulled her jeans off, he undid his button, she pulled the zip, dragged the jeans down, they lay and rubbed skin, making throat and nose sounds. She moved and sat on him, she was weightless. She put her right hand behind her and took him, held him, squeezed him, raised herself and came down on him. In that moment, he could have died of pleasure, he wanted to be as deep in her as was humanly impossible. She pulled her heavy jumper off, threw it away, the spencer gone too, ripped off, discarded. His hands went under her bra and it loosened, he had her breasts in his hands, the inexpressibly lovely weight and feel, and his face was on them, rubbing, a nipple in his lips, a small nipple, sucking it, the other one, back and forth between them. She was riding him, her head back, making sounds, a hand behind his head, a hand behind her scratching him, short nails scratching him.

The fire's light lay yellow and gentle and unstable on the things in the room, the room was smaller now, shrunk to the reach of the flames.

… LONDON …

PALMER SAT behind the desk, hands together, fingers steepled.

'Come in,' he said.

The man came in, looked at Palmer and Charlie Price and Martie and Carrick, looked around with an air of distaste, like a first class traveller allocated a seat in economy by mistake.

'Couldn't we have done this another way?' he said. 'I'm not ecstatic about coming here.'

'I don't have time for the cloak-and-dagger,' said Palmer. 'And I wanted to impress on you this business has been fucked up to high hell. There's shit flying, there's no error margin left.'

'You may consider me impressed,' said the man. His eyes panned over the three other men. 'The committee may also consider me impressed.'

Palmer thought he would like to kick the man's arsehole north of his eyebrows. He said, 'There are possible complications.'

'Life's a vale of possible complications.'

Palmer looked at his reflection in the glass door behind the man. He could just make out the furrows on his forehead and the deep folds flanking his mouth. When the kick urge had subsided, he told him about the problem.

'Well,' said the man, 'that's a pity. And it'll make the laundry work troublesome. Where are we talking about?'

'Right here,' said Carrick.

He had the maps out on the table. 'It's difficult country,' he said. 'I'll talk you through the …'

'Just point, darling,' said the man. 'I was reading maps when you were doing wee-wees and poo-poos.'

80

… WALES …

HE WAS IN the kitchen, filling the kettle. Jess came up behind him and ran a hand up the back of his head, from nape to crown. He shivered like a puppy.

'I meant to say,' she said, 'before you grabbed me and did those awful things to me, Dai at the garage says he'll ring if anyone asks the way here. I gave him my cellphone number.'

'You know him?'

'From the other times I've been here. Four slices be enough?'

He loved her lilting voice. He loved everything about her.

Nothing in his life had prepared him for her. He could not believe that she had happened to him. He knew about luck. He had survived things by luck and chance and fate, if there were such things, Greeks seemed to think so.

He turned and grabbed her by the hips and kissed her.

It went on for a time, it could go on forever. They parted and she drew the back of her right hand across her lips.

'Good kisser. I've been meaning to ask, what does your name mean? Does it have a meaning?'

'It means no one.'

'No one?'

'No one, nobody.'

She raised her right hand and drew her fingers across his mouth.

'Good mouth,' she said. 'You have a very good mouth. Good for many things. You'll never be no one to me. Well, never's a long time. Let me work now. We have a long afternoon ahead. And then there's the night.'

She went to the bench top beside the stove. She was spreading bread when she said: 'Dai at the garage says the bank thinks my card's been stolen.'

Niemand thought the room seemed dimmer, the light through the small windows seemed to have faded.

'Why?' he said.

'What?'

'Why would the bank think that?'

'Don't know.'

'When did you use it?'

'When I filled up. Then I went to the shop and when I was coming out Dai came over and said the bank rang and asked if he knew the person, the cardholder. He said yes, so they said that was fine.'

Niemand went to her, stood behind her, put his hands on her shoulders.

He felt no alarm, no urgency, only a terrible certainty of what his stupidity had wrought and a terrible sadness.

'Jess,' he said, 'you have to go now, soon. Get in the car and go.'

She turned, mouth open. 'Why?'

'They've found us. Your card. They'll be on the way here now.'

She closed her eyes. 'What about you?'

'I'll try to do a deal with them.'

'Then I'll stay.'

Niemand put fingers to her lips. 'No. I can't take that chance. I'll tell you what to do and when it's over, I'll come to you.'

She put her right hand under his chin, pushed his head back.

'I'm in love with you,' she said. Her eyes were closed. 'That's pretty stupid, isn't it?'

His chest was full, his throat was full. He found it hard to speak. He kissed her closed eyes, so soft, so silky, he could have died in the moment, been spared the rest.

'We'll go to Crete,' he said. 'You'll like it.'

81

... WALES ...

WHEN THE old Morris Countryman was out of sight, Niemand reversed the Audi out and parked it in plain sight. He had to assume that there was time, that they were not already there, watching the farmhouse, waiting for dark.

He went back into the barn and took a reel of nylon fishing line off its peg under the rods. He closed the barn doors and went inside the house, put on his own clothes. There was a dark-blue jersey in the dressing table drawer and he put that on. He went to the fireplace and reached in for soot, rubbed it on his face, his throat, his neck, his ears, on his eyelids, into his hair.

He left his hands clean. That would be the last thing.

The gun cupboard Jess had shown him was in the smallest bedroom. He unlocked it and took out the shotgun, a double-barrelled Brno, and the old .303, a Lee Enfield bolt-action with a ten-round magazine. It would have been better to have the machine-pistol he had taken from the man on the roof but Jess needed a weapon in case they were lying in wait along the narrow road. There was an unopened box of shotgun cartridges and five clips of .303 rounds. He filled the magazine, pressing in the cold brass-jacketed shells with a thumb. The other clips he put in his jacket pockets.

The sitting-room furniture had to be rearranged, curtains drawn. After that, he rubbed soap on the barrel of the .303. He found the small sewing-machine screwdriver in the kitchen drawer. He sat at the kitchen table and worked on the shotgun, testing until both triggers were as he wanted them to be.

The light was going fast. He pumped a lamp and lit it, took it into the sitting room, tried several resting places for it until the shadows were right. Then he did the delicate work, not hurrying.

It was dark when he finished. He went to the bedroom and put on the bulletproof apron, adjusted it until it was comfortable. Second-last thing: pocket the packet of nuts and raisins Jess had bought.

Last thing: he went to the fireplace again and blackened his hands, black-ened his wrists and forearms. He rubbed soot into the soap on the .303 barrel

Then he put on the black rolled-up balaclava, took the old .303 and went out the back door.

He went around the barn and up the cold slope into the dark, dark conifer wood. At the place he had chosen earlier, he sat, leaned against the tree, listened to the sounds of the night.

It was a pity it had to end here, like this. But you couldn't keep running away. He thought fleetingly about running away from the boys' home to the railway yards, about the blood, dried black and crusted, that was still on his filthy legs and buttocks and back when the police took him home.

No more running. He had told Jess to wait until morning, then take the film and Shawn's documents to a television station. He should have done that after he was shot.

No point in regret.

He tried not to think about Jess, not to think about anything but to go into the empty trance of waiting and listening.

... HAMBURG–ENGLAND ...

THE ONLY passenger in an eight-seater jet, sitting in a leather chair in the hushed and hissing projectile.

The co-pilot came out, young, short dark hair, released the crackling, buzzing sounds of the cockpit.

'Clear night,' he said. 'That's Gronigen below us. We'll be over the North Sea in a minute. Can I get you anything, sir?'

Anselm shook his head and the man went back.

Sliding on the night towards England. With luck, towards Constantine Niemand and his film. What did it show that made it so sought after? Was it the end of the long line that Caroline Wishart had drawn from Kaskis's reference to a village in Angola?

Anselm closed his eyes. The only sound in the capsule was a gentle sibilance, a steady watery murmur. His mind drifted on the current.

Kill you here, kill you there. Not a fucking thing to lose.

The words of Baader. He was right. It was better to die trying to find out what these people had done than to die ignorant.

The firm's layers of disguise penetrated, their mosaic of inquiries known to someone, laid out somewhere, piece by piece, until the picture appeared. What else had Baader said?

In the end, everything makes sense. You just need enough of it.

He fell asleep and then the co-pilot was saying, 'Starting our descent, sir, would you mind fastening your belt?'

… WALES …

NIEMAND HEARD the sound.

A small sound, a tap.

Close behind him, on the path, a foot had touched something. Perhaps knocked one solid pine cone into another, the path was littered with fallen cones.

Silence.

Niemand rose against the broad tree trunk, inch by inch, not touching it, breathed as shallowly as possible, regularly, just enough oxygen to sustain life.

A breath, a quiet expulsion of air, a hiss.

Someone was almost close enough to touch him. He didn't move his head, kept it back, didn't look sideways. The yellow night glasses might glint, catch some light from a star a trillion miles away and betray him.

The figure was beside him, an arm's length away. He held his breath.

Passing him, moving slowly.

A figure as black as he was, bent forward.

Let him be alone.

Niemand didn't breathe, bent a little at the knees.

He pushed off, swung the Kevlar knife in his right hand. Around and down.

There was an instant when the man's head was turning, disturbed, then the narrow blade entered the side of his throat above the collarbone, penetrated downwards.

The man made a hawking noise, not loud, and Niemand pulled him to earth, dropped him softly, held the knife in him, moved it.

Waited until he was sure.

Then he took the man's weapon out of his left hand, ran his fingers over it. Heckler & Koch machine pistol, MP5K, three-round burst trigger group, he knew the weapon. He wouldn't be needing the old .303. He ran his hands over the man's clothing, felt his footwear.

How many would there be?

Not too many. This man was a soldier. By his weapon and his clothing and his ankle-holster and his knife and his silky night-fighting boots. That was good. Trained to kill, he had been killed. No hard feelings. Soldiers took their chances with death.

How many? Soldiers, trained killers, perhaps four or five, no more. Two from the back, two from the sides, the doorkeeper at the front. One front door, one doorkeeper.

Niemand moved forward, the dead man's black-bladed knife in his mouth, machine-pistol in hand. They would not be able to pick him from the dead man. Just a black figure carrying a weapon coming from where they expected someone to come.

He waited at the forest's dark edge, looking back and forth. A wind from the north now, not much, just enough to disturb the scrubby trees on the slope.

There.

A shadow moved. On his right.

Again.

Keeping low, hugging the shadow of the conifers, not too concerned about being seen from the house, the big barn blocking the line of sight.

Niemand looked to his left. Another one should come from there, around the corner of the trees.

He didn't. He came around the stock pen, near the rough path they had taken on their walk. Just his shoulder and his head in view. He had come up from the stream, crawled up, lots of cover, dead ground.

That was three. Three and the doorkeeper. They were confident, they knew they were good. Just two to take out and one of them a woman.

He waited. He couldn't move first.

The other men weren't moving, frozen. Were they waiting for him?

Did I kill the leader? Am I the leader now? Are they waiting for my signal? Shit.

No. The man on his left came out from behind the stock pen and ran for the side of the barn.

The shadow on the right was moving too, coming down the slope, heading fast for the other side of the barn.

Niemand stepped out of the trees, moved down the slope in a crouch, reached the wall. The man on the right was around the corner. He would be waiting for him now.

He put the H&K in his left hand, took the knife out of his teeth.

He went around the corner fast, bent low.

The man was waiting at the corner, back to the wall, machine-pistol up, at head height.

He turned his head, looked past his upraised arm at Niemand.

He was wearing sleek night-vision goggles.

Oh Jesus, he can see me, he can see a man in a black leather jacket.

The man's weapon was coming down.

Niemand fired the pistol one-handed, fired two bursts at the middle of the body, bullets hit the brick wall, screeched, the man's knees went, he sat down, he didn't get off a shot.

Niemand ran past him, didn't stop at the corner, went around it, got halfway along the barn, at the doors.

The other one appeared, night-vision goggles too, Niemand was running straight for him, the man hesitated for a moment, uncertain, he would have recognised the sound of the H&K.

Niemand shot him at point-blank range, in the chest, a three-round burst, gave him the double tap, the man went backwards and sideways, not dramatically, met the barn and slid.

Two bangs in the house, an instant apart.

The shotgun tripwire.

Someone in the house, the doorkeeper had left his position, come through the front door, into the sitting room.

Four down, that would be it.

Make sure. If I come from the back, he'll think I'm one of them.

Niemand ran for the back door, wrenched it open, ran through the room, through the sitting room door in a crouch, the dim lamplight, a figure on the floor ...

Little pops of flame, he didn't hear the sound, he was punched in the chest, more than once, it was hard to tell, so quick, he stopped in his tracks.

Niemand emptied the magazine into the man on the floor, firing bursts as he went to his knees.

Silence.

No pain.

Not gut-shot anyway, the BB. Good thing I found that in the car. And the knife. That's something positive.

He fell over sideways, felt his head hit the stone floor. As if it belonged to someone else.

Breathing was a problem. Something stuck in his throat.

Funny place to die. Up here in English mountains. Hated the English, the old man. Dumb to take on four of them. Still. Know they've been in a fight. Jess. So lovely. So good.

84

… WALES …

THE FARM gate was open and they drove up the steep drive and turned left, stopped in front of the low stone farmhouse. In the lights, they could see the front door – open, not fully open, ajar.

'Well,' said Caroline. 'It's the place. Here's hoping.'

'Yes. There's a light on.' They sat for a moment.

'Cold to have the front door open,' said Anselm.

'Yes.' She shivered. Her clothes made a sound, her chin against the fabric of her coat.

'Well,' he said. 'Since we're here.'

He got out. Black night, cold wind whining in trees somewhere nearby. They were high here, clean air, it felt like the Balkans.

He went to the front door, reached across the threshold, held the door-knob and knocked.

Nothing. Not a sound.

'Mr Niemand,' he said loudly.

Nothing.

'Jessica.' Louder.

Nothing. Just the wind, the keening wind.

He felt the hair on his neck. He looked around. He could see Caroline in the car, her outline. His chest hurt.

She saw him looking at her and got out, came across the gravel, a tall woman, not unhandsome.

He tried again.

'Mr Niemand. Constantine.'

Nothing.

He pushed open the door and went in. A small hallway, coats and hats. The light was coming from a door to the left.

A smell of something. Not quite of burning, something more acrid. He looked around. Caroline was biting her lower lip.

'I don't know about this,' she said quietly.

Anselm thought he would like to turn and leave, drive down the hill, along the winding road, through the cluster of buildings, get back to the highway.

Too late for that. It occurred to him that he had no panic symptoms. He was uneasy, he was close to fearful, but he was not showing the symptoms.

Caused by fear and violence, cured by the same.

Hair of the dog.

He went through the door, saw the legs first.

A figure in black, absolutely dull black, no head. No, a hood on his head, face down, his black hands around a black weapon, a machine-pistol.

In the middle of the room, a shotgun tied to a chair was pointing at him. Anselm was too shocked to move.

Caroline made a noise, a deep, sobbing intake of breath.

On the other side of the room lay another figure in dark clothing, a man lying on his side, blood run from him over the stone floor to the edge of the carpet, soaked up by the carpet, blotted, blackish blood.

The man made a sound like a hiccup. Again.

Anselm did not think, he went to the man, pulled his poloneck down, put an index finger against his throat, in the collarbone cavity. The faintest pulse.

'He's alive,' he said. 'We'd better do something.'

For want of anything better to do, he took off the man's rolled-up balaclava.

'It's him,' said Caroline in a voice without timbre. 'It's Mackie. Niemand.'

'And a terrible fucking nuisance the man is too,' said O'Malley from the doorway.

85

... WALES ...

HE CAME into the dim room, bent over and picked up the machine-pistol lying near Niemand's head.

Anselm stood up. 'Jesus, Michael,' he said. 'What the fuck is this? What exactly the fuck is this?'

O'Malley had the magazine out, looking into it. He dropped it on the floor and took another one out of his coat pocket. It made a precise snick as it locked in.

'What the fuck is this, John?' echoed O'Malley, looking around the room like a real estate agent being asked to sell something nasty. 'Why do rich people crave this sort of thing? A croft in the Welsh wilderness, wind never stops howling, natives slathered in sheepshit and woad, incomprehensible tongue, nasty secessionist tendencies.'

O'Malley walked over to the shotgun tied to the chair, ran a hand over the trigger guard, pulled at something. It caught the lamplight and Anselm saw that it was nylon fishing line that ran to the leg of an armchair.

'A booby trap so cheap, so primitive, so old. And here lies dead of it a killer with the most expensive and sophisticated training the modern world can provide.'

He tested the triggers with a black-gloved finger. 'Ah,' he said. 'Knew how to make this work, did your Mr Niemand. Breathe hard on the buggers and bang.'

'Michael, what?' said Anselm. 'Tell me. It's late, I'm tired and sober and I've got a knife wound nine inches long. What?'

O'Malley had the Heckler & Koch in his left hand. He transferred it to his right.

'I'm sorry about that,' he said. 'Sorry about this too.' He ran a hand over his curly head. 'Truly, I wish it were another way.'

It came to Anselm, as it had come to him in Beirut, that something had ended, something was over and gone. A still moment, the highest point of the pendulum's swing, the end of momentum, the dead point.

'Kaskis,' he said.

O'Malley was looking at Caroline. She was frozen, hands at her sides, holding herself like a Guardsman on parade, waiting for the Queen.

'I saved you, John,' said O'Malley. 'You and Riccardi. They wanted to kill all three of you, I talked them out of it. I said it wasn't necessary, you knew nothing, the idiot Riccardi less. I've given you eight good years. Well, eight years. Think of it that way. And I told you you weren't a journalist any more. I tried to warn you off.'

Anselm thought that he had never seen this look on O'Malley's face. His handsome poet's face was sad. He was going to kill both of them and he was sad that he had to do it.

O'Malley raised the weapon, held it on its side, weighed it in his hand, bounced it.

'This is awkward,' he said. 'I would really rather not. But. *Necessitas non habet legum.* Know the expression, boyo?'

Anselm nodded. He felt nothing. No panic this time.

'Yes, well ...' O'Malley raised the weapon and pointed it at Caroline.

'Sorry, darling,' he said. 'But think what you did to that poor old bugger Brechan on behalf of MI5.'

Grunts, not loud, several quick grunts.

O'Malley's face below the high cheekbone blew apart, his face seemed to break in two, divide, an aerosol spray of red in the air around his head, a piece of scarlet veil floating.

They stood.

The woman came in, went to Niemand, put her head down to his head, seemed to kiss him.

She jerked her head up.

'He's alive,' she said. 'For fuck's sake do something.'

Anselm looked at Caroline. She was grey-white, the colour of cemetery gravel. She shook her head and put her hand in a coat pocket and took out a cellphone.

'Right,' she said. 'Right.'

And then Caroline, holding the tiny device towards the light to see the keys, she moved her head, her long hair moved, she looked up and said to Jess in her upper-class voice:

'I don't suppose, I don't suppose you know where the film is?'

86

… HAMBURG …

IN THE BLUE underwater gloom of the workroom, Anselm and Baader and Inskip and Carla watched the big monitor.

The television anchor was too old to pull her hair back like a twelve-year-old Russian gymnast. She tested her lips swiftly. They worked. Collagen and cocaine did terrible things to lips.

All front teeth showing, she went through the preamble. Then she said:

We warn that the film contains images of violence that will shock. Please ensure that children are not watching.

The aerial view of wooded sub-tropical country, late in the day.

Angola, 1983. The oil-rich African country is in the grip of a long-running civil war in which the United States has intervened, spending millions of dollars in an attempt to counter Russian influence. This film was taken from a helicopter. Analysts say from the co-pilot's seat. They believe the film was unauthorised and the person filming took care not to be seen.

A village burning, thatched huts burning, several dozen huts, cultivated fields around them marked by sticks.

This nameless village is in northern Angola. There is no evidence of military activity.

On the ground now, another helicopter in view, no markings visible.

The filming is through the open door of the helicopter. Notice the dark edge to the right. The other helicopter is a Puma of a type used by the South African Defence Force.

Now a long panning shot, bodies everywhere, dozens and dozens of bodies. An enlarged still of a group of bodies.

These people have been overcome by something. There are signs of vomiting, stomach cramps and diarrhoea.

Another enlarged still. At least a dozen people lying near a crude water trough. Black people in ragged clothes, mostly women and children, a baby. Some have their hands held to their faces, some are face down on the packed dirt.

Medical experts say the signs of poisoning are even more apparent here. They are consistent with those produced by the biological poison ricin, which is made from a toxic protein found in castor oil seed.

Motion again, white men in combat gear carrying automatic weapons, standing around, six of them, relaxed, weapons cradled.

The frame held still, enlarged.

These men are American soldiers, part of a super-secret unit called Special Deployment, also known as Sudden Death. They were drawn from Special Forces Operational Detachment Delta Airborne stationed at Fort Bragg, North Carolina. Although they wear no insignia, they are armed with the Heckler & Koch MP5K, first issued in 1977. The man on the left carries a Mossberg Cruiser 500 shotgun, and Beretta 9mm handguns are visible on three of them. Their boots are Special Forces tropical issue.

We also know the names of four of these soldiers.

Circles around four heads.

Enlargements.

From the left, Maurice Tennant Gressor, Zoltan James Kaldor, Wayne Arthur Fitzgerald, and Joseph Elias Diab. These men are all dead, in circumstances that can only be called suspicious. It is thought that all except two of the Special Deployment members in this shot are dead.

The film moving again, two men in coveralls talking to a tall soldier, the only one without headgear, his back to the camera. The camera zooms in on the group, the soldier is talking to one of the civilians, a man with a moustache.

Freeze.

Enlargement.

This man is Dr Carl Wepener Lourens, then head of a South African company called TechPharma Global, an importer of chemicals. Lourens moved in white South Africa's highest military and political circles and travelled the world, frequently visiting Britain, the United States and Israel. His death in a fire at his company's premises outside Pretoria was reported recently. He was under investigation for currency and other offences committed under the apartheid regime.

Dr Lourens is also linked with an Israeli company called Ashken, said to be an Israeli military front engaged in defence research.

The film moving again. Lourens is speaking to the person next to him, a short man, balding, a mole on his cheek. The man shakes his head, gestures, palms upward.

Freeze. Enlargement.

This man is Donald Trilling, president of Pharmentis Corporation, fourth largest US pharmaceutical company, convenor of Republicans at Work. He is often described as one of the most influential men in America. When this film was taken, Trilling, a Vietnam veteran, was head of Trilling Research Associates of Alexandria, Virginia. Trilling Research was taken over by Pharmentis Corporation in 1988 and Trilling became head of Pharmentis. In 1989, a Congressional hearing was told that Trilling Research received US Defense Department contracts worth more than $60 million between 1976 and 1984. The details remain classified. These contracts are now believed to have been for research into chemical weapons, including one called Eleven Seventy, apparently a ricin-like poison.

It is now clear that millions of dollars found their way from the US Defense Department to Trilling Research and then to bank accounts linked to Dr Carl Lourens.

They are thought to be payment for the manufacture and testing of chemical weapons developed by Trilling.

The film moving again. The soldier is turning towards the camera when the picture goes dark.

Here film analysts think that the cameraman is trying to avoid being seen.

When the film resumes, the tall soldier is standing at the bodies lying around the water trough. He moves a man's head with his boot.

The man on the ground is alive.

The man moves his arm, his fingers move. The soldier shoots him in the head from a few inches, gestures with his left hand, a summoning gesture.

The soldier takes off his dark glasses, wipes his eyes with the knuckle of his index finger. His face is seen clearly.

Freeze.

Enlargement.

This is the Special Forces Delta Force officer in command of Special Deployment on this mission.

A still photograph of five smiling young soldiers in dress uniform. One head is circled.

This is the same young soldier photographed on graduation day with other members of his West Point class.

A montage, the soldier in the film side by side with the smiling West Point graduate.

This young American soldier is Michael Patrick Denoon, later a four-star general and, until three days ago, US Defense Secretary and aspirant presidential candidate.

Michael Denoon resigned as Defense Secretary of State shortly after being shown parts of this program. He will not be seeking the Republican nomination.

The Angolan film running again, Denoon and the soldiers going around shooting people where they lie, shooting them in the head – men, women, children, a baby.

The Angolan village is believed to have been targeted by mistake. Fifteen kilometres away was an encampment housing hundreds of military personnel. It is believed that no one in the village survived, dying either from the chemical weapon used or executed by the men of Sudden Death. The bodies are thought to have been loaded onto C-47 transport aircraft by the unit and dropped at sea off the South-West African coast.

There is today no trace of the nameless village. Not a sign that people, families, lived there. The victims have no monument. Documents we have seen place the blame for this terrible experiment, this atrocity, squarely with the military in the United States, South Africa and Israel.

The program went on, putting together the pieces. Kaskis, Diab, Bruynzeel, Kael, Serrano, Shawn, all had their moments.

'No mention of O'Malley,' said Baader. 'Why am I not surprised?'

In the last minutes of the television special, they watched Caroline Wishart, tall and elegant in chinos and a leather jacket. Ringing a bell in a white wall beside a wooden gate. No one comes but the camera peers over the wall and, for a moment, captures a picture of a tall, grey-haired man with a moustache standing by a swimming pool and shouting something, angry.

Then Caroline:

This millionaire's villa in Madeira is owned by a company called Claradine. Its directors are two Swiss lawyers. The man in the picture calls himself Jürgen Kleeberg. His real name is Dr Carl Lourens and he has been staying in this luxury home since shortly after his death in a fire was reported in South Africa.

'I take it that's the Jürgen Kleeberg once a guest at the Hotel Baur au Lac, Zurich,' said Inskip.

'That is the Jürgen,' said Anselm.

The program finished. The credits described Caroline Wishart as the chief investigative reporter of her newspaper.

'Well, you'll probably live,' said Baader. 'For a while.'

He left the room.

'Sound of polite cough,' said Inskip. 'What did that mean?'

'He thinks I may see Christmas,' said Anselm.

'I wasn't told this job was life-threatening.'

'Only for the living,' said Carla. 'You have nothing to fear.'

87

... BIRMINGHAM ...

HE WAS dreaming about walking down a mountain path. There was someone ahead of him, talking to him in Greek, a boy, his cousin Dimi. And then Dimi started speaking in Afrikaans. He stopped and turned, and it wasn't Dimi. It was his father, the lined brown adult face on a boy's body. The sight frightened Niemand, brought him awake. He opened his eyes, blinked, his vision blurred.

For a moment, he was without memory. Then he saw the tubes in his arms and chest, tubes taped down, realised. Joy at being alive flooded him until he thought of Jess. He had sent her away, hoping that they were not watching the farmhouse, not waiting beside the lane. But even if she had got away from the farm, they would have found her. They could find anyone.

He closed his eyes and tears welled behind the lids, broke through the lashes, ran down his face, down his neck.

'You're crying,' said the voice, the lilting voice. He could not believe he was hearing it. He opened his wet eyes and she was there, leaning over him, inches from him, and then she was kissing his eyes, kissing his tears, he felt her lips and he hoped he was not dreaming. Life could not be that cruel.

'Crete,' said Jess. 'I'm going to take you to Crete. Get you well.'

'Yes,' said Niemand. 'I love you. You can take me to Crete.'

88

... HAMBURG

FRÄULEIN EINSPENNER'S last rites were at the crematorium in Billstedt. Anselm, four elderly women, and a middle-aged man were the only mourners. He knew one of them, Fräulein Einspenner's neighbour, Frau Ebeling.

Afterwards, she came up to him and they shook hands. She was carrying a parcel wrapped in brown paper.

'It was very peaceful,' she said. She had a round face, curiously unlined.

'I'm glad,' said Anselm.

'She went to the doctor and in the waiting room, she was sitting there, and she closed her eyes and she died. They didn't notice for a while. Her heart.'

Anselm nodded.

'It was as if she didn't expect to come home again. Everything was packed. Her clothes, everything.'

Anselm didn't know what to say.

'She was so fond of you,' said Frau Ebeling, putting her head to one side and studying him as if to find the reason.

'I was very fond of her,' said Anselm. 'I loved her.'

'Yes. Your whole family was very dear to her. She spoke often of them. Frau Pauline and Herr Lucas. Frau Anne and Herr Gunther and Herr Stefan and Fräulein Elizabeth and Herr Oskar. I know all the names, I heard them so often.'

'Did she ever speak of Moritz?'

'Moritz? No, not that I can recall.' She held out the package. 'This has your name on it. Perhaps she was going to give it to you when you visited again.'

Herr John Anselm was written on the top in a fine crabby hand, big letters.

It was almost dark when he got back to the office. He parked outside the annexe. Cold but no wind, it was going to be a clear night.

In his office, he unwrapped the parcel. A cardboard box, the size of two shoeboxes. It held five framed photographs of different sizes, unframed photographs, a dozen or more, old letters tied with a blue ribbon.

The face jumped out of all the photographs. A blond boy growing into a tall, fair-haired young man. In one of the framed pictures, he was in a

547

dinner jacket, elegant, laughing, cigarette between long fingers. The dark-haired young woman at his side had a nervous look, as if she wasn't quite sure what was happening.

The unframed pictures would fit the empty spaces in the old albums, fit neatly back into the corners that once held them.

It would be restoring the albums, Anselm thought, filling the gaps, making the record whole. He could put Moritz back into the family memory.

He untied the ribbon around the letters. They were all addressed to Fräulein Erika Einspenner in a slashing hand.

Not only letters. There was a photograph.

A group of soldiers, hands on each other's shoulders, a truck behind them.

Moritz was in the centre, bare-headed, smiling.

Anselm turned the picture over. On the back was written in the same bold handwriting:

Dienst bei die Fahne. Riga, August 1943. Moritz.

On service with the colours.

What colours?

He went down the passage. Baader, one leg on his desk, was reading a file.

'What do you know about World War Two uniforms?' said Anselm.

Baader looked at him, at the picture he was holding. 'What's that?' he said.

'A photograph.'

Baader held out his hand, looked at the picture. 'Himmler's scum,' he said. '*Waffen SS SD.* See the collar tabs on the *Sturmbahnführer*, this blond one in the middle? Black felt with silver piping.'

He turned the photograph over. 'Even worse. *Einsatzkommando.* Extermination squad. Scum's scum.'

He turned it back, studied it, looked at Anselm, back at the photograph. 'Looks a bit like you, the blond major. What's the interest in these murderers?'

Anselm held out his hand, took the photograph.

'Just something I found,' he said.

He went onto the balcony and smoked a cigarette. He stood in the corner, looked at the winter city, the white tower and the glowing skyscraper, the low lights of the Pöseldorf shore, a ferry heading for the Rabenstrasse landing. The light from Beate's desklamp lay across the balcony in a shaft, lay on him. His smoke drifted across it, sheet white, met the darkness, vanished in a straight line.

He took the final draw, arched the stub into the night, a dying star falling on the old, forgotten roses. Roses without names.

In his office, the phone rang.

'Are you running?' she said.
'I'm running.'
'When?'
'Five minutes.'
He waited for her to say it.
'Don't let me pass in the dark,' she said.
'Not if I can help it.'
'You can,' she said. 'You can.'

AN IRON ROSE

For Josephine Margaret Temple and
Alexander Roydon Harold Wakefield Temple:
first and best influences

'MAC,' THE VOICE said. 'Ned's dead.'

I couldn't take it in. I screwed up my eyes and tried to focus, head full of sleep and beer dreams.

'What?' I said.

He said it again.

'Jesus, no. When?'

'Don't know.' There was a pause. 'He's hangin in the shed, Mac. Can you come?'

Dead? Ned? What time was it? Two forty-five am. Sunday morning. I pulled some faces, fighting the fog and the numb incomprehension. Then I said, 'Okay. Right. Right. Listen, you sure he's dead?'

There was a long silence. Lew sniffed. 'Mac. Come.'

I was starting to think. 'Ambulance. You call the ambulance?'

'Yeah.'

'Cops?'

'No.'

'Call them. I'll be there in ten,' I said.

In the passage, Drizabone off the hook, straight out the door. Didn't need to dress. I'd fallen asleep in a cracked leather armchair, fully clothed, half-eaten pie on the arm, television on.

I didn't see the dog but I heard him land on the tray. Little thump. Short route through Quinn's Marsh, saved a few minutes by bumping open the gate with the roobars and putting the old Land Rover across the sheep paddock behind Ned Lowey's house. You could see the house from a long way off: all the lights were on.

I slewed around the corner and Lew was in my headlights: arms at sides, hair wild, stretched tracksuit top hanging over pyjama pants, barefoot.

I got out at a run. 'Stay there,' I shouted over my shoulder to the dog. 'Where?'

Lew led me down the path between the garage and the chook run to the big machine shed. The double doors were open and a slab of white light lay on the concrete apron. He stopped and pointed. He didn't want to go in.

'Wait for the ambulance in front,' I said.

For a moment the light blinded me or I didn't want to see. Then I focused on Ned, in striped pyjamas, arms neatly at his sides, hanging against the passenger side of the truck. His head was turned away from me.

553

When I got close I saw why Lew had not answered my question about whether he was sure Ned was dead.

I looked up. The rope was tied to a rolled steel joist about two metres above the truck cab. Ned had climbed up onto the cab roof, tied the rope to the joist, slid it along, tied a slipknot around his neck. And stepped off the cab roof.

'Mate, mate,' I said helplessly. I wanted to cry and be sick and run away. I wanted to be asleep again and the telephone not to ring.

Lew was sitting on the verandah step, shoulders slumped, head forward. I found the makings I kept in the Land Rover for when I needed a smoke, rolled a cigarette, walked the fifty metres to the gate. The night was black, absolutely silent. Then, far away, a speeding vehicle crossed the threshold of hearing.

I walked back, went into the house, down the long passage to Ned's bedroom. It was neat, like a soldier's quarters, the bed made drum tight.

Why was Ned in pyjamas?

On the way out, I paused in the sitting room, looking around the familiar space for no good reason. It was warm, the wood heater down low and glowing.

My eyes went to the photograph on the mantelpiece: Ned and my father, two big men in overalls, laughing, each with a king brown in hand. Between them the camera froze a thin boy in school uniform. He had a worried look. It was me.

I went outside and sat down beside Lew, looked at his profile. He was a mixture of Ned and his mother: long face, high cheekbones, strong jaw. 'How'd you find him?' I said.

He shivered. 'I came back about eleven. He's always asleep by then. Went to bed. Woke up, I don't know, half an hour ago, went to have a leak. Then when I got back into bed, I thought: he didn't say anythin.'

'Say anything?'

'You can't walk past his door without him saying somethin. Doesn't matter the time. Middle of the night. He hears everythin. And he didn't say anythin either when I went to the bathroom before I went to bed. But I didn't think about it then. So I got up and he wasn't in bed.' He paused. 'Then I went to look for the car and it was there, so I went to look for the truck. And ...'

He put his head in his hands. I put my arm around his shoulders, gave him a squeeze, helpless to comfort him, to comfort myself. We sat like that until the ambulance arrived. The police car was about a minute behind it. Two cops. By the time Lew and I had given statements, it was after 5 am and there were two police cars and four cops standing in the warm sitting room, smoking cigarettes and waiting for someone from forensic to arrive.

I BROUGHT Lew home with me. He couldn't stay there, in that familiar house made strange and horrible. We drove in silence in the silver early dawn, mist lying in the hollows, hanging in the trees, dams gleaming coldly. The first smoke of the day was issuing from farmhouse chimneys along the way.

I felt that I should speak to him, but I couldn't. He's just a kid, I said to myself. Two weeks from now he'll be over it. But I wouldn't be over it. Ever. Edward Lowey had been part of my life since I was ten. He was the link with my father. There were lots of questions I wanted to ask Lew, but this wasn't the time.

At home, I made scrambled eggs, but neither of us could eat. We sat there like people in an institution, not saying anything, looking at the table, not seeing anything. Finally, I shook myself and said, 'Let's get some wood in. They say it's going to get colder.'

I fed the dog the scrambled eggs and we went out into the raw morning, low cloud, spits of rain. While Lew walked around, hands in pockets, kicking things, I found another axe and put an edge on it on the grindstone. Then we chopped wood solidly, an hour, one on each side of the woodpile, not speaking, pausing only to take off garments. Chopping wood doesn't take your mind off things but it burns off the adrenalin and it sends you into a trancelike state.

Lew had just turned sixteen, but he was lean and muscled in the upper body and he matched me log for log and he didn't stop until I did. He was fetching a drink and I was standing there, leaning on my axe, sweat cooling, when an old red Dodge truck came up the driveway.

A tall woman, around thirty, dropped down from the cab: slim, long nose a little skew on her face, some weight in her shoulders, crew-cut dirty-blonde hair, overalls, pea jacket, no make-up.

'G'day,' she said. 'Allie Morris.'

I'd forgotten about our arrangement for today. I walked over and shook hands. 'Mac Faraday.'

Lewis came out the house carrying two glasses.

'We've had a bit of a shock,' I said. 'His grandfather …'

I didn't want to say it. 'He found his grandfather dead this morning.'

'I'm sorry,' she said. 'That's terrible.' She shrugged. 'Well, the other thing. I don't suppose this is the day for it …'

I said, 'It's the day. Never a better day.'

I introduced Lew and we left him to stack the wood and went into the smithy. I'd cleaned out the forge on Saturday morning and laid the fire: paper and kindling over the tue hole, coke around that and green coal banked around the coke. I lit the paper and started the fan blower. Allie Morris came over with the watering can and dampened the green coal. She'd taken off her coat. Under her overalls, she was wearing a shirt with heavy canvas sleeves.

'Useful shirt,' I said.

'Blacksmith's wife in England makes them. Got tired of looking at all that burnt skin.'

'It's not a good look.'

'Sure you know what you're doing here?' she said. 'Never heard of anyone doing it.'

'People did it for hundreds of years.'

'Well, maybe they didn't have any choice. You could get a new one. Stick this thing in a museum.'

'Making things on this when Queen Victoria was a baby,' I said.

'Yes,' she said. 'And it's outlived its usefulness. Might as well hang on to your old underpants.'

I thought about this for a moment. 'Wish someone else would hang on to my old underpants,' I said. 'While I'm wearing them.'

Allie was pushing coal towards the glowing coke. She looked up, bland. 'Surprised to hear that position's vacant,' she said. 'Give it a blast. We'll be here all day.'

I gave the fire a blast. Allie Morris was a quali?ed farrier and blacksmith, trained in England. For a long time I'd been looking for someone to do the horse work and help in the smithy. Then I saw her advertisement in the Situations Wanted.

'I'd be in that if the terms were right,' she'd said on the phone. 'But I've got to tell you, I'm not keen on the business side.'

'You mean extracting the money?'

'In particular.'

'You want to come around on Sunday? Eight–thirty? Or any time. Give me a hand with something. We'll talk about it.'

I'd explained what I wanted to do.

It took a good while to get the fire right: raking and wetting until we had a good mass of burning coke that could be compacted.

'What I had in mind,' I said, 'you do the horse work, I take the bookings, keep up the stores, send out the bills, and get the buggers to pay.'

'Last item there,' said Allie. 'That's the important function. That's where I fall down.' She shook her head. 'Horse people.'

'Tight as Speedos,' I said.

'I had to tell this one bloke, I'm coming around with two big men and we're going to fit him with racing shoes, run him over the jumps. And he still took another week to pay up.'

'I'll need your help with some general work too,' I said. 'Sometimes I can't cope. And I'm not all that flash on the finer stuff.'

'Sounds good to me,' said Allie, banking coal around the coke. 'Got to get even heat for a job like this. Get the heat to bounce off the coal, eat the oxygen. Reducing fire, know the term?'

'Use it all the time,' I said.

Lew and the dog came in to watch. The dog went straight to his spot on a pile of old potato sacks in a corner, well away from sparks and flying bits of clinker.

Finally, Allie said, 'All right, let's do it.' She was flushed from the heat. It was an attractive sight.

I had a sliding block and tackle rigged from the steel beam in the roof and a chain around the battered anvil's waist. Lew and I pulled it up, an unwieldy 285 pounds of metal. You could tell the weight from the numbers stamped on the waist: two-two-five, standing for two hundredweights, or 224 pounds; two quarters of a hundredweight, fifty-six pounds; and five pounds. To get it under the smoke hood and onto the coke bed, Allie slid it slowly down a sheet of steel plate.

When it was in place, I unshackled the chain.

'Got any tea?' Allie said. 'This'll take a while.'

'I'll make it,' said Lew. He looked glad of something to do.

It took about an hour in the intense heat to get the face of the anvil to the right colour. We put on gloves and I got the chain around its waist, pulled it to the lip of the forge and Lew and Allie hoisted it. The day was dark outside and we had no lights on in the smithy. But when the anvil came out and hung in the air, turning gently, the room filled with its glowing orange light and we stood in awe for a moment, three priests with golden faces.

Carefully, we set the dangerous object down on the block of triple-reinforced concrete I used for big heavy jobs.

'Well,' said Allie, 'the thing will probably break in half. Put your helmet on.'

I handed her a six-pound flatter and a two-pound hammer and we went to work, hammering, dressing the face and edges of the anvil, trying to get the working surface back to something like its original flatness.

'Lew's grandfather found this anvil,' I said. 'In the old stables at Kinross Hall. Bought it off them for twenty dollars. Gave it to my old man.'

ALLIE MORRIS had just left when they arrived, two men in plainclothes in a silver Holden. I heard the car outside and met them at the smithy door. The dog came out with me. His upper lip twitched.

'Lie down,' I said. He turned his head and looked at me, lay down. But his eyes were on the men.

'MacArthur John Faraday?' the cop in front said.

I nodded.

'Police,' he said. They both did a casual flash of ID.

I put out my hand. 'Look at those.'

They glanced at each other, eyes talking, handed over the wallets. The man who'd spoken was Detective Sergeant Michael Bernard Shea. His offsider was Detective Constable Allan Vernon Cotter. Shea was in his forties, large and going to flab, ginger hair, faded freckles, big ears. He had the bleak look men get on assembly lines. Cotter was dark, under thirty, neck muscled like a bull terrier's, eyes too close, hair cropped to a five-o'clock shadow. Chewing gum.

I gave them the wallets back.

'Lewis Lowey here?' Shea said.

'Yes.'

'Like a word with you first, then him. Somewhere we can sit down?'

'What kind of word? We've given statements.'

Shea held up a big hand. 'Informal. Get some background.'

I put my head back in the door. 'Police,' I said. 'Don't go anywhere, Lew.'

I took them over to the shed that served as the business's office. It held a table, three kitchen chairs, and a filing cabinet bought at a clearing sale. I sat down behind the table. Cotter spun a chair around and sat down like a cowboy.

Shea perched on the filing cabinet behind Cotter. He looked around the room, distaste on his face, sniffing the musty air like someone who suspects a gas leak. 'So you been here, what, five years?' he said.

'Something like that,' I said.

'And you know this bloke?'

'A long time.'

'First on the scene.'

'Second.'

'You and the kid. First and second.'

I didn't say anything. Silence for a while. Shea coughed, a dry little cough.

'You, ah, friendly with the kid?' This from the offsider, Cotter. He was staring at me, black eyes gleaming like sucked grapes. His ears were pierced, but he wasn't wearing an earring. He smiled and winked.

I said to Shea, 'Detective Constable Cotter just winked at me. What does that mean?'

'I'll do this, Detective Cotter,' Shea said. 'So Lewis rang you at...?'

'Two forty-five. It's in the statement.'

'Yeah. He says you got there about two fifty-five. Looking at his watch all the time.'

'About right.'

'Clarify this for me,' Shea said. 'It's twenty kilometres from here. You get dressed and drive it in ten minutes. Give or take a minute.'

'It's fifteen the short way,' I said. 'I didn't get dressed. I was dressed. I fell asleep dressed. And I didn't obey the speed limit.'

Shea rubbed the corner of his right eye with a finger like a hairy ginger banana. 'Old bloke worth a bit?'

'Look like it?'

'Can't tell sometimes. Keep it under the mattress. That his property?'

I nodded.

'Who stands to benefit then?'

'There's just Lew, his grandson.'

'Then there's you.'

'I'm not family.'

'How come you inherit?'

I said, 'I'm not with you.'

'We found his will,' Shea said. 'You get a share.'

I shrugged. This was news to me. 'I don't know about that.'

Cotter said, 'Got any gumboots?' Pause. 'Mr Faraday.'

I looked at him. 'Dogs got bums? Try the back porch.'

Cotter got up and left.

'We'll have to take them away,' Shea said.

I got up and went to the window. Cotter had the Land Rover passenger door open and was poking through the mess inside.

'Your man got a warrant?' I said.

'Coming to that,' Shea said. He took a folded piece of paper out of his jacket pocket. 'Here's your copy.'

'Got something in mind?' I said.

It was Shea's turn to say nothing, just look at me, not very interested.

I heard the sound of a vehicle, then another car nosed around the corner of the house. Two men and a woman.

'The gang's all here,' I said. 'Go for your life.'

Shea coughed. 'I'm going to ask you to come into town for an interview.

When we're finished here. The young fella too. Don't want you to talk to him before. Okay? So you can't travel with him. He can come with me or you can make some other arrangement, get a friend. You're entitled to be represented. Kid's gotta have someone with him. You don't want to come of your own accord, well, we do it the other way. Believe me.'

There wasn't a way around this. 'Let me explain this to Lew,' I said.

Shea nodded. We went over to the smithy. Lew was where I'd left him, puzzled and frightened. I sat down next to him.

'Lew,' I said, 'listen, mate. They're going to search the place. Then they want us to go into town so they can ask us some more questions. They'll record everything. You'll have a lawyer with you, just so everything's done right. All right?'

'We told them,' Lew said.

'I know. It's just the way they do it. I'll tell you about it later. I'm going to arrange for your lawyer now. We can't talk to each other again before the interviews. I'll be there when you finish.'

He looked at me, looked away, just a child again in a world suddenly turned from stone to water. He was on the edge of tears. I gave him a little punch in the arm. 'Mate, this'll be over in next to no time. Then we can have a feed, get some sleep. Hold on. Right?'

He moved his head, more tremble than a nod. He was exhausted.

I rang the lawyer who'd handled my father's estate. 'You're better off with someone who specialises in crime,' he said. 'What's your number?'

I waited by the phone. A tall cop came in, opened the Ned Kelly stove and poked around in the ashes. When he'd finished, he started on the chest of drawers, working from bottom to top like a burglar.

The phone rang.

'Mr Faraday?'

I said yes.

'I'm Laura Randall.' Deep voice. 'Mike Sherman said you had a matter.'

I told her what was happening.

She said nothing until I'd finished. Then she said, 'Ring me just before you leave. I'll meet you there.'

The search took nearly two hours: house, smithy, all the outbuildings. When they'd finished, the five of them had a conference outside. Shea came into the office and said, no expression, 'Firearm on the premises.'

I nodded.

'.38 Colt Python.'

I nodded again.

'Licence?'

'No.'

'Unlicensed firearm?'

I savoured the moment. 'Special permit.'

'Special permit. That's for what reason?'

I said, 'See if they'll tell you, Detective Sergeant.'

He didn't like this. 'I will. I will.'

When they'd bagged the gun we set off for town, Shea and Cotter in front with Lewis, then me in the Land Rover, then the other car. It began to rain as we crested the last hump of the Great Dividing Range, all sixty metres of it.

I parked behind Shea and Cotter in front of the police station, an old two-storey redbrick building with an ugly new annexe. The other cops drove through an entrance marked official parking only.

As I got out, the door of a BMW on the other side of the narrow street opened and a tall woman with dark hair pulled back in a loose ponytail got out. She took a leather briefcase out of the back seat and came over.

'Mr Faraday?' she said. 'Laura Randall.' Her breath was steam in the cold afternoon. She was in her thirties, thin, plain, pale skin, faintly amused twist to her mouth. The clothes were expensive: brown leather bomber jacket, dark tartan trousers over gleaming boots.

We shook hands. Shea, Cotter and Lew were out of the car, standing on the pavement. Cotter had his hands in his pockets and a cigarette in his mouth. He looked like a bouncer on his break.

I moved around so that I had my back to them. 'That's your client,' I said. 'The young fella. He told them the story this morning. He doesn't know anything. The fat one over there, Shea, he's hinting he thinks the kid and I might be in it, killed Ned for the inheritance. Maybe more than just friends, too.'

She looked me hard in the eyes. 'Sexually involved?' she said. 'Are you?'

'Only with the opposite sex,' I said. 'And that infrequently.'

She didn't smile.

I said, 'There's nothing like that. Lew's a good kid, been messed around by his mother. His grandfather was my father's best friend.' I paused. 'He was my best friend too.'

Laura Randall said, 'You need to understand, if he makes an admission in this interview, they'll call me as a witness. I won't be able to represent him.'

I shook my head. 'Can't happen. Nothing to admit. I just want someone with him, make him feel he's not alone with these blokes.'

'You'll need someone with you too,' she said.

'No,' I said. 'Not with this lot. I've been on fishing trips with pros.'

She gave me an interested look. 'Talk to you later,' she said. 'Mr Faraday.'

'Ms Randall.' To the dog, I said, 'Stay.'

It was dark before we got home and we were both staring-eyed with fatigue. After I switched off the engine, we sat in silence for a while. Finally, I shook myself into action. 'Okay. Lew, that's over. There's two big pies in the top rack of the freezer. Bang them in the microwave, twenty minutes on defrost. I'll get the fire going.'

We ate lamb pies, made for me by the lady down the road, in front of the fire, watching football in Perth on television. Lew drank half a glass of beer. I drank half a bottle of red. He had barely stopped chewing when his head fell onto his shoulder. I made the bed in the spare room, put a pair of pyjamas on the pillow, woke him and pushed him off to bed. Then I started work on the second half of the bottle.

In the night, far from dawn, I sat up, fully awake, swept the blankets from my legs. Deep in sleep, some noise had alarmed me. Not the wind nagging at the guttering and the loose tiles, shaking the windows, making the trees groan like old men being massaged. Not the occasional slash of rain hitting the panes like pebbles. Not the house timbers creaking and ticking and uttering tiny screeches, not the plumbing gargling and knocking, not the creatures moving in the roof.

Something else.

When I'd first come from Melbourne, to my father's house at the crossroads, the old life's burden of fear and vigilance heavy on my back, I'd sat in the dark in every room in turn, eyes closed, listening, pigeonholing sounds. And I had slept fitfully for weeks until I knew every night noise of the place. Only then was I sure that I would hear the sounds that I was always listening for: a vehicle stopping on the road or in the lane, a squeak of the new gravel I'd put around the house, the thin complaint of a window being forced.

Now I heard the sound again: the flat, hard smack of a door slamming.

It was the smithy door. Once or twice a year I'd forget to slide the bolt. The wind would gradually prise the door open, then slam it triumphantly and start prising again.

I got up and went into the black, wet night. The dog came from nowhere to join me, silently.

FRANCIS KEANY was waiting for us in front of the dilapidated mansion called Harkness Park, sitting in his warm Discovery, smoking a panatella and listening to *La Traviata* on eight speakers. When the window slid down, the warmth and the aromatic Cuban smoke and the music floated out to us where we stood in the cold and the rain and the mud.

'Boys,' he said. 'You know I don't like to wait around when you're on my time.'

Stan Harrop cleared his nose and spat, a sound like a blow dart being fired. The missile hit the right front hubcap. 'We're not on your fucking time, Frankie,' he said. 'We're here to look at a job. Don't like it, off we fuck.'

Francis's eyes narrowed. Then self-interest clicked in and he cocked his head and smiled, the smile that had won many a society matron's heart. And the rest, so the word went. 'You're absolutely right, Stan,' he said. 'I'm getting ahead of myself. Let me show you the magnitude of the task.'

He got out of the vehicle, put a Barbour hat on his sleek head to complete his Barbour outfit, and led us down the driveway and into the wilderness. We couldn't get far: this was a garden gone feral. Francis started down what was once a path and was now a dripping tunnel that narrowed rapidly. He wrestled with branches for a few metres, gradually losing confidence. Finally, faced with an impassable thicket, he gave up. We reversed out, Lew in front, then me, then Flannery, then Stan, then Francis.

Francis pushed his way past us and tried another matted and sodden avenue. A few metres in, he missed an overgrown step, fell forward and disappeared into a dank mass of vegetation. His shriek hung in the cold air, wild enough to send hundreds of birds thrumming skywards.

We all stopped. Stan began to roll a cigarette one-handed as we waited for Francis to emerge. 'Hurt yourself?' he said, no trace of sympathy in his voice, as the wet figure struggled upright, cursing.

'Course I fucking hurt myself,' Francis said, each word a small, distinct explosion. 'Look at this shit on my trousers.'

'On?' Stan said. 'We know there's a shit *in* your trousers. What are we looking for here, Frankie? Don't have to hack my way with a bloody machete to see it's a jungle.'

563

Francis was examining the slime on his palms, mouth pursed in disgust. 'My clients want it restored,' he said. 'I was trying to show you the enormity of the task.'

'Enormity? That's not the word you want, Frankie,' Stan said. He was a pedant about language. 'Try enormousness. And if they want it bloody restored, what do they want it bloody restored *to*?'

'I don't know,' Francis snarled. 'Don't fucking care. Its former fucking glory. That's your department.'

'Francis Keany doesn't know and doesn't fucking care. You should put that on your business cards.'

Stan took pleasure in giving Francis this kind of needle. The only reason Francis tolerated it was because without Stan he wouldn't be able to take on jobs like this. Francis had started out as a florist and conned his way into the garden design trade. He apparently wasn't too bad at doing little squares of box with lollipops in the middle and iceberg roses lashed to dark-green trellis. But then one of his satisfied society matrons commissioned him to do a four-acre garden from scratch near Mount Macedon. Francis panicked: you couldn't fill four acres with little squares of *Buxus semper-virens*. You couldn't copy another big garden. People would notice. And then, somehow, he heard about Stan Harrop.

Stan had started work at twelve as a garden boy at Sefton Hall in the south of England. Four years later, he lied about his age and went off to war. When he came back, five years on, he was all of twenty-one, sergeant's stripes on his arm, the ribbon of the Military Cross on his chest, and a long bayonet scar on his right forearm. It was twenty years before he left Sefton Hall again, this time to catch the P&O liner to Sydney to be head gardener on an estate outside Mittagong. Over the next twenty years, he ran four other big gardens. Then he bought fifty acres with a round hill on it down the road from Ned Lowey and started a nursery. That was where Francis Keany found him. It was the luckiest day of Francis's life. And for Ned and Flannery, and later for me, it meant fairly regular work at a decent rate of pay.

'There's a little clear bit over there,' Lew said. We followed him through a grove of plane trees into a clearing. For some reason, rocky soil perhaps, nothing had grown here. You could at least see some way into the jungle. Overgrown shrubs were everywhere. Mature deciduous trees – oaks, ashes, elms, planes, maples, birches – stood in deep drifts of rotting leaves. To the left, what might once have been a tapestry hedge of yew and privet and holly was a great impenetrable green barricade. Rampant, strangling holly had spread everywhere, gleaming like wet plastic. All trace of the garden's form, of its design, had been obliterated by years of unchecked growth.

'These clients of yours,' Stan said, 'they understand the *magnitude* of what they're getting into here? Financially speaking.'

'Leon Karsh,' Francis said. 'Food. Hotels. Travel. Leon and Anne Karsh.'

Stan looked at me. 'Food. Hotels. Travel. How do you suggest we approach this thing, Mac?'

I said, 'Food. Hotels. Travel. From the air. We approach it from the air. Aerial photography.'

'My feelings exactly,' Stan said. 'Francis...?'

'Aerial photographs?' Francis said. 'Are you mad? Can you imagine the expense? Why don't you just poke around and ...'

'Aerial photographs,' said Stan. 'Aerial photographs and other research. Paid by the hour. Or we fuck off.'

You could see Francis's fists clench in the Barbour's roomy pockets. 'Of course,' he said through his capped teeth. 'Whatever it takes.' Pause. 'Stan.'

Before we left, we went down the road and looked at the derelict three-storey bluestone flour mill on the creek at the bottom of the Karsh property. Flannery went off to look at the millrace pond. He was obsessed by machinery, the older the better. When he came back, he had a look of wonder on his face, the face of a naughty thirty-five-year-old boy. 'Sluicegate'll still work,' he said. 'Someone's been greasing it.'

The wind had come up and, while we looked at the building, a slate tile came off the roof and sailed down into the poplar thicket along the creek.

'Dangerous place to be, down the creek,' Flannery said.

We drove back via the country cemetery where we'd buried Ned. It was a windblown acre of lopsided headstones and rain-eroded paths on a hill-side above a weatherboard Presbyterian church. Sheep grazed in the paddock next door, freezing at the sight of the dog.

'I'll just pop this on,' Stan said. He'd made a wreath out of ivy and holly for Ned's grave. He hadn't come to the funeral. 'I can't, Mac,' he'd said on the phone. 'I can't go to funerals. Don't know what it is. Something from the war. Ned knew. He'll understand. Explain to the boy, will you?'

We all got out, into the clean, biting wind. This was my third visit to the place. My father's grave was here too. You could see for miles, settled country, cleared, big round hills with necklaces of sheep, roads marked by avenues of bare poplars. Ned's grave was a bit of new ploughing in the cemetery. Two magpies flew up angrily at our approach, disturbed at the rewarding task of picking over the rich new soil for worms.

Stan put the wreath on the mound. 'Sleep well, old son,' he said. 'We're all better for knowing you.'

I walked around to my father's grave. It needed weeding and the silver paint in the incised inscription was peeling. *Colin MacArthur Faraday, 1928–1992*, it said. Under the date, a single line, Ned's choice: *A free and generous spirit come to rest.*

Ned had made all his own arrangements for his burial: plot, coffin, picked and paid for. It was typical. He was organised in everything, probably why he got on so well with my father, who made life-changing decisions in an instant at crossroads and regarded each day as the first day of creation.

'You ask yourself why,' Stan said as we neared his gate.

'You ask yourself who,' I said.

ALLIE MORRIS had just arrived when we parked next to the smithy. She was wearing her bluey and a beanie and yellow leather stockman's gloves. Although she hadn't known Ned, she'd come to the funeral.

'I saw your legs at the funeral,' I said. 'First time.' She'd worn a dark-blue pinstripe jacket and skirt and a black shirt and black stockings. Ned would have approved. All the other men at the funeral did, many of them sober.

She scratched her forehead under the beanie with a thumbnail. 'Legs?' she said. 'You only had to ask. What's happening today?'

We went over to the office to look at the bookings and check the answering machine.

'You've got two over at Miner's Rest, then the Shetland lady wants you. After that, there's a new one at Strathmore. In the badlands.'

'Badlands,' she said. 'Take the badlands before the Shetlands. Last time one of the things tried to bite my bum.'

'The Shetland,' I said. 'A discerning creature. Knows a biteworthy bum when it sees one.'

'I'm not sure how to take that.'

'The right way. Leave you free on Thursday? Bit of hot work here.'

After she'd gone, I got the forge going, got to work on some knifemaking.

We had the reading of the will the day after Ned's funeral. He'd made it soon after I reopened the smithy opposite the pub in the potato country, an hour and a half from Melbourne. It was the year Lew came to live with him following his mother's drowning off Hayman Island. Monica Lowey tried a lot of strange things in her time but scuba diving on speed was the least well-advised. The property was Ned's main asset. He wanted it sold and the proceeds divided 60:40 between Lew and me, Lew to get his share when he was twenty-five. I got the tools and the backhoe. Lew got everything else. And then there was a little personal matter: he asked me to use some of my share to look after Lew.

I was working with the file when I heard the vehicle. I went to the door. Silver Holden. Shea and Cotter. Shea got out, carrying a plastic bag.

'They say you can have this back,' he said.

I took the bag. I'd forgotten how heavy the Python was.

Shea looked around as if contemplating another search. 'Buy any rope recently?'

'Fuck off,' I said.

He gave me the look. 'Not helpful, the Feds,' he said. 'Fucking up themselves.'

'That right?'

Shea put both his hands in his pockets, hunched his shoulders, shuddered. 'Jesus, how d'ya live out here? Santa's dick. Fella down the road here, he can't sleep. Knows your noise. Puts a time on you goin past. Good bit after the kid called the ambulance.'

'Amazing what best practice detective work will reveal,' I said. 'What's forensic say? There's no way Ned would top himself.'

He sighed, moved his bottom jaw from side to side. 'Listen, I asked before. In his background. Anything we should know? Old enemies, new ones, anything?'

I shook my head. 'I never heard anything like that.'

'Well,' Shea said. He took his hands out of his pockets, rough, ruddy instruments, and rubbed them together. 'It's not clear he done himself or there's help. Anyway, doesn't look like he had health worries. Ring me you think of anything.' He took out his wallet and gave me a card. As he was getting into the car, he said, 'So there's life after, hey?'

'After what?' I knew what he meant.

'After being such a big man in the Feds they let you keep your gun.'

'You've got to have life before to have life after,' I said.

He pursed his lips, nodded, got in.

I went back to work on the knife, thinking about Ned. Suicide? The word burned in me.

IT TOOK me three days to clean out Ned's house. I started outside, working my way through his collection of sheds, carting stuff back to my place. On the morning of day three, I steeled myself and went into the house. There had been no fire for more than a week now and the damp cold had come up from under the floorboards and taken hold.

I did Ned's room first: there was no other way. I packed all the clothes into boxes, put the few personal things in Ned's old leather suitcase. Then I started to pack up the rest of the house. It wasn't a big job. Ned's neatness and his spartan living habits made it easy. I left the sitting room for last. It was a big room, made by knocking two rooms into one. There were two windows in the north wall, between them an old table where Ned had done his paperwork. There were signs that the cops had taken a look. Both drawers were slightly open.

I took the deep drawers out. One held stationery, a fountain pen, ink bottle, stapler, hole punch, thick wads of bills and invoices held together with rubber bands, a large yellow envelope, Ned's work diary, a ledger. The other one held a telephone book, a folder with all the papers relating to the purchase of the property and the regular outgoings, three copies of the *Dispatch*, string, a magnifying glass, a few marbles, and a wooden ruler given away by a shop in Wagga Wagga. The yellow envelope was unsealed. I looked into it: staples, rubber bands, string, assorted things. I stuffed the newspapers into a garbage bag and packed everything else into a box.

At the end of the day, I had all the things to go to the Salvation Army in one shed, the things to keep in another, and the contents of Lew's room and Ned's personal things on the back of the Land Rover. I also had two large bags of stuff to be thrown away.

I drove home via the shire tip and dumped the bags. Then it was all speed to the Heart of Oak, the pub a few hundred metres from the smithy. I was parked outside, taking out the key, taste of beer in my mouth, when the question came to me.

Why would Ned keep three copies of a newspaper in his drawer? All the other papers were in the shed, tied in neat bundles for the recyclers.

Forgot to throw them out.

No. Everything else in that drawer had a purpose.

I turned the key. Back to the tip. The man was closing the gate as I arrived.

'Don't tell me,' he said. 'You want it back.'

The bags were where I'd left them, and the papers were on top of the one I opened.

I took them into the Heart of Oak with me. It was just me and Vinnie the publican and a retired potato farmer called George Beale. Vinnie and George were playing draughts, a 364-day-a-year event contested in a highly vocal manner.

'Now that's what I call a dickhead move,' George was saying as I came in. 'Told you once, told you a thousand times.'

'Funny how I keep winnin',' Vinnie said.

'Sometimes,' said George, 'the Lord loves a dickhead.'

They said Gidday and Vinnie drew a beer without being asked.

The papers were about six weeks old, the issues of a Monday and Tuesday in April and a Thursday in June. The front-page lead in Monday's paper was headlined: BODY IN OLD MINE. I vaguely remembered reading this, people talking about it in the pub. The story read:

Police are investigating the discovery of a skeleton at the bottom of an old mine shaft at Cousin Jack Lead in the State forest near Rippon.

The macabre find was made by Dean Meerdink of Carlisle, whose dog uncovered the shaft entrance and fell about ten metres, landing on a ledge.

'We were out with the metal detector,' Mr Meerdink said. 'Deke was off looking for rabbits and he just vanished. I was calling his name and I heard a faint bark. Then I saw this hole and I thought: he's a goner. I didn't want to get too close in case there was a cave-in, so I went back and rang the shire.'

Three CFA firemen with a ladder went to the scene and shone a spotlight down the shaft.

'The shaft goes almost straight down and then branches off parallel to the surface,' said CFA fireman Derek Scholte. 'The dog was fine and I was about to go down when I saw the skull. We called in the police.'

A police spokesman said the remains were human and had been taken to Melbourne for forensic examination.

I turned to Tuesday's paper. The follow-up story was also on the front page, under the headline: MINE BODY IS YOUNG WOMAN.

It began:

The remains of a body found in an old mine shaft near Rippon yesterday have been identified as those of a young woman.

Melbourne forensic scientist James LaPalma said yesterday the skeleton was that of a woman, probably under twenty. It was at least ten years old. The cause of death had not been positively ascertained but an initial examination suggested that her neck had been broken.

A spokesman for the Victoria Police said the discovery was being treated as a murder. An inquiry was underway.

The third paper, published on a Thursday in June, didn't have a front-page story on the skeleton in the mine. The story was on page three, under a photograph of a chain with a broken catch. On the chain was a small silver star.

MAN'S CHAIN FIND NEAR DEATH MINE

A man fossicking for gold with a metal detector near the mine shaft where the remains of a young woman's body were discovered last month yesterday found a silver ankle chain police say may belong to the woman.

The man, who does not wish to be identified, found the broken chain about one hundred metres from the entrance to the mine shaft and two hundred metres from the track through the State forest near Rippon.

The story went on to repeat the information in the two previous ones. The police asked anyone who recognised the chain to come forward. I read all three stories again, finished my beer and went home.

I RANG the newspaper and asked for Kate Fegan, the name on the stories about the skeleton.

'Kate, my name's Milton, Geoff Milton. *Canberra Times*. I wonder if you can get me up to date on a story you handled about six weeks ago?'

Lying comes easily when you've lived my kind of life.

'Well, sure. If I can.' She was young, probably just out of her cadetship.

'The body in the mine shaft. Has that been identified?'

'No. The teeth are really all they've got to go on and they're no help. She had all her teeth, no fillings. She probably never saw a dentist, so there wouldn't be any dental records. They're pretty sure it isn't someone local. That's about all.'

'Why's that?'

'There's no-one missing from around that time. No-one that age.'

'They've put a time on it?'

'Within a year, they reckon. Around 1985.'

'How'd they do that?

'The shire put a track in there in late 1984. Before that you had to walk about five kilometres through dense bush to reach the mine. Then there's the decomposition. There's a scientist in Sydney who specialises in that. Reckons no later than 1985 to '86. Firm on that.'

'And her age?'

'Around sixteen. They can tell from the wrist bones.'

I said, 'So there's nothing with the remains? Clothes, stuff like that?'

'Nothing. No trace of clothes or shoes, no jewellery. She was probably naked when she was thrown down.'

'And the cause of death?'

'Difficult to say. Her neck was broken. But that might have happened after death. That was in another story I wrote. Are you doing a story?'

'Just a general piece on missing girls,' I said. 'So they don't hold out much hope of identifying her?'

'It would be pure luck, they say. I could fax you the clippings.'

'Thanks, but I think I've got everything I need. You've been a big help.'

As I put the phone down, Lew came in, tracksuit and runners, hair wet with rain, sallow skin shining.

'You play in this?' I said.

'Just the short game. He made me hit about a million.'

'He's a hard man. Hope it's worthwhile. Listen, I want to talk to you about school.'

Lew had dropped out of school at the beginning of the year. I knew Ned had tried everything to prevent it happening but the boy became withdrawn and Ned gave up. I think his fear was that Lew would end up running away, as his mother had.

'School.' Lew took on a wary look. 'I've got to shower.'

'Hold on, mate,' I said. 'Ned asked me to look after you. That doesn't give me any rights. But I want you to know what I think, okay?'

He didn't look at me. 'Okay.'

'Leaving school at sixteen is for people who for some reason don't have any choice. That's not you. I want you to think about going back.'

He screwed up his face. 'Mick says I could be a pro.'

'Millions of kids want to do that, Lew. Maybe it'll happen. But give yourself some other options.'

He looked at me for a moment, in his dark eyes something I couldn't read. 'Got to shower,' he said and left the room.

I'd done my duty. Ned would have wanted me to try, but pushing it wouldn't work. I wasn't much and I wasn't family but I was all Lew had now and he was at the age when the testosterone and the self-doubt turn some boys into unpredictable explosive devices. I couldn't be a parent to him. The best I could hope for was that he would value my friendship, trust me. I had always been comfortable with him, liked the dry sense of humour he'd got from his grandfather's genes and example. From the moment he came into my house to stay on that grim early morning, he'd fitted into the routines of the place. He helped out without being asked, washed clothes, vacuumed, made fires, cooked. By Ned's account, Lew's life with his mother had been anything but easy. You could read some of that in his self-contained manner, but he was still just a boy in most ways.

I started work on supper: beef and vegetable stew. Open freezer door, take out two portions of beef and vegetable stew, made two weeks before. Place in microwave to defrost. Open bottle of beer. All the while I was trying to recall myself at Lew's age. But I couldn't remember where I'd been then, the places came and went so quickly.

I took the beer to the sitting room, lit the fire and switched on the early television news. A man with a face immobilised by cosmetic surgery said: *Heading tonight's bulletin: Victoria goes to the polls in five weeks. The Premier, Mr Nash, today called a snap election fourteen months before the end of the government's term.*

James Nash appeared on the screen seated next to his deputy, the Attorney General, Anthony Crewe, who was the MP for these parts. Nash was short and balding, with a worried expression. His suits had an inherited look. Crewe, on the other hand, looked like the advocate you want to plead your case to an all-female heterosexual jury: sharp features, smooth hair, dimpled chin. He had a wry, knowing smile and his suits lay on him like a benediction.

'The Nash government hasn't been afraid to take the hard decisions,' the Premier said. 'We're confident that the people of Victoria value that and want us back for a third term of office.' He didn't look at all confident.

'Premier,' said a male voice, 'how do you react to allegations within your own party that this election is designed to stave off a leadership challenge from Mr Crewe, the Attorney General?'

Crewe smiled his wry smile and said, 'I'll answer that if I may, Premier. Mr Nash has my complete support and loyalty. There is no leadership challenge, election or no election. I'm happy to repeat that as many times as you want me to.'

The rest of the news was the usual line-up of accidents, strikes, bomb threats and businessmen in court, concluding with the heartwarmer: a man had rescued a guinea pig from a burning house.

Lew was silent during our meal but I couldn't feel any tension in him, so I didn't make an effort to talk. When we'd finished, he said, 'Good stew. Gotta show me how to do it. I'll wash.'

I left him washing up and went out to the office, picking up the dog on the way. The night was still and clear. I heard a car door slam down at the pub and a woman's laugh. I thought about the naked girl falling down the mine shaft, into the absolute blackness of the earth. Was she still alive when she was stuffed into the opening in the ground?

I'd put the boxes with Ned's papers and personal things in a corner. The one holding the work diary was on top. I took the old ledger over to the table and leafed through the pages recording about twenty years of Ned's working life. In his neat, slanting hand, he had noted every job he did: date, client, type, number of hours worked, amount charged, expenses. The last entry read: *July* 10. *Butler's Bridge Nursery. Rip subsoil approx acre. Four hours.* $120.00. *Fuel 36 km.*

I turned back to 1985. The first half of the year had been lean, sometimes no more than three or four small jobs a week, entries like: *Mrs Readshaw. Fixed garage door. Half hour.* $5.00. *14 km.*

In July, things began to pick up. He had three weeks fencing a property at Trentham, then he did a big paving job, demolished a house, spent five weeks putting in a drive-way, gates and fences on a horse property. In October, he built a wall at Kinross Hall, the first of a series of jobs there that took up most of his time until late November. That was where he had found the old anvil. December and January were quiet, but from mid-February, for most of 1986, Ned worked on an old school being turned into a conference centre.

I read on, through 1987 and 1988, 1989, 1990. I went back and read 1982 to 1984. Then I sat back and thought. About fifteen employers' names occurred regularly across the years, people who gave Ned jobs big and small. I looked at 1982 again. Two employers appeared for the first time: J. Harris of Alder Lodge, the horse property, and Kinross Hall. I read forward. Alder Lodge became a regular source of work, most recently in May when Ned repaired a kicked-about stable. Kinross Hall employed him three times in 1982, for two long periods in 1983, for almost three months in 1984, and in 1985 he did five separate jobs there, the last a three-week engagement ending on 22 November. That was the end of Kinross Hall. Ned never worked there again.

I told Lew where I was going and the dog and I walked over to the pub. Half a dozen or so regulars were in place, including, down at the end of the bar talking to Vinnie, Mick Doolan. He was a small man, chubby, florid, head of tight grey curls and eyes as bright and innocent as a baby's. Everything about Mick was Australian except his Irish accent. I sat down next to him.

'Well, Moc,' he said, 'just sayin to Vinnie, can't get over Ned goin out like that. No sense in it. Not Neddy.'

'No,' I said.

He drank some stout. 'Had these police fellas around today. Murderers roamin the countryside and they're out makin life difficult for small businessmen such as misself.'

Mick was a dealer in what he called Old Wares, mostly junk, and the police took a keen interest in the provenance of his stock.

I said, 'Small businessman? The police think you're a small receiver of stolen property.'

He sighed. 'Well and that's exactly what I'm sayin, Moc. They form theories based on nothin but ignorance and then they devote the taxpayers' time to provin them. And naturally they can't. Vinnie, give us a coupla jars and a bag of the salt and vinegar. Two bags.'

'One, Vinnie,' I said. 'Mick, what's Kinross Hall?'

'Kinross Hall? It's what they used to call a place of safety. For naughty girls. They won't let you in, Moc.'

'Did Ned ever talk about working there? Late '85?'

He scratched his curls. 'Well, you know Ned. Not one to gossip.'

Vinnie arrived with the drinks and the chips. I paid.

I persisted. 'Did he ever say anything about the place?'

Mick munched on chips, washed them down with a big swallow, wiped his mouth. 'From what I could gather,' he said, 'he thought the place should be closed down. He said he wouldn't work there again.'

'Why?'

'He heard some story. Went to see the police about it and they told him basically piss off, mind yer own business. That's how I remember it.'

'What kind of story?'

'I couldn't tell you. He never said. You know Ned. Y'had to read his mind.' He offered me the chip packet. 'Now you're a cert for Satdee? And you'd be settin an example to the young fellas by attendin Wednesday trainin. I've bin workin on a new strategy, could be revolutionary, turnin point in the history of the game.'

I said, 'New strategy? What, we kick a goal? That'll shock 'em rigid.'

A GIRL with a broken neck, a naked girl, thrown down a mine shaft and the entrance covered. I couldn't get it out of my mind.

I thought about these things all through the morning as Allie Morris and I worked at the forge on an order for four dozen garden-hose hooks. It was pleasant enough work once we had forty-eight lengths: heat the flat steel to glowing red, use jaws in the anvil hardie hole to put a bend in one end, bend sixty centimetres down to make a flap, squeeze the top half in the vice to make a doubled length. Then curve the rest into a three-quarter circle over the anvil horn. The job was finished by putting a stake point on the end that went into the ground. Two people working with red-hot metal can be awkward, but we found a rhythm quickly, taking turns at heating, bending and hammering, Allie's deftness compensating for my occasional clumsiness.

We finished just before one pm: four dozen hose hooks, neatly stacked on Allie's truck to be dropped off for priming and painting.

'That's a day's work,' Allie said. 'Does the pub do a sandwich?'

We took turns to clean up in the bathroom I'd built on to the office so that I didn't have to traipse into the house in a filthy condition, and walked down the road in silence. The dog appeared ahead of us: taken a short cut through the neighbour's paddock. The sky was clearing, the cloud cover broken, harried fragments streaming east in full retreat.

Suddenly the world was high and light and full of promise. I hadn't talked much to Allie since she started. She had a reserved way about her, not rude but not forthcoming. And I didn't have any experience of working relationships like this. Man and a woman working with hot metal.

At the pub, it was just us and Vinnie and two hard-looking women in tracksuits playing pool. The fat one had a lipstick smear at the edge of her mouth. It looked like a bruise when she bent her head. Allie put the beers down and said, 'Know someone called Alan Snelling?'

'Know who he is.'

'What's he do?'

'Runs a few horses. Nice house. Nice cars. Gets married every now and again.'

'He asked me out.'

'Available to be asked out?' I instantly regretted the question.

She smiled, drank some beer, wiped away a thin tidemark of foam on her upper lip with a fingertip. 'I'm between engagements. He was at Glentroon Lodge yesterday, looking at a horse. Asked my opinion.'

'Who wouldn't,' I said. 'An older man. They can be attracted to capable young women.'

She put her head on one side. 'Older man? He's about your age.'

'That's what I mean.'

She laughed. Vinnie arrived with the toasted sandwiches.

'That was quick,' I said.

'Cook's day off,' said Vinnie. 'Everything's quicker on his day off. Including the time. Passes too fast.'

We talked business while we ate. On our way back, I said, 'About Alan Snelling.'

'Yes?'

'You want to think.'

'Meaning?'

'Alan's lucky,' I said. 'His old mum popped off. Nobody thought she had much, just the house, falling-over weatherboard. Not so. She had lots of things. Jewellery, coin collections, stamp collections, and a box with about $100,000 in cash in it. All up, worth about $400,000.'

'Well, I suppose there's an explanation,' said Allie.

I said, 'Also, Alan had a business partner, ran their little video hire business in Melbourne. Top little business, big as a phone booth, cash flow like Target. Then the partner was working out in his home gym and the machine collapsed on him. Fatal.'

'That's not lucky,' Allie said.

'They had key executive insurance,' I said. 'Half a million.'

We were going down the lane, when Allie said, 'What's that about his mother mean? I don't get it.'

'People could think Alan was parking invisible earnings with his mother.'

'Invisible? You mean illegal? Like drugs?'

I shrugged. 'Among the possibilities.'

'Jesus,' Allie said. 'How do you know this stuff?'

'I forget where I heard it,' I said.

Allie went off to a job. I should have worked on the knives but instead I rang the library at Burnley Horticultural College and asked them if they had any information on Harkness Park. The woman took my number. She rang back inside half an hour.

'I've tracked down a dozen or so references to it,' she said. 'There'll probably be more.'

'Any pictures or drawings?'

'No. It was designed by a man called Robert Barton Graham, an Englishman. It's not clear but he seems to have been brought out by a Colonel Stephen Peverell in 1896 to design the garden. He designed other gardens in Victoria while he was here, but they're all gone as far as we know.'

'Anywhere else I could try?'

She sighed. 'Our collection's pretty good. The State Library doesn't have anything we don't have. Not that you can get to, anyway. I'll keep looking.' As an afterthought, she said, 'Sometimes the local history associations can help. They might know who has information.'

I drove over to Brixton, the town nearest Harkness Park. I knew where the local history museum was, a brick and weatherboard building near the railway station. It had once been a factory with its own rail siding. Two elderly women sitting behind a glass display counter in the front room of the museum looked surprised to see a visitor.

'G'day,' said the smaller of the pair. She was wearing a knitted hat that resembled a chimney pot. Wisps of bright orange hair escaped at the temples. 'You're just in time. We're just having a cup of tea before we close.'

A hand-lettered sign said: Adults $2, Children $1, Pensioners Free. I put down a coin.

The second woman took the money. 'On your own, are you?' she said. She looked like someone who'd worked hard outdoors: ruddy skin, hands too big for her wrists.

'I'm interested in gardens,' I said. 'Old gardens.'

The women looked at each other. 'This is a local history museum,' the smaller one said apologetically.

'I thought you might be the ones to ask about old gardens around here,' I said.

They exchanged glances again. 'Well, there's a good few that open to the public,' the taller one said. 'The best'd be Mrs Sheridan's, wouldn't it, Elsie? Some very nice beds.'

'You don't know of a place called Harkness Park?' I said.

'Oh, Harkness Park,' she said. 'Mrs Rosier's house. I don't think that's ever been open. She had nothing to do with the town. Didn't even come to church. People say it was a grand garden once, but you can't see anything from the road except the trees. It's like a forest.'

'Old Col Harris used to work there,' the other woman said. 'Him and that Meekin and another man – I can't remember his name, lived out on Cribbin Road. Dead now. They're all dead.'

'There wouldn't be photographs, would there?' I said.

The taller woman sighed exaggeratedly. 'Don't talk about photos. There's a whole room of unsorted photos. Mr Collits was in charge of photographs. Wouldn't give anyone else a look-in, would he, Elsie?'

'He's not around anymore?'

She shook her head. 'Blessing, really. Had a terrible time.'

'I told the committee we needed to appoint someone to sort the photos,' Elsie said. 'But will they do anything practical?'

'These men who worked at Harkness Park,' I said, 'do they have family still here?'

'Why don't you just go out there and knock on the door?' Elsie said. 'It's still in the family. Some cousin or something got it.'

'They sold it. I'm interested in knowing what it was like twenty or thirty years ago.'

'Col Harris's boy's here,' the taller one said. 'Dennis. Saw him a few weeks ago. Wife went off with the kids. Shouldn't say that. He works for Deering's. They're building the big retirement village, y'know.'

I said thanks and had a look around the museum. It was like a meticulously arranged garage sale: nothing was of much value or of any great age, but assembling the collection had clearly given the organisers a lot of pleasure.

Finding the new retirement village wasn't a problem. It was at an early stage, a paddock of wet, ravaged earth, concrete slabs and a few matchstick timber frames going up.

A man at the site hut pointed out Dennis Harris on one of the slabs, a big man in his forties with long hair, cutting studs to length with a dropsaw. At my approach, he switched it off and slid back his ear protectors. Dennis's eyes said he didn't think I was the man from Tattslotto.

'Sorry to bother you,' I said. 'Ladies at the museum thought you could help me.'

'Museum?' Deep suspicion, stiff shoulders.

'They said your father worked at Harkness Park. I'm trying to find old photos of the place.'

Dennis's shoulders relaxed. He nodded. 'There's pictures in his old album. Lots. He used to work in the vegie garden when he was a young fella. Before the war. Huge. Wall around it. There was five gardeners there.'

We arranged to meet at the pub after knock-off. Dennis brought the album. 'Take it and copy what you want,' he said.

'I could give you some kind of security for it,' I said.

'Nah. What kind of bloke pinches old photos? Just bring it back.'

I bought him a beer and we talked about building. Then I drove home and rang Stan.

'Research,' I said. 'Paid for by the hour. I've got photographs from the 1930s.'

'No you haven't, lad,' he said. 'Not yet. Not enough hours.'

TEN MINUTES into the last quarter, it began to rain, freezing rain, driven into our faces by a wind that had passed over pack ice in its time. We only needed a kick to win but nobody could hold the ball, let alone get a boot to it. We were sliding around, falling over, trying to recognise our own side under the mudpacks. Mick Doolan was shouting instructions from the sideline but no-one paid any attention. We were completely knackered. Finally, close to time, we had some luck: a big bloke came out of the mist and broke Scotty Ewan's nose with a vicious swing of the elbow. Even in the rain, you could hear the cartilage crunch. Scotty was helped off, streaming blood, and we got a penalty.

'Take the kick, Mac,' said Billy Garrett, the captain. He would normally take the kick in situations like this, but since the chance of putting it through was nil, he thought it best that I lose the game for Brockley.

'Privilege,' I said, spitting out some mud. 'Count on my vote for skipper next year. Skipper.'

I was right in front of goal but the wind was lifting my upper lip. I looked around the field. There were about twenty spectators left, some of them dogs sitting in old utes.

'Slab says you can't do it,' said the player closest to me. He was just another anonymous mudman but I knew the voice.

'Very supportive, Flannery,' I said. 'You're on, you little prick.'

Squinting against the rain, I took my run-up into the gale, scared that I was going to slip before I could even make the kick.

But I didn't. I managed to give the ball a reasonable punt before my left leg went out under me. I hit the ground with my left shoulder and slid towards goal.

And as I lay in the cold black mud, the wind paused for a second or two and the ball went straight between the uprights.

The final whistle went. Victory. Victory in round eight of the second division of the Brockley and District League. I got up. My shoulder felt dislocated. 'That'll be a slab of Boag, Flannery,' I said. 'You fucking traitor.'

'Brought out yer best,' Flannery said. 'Psychology. Read about it.'

I said, 'Read about it? *Psychology in Pictures*. I didn't know they'd done that.'

We staggered off in the direction of the corrugated-iron changing room. On the way, Billy Garrett joined us. 'Pisseasy kick,' he said.

'That's why you didn't want it, Billy,' I said. 'Not enough challenge.'

After we'd wiped off the worst of the mud and changed, we drove the hundred metres to the Heart of Oak. Mick Doolan had about twenty beers lined up.

'Magnificent, me boyos,' he said. 'Out of the textbook. And good to see you followin instructions, Flannery. Hasn't always bin the case.'

'Instructions?' Flannery said. 'I didn't hear any instructions.'

The outside door opened and the big bloke who'd broken Scotty Ewan's nose came in. Behind him were four or five of the other larger members of the Millthorpe side, just in case. He came over to Mick.

'Bloke of yours all right?' he said. 'Didn't intend him no harm. Sort of run into me arm.' He looked down at his right forearm as if inquiring something of it.

'Perfectly all right,' Mick said. 'Hazard of the game. Nothin modern medical science can't handle. Won't be out for more than three or four. Shout you fellas a beer?'

'Thanks, no,' the man said. 'Be gettin back. Just didn't want to go short of sayin me regrets.'

'You're a gentleman, Chilla,' Mick said. 'There's not many would take the trouble.'

After they'd left, Flannery said, 'There's not many would have the fuckin front to come around here afterwards. Might as well've hit Scotty with an axe handle.'

'Think positively,' Mick said. 'Some good in the worst tragedy. Got the penalty. And we won.'

'Bloody won a lot easier if you'd play Lew,' Billy Garrett said. 'Be the only bloke under thirty in the side.'

I said, 'Also the only bloke who can run more than five metres without stopping for a cough and a puke.'

Mick took a deep drink, wiped the foam from his lips, shook his head. 'Don't understand, do ya lads? Young fella's pure gold. Do ya put your young classical piano player in a woodchoppin competition? Do ya risk your young golf talent on a frozen paddick with grown men, violent spudgrubbers and the like? Bloody no, that's the answer. Boy's goin to be a champion.'

'Speakin of champions,' said Flannery. 'Reckon I'm givin away this runnin around in the mud on Satdee arvos, big fellas tryin to bump into me. All me joints achin.' He scratched his impossibly dense curly dog hair. 'Could be me last season.'

Mick's eyes narrowed. He rubbed his small nose. 'Last season? That so? Well, Flanners me boyo, get to the Grand Final, I'll point out a coupla fellas ya can take into retirement with ya.'

I took the next shout. Then Vinnie came in from fighting with the cook and sent the beers around. Flannery's younger brother came in with the lovely and twice-widowed Yvonne and shouted the room. Things were good in trucking. Other rounds followed. In due course, Mick broke into 'The Rose of Tralee' and Flannery's voice, shockingly deep from the compact frame, joined him. The air warmed, thickened, became a brew of beer fumes, breath, tobacco smoke, cooking smells from the kitchen. The windows cried tears of condensation and my shoulder was healed of all pain. It was after ten, whole body in neutral, when I decided against another drink. I was saying my farewells when Mick put his head close to me and said, 'Moc, other day. That Ned thing we were discussin. Met the fella today, works on the gate at Kinross Hall. Says Ned was there a coupla days before. Before he— y'know.'

I wandered out into the drizzle, cold night, black as Guinness, smell of deep and wet potato fields. The dog appeared and we found our way across the road. I stopped for a leak beside the sign that said *Blacksmith, All Metalwork and Shoeing*. Flannery had done it for me in pokerwork and it wasn't going to get him a place in the Skills Olympics. Down the muddy lane the two of us went home, both happy to have a home. Homes are not easy to come by.

THE SIGN saying *Kinross Hall, Juvenile Training Centre* directed you down a country road. Five kilometres further, another sign pointed at a long avenue of poplars. At the end of it, huge spear-pointed cast-iron gates were set in a bluestone wall fully three metres high. Above them, an ornate wrought-iron arch held the words *Kinross Hall*, the two words separated by a beautiful wrought-iron rose. Through them you could see a gravel driveway flanked by bare elms. An arrow on the gate took the eye to a button on the right-hand pillar. A sign said: RING.

I got out of the vehicle, admired the craftsmanship of the iron rose on the arch, and pushed the button. After a few minutes, I rang again. Then a man in standard blue security guard uniform came walking down the drive – moon face, fat man's walk, not in any hurry.

'Yes,' he said.

'I'm trying to find about someone who was here about two weeks ago,' I said.

He didn't say anything, just looked at the Land Rover and looked back at me blankly.

'Bloke called Ned Lowey,' I said.

He nodded. 'I heard about him. He was here. Hold on, tell you when.' He went off to my right, out of sight. When he came back, he had a black and red ledger, open. He riffed through it, then said, 'Tuesday 9 July, nine twenty am.'

I said, 'What was it about?'

Still expressionless, he said, 'Wouldn't know, mate. Had an appointment with the director at nine-thirty am.'

'How do you get to see the director?'

'Ask. Want me to?'

I nodded.

'Name and purpose of visit.'

I gave him my name and said, 'Inquiry about Ned Lowey's visit.'

He wrote it in the book and went off again. He was away no more than two minutes. 'Better put the dog in the cab,' he said. 'Park in front of the main building. Turn right as you go in the front door. Down the passage. There's a sign says Director's Office.'

I opened the passenger window and whistled. The dog jumped onto the cab roof. His back legs appeared, scrambled their way over the windowsill, and then the whole animal dropped into the cab. The guard shook his head and opened the gate.

No inmates were to be seen, only a man on a ride-on mower in the distance. The main building was stone, someone's house once, a mixture of castle and Gothic cathedral with a hint of French chateau, set in immaculate parkland. It could have been an expensive country hotel but it had the feeling of all places of involuntary residence: the silence, the smell of disinfectant, the disciplined look of everything, the little extra chill in the air.

The secretary was a pale, thin woman in her thirties with very little make-up. Her bare and unwelcoming office was cold and she had her jacket on.

'Please take a seat,' she said. She tugged an earlobe. Blunt nails. 'Dr Carrier will see you shortly.'

It was a ten-minute wait in an upright chair, probably an instructional technique. The secretary pecked at the computer. There wasn't anything to read, nothing on the walls to look at. I thought about Ned. Had the director kept him sitting here, too? On this very chair? Finally, the secretary received some kind of a signal.

'Please go through,' she said.

The director's office was everything the secretary's wasn't, a comfortable sitting room rather than a place of business. A fire burned in a cast-iron grate under a wooden mantelpiece, there were paintings and photographs on the walls and chintz armchairs on either side of a deep window.

A woman sat behind an elegant writing table. She was in her mid-forties, tall, and groomed for Olympic dressage: black suit with white silk cravat, dark hair pulled back severely, discreet make-up.

'Mr Faraday,' she said. She came around the table and put out her right hand. 'Marcia Carrier. Let's sit somewhere comfortable.' There was an air of confidence about her. You could imagine her talking to prime ministers as an equal.

We shook hands and sat down in the armchairs. She had long, slim legs.

'I understand it's to do with Mr Lowey,' she said. 'What a shock. A terrible thing. Are you family?'

'Just a friend,' I said. 'I wonder if you can tell me why he came to see you?'

She smiled, put her head on one side in a puzzled way. 'Why he came to see me? Is this somehow connected with what happened?'

'I don't know.'

'It was about work,' she said.

I waited.

'He'd done some work for us before. A long time ago. I confess I didn't remember him. He was inquiring about the prospect of future work.'

'You hire the casual workers yourself?'

'Oh no.' She shook her head. 'Our maintenance person does that. But

Mr Lowey asked to see me.' She smiled, an engaging smile. 'I try to see anyone who wants to see me.'

'So he was looking for work?'

'Basically.'

'He did quite a lot of work here in 1985. Can you tell me why you didn't use him again?'

She shrugged, puzzled frown. 'I really can't say. Lots of people work here. The maintenance person may have had some reason. Then again, we didn't use many outside contractors from '86 to '91. Budget cuts every year.'

I looked out of the window. You could see bare trees, gunmetal clouds boiling in the west. 'Did you know that he went to the police about something to do with this place?' I said.

Her eyes widened. 'No.' She appeared genuinely surprised. 'You mean in 1985 or now?'

'In 1985.'

'Do you know what about?'

I shook my head.

'Well,' she said, 'he certainly didn't mention anything a few weeks ago. I can't imagine what it could have been.'

'You had no inquiries from the police in 1985?'

'The local police? I'd have to check the records. I can't recall having anything to do with them.'

'There wasn't anyone missing?'

'Missing?'

I said, 'I presume some of your charges do a runner occasionally.'

She laughed. It brought her face alive. She was very attractive. 'They do from time to time, and we notify the Department of Community Services and they handle the business of looking for them. They generally find them in a few days, back in their old haunts.'

'And you didn't have one like that in late '85?'

She clasped her hands. 'Mr Faraday, I'm happy to answer your questions but I'm not sure what this is about.'

I wasn't sure either but I said, 'I had the vague thought that Ned's death might be connected with something that happened here in 1985.'

She was looking at me in a way that said she had grave doubts about my grip on reality. 'I'll find out,' she said. 'It'll take a few minutes. Can I offer you coffee? Tea?'

I declined and she left me. I walked around the room looking at the pictures. The paintings were all oils, small, signed by the same hand – B.I. or B.L. From a distance they looked like bush campfire scenes. Close up, they had the power to disturb. Something unpleasant seemed to be happening in them, primitive sacrifice or torture, people in poses of prayer and supplication and indistinct flesh-toned objects in the flames. There were six of them, not markedly different, not hung in any order I could detect.

Marcia Carrier was in most of the photographs, family scenes with another dark-haired girl and a couple who might have been their grandparents. The man was stern-looking, handsome, hair intact, cleft chin. The woman was overweight, dowdy. I went back to looking at the paintings.

'Painted by my father,' Marcia Carrier said. 'Just a weekend painter.'

'Very dramatic weekend painter,' I said.

She laughed again. 'I must say I don't quite understand them. Now. There was no-one absent without permission from here in late 1985. In fact, no-one strayed in 1985. Two girls took unofficial leave in 1986, both returned to us within a fortnight. Is that helpful?'

I said, 'Thanks. I won't waste any more of your time.'

'Coffee's on its way,' she said. 'I insist.'

I sat down. The secretary came in with a tray holding a silver coffee jug, big French coffee cups, warm milk, shortbread. Marcia Carrier poured.

'What sort of work do you do, Mr Faraday?'

'I'm a blacksmith, metalworker.'

'Really? I've never met a blacksmith. How do you become one?'

'Years of training under a master craftsman. Intensive study of the properties of metals. Also, you have to be able to hit hot things with a really heavy hammer. How do you get to run a place like this?'

Her serious look did not leave her. 'Well, you have to be a public-spirited person, utterly selfless, with an abiding faith in the essential goodness of human beings. You also need a deep understanding of psychology. Then you have to be a superb administrator who thinks nothing of working long and unpredictable hours.'

'So,' I said, 'basically anyone can apply.'

She had an engaging laugh. 'Your inmates ...' I said.

'Clients.'

'Clients. How do they get here?'

She was serious now. 'The courts send us all sorts of girls – rich kids, poor kids, kids you can help, kids you can't. They've all got one thing in common. No-one wants them except for the worst reasons. They've usually landed up on the street and someone, sometimes a number of people, is pushing them towards drugs and prostitution. If no-one intervenes, most of them won't see twenty. If the department can convince a court that a girl's in significant danger, she might get sent here.'

'Then what happens?'

'We try our best to help them. You have to understand, some of these girls have had no childhood. Shunted around, never felt wanted, sex at an early age, often raped. They're fifteen going on forty. Our aim is to convince them that their lives have worth and that they can live worthwhile lives.'

I had the feeling she'd said all this before. Many times. 'Doesn't sound easy,' I said.

'No.' She looked out of the window. 'Mostly we're too late. And for some girls I sometimes think it's always too late.'

I didn't say anything.

She turned her eyes on me. 'Do you believe in evil, Mr Faraday?'

I thought about this for a while. It wasn't the kind of question people often asked me. Finally I said, 'I don't doubt that some people are evil. I'm not sure there's an evil that's independent of evil people.'

Marcia Carrier nodded. 'Have you noticed,' she said, 'that evil people have a kind of force about them? A kind of independence? It's a very powerful thing to have. It's a stillness, an absence of doubt, an indifference to the world. It draws people to them. The moral vacuum sucks people in. The weak go to the strong. We see girls like that here. Some of them come on like victims, like wounded creatures. But sooner or later the other side shows through. The side that's the predator, the side that inflicts wounds. The evil side.'

She shook her head, quick self-chastising movement. 'But that's all too serious,' she said. 'We do what we can for the girls. They can study if they want to. Some do. For others, it's too late. For now anyway. For them, we have a range of programmes. Self-esteem. Life skills. Job skills. That sort of thing.'

That was the end of talking about Kinross Hall. She moved the conversation over to the possibility of spring ever coming. We talked about coffee-making, her ignorance of football, the effects of sun deprivation. It was an easy exchange. When I got up to go, she said, 'This is going to nag at me. I'll have another look at the records, see if there's anything I didn't spot that might have worried Mr Lowey. What's your phone number?'

At the door, we shook hands. She had a nice, dry grip and she held it for a second.

'I'm pleased to have met a blacksmith, Mr Faraday,' she said.

'Mac.'

'Marcia.'

The security man had the gate open when I rounded the corner. He gave me a little wave.

I went home, lit the Ned Kelly in the forge and got back to work on the knives. I had made my first knife for George Tan, a chef friend of Vinnie the publican. He'd lost the index finger on his chopping hand to a boat winch. When he got back to work after two months off, he found his knives unbalanced in his hand. George showed me the problem in the pub one Monday night, and I drew a knife shape that might compensate for the missing finger. It took four or five versions to get the distribution of weight right. George was ecstatic. He rang me to say he wanted a full set. Another chef in his kitchen, a ten-fingered one, tried the knives and ordered three. He showed them to a chef in Sydney, who ordered a full set. I now had orders for about thirty knives.

Filing and fitting, stove gradually warming the room, I thought about my visit to Kinross Hall.

I couldn't believe Ned had gone to see Marcia Carrier about work. Ned never asked anyone for work. And leaving aside Ned's nature, he had no need to drum up work. His diary showed an almost full workload of bookings for two or three months.

Marcia Carrier had not told me the real reason for Ned's visit to Kinross Hall the day before he died. Why? I kept turning my meeting with her over in my mind. Then I went to the office and rang Detective Sergeant Michael Shea. He was out. They would pass on a message. I left my number. I was sorting out Allie's appointments when the phone rang.

'Shea.'

I said, 'There's something. Ned Lowey complained to the cops about Kinross Hall in late 1985. November. Can you check that?'

Silence. He cleared his throat. 'November '85? Why the fuck would I want to check that?'

'You might find out something.'

There was a long silence. I could hear traffic noises. Then he said, 'I'm the policeman.'

'Trying to help,' I said. 'Don't want that, fine.'

Silence again. Someone said something in the background. Probably skinhead Cotter. 'Get back to you,' Shea said.

IN THE half-awake dawn, rain hissing in the downpipes, I lay on my back and, for the first time in years, thought about the old life. When I'd come to my father's house and the smithy to stay, I had schooled myself to shy away from thinking about my recent past until the people in it seemed unreal and unimportant, as if I'd created them or seen them in a film. In my mind, I called that the old life. I wanted a new life, a life among ordinary people, people like Ned and Stan Harrop and Flannery. Now Ned's death had shaken everything loose and I didn't try to fight the thoughts.

The old life. It had been my life for thirteen years. The old life. The Job. The endless, seamless job that had no clear beginning and was never finished. 'Your job!' Susan had screamed one night. 'Don't call it your fucking job! It's not a job. It's your fucking life! It's your fucking person-ality! It's *you*. It's what you are. You don't exist without it. There isn't anything fucking else in your world, don't you understand that?'

I did understand that. And then again I didn't. Not that it made any difference. She left me anyway. I came home one day and she was on the pavement putting suitcases into her car. It was a sunny day in early spring and, from a full block away, I saw the gold of her hair catch the light. A flash, like sun on a helmet.

Another departure. My whole life seemed to be about departures. My father and I changing towns every year or two, the two of us packing every-thing into the truck, sometimes no-one to say goodbye to, driving away from some forlorn fibro house in the grey dawn. I used to put myself to sleep thinking about the towns, trying to picture the few friends I'd made. Wal in Cunnamulla who gave me a Joseph Rodgers pocketknife. Sleepy-eyed Gibbo in St George whose mother always wanted to feed me. Russell in Baradine whose dog had spotty pups. For many years, I had the feeling that it was vitally important to keep the memories of these and other people and places alive. To let them fade away would somehow be an act of betrayal, of disloyalty. Perhaps this was because I had no recollection of my mother, and I felt that this was somehow my fault, as if I had not cared enough about her, as if I had cast her off, thrown away her memory. Your mother. Other people's mothers ask you about your mother. The fathers ask: 'So what's yer father do?'

Why did we keep moving? I never really understood. I asked my father once, one night in my first university vacation, watching him work in the smithy. He didn't stop what he was doing. After a while, he said, 'Never wanted to stop anywhere long after I lost your mum.' There was a long silence, then he said, 'Nothin's forever, John. Enjoy what you can and don't be scared to move along.'

Before I was in my teens, I could tell when we were going to move. My father became morose, pacing around at night, not fishing, not reading, saying things like: 'Jesus, imagine endin up in a dump like this.' Once that started, it was over. Mentally, he was already somewhere else. It only remained for me to tell the teacher and get my sealed envelope. And prepare myself for the fight.

That's the thing I remember most clearly about the string of tiny towns that looked as if they'd been dumped on the site from the air. The fight in the first week. They trailed you after school like mongrels following a bitch on heat. Big boys, small boys, fat boys, thin boys, all aroused by the prospect of violence, strutting, jostling. You walked on, whole body tense, heart like a piston in your chest, feeling them getting closer, half hearing the taunts through the blood noise in your head. Then someone would try to trip you, usually a small one, over-excited, wide-eyed, flushed. Or a few would run past you, turn and block your path or dawdle along, finally stopping. That was the moment.

By the time I was twelve, I'd learned to short-circuit the process, stop, turn, issue the challenge, draw out some pale-eyed, mouth-breathing boy, spitty lips, hands too big for his wrists. You couldn't win these fights. Some bigger boy always dragged you off if you got the upper hand. But what my father taught me was that you had to show the whole baying mob that you were a dangerous person, a person prepared to kick, bite, pull hair, tear ears, gouge eyes, squeeze testicles, anything. 'Don't worry about fair,' he said. 'Dangerous is what you want to be. Go mad. Nobody wants to fight a mad person. Nobody wants fingers stuck up his nose.'

He was right. He also taught me the barfighters' tricks: the quick chest shoves to get the opponent off balance, the heel scraping down the shin and stamping on the instep, the Adam's apple punch, the thumbs pressing under the ears, the chop under the nose, the many painful uses of the elbow, the double ear slap, the protruding knuckle in the chestbone. I learned these things and I survived.

Ned Lowey. In all this movement, this rootlessness, this life in shabby houses and scuffed caravan parks and shearers' quarters that smelled of sweat and ashes, Ned Lowey was the still point. We were on our way to another town, another fight, another departure, when I met him for the first time. It must have been some time after my ninth birthday, but I had been hearing about Ned as far back as I could remember, things like 'We need bloody Ned Lowey for work like this', or 'Here's a little trick Ned Lowey showed me', or, at picnic races, 'Back Ned Lowey ridin sidesaddle against this lot'. We drove into Ned's backyard and he came out and shook hands with my father. They stood there smiling and slapping each other's arms.

'This is the young fella,' my father said. 'John. We named him for the wife's father.' I remember my surprise at two things. One was that Ned was Aboriginal. My father had never mentioned it. The other was that Ned Lowey was not a giant. I remember that he took me by the shoulders, picked me up and held me to his chest. Then we went into the house to meet his wife. She was sitting in a patch of sun in the kitchen, not doing anything, a gaunt woman with faded blonde hair. I knew without being told that there was something wrong with her.

Ned Lowey. I shook the thoughts away and got up. By seven am, I was in the smithy getting ready to start work on Frank Cullen's latest contraption. Frank inherited the huge property that had been in his wife's family, the Pettifers, for generations. That was the end of farming. Now he spent all his time designing strange and usually counterproductive devices. Every six months or so, he came in with a set of plans for another machine that was going to change the face of rural life. The first one I made for him was designed to help elderly farmers mount horses. It featured a hydraulic piston and was said to have enabled the test jockey to mount a tree. The latest one was a sort of tray on wheels that fitted on the back of a ute. By fitting tracks, the tray could be run off the back and loaded. A winch operated by the driver then pulled it back up.

'Came to me in a flash, Mac,' Frank said. 'Can't think why no-one's ever thought of it.'

'Takes a special kind of mind,' I said.

It was almost noon and I had just finished welding the heavy-gauge steel mesh into the angle-iron base when Frank and Jim Caswell arrived. Jim was rumoured to be old man Pettifer's illegitimate son. Frank was somewhere in his seventies with a big, bony head, patches of hair, exploding eyebrows and ears like baseball mitts. Jim was about fifteen years younger, full head of grey hair cut short, small-featured, neat. He looked like a clerk in some old-fashioned shop. Usually they both wore the squatter's uniform: tweed jacket, moleskins, blue shirt and tie. Today Jim was in a dark suit, white shirt and navy tie.

They sat down on the bench against the wall and watched me marking the position of the axle mountings. These visits were a feature of the construction period.

'Nice job so far, Mac,' Frank said. 'Paying attention to the plans? Worked out in every detail.'

'Like I was building a Saturn VI,' I said.

'Good man.' He turned to Jim. 'So who was there?'

'Langs, Rourkes. Carvers, Veenes, Chamberlain, Charlie Thomson, Ormerods, Caseys, Mrs Radley, Frasers. Just about everyone. Old Scott.'

'Old Scott?' Frank said. 'Danny Wallace hated the miserable old bastard. What did he want?'

'Same as everyone else, I s'pose. Came to pay his respects.'

'Anybody ask after me?'

'No.'

Frank scratched a moulting patch of hair. 'Not a word? What about old Byrne? He must've noticed I wasn't there.'

'Didn't say anything.'

'Well,' said Frank. 'That's that bloody mob for you. I knew Danny Wallace since '47, day I king-hit him in the Golden Fleece. Used to put him to bed. That drunk he'd get on a horse backwards.' He patted his jacket. 'What happened to my smokes?'

'I though he was cryin a bit at the end,' Jim said. 'By the grave.'

'Who?'

'Old Kellaway.'

Frank found his cigarettes and lit one with a big gold lighter. He coughed for a while, then he said. 'Old Kellaway? Bloody crocodile tears. Sanctimonious old bastard. Spent his whole life crawlin up the cracks of the rich. You know where the bastard was in the war? Y'know?'

'I know,' Jim said.

'Chaplain in the Navy, bloody Australian Navy, two pisspots and a tin bath. Hearin the bunnyboys' confessions.' He put on a high voice. '"Forgive me, father, I cracked a fat at Mass."' Then a deep voice: '"My son, the Lord forbids us to lust after petty officers' bums. Say fifty Hail Marys and report to my cabin after lights out."'

'He's all right,' Jim said. 'Hasn't been much of a life for him.'

'All right?' said Frank. 'All right? He's far from bloody all right. If he was all right he'd never have landed up here so he wouldn't have much of a life. He'd a been a bloody cardinal, wouldn't he?'

Frank took a small leather-bound flask out of his inside pocket. 'Just thinkin about bloody Kellaway gives me a need for drink,' he said. He took off the cap and had a good swig.

Jim muttered something.

'What's that?' Frank said, wiping his lips. 'You say somethin?'

'Nothin.'

'Don't bloody nothin me. Somethin to say, spit it out.'

'Bit early for the piss, innit?'

Frank nodded knowingly. 'Sonny,' he said, 'don't come the fuckin little prig with me. I've had disapproval from a whole family of disapproval experts. I feel like it, I'll give myself a whisky enema for breakfast.'

I was looking at the plan. 'What's this twisty thing you've drawn here, Frank?'

He eased himself up and came over. 'It's a spring, Mac. A shock absorber.'

'Right,' I said. 'That horse mounter needed a shock absorber.'

'I need a bloody shock absorber,' Frank said. 'Shares goin down like the *Titanic* and the bastards call an election. This country's buggered, y'know that, Mac. Get butchered for bloody king and country twice, then it's for the Yanks. Now everythin's for sale. Power stations. Telephone. Bloody airports. Negative gear this bloody Parliament buildin chock-a-block with liars, thousands of bloody bent police thrown in. Buy the whole country.'

'What about Crewe?' I said. 'Going to get back, is he?' I went over to the cabinet to look for some suitable springs for the shock absorber.

'Anthony Crewe,' Frank said. 'Lord only knows how they made that bastard attorney-general. Bloody miscarriage of justice if ever there was one. Done that shonky will for old Morrissey.'

'That's enough, Frank,' Jim said.

Frank turned his big head slowly. 'What?' he said. 'What did you say?'

Jim looked away. 'You know what Mr Petty always said about repeatin gossip.'

A look somewhere between pleasure and pain came over Frank's face. 'Little man,' he said, 'don't quote The Great Squatter to me. I've told you that before. I had those sayins straight from the horse's arse for thirty-five years. Now a miniature ghost of the old shit follows me around repeatin them. Is that what they mean by everlastin life? You're dead but your miserable opinions linger on to haunt the livin?'

He turned back to me. 'Now, as I was sayin, the bastard Crewe shoulda been in jail over that will.'

'What will?' I was looking in the box for springs.

'Will he produced after old Morrissey turned up his toes. Half the bloody estate to the physiothingamajig. Who happens to be Mr Shonky Crewe's current rootee. Lorraine was her name, I recall. Latest in a long line. Once he got his cut, he was into that Kinross Hall warder. Dr Marcia somethin or other. All legs and hair.'

I looked up. 'Crewe had an affair with Marcia Carrier?'

'That's what they say,' Frank said. 'He's the boss cockie out there, y'know. Chairman of the council, whatever. They should take a bloody good look at that place. God knows what goes on there. I see the quack switched off his lights the other day. Hanged himself down there in Footscray. Least he picked a place with a decent footy team.'

'Frank,' Jim said. He had a habit of sitting with his hands clamped between his knees, palms together.

'Shut up,' Frank said. 'Dr Barbie. Good name, eh? I'd take the wife rowin, though. That Irene.'

'What's he got to do with it?' I said.

Frank lit another cigarette. It started a coughing fit. When it ended, he wiped moist eyes and said, 'Where was I?'

'Dr Barbie. Where's he fit in?'

'Kinross quack. Inherited the job from old Crewe. Looks just like old Crewe, too. Now Dr Barbie's mum, she was the receptionist for umpteen bloody years.'

'You never bloody stop, do you?' Jim said.

'Take that girl Sim Walsh picked up,' Frank said. 'Now where did she come from? Naked as your Eve. On Colson's Road. Out there in the middle of the night. Covered in blood. Been whipped like a horse.'

'That's serious,' I said.

'Bloody oath. Told me about it one night he'd pushed the boat out to bloody Tasmania.'

'Drunk talk,' said Jim. 'Sim Walsh was drunk for forty years. Most likely made the whole thing up.'

I said, 'When was this?'

'Good way back,' Frank said. 'Around '82, could be '83. Thereabouts.'

'What happened?'

'Nothin. Said he took her home, cleaned her up. Girl wouldn't go to hospital, wouldn't go to the police. Scared out of her wits. Put her to bed. Next day, gone.'

'She tell him what happened?'

'No. Kept talkin about a bloke called Ken. You got springs, then?'

'I want the right springs,' I said. 'Not any old springs. Who was the girl?'

Frank stumped over to the door and flicked his cigarette end into the yard. 'Juvenile harlot from Kinross Hall,' he said.

'She told him that?'

Frank thought about this. 'Well,' he said, 'near enough. Sim said she was ravin. Drugs, he reckoned. Mind you, he was ravin a bit himself that night.'

'Never reported it?' I said.

'Don't know,' Frank said. 'Come round the next day, eyes narrer as bloody stamps side-on. Said, do me a favour, what I said about that girl, forget it. Load of rubbish I made up.'

'And here you are doin it,' said Jim. 'He told you it was a load of rubbish. What more d'ya want?'

'I want you to keep your mouth shut,' Frank said. 'Sim didn't make it up. He could bloody bignote himself – me and Douglas Bader and Sailor Malan saved the world from the bloody Nazis – but he wouldn't make anythin up. Not out of nothin. Not in his nature. Oh no, it happened. Believe you me. He never came near me after that. Saw me comin, he'd cross the street. Another bugger I wouldn't go to his bloody funeral.'

ALEX RICKARD was ten minutes late but that was a misdemeanour by his standards. 'Mac, Mac,' he said, sliding onto the plastic barstool seat. 'Back from the fucking dead. Where you been, mate?'

'Here and there,' I said. 'What is it with you and these grunge pits?'

Alex looked around at the pub: yellow smoke-stained walls, plastic furniture, scratched and cigarette-burnt formica-topped bar, three customers who looked like stroke victims. It was on Sydney Road and John Laws was braying at full volume to overcome Melbourne's worst traffic noise. The house smell was a mixture of burnt diesel, stale beer, and carbolic. 'I dunno,' he said, shrugging his boxer's shoulders in the expensive sports coat. 'It's the kind of bloke I am. True to my roots.'

'That's the thing they all value most about you,' I said.

'You drinking?' said the barman. He'd modelled his appearance on the barmen in early Clint Eastwood westerns.

'Beer,' said Alex. I ordered a gin and tonic. I wasn't going to drink anything that came up from this pub's cellar.

'No tonic,' said the barman. 'No call for it.'

'What do they drink gin with?' I said.

'Coke,' said the barman. 'You drink Coke with gin.'

'Whisky and water,' I said. 'You got any call for water?'

He muttered something and left.

Alex rubbed the tip of his long nose between finger and thumb. 'Y'know a Painter and Docker got it right where you're sitting?' he said. 'Bloke walked in the door, up behind him, took this big fucking .38 out the front of his anorak. Three shots. Bang. Bang. Bang. Back of the head, two in the spine. Walks out the door. Gone.'

'They get him?' I said.

'No witnesses,' Alex said. 'Sixteen people in the pub, no-one saw a fucking thing.'

'Funny that,' I said. 'You get so wrapped up talking footy, they shoot someone next to you, covers you with blood, you don't notice a thing.'

The drinks arrived. Alex paid, keeping his wallet well below the counter. 'So they say you looked the other way on Lefroy,' he said, not looking at me.

'Who's they?'

'I done a few jobs for Scully.'

'Scully tell you?'

'Nah. The offsider.'

'Hill? Bianchi?'

'Hill. Bianchi's dead. Went to Queensland and drowned.'

'Wonderful news,' I said. 'Saves me killing him. Listen, your boy any good on the Human Services Department?'

He flicked his eyes at me, away, back. 'Human Services? What the fuck you want with Human Services? They dealing now?'

'It's a private thing. I need the records of a place called Kinross Hall for 1985. It's a kind of girls' home. Who went in, who came out. All that.'

Alex drank some beer, took out a packet of Camel. 'Smoke?'

I shook my head.

He lit up, blew plumes out of his nostrils. 'Could be easy. Could be fucking hard. It's in the database, my boy's probably in there like a honeymoon prick. Not— well, there's ways. But it'll cost.'

'How long to find out?'

Alex took out a grubby little notebook and a pen. 'How d'ya spell this place?'

I told him.

'Eighty-five. What's the mobile?'

I gave him my number.

'He can probably get in and look at the database inside an hour. Not there, I'll have to think. I've got this sheila in the archives, knockers absent but Jesus, the arse on her. She can get all kinds of stuff. Thinks it's sexy. Like I'm a spy.'

'In your special way, Alex,' I said, 'you are. Want to talk about money?'

He gave me a long look, drawing on the cigarette. There was something of the fox about him. 'Not now,' he said. 'Maybe if we have to go the next step.'

I was looking at the military history shelf in Hill of Content bookshop when the phone rang. I went outside into Bourke Street. It was lunchtime, street full of smart people in black.

'That thing we were talking about,' Alex said.

'Yes.'

'Don't have to go the next step. Where are you?'

'Bourke Street. I'm parked in Hardware Lane.'

'The one on the corner?'

'Right.'

'I'm closer than you are. See you outside the side door.'

I spotted him from a long way away, across the lane, back to the car park, brown packet under his arm. When I got close enough, I saw him watching me in the shop window. I gave a spy-type wave, close to the hip. He turned and came over.

'Here,' he said. 'Fucking phone book of stuff. Boy downloaded all the '85 material in the file.'

I took the packet. 'How'd he get in?'

Alex smiled his foxish smile. 'They've got a link with Social Security. He reckons their data protection's good as a knitted condom.'

'What's the bill?'

'I'll put it in the bank,' Alex said. 'Day will come.'

We shook hands. He looked at me for a while, deciding something. 'Look after yourself,' he said. He walked off, hands in pockets, chin up, at ease with himself.

IT WAS just before dark as I entered the home straight, the long avenue of bare poplars, the light turning steely blue-grey, the wet road shining like a blade. I was thinking about the girl in the mine shaft. Could she have been brought from far away? Whoever pushed her into the hole in the ground had to know that it was there: you wouldn't travel a long distance with a dead body unless you had some burial spot in mind. Perhaps a local person, someone who knew the area, had murdered the girl in Melbourne. Had the police eliminated all the girls missing in Melbourne around that time? Surely not.

But why would Ned be interested in the finding of her body? Why did he go to Kinross Hall?

Allie was still working in the smithy. Face shining, she was making curtain poles, bending and twisting the red-hot iron into shepherd's crook shapes with smooth, economic movements. I stood in the doorway watching her. She reminded me of my father at work. I was never going to be that good.

'Looking smart,' she said, putting the last pole in the rack. 'Debonair, even. That's the first time I've seen you wearing a tie.'

'You only had to ask,' I said, taking it off and putting it in a jacket pocket. 'Everything all right here?'

'Booming,' she said. 'Woman over at Kyneton wants two sets of gates. She saw the ones you made for Alan Frith.'

'That's nice,' I said. 'Frith doesn't pay for his inside a week, I'll take them round to her.'

'And a man called Flannery was here. He put a case of beer in the office.'

'That's nice too,' I said. 'How many did he drink?'

'Just one.'

'Must be Lent,' I said. 'You in a hurry?'

She looked at me speculatively. 'No.'

'Mind helping me read something?' I told her about Ned working at Kinross Hall in 1985, Mick Doolan's story about the complaint to the police, Ned's visit four days before his death, and my meeting with Marcia Carrier.

'Pretty weird,' she said. 'What's the reading matter?'

'Kinross Hall records.'

'How'd you get them?'

'Some bloke gave them to me. I forget who.'

She scratched her short hair, face impassive. 'Maybe it was the same bloke who told you about Alan Snelling and you've developed a block about remembering him.'

I tore the continuous print-out Alex had given me into pages while Allie showered. She came back in jeans, a grey polo-necked sweater and her half-length Drizabone, and we walked down the road. Her skew nose and wet and shiny crew cut gave her the look of a boxer. A rather sexy female boxer. She caught me looking at her.

'What?' she said.

'Nothing.'

The pub was empty except for Vinnie and George Beale playing draughts and a farmer reading the *Weekly Times* at the bar. We got two beers and went into the small lounge where a fire was dying in the grate. I fed it some kindling and a log from the bin.

'I'm hoping there's something that'll jump out at you,' I said, giving her half of the print-out pages.

'Like what?'

'Christ knows. Something happening to a girl. Trouble of some kind. Anything out of the ordinary.'

We settled down in the sagging armchairs and started reading. I'd taken the first half of 1985 and it quickly became clear that the department liked paperwork. Kinross Hall filed monthly accounts, fortnightly pay sheets, weekly lists of admissions and discharges, and reports by Dr Ian Barbie on medical visits. Every three months, it produced a budget operating statement and a report card on each inmate. The department filed full personal dossiers on all new admissions. Once a month, Kinross Hall was visited by two senior department staff and they filed a report.

It took us more than an hour to skim through the print-outs. Midway, I fetched more beer. Finally, Allie said, 'Well, nothing sticks out to me. I mean, here's a major event. The inspectors had four written complaints about the food in October. Dr Carrier says the reason was the cook was off sick and the second in charge was having domestic troubles and basically couldn't give a bugger about the food.'

'No-one jump the wire in November?' I said.

'No. There were five admissions and three discharges in November. The three had all turned seventeen. They don't seem to be able to hold them after that.'

'Nothing else?'

'The hot water system broke down.'

'You hungry?'

'Why?'

'I've got a farm chook, raised on insects and berries in the wild.'

'Now you tell me. I'm going out.'

'Well,' I said, 'hot date with Alan Snelling could be better than a hot chook.'

'It's not Alan Snelling. You took the shine off Alan Snelling. A vet.'

'Pure animal, some vets,' I said.

She smiled at me. 'This one comes on like he's got a Rottweiler stuffed down the front of his jeans.'

'Probably a Jack Russell thinks it's a Rottweiler.'

'It's not the size of the bite that counts.'

'What counts?'

'How long they gnaw at you.'

At home, Mick Doolan and Lew were watching a golf video. As I came in the door, Mick was saying, 'It's all that wantin to hit the ball to kingdom come, lad. Bin the ruination of many a great talent. What I'm tryin to do is to get you to play the game backwards.'

'But drivin's where the game starts,' Lew said.

'And ends fer a lotta the fellas. We'll get to the drivin. We've got the puttin down flat. Now we've got to get the approach right. Not twice outta ten, not three times. Ten outta ten. Lookit this fella on the screen here. Ya can't putt like that. See. Bloody country mile.'

'Can't you watch porn videos like everyone else?' I said.

Mick looked around. 'When I'm done coachin this lad,' he said, 'they'll be askin us to *star* in the porno videos.'

'Golf porn,' I said. 'There could be a market for that.'

I went to work on the chicken. My father's recipe, made a hundred times: rub the skin with butter, stuff with a mixture of breadcrumbs, finely chopped onion, Worcester sauce, grated lemon rind, chopped raisins, half a cup of brandy. Stick in oven until brown.

I opened a bottle of the Maglieri. Mick came in to say goodnight and had a glass. He studied the label. 'Lay this drop on,' he said, 'they'd be fightin to get in for communion.'

After supper, Lew and I played Scrabble. He was good with small words, quick to see possibilities.

'"Zugzwang"?' I said. 'Two zs. What kind of a word is "zugzwang"?'

'You challengin it?'

'Zugzwang? I am most certainly challenging zugzwang.'

'We playin double score penalty for failed challenges?'

'We are. And we are playing minus-score penalty to a player who doesn't take the opportunity to withdraw when challenged. Are you withdrawing zugzwang?'

'Surprised at you, Mac. Everybody knows zugzwang.'

'Withdrawing, Lewis? Last chance.' I put my hand on the *Concise Oxford Dictionary*.

'Open it,' he said. 'At "z".'

I did. 'Zugbloodyzwang,' I said. 'You little ...'

There was no recovering from zugzwang. We were packing up, when I said, 'Think about what I said about school?'

He didn't look at me. 'Thinkin about it,' he said. 'Thinkin about it a lot.'

When Lew went off to bed, I put another log on the fire, fetched a glass of the red, got out a book Stan had lent me called *The Plant Hunter: A Life of Colonel A. E. Hillary*. I was on page four when Lew came in wearing pyjamas.

'Forgot to tell you,' he said. 'I was lookin in Ned's Kingswood for my stopwatch. He used to take me out on the road and drop me for my run and I left the watch in the car one day.' He held out a piece of paper. 'This was on the floor.'

I took it. It was a ticket from a parking machine, a Footscray Council parking machine in the Footscray Library parking area. It was valid until 3.30 pm on 11 July. That was two days before Ned's death.

'Make sense to you?' I said.

Lew shook his head. 'Ned had to go to Melbourne, he started complainin a month before.'

'Must be some explanation,' I said. 'Sleep well.'

When he'd gone, I got out the Melways street directory and found the Footscray Library parking lot. Then I got the Melbourne White Pages and looked up Dr Ian Barbie.

I put the Melways and the phone book away, refilled my glass in the kitchen, slumped in the armchair staring at the fire.

Ned had parked within two hundred metres of Dr Barbie's consulting rooms. Two days later, Ned was dead. Hanged. Two days after that, Dr Barbie was dead. Hanged.

The wind was coming up, moaning in the chimney, sound like a faraway wolf. The dog and I went out to the office in search of a telephone number I hadn't used in years.

I SAW Brendan Burrows from a long way away. He had a distinctive walk, his left shoulder dropping as his left heel hit the ground. Even from fifty metres, I could tell that he'd aged about twenty years since I'd last seen him. You could count the straw hairs he had left, deep lines ran down from the thin, sharp nose. It's hard to be a policeman and an informer on your colleagues. The days are cold, the nights are worse.

'Fuck,' he said, sitting down next to me. 'Used to be able to do this stuff on the phone. How ya goin? Fair while.' We shook hands. The country train platform at Spencer Street Station in Melbourne held us and a fat woman, exhausted, and two small children bouncing off each other like atoms in some elemental physical process that produced tears.

He put his hand into his leather jacket and took out a sheet torn from a notebook. 'Ian Ralph Barbie, forty-six, medical practitioner, 18 Ralston Street, Flemington, hanging by the neck in disused premises at 28 Varley Street, Footscray. Your man?'

I nodded.

'Got this on the phone in a hurry. Body found approx eleven am, 16 July. Estimated time of death between nine pm and midnight, 15 July. Cause of death, a lot of technical shit, but it's strangulation by hanging. Significant quantity of pethidine. Lots of tracks. No injuries. Last meal approx eight hours before death.'

'On him?'

'Wallet. Cards. No cash. Car clean like a rental. Jumped off the top. Drove inside the building, got on the roof, chucked the rope over a beam.'

'Don't you need some special knot for a noose?'

'Something that'll slip. Must've looked it up. There's nothing isn't in books.'

'Note?'

'No.'

'Any interest?'

Brendan's head turned slightly. A shaven-headed man in an anorak carrying a bulging sports bag was coming down the platform. His eyes flicked at us as he passed. You could hear Brendan's jaws unlock.

'They look at you,' he said, 'they're not on.' But he watched the man go down the concrete peninsula. 'Need a break. You get para. You bastards owe me. No, no interest. Another medico on the peth, can't take the lows anymore, goes out on a high. Happens with the quacks a lot. Guilt. Feel a lot of guilt. Pillars of fucking society sticking stuff up the arm. Don't call peth the doctor's drug for nothing. Still, dangling's a worry. Unusual. Needle, that's the way they go. You got it, you use it.'

'That's it, then?'

'Well, watch's gone, clear mark of watch on left wrist. Probably nicked by the deros.'

'Deros?'

'They found him.'

'Right. Brendan, listen. Scully – what's happened to him?'

'Been livin in Queensland? Outer space? Good things only for the man. Next deputy commissioner. To be anointed soon.'

'I've been away. How'd he do that?'

'Plugged a bloke into Springvale, suburb of smack. Smackvale. Three years in the making. Had to import this cop from Vietnam. Any day now they'll announce he's delivered half the Vietcong and a fucking mountain of smack. Scully's going to be the hero of the day. Course, most of the stuff 'll be back on the street by dark. Catch the upward move in price.'

'He's a lucky man.'

'Blessed.' Brendan looked around, scratched his scalp. 'You heard the shit's flying sideways about surveillance records? About ten years' worth gone missing in Ridley Street.'

'They're on disk, right?'

He made a snorting sound, like a horse. 'They scanned everything onto a hard drive, three sets of backup floppies. But the bloke taking the floppies over to Curzon Street for safekeeping, he got hit from behind by a truck. And while they're sorting it out, his briefcase gets nicked. Can you believe that? Oh well, there's always the paper. But no, all the paper has vanished. Fucking truckload. Well, this is bad, but thank Christ there's the hard disk.'

Brendan paused, looking as happy as I'd seen him.

'Guess,' he said.

I'd guessed. 'Don't know.'

'Hard drive's like the Pope's conscience. Not a fucking thing on it. Hacked into, they reckon. Supposed to be impossible.'

'So?'

'Lots of people happy.'

'You reckon what?'

'Dunno. People don't get together to make something like that happen. More like one very big person got together with some friends. Couldn't just take out the bit the person wanted, they took the lot.'

I said, 'And you take the view one friend could be Scully. How come the Commissioner doesn't think that too?'

Brendan gave me a long, unblinking stare. 'Yeah, well, the view's different from the thirtieth fucking floor. Ground level's where you smell the garbage. They're all overdue, that mob.'

'I hear Bianchi drowned.'

'A fucking tragedy. Cop resigns, buys waterside mansion in Noosa with modest pension and savings. Found floating in river. New wife says he went out for a look at the new boat, she falls asleep. Exhausted from a marathon dicking probably. Next morning the neighbour sees poor Darren bobbing around like a turd.'

'What about Hill?'

'Bobby's making lots of money in the baboon hire business. Calls himself a security consultant. Need muscle for your rock concert, nightclub, anything, Hill Associates got baboons on tap, any number. Also provides special security services for rich people. Drives this grey Merc.'

'I knew the boy would amount to something.' We shook hands. 'Thanks,' I said. 'Appreciate it.'

'I only do it because you can get me killed,' he said, unsmiling. 'You go first. I'll just have a smoke, watch the trains a bit.'

I was a few paces away when he said, 'Mac.'

I turned.

'The Lefroy thing,' he said. 'I heard Bianchi was in that pub in Deer Park one day around then.'

'Yes?'

'Mance was there too. That's all I heard.' He looked away.

'MUCH MALIGNED creatures, chooks,' said Dot Walsh, frisbeeing out another precise arc of grain to the variegated flock of fowls. 'Quite intelligent, some of them. Unlike sheep, which are uniformly stupid.'

She pointed to a large black-and-white bird. 'That's Helen, my favourite. After Helen of Troy.'

By her voice, Mrs Walsh was English, in her seventies, deeply lined but unbowed and undimmed, with hair cut short and sharp. I'd told her my business at the front door. She'd shown no interest in why I wanted to know more about the story her husband had told Frank Cullen.

'I'm surprised Frank remembers it,' she'd said. 'I used to make a special trip to the tip with bottles after one of their sessions. Anyway, I don't suppose it matters now that Simon's gone. Come through. It's chook feeding time.'

When she'd exhausted the grain, we went on a tour of the garden. Even in the bleak heart of winter, it was beautiful: huge bare oaks and elms, black against the asbestos sky, views of farmland at the end of long hedged paths, a pond with ducks, a rose walk that narrowed to a slim gate just wide enough for a wheelbarrow.

'How big?' I said.

'Two acres,' she said. 'All that's left of nearly a thousand. From a thousand acres to two in a generation. That was my Simon's accomplishment. Simon and Johnny Walker Black Label. The old firm, he used to say. Still, he was a lovely man, lovely. Just unfirm of purpose.'

She moved her head like her hens as she talked, quick sideways jerks, little tilts, chin up, chin down, eyes darting.

I got on to the subject. 'You never saw the girl that night?'

'No,' she said. 'I was in Queensland with Fiona, our daughter. She was having domestic trouble. Temperament like Simon, I'm afraid. Forty-six and still thinks that responsibility is something for grown-ups.'

'Could you put a date on that trip?'

'Oh yes. October 1985. My granddaughter had her tenth birthday while I was there.'

'May I ask you what your husband told you happened?'

'Simon ran out of cigarettes at about ten o'clock. It often happened. It was a Thursday night I think, my first night away. He drove down to the Milstead pub. He used to take the back roads. He was coming back down Colson's Road, do you know it?'

I nodded.

'Well, he came around a bend and there was this girl by the side of the road. Not a stitch on. Naked. She'd been beaten. He got her into the car and brought her back here.'

'He didn't think of going to the police?'

'The police? No. He thought she needed medical attention.'

'She was badly hurt?'

'He thought so at first. Lots of blood. But most of it had come from her nose. That was swollen. Simon thought it might be broken. There were red puffy welts all over her body as if she had been whipped, he said. And she had scratches everywhere and dust and what looked like cement stuck to her. But he didn't think she was seriously hurt.'

'Why didn't he take her to casualty?'

She gave me her sharp little look. 'Simon was a drunk, Mr Faraday,' she said, no irritation in her voice, 'but he wasn't a fool. It was half past ten at night. He would have had at least half a bottle of whisky under his belt by then. He'd already had his licence suspended once. The safest thing for both of them was to bring her here and get someone else to take her to hospital.'

'Did he find out how she got her injuries?'

She didn't answer for a while. We were walking between low walls of volcanic stone towards the back of the old redbrick farmhouse. The sky had cleared in the west and the last of the sun was warming an aged golden Labrador where it sat watching us, fat bottom flat on the verandah boards.

'In the beginning, in the car, Simon said she was crying and babbling and saying the name "Ken" over and over again. He couldn't get any sense out of her. He thought she was on drugs. When they got here, he gave her a gown to put on and he went to the telephone to ring Brian. That's his nephew, he farms about ten minutes from here. He wanted Brian to take her to casualty. That's when the girl attacked him.'

'Attacked him?'

'Tried to get the phone away from him and punched him.'

'He'd told her what he was doing? Phoning someone to take her to hospital?'

'I suppose so. He said she shouted, "Don't tell anyone. I'll say you raped me". Her nose was bleeding again and her blood got all over him. I saw his jumper when I got back.'

'So he didn't phone?'

'No. It wasn't the sort of thing he was used to, Mr Faraday. Went into shock, I imagine.'

We'd reached the verandah. The dog came upright by sliding its forelegs forward until they went over the edge and dropped to the first step.

'This bloke's in worse shape than I am,' Mrs Walsh said. 'Needs two new hips. Can I offer you a beer? I have a Cooper's Sparkling this time every day.'

We sat on the side verandah in the weak sun and drank beer. I had a pewter mug with a glass bottom and an inscription. I held the mug away from me to read it: *To Sim, a mad Australian, from his comrades,* 610 *Squadron, Biggin Hill,* 1944.

'He was in the RAF,' Mrs Walsh said. 'He was in England doing an agriculture course when the war broke out, so he joined up. He was billeted with my aunt for a while. That's where I met him.'

I said, 'Biggin Hill was a fighter station, wasn't it?'

'Yes,' she said, looking up at the sky as if expecting to see a Spitfire come out of the sun. 'He never got over the war. None of them did, really. All that expecting to die. Every day. For so long. And they were so young.'

A silence fell between us, not uneasy, until she said, 'The girl calmed down after that, said she was sorry. Simon found some of Fiona's pyjamas and a pair of her riding jeans and an old shirt. She showered and went to bed in the spare room. The bed's always made. Simon said he brought her a mug of Milo but she was asleep. The next day, she asked if he could take her to a station and lend her the fare to Melbourne. Simon said she looked terrible, swollen nose, black eyes. He took her to Ballan, bought her ticket and gave her fifty dollars. And that was that.'

'Did he find out her name?'

'No.'

'And he never reported it to anyone?'

'No. He should have. It was too late by the time I got back.'

'Did he think she was from Kinross Hall?'

'Well, she wasn't a local. You get to know the locals.'

'But there wasn't any other reason to think that?'

'No.'

'Do you ever think about how she might have found herself in Colson's Road?'

She shrugged, took a sip of beer. 'Simon thought she might have been pushed out of a car.'

I finished my beer, got up, said my thanks. At the front gate, Mrs Walsh said, 'Things left undone. Sins of omission. Most of us err more on that side, don't you think, Mr Faraday?'

Howard Lefroy's apartment, the blood up the tiled walls, came into my mind.

'Amen,' I said.

A naked girl, neck broken, thrown down a mine shaft, some time after 1984. A naked girl, beaten, by a lonely roadside in October 1985.

Ned worked at Kinross Hall in November 1985.

And never set foot there again. Until a few days before his murder.

I took the long way home, down Colson's Road to Milstead in the closing day. There was a pine forest on the one side, scrubby salt-affected wetlands on the other. Dead redgums marked the line of a creek running northwest. The last of the light went no more than four or five metres into the pines. Beyond that, it was already cold, dark, sterile night. Nothing cheered the heart on this stretch of Colson's Road.

Neither did anything in the bar at the Milstead pub. An L-shaped room with a lounge area to the right, it had fallen in the formica wars of the seventies. The barman was a thin, sallow man with greased-back curly hair and a big nose broken at least twice. A small letter J was crudely tattooed in the hollow of his throat. As an educated guess, I would have said four or five priors, at least one involving serious assault, and a degree or two from the stone college. He hadn't studied beer pulling either.

'Helpin out,' he said, putting down the dripping glass. 'Owner's on the beach in fucking Bali, regular bloke got done this arvo, wouldn't take the breathie, the bastards lock him up.'

'Thought you had some rights,' I said. 'You local?'

He gave me a long look and made a judgment. 'Wife,' he said. 'Well, ex, pretty much. Bitch. Fuckin family swarm around here. Get the motor goin, I'm off to WA. Bin there? Fuckin paradise.'

He took my five-dollar note and short-changed me without going near the till.

'Who owns the pine forest down the road here?' I said.

He was pouring himself a vodka. Three vodkas, in fact.

'Wooden have a fuckin clue, mate.' He raised his voice. 'Ya breathin there, Denise? Who owns the pine forest?'

'Silvateq Corporation,' a husky voice said from around the corner. 'S-i-l-v-a-t-e-q.'

I took my glass and made the trip. A woman somewhere out beyond seventy, face a carefully applied pink mask matching her tracksuit, was sitting at a round table playing patience. She was drinking a dark liquid out of a shot glass.

'G'day,' I said. 'John Faraday. What's Silvateq Corporation?'

She looked me over and went back to the cards. 'A company,' she said.

'Right,' I said. 'Is it local?'

'Collins Street,' she said. 'They sent me a letter tellin me not to use their road. *Their* road. It's bin a public track since God was in nappies. Wrote back, told 'em to bugger off. Not another word.'

'They backed off?'

'No. Put a bloody great barbed-wire fence across the road and dug a trench behind it. Looks like the bloody Somme.'

She took a sip of the black liquid and ran her tongue over her teeth. 'Course the shire's bought off. Only takes about ten quid.'

'This was when?'

She flipped a card. 'More than ten years. When did that Hawke get in?'

'In '82.'

'Round about then. Bought it from old Veene. He planted the trees along the road. Twenty rows, I remember. This other bunch planted the rest. Know what they call bloody pine plantations? Green graveyard. Nothin lives in 'em.'

Green graveyard. I thought about that on the trip home. The mine shaft the girl was thrown down was in a pine forest near Rippon. How far was that from Colson's Road?

On the way home, gloomy, I stopped at Flannery's place, a small village of dangerously old sheds surrounding a weatherboard house. He lived with a cheerful nurse called Amy who wouldn't marry him. 'Marry a flogged-out backyard mechanic whose first wife walked off with a water diviner?' she once said. 'I'd need time to think about that. A lifetime.'

'Just as easy been the fence bloke,' Flannery had said, 'but then I'da had a new fence. This bugger's got a bit of wire, coathanger wire, picks three spots, bloody wire's vibrating like a pit bull's chain. Down we go, drillin halfway to the hot place, fifty bucks a metre. Two holes bone dry, third one a little piddle comes out, takes half an hour to fill the dog bowl. Still cry when I think about it.'

Flannery was in one of the sheds working under the hood of a Holden ute by the light of a portable hand lamp. The vehicle was covered in stickers saying things like *Toot to Root* and *Emergency Sex Vehicle* and *Bulk Sperm Carrier*.

'My cousin's boy's,' he said. 'Virgin vehicle. Never had a girl in it.'

'I can see he's waiting for someone special,' I said. 'Listen, you know of Ned ever going around asking for jobs?'

Flannery was wiping his large hands on his jumper, a garment that qualified as a natural oil resource. 'Ned? Ask for a job? You smokin something?'

'Second question. He ever talk about a doctor called Ian Barbie?'

'What's this? Doctor? Ned wouldn't know a doctor from a brown dog.'

I looked into the engine. 'Dirty.'

'Clean inside that matters,' Flannery said. 'Let's go a beer. Got some in this little fridge over here, bought it off Mick.'

'I can see the dent.'

'What dent?'

'Dent it got falling off the truck.'

THE PERFECT is the enemy of the good. Making knives would be easy if all you wanted was a good knife. But you don't. You want a perfect knife. And so, in the endless grinding and filing and fitting and buffing, the mind has plenty of time to dwell. Today, moist Irish day, sky the colour of sugar in suspension, I dwelt on Brendan Burrow's parting words. All I wanted from Brendan were the details of Ian Barbie's suicide. And then he said: *The Lefroy thing. Heard Bianchi was in that pub in Deer Park one day around then.* And I said: *Yes?* And he said: *Mance was there too.*

Mance was there too.

The feeling of missing a step, of walking into a glass door, of being shaken from deep sleep. With Bianchi? At the same time as Bianchi? I knew the answer. Just before noon, I finished polishing a small paring knife and the dog and I went over to the office.

The file was at the back of the cabinet, not looked at for years. I sat down at the table and took out the record of interview. I didn't want to read it again. I read it.

RECORD OF INTERVIEW

DATE: 5 June 1994.
TIME COMMENCED: 3.10 pm.
TIME TERMINATED: 3.25 pm.
NAME: MacArthur John Faraday, Detective Senior Sergeant, Australian Federal Police.
OFFICERS PRESENT: Colin Arthur Payne, Inspector, Australian Federal Police. Wayne Ronald Rapsey, Detective Inspector, Internal Affairs Division, Australian Federal Police. Joseph Musca, Detective Inspector, Victoria Police.
SUBJECT: Matters relating to the surveillance of Howard James Lefroy.

D-I RAPSEY: For the record, this is a resumption of the interview with Detective Faraday terminated at five forty-five pm yesterday. Detective, do you have anything to add to your statements yesterday?
DSS FARADAY: No. Sir.
D-I RAPSEY: I want to go over a few things. The decision to wait for Howard Lefroy to dispose of the heroin. You made it.

DSS FARADAY: Yes.

D-I RAPSEY: Did you inform your superiors that Lefroy was in possession of the heroin?

DSS FARADAY: No.

D-I RAPSEY: Why was that?

DSS FARADAY: I was afraid it would jeopardise the operation.

D-I RAPSEY: Reporting something to your superior officer would jeopardise an operation. Serious statement, detective.

DSS FARADAY: Yes, sir. As I said last time and the time before, it was not my superior officer I was worried about but other officers.

D-I RAPSEY: Equally serious. What was your reason for waiting?

DSS FARADAY: I believed Lefroy was dealing with a top-level distributor. We had no idea who. Just take Lefroy out, some other importer takes his place. Nail everyone at the pick-up, we at least have a chance of finding out who's buying. Small chance, but a chance.

D-I RAPSEY: You say you discussed this with Inspector Scully.

DSS FARADAY: I told him. Correct.

D-I RAPSEY: What was his view?

DSS FARADAY: I don't recall him offering a view.

D-I RAPSEY: Did he disagree?

DSS FARADAY: I don't recall that he offered an opinion.

D-I RAPSEY: What if Inspector Scully says that he made it clear to you that he strongly opposed waiting for Lefroy to dispose of the heroin and wanted to…?

DSS FARADAY: He did not.

D-I RAPSEY: So he'd be lying?

DSS FARADAY: Draw your own conclusions.

D-I RAPSEY: Moving on. Howard Lefroy's flat. Visual contact?

DSS FARADAY: Three windows. Only the dining room blinds were left open at night.

D-I RAPSEY: And audio?

DSS FARADAY: All rooms except the hall. Sitting room was weak. Had been for a couple of days.

D-I RAPSEY: Why didn't you fix it?

DSS FARADAY: Too risky. Too close.

D-I RAPSEY: Too close to what?

DSS FARADAY: The pick-up.

D-I RAPSEY: There was going to be a pick-up at Lefroy's place?

DSS FARADAY: According to my information.

D-I RAPSEY: Source?

DSS FARADAY: I had information.

INSP. PAYNE: Answer the question, Mac.

DSS FARADAY: Lefroy's woman, Carlie Mance.

D-I RAPSEY: She was a registered informant?

DSS FARADAY: No. I believed registering my informant would endanger her.

D-I RAPSEY: You going to stick with this line?

DSS FARADAY: Yes, sir.

D-I RAPSEY: We'll come back to it. Believe me, we'll come back to it. Moving on. So Lefroy had five kilos of heroin in the flat and you were waiting for someone to come along and collect it?

DSS FARADAY: That's correct.

D-I RAPSEY: How long were you going to wait?

DSS FARADAY: As I said before, I had reason to believe that we didn't have long to wait.

D-I RAPSEY: How long had you been waiting?

DSS FARADAY: It's on record.

D-I RAPSEY: Tell me.

DSS FARADAY: Two days.

D-I RAPSEY: According to Inspector Scully, you initially informed him that the pick-up would take place within four days of the heroin's arrival at Lefroy's flat. Is that correct?

DSS FARADAY: Yes.

D-I RAPSEY: How did you know?

DSS FARADAY: Informant.

D-I RAPSEY: Ms Mance? The unregistered informant?

DSS FARADAY: Correct.

D-I RAPSEY: We'll revisit this. Moving on. Let's talk about the night.

DSS FARADAY: This'll be the third time.

INSP. PAYNE: Don't be an arse, detective. You're in serious trouble here. This isn't about dry-cleaning on the house or free screws.

D-I RAPSEY: What time did Ms Mance arrive?

DSS FARADAY: Just before Howie went for his walk. Around noon.

D-I RAPSEY: What did they talk about?

DSS FARADAY: The usual. Nothing. Howie didn't talk business to her.

D-I RAPSEY: So how did she know his business?

DSS FARADAY: She didn't. All she knew was that the pick-up was going to be at Howie's.

D-I RAPSEY: So Howard's on his walk? What then?

DSS FARADAY: Dennis rang. Said he was coming around. Eight-thirty sharp.

D-I RAPSEY: You were listening?

DSS FARADAY: It sounded like Dennis. It still sounds like Dennis.

D-I RAPSEY: Dennis been to Howard's place before?

DSS FARADAY: Not while we were on him, no.

D-I RAPSEY: Didn't think it strange Dennis suddenly decides to visit Howard?

DSS FARADAY: They're brothers. Their mother needs to go into a home and she doesn't want to. Howie takes her side. Dennis is on the phone to Howie for weeks trying to talk him round and he's getting nowhere. No, I didn't think it was strange he wanted to see Howie.

INSP. PAYNE: Your people made a positive ID of Dennis when he showed up?

DSS FARADAY: Good as they could. Mackie knew him. His car. Tinted glass. We took pictures. We've enhanced them. Looks like him.

INSP. PAYNE: But they didn't get a good look at him.

DSS FARADAY: They saw him for about thirty seconds. He drove up, the garage door opened, he drove in.

D-I RAPSEY: Opened?

DSS FARADAY: It's a high-security building. You need a remote control with your own code to open the garage door. Or someone in the building can press a button and open it.

D-I RAPSEY: So someone was watching for Dennis?

DSS FARADAY: They knew when to expect him.

D-I RAPSEY: Who was on duty?

DSS FARADAY: Mackie and Allinson.

D-I RAPSEY: You didn't think this was important enough for you to be there?

DSS FARADAY: No. Mackie knew Dennis. He knew Dennis better than I did. What would me being there help?

D-I RAPSEY: And with hindsight?

DSS FARADAY: With hindsight, I should have spent twenty-four hours a day on the job instead of just twenty.

D-I RAPSEY: Let's go on. Mackie rang you.

DSS FARADAY: Correct. I was asleep.

D-I RAPSEY: What did he say?

DSS FARADAY: He said Dennis'd turned up.

D-I RAPSEY: And you said?

DSS FARADAY: I said: So?

D-I RAPSEY: Mackie suggested a tail on Dennis when he left. What was your response?

DSS FARADAY: I said no.

D-I RAPSEY: Didn't even consider it? Five kilos of smack up there, brother shows up on short notice.

DSS FARADAY: Dennis is clean, no history, no connections. Rotary clean. In the time we covered him, he did nothing. He thinks Howie made his money on the stockmarket. He's not going to courier smack for Howie.

D-I RAPSEY: So Dennis drives off. When did Mackie call you again?

DSS FARADAY: Nine o'clock. Just after.

D-I RAPSEY: The reason?

DSS FARADAY: He was worried about a call Howie made as Dennis came out.

D-I RAPSEY: Listened to it?

DSS FARADAY: I've listened to it.

D-I RAPSEY: Howard's voice.

DSS FARADAY: Howie's voice.

D-I RAPSEY: Sound a bit stagey?

DSS FARADAY: Yes.

D-I RAPSEY: Know the person on the other end?

DSS FARADAY: As you know, the person doesn't say anything.

D-I RAPSEY: One-way conversation.

DSS FARADAY: Not unusual for Howie. They pick up the phone, he talks.

D-I RAPSEY: Never raised a doubt in your mind?

DSS FARADAY: Not when Mackie described it, no.

D-I RAPSEY: What did you tell Mackie?

DSS FARADAY: Told him I'd listen the next day.

D-I RAPSEY: Ten minutes later, he rings you again. What did he say this time?

DSS FARADAY: Someone rang Howie. Howie didn't make any sense, didn't answer questions, said goodbye in the middle of something the guy was saying.

D-I RAPSEY: That didn't alarm you? Didn't interest you?

DSS FARADAY: No. Sounded like vintage Howie.

D-I RAPSEY: And when you listened to the tape?

DSS FARADAY: I had the benefit of hindsight.

D-I RAPSEY: Would you have picked it if you'd been there?

DSS FARADAY: Yes.

D-I RAPSEY: And exactly when did you listen to the tape?

DSS FARADAY: The next day.

D-I RAPSEY: Mackie says he asked you to come back and listen. Is that right?

DSS FARADAY: He did.

D-I RAPSEY: And you didn't.

DSS FARADAY: I didn't see any reason to.

D-I RAPSEY: So let's get this straight. Lefroy is sitting in his flat with five kilos. You believe that a pick-up could take place at any time. He gets a visit from his brother. Something that hasn't happened before. Your man calls you to suggest a tail because he didn't get a good look at Dennis. You say no. Howard makes a phone call to someone who doesn't talk back. Your man calls you. Forget it, you say. Then someone calls Howard and it sounds weird to your man. He calls you. You say, I'll listen tomorrow. Is that a fair account?

DSS FARADAY: You have to understand, Mackie was new on Howie. I've listened to hundreds of Howie's conversations. This stuff wasn't weird for him.

D-I RAPSEY: Nothing else happened that night?

DSS FARADAY: No. Loud music. Stopped about midnight. Often that way.

D-I RAPSEY: No more calls.

DSS FARADAY: No.

D-I RAPSEY: Let's go to the morning. What kind of routine did Lefroy have?

DSS FARADAY: Call to his broker. Six forty-five, Monday to Friday.

D-I RAPSEY: This Thursday he didn't.

DSS FARADAY: No.

D-I RAPSEY: What else did he always do?

DSS FARADAY: Open all the curtains. Make coffee. Walk around naked. Phone people.

D-I RAPSEY: Didn't happen either.

DSS FARADAY: No.

D-I RAPSEY: Who was on duty?

DSS FARADAY: O'Meara. Stand-in.

D-I RAPSEY: Briefed on Lefroy's habits? Knew what to expect? Shown the log?

DSS FARADAY: He was a stand-in. He was covering for two hours.

D-I RAPSEY: What time did you show up?

DSS FARADAY: Just after seven am.

D-I RAPSEY: Was that late?

DSS FARADAY: Depends. I had a flat. Happens.

D-I RAPSEY: What did you do when you finally arrived?

DSS FARADAY: Listened to the tape. Two minutes. We went straight in.

Howard Lefroy was in the wide hallway, near the sitting room door. He was wearing one of his big fluffy cotton bathrobes, the one with navy blue trim. The carpet was pale pink, the colour of a sexual blush. Except around Howie's head and upper body, where it was dark with his blood. He'd been killed where he lay, his head pulled back by the ponytail and his throat cut. More than cut. He was almost decapitated. The bathrobe was bunched around his waist, displaying his short hairy legs and big buttocks.

Carlie Mance was in the bathroom, naked. She had tape on her mouth and her wrists were taped to the chrome legs of the washbasin. The man had been behind her when he cut her throat, kneeling between her legs, a fistful of her dark, shiny hair in his right hand, dragging her head back.

Her blood went halfway up the mirror over the basin, a great jet that hit the glass and ran down in neat parallel lines.

I should have stayed to ID Dennis. Or I could have put Mackie in a car right outside the garage to ID him. Or we could have had Traffic Operations pull him over nearby and had a good look at him. Carlie would have been alive. Lefroy too, not that I cared about that: cheated, that's all I felt when I saw him.

But I didn't do any of those things ... And I didn't put a tail on the car. Thirteen years on the job and I didn't do any of those things.

The portable phone had a device that looked like a dictation machine attached to it. Howard Lefroy was on the tape, the two phone calls that had made Mackie suspicious. They were composites.

D-I RAPSEY: Tell us about this lockup of yours.
DSS FARADAY: As I've said about twelve times, it's not my lockup. I hired it for my wife. I took some of her stuff there. Once. I gave her the key.
D-I RAPSEY: We're assuming here that it would be out of character for your wife to keep 100 grams of smack and $20,000 in cash in her lockup. Fair assumption?
DSS FARADAY: I'd go with it.
D-I RAPSEY: So it would belong to someone else. Right?
DSS FARADAY: Jesus, charge me, why don't you?
D-I RAPSEY: In good time. You've had dealings with Howard Lefroy, haven't you?
DSS FARADAY: Dealings? I don't know about dealings. I was on a job where we tried to get in touch with him. Seven, eight years ago.
D-I RAPSEY: You tried to roll a bloke. One of Lefroy's runners.
DSS FARADAY: We rolled him.
D-I RAPSEY: But it didn't work out.
DSS FARADAY: No. We put him in a safe house and somebody came around and took him away.
D-I RAPSEY: Dead, would you say?
DSS FARADAY: I would say.
D-I RAPSEY: You aware the talk was Lefroy was tipped off?
DSS FARADAY: That is what generally happens in Sydney. People get tipped off.
D-I RAPSEY: By you?
DSS FARADAY: I'll say yes? I'm supposed to say yes, am I? Trick question, is it?
D-I RAPSEY: So first Lefroy gets lucky with you around and then he gets unlucky.
DSS FARADAY: I'm sorry, is that a question?
D-I RAPSEY: It's the central question on my mind, Detective Faraday. It's the central question on many people's minds. And we'll answer it before we're finished. Interview terminated at three twenty-five pm.

That wasn't the last interview, not by a long way. But as I had sat there, looking at the men who weren't looking at me, I had known without doubt that I wasn't one of them anymore. It was the end of that life. Thirteen years. Thirteen years of belief and self-respect. Pride, even. Come to an end in a grubby little formica-lined office reeking of disbelief.

I could have lived with that. What I couldn't live with was that my negligence, my confident negligence, killed Carlie Mance.

I put the file away, made a phone call and set off for Melbourne to look for the scene of Dr Ian Barbie's end.

IT TOOK me the best part of two hours to get to Varley Street, Footscray. And when I got there, I didn't want to be there. It was a short narrow one-way street that ended in the high fence of some sort of container storage depot. Newspaper pages, plastic bags, even what looked like a yellow nylon slipper had worked their way into the mesh.

The right side of the street was lined with the high rusting corrugated-iron walls of two factories. The steel doors of the first building appeared to have been the target of an assault with a battering ram, but they were holding. At the end of the street, one of a pair of huge doors to the second building was missing, leaving an opening big enough for a truck.

The left side of Varley Street consisted of about a dozen detached weatherboard houses, small, sad structures listing on rotten stumps behind sagging or collapsed wire fences. Several of them had been boarded up and one was enclosed by a four-metre-high barbed-wire fence. About a tonne of old catalogues and other pieces of junk mail had been dumped on the porch of the house three from the corner.

My instinct was to reverse out of Varley Street and go home. There was nothing to be gained here. But I parked at the end of the street outside a house that showed a sign of being lived in: a healthy plant was growing in a black nursery pot beside the yellow front door. I got out, locked the door, put on the yellow plastic raincoat I kept in the car, and crossed the street.

The missing door had opened on to what had probably been a loading bay, a large concrete-floored space with a platform against the right-hand wall, which had two large sliding doors in it.

Opposite the entrance was another doorway with both doors open. Trucks had once driven through to the tarmac courtyard visible beyond.

I walked out into the courtyard. There was a blank corrugated wall to the left, a low brick building that looked like offices to the right and ahead a high cinder-block wall. The day of the weeds had come. Everywhere they were pushing contemptuously through the tarmac and their reflections lay in the cold puddles in every depression.

To my right, about twenty metres along, there was another doorway, big enough for a vehicle.

I walked over and stood on the threshold.

It was a big space, dimly lit from small windows high in the street wall. People had been using it recently: there were deep ashes in a corner, surrounded by empty cigarette packets, beer cans and the ripped cartons and wrung-out bladders of wine casks. In the air was the chemical smell that comes from burning painted wood.

I walked into the middle of the space and looked up. The beams were low.

A voice said, 'Not there, mate. Over to ya right, that's where.'

There was a man standing in the doorway, a dark shape against the light. He came towards me, his details emerging as he moved into the gloom: long, unkempt grey hair, grey stubble turning to beard, thin body in a black overcoat over a tracksuit, battered training shoes, one without laces.

'Ya come to see where the bloke strung hisself up, have ya?' he said, stopping about five metres away.

'That's right,' I said.

'Not a cop,' he said. It was a statement of fact.

'No.'

'Got a smoke on ya?'

I shook my head.

'Should be chargin admission. See that beam up there?'

He pointed at the roof to my left, to one of the trusses. The crossbeams were about four metres up. 'Rope went over there. Jumped off the car roof.'

'How d'you know that?'

'No other way, mate. He was hangin there right up against the car, bout three feet off the ground. Head looked like it was gonna pop.'

'Did you find him?'

'Na. Me mate Boris. But I was right behind.'

I took a short walk, looking up the beam, looking at the floor, looking at the campfire zone. I came back and stopped a short distance from the man. The skin under his eyes was flaking.

'The bloke's mum asked me to take a look,' I said.

He nodded. 'Be a bit upsettin, rich bloke an all.'

'What's your name?'

'Robbo, they call me. Robert's me proper name.'

'Robbo, how do you know he was a rich bloke?'

He thought for a moment. 'Had a tie on, y'know. Funny that.'

'Anything else catch your eye?'

'Na. Tell ya the truth, I'd had a few. Went down the milk bar to call the cops.'

'You and Boris know this place well?'

He looked around as if seeing it for the first time. 'I reckon,' he said. 'Make a bit of a fire, have a drink.'

'You do that often? Every night?'

'When it's warm we just stay in the park.'

'Must have been pretty cold that night. How come you weren't here?'

'When?'

'The night the bloke hanged himself.'

'Dunno. Can't remember.'

'So you came here the next day. In the morning?'

Robbo fingered the skin under his left eye. 'I reckon,' he said. 'Boris'd know. He's a youngster.'

'I might like to talk to Boris,' I said. 'Is he going to be around some time?'

Robbo looked off into the middle distance. 'Well,' he said, 'ya see him and ya don't.'

I took out my wallet and found a ten-dollar note. 'Where do you buy your grog?' I said.

'Down the pub. Geelong Road. Just near the park.' He waved vaguely.

'They know your names there?'

He thought about it. After a while, he said, 'Reckon.'

I gave him the ten dollars. 'I'll leave a message for you at the bottle shop. Be sure you tell Boris. I'll give you another twenty each when I see him.'

He gave me a long look, nodded and shuffled off.

I carried on with my look around. The wood for the fire came from cupboards and counters in the office building. Only bits of the carcasses remained. Ripping up of the floorboards had started. To the left of the office building was a laneway ending in a gate, its frame distorted and with large pieces of mesh cut out.

There wasn't anything else to look at, so I left. As I was driving away, I looked in the rear-view mirror and saw a boy of about twelve, one foot on a skateboard, watching me go. I hoped he didn't have to do all his growing up in Varley Street.

THE STREETON pub. Solid redbrick building, twenty metres long, small lounge on the left, bar on the right, standing at a skew crossroads on a windy hill. I made a hole in a steamed-up pane of a bar window and watched a Volvo pull up outside: Irene Barbie, short red hair lighting up the sombre day like the flare of a match. What daylight was left was retreating across the endless dark-soiled potato fields. She was wearing a tweed jacket and jeans, didn't seem to notice the thin rain falling, took a small black suitcase from the front passenger seat and locked it in the boot. Vet's bag, full of tempting animal drugs. It wasn't an overly cautious thing to do: there were men drinking at the bar who looked capable of snorting Omo if it promised a reward.

I drained my glass and went through to the empty lounge to open the door for her. She was medium height, slim, nice lines on her face. It was hard to guess her age – somewhere in the forties. There was no grey in the springy red hair.

'Mac Faraday,' I said. 'Irene?'

We shook hands.

'I'll take a drink,' she said. 'Double scotch. Just had a horse die on me. Perfectly healthy yesterday, now utterly lifeless. Massive bloody things go out like butterflies. Thank God there's a fire.'

When I came back, she had her boots off and her feet, in red Explorer socks, warming in front of the grate.

'Thanks,' she said. 'Disgusting to take off your shoes in public, but I feel like I've got frostbite.'

'I'd join you,' I said, 'but I'm not sure my socks match.'

'I changed mine at lunchtime,' she said. 'I had a gumboot full of liquid cow shit.' She moved both sets of toes, waving at the fire.

We drank. I'd spoken to her on the phone. Allie knew her from working around the stables and that got me over the suspicion barrier.

'She's a real asset around here, Allie,' she said. 'District's full of self-taught farriers.' She had another large sip, put the glass on the floor beside the chair. 'Well,' she said, 'the pain is receding. I'll tell you straight away, I had very little to do with Ian in the last two years.'

'Something involving Ian puzzles me,' I said. 'A friend of mine, man called Ned Lowey, not a patient of Ian's, went to see him in Footscray. Now they're both dead. Both hanged. Ned, then Ian. Two days in between them.'

She was silent. Then she said, 'Well, that's hard to explain.'

'I'm not convinced Ned killed himself,' I said. 'Can I ask you whether you could see Ian killing himself?'

She considered the question, looking at me steadily, grey eyes calm under straight eyebrows. 'Yes,' she said. 'Yes, I could.'

'Why's that?'

Sip of whisky, audible expulsion of breath, wry face. 'It's not easy to talk about this.' She looked into my eyes. 'Are you married?'

'Not any more. Does that disqualify me?'

'People who haven't been married have trouble understanding how things can change over the years. I was married to Ian for nearly twenty years and I knew less about him at the end than I did at the beginning. Yes, he could kill himself.'

Now you wait.

'If you ask around about Ian, you won't hear anything but praise. Everywhere I went, people used to tell me how wonderful he was. It's worse now that he's dead. People stop me in the street, tell me how they could ring him in the middle of the night, never get a referral to a duty doctor, never get an answering machine. How he'd talk to them for twenty minutes, calm them down, cheer them up, make them feel better, traipse out at two am to comfort some child, reassure the parents, hold some old lady's hand. And it's all true. He did those things.'

'Sounds like the old-fashioned doctor everyone misses,' I said.

She smiled, without humour. 'Oh, he was. Like his partner, Geoff Crewe, seventy-nine not out. And Ian wasn't just a good doctor. He was wonderful company. Mimic anyone, not cruelly, sharp wit. He noticed things, told funny stories, good listener.'

She looked around the room, looked into her glass.

'But,' I said.

'Yes. The But. That was Ian's public face. Well, it was his private face too. In the beginning. There was an unhappiness in Ian and it got worse over the years. After about five years, it was like living with an actor who played the part of a normal human being in the outside world and then became this morose, depressed person at home. He'd come home full of jokes, talkative, and an hour or two later he'd be slumped in a chair, staring at the ceiling. Or in his study, head on his arms at the desk, or pacing around. He cried out in his sleep at night. Almost every night. I'd wake up and hear him walking around the house in the small hours. He used to love skiing, one thing that was constant. Went to Europe or Canada every year for three weeks. Then he just dropped it. Stopped. If he'd been drinking, he'd try to hurt himself, hitting walls, doors. He put his fist through a mirror once. Forty stitches. You couldn't reason with him. All you could do was wait until the mood swung. It happened a few times a year when we were first married. I was in love. I sort of liked it. It made him a romantic figure. In the end, we didn't speak ten words a day to each other. I stuck it out until our daughter left home and then I left him.'

'Did he have treatment?'

'Not while I was with him. I'd try to talk to him about it but he wouldn't, he'd leave the house, drive off, God knows where. And I was always too scared to push it for fear he'd do something in front of Alice.'

'He wasn't like that when you met him?'

'You had to live with him to see that side. People who'd known him for donkey's years had no idea. I met him at Melbourne Uni. He was fun, very bright, near the top of his class. We went out a few times, but I didn't impress his friends and he dropped me. Then I met him again here when I started practice.'

'He was a local?'

'Oh yes. Part of a little group from here at uni. Tony Crewe, Andrew Stephens, Rick Veene.'

'Tony Crewe – is that the MP?'

'Yes. All rich kids. Except Ian. His father was a foundry worker. Left them when Ian was a baby. His mother was Tony's father's receptionist for about forty years. I think Geoff Crewe paid Ian's way through St Malcolm's and through uni. They ended up partners.'

'And the group? Did Ian stay friends with the others?'

Irene had a sip of whisky, ran a hand through her hair. 'It's not clear to me that they ever were friends. Not friends as I understand friends. Mind you, I'm just a Colac girl. Ian was sort of … sort of in their thrall, do you know what I mean?'

'Not exactly.'

'Andrew Stephens was a golden boy. Clever, rich, spoilt, got a sports car when he turned eighteen. Scary person, really. Completely reckless. His father was a Collins Street specialist, digestive complaints or something, friend of Geoff Crewe's from Melbourne Uni. They were very close once, I gather. Andrew was sent to St Malcolm's because Geoff's boy went there. The Stephenses had a holiday place outside Daylesford called Belvedere. Huge stone house, like a sort of Bavarian hunting lodge. Andrew lives there now. With the gorillas. Sorry. Shouldn't say that.'

'Why not?'

She emptied her glass. 'I'm going to risk another one. What about you?'

'I'll get them,' I said.

She shook her head and went to the serving hatch. I was admiring her backside when she turned and caught me at it. We smiled.

'The gorillas?' I said when she came back with the drinks.

'Doesn't do to talk about valued clients. I'm due out there to look at a horse tomorrow. Still. Andrew's got two large men with thick necks living on the property. We call them the gorillas.'

'What do they do?'

'Nothing as far as I can see. Well, except take turns to drive the girls around.'

'His children?'

She laughed. 'Right age. No. He doesn't have children. Two marriages didn't take. There's always a new girl at Belvedere, two sometimes. Some of them look as if they should be at school. Primary school, my partner once said.'

'What's Andrew do for a living?'

'It's not entirely clear. Developer of some kind. They say he owns clubs in Melbourne. His father apparently left him a heap. He used to talk shares with Tony Crewe – shares and property and horses.'

'So you've been with them?'

'Oh yes. We'd go to dinner with Tony and current woman and Andrew and sometimes Rick Veene and his wife two or three times a year. I have to say I hated it. I think Ian did too. He turned into a kind of court jester when he was with Tony and Andrew and Rick. I once suggested we turn down a dinner invitation and Ian said, "You don't say no to Tony and Andrew". I said, "Why not?" and he said, "You wouldn't understand. They're not ordinary people". Anyway, Andrew and Tony had some kind of falling out and the dinners stopped.'

'Did Ian ever talk about Kinross Hall?'

'No. Geoff Crewe was the place's doctor for umpteen years and I think it sort of passed on to Ian. The director came with Tony Crewe to dinner a few times. Marcia Carrier. Very striking. Ian didn't get on with her so he gave up the Kinross work.' She swirled her drink around and finished it. 'Night falls,' she said. 'None of this helps in finding out why your friend went to see Ian, does it?'

'No,' I said. 'Why did Ian give up his practice and move to Footscray?'

Irene shrugged. 'No idea. Seems to have happened overnight. About a year ago, he phoned Alice, our daughter, and gave her a new phone number. She rang me.'

'Thanks for taking the time,' I said, getting up.

She gave me a steady look. 'If you want to talk again, give me a ring.'

We went out to her car in the deepening dark. There was a house across the road and I could see into the kitchen. A man in overalls was staring into a fridge as if he had opened a door on hell. As she was getting in, I said, 'Ian's pethidine habit. How long did he have that?'

Irene closed the door and wound down the window. The light from the pub lit half her face. 'What makes you think Ian had a pethidine habit?'

'Heard it somewhere,' I said.

She looked away, started the car. 'News to me,' she said. 'Give me a ring. We'll talk about it.'

I watched the cheerful Swedish tail-lights turn the corner where the ploughed paddock ran to the road and nothing interrupted the view. The line between night and day was the colour of shearers' underwear. Far away, you could hear the groan of a Double-B full of doomed sheep changing gear on Coppin's Hill. In the pub, a hand grenade of laughter went off.

The man across the road slammed the fridge door: hell contained. For the moment.

'WELL, GET on with it. What d'you want to know about Ian Barbie?'

'Why would he kill himself?'

Dr Geoffrey Crewe, age seventy-nine, gave me a sharp look from under eyebrows like grey fish lures. He was a big man, parts of whom had shrunk. Now the long face, long nose, long ears, long arms did not match the body. The body was dressed in corduroy trousers, what looked like an old cricket shirt, an older tweed jacket, and a greasy tweed hat. What had not shrunk was the value of his house. He lived across the road from the lake, redbrick double-storey facing south. I'd arrived as he was leaving on a walk. He set a brisk pace, even though his left leg buckled outward alarmingly when it met the ground. It occurred to me to ask him whether he fancied a game of football on Saturday. He could certainly outpace Flannery over a hundred metres.

'Don't know if there's a sensible answer to the question,' he said. 'What's it matter anyway? Made his choice. You make your choice. Serious choice, but just a choice.'

'His wife says he was often depressed.'

He gave me a look that said he'd met smarter people.

'Could be said about half the people in the line of work – more. Not shuffling bloody paper, y'know. Pain and suffering and bloody dying.'

A fat pink woman in a lime-green towelling tracksuit, large breasts swaying and bouncing out of control, lurched around a corner. 'Gidday, Dr Crewe,' she panted.

Dr Crewe touched a finger to the brim of his tweed hat. 'Don't know what they think they're doing,' he said. 'Do herself a lot more good jumping up and down naked on that miserable bloody shopkeeper she's married to.'

I rolled up my right sleeve. The day was clear, almost warm. I'd left my jacket in the car. 'Didn't surprise you?'

'Too late for surprises. Precious bloody little surprises me. What's that on your arm?'

I looked down. 'Burn.'

'Burn? What kind of work d'you do?'

'Blacksmith.'

He nodded. 'Reasonably honest trade.' Pause. 'This interest in Ian Barbie, say it again.'

I told him about Ned's visit to Footscray.

'Sure he went to see Ian?'

'The receptionist remembered him. He didn't have an appointment, said it was a private matter. She told Ian and he saw him after the next patient. He was with Ian for about ten minutes.'

Dr Crewe didn't say anything for a while. Out on the calm water, a man in a single scull was sitting motionless, head bowed, shoulders slumped, could be dead. Then he moved, first stroke slow and smooth, instantly in his rhythm, powerful insect skimming the silver surface. At the end of each stroke, there was a pause, missed in the blink of an eye.

'This Ned,' he said. 'Any drug problem there?'

'No.'

We walked in silence for perhaps fifty paces. 'Ian had a drug problem,' I said.

He didn't say anything, didn't look at me. We passed a scowling group of seagulls on a jetty, identical commuters waiting in anger for an overdue train home.

'I left the practice on my seventieth birthday,' said Dr Crewe. 'Nine years ago last month. Saddest day of my life. Second saddest. Nobody feels seventy, y'know. Not inside the heart. Always twenty-five inside.'

More silence. Two runners came from behind, short chunky men, hair cut to stubble, big hairy legs. Footballers. Then a tall blonde came into view, white singlet, tight black stretch shorts, hair pulled back. She was at full stride, moving fast, balanced, arms pumping. As the balls of her feet touched the ground, her long thigh muscles bunched above the knee. Her legs and torso were flushed pink, her head was back, mouth open, eyes slits.

We both turned to watch her go. Our eyes met.

'Always twenty-five inside,' he said. 'And sometimes you feel you could be twenty-five outside too.'

'Eighteen,' I said. 'Eighteen.'

He gave a snort and picked up the pace. We were going up an incline between two huge oaks when he said, 'You don't want to accept your friend's suicide.' A statement.

'No.' It came out sharply.

'I won't talk psychological bullshit to you, but some questions you have to leave alone. They didn't do it to hurt you. They did it because something hurt them and they wanted to put an end to that pain.'

'Dr Crewe,' I said, 'I don't know about Ian, but Ned wouldn't kill himself.'

He stopped. I was taken by surprise, went a pace further.

'They don't end up hanging by accident,' he said. 'So I don't know what you're saying.'

I said, 'I think Ned's suicide was staged. I think he was murdered.'

He put his head back and looked at me down the long nose. 'Police think what?'

'Investigating officer seems to think it's a possibility.'

'Probably humouring you. You reckon the same might hold for Ian?'

'If I'm right about Ned, it's possible.'

Dr Crewe sighed and started walking. After a while, he said, 'Loved the boy, y'know.'

I didn't say anything.

'Loved his mother, too, might as well tell you. People say he's mine, but he's not. Often wished he was. Instead I've got Tony – every inch a Carew, not a trace of Crewe in him. Mean-spirited, selfish, whole bloody clan's like that. Mean-spirited and selfish genes pass on to every generation, doesn't matter who they marry. Tony's mother was a prime example.'

A small, round man in a tracksuit overtook us, wobbling as he ran. 'Doc,' he gasped. It sounded like an appeal for help.

'G'day Laurie. Walk, you bloody fool.'

The man gave a feeble wave.

'Three Carews joined up the same day I did,' said Dr Crewe. 'Wife's brother, two of his cousins. You'd think one of 'em would see some action. Hah. Whole war in Canberra, fighting the paper, all three. More than luck involved, I can tell you. Tony's the same. If there's an easy way, he'll find it.'

'Ian was at Melbourne Uni with Tony,' I said. 'Little group of local boys, I gather.'

Dr Crewe looked at me, shook his head. 'Done anything to keep Ian away from Tony and Andrew Stephens and the Veene boy. Andrew's father was a good man, fine man, fought with the Greek partisans in the war. Good doctor too. Andrew. Young Andrew's just rubbish. Too much too soon. Like Rick Veene. Rick's got Carew in him somewhere down the line. His mother's Tony's mother's third cousin or something. Poisonous breed. Buy their way through life. Bought off bloody Carew, that was easy enough.'

'Carew?'

'Carew College, University of Melbourne. Tony's mother's grandfather paid for it. Out of ill-gotten gains. Unjailed criminal. College. Place you stay in. Know about that?'

'Only just,' I said.

He gave me a look and an appraising nod. 'Blacksmith. Name again?'

'Mac.'

'Mac. I remember. Mac.'

There was a sound like sandpapering behind us and a group of male runners split to pass us, came together, all one physical type, a big pack of brothers sent out to run until supper time.

'So,' I said, 'Carew.'

'Carew?'

'Bought off. Carew.'

'Bought off?'

'The college.'

'Oh. That's right. Bought off. Andrew Stephens, Carews and the Veenes. Bloody Carew family trust gives the college some huge sum every year. Clive Carew and Bob Veene were on the council then. Bob Veene. Bloody rabbit. Pathetic. Rick's the only son. Four girls. Nice things, bit on the big side mark you, but nice, healthy girls, never heard a bad word about them. One's married to a carpenter. That'd make the bloody Veenes' foreskins curl.'

'Why did they buy off the college?'

'Business with a girl. Didn't hear about it till years later. Tony's mother and the rest of them did the dirty work. Kept me in the dark 'cause they knew me. I'd have let the buggers take the consequences. Jail if necessary. Never been any consequences for Tony and Andrew. Never. Not in their lives. Now Tony's the bloody attorney-general. Unbelievable. Makes you think even less of politics. Never thought that'd be possible. Not an ounce of respect for anything. Went into politics because he saw it was easy money. All talk and some bloody public servant does the work. Or doesn't.'

He shook his head. 'Shocked me that old Andrew'd get involved in something like that. Doted on that bloody boy of his. We had a big blue, not the same after that. Friends for going on thirty years. Still, bribery's bloody bribery. Can't brush over it.'

'So Ian was involved in this Carew business?'

'Don't know. Suppose so. Time I found out, it was pretty pointless to ask.'

We had reached a marker that said two kilometres. Dr Crewe said, 'Turnaround time.'

'Kinross Hall,' I said. 'Why did Ian stop being Kinross Hall's doctor?'

His shoulders seemed to sag a little at the mention of the place.

'Don't know. Gave me the brushoff when I asked him. That Carrier woman, probably. Picked her for a cast-iron bitch moment I laid eyes on her. Another brilliant piece of work by Tony.'

'Tony?'

'Chairman of the management committee. Got her appointed instead of Daryl Hopman. He was deputy when old Crosland retired. Good man, sound. Well, he didn't last long after Carrier arrived. Took early retirement, died. Inside a few years, all the old staff gone.'

'Did you know about Ian's pethidine problem?'

He glanced at me. 'Ian had a lot of problems. Not a well man.'

'Physically not well?'

'Mind, body, all the same. Not a well man.'

I had a stab in the dark. 'Someone said he might have had some sort of sexual aberration.'

He didn't reply. We walked in silence. At his gate, Dr Crewe said, 'Big word for a blacksmith, aberration. Well, Mr Blacksmith, I'd like to think that Ian didn't kill himself. But I can't. For your man, maybe you're right. I'll say good day.'

I said thank you.

He nodded, opened the gate and went down the path without looking back.

On the way home, in minutes, the day darkened and it poured, solid sheets like a monsoon rain. A freezing monsoon rain. Then it stopped, the clouds broke, the sun came out and all along the road the shallow pools were full of sky.

KEN BERGLIN was in his mid-thirties when I went to work for him, but to me he seemed to be of my father's generation. He was tall and gaunt, bony-faced, with colourless thinning hair combed straight back, and he always wore a dark suit with a white shirt and dark tie.

On my first day back from training in Chicago, waiting to go undercover, we met at the War Memorial at opening time. It was autumn in Canberra, cold, the flaming leaves changing the colour of the air. We were looking at a World War I biplane in a towering near-empty gallery when he said to me in his hoarse voice, 'So you seen all the shooting galleries and the crack shops?'

I nodded.

'They tell you you can't do this work without a sense of moral superiority?'

'They mentioned it in passing,' I said. 'Few hundred times. I'm shit-scared to tell you the truth.'

'Always will be. That's the job. Listen, Mac, this moral superiority, holding the line against the forces of darkness stuff, that's useful out there. Like a swag full of arseholes. Believe me. I know. I've been there. Let's have a smoke.'

We went out into a courtyard. I offered him a Camel.

'There's some good comes from the Yanks,' he said. The air was still and the blue-grey smoke hung around us like a personal mist.

Berglin studied his cigarette. 'You live with the scum,' he said. 'One of them, in their world, they can buy anything, buy anyone. You forget what you are. Some of them you even like after a while. Then you start to think like them. The whole thing starts to look normal. Like a business, really. Ordinary business. Like being a man buys and sells fucking meat. So the vegetarians don't like the business. They don't even like to look in the shop window. Half a chance, they'd put you out of business. You think, what the fuck does that matter? There's plenty who want a thick, juicy steak. And all these friends of yours are doing is selling it to them. Should that be a fucking crime?'

Berglin paused and looked at me inquiringly. 'Making sense to you, this?'

'So far.'

Something caught his eye. He pointed. 'Eagle,' he said. We watched it for a while, bird all alone in the vast blue emptiness, dreaming on the high winds.

'Anyway,' Berglin said, 'when you start thinking like the other side, you're on the way to changing sides. And that will make you a worthless, faithless person. Agree?'

It was hard not to. I nodded.

Berglin took a deep drag and blew a stream of perfect smoke rings, like a cannon firing tiny grey wreaths.

'Worthless, faithless, that's bad,' he said. 'But there's worse. Dead is worse.' He stood on his cigarette butt. 'Let's have a look at Gallipoli. My favourite.'

He led the way to a gallery that featured a huge diorama of the disastrous Gallipoli landing. Two young Japanese tourists in expensive ski wear were studying it, faces impassive.

'Always have a look at this,' Berglin said. 'Bloody marvellous, not so?'

We admired the huge scene.

'You think you're scared?' he said. 'Consider these poor bastards. Boys led to the slaughter.'

It occurred to me that our meeting place was more than a matter of convenience.

The Japanese left. They were holding hands. 'Dead, Mac,' Berglin said again. 'One inkling that you've moved across, you're just a picture in an album. And we'll know, believe me. You cross over, you can't go home anymore. Know that line? American book. This is like marriage except that when we say "Till death do us part", we mean it. And it's you who's dead. You religious?'

I shook my head.

'No. Me neither. They say it can help with the fear. I deeply fucking doubt that. Well, we've got to talk some details. Got a little room here I sometimes use.'

Later, before he sent me off, Berglin said, 'How to be a halfway decent person. That's the main question in life. The work, the job, it's on the side of the fourteen-year-olds. Get a few free tastes – two years later, they're in the cold filing cabinet, tracks all over 'em like a rash. This scum, they are way over on the other side. Across the dark river. Keep it in mind, Mac. Won't, of course. Wouldn't be any fucking use if you did.'

He was absolutely right. I never gave it a thought over the next few years, living under the gun, sweating on the moment of discovery. But I often thought about that meeting with Berglin later. And I thought about it again, driving home from talking to Dr Crewe.

I parked outside the smithy and went to have a piss in the bathroom alongside the office. Still thinking about Berglin, I was in the room before I heard the shower.

Allie was in the big open shower stall facing me. She had her head back under the spray, arms raised to shampoo her hair. Before I backed out, I registered sleek pubic hair, flattened breasts with prominent nipples, defined ribcage, long muscular thighs.

I was in the smithy, shaken, lustful, looking at a sketch of gateposts a hobby farmer outside Wallace wanted when Allie came in, shiny clean, spiky, no make-up.

'Sorry,' I said. 'No truck. Didn't occur to me you'd be showering.'

'That's okay,' she said without a trace of embarrassment. 'They told us at school to lock the cubicle. I was feeling filthy. Alarm didn't go off this morning, twenty minutes to get to the job.'

'Where's the truck?'

'Lent it to Mick. Met him in the pub at lunchtime. He's broken down other side Newstead.'

'Overloaded with furniture ripped off the rural poor,' I said. 'That's the first time I've seen you naked.'

She smiled. 'You only had to ask.'

We looked at each other for a moment, a trace of awkwardness.

'You working?' she said.

'Gateposts for a bloke at Wallace.' I handed her the sketch the man had given me.

She whistled. 'Gateposts? These are gateposts? What is the place? Some kind of agribrothel?'

'Hardiplank house on two acres. He says his wife saw gateposts like this in America. Went to Disneyland with her first husband.'

Allie scratched her head. 'Disneyland and Cape Kennedy, Cape Canaveral, whatever it's called. Does he see that they look like two giant wangers?'

'Wanger? That's the current term is it?'

She nodded. 'This week's term. Wanger.'

'He's under no illusions,' I said. 'I suggested to him that they looked like a pair of pricks and he said, there's been two of us. When my wife marries again, she can come around and get you to make a third prick.'

'No illusions,' Allie said.

'Any idea how you'd make something like this?'

She shrugged. 'You work behind closed doors. Then you transport them at night, under a tarp. And you don't have anything to do with their, ah, erection.'

When we stopped laughing, we went over to the office and worked out how to make the posts and what to charge.

'Add twenty per cent to cover embarrassment and possible prosecution,' Allie said.

'We may have priced ourselves out of the market here,' I said.

'For this kind of work,' Allie said, 'we *are* the market.'

I rang the man and gave him the quote. When I put the phone down, I said, 'Didn't blink. Wife wants them up in time for the Grand Final. They have a big gathering every year.'

Allie frowned.

'No,' I said. 'Stop now.'

We went out into the rapidly chilling day to inspect the steel store.

'MACARTHUR JOHN Faraday,' Berglin said. 'Nothing for four years, then twice inside a month.'

I could picture the long, sardonic face, the narrow black shoes on the desk, the cigarette dangling from the jaundiced fingers.

'Twice?'

'Had your local jacks on the line about that special permit. Been firing the cowboy gun at the neighbours?'

'What'd you tell them?'

'Piss off. How've you been?'

'Fair. You?'

'So–so. Creeping age. What's on your mind?'

'Two things. One's a favour.'

'"And every favour has its price/paid not in coin/but in flesh/slice by slice." Know that poem?'

'Engraved on the mind,' I said. 'After two hundred hearings. I need to find someone.'

'We all do. It's the human condition.'

'Melanie Loreen Pavitt.' I spelled the surname. 'Born November 1966. Discharged from Kinross Hall November 1983. No known family. No fixed address after 1979.'

I'd gone back to the Kinross Hall print-out after talking to Dr Crewe. It said that in October 1983, in the week that Simon Walsh found the naked girl on Colson's Road, a girl called Melanie Pavitt turned seventeen and reached the end of her two-year stay at Kinross Hall. It was a straw.

'Thirty-two now,' Berglin said. 'What's Kinross Hall?'

'Place of safety, girls' juvenile detention centre, whatever they call them now.'

'Out your way?'

'Yes.'

'So what line you in now? Blacksmith and missing persons?'

'It's personal.'

'And the second thing?'

'I hear Carlie Mance was in that pub in Deer Park with Bianchi close to the day.'

There was a long silence. I could hear smoke expelled. Then Berglin said, 'Bianchi's dead, you hear that?'

'Carlie's dead too.'

'I think this thing's pretty much closed, Mac.' Berglin's voice was as close to sympathetic as it got.

'Closed? Someone cuts Lefroy's throat, rapes Carlie Mance, cuts her throat, walks away with a few million bucks in smack. On my watch. It's closed? It's a fucking unsolved crime. How does it get to be closed?'

Silence again. Then he said, 'Where'd you hear this Deer Park stuff?'

'Don't ask.'

'Jesus. And you want me to what?'

'Tell them to get out the file and start looking at Bianchi. Nobody looked at Bianchi.'

Berglin blew smoke. 'Mac, you look at Bianchi, who else are you looking at?'

'That's what I mean. I hear he's about to make deputy Pope.'

'You hear right. And you're suggesting I dump a bag of fresh dog shit in the Vatican air conditioning. I'll have to think about that. Give it a little thought. What's your number? This Pavitt, I'll tell you in the morning.'

I gave him the number. Then I said, 'I'm clean. You know that, don't you?'

Silence. A sigh. 'In so far as I can be said to know anything,' said Berglin. 'Yes.'

I was cutting twelve millimetre steel rods with the power hacksaw when the nose of a red Porsche appeared in my line of sight through the open smithy door. I cut the power, took off the helmet and went outside.

A big man, in his forties, overweight, bald, little ponytail, dark beard shadow, corduroy bomber jacket with leather collar, was getting out of the car. Another man was in the passenger seat. 'Afternoon,' he said. 'Mac Faraday?'

I said yes. He came over and put out a big hand. I shook it. Soft hand, gold chain around his wrist.

'Andrew Stephens,' he said. 'Sorry to butt in. Passing by. Can we talk for a minute?'

It took a second for the name to register. 'It's warmer inside,' I said.

We went into the smithy. He looked around like someone seeing for the first time a place where people worked with their hands.

'So what do you make here?' he said.

'Anything. Gates, fences, fighter aircraft.'

Stephens laughed, a girlish giggling laugh showing perfect teeth, capped. His head was pear-shaped. 'That's funny,' he said. He went over to the bench, took out a white handkerchief, wiped the bench, sat down, thighs wide apart.

'Saw Irene Barbie this morning,' he said. 'She told me you were interested in Ian's death, whether it was suicide.'

I nodded.

Stephens pulled at his ponytail. 'Great friend of mine, Ian,' he said. 'Can't believe he's gone.'

I didn't say anything.

He took a packet of cigarettes out of his jacket, waved it at me inquiringly, lit one with a slim gold lighter, blew smoke out of his nose. He was wearing a Rolex wristwatch. 'I'd like to think he didn't commit suicide,' he said. 'Irene said you asked about pethidine. What made you ask that?'

'Heard it somewhere,' I said.

Stephens took a drag, sighed smoke. 'It's true,' he said. 'Poor bastard. Irene didn't know. Ian suffered from depression, came on him in his twenties. We all tried to help, all his friends. Wasn't anything you could do. Nothing. Out of anyone's control. Pethidine's the only reason he didn't kill himself years ago.'

He took out the handkerchief and blew his nose. 'I gather a friend of yours was found dead recently too,' he said. 'I'm sorry. You don't know what it's like until you lose someone like that. Rather bloody not know.'

'Yes.'

He stood up. 'Well,' he said, 'I was coming this way, thought I'd stop and say, you find out anything that makes you think Ian didn't kill himself, I'd be grateful if you'd tell me. We all would. I know Tony Crewe – y'know Tony Crewe, the Attorney General? Close friend of Ian's, of mine. Tony would appreciate hearing anything like that.'

'I'll do that,' I said. 'But I think he killed himself.'

'Yes. That's what's most likely. Wonderful bloke, lovely. Well. That's life.'

We went outside. The other man was out of the Porsche now, leaning against it, smoking a small cheroot. He was big, thick-necked, face like a ten-year-old on steroids.

'While I'm here,' Stephens said, 'I'm thinking of getting someone to look after the maintenance on my properties. Big job, mainly supervision. Well paid. Think something like that would suit you?'

'Not really,' I said.

He nodded, put out his hand. 'Anything makes you think Ian's death's other than the way it looks, you let me know. I mean first. Before you tell anyone else. That way, we make sure everything's properly investigated. Quickly, too, I can guarantee that. Tony Crewe will see to that. Okay? And I'll make sure you're not out of pocket for any expenses. My duty to the family.'

'You'll be the first to know,' I said.

'Good man.' He took out a wallet, gave me a card, tapped me on the arm.

They got into the car and drove off. I heard the engine note turn to a howl as they took the first hill.

I STARTED at full forward, a position in the Brockley side where the ball was seen so rarely that a full forward had once gone home at the end of the third quarter and no-one noticed until the team was in the pub.

This Saturday was different. We were playing Bentham. I arrived about thirty seconds before the start, missing Mick Doolan's tactical briefing and inspirational rev-up. He got his motivational material from studying a six-pack of videos called *Modern Meisters of Motivation* bought for $2.50 at a trash and trivia market. The players, many having their last cigarette before quarter-time, found messages such as *Sell the SIZZLE not the STEAK* and *Don't SEE to BELIEVE, BELIEVE to SEE* extremely powerful: aflame, the Brockley side would stroll out, tugging at their jocks. The usual result: five goals down at quarter-time.

Not today. Either a new video found or Mick had fed the men elephant juice. Billy Garrett was, without effort, leaping free of the earth's grip. Players who routinely handballed into the ground or to the other side were sending the ball to within metres of team-mates. Even Flannery seemed fresh from a Swiss rejuvenation clinic, backing into packs and coming out with the ball. From all over the field, players were kicking the ball in my direction. It was unnerving but I took four marks, kicked two goals and a behind. At quarter-time, we were four goals up.

As we trooped off, I saw Allie on the bonnet of her truck, leaning back against the windscreen, legs crossed at the ankle. She was wearing a red quilted jacket and a scarf, and you could see the colour in her cheeks from thirty metres. There was a man lounging next to her, floppy dark hair, sallow, young. She gave me the thumbs up, hand cocked forward. Three things went through my mind. One, she'd come to watch me play without being asked. Two, she'd come with another man. Three, don't be a stupid prick.

In the second quarter, Bentham put a man called String Woodly at full-back. He consisted almost entirely of thin rubbery arms that he wound around you like pipe cleaners while pretending to be interested in taking a mark. No-one had ever seen him take a mark, but very few opposing players had got one while wrapped in String. Carrying him around was exhausting. Billy complained to the umpire. This didn't work. I resorted to falling over in his embrace, trying to land on him with an elbow in some painful spot. This didn't work either. I kept landing on my elbow with String on top of me. Finally, I had Flannery sent over and we had a chat.

The next time the ball came our way, coming down through the mist, Flannery got close behind the two of us, pulled out the back of String's shorts. Using the waistband elastic as a step, he ran up String's back and plucked the ball from the sky. String let me go, falling over forward, clutching at his shorts, now around his knees.

'That's not in the bloody game,' he said, offended, as Flannery landed on his right shoulder.

'Stick around, beanpole,' Flannery said, getting ready to kick. 'Show you lots not in the game.' He took two paces and kicked the ball through the middle. He looked around at me, astounded by his feat. 'Shit,' he said. 'Haven't kicked a goal since school.'

'That long,' I said. 'Since you were twelve.'

String wasn't the same after his experience, and Flannery and I saw off a few other Bentham spoilers before the day was over. We ran out ten-goal winners. No-one could remember Brockley winning by ten goals. We went back to the Oak in a state of high excitement, singing one another's praises. Nothing disturbed our joy until only the hard core remained.

'Was a time,' said Trevor Creedy, 'when Brockley won by bloody ten goals every second week.' He was a small man with close-set eyes, now murky, the kind of supporter who finds victory deeply unsatisfying. 'That was,' he said, 'before they starting pickin girls. And makin blokes coach never kicked a footy.'

'Trev,' Mick said, 'been meanin to ask ya. How'd ya like to share the coach's job? I mean, with a view to takin it over?'

Creedy's eyes narrowed. 'Ha,' he said. 'Tryin to bloody buy off ya critics. Won't bloody work with me.'

He left, now a happier man.

'Lovely fella,' said Flannery. 'Fixed his car for him, took it for a spin, see how it goes. When I give him the bill, he takes off fifty cents for petrol. Don't expect me to pay for your joyridin, he says.'

Mick's mobile trilled. He had a brief conversation, then he said, 'Vinnie, me own Gestapo's on the way. Let's have a lightnin round for the survivors.'

The dog joined me as I stepped out of the door, suddenly aware that no area of my body was without its own dull pain. A full moon gave a pale and cold daylight when the clouds parted. Both limping a bit, the dog and I walked down the road and down the lane.

I WAS in the office, going through Allie's work diary and writing up invoices, when I heard the car. Marcia Carrier was getting out of her BMW when I reached the door. She didn't look like an Olympic dressage contestant today. Today she looked like an Olympic skier *après ski*: dark hair loose, big cream polo-necked sweater, camel-coloured pants. She looked healthy and fit, like someone who ran and swam and had a lot of wholehearted sex in front of open fires, followed by yoghurt milkshakes.

'Mac,' she said, 'I rang the number you gave me, no reply. So I drove over on the off-chance.'

'Nice to see you,' I said.

'Got a few minutes?'

'Hours. Days. Kitchen's the only warm room in the house.'

'I was hoping for the forge.'

'Forge's having a rest today. Sunday is forge's day of rest.'

The kitchen didn't look too bad. Spartan but clean. I pulled another captain's chair in front of the stove. Mick Doolan had sold me six for two hundred dollars: 'To you, Moc, a gift. What I paid for them. Less. I think about it now, less. Much less.'

'I'll make coffee,' I said.

'Mac, sit,' she said, lacing her fingers. 'I have to tell you something and I'm embarrassed about it ...'

I sat down.

'When you came to see me about Ned Lowey, I think I said it was going to nag at me.' She was studying her left hand on the arm of the chair. It was older than her face.

'I remember.'

A spray of rain, like gravel thrown, hit the window. She tensed. Our eyes met.

'Well, it did. I went back to the files, looking for something that might have happened while Mr Lowey was working at Kinross. I found something. About an hour ago.'

'Happened to a girl?'

She nodded. 'Two girls.'

'When you were in charge?'

'I was new. Took over in 1983, into a nightmare. The place was run like a mini-kingdom, all these places were, minimal record-keeping, incompetent staff, all sorts of kickbacks with suppliers and contractors, ghosts on the payroll, you name it. My predecessor might have been a wonderful man but he was completely out of touch with what was going on around him. And to make things worse, Kinross wasn't even getting the funding it was entitled to. So I cleaned up the obvious rorts and got a proper reporting system going. Then I left the day-to-day running to my deputy. He seemed to be an honest person. I devoted most of my time to working on the department and the minister to get Kinross's funding up to speed.'

'The girls,' I said.

She clasped her hands, face unhappy. 'Mac, I found a report in Daryl Hopman's confidential file. He was my deputy. I've never seen the file before, didn't know it existed. And I only found it by chance.'

'What kind of report?'

'It involves two girls. I should have been told about it and I wasn't.'

She paused. I waited.

She sighed again. 'It also involves Mr Lowey. I'm sorry to tell you that. I know how much he meant to you.'

'Involves?' I could feel the blood in my head.

Marcia put her hands through her hair. 'I'll just say it. The girls were caught coming back into the Kinross grounds shortly before four am one night in November 1985. They said they had been at Ned Lowey's house and had been given drugs, amphetamines, speed, for sex.'

I stood up. 'Not possible, a mistake. Not Ned. Absolutely not.'

'I'm sorry,' Marcia said. 'I'm really sorry. I felt I had to tell you.'

I went to the window, looked out, saw nothing. 'What was done?'

'Nothing. It's unbelievable. Nothing was done about a serious allegation of criminal conduct. Nothing. It says everything about the way Kinross was run in the old days. I shudder to think what else may have been ignored like this. In the maintenance supervisor's file I found a note from Daryl saying that Ned was not to be employed again. I presume Daryl wrote the report as some kind of insurance if word leaked out.'

'Insurance?'

'He may have planned to say that he had made a report to me and that I was the one who failed to act.'

'The girls said Ned gave them drugs?' Ned having anything to do with any drug other than a stubbie of Vic Bitter was inconceivable. But my treacherous inner voice said: *What do you really know about Ned?*

Marcia unclasped her hands, pushed back her hair, started to speak, hesitated. 'I shouldn't tell you this, Mac,' she said, 'but that's not the whole story.'

I shook my head in disbelief. I didn't want to hear any more. I wanted to hold on to the Ned I loved.

'The girls said Dr Barbie was at Ned's house and had sex with them. Violent sex.'

Ned going to see Ian Barbie in Footscray.

Ned and Ian Barbie, both dead, hanged.

The girl's skeleton in the mine shaft. The newspapers Ned kept.

Melanie Pavitt, naked and bleeding in Colson's Road. About four kilometres from Ned's house.

'What are you going to do?' I said.

Marcia got up, tugged at her sweater. 'Nothing. I'm not going to do anything. They're dead. Both men. What's the point of doing anything now? The families have had enough pain.'

She came over, put her hand on my arm. I could smell her hair, a rose garden far away.

'Mac, I've destroyed Daryl's report,' she said in a low voice. 'I think you and I are the only people who know about this. The two of us and the girls. They probably don't even remember it. I'm protecting myself, I can't deny that. I was in charge, I'm responsible for the girls' welfare. But I'm a victim here too. I knew nothing about what happened. Daryl left this thing behind like a time bomb.'

I didn't say anything.

Marcia squeezed my arm gently. 'Mac, I think I'm doing the right thing for everyone. Is it the right thing? If you think it isn't, I'll go public, take the consequences. If you think it is, we never speak of the matter again. To anyone.'

What else was there to say? 'Yes.' I said. 'It's the right thing.'

At her car, engine running, window down, she said, not looking at me, 'God, I'm glad that's over. Would you like to have a drink some time, dinner? Anything?'

I pulled myself together. 'Drink, dinner, followed by anything. And everything.'

'I'll call you,' she said, hint of a smile.

I watched the car go down the lane, turn, heard a little growl of acceleration. I didn't want to go inside, didn't know what to do with myself, got into the Land Rover and drove.

STAN HARROP and his son, David, were in the northwest corner of the field nursery on Stan's property, talking to the driver of a tip truck carrying a load of stones. I parked at the gate and made my way along the paths between raised north–south beds. David gave me a salute. He was about twenty-five, thin and sandy, with Stan's big hands. Stan had waited until he was nearly fifty to take his shot at immortality with David's mother.

'A wall, Mac,' Stan said. 'A drystone wall. Twenty metres of wall. Know anything about drystone walls?'

'Been a while,' I said. When I was sixteen my father and I built two hundred metres of drystone wall on a property called Arcadia near Wagga. In my mind I saw a man and a boy and a pile of stones in the burning day, and heard my father say: *Stone you need's at the bottom of the bloody pile. That's the way nature works. In bloody opposition to man.*

'So where d'ya want 'em?' the driver said. He was a fat, sad-looking man in overalls and a baseball cap with 'Toyota' across the front.

Stan scratched his head. 'Well, I suppose they can go just here.'

'Want my advice?' I said.

'Quick,' Stan said.

'What's the line of the wall?'

'North–south,' David said. He pointed. 'In line with that post.'

'Take it slow and tip 'em out down the line,' I said to the driver. 'You don't want any piles. Do that?'

'At the limit of the technology,' the man said. We got out of the way and he went into action.

'The right stone,' I said. 'Finding it's the problem. Much easier if they're spread out.'

'What about the footing?' said Stan.

'How high's the wall supposed to be?'

'Not high,' said David. 'Metre and half.'

'High enough,' I said. 'Needs a trench about half a metre deep, metre and a quarter wide. Then you taper the wall to about fifty centimetres at the top. Put a bit of cement in the bottom layers. Purists don't like that.'

'Purists be buggered,' Stan said. 'Get the machinery, lad.'

I got gloves out of the Land Rover, put on boots. David ripped the footing in half an hour. We shovelled out the earth, hard work, and then we got the strings up. I showed Stan how to arrange the bottom rocks, then

David and I carried and Stan laid. It was punishing work, moving heavy objects not created with human hands in mind.

'Wanted to give the women a surprise,' Stan said. 'Gone to Melbourne. To shop. What kind of bloody activity is that?'

'I could learn to shop,' I said. 'Can't be that hard.'

I was glad to be there, glad that there was somewhere I could be, glad to be doing something that prevented me from thinking about Ned. I desperately didn't want to think about Ned.

We stopped when the light was almost gone, cold biting the face.

'I think I see a drink in your future,' Stan said, patting my shoulder. 'Thought metal was the area of expertise. Now you turn out to know a bit about stone.'

We sat in Stan's office next to the low whitewashed brick house he had built in the lee of the hill. A fire was burning in a Ned Kelly drum stove. David drank his beer and went off to feed the chooks. Stan took two more bottles of Boag out of the small fridge in the corner and opened them.

'Something on your mind,' he said.

I drank some beer out of the glass mug and looked at a botanical print on the wall. 'Heard a story about Ned today,' I said.

'Yes.' He was lighting his pipe with a big kitchen match.

I told him what Marcia had said.

Stan blew out smoke, drank beer, put the mug and pipe down. He didn't show any sign of shock.

'Ned. Drugs. Sex with teenage girls.' He looked at me over the big hairy knuckles of his clasped hands. 'Go to my grave not believing it.'

'Who'd invent something like that?' I said.

'You believe it?'

'Rather not think about it. Wouldn't have had to think about if I hadn't gone poking about.'

'What poking about?'

I told him about Ned's visit to Kinross Hall, how my questioning of Marcia Carrier had led to her finding of Daryl Hopman's report.

'Just her word for it, then,' Stan said. 'Could be trying to shift the blame from the doctor to Ned.'

'Then why mention the doctor at all?'

We sat in silence, Stan generating smoke. For a moment I had been going to tell him about the other things that haunted me: the skeleton in the mine shaft, Melanie Pavitt naked in Colson's Road, Ned's visit to Ian Barbie in Footscray. But Daryl Hopman's report offered an explanation for all of them that was too chilling to speak about.

'Better get moving,' I said, getting up. 'Boy's at home without food.'

'Boys find food,' Stan said. He walked to the vehicle with me. When I'd started it, he said: 'Learned a lot about men in the war. Scoundrels and saints, met 'em both. Don't believe this about Ned, so it's not going to change anything.'

We looked at each other, united in our desire to hold on to the Ned we knew.

'Another thing, Mac,' said Stan.

I could barely see his face.

'Ned was like a brother to your father. Something like this, he would have known. See you tomorrow.'

As I drove away, I thought perhaps my father did know. Perhaps that was what he wanted to tell me on the night he shot himself.

WE'D PUT in five hours in the grounds of Harkness Park – me, Stan Harrop, Lew and Flannery – before Francis Keany's Discovery murmured down the driveway. What we were trying to do was uncover paths, using a large-scale plan Stan and I had drawn from exploration and aerial photographs and the old photographs I'd found.

'They're bloody there,' Stan said. 'Get the paths, we've got the garden.'

It was hard going: the place was one big muddy thicket. The elms in particular had embarked on world conquest, sending out armies of suckers, densely colonising large areas. Some of the suckers were mature trees, now spawning empires of their own.

'Dutch elm disease might be the answer,' Stan said. 'Nature's way of saying fuck off.'

Stan had assembled us at 8.30. We were armed with two chainsaws and a new thing, a brushcutter with a circular chainsaw blade. Flannery liked the idea very much.

'Tremble, jungle,' he said.

I said, 'The point is, Flannery, we apply the technology with some purpose in mind. We don't apply it simply because we like laying waste to large areas of nature and seeing big things fall over.'

'Wimp,' said Flannery.

Stan went for a long walk through the muddy paddocks around the house. We were on smoko, sitting on Flannery's ute, when he came back. 'Major thing,' he said, hitching his buttocks onto the tray, 'major thing is, gardens like this, they're designed for vistas. Looking *from* the house and the garden, looking *at* the house and the garden. But if the bloody vista's gone, all brick-veneer slums crowding it, you can't see what the designer saw.'

'So you got it worked out,' Flannery said. He was eating a pie. A viscous fluid the colour of liquid fertiliser was leaking down his unshaven chin. This and the Geelong beanie pulled down to a centimetre above his eyebrows gave him a particularly fetching appearance.

'More or less,' Stan said. At that moment, Francis Keany's vehicle came into view.

Francis got out, the picture of an English country gentleman. He nodded to the peasants and said to Stan: 'Good morning, Stan. So what do we now know? Enough research to write an entry in the *Encyclopaedia Britannica.*

Paid by the hour. Photographs taken from a great height. At a cost of about five dollars a metre. Charged both going up and coming down, as far as I can tell. So what do we now know about this garden?'

Francis had clearly been working on his opening lines during the drive from Melbourne.

Stan was patting pockets for his pipe. 'Not much,' he said, sadly.

Francis's face went tight. He pursed his full lips, lifted his chin and slowly turned his face away from us until he was in full profile. This was a mistake. Stan had a clipping of a magazine article in which Francis's profile was described as that of a Roman senator on a coin.

'What Roman senator do you think that magazine twat had in mind?' Stan said in a musing tone. 'Pompus? Was there a Priapus? What about Fartus?'

Francis came back into full face. He blinked several times, willing himself to remain composed. 'In a few minutes,' he said, voice edging on the tremulous, 'Mr and Mrs Karsh are going to drive. Through that gate. I'd like to have something to tell them. If that's at all possible.' Pause. 'Stan.'

Stan found the battered and blackened object resembling a piece of root rescued from a bonfire. He applied a yellow plastic lighter with an awesome flame. Smoke gathered around him until he looked like a smouldering scarecrow. Francis took two paces backwards to get away and was starting to speak when a black Mercedes station wagon with tinted windows nosed around the corner of the drive.

'Oh shit,' he said.

The car stopped next to Francis's Discovery. The front doors opened. The driver was a tall woman, thirties, lightly tanned, sleek dark hair to her shoulders, minimal make-up. She was wearing a camelhair donkey jacket, thin cream sweater, jeans and walking boots. The passenger was in his late fifties, stocky, pale, small features, dark suit, tired eyes. He ran fingers the colour of chicken sausages through his thick grey hair and loosened his striped tie.

'Jesus,' he said. 'Why isn't it snowing?'

Francis coughed. 'Leon,' he said. 'Anne. Good to see you. Filthy weather, I'm afraid. I'd like to introduce Stan Harrop. He's one of my associates with a special knowledge ...'

Leon Karsh ignored this and came around to shake hands with all of us, starting with Flannery. 'Leon Karsh. Thanks for your help here.' Soft voice, unusual accent, upper-class English over something else. When he got to Stan, he said, 'My wife tells me you were responsible for Faraway in Bowral. I knew the family. Wonderful garden.'

'Responsible, no,' Stan said. 'I was the maintenance man.'

Leon Karsh smiled. 'Excellent maintenance, then.'

'Thank you,' Stan said.

'What I'm trying to do here, Leon,' Francis said, 'is to recapture the essence of the original garden without necessarily being constrained by the more obvious limitations of the original designer's vision. To do that ...'

'What limitations are those?' said Stan.

Francis gave him a look, a laser beam of hatred. 'To the trained eye,' he said, 'it's obvious that the absence of a central axis ...'

'To the trained eye,' Stan said, 'there is a central axis. Mac, explain. I've got to get these expensive craftsmen back to work.'

It was amazing to me that Stan had managed to work for other people for so long. I fetched the plan and the copies of the photographs from the truck and laid them out on the tray. Anne Karsh was at my left elbow, Leon Karsh at my right. I could feel Francis behind me, trying to see over my shoulder. Anne smelled faintly of rosemary and cinnamon, a clean smell.

I said, 'The garden was designed around 1885 by an Englishman called Robert Barton Graham for the Peverell family. The Peverell brothers were on the Ballarat goldfields until they realised there was more money in supplying timber and then flour to the miners. They built a mill on the creek here in 1868 and the house later. It was in the family till the 1950s. Lots of them are buried down the road here, next to the church.'

I found the right photograph. 'This is dated December 1937. Two gardeners clipping a low circular hedge. It's box. If you look carefully, you can see there's a circle of hedge inside another circle. Paths run to the centre. A cross of paths.'

Anne Karsh leant forward to look at the photograph. 'A sort of double mandala,' she said. 'One path's wider than the others.' A breast touched my arm.

'Exactly,' Francis said. 'Mac has been very useful ...'

'The luck here is the sundial,' I said, pointing at the photograph. 'It tells us this picture was taken looking north.'

'That's important,' Francis said. 'Obviously ...'

'It also tells us the time of day,' I said. 'It's late afternoon. This dark at the top left of the photograph – we couldn't work that out. That's because we assumed that the wide path would be the key to the long sightline. You can see the path runs north–south, and that puts the house behind the photographer.'

'It's the shadow of the house,' Anne Karsh said, the pleasure of discovery in her voice. 'That's the big chimney.'

I said, 'That's right. It made Stan think that perhaps the long axis of garden ran across the front of the house.'

'Odd thing to do, isn't it?' Leon Karsh said. 'Not that I know anything about garden design.'

'You have an instinct for form, Leon,' Francis said. 'It's a gift.'

'It is odd,' I said, 'and unlikely, according to Stan. Then we got the aerial photographs.'

'I insisted on aerial photography,' Francis said. 'One of the most valuable tools in the armoury of the garden restoration architect.'

'Tools in an armoury, Francis?' Anne Karsh said. Stan was going to like her.

I unrolled the big enlargement. 'Here's the house. Here's the creek. Here's the old mill. Now, from the length of the house shadow in the old photograph …'

'You can pinpoint the sundial,' Anne Karsh said, pointing. She had strong hands, no rings. 'God, it's just jungle.'

'We've found it,' I said. 'Box and yew trees now. Something else puzzled us.' I pointed to a large area, bare in comparison with the rest of the garden, to the right of the house.

'Not a natural shape,' Anne Karsh said. She bent over the photograph and her hair swung like a silk curtain and touched my cheek. I flicked a glance at her. I wished I'd shaved.

'Not at all natural, Anne,' Francis said. 'Very perceptive of you.'

'No-one had mentioned,' I said, 'that the original house burned to the ground in 1904.'

'The shape of a house,' Leon Karsh said. 'You fellows have done well.'

'Thank you, Leon,' Francis said, modestly.

'The mark of the house still shows because, for some reason, they didn't finally demolish the ruins until the late 1940s,' I said. 'They built the new house as a replica of the old one, but it was too late to change the main axis of the garden. You'll also have to live with it.'

'A pleasure,' Anne Karsh said. I didn't look at her. I wanted to.

'Stan's worked out the focal point of the main axis,' I said. 'The main sightline leads the eye to the church steeple in Brixton. You can't see it now because of those pines planted about forty years ago. Stan found out that while Graham was working on the garden, he also designed the church. Colonel Peverell paid for it.'

'One cheque satisfied both man and God,' Leon Karsh said. 'In that order. Things don't change much.'

'So,' Francis said, 'you can now appreciate the enorm … the magnitude of my task here.'

'Can we see what's happened so far?' Leon Karsh said to me. I looked at Francis. He was not a pleased person.

'Go ahead, Mac,' he said. 'I have planning to do.' He turned to Anne Karsh. 'My dear, you have no idea – the logistics of a project like this resemble fighting the Gulf War.'

The Karshes put on gumboots and I showed them what we'd found so far, including paths, a sunken tennis court and a pond that was gravity-fed through a stone aqueduct from a spring on the hillside behind the house.

'Where does the water go from here?' Anne Karsh said.

'Haven't got to that yet,' I said. 'Probably channelled down to join the creek above the pond that feeds the millrace.'

'There's a millrace?' She checked herself, delighted. 'Well, since there's a mill, I suppose there is.'

'In good shape,' I said. 'Locals say the mill produced flour until World War II. The creek's dammed down there to create a millpond. You open a sluicegate to let water into the headrace.'

'I'd like to see that,' Anne Karsh said.

'Next time,' Leon Karsh said. 'The architect should be here. Should have been here before us.' He turned his weary eyes on me. 'So you're a landscape gardener?'

'No.'

Leon looked at me. Not a glance. A look. In his eyes you could see instinct and intelligence. I was being evaluated. God knows what he saw in my eyes. Attraction to his wife perhaps.

'No,' I said, 'I'm a blacksmith. I work for Stan when things are slow. Which is quite often.'

'But you haven't always been a blacksmith.'

'Leon,' Anne said, 'you're prying.'

'That's right,' Leon said. 'I'm prying. My whole life is spent prying.'

'I've done a few things.'

'And you're not easily pried. We'll need an estate manager here when we're finished. You might be interested.'

'Bit too independent these days,' I said. 'But that might change. I'll show you what's left of the walled garden on the way back.'

The architect was waiting at the house, a thin middle-aged man, wispy chicken-feather beard, dressed for an Atlantic crossing in an open boat. With him was a clone, cloned smaller, presumably the assistant architect. In my days among the rich, I'd observed that nothing they paid for came in ones: not lawyers, not gardeners, not architects, not whores. Even their women came with a mother or a sister or a friend, usually fat, often ugly, always resentful.

I excused myself to rejoin the labourers, to go back to my place. Leon shook my hand. Anne said, 'I'd like to see the mill some time if that can be arranged.'

'Any time you want to see it, it's down there,' I said. 'It's your mill.'

'Mac,' Leon said, 'I'll tell Francis to build in the time for showing Anne the mill. Keep her away from the dangerous places. These old buildings, everything's rotten.'

'Any time,' I said.

I found Flannery and Lew on their hands and knees looking for a path. 'Glad to see you're safe,' Flannery said. 'Thought you'd slipped over onto the managerial side. Notice that woman's mouth? Very powerful. Suck the grips off your handlebars. She give you an indication of anything?'

'Said she found the bloke with the pie gravy running down his chin irresistible. Turned her on.'

'I've heard it can do that,' Flannery said. 'Chittick's pie.'

*

At the end of the day, we had a few beers at the Heart of Oak and then I went home, dog-tired, still hurting from Saturday's football, sick at heart about Ned.

It was Lew's turn to make the meal. I poured a big glass of red wine and went out to the office to finish making out Allie's invoices. There was a note from her on the desk:

> You are my No 1 football hero. Can I wash your jumper, anything that has been close to you? On second thoughts, perhaps not anything. To business. You'll see I'm booked up tomorrow but can give you a hand with the, um, gateposts on Wednesday. See you tomorrow evening.
> Your devoted fan, Allie.

Something was nagging at me as I worked. November 1985. Ned and Dr Barbie. The depressed Dr Barbie. Barbie the skier.

Skiing.

I stopped writing mid-invoice and looked up Irene Barbie's number. She answered on the second ring.

'Irene, Mac Faraday. Sorry to bother you at night.'

'That's all right. I've been thinking about our conversation.'

'I want to ask you about Ian and skiing.'

'Yes.' Puzzled.

'When did he give it up?'

'When? Oh, I'll have to think— um, it would have been around 1986 or '87.'

'You said he went to Europe or Canada every year. What time of the year?'

'Usually from mid-November. He'd get back in time for the start of the school holidays.'

'You wouldn't be able to say whether he went in November 1985, would you?'

'I'm sure he did. I can find my diary if you want to hold on.'

'Take as long as you like.'

I drank some wine and waited, feeling the tension in my neck and shoulders.

Irene Barbie was back within three minutes.

'Mac? Still there?'

'Yes.'

'One second while I ...'

I held my breath.

'Left for Canada on November 13, came back December 5.'

I breathed out. 'You're sure that's 1985?'

'Oh yes. This is from my diary. Can you tell me why you want to know this?'

'I'd like to talk to you again,' I said. 'If that's possible. And I'll tell you then.'

'Ring me,' she said.

I set off to get another glass of red. The pain had left my body. I felt a sense of relief and elation.

Marcia Carrier was lying about Ned and Ian Barbie.

BERGLIN TRACED Melanie Loreen Pavitt to an address in Shepparton, out where the neat town begins to fray. You drive past the restumped houses, disciplined yards, steam-cleaned driveways, tools hung on pegboard in swept garages, retired men in caps, full of empty purpose. Then the brick veneers, low, brown, ugly, lawns shaved, big windows blinded. At the end of the concrete drive, fixed to the two-car garage, a hoop. It waits for the sad boy to come home and throw the meaningless ball, pass the time until summoned to eat the processed food, watch the manufactured world, sleep.

Further out, on bigger blocks, windswept, treeless, beyond mowing, stand exhausted weatherboards, at the end of their histories, all hope gone, boards sprung, stumps rotten, roofs rusted.

Melanie Pavitt's weatherboard house stood in a sea of long yellow grass, leaning with the prevailing wind, bright junk mail blowing around. The brick chimney on the right was bulging at the bottom and swaying inwards at the top. The windows' sashcords had disintegrated and pieces of weatherboard fallen off the side of the house held up the top panes. I felt the verandah boards, grey, eroded like Ethiopian hillsides, sag under my weight. Next door was a work in progress, a long brick-veneer train carriage of a house with two window openings blocked with plywood and the end wall half-built. Silver insulation foil caught the light. Behind the house was a huge shed, more factory than garage. A newish red Nissan, dusty, stood at the end of a paved section of driveway facing the shed across a riverbed of bluestone dust.

There was no response to my knocks. Inside a radio was on at full volume. Country and western. I thought of going around the back, then a vertical blind in the unfinished house moved. I went over and knocked on the unpainted front door. It opened instantly, on a chain. A woman in her forties, pretty face, plump, long dyed auburn hair, sleep in her eyes, lipstick a little smudged, said, 'Yes.'

'Sorry to bother you,' I said. 'I'm looking for Melanie Pavitt. Does she still live next door?'

There was a wary silence. Finally, she said, 'Police?'

'No. I'm not selling and I'm not collecting either. It's a personal matter.'

She put a finger to the corner of her right eye, pulled the skin back. 'Yeah, she's next door.'

'She doesn't seem to be home. Any idea when she might be back?'

The woman closed the door briefly to take off the chain. She was wearing a purple dressing gown. 'Didn't hear her go,' she said. 'The car makes a helluva noise, exhaust shot. She might be in the back. Let me put something on, I'll come with you.'

I waited on the verandah. It was quiet here, just a faraway hum of traffic. The woman came out wearing tight jeans, a fluffy blue mohair-like top with three-quarter sleeves and black pumps. She had repaired her make-up. She walked ahead of me, buttocks jiggling.

'Doesn't go out much, Mel,' she said. 'Not since the boyfriend moved in. Nice bloke. Used to be in and out of my place. Not anymore.'

We tried knocking again. Nothing. Just the music.

'Try the back,' said the woman. 'By the way, my name's Lee-Anne, two words with a hyphen.'

'John,' I said. We walked down the car tracks beside the house. The kitchen was a lean-to at the back, younger than the main house.

Lee-Anne knocked on the back door. The music was louder here. 'Stand by Your Man'.

'Won't hear anything over that racket,' Lee-Anne said. She tried the doorknob. The door opened. She took a step inside.

'Mel? You there? Someone for you.'

Nothing. Just the music.

Lee-Anne took another step in. I followed. The kitchen was neat, a smell in the air of something burnt. 'Mel!' Lee-Anne shouted. 'Barry!'

The door to the rest of the house was closed. Lee-Anne opened it and called out again.

We went down a short, dark passage, past a door on the left, towards a closed door and the music. At the door, Lee-Anne paused, turned to me. 'You go first,' she said. She bit her lower lip.

I opened the door.

It was a sitting room, also dark, curtains drawn, old blond-wood furniture, a big television, radio on top of it. A fairground barker's voice was saying, 'Wangaratta Ford. Where the best deals are waiting for you.' The burnt smell was gone now. Replaced by something else.

I knew what it was. Before I saw the man.

Lee-Anne came in behind me and screamed.

He was sitting in the chair facing the television. A big part of his face was missing, a black, congealing cavity, and his whole chest was dark with dried blood. Behind his head what looked like a gallon of blood had seeped into the chair upholstery.

That was the other smell: the salty, sickening slaughterhouse smell of blood.

I stepped forward for a closer look at the man. He was holding a revolver in his right hand.

'Barry?' I said.

Lee-Anne nodded, face chalk-white, lipstick startling against it.

'Don't touch anything,' I said.

Two other doors, closed, led from the room. I opened the left-hand one: a small bedroom, empty.

I turned. Lee-Anne was looking at the floor. 'Through there?' I said, pointing.

'Mel's bedroom,' she said softly, without looking up.

I opened the door. Double bed, made. Wardrobe, dresser. No-one there.

I went back, down the dark passage, to the other door.

'Bathroom,' said Lee-Anne from close behind me.

I opened the door.

The bath was directly in front of me. A woman was in it, naked, floating in dark water. Shot once, through the left eye. She had been sitting upright and the bullet had sprayed the contents of her head over the wall behind and beside her.

'Don't look,' I said. 'Call the cops from your place.'

I heard her run down the passage. Then I had a look around. An old suitcase was on top of the wardrobe in Melanie's bedroom. I took it down, gripping the handle in a tissue from the dressing table, and opened it on the bed: perhaps a dozen letters, an empty perfume bottle, a pair of gold high heels, a gold chain belt, three packets of photographs, a bead purse with some Fijian coins, a small velvet box that had held a ring, a black-covered book.

I opened the book. On the first page was written large: *My Life. By Melanie Loreen Pavitt.*

I put the letters, the photographs and the book into my shirt, replaced the suitcase, left the house. At the car, I made sure Lee-Anne wasn't watching and put the stolen goods under the front seat. Then I drove the car into Lee-Anne's yard, over the bluestone dust and parked behind the house. I found the emergency cigarettes and went round the front and sat on the front step.

'Get a smoke off you?' she said from behind me, voice tremulous. 'I'm shakin.'

'Natural,' I said, offering her the packet and the matches. She lit up and sat down beside me. We sat there smoking, not saying anything, waiting for the sirens and the police. When I heard the first wail, I said, 'Inside's better. There'll be television people and other journos coming. They tip them off.'

We went in and stood at the breakfast bar in Lee-Anne's kitchen. This room was finished, all pale gleaming wood and stainless steel.

'Nice room,' I said. 'Listen, I'll explain afterwards but I'm going to arrange it with the cops that they tell them the bodies were found by a neighbour. They'll want you on camera. You want to do that? It'll get rid of them.'

She nodded. The idea didn't displease her.

'Okay. Don't say anything about what you saw. Don't mention me. Just say something like, "I've lost a good friend and neighbour and I'd appreciate being left alone to grieve".'

She nodded again, eyes brighter. Then the cops knocked.

I was lucky. I got an intelligent plainclothes cop straight off. He listened to me, wrote down my name and the number I gave him to ring, rang his station commander, gave him the number. The superior rang back inside five minutes, they exchanged a few words, the cop came over.

'That'll be in order, Mr Faraday. Mrs Vinovic's giving a statement in the sitting room. I'll take yours here.'

We heard the sound of a helicopter. 'Vultures here,' the man said. I looked out of the window. The helicopter was above Melanie's house, camera protruding like a gun.

It was dark before the circus was over. We stood in the sitting room. 'Helluva way to spend an afternoon,' I said. 'Anyway, it's over. Time to get moving.'

'A drink,' she said. 'Have a drink.' The high colour brought on by the television appearances was fading. She tried out the name. 'John.'

'I've got a long way to go.'

'Just a drink. One drink. What d'ya drink? Beer? I've got beer. Wine? Lots of wine. Bobo didn't drink anything except wine. All kinds of wine. There's a cellar y'know. Proper cellar. Bobo had to have a cellar.'

'Beer would be good.'

'Beer. I'll have a beer too. Don't often drink beer. Fattening. What the fuck.'

At six thirty, we watched the news on television. Melanie's house from the air, the voice-over. 'A thirty-two-year-old Shepparton woman and her de facto husband were found dead of gunshot wounds in their house outside the town today.' We saw a lot of police coming and going and a young male reporter with receding hair identified the dead man as Barry James Field, twenty-seven, an unemployed building worker. Lee-Anne came on and said her dignified piece. The camera liked her.

'Good,' I said. 'Just right.'

'Police are treating the deaths as a murder–suicide,' the reporter said.

At eight o'clock, I rang Lew. 'I'm held up here,' I said. 'Back tomorrow.'

Lee-Anne came into the kitchen with a bottle of champagne. The heating was on high, she'd taken off the fluffy top to reveal a Club Med T-shirt strained to its limits, her colour was back. 'Perrier Something,' she said. 'Fucking case of it down there. All right, y'reckon?'

'I reckon.'

I opened it gently. I'd have to get a cab to a motel.

'Bobo had the cleaning contract at my work,' Lee-Anne said. 'Clean, clean, clean, it was like a religion. First place we lived in, rental, you won't believe this, he used to get in the roof with this industrial vacuum. Huge fucking thing, noise like a Boeing, suck a rat out of a drain.'

I poured. Lee-Anne drank half a glass.

'Dust in the ceiling. Couldn't bear the idea. Can you credit that? I mean, who cares you don't even know it's there? Mind you, look at this place now. Bobo'll be spinning.'

'Looks fine,' I said. Somehow I'd forgotten that we were twenty metres from a house where we'd found two people dead.

'Light's too bright.' She went to the door and turned a knob. 'Better. Dimmers in every room. Toilet, even. I thought dimmers were about bloody romance. Shouldn't talk like this about Bobo. Drove the ute under a semi outside Wang. Horror crash, the paper said. Could've posted it. What I want to know is what the fuck he's doing outside Wang when he tells me he's in Bendigo overnight, big cleaning contract coming up?'

Lee-Anne came back to her seat opposite me. She put her elbows on the counter, held out her glass and looked into my eyes. She was looking startlingly attractive. 'Bobo was number two. First was Steve. Don't even think about him. Photographer. Just a kid when I met him. Coburg girl. Very strict family. My God, strict. You don't know strict. You have to be Coburg Lebanese to know strict.'

I filled her glass, added Perrier Jouet to mine. Very good drop. Howard James Lefroy liked Perrier Jouet. Not the drink you'd expect to be having outside Shepparton on a freezing night in June, wind coming up outside, silver foil insulation on the unfinished wall vibrating like a drum skin, blood still on the tiles in the shaky weatherboard next door.

'Not that it kept you fucking pure,' said Lee-Anne. She put her hands on the counter. They were good hands, long fingers, nails not painted. 'Not when you met a photographer. Called himself a photographer. Not what a lot of people called him.'

Lee-Anne put an arm up her T-shirt to adjust her bra. I was hypnotised.

'Wedding pictures. Half the time they didn't come out. Whole fuckin weddings, excuse me. Vanished like they never happened. Steve was always on the run from fathers, brothers, uncles. I donta wanta my money back, I wanta my daughter's pictures, watta fuck you do with them? Not a street he could walk in safety, Steve, that many people lookin for him.'

We opened another bottle of the French. It seemed to last five minutes.

'Listen, Lee-Anne,' I said. 'Reckon we can get a taxi out here? Take me to a motel?'

She put her glass down, got up, took off her T-shirt, threw it over her shoulder, put her hand behind her back, unclipped her virgin-white bra, tossed it away. It landed in the sink.

'I don't suppose you'd have a spare bed,' I said, mouth dry.

'It's been four years,' she said, coming around the counter. 'I've still got Bobo's condoms.'

In the night, she woke me and asked, 'You seen dead people before?'

What do you say?

I left before dawn, kissed her on the mouth.

THE TITLE of Melanie Pavitt's handwritten autobiography promised more than it delivered. It didn't go beyond the age of thirteen. She stopped in the middle of a page with the words: *I did not see Mum again. I herd she went to Perth with a man but I dont no if its true. She never loved me so it dosent matter.*

All the letters except one were from a man called Kevin, written from Darwin and Kalgoorlie, never more than a page: weather, job, miss you, love. The most recent one was five years old.

The other letter was brief, too, in a sloping female hand, signed by someone called Gaby, dated 12 July 1995. No address. It read:

Mel!!! You rememberd my Mums adress!!! She sent the letter to me here in Cairns. Im living here with a man called Otto, hes a German mechanic and very nice and kind altho a bit old. Still you cant have everything can you. I was really shocked to see the things you wrote. The barstards shoud be locked up!!! You are pretty lucky to be alive I reckon, its like those backpackers mudered near Sydney, Otto new one of them, a girl. Id never have said that Ken woud do something like that, they are people you are suposed to be abel to trust!!! I suppose they think there money makes it alrite. Now you now where I am come and stay, theres lots of room. Otto wont mind. Its hot all year here. To warm a lot. Write soon. Love Gaby.

I read the letter twice.
Ken?
That was the name Dot Walsh said the naked girl in Colson's Road had said over and over.
… saying the name Ken over and over again.
I read Gaby's letter a third time. I was in the kitchen, sitting near the fired-up stove, but I felt a chill, as if a window had been opened, letting in a gust of freezing air.

I opened the stove's firebox and fed in the letters from Kevin. If he was Melanie's killer, he was probably going to go unpunished, courtesy of me. Then I went out and got the Kinross Hall records. They listed a girl called Gabriele Elaine Makin, age sixteen, at Kinross Hall at the same time as Melanie Pavitt in 1985.

I found the staff list and went through it. No Ken.

At least two people knew who Ken was and what happened on the night Sim Walsh, World War II fighter pilot and drunk, found Melanie Pavitt naked in Colson's Road.

One of them was dead, one bullet through the left eye from a .38 Ruger from at least two metres away. If my judgment was worth anything, Melanie Pavitt had not been shot by her boyfriend, Barry James Field, unemployed building worker. Lee-Anne described Barry as a calm, sensible person who was the best thing that had ever happened to Melanie. He also seemed an unlikely owner of a weapon the cops had in ten minutes identified as stolen from a Sydney gun shop in 1994.

The other person who knew what happened to Melanie in 1985 was Gaby Makin.

I went over to the pub and rang inquiries. Then I rang Berglin. I gave them my name, we went through the rigmarole and they connected me.

'Wanting to ask you,' he said without preamble. 'What is it with you and dead people?'

'Raised the subject of Bianchi?' I could see Flannery at the bar, hunched, staring into a glass of beer, just a shadow of Saturday's hero.

'I mentioned it, yes.'

'So what's going to happen?'

'Don't think it's going on the priority list.'

'It should.'

Berglin sighed. 'Mac, listen. We talked about this before. Things blow up on you, it happens. The smack lost, the woman in the wrong place. Lefroy, that was a plus. Nailed him, he'd own the whole fucking prison system now, living like King Farouk, meals from Paul Bocuse, hot and cold running bumboys. Do a line anytime he likes. You've got another life now. Forget about the shit. Any brains, if I had them, I'd ask you can I join you out there in chilblain country, making candlesticks, whatever the fuck it is you do.'

I let the subject lie. 'I need another trace.'

'Jesus, I don't know about you.' Pause. 'Who?'

I spelled it out: Gabriele Elaine Makin, born Frankston 1967, juvenile offender last known in Cairns. Not in the phone book.

'Hope she survives your interest in her,' Berglin said. 'Don't call me.'

'Something else.'

Silence.

I changed my mind. I had been going to ask about Bianchi's widow.

'Forget it, not important.'

'I'm glad.'

I went to the bar and sat down next to Flannery.

'I like the next day more when we lose,' he said. 'Whole week more. I don't think we should win again this Satdee.'

'Three in a row?' I said. 'In another life.'

'Beer's on the house,' Vinnie the publican said. 'Few more Satdees like that, I'm takin the place off the market.'

'Didn't know it was on the market,' Flannery said.

'Pub without pokies?' Vinnie said. 'Pokieless pub is on the market.'

'Tabletop dancers,' Flannery said. 'That's the go. Uni girls shakin their titties, showin us the business. Have a pickin-up-the-spud competition.'

Vinnie looked over to where two elderly male customers were grumbling at each other. 'Tabletop dancers? Need a bloody ambulance on standby outside. Mind you, that fuckin' cook'll need an ambulance if he doesn't come in the door in two minutes.'

When the cook arrived, Flannery and I ate steak and onion sandwiches. From where we were sitting, I could see the wet road and the entrance to my lane. I was washing down the last bite when Allie's truck turned in. We had work to do on the gateposts.

I WOKE early, stood in the shower thinking about the heft of Lee-Anne's breasts, the sight of Allie naked. Then I thought about being fifteen, digging out rotten stumps from grey rock and unyielding clay, face down in fifty centimetres of damp and cold crawl space, breathing the dank, dead air under a farmhouse near Yass. Crawling out, hearing footsteps on the boards above me, turning over and looking up through a gap between old floor-boards, parched boards, tongues shrunk, parted from their grooves, unmated. Seeing from below a woman, a naked woman, mature woman, my eyes going up the sturdy legs, parted legs, pink from the bath, seeing at the junction the secret hair, the dark, curly, springy, water-beaded hair that marked the place, the little folds of belly, the plump wet undersides of breasts, a glimpse of chin, of nose. Of seeing her move her buttocks against a towel, run it over her breasts, breasts swaying, long nipples, of seeing her open her legs, wipe the towel casually between the thighs, wipe the dark, intimate folds of skin …

Time for breakfast. I was sitting in a patch of weak sunlight eating break-fast, grilled bacon and a poached egg, when the phone rang. It was Berglin.

'That inquiry,' he said. 'Party's no longer with us. Motor accident in 1993, dead on arrival.'

I swallowed my mouthful. 'Sure about that?'

There was silence, then he said, 'As sure as one can be on the basis of the information supplied and the absence on all available records of anyone else with identical particulars. Yes.'

'Sorry. Thanks.'

'One more thing. The person in the Vatican we spoke of. You with me?'

'Yes.'

'Extremely resistant on a number of grounds to revisiting the matter in question.'

'So?'

'So the future of this course of action is uncertain.'

I went back to my breakfast. A cloud extinguished the sunlight like a door closing on a lit room.

When I'd finished, I got Gaby Makin's letter out again. It was dated 12 July 1995.

Written from beyond the grave. Either that or Berglin was lying to me. Everything was starting to remind me of the old days.

I drove into town and consulted the Cairns Yellow Pages. I tried the Mercedes dealership first, asking for the workshop.

'Have you got a mechanic called Otto?' I said. 'German?'

'Otto the Hun. Otto Klinger. Not any more. He's at Winlaton Motors in Brissy. Couple of years now. Miss him, too.'

He gave me a number.

The workshop office at Winlaton Motors got Otto Klinger on the line inside a minute.

'Ja, Klinger,' he said.

'Otto, I'm a friend of Gaby Makin …'

'Gaby and I are no longer together,' Otto said. 'She has gone with another person.'

'I heard she was killed in a car accident in 1993.'

'Gaby? Incorrect. She has only gone approximately one year.'

'Any idea where?'

'No. It is no concern of mine.'

'Do you know anyone who would know?'

Otto sighed. 'I suppose her girlfriend down the road would know. This is important, yes?'

'Otto,' I said, 'it could be a matter of life and death, yes.'

He sighed again. 'Give me a number for you and I will speak to the woman today if I can find her.'

I gave him a name and number. On the way home, I thought about how I'd got Melanie Pavitt's address from Berglin. Would Melanie be alive now if I hadn't? It wasn't a thought I wanted to entertain. Why would Berglin lie to me about Gaby? He had never heard of Kinross Hall until I rang him to trace Melanie.

But, before that, why had Marcia lied to me about Ian Barbie and Ned?

Allie was dampening the green coal in the forge when I came in the door. The dog was watching her. She was wearing jeans, a leather apron and one of her shirts with canvas sleeves.

'Okay to fire it when you're not here?' she said. 'We didn't discuss that.'

I gave the question some thought. It had meaning. Significance. 'You mean, can you play with my toy when I'm not here. Is that it?'

'Pretty much,' she said. 'I should have raised it. Some smithies are like petrolheads, only the forge is the car. One vehicle, one driver. One toy, one boy.'

'The toy can be played with,' I said. 'Day and night. And the bits in between.'

She gave me her slow, one-sided smile. 'Day'll be fine. I've got till four. Reckon we can get these giant wangers out of the way?'

We finished the things just before three pm, no feeling of achievement, just relief. I made corned beef and cheese sandwiches and we ate them sitting on the office step, reading bits of the paper, not saying much.

'That vet,' I said. 'Rottweiler or Jack Russell?'

Allie frowned. 'Labrador, it turned out. Nice but not too bright.'

'Sometimes,' I said, standing up and taking her plate, 'that's what you want in a dog.'

She looked up at me from under her straight eyebrows. 'Maybe it's a mongrel I'm looking for.'

'Flannery's between engagements.'

'Then again, maybe it's not. Do we have to deliver these monstrosities?'

'No. Spared that. He's picking them up. Feel like a beer later?'

She pulled a face. 'Would be good but I'm heading way over the other side of town. Tomorrow?'

I suddenly remembered it was Friday. Football tomorrow. No, thank God, we had a bye. 'Tomorrow.'

'I'll ring,' she said.

I worked on a chef's knife until the drink called. Mick Doolan and Flannery were at the bar.

'Tactics, Moc, we're talkin tactics,' Mick said. 'Just a couple more wins and we'll be bookin a finals berth. Wouldn't that be grand?'

Flannery groaned. 'Extra games,' he said. 'We'll be playin on cortisone. Can they test for that?'

I WAS watching the Saints beating the Eagles in Perth when the phone rang.

'Klinger,' Otto said. 'This stupid girlfriend of Gaby's wishes to telephone Gaby and to tell her why you wish to speak with her, and to get permission to give you Gaby's telephone number. I think she thinks that it is I who wishes to find out Gaby's number. That is a very foolish thing to think, I can tell you.'

'Thanks, Otto. Can you tell the friend I want to talk to Gaby about someone called Melanie Pavitt.' I spelt the name.

'I will call again,' Otto said.

He rang back in twenty minutes.

'That is all okay. Here is Gaby's telephone number.'

I thanked him, wrote it down. It was in Victoria. I dialled it. A woman answered: 'Yes.' Wary.

'Tony Mason,' I said. 'I sent you the message through Otto. I'd like to talk to you about Melanie Pavitt.'

'What about her?'

'About her experiences after leaving Kinross Hall. Immediately after she left.'

She thought about this for a while. 'Who are you?' she said.

'Investigator for the Department of Community Services.'

'Why doesn't she tell you?'

Gaby didn't know that Melanie was dead. This wasn't the time to tell her.

'She has, but I'd like to talk to someone who was at Kinross at the same time and who heard about what happened directly from Melanie. It won't take long.'

'On the phone?'

'No. I'll come and see you. Or we can meet somewhere, whatever suits you.'

'Well,' she said, 'I suppose so. But I'm out in the country.'

'That's not a problem.'

I LEFT long before dawn in the freezing and wet dark, trees stirring in the wind, huddled sheep caught by my lights on the bends. By 9.15 am I was in the high country, in Mansfield, eating a toasted egg-and-bacon sandwich and drinking black coffee. It was cold up here, hard light, pale-blue cloudless sky. The coffee shop was full of people on their way to ski, groups of rich-looking people: sleek but slightly hungover men, just edging pudgy; women with tight smiles and lots of blonde hair; vicious children, all snarls and demands, woken early for the trip. The women had a way of tossing their heads and flicking their hair from below with their fingertips as if it were tickling their necks. In the street, it was all four-wheel-drives, BMWs and Saabs.

I wasn't going towards Mount Buller. I was going north-east. On the way to Whitfield, following Gaby's instructions, I turned right onto a dirt road, turned again, again, thought I'd missed the place, found it, a brick, stone and weatherboard house, low, sprawling, expensive, a long way from the road, at the end of a long curving avenue of poplars, bare. Off to the right was a corrugated-iron barn and beyond that what looked like stables. Gaby had done well for herself.

Going through the gate either triggered something or sound travelled long distances in this air. A woman was waiting near the barn when I came around the final bend. She pointed to the road that led to the stables and turned to walk in that direction. She was big, tall, not fat yet, pale hair in a ponytail, dark glasses, sleeveless quilted jacket.

There was a house beyond the stables, an old stone building with a weatherboard extension. It said *Manager's House*. Gaby hadn't done as well as I'd thought. I parked next to a clean Toyota ute and got out.

Gaby took her dark glasses off. She was reaching the end of pretty, face not sure what to become. No make-up, eyes that had seen things. You wouldn't want to mess with her.

'Tony Mason,' I said, putting out my hand.

She shook, no grip, ladylike. No smile.

'Let's go inside,' she said. 'I have to be in town in an hour.'

She took off her boots at the front door. 'You don't have to,' she said. 'Been in the stables. You smell it in the warm.'

The house was warm, uncluttered, smelling pleasantly of something I couldn't recognise.

I followed her down a passage lit by two skylights into a sitting room full of light, foothills in the windows, pale grey hills beyond.

A baby cried, small sound, pulling power of a regimental bugle.

Gaby said. 'Feedin time. Sit down.' She was taking off her waistcoat as she left.

I sat down in the most upright chair in the room. She came back with something wrapped in a pink blanket, sat down opposite me, unbuttoned her checked shirt, fiddled and produced a breast, aureole the colour of milky instant coffee and the size of a small saucer. She revealed the baby's head. It was a big head, covered in fuzz.

'Never thought I'd just take out a tit in front of a stranger,' she said, no expression. The child ship docked with the mother ship. Gaby's expression softened.

'Well,' she said, little smile, not looking at me. 'Not just one tit anyway.'

I laughed. She looked at me, her smile opened and we were both laughing.

I said: 'Melanie's dead. I think she was murdered.'

The smile went. We sat in silence for a moment. Gaby had the look of someone who'd had a new and untrue and malicious charge levelled at her.

'Dead?'

I told her how.

She pulled the baby closer. 'You're not from the fucking department,' she said, matter-of-fact, not alarmed. 'That was all bullshit.'

'No,' I said. 'Gaby, I'm a friend of someone who sometimes worked at Kinross. They're trying to shaft him with molesting girls.'

'Who?' she said.

'He was a handyman. Ned Lowey.'

She said, 'No, I never heard that. Barbie, yes.'

'Tell me about Melanie's letter. What happened to her?'

She shifted in the chair, adjusted the baby. 'Didn't keep the letter. She came to see me, y'know? In Cairns.'

'No, I didn't know.'

'Yeah. After the letter.' She tilted her head, thoughtful. 'How'd you get my letter?'

'I found it in her bedroom.'

'Before she …'

'After. I found the body. Me and the woman next door.'

She nodded.

'So she came to see you?'

'In Cairns. Stayed for a week. Was going to be longer. Otto started playin up, so she left.'

'You talked about what happened?'

'Yeah.'

'Someone called Ken was involved. Who's he?'

Gaby looked down at the suckling. 'I don't want to get in any trouble,' she said. 'Had enough trouble.'

'There'll be no trouble,' I said. 'No-one's going to hear anything you tell me.'

'Well.' She sighed. 'We were pretty pissed when she told me. Don't remember all that much. Couldn't hear a lot of what she said anyway. Cryin and sniffin.'

'Ken,' I said. 'Who's he?'

'The doctor.'

'Dr Barbie?'

'Yeah.'

'Why do you call him Ken?'

'The dolls? Barbie and Ken. There was Barbie and Ken.'

'Right. Barbie and Ken. How was Ken involved?'

Gaby sighed again. 'Day Mel was leavin, he examined her. Said he was goin to Melbourne, he'd give her a lift, save her goin by train. Only she mustn't tell anyone cause he'd get into trouble. She thought he was a nice bloke. We all did. Anyway, they took her to the station and dropped her and Ken picked her up. Gave her a can of Coke.'

She stopped and fiddled with her breast, shifted the baby. 'Mel said she remembered drivin along, gettin dark. Next thing she woke up, she was bein dressed in schoolgirl clothes, y'know, a gym and that.'

'Who was doing that? Ken?'

'She wasn't sure. Two men. They did all kinds of sex things to her. Not normal, know what I mean? Tied her up. Hit her with something. Made her do things to them. She cried when she told me.'

'She saw their faces?'

'Not properly. They didn't hide their faces. That's why she knew they were going to kill her. But she didn't get a real good look at them. The room was dark and she felt dizzy. And they had a light in her eyes all the time.'

'She couldn't describe them at all?'

'Not really.'

'So one could have been Dr Barbie?'

'Well, he's the one gave her the Coke.'

'How'd she get away?'

'They went off. The one man goes, "Back soon, slut, with a friend for you. She's been looking forward to this."'

'She?'

'Yeah. She. Anyway, Mel's in this room, stone room, bars on the window, it's upstairs. There was a bed and she stood it up on its end, got on it and she ripped a hole in the ceiling. There was a small hole and she made it bigger. Got into the roof, pulled off some tiles and got out onto the roof and climbed down a drainpipe. Pretty incredible, hey? She's just a little thing but really strong. Barbie liked the little ones.' She stopped. 'She was. Really strong.'

'And she got away.'

'She said she ran for ages, like through some kind of forest. Pitch–dark and she was dead scared they were coming after her. She got to a road and she hid from cars. Then it was so cold she thought she'd die, so she started walking along the road. Naked. Then an old man stopped and took her to his house.'

'I know what happened from then,' I said.

I went over the story with her. There wasn't any more to tell. Outside, cold a shock after the warm house, Gaby said, 'I don't want any trouble. Really. I've got a good bloke now and the baby.'

'Don't worry,' I said. 'You won't hear anything about this again. But if you remember anything else, ring me.'

I wrote my number on the back of an automatic teller machine receipt.

In the rear-view mirror, I saw her watching me go, standing in the universal stance of mothers, baby on hip, pelvis tilted, knees slightly bent. I thought, what right have I to give her any assurances?

The last person I had given assurances to was Carlie Mance.

DRIVING BACK, my mind drifted over what I knew and what I didn't know. The two men who assaulted Melanie could be the killers of the girl in the mine shaft. Who were they? Ian Barbie and someone else.

Barbie the delivery man. Had he delivered other Kinross Hall girls? How could he do that without the girls being reported missing?

And that raised the issue that I didn't much want to think about. Had my inquiry about Melanie led to her death? How could that be? I ask Berglin to trace someone and then I find the person shot dead. Melanie Pavitt, not shot dead in the messy way of domestic killings everywhere. No. Shot dead with fussy precision. One shot in the eye. Was this the work of her gentle unemployed builders' labourer? This I could not believe. Then Berglin lies to me about Gaby Makin. Why? What conceivable interest could Berglin have in my inquiries? He was a federal drug cop and drugs didn't seem to enter this puzzle.

Berglin lie to me? Of all the things he said to me over the years, when I thought of him, two sentences spoken in his hoarse voice at our first meeting always echoed in the mind: *How to be a halfway decent person. That's the main question in life.*

In the shitstorm after the Lefroy and Mance killings, when all fingers pointed at me, Berglin had been impassive. He never said the words I wanted him to say, never patted my arm, never invited me to confide in him. You could read nothing in his eyes. One morning, suspended from duty, wife gone, unshaven, hungover, I went to his office. He looked at me with interest while I shouted at him: abuse, recriminations, accusations of betrayal. When I ran out of things to say, Berglin said, no expression, 'Mac, if I think you've moved across, you'll be the first to know. I'll come around and kill you. Enjoy the vacation. Now fuck off.'

I left, feeling much better.

Now I'd have to see him, confront him with the lie he'd told me. I hoped very much that he could explain it away, but I couldn't see how.

I was still brooding on this as I drove down the damp and overgrown driveway at Harkness Park. Stan had rung to say that Francis wanted him to put on extra hands, presumably so that he could send out his bills sooner. Stan was reluctant: he didn't like big crews. I'd suggested that instead of bringing in more workers we draw up a work schedule that provided incentives for meeting targets early. Flannery and Lew liked the idea. They were to have spent the morning clearing the main path down the sightline. Stan had estimated hours for the job and I wanted to see how far they'd got.

They'd done well, pushing at least thirty metres beyond Stan's expectation, neat work, greenery piled ready for chipping. I was admiring the elaborate brick and cut stone path uncovered, thinking about where to establish the compost heaps, when I heard a vehicle in the driveway, just a hum. I didn't think about it, backed into the dense overgrown box hedge beside the path, looked back towards the house. A month earlier, I wouldn't have done this. Fear had come back into my life, uninvited.

I waited.

Anne Karsh, hair pulled back today, jeans, battered short Drizabone, looking around. I stepped out of hiding. We walked towards each other down the path, eyes meeting, looking away, coming back.

'Checking on progress,' I said when we were close enough.

'You or me?'

'Both?'

'No, not me,' she said. She smiled. 'Just wanted to be here, really. In love with it. What were you doing in the hedge? If that's a hedge.'

'Hedge examination. How about this path?'

'This is an unbelievable path. It's so ornate.'

I turned and we walked to the edge of the known garden. Beyond was wilderness. 'It's like archaeology,' she said. 'For the first time, I can understand the thrill.'

'Thrill time next week,' I said. 'The pines come down. Then we see the steeple. See what the man wanted us to see.'

'Who cuts them down?' We were on our way back.

'A professional. The biggest one's nine metres around at the base. Death to amateurs. We could bring in a portable sawmill, turn them into planks. You could have something made out of them. Terrible waste otherwise. All those years of growing.'

She looked at me. 'Leon'll like that. Could you do it?'

'If you tell Francis that's what you want.'

She held out her right hand. We stopped. 'I'll tell him now.' She took out a small leatherbound book, found a page, took a mobile telephone, minute, from another pocket, punched numbers. After a short wait, she said. 'Francis, Anne Karsh ... Well, thank you. Francis, the pines blocking the view to the church steeple are coming down next week. Can you arrange to have them turned into usable timber? ... Leon will be thrilled. Stan will arrange it, I'm sure. Thank you, Francis ... I look forward to that too. Bye.'

We walked, explored the thicket around the site of the original house, forced our way through to the old orchard, desperate-looking fruit trees but the least overgrown place because of the deep mulch of fallen fruit.

'You can prune these buggers back to life,' I said. 'If you want them.'

'I want them,' she said. 'I want everything the way it was.'

I looked at her.

'I've got a flask of coffee,' Anne said. A thorn had scratched her cheek-bone, delicate serration, line of blood like the teeth of a tiny saw. 'Drink coffee?'

'Got enough?'

'I've got enough.'

The Mercedes boot held a wicker basket with a stainless-steel flask and stainless-steel cups. We sat side by side on the front steps of the house, huge, dangerously aged poised portico above us, drinking coffee, talking about the garden. She had an easy manner, sense of humour, no hint of rich lady about her. A weak sun emerged, touched her hair.

'Nice,' she said.

'Good coffee.'

'The day, the place, the moment.'

'Those too.'

We didn't look at each other, something in the air. Then our eyes met for a moment.

'Mr Karsh working today?' I said, regretted the question.

'No. He's in Noosa for the weekend. His new girlfriend goes to Noosa for the winter.'

I looked at her. 'I understand it's wall-to-wall girlfriends in Noosa.'

She leaned sideways, studied me, smiled a wry smile. 'I've been a girl-friend. There's no moral high ground left for me.'

'Not for any of us,' I said.

'Leon's a charming person,' she said. 'His problem is chronic envy. Non-specific envy. His greatest fear is that he's missing something, that there's something he should be doing, that there's something he doesn't know about or hasn't got that will make him happy and complete. If he saw a man leading a duck down the road on a piece of string and looking at peace, Leon would send someone out to buy a duck and give it a try for fifteen minutes. Then he'd say, fuck this duck, why's that woman on the bicycle look so pleased?'

'Why did you?'

'What?'

'Look so pleased?'

'So,' Anne said. 'Blacksmiths are not without insight. I worked for a merchant bank that was hired by a company to fight off a takeover bid by one of Leon's companies. Very messy business, went on for months, working seventeen, eighteen hours a day, seven days. One Sunday I got home and my husband had gone off with my best friend. Anyway, we fought off Leon and we had a no-hard-feelings drink with the other side and Leon showed up. I think he then began to see me as a substitute for the company he couldn't have. Anything Leon can't have leaps in value in his eyes.'

'So he took you over.'

She smiled. 'Well, as I said, he's a charming person. He has the gift of charm. It was a totally uncontested takeover. But as I found out, for Leon, you conquer the peak, another peak beckons. More coffee?'

'Just a drop.'

'There's plenty.' She poured. 'That's me. And I'm not complaining. What about you?'

'My wife didn't like my hours either.'

'Blacksmiths work long hours?'

'Pre-blacksmith.' I stood up. 'Time to go. Thanks for the coffee.'

She stood up too. Standing on the step above me put her eyes level with mine. We looked at each other. 'Let me know when you'd like to see the mill,' I said.

Anne nodded. 'Can you give me a number?' She wrote it in her leather-bound book.

'Well,' I said. 'See you soon then.'

She put out a hand and straightened my shirt collar, pulled her hand back. 'Thank you,' I said. I thought she blushed a little.

'Terrible urge to straighten pictures,' she said. 'I'll call you. Next week.'

I drove home in the waning day. Towering dark clouds on all horizons made it seem as if I were crossing a valley floor. It was dark by the time I stopped outside the Heart of Oak to see if Flannery was there. He wasn't.

'Car went in your drive just before dark,' Vinnie said.

I left the vehicle where it was, walked up the road, climbed the paddock gate in the far corner and crossed the sodden field so that I could come at the house from the back, from behind the smithy.

The caller was still there: a car was parked in front of the office. I went across the gravel, slowly, my gravel, gravel put down so that I could hear it crunch. All senses on high-beam, I looked into the kitchen window.

Something touched my leg. I froze.

The dog, puzzled.

Inside, Lew was feeding the stove. He turned and said something to someone out of my field of view. The person laughed.

I let out my pent-up breath and opened the back door.

Berglin was in my favourite chair, long shoes on the table, cigarette dangling from a hand.

'MacArthur John Faraday,' he said. 'Home is the hunter.'

THERE WAS no other way to do this. 'Lew,' I said, 'I need to talk to this gentleman alone.'

When he'd gone, I said, 'You lied to me.'

'Come again?' Berglin's eyebrows went up in the middle.

'That trace. Gabriele Makin.'

'Yeah. Dead.'

'Not dead. Undead. Not a million fucking kilometres from here.'

He blew smoke towards me, eyes narrowed. 'You sure?'

'Of course I'm fucking sure.'

'How'd you find her?'

'Phone book. What the fuck did you use?'

'Contractor.'

'Why?'

He blew smoke. 'Why? I'm going to put some personal request through the system? I'm going to do that? I put that Melanie Pavitt through the system, Canberra'd be asking me why I wanted to find a person turns up dead. Make sense to you? Fresh air's slowing the brain out here.'

'Who's the contractor?'

Berglin mashed his cigarette into the ashtray Lew had found for him. 'It's my worry. I'll talk to him. Believe me, I'll talk to him.'

From nowhere the thought came to me. 'Alex Rickard,' I said. 'You're using Alex Rickard.'

Berglin was lighting another cigarette, lighter poised. He lowered it. 'I'll stand on the cunt's head,' he said. 'We'll know why in quick time.'

'What about a beer?' I said, slack with relief. Not Berglin to blame but Alex Rickard.

'Thought you'd never ask.'

I opened two Boags, found two glasses, sat down at the table.

Berglin took a big draught from the bottle. 'Listen,' he said, 'two reasons I'm out here in the fucking tundra. One is, from your time on the Lefroy fuck-up, the name Algie mean anything?'

'Algae? As in blue-green slime?'

'Don't know. Could be. Not likely. Could be A-L-G-I-E. Could be two parts: Al G, like a first name and a surname initial. Maybe Al Gee.'

'No. Never heard it. It's someone's name?'

'Calls himself that, yeah.'

'How's this come up?'

'Run-through last night, Bulleen of all fucking places. Nothing's sacred. Person we had an interest in last year. Local jacks turned over this low-level garbage in Footscray, he tells them this weed bloke's grown overnight. Now he's a smack supplier, found some fucking original channel – big, not your arse full of condoms at all. Scully's cockbrains wire the place up like a recording studio, move in across the road. Nothing to report. So they say. Stereo-quality farting, got the man mango-kissing his sister-in-law, very vocal performance, that's about it. Waste of public money.'

He drank some more beer. 'This is good,' he said, looking at the bottle. 'The pointyheads can make beer. Anyway, subject closed until last night. Then the serene Bulleen household is severely disrupted. Man alone at home, wife at the Chadstone shopping centre. He's beaten, badly knocked about, teeth dislodged, flogged. Worse. Throat cut.' He paused. 'Don't say anything, the thought occurs.'

We sat in silence for a few seconds. Berglin drank most of his beer, wiped his thin lips. I got out two more.

'Good dog,' he said. 'Now the reason for all this unpleasantness might have remained obscure, MacArthur. But for one thing. False wall in the back of the house, space about a metre between the kitchen and the laundry. Get into it through the ceiling. Up the ladder in the garage, through the inspection hole. Last night, half the fucking kitchen wall kicked in.'

Berglin put out the cigarette, more gently this time, found another one, looked at it, put it down on the table. 'Christ knows what these cunts went off with,' he said, 'but they left behind, down there in a corner, up against the plasterboard, a quarter kilo of outstanding, medal-winning-purity product. Melbourne Show quality.'

'How come?'

'Just bad light, they reckon. Pricks in a hurry, got plenty, never saw it.'

'Algie,' I said. 'Where's that come in?'

'The wife says, she is a very scared person, that the deceased said to another man, person she doesn't know, she was near them in a public place, he said, "Algie's on, the lot".'

'That's it?'

'She heard that. Algie.'

'Four words. What public place? Street? Shopping centre? Lots of noise?'

'Noisy, but Algie, yeah. She says, she said to him in the car, who's Algie? He said, just a bloke I'm doing business with.'

'Could have been clearing his throat. Said it fast? *Algiesonthelot*. Native English speakers these Bulleen people?'

'Since your departure,' said Berglin, 'we find ourselves bereft of ideas. But we stumble on. He's Turkish, old man's a Turk. We've run Algie by umpteen Turks. More Turks than Gallipoli. Doesn't make sense in Turkish.'

'But it's come up before.'

'What?' He was studying the beer bottle again.

'Algie. Algie – the word in question.'

He shrugged. 'It's been around.'

'Around? Well, familiar word. Algie. Since when? Since before Lefroy?'

'No. That's why I'm here. Asking you.'

'So when's it come up? How long after Lefroy?'

'Not long. Soon. On some drug bug, these spiders are talking. Appears to be about Lefroy. The one says, heard it was Algie.'

'I've never heard that,' I said. 'How come I don't know that?'

'Mac, no-one needs to know everything.'

'What does that mean? Exactly?' I said.

'What it says.'

I took a deep breath. 'Soon after Lefroy I had a definite need to know about anything like that, Berg,' I said. 'But moving on, you're here because you're in some kind of shit, second Lefroy-style run-through, new boys in Canberra think it's time you kicked on to that block at Batemans Bay. That it?'

'Third,' said Berglin.

'Third?'

'Third Lefroy-style run-through. There's lots of them go on but not killing. Three years ago, we had two Chinese blokes, property investment advisors for Hong Kong syndicates, that's the story. Rent a flat in St Kilda, ground floor, beachfront, big flat, four bedrooms, gold taps, that sort of thing. They come and go, Hong Kong, Taiwan, Bangkok, Hawaii, Sydney, Brisbane. Never stop for more than a few days, real estate people show them around buildings. Hong Kong clears them, Scully's people give them a clean bill. Operation terminated. I had a bad feeling, but we couldn't go on without the local jacks.'

Berglin lit his cigarette. 'About eighteen months ago, the lady lives upstairs looks down from her balcony, sees a pool of blood on the balcony below. From under the door. It's all tiles, inside and out. Blood runs free. She calls jacks. Chinese bloke's taped up, throat cut.'

He looked at me in silence for a while.

'What?' I said.

'Woman there too. A hooker. In the bathroom. Same treatment as the bloke. And worse. Much worse. We kept the details quiet.'

I swallowed. 'This means what?'

He shrugged. 'Don't know. Stuff, money, probably money. Pick-up, pay off. Someone knew.'

'Algie?'

'Yesterday was a big day for shit floating up. There was another hooker these Chinese blokes liked. Hired by the day on other visits. Woman called Lurleen. We couldn't ever find her. Yesterday she rings a number we gave this other hooker, her friend, back then. Lurleen's back in town and she's scared. I had a little walk and talk with her. Guess what?'

'No.'

'She's in the flat too on the night. She's got a key, been there all afternoon. Now she's in the kitchen, hears the doorbell, hears the Chinese open the door, he says something and then she hears him scream. She doesn't fuck around, knows shit when she hears it coming, out the door to the garage, gone. Next day she reads the bit in the paper, moves interstate. Wollongong. She reckons anyone looking for her, they won't look there. I reckon she's right.'

'How does she help?'

'Algie,' Berglin said. 'That's what the Chinese said at the front door. He said, "You are Algie?" A question.'

'She heard that from the kitchen?'

'He had a high voice, the Chinese, she says. Clear voice. And there was a half-open door to the hallway and the sitting room. Open-plan place.'

'You give her the name before she told you what she heard?'

'Don't be a dork. This woman's kosher. Lefroy and the Chinese, same visitors. And if this Algie in Bulleen is Lefroy's Algie ...'

I finished my beer, fetched two more. 'So that would just about get you to the second thing that brings you here,' I said.

'Yes,' said Berglin. 'Bianchi and Mance at the pub in Deer Park. You need to tell me who told you that.'

'No,' I said. 'My telling days are over. Anyway, person can't take it any further. Just heard it.'

Berglin nodded, drank some beer, scratched his head. 'Need a pee,' he said. 'Let's go outside. I like an open-air pee when I'm in the country. Pee, a cigarette and a look around. The stockman's breakfast.'

We went into the night, over to the paddock fence and pissed on the weeds.

'Wouldn't want to expose the pork out here too long,' Berglin said. 'Lose it to frostbite. Listen, should be clear to you if Mance was playing both you and Bianchi, the idea came from Scully. Bianchi was just a cockbrain, messenger, fetch the hamburgers, get us a pie.'

'And then,' I said, 'you have to begin to think the unthinkable.'

He zipped his fly. 'A possibility, no more.'

'Here's another possibility. Three separate surveillance operations, three targets dead, stuff gone. And it's all got nothing to do with the surveillance.'

'Odds higher there,' Berglin said. 'It gives me the same worry you had and that makes doing anything very difficult.'

'And I hear the surveillance records vaporised.'

Berglin looked at me, head tilted. 'For a bloke way out of the loop, you hear a lot.'

'What about the spring cleaning after I left?'

'Did that, but houses get dirty again. Christ, let's get inside.'

At the back door Berglin stopped, tapped my arm, took out a cigarette. 'Mrs Bianchi, she went on protection, new name, new everything, new tits even if I read the expenses right. Got a bloke looking for her now, reliable bloke, one hundred per cent, reports only to me. He says he's warm. We find her, you want to talk to her?'

'You know an expression I always hated in the old days?' I said. 'The loop. Well, I don't want to be back in the loop.'

Berglin lit the cigarette, flame cupped, eyes narrow in the flare. 'This loop is you and me, Mac,' he said. 'You don't come into it, you want to think about sending that nice young fella away, put the dog in the kennels, sleep under the bed with the big gun. The old days aren't over yet.'

ALEX RICKARD was a creature of habit and that is not a wise thing to be when people you may not want to see want to see you. The habit meant he would be at Flemington Racecourse on Wednesday afternoon. On another day, it might have been Moonee Valley or Caulfield. What was certain was that on a Wednesday afternoon Alex would be at the city races.

I got there early and found a place where I could watch the turnstiles. It wasn't going to be hard to spot Alex in the crowd. There wasn't a crowd, just a trickle of depressed-looking men in jail-release clothes. Ten minutes before the first race, Alex and a short, bald man in a raincoat who looked like Elmer Fudd came through. Alex raised the standard of dress by a few hundred points. He was very Members' Enclosure: grey flannels, a grey tweed sports jacket, blue shirt, red tie.

The pair stopped off for a quick hot dog and read their race books. Elmer Fudd had two quick hot dogs. He talked a lot, waving the race book and the hot dogs around. Alex found him amusing, smiling as he ate, and then carefully wiped his lips and hands on the little paper napkin.

I kept a good distance from them in the betting ring. They favoured different bookies. Alex knew his firm well: he got a pat on the arm from the man with the laptop computer and the slip writer whispered something in his ear. Alex had a good laugh, Fudd came over and the pair went onto the grandstand. I found something to lean against and settled in.

After the first race, the two came down, pleased with themselves, visited their bookies. Same after the second race, not as pleased now. It was going to be difficult to talk to Alex if he went everywhere with Fudd.

I almost missed Alex after the third race. He was alone and I was looking for the pair of them.

He wasn't going to his bookie this time. When I realised he was heading for the toilets, I picked up speed, got too close to him, prayed he wouldn't look around.

But he didn't. And there was more luck in the toilet. Only one cubicle door was closed and Alex was alone at the urinal, in the right-hand corner, getting his prick out.

He didn't see me coming.

I ran the three steps, slammed him into the stainless steel with my left shoulder, punched him in the kidneys three times, one full shot with everything, two short chops.

Alex made a vomiting noise and sagged. I held him up by his left shoulder, took a handful of his smooth hair at the crown and smashed his head into the wall several times.

I let him go and he dropped to his knees. There was blood on the stainless steel at head height. I put a knee between his shoulder blades and jerked his head back by his long front lock until he was looking up into my eyes.

'Alex,' I said. 'Didn't keep my inquiry confidential. Who'd you tell? Quick, they'll find you dead here.'

He opened his mouth wide. Blood from his forehead ran into it and he coughed, spraying red onto the stainless steel. 'No, Mac, no ...'

I heard a sound behind me. A tall man with black rimmed glasses had come out of one of the cubicles.

'Back in the dunny or I'll kill you,' I said.

He went back like a film in reverse. The lock clicked.

'Quickly, Alex,' I said, banged his head against the urinal again. Blood dropped onto the white disinfectant balls in the trough.

'Mac, no ...'

I banged his head again, took his ears in my hands, small ears, not easily grasped, and began to twist them off. It was difficult. They were slippery.

'Last chance, Alex. Who?'

'Bobby Hill,' he said, barely audible. 'Didn't think it mattered, thought you were out of it.'

I let go of his ears, pulled his head back by the hair, strong hair, and looked into his eyes from close range. 'Alex,' I said, 'who told you to tell Berglin that Gaby Makin was dead?'

'I'm dead.'

I bounced his head off the urinal again, once, twice, blood spattering. 'Right, you prick,' I said. 'Dead now if you don't tell me.'

Alex groaned. I gave him one more smash. Harder.

'Bobby.'

'Why? Quick.' I pulled his head back again.

'Anything you or Berglin wanted to know, pass it on.'

'Listen carefully, Alex,' I said, jerking his head back again so that he could look at me. 'You're a little man in deep shit. Tell Bobby Hill you've told me, Bobby kills you. Then I dig you up and kill you. Repeatedly. Then it's Berglin's turn. No matter what happens, you tell Bobby, you die. Painfully. Understand me?'

I let him go. Alex's head hit the urinal again and he collapsed sideways, slowly. I pushed his head into the trough with my right foot and pressed the flush button. A gentle spray of water dampened his face and hair. Trickles ran down his bleeding forehead and the trough turned bright pink.

'"Let the water and the blood from his riven side which flowed be of sin the double cure",' I said. Was that the way it went? It just came to me.

Four men, different sizes, all wide-eyed, were blocking the passage.

'Gentlemen,' I said, 'an emergency. Need St John Ambulance here. This man has had a serious pissing accident.'

They flattened themselves against the walls. I passed between them, left the racecourse, went home, fed the dog, made supper, played Scrabble with Lew, got beaten again.

I was washing up, thinking: open another bottle, go to bed. Lew appeared in the door.

'Mac,' he said, moved his shoulders, looked at the floor. 'Think I'll go back to school. That's what Ned wanted.'

I looked at the boy: father unknown, mother unknowable, grandfather allegedly something I didn't want to think about. And nothing bad in this quiet and gentle person.

I wished I could hug him.

'I'll take you to the bus,' I said. 'That's easy.'

He did a ceiling examination.

'Down the road,' he said. 'The girl. They go in every day. I asked. Will you talk to the school? And tell Stan I'll work at weekends?'

'Sure. Talk to them tomorrow.' There was a new family down the road. I'd seen the girl on a horse from a distance. Perhaps both Ned and I and the girl all wanted Lew to go back to school. I had a feeling dawning about which one had had the deciding influence.

Before I went to bed, I put the Colt Python, safety catch off, in a Blundstone boot next to the right back leg of the bed.

I lay on my back for a long time, thinking about Bobby Hill, thin and handsome Bobby Hill, straight dark hair combed back, metal-rimmed dark glasses. Of the trio of Scully, Hill and Bianchi, Hill had been the watchful one, little disbelieving smile never far from his lips. He was Scully's offsider but managed to give the impression without saying anything that pudgy Scully worked with him.

Bobby's making lots of money in the baboon hire business. Those were Brendan Burrows's words. What interest would Hill have in my Kinross Hall inquiries? Something Berglin once said came to mind: *He who says Hill says Scully.* Would that still be the case? Could it be Scully who was interested in me? I was history, he was about to be made deputy commissioner.

Was I history? What had Berglin said?

The old days aren't over yet.

Not a thought to fall asleep on.

I DREAMT I was in the old factory in Footscray, Dr Barbie's point of exit. It was cold, dark in the corners spreading out. I was walking from cavernous space to cavernous space, looking for something in the gloom, uneasy. I pushed open a huge sliding door and I was in a room filled with light, the ceiling seemed to glow, one huge skylight. People were standing in groups, talking and drinking, laughing. The nearest group had their backs to me. As I approached, one by one they turned, smiling, greeting me: my father, that shy smile, Ned, Alex, forehead bloody, Brendan Burrows, Berglin, Scully, Hill, Bianchi, Lefroy. The group parted and Carlie Mance appeared, radiant, took my arm, tucked it under hers. We walked together to the centre of the chamber and she pointed. A body, elongated, was dangling from the roof, slowly turning. I waited, full of dread, to see the face. It came around slowly, slowly, familiar profile ...

I woke, sweating, still filled with the dream's apprehension. Just like the old days, I thought.

It was almost five am. I got up, no point in staying in bed, washed my face, revved up the kitchen stove, made a pot of tea, read *The Plant Hunter* till it was time to shower, cook, eat and start work. Today was committed to finishing Frank Cullen's contraption, long overdue. But Frank was a patient man. He never hurried the realisation of his inventions because it gave him time to think about modifications. Not big ones: tweaks of the brilliant concept.

I was tidying up the welds with the anglegrinder when Allie arrived. I switched off and lifted the helmet. She knew about the contraption.

'What I don't understand,' she said, 'is why you wouldn't simply put whatever it is you want to load onto the back of the ute. Why would you put it on this thing and haul it up with a winch?'

'The idea, as I understand it, and I may be utterly wrong here, is that you can take this thing where utes fear to go. Reach the parts ordinary utes cannot reach. Then you haul it back and wham! It's on board.'

She rolled her eyes. 'Haul it back? How much cable is there going to be?'

'Brilliant idea or scrapmetal in the making,' I said, 'the man doesn't blink at the bill, writes out the cheque right here in front of me, very neat and legible hand, and the bank doesn't blink either. Which is a lot more that can be said for many of our clients.'

'Which is why I'm glad I don't have to send out my own bills anymore.'

'Not gladder than I am,' I said. 'Listen, this extensive training of yours equip you to make a knife blade?'

'You don't have to be a Rhodes scholar,' she said, 'to make a blade. All you have to do is take pains.'

I put up my gloved hand. 'Point taken, to the hilt. I'm weeks behind with the knives. Fit it in? I'll show you what's needed.'

'Let's look at the diary,' she said. 'Has to be time this week.'

I was fitting the wheels when Frank Cullen and Jim Caswell arrived, today in full squatter's uniform. Jim took his seat on the bench, Frank came over to inspect the work.

'Nice wheels, Mac,' Frank said. 'Where'd you get 'em?'

'Place in town sells bearings,' I said. 'Cost a fair bit.'

'Quality,' Frank said. 'Remembered when price is forgotten.'

'Very true,' I said. 'Motto of this workshop.'

'Now these tracks,' Frank said. 'Bin givin 'em some thought, woke up this mornin with the answer.' He took a folded piece of paper from his shirt pocket and carefully opened it. 'This diagram shows what I've come up with.'

I looked at it. The tracks now had angled projections at each end.

'Beauty of it,' Frank said, 'is these top bits. They slide into these housings you bolt to the tray. What d'ya think?'

'Like all the best ideas,' I said, 'you wonder why you didn't think of it earlier.'

Frank took a seat, lit a cigarette, had a good cough.

'Don't know how you can do it,' Jim said, shaking his head.

'Do what?' Frank said.

'Smoke. You know what the doctor said.'

'Bloody doctors,' Frank said. 'What do they know? Know buggerall, that's why they blame the fags. Could be somethin else entirely. Could be— could be bloody potatoes kills ya. Carrots. I read where everybody in China smokes, from babies upwards, they don't bloody die any more than anyone else. Look at that Mao Tsebloodytung, used to smoke in his sleep, couldn't get him to die. Same with the other bloke, whatsisname, thingummy, shot them students, eighty fags a day, still runnin the place at ninety, whatever.'

'The Veenes,' I said. 'What do you know about the Veenes?'

'Veenes,' Frank said. 'Don't talk to me about Veenes. I know Veenes. Worked for bloody old Clarrie Veene, the most miserable bastard ever to walk God's earth, bar none. Used to look at you like you were a sick dog he wouldn't waste a bullet on, kill it with a spade. Little bastard used to come up to me, didn't reach my top button, course I was six-three then ...'

'You were never six-three,' Jim said.

'You bloody dwarf, what would you know? You couldn't see that high. Come up to me, the old bastard, wasn't all that old then either, come right up to me, under me nose, say something like, whining bloody voice,

"Cullen, when you going to do something about that slate you're running over at Meagher's?" Coulda killed him right there, one blow.'

'A Veene had some land near Milstead,' I said. 'Pine forest now.'

'That was Ernest's,' Frank said. 'Clarrie's brother. Another miserable bastard. Went to his son. Donald.'

'Some Melbourne company owns it now,' I said.

'Rick Veene's got a share in the company,' Frank said. 'Heard that. He's Donald's boy. Looks a lot like Ernest. Rick's tied up with that Stefanidis from over near Daylesford. RSPCA went there, heard he was shooting pigeons. Bloke behind a wall throws 'em in the air, Greek shoots 'em with a twelve bore from about four yards. Sticks it up their arses practically. Couldn't prove it. Not a feather to be found.'

'What's on the land apart from trees?'

'Old house. Bluestone place. Solid. Never lived in I don't think after Donald moved to town.'

'When was that?'

'Oh, donkey's. Died about twenty years ago.'

Just before noon, I finished the contraption. We fitted the housings to Frank's ute, attached the tracks and ran the tray up them, not without difficulty.

'Good work,' Frank said. 'Excellent work. Craftsmanship of the highest order.'

We went over to the pub for a sandwich. I had a beer. Jim had a glass of milk. Frank had three brandies.

The phone was ringing as we came up the lane. I ran for it.

Irene Barbie.

'Mac,' she said, 'I've had a call from my daughter. From London. She's just got back from Italy and Greece and she found a letter from Ian waiting for her. It's been to about five of her previous addresses.'

I was still panting.

'Are you all right, Mac?'

'Fine. Been running. Go on.'

'Well, I think it puts Ian's suicide beyond doubt. Alice was in tears and the letter sounds a bit disjointed, but Ian says he's leaving a note explaining everything and apologises for the pain he's caused.'

'Leaving a note where?'

'He doesn't say.'

'Police ever mention a note to you?'

'No. Well, they asked me if I knew of any note Ian might have left. They didn't know of one.'

Ian's wristwatch. Brendan Burrows on the station platform.

Well, watch's gone, clear mark of watch on left wrist. Probably nicked by the deros.

Could they have taken anything else?

'It'll probably turn up. Thanks for telling me, Irene.'

'About Ian and pethidine …'

'Yes.'

'You were right. Andrew Stephens told me. I never knew. Must have been blind.'

'Most of us are blind some of the time,' I said. 'Some of us most of the time. There wasn't anything you could have done.'

'No, well, I suppose not. Thanks, Mac.'

I went out to see Frank and Jim off. Frank said: 'Gettin the winch tomorrow. Big bugger. More pull than a scout-master. I'll come round, you can bolt it on for me, we'll settle up.'

Frank and Jim had to wait at the entrance to the lane to let another vehicle in. A silver Holden. I stood where I was outside the smithy and Detective Sergeant Shea drove the car to within twenty-five centimetres of my kneecaps.

DETECTIVE SHEA was alone, the lovable Cotter presumably engaged in bringing cheer elsewhere. He got out of the car, looked at me, looked around, not approving. 'Bloody freezing as usual,' he said.

'I'm stuck here,' I said. 'You on the other hand are free to leave for warmer parts any time you like.'

'Don't take it personal,' he said. 'Talk inside?'

We went into the office. It wasn't much warmer there. I sat behind the desk, Shea looked at the kitchen chair disdainfully and sat on the filing cabinet.

'Suppose you thought we weren't doin anything,' he said.

'No,' I said. 'Thought you weren't achieving anything.'

He smiled his bleak smile. 'Takes time,' he said. 'You'd know. That complaint you told me about. One Ned made. About Kinross Hall, 1985. I looked that up. Investigated and found to be without substance. No further action taken.'

'What was the complaint?'

Shea looked awkward. 'Well,' he said, 'y'know I'm not allowed to divulge this kind of stuff. Lots of complaints, they've got no basis in fact, cause innocent people harm if the word got around ...'

'Ned's dead,' I said. 'And it's a long time ago.'

He rubbed his jaw with a big red hand. 'This's off the record, I never told you this, flat denial from me.'

'I never heard it from you.'

'Ned said a girl at Kinross told him the director, her name's Marcia something ...'

'Carrier.' A sick feeling was coming over me.

'That's right. The girl said this Marcia got her alone and made sexual, y'know, advances to her. She didn't want to and the woman slapped her up, blood nose, hit her on the body with somethin she said, stick, cane.'

I kept my voice neutral. 'This was investigated?'

Shea nodded. 'Oh yeah, two officers investigated. No substance. Girl said she'd made up the story to get some smokes from Ned. Marcia whats-hername, she said the girl was always makin up stories, been to her with wild stories, fantasy artist, something like that.'

'Fantasist.'

'That. So end of story. Scully and the other officer said no grounds to do anythin.'

The light from the window seemed suddenly brighter. I had difficulty seeing Shea's features. 'Scully?' I said.

'Yeah. Big noise now. You'd know him. In drugs. They say he's going to be deputy commissioner. Stationed here for three, four years in the eighties.'

'I know him,' I said. 'Who's the other officer?'

Shea got out his notebook, found the place. 'Bloke called Hill,' he said.

I nodded, got up. We went out into the rain. At the car, I put out my hand. We shook.

'Not finished with Ned,' he said. 'There's stuff I'm workin on. Be in touch.'

I went back to the office, sat down, stared at the desktop: Scully and Hill at Kinross Hall investigating Ned's complaint about Marcia Carrier.

I thought about the paintings in Marcia's office, small paintings of what looked like primitive sacrifice or torture.

The skeleton in the mine shaft. A girl. Around sixteen.

Ned's work diary, that was where it all began. I got out the box holding everything from Ned's desk: the newspapers, the marbles, the old wooden ruler from the grocer in Wagga, the big yellow envelope full of stuff.

I read the diary again. It was 1985 that had started me on Kinross Hall. As I went through it, I was thinking about Berglin. Berglin on making sense of scraps of information, on knowing people:

What you ask yourself is: what will this stuff I'm hearing about look like in hindsight? What kind of sense will it make then? You've got to think like an archaeologist, digs up this bit of something, fragment, could be bit of ancient pisspot, could be bit of the Holy Grail. The archaeologist's got to see the whole pot in the fragment. It's called using your imagination. They don't pick you people for this kind of ability, so we're working against type.

Same thing with targets. You think you know them. Seen the pictures, maybe watched them in the street, public places, read the file, know their histories. But you don't know them until you can predict what they'll do in given circumstances. Till then, they're just cardboard people to you. That's why you've got to listen to the tapes. Everything. Every boring word, never mind it's about who's picking up the kids from school or who did what at fucking golf. You don't know a target until every grunt has meaning for you. And lots of it, it's just grunts. People just grunt at each other. Grunts with meaning.

It came out of the page in Ned's diary, lifted out at me, 1987: *March* 12. *Veene house, Colson's Road. Fix gutters, new downpipes. Six hours.* $100.00. *Materials* $45.60. *Found silver chain.*

Under this entry, Ned had written: *Forgot to put with invoice.*

Silver chain. I remembered something about a silver chain. In the news-papers from Ned's drawer. I got them out. Page three, a Thursday in June, a photograph of a chain with a small silver star and a broken catch. An ankle chain.

Was the chain Ned found at the Veene house an ankle chain? He hadn't returned it with the invoice. Had he handed it in later?

Perhaps he forgot to. Perhaps he still had it when he saw the picture in the newspaper.

My eye fell on the big yellow envelope. I'd looked in that.

Hadn't I? I remembered seeing staples and string. I took the envelope out of the box and tipped its contents onto the desk.

Staples, a bulldog clip, box of rubber bands, neatly coiled length of string, small penknife.

And then the chain slid out like a thin silver snake. A silver chain, broken catch.

I shook the envelope.

Something dropped out, fell onto the newspaper, bounced, came to rest a few centimetres from the photograph.

A small silver star, the twin of the one in the picture.

I HADN'T noticed the message on the answering machine, left while we were having lunch at the pub. It was Anne Karsh.

Mac, hi. Anne Karsh. I've got nothing on this afternoon. I'll be at the house from about three pm if you're free to show me the mill. If you can't make it, don't worry, we'll do it another day.

Ned thought he knew where the girl in the mine shaft was killed: the Veene house, where he'd found the ankle chain. He didn't trust the police, so he went to see Marcia. Then he went to see Dr Ian Barbie. And then he was murdered.

Marcia Carrier, Dr Marcia Carrier, Director of Kinross Hall, attacking a girl ... *blood nose, hit her on the body with somethin she said, stick, cane.*

One of the men who abused Melanie Pavitt told her: *Back soon, slut, with a lady friend for you. She's been looking forward to this.*

Was it possible?

I thought about these things, dark things, on my way to Harkness Park, slit-eyed streamlined dog face in the outside rear-view mirror, wind baring the fangs.

Anne Karsh's small black Mercedes was parked in front of the house and she was sitting on the steps where we'd sat drinking coffee. She got up at my approach, walked to meet me. Not the outdoor look today: hair down, long black and green tartan skirt with pleats, green shirt, black V-necked sweater.

'Mac,' she said.

We were close. I moved back.

'Thought you wouldn't come,' she said. 'I had business things, they fell through. Suddenly couldn't bear the city. I'm on my way to becoming a country person.'

'I'm glad,' I said.

'Are you? Ripped away from the blazing heat of the forge?'

I hadn't registered her eyes before. Hazel.

'Not blazing today,' I said. 'Today was welding, grinding and fiddling.'

She smiled. 'Oh, is that the blacksmith's burden? To weld, grind and fiddle.'

'By and large,' I said, 'I'd rather blaze.'

Silence for a moment, looking at each other. I wished I was better dressed.

'Have you seen the house?' she said.

'No,' I said. 'What entrance do I have to go in?'

She appraised me, serious face. 'Take your boots off, you can come in the front.'

We went through the front door, boots and all.

'Almost everything's here except the clothes and the pictures,' she said. 'It's as if they went on holiday and never came back.'

We started downstairs, went from huge room to huge room, looked out of the dirty windows at a dim day growing duller. Everywhere, we bumped into each other; in big spaces, we bumped into each other, sorry, sorry, hands unsure of where to go.

Upstairs. More bedrooms than a country pub, beds in all of them, clean coir mattresses, striped, some with neatly folded blankets on them.

In a large bedroom, not the master bedroom but big, wooden double bed, we looked out of the window, down at the newly cleared garden.

'It's going to look beautiful from here,' Anne said. We turned inward at the same moment, looked at each other.

'Beautiful,' I said. She was beautiful.

There was a moment of decision, indecision.

I put out a finger and touched her lips, in the centre.

'Oh Christ,' she said, reaching up and taking my head in her hands.

I put my hands on her waist, long, strong waist, drew her to me. As our mouths and our bodies met, she tilted her hips and pushed her pelvis against me. My hands slid down over her buttocks, lifted her, pulled her.

When our mouths parted, I said, close to her skin, 'Terrible urge to take off your clothes.'

'Terrible urge,' she said, 'to have you take them off.'

Kissing again, lost in her mouth, my hands on the bottom of her sweater, pulled it up. We broke free just long enough for it to pass over her head. I started unbuttoning her shirt from the collar, she took her fingers out of my hair and unbuttoned her cuffs, pulled the shirt over her head.

White lacy bra. I held her by the shoulders, looked, kissed the round tops of her breasts, put my tongue into the half cups, felt the nipples, risen, insistent.

'Oh sweet Jesus,' she said. Her hand went behind her back and the bra fell away, trembling breasts, not small, not big, lolling in my hands, mouth torn between three places, more, nipples, hollows of the throat, ears, eyes.

She loosened my belt, waistband, silky hand sliding over my stomach, gripping me, chamois grip, pulling, squeezing. I groaned.

The bed drew us, shoes, socks, pants, underpants went. I was naked first, five-limbed. Cold, hot. Anne was on her back, mouth open, loose, lovely. I pushed up her long skirt, pulled her pantyhose down her legs, over the long thighs, tense, the curve of calves, delicate ankles. Small white lace knickers, dark and springy promise beneath. Off. Pale stomach, hollow. I rubbed my face against it, kissed it, felt a pulse against my lips, buried my face in her dense pubic hair, thighs opening, sweet musk, the place, moist, salty, impossibly delicate rose petals of flesh, my hands under her buttocks lifting her, feeling the muscles clench, her hands in my hair pushing me down, hips moving.

Anne brought me up, my tongue tracing a line to her belly-button, tip pushing into the whorl, turned me over, tartan skirt off and in the air, floating to the ground, knelt above me, pushing her hair back with one hand, holding the engorged thing with the other, leaning forward, shoulders, breasts bigger, flushed with blood, kissing me, sucking my lips, her lips pulling mine in, her hand drawing the thin foreskin back, down, slowly, tight, drum tight, edge of pain, exquisite. And then the instant beyond pleasure, the touch, the warm, wet, tight, yielding, nipping, teasing, enfolding, gripping.

'Yes,' she said, sliding down, sitting on me to the hilt, ecstatic pubic junction. Beautiful, abandoned, impaled jockey, grinding, bending backwards, breasts flattening, nipples, ribs, hipbones, tendons in her neck sticking out, 'Yes. Yes. Yes. Oh fuck, Jesus Christ, yes.'

We didn't do the mill inspection; it would have to wait. We kissed goodbye outside, against her car, lingering kiss, kisses, almost started the whole thing up again.

I was about ten kilometres from home, happy, at peace for a moment, driving in the dark down a winding lonely stretch without farmhouses. A siren came on behind me, harsh, braying sound, happiness disrupted, rear-view mirror full of flashing orange light.

I slowed, went onto the verge, stopped.

The car pulled up close behind me but much further off the road.

I rolled down the window, waited.

A middle-aged cop, moustache, leather jacket, no cap, appeared at the window.

'Licence,' he said, tired voice.

'What's this about?' I said. 'I wasn't speeding.'

'Licence, please,' he repeated.

I found it in my wallet, handed it over.

He shone his torch on it. 'MacArthur J. Faraday?'

'Yes.'

'This your current address?'

'Yes.'

'Mind stepping out of the vehicle. Sir.'

'Jesus,' I said, got out. Bitter cold outside, no moon, north wind humming in the trees. The dog made his warning sound.

'Quiet,' I said 'Stay.'

'Turn and face the vehicle, please, hands on top,' the cop said.

'What's going on here?' I said. 'There's no ...'

'Do as I say, please. This'll only take a minute. We're looking for stolen goods.'

I turned and assumed the position.

'Pace back, please.'

I took the pace, weight on my hands, unbalanced, leaning on the freezing vehicle.

A second cop came around the back of the Land Rover, short, pale hair slicked down, head just an extension of his thick neck. He had no visible eyebrows and a nose like the teat of a baby's dummy.

He walked straight to me, swung his left leg, kicked my left leg out backwards, hit me in the back of the neck with a round side-on swing of his fist.

Everything went red, black, white, unbearable pain behind the eyes, in the bones of my head. I didn't even feel myself fall, land on the wet tarmac.

The next thing I registered was a heavy weight, a foot between my shoulder blades, something cold and hard pressing against the cavity under my left ear.

The muzzle of a revolver.

The pain seemed to dissolve. Cold and rough tarmac against the face, chill wind down here at ground level, smell of Anne on my shirt, French perfume, delicious Anne. I registered that but all I felt was sad. Sad and stupid. The watchful years, the looking for the signs, the ingrained disbelief about everything. For nothing. This is a stupid way to go, I thought. Careless. What would Berglin say?

'Bobby said to say goodbye,' said the middle-aged cop. 'Be here to say it himself, only he's got better things to do.'

He pulled my head back by the hair, painful, changed the angle of the muzzle to make sure he blew my brain away.

Headlights. Coming the way I'd come.

'Fuck,' said the man. 'Don't move.' He took the barrel away from my ear, pushed down harder on my spine with his foot.

A vehicle slowed, slowed, almost stopping. Went past us. Stopped.

I turned my head, saw the driver's door of a ute open, stocky frame come out, curly hair.

Flannery. On his way to the pub.

'What's this?' he said. 'What the fuck's this?'

'It's an arrest, sunshine,' the neckheaded cop said. 'Get back in your vehicle and drive on immediately. Now. Or you're under arrest for obstructing a police officer.'

I couldn't see the expression on Flannery's face but I could see the shrug.

'Okay, okay, I'm going,' he said. 'You could've asked nicely.'

He got back into the ute. Trouble getting it into gear, clutch grating.

'He ID us?' the middle-aged cop said.

'This light?' Neckhead said. 'No fucking way. He gets round the bend, buzz this cunt.'

Flannery revved his engine.

Hope gone.

And then Flannery's ute was coming at us in reverse, engine screaming.

'Jesuschrist!' the cop standing on me shouted.

His foot came off my spine.

I tucked my legs in, rolled to my right, heard Flannery's ute hit flesh and bone, brakes squeal, shouting.

I got around the front of the Land Rover, stood up. Flannery in first gear, coming back past me.

The cop he'd bumped was up, walking towards the police car, holding his left arm up by the elbow, screaming, 'Kill the fucking cunts!'

Neckhead, where?

I was backing off in Flannery's direction.

Neckhead popped up behind the Land Rover tray, revolver combat grip, two-handed, steadied himself to shoot me.

The dog jumped three metres onto Neckhead's out-stretched arms, jaws lunging for his throat, silent.

Neckhead made a shrill sound, went over backwards, rolled, knocked the dog off with the revolver barrel, tried a shot at it, two shots, missed, lead singing off the tarmac.

I screamed for the dog, ran for Flannery's ute, wrenched open the door, ute moving, half-in, foot dragging, heard the dog land on the back.

Flannery put his foot flat.

There was sound like a hard doorknock on the back window, followed by a smack on the roof above the rearview mirror.

I ducked, looked at the window: neat bullet hole, spider-web of cracks around it.

'Fuck,' said Flannery. 'Couldn't they just give you a ticket?'

I breathed heavily for a while, got my breath back. 'One tail light out,' I said. 'Attracts the death penalty. They coming?'

'No,' he said. 'Reversed over, attacked by dog, probably think, shit, let him off this time.'

I got out the mobile phone Berglin had insisted on leaving with me, found the number he'd written on a blank card, punched it in. Berglin answered immediately.

'Listen,' I said, 'that loop you were talking about.'

'Yeah?'

'Count me in. Two blokes in cop uniforms just tried to kill me. Told me Bobby said to say goodbye.'

'Bobby? That's our Bobby, is it?'

'I only know one Bobby.'

'Yeah. One Bobby's enough. Bears thinking about this. Good timing though. We've found the lady in question. Today. This afternoon.'

'Far?'

'From you? Five, five and a half hours.'

'Let's have it.'

When I'd put the phone away, Flannery said, 'What was it you said you did before you took up the metal?'

You couldn't lie to a man who would reverse over a policeman for you.

'I didn't say. Federal cop. Drug cop.'

'That's was, is it?'

'Very was. But there's stuff left over, unfinished stuff. Some stuff's never finished. Glad you came along then. Thanks.'

'Done it for a blind bloke,' Flannery said. 'What now?'

Home wasn't safe anymore. The only real home I'd ever had. My father's house, his workshop, his forge, his tools. The only place he'd ever felt settled, his demons banished. For a while at least. And bit by bit, over the years I'd lived there, I'd banished my demons too. Found a life that wasn't based on watching and lying and plotting, on using people, laying traps, practising deceit. But I'd brought a virus with me, carried it like a refugee from some plague city, a carrier of a disease, hiding symptoms, hoping against hope they would go away. And for a time they had. And I was happy.

But that life was over. Men in police uniforms came to execute you on the roadside beside dark potato fields. That was a definite sign the new life was over.

'Reckon you could drive me and Lew over to Stan's? I want him to stay there. We can pick up the Land Rover on the way back?'

'If I get a drink after that.'

'For you, Flannery,' I said, 'it's a possibility. I'm considering rewarding you with a few bottles of Boag's. Tasmania's finest.'

'Foreign piss,' Flannery said.

I didn't go into the house until I'd stood in the dark and watched Lew moving around, making supper, normal behaviour. Then I went in and made the arrangements.

BEACHPORT IN winter would be a hard thing to sell: dirty grey sky, icy wind off whitecapped Rivoli Bay whipping the tall pines, seven cars, two dogs, and a man on a bicycle in half an hour. But no-one had to sell the little boomerang-shaped town to Darren Bianchi's widow. She chose it.

I slept in a motel in Penola, little place out on the flats, vine country, turning on the too-soft mattress, half-awake, feeling the gun behind my ear, hearing the man say *Bobby said to say goodbye*.

I got up early, feeling as if I'd never been to bed, put on a suit and tie, ate eggs and fatty bacon at a truck stop, got to Beachport in time to see the former Cindy Taylor, former Mrs Cindy Bianchi, present Marie Lachlan, open her hairdressing salon. It was called Hair Today and it was a one-person show.

Marie was dressed for the climate: red ski pants, boots, big red top with a hood. I gave her twenty minutes to settle in, walked across the road, opened the door.

It was warm inside, clean-smelling, hint of coffee. Marie was in a sort of uniform now, pale pink, talking on the phone, back to me, didn't seem to hear me come in. She put the phone down, half turned and caught sight of me in the mirror. Her head jerked around. She was in her late thirties, short dark hair, pretty in a catlike way, little too much make-up.

Her eyes said *Oh shit*.

'G'day,' I said. 'Do men's haircuts? Got a meeting in Adelaide this afternoon, looking pretty scruffy.'

She was going to say no but she hesitated, changed her mind. 'Sure do,' she said. 'Come and sit down at the basin.'

I went over and sat in a low chair, back to a basin.

'You're out early,' she said.

'Too early. Drove from Geelong yesterday, stayed over in Mount Gambier. Thought I'd come down, have a look at the coast along here. First time I've been this way.'

'Pretty ordinary in winter,' she said. 'Lean your head back.'

She wet my hair with warm water, began to shampoo it, a kind of scalp massage with fingertips, soothing.

'Mind you,' she said, 'it's pretty ordinary in summer too.'

She was relaxing. I could hear it in her voice. People who come to kill you don't take time out for you to give them a shampoo and haircut first.

'So what do you do?' she said.

'Liquor rep,' I said. 'Well, wine rep these days. Mostly wine. Like wine?'

'Don't mind a few wines,' she said, fingers working in my hair. 'Like champagne. You carry champagne?'

'We're agents for Thierry Boussain, French. Terrific drop. No-one's ever heard of it, small firm. All people know is the Moët, Bollinger, that stuff, produce it in the millions of bottles. Thierry's exclusive, few thousand cases.'

'Never heard of it,' she said. 'Might try it one day.'

She dried my hair with a towel. 'Cutting time. Sit in the first chair. Warmest place.'

I changed chairs.

'Now,' she said, 'how do you want it?'

'Actually,' I said, looking at her in the mirror, 'I think I'll give the cutting part a miss, Cindy.'

Cindy froze. Terror in her eyes, tiny step backwards.

'No,' I said, 'I'm not bad news. Bad news doesn't have a shampoo first, anyone can come in, see me in the chair, get a good look at me.'

'Who are you?' she said, voice controlled, scared but under control.

'A friend,' I said. 'Someone who wants you to stay alive. We want to talk to you about Darren. You talked to the police, I know. This is different.'

'How different?' She wasn't looking at me, looking towards the door, possibly calculating her chances of reaching it.

'Cindy,' I said. 'Look at me, look at me. Don't be a dork, think you can run out the door, that'll save you. Nothing to fear from me. I'm your best chance of staying alive. Forget witness protection, that number they gave you to ring. Rang it now, you'd be saved, would you? Batman, out of the sky, saves you?'

She swallowed. 'That's Superman. Batman comes in the Batmobile.'

'Superheroes. Can't get my superheroes straight. Darren had a big trust in cops, did he? Did he?'

'No,' she said, meeting my eyes in the mirror. 'Didn't trust anyone. Specially not cops.'

'Wise man,' I said. 'Wisdom of an ex-cop.'

'So wise he's dead.'

'No-one's wise enough. Unfortunately.'

Cindy hugged herself. 'What more can I tell?'

'Things you didn't tell the cops, right?'

'Maybe. Some. I don't know?'

'Darren ever talk about someone called Algie?'

'Algie? Didn't say it like that.'

'Didn't say it like what?

'Algie. Said it like El G.'

'El G?'

'Yeah, y'know, like El Torro?'

'I get it. El G. Darren talk about El G?'

She shrugged. 'Well, after the burg ...'

'What burg's that?'

'More like a hurricane than a burg,' she said. 'Place destroyed. Fifteen grand's worth of damage.'

'Darren said what?'

'I dunno, El G. He said, fucking El G.'

'He said, fucking El G. Like El G did it? You tell the cops that?'

'No.'

'What else didn't you tell them?'

She hesitated.

Two cars went by in quick succession. Rush hour in Beachport.

'Cindy,' I said, 'they've done the show. This is the tell.'

'He said – Darren said – don't worry, what they want, the lawyer's got.'

'The lawyer. Who's the lawyer?'

'In Melbourne. Fielding something, they used to write. I don't know. I was out the house so quick. Fielding, three names. You want some coffee?'

'Coffee would be nice, Cindy,' I said. 'Black.'

'Sugar?'

'Just the one. Thank you.'

There was a glass percolator on a warmer at the back of the room. She came back with coffee in glass cups.

'Want to move?' she said.

'This is comfortable. Nice chair. You happy standing?'

'Stand all day.'

We drank coffee. 'Good, this,' I said.

'Real coffee,' Cindy said. 'Miss coffee places. Nescafé, that's what they give you around here.'

'Darren ever talk about someone called Lefroy?'

She didn't hesitate. 'Yeah. Saw him killed. Throat cut.'

My skin seemed to shrink, pull tight around my mouth, eyes. 'Darren saw him killed?' I said.

Cindy had a sip of coffee. 'Video. This bloke showed them a video. Girl killed too.'

Never change your tone. Berglin's rule. Start with it, stay with it. Want another tone, get someone else. 'What bloke is this?'

'El G. Took them to this place, big house, with like a little cinema.'

'Who's they?'

'I dunno. Darren and his mates, I dunno. Cops. We stayed in a hotel after the burg, Darren got so pissed, just talked. I didn't ask questions. Didn't know about that part of his life.'

'So they saw a video of a man called Lefroy and a woman being killed? That's what you're saying?'

'Yeah. Darren told me that. Said it made him sick. The man laughed.'

'El G?'

'Yeah. El G laughed. Showed it twice, Darren said. Funny name that. Stuck in my mind.'

'El G?'

'No. Lefroy. Spell it how?'

'Wouldn't have a clue,' I said.

A customer came in the door, elderly lady, head wrapped in a woollen scarf.

'Not late am I, Marie?' she said. 'Lovely and warm in here.'

'Have a seat, Gwen,' Cindy said. 'Won't be a moment.'

'On the night,' I said, 'Darren went out to the boat, never came back. That's it?'

'Where'd you hear that?' Astonishment. 'Cop said it must've gone on for an hour, more. Cut his ears off, burnt his hair off, don't you know that?'

'Yes,' I said. 'Just testing. The lawyers – Fielding, Something, Something?'

'Yes.' She picked up a comb and combed my hair. 'Nice hair.'

'My father's hair,' I said. 'Couldn't give him anything back.'

I HAD plenty of time to think on the trip back. El G, Scully, Hill and Bianchi watching a video of the killing of Howard Lefroy and Carlie Mance. A quick video, home movie really. Made while I was telling Mackie there wasn't any point in tailing Howard's brother when he left. El G enjoying it, laughing, showing it again. Did it show the moment of Carlie's execution? The man in rut behind her, between her legs, her head pulled back, blood squirting up the tiles?

One to do the killing, one to film it. Was that the way it had worked? Was the killer the driver, the man made up to look like Dennis Lefroy? Or was it the man who must have been in the boot when Dennis drove into the garage? Perhaps there were two men in the boot?

Years later, Bianchi burgled, then tortured and killed. Tortured for what? Pleasure? Something else?

Don't worry, what they want, the lawyer's got.

The killers Bobby sent had come up behind me on a country road. How could they know where I'd be?

I had a hamburger at a McDonald's on the outskirts of Geelong, read the *Age* I'd bought in Hamilton, rang inquiries for the Law Institute of Victoria on Berglin's mobile. An obliging woman took about two minutes to find the only three-name law firm in Melbourne beginning with Fielding: Fielding, Perez, Radomsky. She gave me an address in Rathdowne Street, Carlton.

I found a park across the street, outside a bookshop. As I crossed, the sun came out, took the edge off the wind. The gang of three had a shopfront office, two women behind a little counter. I said I'd like to see one of the lawyers. A five-minute wait produced a man who looked like the young Groucho Marx.

'Alan Perez,' he said, hand outstretched. 'Come into my office.'

It was a very basic office, desk, computer, two client chairs, degree certificate.

'Now. How may I help you?' he said. 'Mr...?'

'Bianchi,' I said, 'Craig Bianchi. I'm helping my sister-in-law tie up the loose ends of her husband's estate. He was a client of your firm.'

'Who was that?' he said, furry black eyebrows coming together.

'Darren Bianchi.'

'Not a client of mine. I'll just look him up. Spell it how?'

He swivelled his chair, did some computer tapping, peering at the screen. He needed glasses. 'Bianchi. Yes. Client of Geoff Radomsky's.' He swivelled back to look at me. 'Deceased, did you say?'

'Dead, yes.'

'Well, both of them.'

'Both of them?'

'Geoff's dead too. Here, in his office.'

'Heart?' I said. But I knew what was coming.

'No. Abducted at his house, just around the corner, Drummond Street. Parking his car, garage's off the lane. They, well, no-one knows, could be one person, brought him here, made him open the safe. Shot him. In the eye.'

Melanie Pavitt, lying there in her bath, gaping wound where her eye had been.

'Nothing of value in the safe,' Perez said. 'Druggies, they think. Thought we kept money here.'

'Things taken from the safe?'

Uncomfortable, pulling at a ring on the little finger of his left hand. 'Don't think so. Safe's register of contents wasn't up to date. Oversight, happens in a busy office. Everything thrown around, of course.'

'When was this?'

'More than a year ago now.'

'And you wouldn't know if there was anything concerning Darren in the safe. Right?'

Perez gave me a reassuring smile. 'We can check that. I'll get Mr Bianchi's file.'

He went away. I got up and looked out the window. Two men, both balding and bearded, expensive clothes, were leaning on cars, BMW, Saab, parked next to each other on the median strip. They were talking across the gleaming metal, lots of gestures.

Alan Perez came back with a folder, sat down, went through it, eyebrows again trying to merge. There were only two pages as far as I could see.

'Yes,' he said, eyes down. 'That's unfortunate.'

'What?'

'File's confidential, obviously, but there is a record here of a tape, audio tape, left with Geoff for safekeeping.'

'Where would that be kept?'

'Well, in the safe I imagine. In the absence of other instructions.'

'Are there other instructions?'

Perez drew his furry upper lip down. 'No. So that's where it would have been put. I'm sure.'

'Still there?'

'I'll check,' he said, left again.

He was back inside a minute.

'No. Not there. No tapes.'

'So it could have been taken?'

Eyebrows again, black slugs trying to mate. 'If it was in the safe. Where we would expect it to have been. But we don't know. Yes. It could have been.'

I tried him on. 'My sister-in-law says my brother left clear instructions with you about something. That would be about the tape, would it?'

He wasn't happy. 'Client's instructions are confidential, we can't ...'

'Client's dead,' I said. 'And you don't know what you had in your safe. Followed his instructions, have you? I'm happy to have the Law Institute take this up.'

I got up.

Perez said, 'Mr Bianchi, you'll appreciate our problem here. With Geoff dead, no-one was aware of his client's instructions. We could hardly go through all his files to see ...'

'He's my brother,' I said. 'All I want to know is what he wanted you to do. There's something says you can't tell me that?'

Pause. Perez shrugged. 'Well, I suppose not. He wanted the tape handed over to the Director of Public Prosecutions. With copies to the media.'

'In the event of what? When was this to be done?'

He couldn't back off now.

'In the event of his death from other than natural causes.'

'He's dead. Of unnatural causes.'

'We didn't know that. Unfortunately.'

'Followed the instructions?'

He shrugged, crossed his legs. 'You'll understand our position, Mr Bianchi. The circumstances are such that we find ourselves ... it would be unreasonable ... we didn't even know he was dead.'

'Okay, I'll accept that. Is there a Mrs Radomsky?'

'Yes.'

'I'd like to talk to her. He may have said something to her about the tape.'

'Very unlikely. And I'm not sure that she ...'

'Alan,' I said, 'you owe this to Darren's widow. You were negligent in your handling of a client's affairs. You did not have procedures for ensuring that a client's instructions were followed and ...'

'I'll ring her,' he said. 'Would you excuse me for a moment?'

I went out and sat in the waiting area for a few minutes. Perez came out and beckoned me back into his office.

'Helen Radomsky says she knows absolutely nothing about any tape. Geoff never talked about clients' affairs – never.'

'What about his secretary? She here?'

'No. She took Geoff's death badly. Both secretaries did. They both resigned. You can understand ...'

'Got a number for her?'

Perez looked unhappy again.

'Ring her,' I said. 'Explain what it's about.'

I didn't have to leave the room this time. He got out the phone book. 'I got a call from some solicitors in Hawthorn asking about Karen,' he said. 'Blandford something. Here we go.'

He dialled a number. 'Alan Perez, Fielding, Perez, Radomsky. Do you have a Karen Chee? Yes, thank you ... Karen, Alan Perez. Good thank you. You're well, settling in? ... It was a pleasure. Karen, we're trying to find out about a tape that should have been in the safe. Audio tape.'

He listened for several minutes, saying 'Yes. Right'. Finally, he said, 'Didn't see them again. Sure about that? ... Yes. Well, thanks. Look after yourself ... I'll certainly pass that on. Bye.'

He put the phone down.

I held my breath.

'She says Geoff asked her to get the tape copied, two copies. There was some urgency about it. The copying was done by DocSecure – they do confidential copying. She went into the city by taxi, the job was done, she came back and put the master tape in the safe.'

'She had a key?'

'No, there's a slot. Anyway, she then dropped the copies off at Geoff's house. It was after five. The arrangement was for a courier to pick up the package at Geoff's to deliver to Darren Bianchi in Noosa. She assumed both copies were being sent.'

'I'd like to talk to Mrs Radomsky.'

Perez sighed, hesitated, caught my look, dialled. 'Helen, Alan, sorry to disturb you again. Look, it really would be a great help if Mr Bianchi could talk to you for a few minutes ... I know, I know. It'll put his mind at rest. I'd appreciate it ... Great, fine, yes. Thanks, Helen.'

The Radomsky house was a minute away, a freestanding brick two-storey, lace ironwork in need of paint. But not for much longer: a panel van with Ivan De Groot, Painter written on the side was parked outside. I pushed a brass button on the front door. It was opened by a short blonde woman, chubby, in her early forties.

'Mr Bianchi? Helen Radomsky. Come in. We'll have to go into the kitchen, everything else is being painted.'

We went down a wide passage and turned left into a kitchen, a big room with windows looking onto a walled garden.

'Sit down,' she said. I sat down at a scrubbed table. She leant against the counter under the windows.

'I'm sorry about your husband,' I said.

'Thank you. The most senseless thing.'

I nodded. 'Mrs Radomsky, Alan Perez may have explained. My brother left an audiotape with your husband and it's gone, not in the safe.'

She nodded.

'His secretary says she had the tape copied late one afternoon and dropped off two copies here. A courier was going to pick them up.'

'I remember a courier coming one evening. About six thirty. That's two or three weeks before Geoff ... I didn't see what Geoff gave him.'

I put my elbows on the table, palms together. 'It's most likely Geoff sent off both copies. But I'd like to ask you something, just to be certain.'

'Yes?'

'If Geoff didn't give the courier both tapes, where would he have put the second one?'

She smiled. 'Well, he'd have put it on the side table in the study to take to work, forgotten all about it, put a newspaper on top of it the next day. Six weeks later there would be a panic search and we'd find it under sixteen copies of the *Age*, three books and four old *Football Records*.'

'Is it possible?'

She pulled a face. 'I haven't been into the study for more than ten seconds since the night. Actually, I haven't been into it for more than ten seconds in years. And Geoff wouldn't let the cleaning lady near it. He attacked the mess himself about twice a year.'

'Could you bear to ...'

'Of course,' she said. 'Come.'

We went back down the passage. She opened the second door on the left, went in, pulled open heavy red curtains. It was not the study of a tidy person: books, newspapers, files on all surfaces, two bags of golf clubs leaning against the fireplace, a filing cabinet with the bottom drawer pulled out, two full wastepaper baskets, a team of old cricket bats meeting in a corner, empty wine bottles and several wine glasses and mugs on the mantelpiece.

The side table was to the left of the door, no centimetre of its surface visible under a haystack of printed material.

I looked at it. 'So far the hypothesis holds,' I said.

Helen Radomsky began clearing the table, dropping the material on the carpet. She got down to a final layer of newspapers.

'Well,' she said, 'if it was put here ...' She lifted the stack.

A Game Boy, paperback entitled *The Mind of Golf*, gloves, set of keys, dictation machine, coins, ballpoints, two Lotto tickets, window envelopes, dark glasses, a small silver torch, a pocket diary, small dark-coloured plastic box.

Helen Radomsky picked up the box. It had a sticker on the side. She read: 'DocSecure.'

I said, 'Anything in it?'

She shook it. It rattled.

She opened it: one tape.

I said, '"And when it seemed that destiny sought them slain/ Came from the legion's throat one joyous sigh / All eyes gazed up from that blood-stained plain / To see a white dove beneath a salamandrine sky.'"

'What's that?' she said.

'Some poem,' I said. 'All I remember. It's about salvation.'

I FOUGHT against it and then I did it: I rang Anne Karsh. If Leon answered, I'd say Francis wasn't answering and we needed instructions about the pine trees at Harkness Park.

It rang and rang. I was about to give up when she said, 'Hello. Anne Karsh.' Short of breath.

I didn't have much breath either. 'Mac. If this is a bad idea, for any reason, say wrong number and put it down.'

She laughed. I knew the laugh. 'It's a good idea. It's the kind of idea you desperately hope someone else will have because you're too uncertain to have it yourself. And you're walking around feeling like a schoolgirl with a crush. A thirty-four-year-old schoolgirl.'

'I'm in the city,' I said. 'Business.'

I could hear her breathing.

'Is that in the city staying over or in the city going back?'

'In the city staying over. Not sure where yet.'

'I can suggest somewhere,' she said.

'I'm open to suggestion.'

'I still have my flat in East Melbourne. It could use an airing. We could meet there, cook something, eat out, order a pizza, not eat anything.'

'I think eating's important,' I said. 'Not so much what but the social act.'

'So do I. I think social acts are very important. We'll think about the social act when we're there. Make a joint social act decision.'

'You're free this evening then?'

'I'm free for the next two hours, then I've got a brief engagement, then I'm free again. Leon came back from Queensland last night, flew to Europe this afternoon. In hot pursuit of something. Possibly a small European country. Smaller than Belgium, bigger than Andorra.'

'So we could meet quite soon?'

'I think we should get off the phone now,' she said, 'and make our separate ways to East Melbourne at the maximum speed the law allows. Slightly over the maximum speed. When you get there, press the button for A. Lennox.'

'Give me the address,' I said. It was unusual for me to become aroused while talking on the telephone in a car parked outside a newsagency.

The address was a Victorian building, a huge house, three storeys, converted to apartments. I parked across the road, waited. Quiet street. It began to drizzle.

The black Mercedes took ten minutes to arrive, went down the driveway beside the house. I waited two minutes, got out.

I pressed the button next to the name A. Lennox. Anne Lennox. Her name before she took Karsh. There was a lift to the third floor. I walked up, glad to stretch after a day of driving, found the elegant door.

Before I rang, I unsnapped the shoulder-holster button under my right arm. The door opened instantly.

Anne was wearing a trenchcoat over jeans and a camel-coloured top, hair pulled back, dark-rimmed spectacles. I hadn't seen her in glasses.

She brushed my lips with the fingertips of her right hand.

'Suit,' she said. 'Sexy in a suit, Mr Faraday.'

Inside, door closed, we looked at each other.

'Sexy in the glasses,' I said.

'Thank you. For driving.' She took them off, put them in an inside pocket.

I touched her hair. 'Wet,' I said.

'Everywhere. I was in the shower.'

'Rang and rang. Almost gave up.'

'Pays to wait the extra second.'

'Pays like Tattslotto,' I said.

She took off the trenchcoat, hung it on a hook behind the front door, adjusted the central heating dial on the wall.

She kicked off her shoes, unbuttoned her top at the throat and pulled it over her head.

'Pays better than Tattslotto,' she said.

She was naked underneath, nipples alert. She cupped her breasts for me. I bent to kiss them, feverish.

'Didn't have time to get dressed properly,' she said.

'Like you dressed improperly. Very much.'

Kissing, undressing, touching, we found our way down the passage and into a bedroom. I managed to get my jacket and the shoulder holster off together.

'First in quick time, I think,' Anne said, voice blurred. 'Then in slow. Very slow.'

Later, lying naked, sated, in the warm room, Anne side on to me, head on my chest, my hand between her thighs, she said, 'Leon tells me you have an unusual background for a blacksmith, Mr Faraday.'

I felt the sweat on my neck chilling. 'What does Leon know about my background, Ms Karsh?'

She laughed. 'When you turned down Leon's job offer, you became an unobtainable object. And therefore an object of interest.'

'A man with a duck on a string.'

'Exactly.' She bit my right nipple gently, worried it, put her fingertips in my pubic hair, scratched gently.

'And so he made inquiries about me. Is that it?'

'That's it. He couldn't bear not to know.'

'What did he say about my background?'

'Unusual. That's all. Leon never reveals everything he knows. Not at once. He likes you to know he knows and to tell you what he knows when it suits him.'

'And how does Leon find out what he knows?'

'Oh, I think Leon could find out what toothpaste the Pope uses.'

'Would you say,' I said, 'that Leon was a jealous man?'

'No, not jealous. Envious. Of everything he doesn't have.'

'If he thought you were having an affair, would he want to know the details?'

'Probably. Not out of jealousy. Just for the knowledge. Knowledge for its own sake.' She moved her lips onto my ribs. 'Talking of knowledge,' she said, 'carnal knowledge of you is nice. And not just for its own sake.'

She reached over and got her watch off the bedside table, looked at it with her head on my stomach. 'Christ!' She sat upright. 'Have to postpone the learning for a while. I'm due to represent Leon at this charity thing ...'

I lay on the bed and thought while she showered. She came back into the room, unselfconsciously naked, walked around, found clothes.

'Suspender belt tonight, what do you think? Black or white?'

'White. I like the virginal associations.'

She was wearing just the suspender belt and stockings, towelling her hair, breasts jiggling, when she said, 'Leon's got a man called Bobby who can find out anything. I think he called in Bobby to give the once-over when he decided he fancied me.'

I went cold everywhere now. 'What's Bobby's full name?'

'Never heard it. Leon calls him Bobby the Wonder Dog.'

I swung my legs off the bed, reached for my clothes.

'Mac? What? What's wrong?' Alarm in her voice.

I said, 'Anne, it's complicated. Leon's Bobby is likely to be a man called Bobby Hill. After I left you last night, two men sent by Bobby tried to kill me.'

'Kill you? Kill you? Why?'

'Goes back a long way,' I said, putting on my shirt. I sat down to put on my shoes. 'Sordid stuff. Couldn't work out how they knew where I'd be last night. Now I think I know.'

Anne came around the bed, put her hands on my shoulders, kissed me on the lips. 'I'm out of my depth here, Mac,' she said. 'Who are you?'

I kissed her back. 'When it's over,' I said, 'tell you the whole sad story. I have to get out of here. The best thing is for you to leave and then I'll wait a while and go. Is there a back door?'

'To the building? Yes.'

'To this flat?'

'To the fire escape. Yes.' She sat down next to me, put her hand on my thigh. 'Going to be all right, isn't it?'

I kissed her again, soft, hard, hand on her silky neck. 'Has to be. Haven't got to the very slow part yet.'

I stood, found the shoulder holster in my jacket and put it on.

Anne looked at the revolver, looked at me, bit her lower lip. 'Tell me I shouldn't be regretting this,' she said.

I touched her lips. 'No regrets,' I said. 'I'm flying with the angels. Scout's honour.'

While she was putting on lipstick, I said, 'If I'm right, the flat is being watched. If you leave alone, they'll wait for me to come out, jump me outside. If I don't come out and there's still a light on in the flat, they'll think I'm planning to stay here overnight and they'll come to get me later. So I'll leave a light on when I go.'

She was ready. I took her face in my hands, kissed her. She kissed me back, took a hand and kissed it. 'It isn't just lust – you know that, don't you?'

I nodded. 'Yes. I know that. This thing, it's almost over.'

I didn't believe that. Not for one instant.

Anne went out the front door. In the kitchen, by the light from the passage, I found a dark dishcloth, tied it around my neck like a napkin to hide my white shirt. I went out the door, quietly closed on the latch, stood against the wall on the steel fire escape landing and looked down on the parking area.

It was dark, half moon hidden by cloud, the only light coming from a long open-fronted tenants' garage at the back of the property. There were only a few lights on in the building, most people not home yet. In this area, they'd all be working fourteen hours a day to pay for the flat and the BMW and the holiday in Tuscany.

Music coming from one of the flats: Miles Davis.

Anne came into sight briefly, long legs, walking briskly towards her car. Moments later, she reversed out, bathing the yard in blood red light, drove around the corner of the building.

Bobby's boys would not touch Anne, had no reason to. It was me Bobby wanted.

I unclipped the holster, drew the Colt. Time to go.

I took a step towards the stairs, hesitated, moved to the landing rail, back and right cheekbone against the wall, looked down at the landing below.

Nothing. I leaned my head a little further over ...

The tip of a shoe, a black running shoe, in the doorway.

Can't go down. Can't go back. The man below's partner would be in the building now, possibly already in the flat.

I opened the back door, thankful that I'd put it on the latch, backed into the kitchen.

No sound in the flat.

I looked around. Espresso machine on the counter. I holstered the Colt, unplugged the machine, picked it up, solid, heavy, cradled it in one arm, stepped out the door again, closed it quietly.

I stepped carefully to the front edge of the landing, coffee machine held above my head, leant forward until I could see both shoes below.

'Hey,' I said, gruffly, urgently.

He came out of the doorway fast, in a crouch, looking up, silenced weapon coming up in the two-handed grip.

Neckhead. I saw his face for a split second before I threw the coffee machine at him with all the force I could muster. He fired, just a 'phut' noise, no louder than a clap with cupped hands.

But I was already on my way down, one jump to the intermediate landing, painful contact with the railing, left turn ...

Neckhead was on his knees. The coffee machine appeared to have struck him full in the face, blood down the right cheek, the appliance lying in front of him.

He brought the pistol up – one-handed now, not fast, puzzled look on his face – as I dived at him.

Another phut.

I felt nothing, just the impact of crashing into him, knocking him backwards. I was feeling for his throat, found the hand holding the pistol, forced the barrel back towards him, back, back, tried to find the trigger. He was making a strangling noise, I could smell his hot breath: cigarette smoke and meat.

Close up, the sound was loud, I felt the heat, smelt the acrid cordite. His body went limp instantly.

I pulled away, stood up. The bullet had gone in under his left nostril, the back of Neckhead's head was gone. Even in the dark, I could see the blood spreading out from him onto the steel deck.

It had all taken a few seconds. No-one was shouting. Miles was still playing. Probably a tape on a time switch to deter burglars.

Above me, I heard Anne's kitchen door open.

I took the silenced pistol out of Neckhead's hand, shrank back against the door of the second floor flat. Where Neckhead had waited.

Waited.

Heard the soft feet on the steps. Rubber soles.

Saw the shoes, big, the trousers, dark, the waistband of the ski jacket. No more.

The legs stopped. He had seen Neckhead's legs.

'Jesus,' he said, came down the steps in a rush, swung onto the landing, sawn-off shotgun in his right hand, its ugly pig-nostril muzzles coming around to face me.

I shot him in the chest, twice, a third time. His eyes registered something, he bounced against the railing, mouth open, made a sound, cheerful, surprised sound, fell over sideways, slid.

I stood there, pistol in hand, feeling sick. The dishcloth was still around my neck. I took it off, used it to wipe the pistol, put it back in Neckhead's hands again, pressed his fingers, utmost care.

I listened. Nothing but the growl of traffic on Hoddle and Victoria and Wellington Parades, and Miles Davis.

I left the scene of the crimes. Left carefully, in case Bobby had sent more than two people to get me. Not that taking care would make any difference in the long run, the short run even.

He who says Hill says Scully.

I couldn't kill armies of people.

I WENT out on the Tullamarine freeway, suddenly hungry, bought a hamburger in the drive-through at a McDonald's in Keilor, sat in the car park, appetite gone, system flooded with adrenalin, mind lurching between clear and blank.

I hadn't listened to the Bianchi tape.

I didn't want to listen to it. I'd left the Radomsky house with it in my hand and what I had done was to telephone Anne Karsh. All the effort to find it, lying to decent people, and then I put it in my pocket, put it out of my mind.

I took the slim plastic box out of my coat pocket, took out the cassette, slid it into the tape player, hit the buttons.

A voice, counting, humming, whistling. Darren Bianchi's voice.

Silence.

What was he doing?

Testing a wire, that's what he was doing.

Noise, traffic noise, tinny music, scratchy sounds.

So what's she supposed to know, I mean, what do I ... Bianchi's voice. Barely audible against the background sounds.

Know the absolute fucking minimum, anything goes wrong, she knows close to fuckall. Scully's voice.

Bianchi is wearing a wire, sitting in a car with Scully. His boss, Scully.

Dennis will ring ... Bianchi's voice.

Then Scully: *If Howie goes for his walk, only if he's out of there. Doesn't go, we wait till he goes somewhere. He goes, we see him, Dennis rings, says he's coming round. At eight thirty. Now she's got to wipe that from the tape, get it? Howie hears it, we're fucked. It's for fucking Faraday's benefit.*

So Howie doesn't know. He's gonna think, who's at the door?

Darren, don't worry about that, right? My department. Just one thing the bitch's got to do, right. Open the garage door at eight thirty on the fucking nail. You make sure she understands that. No fucking margin for error.

Yeah, eight thirty.

Yeah, eight thirty. It's just a run-through. She keeps her mouth shut, she gets wrapped up, they'll be out of there, five fucking minutes, less. No way Dennis will know she's not as surprised as he is. Okay?

Okay.

Something else. You make sure she knows, change of mind now, she's meat.

Too fucking late for that. She's fucking in. Doesn't want to do it, she's seen fucking Daimaru for the last time. She's fucking sushi. Doesn't do it right, same thing. Applies to you, too. And me. And fucking Bobby. You don't know this fucking El G, fucking mad. I know him from way back, kill anything, kill anyone, come in his pants while he's doing it. Totally fucking crazy, makes snuff movies. Fuck it up, we'll be fucking snuff stars.

Scuffling noises, car door slamming, Scully saying something inaudible.

The next five minutes of the tape were recorded somewhere noisy with background voices, laughter, scratchings, scrapings, bangings. The pub in Deer Park? Bianchi, low voice, giving Carlie Mance her instructions.

I listened with my head back on the seat, mouth dry, wishing I had something to drink, a cigarette.

Carlie showed no signs of fear, no desire to call it off. Bianchi told her what would happen to her anyway. Her last words were: *Darren, tell 'em make sure they don't put anything over my nose – can't bear that, can't even have a pillow over my nose.*

Bianchi said: *Not a problem. Won't happen. I'll tell 'em.*

I ejected the tape, put it in its box, put it in my pocket.

Scully. The bastard. Scully and El G. Scully, the deputy commissioner-to-be. Scully, the man who investigated Ned's complaint. Sitting in that car, talking to Bianchi, he knew that someone – El G, someone – was going to murder Lefroy and Carlie. Murder them, rape Carlie, enjoy it. Film it for future pleasure.

The tape might be enough to nail Scully, but I doubted it. I sat motionless for a while, uneaten hamburger on my lap, staring sightless.

Unfinished business.

I shook myself. Ian Barbie's suicide was unfinished business. His letter to his daughter said he'd left a suicide note. Where? At his surgery? He hadn't. Where he lived? He hadn't. Where he committed suicide? People often did.

I got out the Melways, put on the inside light and found the quickest way to Footscray.

VARLEY STREET, Footscray: one streetlight, icy wind pinning the news-paper pages against the container depot fence, somewhere a door banging in the wind, lonely sound.

I thought I heard them as soon as I stepped into the old loading bay: the sound of a classroom where the teacher has stepped out for a minute, not loud, but unruly, a jostling of voices.

I knew where the sound was coming from. I went across the loading bay, out into the courtyard, turned right and walked towards the glow coming out of a big doorway.

There were four of them upright, around a smoky, spitting fire. Other bodies lay as dead outside the circle, one face down. The fire cast a cruel russet light on wrecked faces, shapeless clothes, a swollen blood-filled eye. Two men who could have been a hundred years old were fighting weakly over the silver bladder of a wine cask, speaking incomprehensible words, neither strong enough to win possession. Someone who could have been a woman was nursing another person's head in her lap, drinking beer from a can, golden liquid running down a cracked chin, dripping onto the long, greasy grey hair.

'Robbo here?' I said.

Only two heads turned, looked at me without interest, looked away.

I went a few steps closer. The smell was overpowering, smoke, wet clothes, other animal odours.

'Boris here?' I shouted.

This time a figure to the right of the fire looked at me, dirty bearded face under a beanie, filthy matted jumper like an animal skin. He was drinking a can of Vic Bitter, two more held between his thighs.

'Fuck you want?' he said.

I went over to him. No-one paid any attention to me. 'You Boris?'

He drank some beer, looked into the fire, spat. It ran down his chin. 'Fucksit you?' he said, rocking back.

'You found the bloke hanged himself here?'

He looked at me, trouble focusing. He wasn't more than thirty years old. 'Course I fuckin did,' he said. 'Fuckin hangin.'

I knelt down. 'Boris, you took his watch.'

He blinked, looked away, put the can to his mouth, half missed it. 'Fuckin,' he said.

'Boris,' I said, 'I don't care about the watch. Did you take anything else? From the man? From the car?'

His eyes came back to me. 'Whar?'

'Did you take anything else from the hanging man? Understand?'

'Fuckin,' he said, looked away, head lolled.

I stood up. Some other time perhaps. Not tonight.

I was on my way out when Boris said, quite distinctly, 'Pay me.'

I stopped and turned, went back. 'Pay you for what?'

He was holding himself together with great effort. 'Pay me 'n' I'll show you.'

I got out my wallet, found a twenty-dollar note, waved it at him. 'Show me and I'll give you this.'

Boris focused on the note, craned his neck towards it, fell back. 'Fiffy,' he said. 'Gotta be fiffy.'

I offered him the twenty. 'Show me and I'll give you another thirty if it's worth it.'

He put out a hand, black with dirt, fresh blood on the inside of the thumb, and took the note, stuck it somewhere under his jumper. Then he lost interest, studied the beer can.

'Boris!' I shouted. 'Show me!'

His head jerked around, some life in his eyes, drained the beer can, threw it over his shoulder, put the other cans under a coat on the floor. 'Gimme hand,' he said, trying to get up.

I gripped the shoulders of his jumper and lifted him onto his feet. He weighed as much as a six-year-old.

'Over there,' he said and began to stumble towards the dark left corner of the big space.

I walked behind him. He fell once. I picked him up.

There was nothing in the corner except a rusted sheet of corrugated iron lying on the concrete.

'Under,' Boris said, swaying. He put out a hand to steady himself against the wall, misjudged the distance and fell over onto the corrugated iron.

I picked him up again, propped him against the wall.

'Lift,' he said, waving vaguely.

I bent down and lifted the corrugated iron, shifted it. Under it I could make out some clothes, two Coles plastic bags, a pair of shoes.

'Bag,' Boris said. 'Gimme.'

I picked up both bags, offered them to him. He focused, put out a hand and knocked one away, almost fell over, took the other one.

He couldn't get it open, fumbling at the plastic. I helped him. 'Thangyou,' he said, put his hand in, couldn't get hold of what was inside, turned the bag upside down and tipped the contents onto the concrete.

An envelope, A4 cartridge envelope.

I picked it up. It was unsealed. I walked back to the ambit of the firelight.

Behind me Boris was making sounds of protest. I opened the flap, took out four or five pages, paper-clipped, top page handwritten. I held it up to the light. It began: *I am writing this because I can no longer bear to go on living ...*

I put the pages back in the envelope, went back to Boris, found two twenty-dollar notes, gave them to him.

'Thank you,' I said.

'Gennelman,' said Boris.

I WAS in the pub in Streeton, in front of the same fireplace where I'd talked to Ian Barbie's wife. A tired and dirty man who began the day coming out of fitful sleep in a motel in Penola, out there in the flat vine country, far from home. Sitting in the warm country pub, I could smell myself: sweat, sex, cordite, wood smoke. All curdled by fear. I drank three neat whiskies, dark thoughts.

'Listen, Mac, I'm closin.'

It was the publican. I knew him, welded his trailer for nothing.

'Finish this,' I said.

'No,' he said, coming over and putting a half-full bottle of Johnny Walker on the table. 'Just closin the doors. Sit long as you like, fix it up later. Put the light out, give the door a good slam when you go. Lock doesn't go in easy.'

'Thanks, mate.'

'Back roads, right.'

'Back roads.'

I drank some more whisky, thought about Lew, Ned asking me to look after him. Lew and the dog, my responsibilities. Lew: mother gone, grandfather gone, just me now. I thought about my life, what it had been for so many years: the job and nothing but the job. Utter waste of time. I didn't even remember whether I'd loved my wife. Couldn't remember what it felt like to love her. Remembered that she could give me an erection with one look. What I did know was that all the self-respect that I had lost with one bad judgment had been slowly given back to me by my ordinary life in my father's house. A simple life in a simple weatherboard house. Working with my father's tools in my father's workshop. Feeling his hand in the hammer handles worn by his grip. Walking in his steps down the sodden lane and across the road to the pub and the football field. And knowing his friends. Ned, Stan, Lew, Flannery, Mick, Vinnie – they were all responsible for giving me a life with some meaning. A life that was connected to a place, connected to people, connected to the past.

But now I was back in the old life, worse than the old life because then it wasn't just me and Berglin. It was me, Berglin and the massed forces of law and order.

It was highly unlikely that my life was connected to the future.

For an hour or so, I slumped in the armchair, drinking whisky, clock ticking somewhere in the pub, lulling sound, sad sound. Fire just a glow of gold through grey. Putting off reading Ian Barbie's last testament in the same way I'd put off listening to Bianchi's tape.

Berglin. I needed to talk to Berglin. I got up, stretched, moved my shoulders, pain from tackling Neckhead on the fire escape. I got out the mobile, switched it on, pressed the numbers.

'Berglin.'

'Mac.'

'Mac, where the fucking hell have you been? Point of having a mobile is to have the fucking thing switched on.'

'Sorry,' I said. 'Been busy. This line secure?'

'Well, as secure as any fucking line is these days.'

'Got a tape. Bianchi, Scully, Mance. Before Lefroy. Bianchi had a wire on him. Insurance.'

Berglin whistled. 'Fuck,' he said. 'Where are you?'

'In the sticks. People are trying to kill me.'

'Again?'

'Yeah.'

'Must be learners. I'll meet you. Where?'

I thought for a while, gave him directions. It was as good a place as any.

I took cigarettes, matches from the bar and the bottle of whisky.

Back roads, route avoiding anything resembling a main road.

As I turned the corner of the drive, the clouds parted for a few seconds, the half moon lighting up the house at Harkness Park. It didn't look ghostly or forbidding, looked like a big old house with everyone asleep. I parked around the side, settled down to wait. It would take Berglin another half an hour. I had a sip of whisky, hunched my shoulders against the cold. Tired.

I jerked awake, got out, yawned, stretched, lit a cigarette. It tasted foul, stood on it.

Car on the road. Berglin? Quick driving.

Stopped. At the entrance to the drive.

Typical Berglin. I'd told him to drive up to the house. But Berglin didn't do the expected. He didn't drive the same way to work two days running.

I went to the corner of the house, looked out between the wall and the gutter downpipe. Hunter's moon, high clouds running south, gaps appearing, closing, white moonlight, dark. Waited for Berglin.

He was no more than fifty metres from me when the clouds tore apart.

A coldness that had nothing to do with the freezing night came over me.

Bobby Hill, slim and handsome as ever, dark clothing, long-barrelled revolver, man wants a job done properly, has to go out and do it himself.

And behind him, a few paces back, another man, short man, wearing some sort of camouflaged combat outfit, carrying a short automatic weapon at high port, big tube on top.

Clouds covered the moon. Too dark to see the man's face.

Moonlight again.

Beret on the second man's head. Turned his head.

Little pigtail swinging.

Andrew Stephens. My visitor in the Porsche.

How did he fit in?

No time to think about that.

The car door was open. I found the box of cartridges under the front seat, moved into the heavy, damp, jungle-smelling vegetation beyond the rotten toolshed.

How many? Just Hill and Andrew Stephens?

It wasn't going to be only two again.

Escape. Which way?

Down to the mill would be best. Cross the stream above the headrace pond, follow the stream down to the sluice-gates. Go around behind the mill, up the wooded embankment. Places to hide there, wait for dawn, ring Stan.

The mobile. I'd left it on the passenger seat.

No going back. I was moving in the direction of the site of the house that burnt down, the first house. But the growth here was impenetrable, I'd end up like a goat caught in a thicket.

I had to veer left, pass in front of the sunken tennis court. But to do that I would have to cross the top of the area we had so painfully cleared. In darkness, that wouldn't be a problem. But if moonlight persisted, I'd have to wait. And they'd be coming ...

Steady. They didn't know which way I'd gone. They'd have found the car by now. It was coal dark. I could be anywhere.

Scully's words on the tape came into my head:

You don't know this fucking El G, fucking mad. I know him from way back ...

Way back? How far back? From Scully's days in the country?

El G? El Torro, The Bull. El Greco, The Greek.

The Greek? Who had said something about a Greek recently? Greek. Recently. In the past few days. The past few days were blurred into one long day.

Frank Cullen, man of contraptions: *Rick's tied up with that Stefanidis from over near Daylesford. RSPCA went there, heard he was shootin pigeons. Bloke behind a wall throws 'em in the air, Greek shoots 'em with a twelve bore from about two yards. Sticks it up their arses practically.*

Andrew Stephens. Andrew Stefanidis?

Andrew's father was a good man, fine man, fought with the Greek partisans in the war. Dr Crewe, walking around the lake, talking about Ian and Tony and Rick and Andrew.

Sudden chilling clarity. Andrew Stephens's father was Greek. He'd anglicised his name.

Andrew Stephens was El Greco, The Greek, close-range shooter of pigeons, maker of snuff movies, organiser of murderous run-throughs.

And then the realisation.

Berglin had always known who El Greco was. Berglin had toyed with me. Berglin had given me to Scully, Hill and El Greco.

Naive. You only know about naive when it's too late.

Absolute silence.

I walked into something, old fence, some obstacle, small screeching noise.

Something landed in the vegetation near me, sound like an overripe peach falling. And then a thump, no more than the sound of a hard tennis forehand.

Whop.

The night turned to day.

Blinded.

Flare grenade. I backed away, left arm shielding my eyes.

The bullet plucked at my collar, red hot, like being touched by an iron from the forge.

I fell over backwards, twisted, crawled into the undergrowth, hands and knees, through the thicket, thorns grabbing, scratching face and hands, reached a sparser patch, got to my feet, ran into the dark, into something solid, forehead first.

I didn't fall over, stood bent, stunned, looked back. The flare was dying, white coal.

'Mac.' Shout.

Bobby.

'Mac. Deal. The tape, you walk. Don't need you dead.'

What hope did I have?

'Okay,' I said, 'I'm coming.'

I ran left, northeast, hindered by wet, clinging, growing things, hampered but not blocked. I reached the fringe of the cleared area, exhausted. Knew where I was.

Clouds opened. Moonlight.

The bullet hit something in front of me. Something solid, tree trunk.

Night-vision scope.

That was the fat tube on El Greco's rifle. Light-enhancing nightscope. He could see in the dark.

I threw myself into the denser growth to my right, crawled deeper, deeper, desperate, no breath left, ten metres, fifteen, more. Into, over plants, roots, through ditches of rotten leaves, mud, scrabbling, don't want to die like this ...

I fell into the sunken tennis court, fell a metre, head over heels, got up, dazed, winded, pitch-dark, sense of direction gone, ran, ran a long way, length of the court perhaps, knee-high weeds, swimming in porridge, fell, crawled, a barrier, a wall, the other side of the court, bits of rusted wire, hands hurting, sodden soil, tufts of grass coming away in my hands.

I was out of the court, on my stomach, all strength gone.

The end.

Fuck that.

I was being hunted. I was their victim. They'd had lots of victims. They knew about victims: they run, you find them, you kill them.

Dangerous is what you want to be. Go mad. Nobody wants to fight a mad person. Nobody wants fingers stuck up his nose.

A father's words to a small and scared ten-year-old son.

Yes. I found the strength, crawled around the perimeter of the sunken court, turned north. Waited in the undergrowth.

Whop.

Fireball. In the tennis court. Night sun. Cold, white night sun.

I buried my head in the dank, wet weeds. Flare thrown from the edge of the tennis court, somewhere near where I'd toppled into the court.

Flare dying, fading.

Dark.

Dark.

And then light, cold silver moonlight through the flying clouds.

Bobby Hill, ten metres away, moving through the knee-high weeds, long-barrelled revolver at his side, not anxious, not hurrying, man out for a walk in difficult conditions.

Dark again. Lying on my face, I reached under my chest, found the gun butt, comforting feel, drew the Colt from the shoulder holster. Safety off. Hammer back.

Whop.

In the air, above me, intense sodium-like light.

I cringed, pushed myself down, didn't move, Mother Earth, breathed wet soil, waited for the pain. You bowl these things, I realised, throw them, they float for a few seconds. Not parachute flares.

No pain. White glare dying away. Slowly, slowly. Dark.

I got up. Walked to the edge of the sunken court, slid down on my back-side, stayed down, drew up my knees, rested my outstretched arms on them. Waited.

Look down. Another flare goes off, don't look at the light.

Pitch dark.

The clouds tore, moon revealed.

Bobby Hill.

The length of a ute from me.

I saw him.

He saw me.

Handsome man, Bobby Hill: dense black hair combed back, nice smile, standing in knee-high weeds on a forgotten tennis court.

He was smiling as he brought the long-barrelled revolver up.

I fired first, at his middle, big bang.

The bullet hit him somewhere near the bottom of his fly, massive punch in the groin. His lower body went backwards, feet leaving the ground.

For an instant, I saw the expression on his face. It said: *This is odd.*

In my head, I said, *Goodbye, Bobby*.

From close by, from the thicket above the tennis court, El Greco said, 'Bobby. Got him?'

I went up the side of the court again, crawled through the vegetation, Colt in hand, dark again, ground sloping, stopped for a second, heard the creek below me, full this time of year.

Flare behind me, to my left. El Greco had misjudged my direction. He was looking further up, thought I'd turned north. I holstered the Colt, lay still, crawled again, mud in my mouth.

Creek close, few metres, rushing water, making a noise no problem. I was in the thicket of poplars that lined the creek, dead branches poking at me, cheek torn open.

I fell head-first down the bank into the stream. Freezing water, couldn't find my feet, taken downstream, banged into a fallen tree trunk, turned around, use of only one hand, swallowed water, Jesus Christ, I couldn't drown after all this ...

My feet found the oozy bottom, I got a hold on a branch stump, pulled myself along the tree trunk. Island in the middle of the creek, some moon-light. Hid behind the trunk until it went.

Another flare, even further over. El Greco thought I was trying to get back to the house, to the car.

Relief. I lay on a cold carpet of moss and caught my breath: I could get out of this.

I waded the second half of the stream, much shallower there, up the bank, into another poplar jungle, blundered into a barbed-wire fence, sound of sleeve ripping, climbed through it, caught, jacket ripped.

I knew where I was. I'd walked down here from the mill. The millpond was about two hundred metres downstream and there was a path of sorts along the creek. I could walk upright. El Greco couldn't see me here, poplar thickets on both banks too dense.

It took me about five minutes to reach the brimming millpond. The moon came out and I could see what I had been hearing: water spilling over the dam wall, small waterfall.

Panting, I went over to the rusting sluicegates, looked down into the empty brick-lined millrace. It ran straight to the old mill, slight fall, disap-peared around a corner to where the millwheel was.

If I dropped into it, I could run the hundred-odd metres to the shelter of the mill unseen, climb out, cross the bluestone-paved loading area and climb the embankment, get deep into the trees.

Safe.

Whop.

Sodium daylight.

In the poplars on the other side of the race pond, not thirty metres away. El Greco.

Changed direction, come back. Probably seen me in the nightscope.

Frozen, I couldn't move, reflexes not working. Tired. Tired.

I sank to the ground slowly, lay full length, felt for the Colt.

Gone. No Colt. In the stream. Oh Jesus.

The flare died. The millrace. Get into the millrace. I said this to myself. Get into the millrace and run.

I crawled to the edge of the sluicegate.

Just do this and you're safe. He'll have to go upstream or downstream to cross.

I turned and put a leg over, found a foothold, looked to see how far the drop was ...

Whop.

Flare over the middle of the race pond, white light intensified by the reflection.

El Greco in the poplars, weapon at the shoulder, looking through the nightscope.

Drop. About to let go, fall into the millrace.

Bang, wink of red light at the mill end of the race. Bang on the metal sluicegate, felt the tremor of the metal in my hand.

Someone in the millrace. Shooting at me. Of course, two down the drive, two come from below. I knew there'd be more than two.

Bang, red wink, sound of bullet over my head.

I heaved myself back over the top.

Trapped. Finished.

My hand was on the sluicegate lever. Jesus. Heard Flannery's voice in my head: *Sluicegate'll still work. Someone's been greasing it.*

I grabbed it with both hands, pulled.

Nothing. No give.

Pulled. Oh Jesus.

Moonlight. Two men in the millrace, thirty metres from me. Bang, barrel flame.

Pull!

The lever gave, I fell to my knees. Sound of rushing, falling water, sluicegate half a metre open.

Not caring where El Greco was, I watched the wall of foaming water barrel down the millrace. The men were on either side, trying to climb out, when it hit them, ripped them off the walls, tumbled them down towards the wheel, sweet Jesus ...

'Hands in the air, Mr Faraday.'

El Greco, behind me, five metres away, pear-shaped head behind the fat nightscope. I raised my tired arms. Berglin, you treacherous bastard. All those years.

'I think we have to do a deal,' I said.

He laughed, delighted.

'A deal. What a wonderful idea. Selling something, are we? Gates? Fighter aircraft?'

Laugh again, the girlish laugh.

'Haven't got the tape on me,' I said. 'Somewhere safe.'

'That's not true, John. For telling me lies, I'm going to punish you. Before I kill you.'

The bullet hit me in the left thigh, like a hard blow from a stick, spun me around, knocked me over.

Pain. Intense, burning pain.

I could see him from where I lay. He came closer, weapon still at the shoulder.

'That was the first part of the punishment, John,' he said. 'Now I want you to ask me not to punish you any more.'

Has to be some dignity at the end.

'Fuck off,' I said. 'You disgust me.'

El Greco lifted his eyes from the sight. 'That was a mistake, Johnny. This is going to take much longer now ...'

He sighted again.

He was going to shoot me low down in the body.

Moon free of cloud, silver light, sound of water. You bastard, Berglin.

How to be a halfway decent person. That's the main question in life.

What would you know, Berglin, you worthless, faithless bastard?

'Wait for it, Johnny,' El Greco said. He laughed, the light, little-girlish laugh. 'It's going to hurt, really hurt. And there's more. Much more.'

A shot. Close. Loud. Another shot.

El Greco looked up from the rifle. His mouth opened. I could see his tongue lolling in his mouth.

He fell over forward, rifle barrel digging into the ground, chest resting on the butt, slowly toppling sideways.

Someone came out of the shadows, wet to the waist, arms at his sides, big automatic pistol pointing at the ground.

'Fuck,' Berglin said. His long foot moved El Greco's rifle away from the body. 'Flare grenades, night sight. Think bloody technology's the answer to everything.'

I tried to get up, got to one knee. Pain. Whole left thigh on fire. 'Why'd you do that?' I said. 'Just going to leap at him, knock the rifle away, strangle him.'

'Got bored waiting,' Berglin said. 'Who's he?'

'Algie. El G. El Greco.'

He reached down, turned the body over, licked fingertips, held them to El Greco's nostrils. 'Won't be standing trial,' he said, straightening up. 'Just as well. Guilty fuckers get off half the time.'

I WAS in the smithy getting ready to temper a knife blade when Detective Michael Shea drove up, again without Cotter. He came in and sat on the bench.

I had a thick iron plate on the fire, just about ready, almost red.

'Can't talk,' I said. 'Got to get this right.'

It was red enough. I took tongs and moved it to the cooler side of the fire, picked up the knife blade and put it on the plate. The important thing now was to quench the blade when it showed the right colour.

Shea came over to watch. The blade absorbed heat from the plate, turned strawy yellow, went through orange into brown, began to turn a redder brown.

I picked it up with heated tongs and put it in the quenching bath of water under a layer of clean olive oil, moved it about.

'What's that do?' Shea said.

'Hard steel's too brittle, snaps. Get rid of some brittleness this way,' I said. 'First you have to harden it, then you temper it like this. What's happening?'

'Big morning. They found more bones. Marcia's rolled, Veene's decided to give us Crewe.'

'That's big.'

'Crewe got pulled this morning. Steps of Parliament. Do it that way down there. Tip off Channel Nine, get your face on camera. Excellent for the career. They ran Marcia through the Canadian databases. No Marcia Carrier. But a Marcia Lyons did time for assaulting girls at a girls' home in Montreal. Turns out it's her. That's her married name, Lyons. She says Crewe found out before she got the job, didn't say a word, made sure she got it. Then he had her.'

'Took part?'

'Admits. Very distressed. Blames her old man. Says he used to beat her and her sister. Says she didn't know the girls were killed after she left. Guilty only of assault.'

Gaby Makin had said something. She was talking about Melanie Pavitt, how strong she was for a small person. What was it?

Barbie liked the little ones.

She hadn't been talking about Ian Barbie, she'd been talking about Marcia. Marcia was Barbie to Barbie's Ken.

'What's Rick say?' I said.

'Gone to water. Says he had sex with the girls at the farm, left them with Andrew and Tony. Only found out later that Andrew killed them. On video. We got the videos. In the basement at Andrew's mansion. Safe buried in the floor. Found it with a metal detector. Make you puke, tell you.'

'Crewe's in the picture?'

'Not. But there's enough. Got dates, times from Barbie's last letter. Crewe was up here for all of them. They picked girls being discharged, nowhere to go, no family. So they just vanished, no-one looked for them.'

He came around and looked at the cool blade, picked it up. 'Nice,' he said. 'You do good work. There's something else. Ned. Been waiting for people to get back to me. Cop in Brisbane, he's been trying to nail a bloke called Martin Gilbert for years, reckons he's Mr Rent-a-Rope, priors for assault, attempted murder. Smart guy. Joe Cool. Three hangins up there, all got the smell, plus one in Sydney, one in Melbourne. One Brisbane one, car belongs to mate of Gilbert's, bloke's interstate at the time, car's a block from the scene at the right time.'

'That take us where?'

'Got a picture of Gilbert,' Shea said. 'Nice colour picture. Had the troops takin it around the motels. Slow business.'

He had something to tell me.

'Motel up the top of Royal Parade had two blokes come in on the night, just before midnight. One's Gilbert, bloke's a hundred per cent on it. The two got pissed in the room, made a lot of noise, manager had to get up, copped a lot of abuse from Gilbert. I'm goin down tomorrow, show him the pictures come today. Some of Gilbert's mates.'

I'd got this large, pale, sad-looking man very wrong. 'You do good work too,' I said.

Shea said, 'There's more. We done the car rentals for the day, ran the IDs, got a rental, cash, false ID. Brisbane troops seen it before, think it's used by Gilbert.'

I started to say something.

Shea held up his hand. 'Small rental place this,' he said, 'not too many paying cash these days. They remember this roll of plastic tape, black plastic tape, found in the boot of the rental when they cleaned it. Still got it too, lyin there in the office. Thought it'd come in useful, says the bloke.'

Shea shifted his buttocks, couldn't get comfortable, got up and went over to stand in the doorway. 'Forensic's had another look at Ned's pyjamas, Brissie cops told 'em what to look for. Now they reckon there was tape on the pyjama sleeves, on the pants.'

'You do more than good work,' I said. 'You do excellent work.'

He looked away. 'Forensic think they might have missed some acetone stuff, like nail varnish remover, used to clean Ned's face, round the mouth. Same on two hangins up in Brissie. Reckon this Gilbert knows his stuff.'

'The plastic tape,' I said. 'Match it with the glue?'

'Tomorrow, we'll hear tomorrow, next day. Soon.'

'Be enough?'

He shrugged. 'Get a positive ID from the motel on Gilbert's mate, he might shake loose.'

He looked out of the door. It had started to rain. 'Got to go,' he said. 'Be in touch.'

I went out with him, put out my hand, 'Glad we drew you on the night.'

He shook my hand. 'Gettin there. Any luck, we get the bastards. Then they get a smart lawyer and they walk.'

I was finishing up for the day when the phone rang in the office.

'Gather your local Member's the first item on the news tonight.' Berglin. No greeting.

'So I hear. What's with our friend in the Vatican?'

'That's why I'm calling. Scully resigned this morning.'

'They going to prosecute?'

'No.'

'No? The bastards. He's a murderer, how many times over.'

'Can't prosecute.'

'Can't? Can't? What kind of ...'

'Can't prosecute the dead. He shot himself. In his garage at home.'

I sat in silence for a while, telephone forgotten, looking out of the window at the tattered clouds blowing south, at the willows down at the winter creek sending out the first pale green signal of spring.

Berglin cleared his throat. 'Well,' he said, 'there endeth the lesson.'

I said, 'Amen.'

WE LIMPED off after the third quarter, six goals down, our supporters – now grown by about ten thousand per cent – giving us a sad little cheer. Kingstead got a roar, hooting, small boys jumping and punching one another.

Mick tried his best in the break. 'Six goals is nuthin, fellas. Knock 'em off in the first ten minutes, cruise away to a magnificent victory. Make it all the sweeter, that's all ...'

'You goin to play Lew or not?' Billy Garrett said. 'What's the bloody point of him sittin on the bench?'

'Keeps 'em guessin, Billy, keeps 'em off balance. Expectin any minute we'll bring on the young fella, brilliant talent, legs of steel ...'

'They're not bloody guessin,' Billy said. 'They're not off bloody balance. They're bloody kickin our arses, that's what they're doin. You gonna play him or not?'

Mick put his hands in his anorak pockets, looked around for under-standing. 'Can't, Billy, boy's in the golf tournament of his life tomorrer. Tiger Woods in the makin, how kin I put him out there, some great lump kicks him in the leg, stands on his head? Great career ruined. My fault. Swore I wouldn't play him except in an emergency.'

'Emergency?' said Billy. 'You think a bloody emergency is like what? Only bloody Grand Final I'll ever play in, thirty-six points behind, side's absolutely bloody knackered. Not an emergency? You off your bloody head?'

'No need to shout, Billy,' Mick said. 'Don't want 'em to think we're not of one mind, gives 'em a psychological hold over us ...'

'They don't need a bloody psychological hold over us, you mad Irish prick,' Billy said. 'They've got a hold on our actual balls, squeezin.'

I was at full forward, second game back after four weeks out, leg almost healed. Garrett and company had got along fine without me, winning three out of four.

Flannery and I walked on together. 'Christ, be glad when this is over,' he said. 'It's not the losin I mind, it's havin to play so long after you know you've lost.'

'No time for defeatism, Flannery,' I said. 'We mature players are supposed to set an example.'

Flannery was walking in the direction of his opponent. Over his shoulder, he said, 'You'll see an example if this cockbrain doesn't stop puttin his elbow in my ribs. Example of how to get a two-hundred-game suspension.'

For the first five minutes, Kingstead were all over us, winning the ball everywhere, four shots at goal, four behinds.

Then something happened to them. Billy Garrett won the ball from four consecutive ball-ups, everyone seemed to have found some speed.

Three goals in four minutes.

At the centre bounce, Billy knocked it out to Gary Weaver, who ran twenty metres, kicked the ball to Flannery, who appeared to have stood on his opponent's instep. Flannery played on, kicked it my way. I got in front of my man and took it on my chest.

Goal.

'Reckon they peaked too early,' Flannery said after taking a mark right in front of goal. 'Field's comin back to us.'

He kicked it. Supporters back in full voice.

Ten points behind.

And there we stuck. It began to rain, steady rain. We wrestled with them in the mud, almost everyone ending up in midfield, all mudmen, unrecognisable, exhausted. My thigh was aching, must have opened the wound. The clock ticked on, every second taking Brockley's first Grand Final victory in seventeen years further away.

Out of nowhere, Kingstead kicked another goal. Ball spun free from a collapsing pack, man ran thirty metres and kicked a goal. Supporters in total ecstasy.

Sixteen points behind. Three goals.

As we were picking ourselves up, Billy Garrett said to me, panting, 'Mac, for Christsake, do it. Talk to the little bastard.'

I looked at Lew sitting on the bench, wearing an old overcoat of mine. He didn't look happy. I was his guardian. What would Ned have done? I didn't really have to ask myself the question. I knew what Ned would have done.

I went over to Mick. 'Fuck the golf,' I said. 'Give the boy a run. You only get one chance in life to save a Grand Final for Brockley.'

Mick opened his mouth, looked into my eyes, closed his mouth. He turned towards the bench.

'You're on, fella.'

Lew was up and out of the overcoat, jogging on the spot, big smile.

Minutes to go. Lew on in the centre.

Billy tapped the ball out. It bounced off the shoulder of a Kingstead player, Lew took it out of the air with one hand, slipped between two opponents, perfect balance, ran, one bounce, two bounces, three bounces, sidestepped two Kingstead players, handballed over the head of another one, ran around him, caught his own handball, running, another bounce, kick.

Goal.

Centre bounce. Billy made a superhuman effort, took the ball over his opponent, came down, threw off a tackle, handballed to Lew, who was already running.

Lew ran around three players, stopped, delivered a kick to Gary Weaver, perfectly weighted kick, hit Weaver on the chest.

Weaver kicked the ball to the square, where Flannery and I and several other Brockley players were in hand-to-hand combat with half the Kingstead side now drafted into defence.

The ball came out of the dark-grey sky. Four of us rose to it, tired men, desperate men, men willing their arms to lengthen.

Lew floated across the front of the pack, fully a metre off the ground, took the ball one-handed, landed like a ballet dancer, perfect pivot, no hesitation, cannon shot through the posts.

Goal.

One goal to victory.

Crowd like Visigoths on a rampage. Grown men would weep in the last light of this day.

Umpire looking at watch. Seconds left.

Centre bounce. No-one was going to take this away from Billy Garrett. He rose like someone called to ascend to a higher place, seemed to grip the ball in a large hand, sent it flying to where Lew was waiting, sent it as if he knew exactly where the boy was, sent it as if they'd arranged it.

Lew went through the Kingstead players with the calm arrogance of someone sent to instruct others on the correct way to play the winter game. No-one put a finger on him. They chased, gave up. Two players collided, heads meeting, fell down senseless.

He came down the field towards me, to where I stood alone, my opponents sure that he was going to goal.

Stopped. Goals in front, thirty metres, no-one within reach of him. Crowd suddenly silent.

Lew kicked, perfect swing of the leg, leg born to kick a football.

Kicked not at goal. Not at exposed, waiting goal.

To me.

Like a father kicking to his son in the street. Kick meant to be marked, on the chest, not high, give the boy confidence.

Instead of kicking it himself, could kick it in his sleep, be a hero, he wanted me to kick the winning goal for Brockley. Brockley, seventeen years in the wilderness, object of derision. Lew was handing me the chance to bring the barren years to a close.

I marked the ball under my collarbone. It fell into my hands, stuck there.

The siren went.

Kick to win after the siren. In a Grand Final. People had never recovered from missing one. Moved away. Changed their names. Never played again.

I went back, pulled up my socks.

It looked like a long way, impossible angle.

Flannery walked across behind me.

'Not saying anything,' he said. 'But ...'

There was not a sound from the crowd. Total silence.

I took a deep breath. No-one should be given this kind of responsibility. No-one.

I ran up and kicked.

Closed my eyes.

Flannery grabbed me from behind, seemed to want to dance with me.

Lew came up, punched my shoulder, put his arm around my waist. I put an arm around his shoulders.

'You little bastard,' I said.

We walked off, shaking hands with opponents, ruffling team-mates' hair, listening to the supporters shouting. Mick was kissing players.

In the gloom, I could see Allie, pale head, standing on the bonnet of her truck, fists raised in the air, shouting something. Next to her, Vinnie was doing what looked like the samba.

And then I saw the black Mercedes, person leaning against the grille. Hadn't seen her, spoken to her, since the night I killed two men on her fire escape. Wanted to, scared to, she didn't call.

I cuffed Lew on the back of the head, walked down the line, wet, covered in mud, people patting me on back.

Anne Karsh was in jeans, tartan coat, hair wet, beautiful. Wary eyes, not smiling.

I stopped a metre away. 'Owe you a coffee machine,' I said.

She shrugged. 'Been meaning to throw out that machine for years. Makes really bad coffee.'

We looked at each other.

'Must've read your mind. Threw it out for you. You in the country going back?'

'In the country staying over. Not sure where yet. Leon's divorcing me. Met a neurosurgeon in Switzerland. I get Harkness Park.'

'Nice place,' I said. 'Got the Bobby Hill memorial tennis court. Want to come back to the pub?'

Anne smiled, nodded, touched my muddy arm.

'C'mon, Mac,' Flannery shouted. 'Got to sing the team song. Got to learn it first.'